MARGARET OLIP...

(1828-1897) was born in Wallyford, r...... ...ed in Scotland until the age of ten when ....verpool and then Birkenhead. Her moth.............. ...irth, but little is known of her father, Fr......... ...hat he once "took affidavits" in a Liverpool .... She wrote her first novel at the age of sixteen ....ing her mother through an illness, but her first publish...... ...rk was *Passages in the Life of Mrs Margaret Maitland* (1849), and in 1851 she was introduced to the Scottish firm of Blackwoods, who were to be her principal publishers, and to whose *Blackwood's Magazine* she remained a regular contributor until her death.

In 1852 she married her cousin Francis Oliphant, an architectural glass painter and associate of Pugin. The greater part of the family income, however, came from her journalism and Scottish regional novels such as *Katie Stewart* and *The Quiet Heart* (1854). In 1859 she found herself a widow with three small children and £1000 in debt: from then on she was always under pressure to write to educate her sons (her daughter died in 1864), and also to support her brothers, nephew and nieces.

One of the greatest women of the Victorian Age, Mrs Oliphant eventually published almost 100 novels, of which the best known are the "Carlingford Chronicles": *The Rector and The Doctor's Family* (1863), *Salem Chapel* (1863), *The Perpetual Curate* (1864), *Miss Marjoribanks* (1866), and *Phoebe Junior* (1876). Other important works include *Harry Joscelyn* (1881), *The Ladies Lindores* (1883), *Hester* (1883), *A Country Gentleman and His Family* (1886), *Lady Car* (1889), *Kirsteen* (1890) and *Sir Robert's Fortune* (1895). She also wrote supernatural tales, biographies, literary histories, translations and travel books. Her last years were overshadowed by the deaths of her nephew Frank in 1879, and her sons Cyril and "Cecco" in 1890 and 1895. Remembered by J. M. Barrie as "of an intellect so alert that one wondered she ever fell asleep", Mrs Oliphant died in Wimbledon at the age of sixty-nine.

Virago also publishes *Hester*, *The Rector and The Doctor's Family* and *Salem Chapel*.

VIRAGO
MODERN
CLASSIC

NUMBER
243

𝕮𝖍𝖗𝖔𝖓𝖎𝖈𝖑𝖊𝖘 𝖔𝖋 𝕮𝖆𝖗𝖑𝖎𝖓𝖌𝖋𝖔𝖗𝖉.

THE
PERPETUAL CURATE

MRS OLIPHANT

WITH A NEW INTRODUCTION BY
PENELOPE FITZGERALD

Published by VIRAGO PRESS Limited 1987
41 William IV Street, London WC2N 4DB

First published in Great Britain 1864 by Wm. Blackwood

Introduction Copyright © Penelope Fitzgerald 1987

British Cataloguing in Publication Data
Oliphant, *Mrs.*
Chronicles of Carlingford.—(A Virago
modern classic)
Vol. 3: The perpetual curate
I. Title
823'.8[F]'   PR5113.C5
ISBN 0-86068-786-4

Typeset by Goodfellow & Egan of Cambridge
Printed in Finland by Werner Söderström Oy

ALLA PADRONA MIA;

ED A TE, SORELLA CARISSIMA!

CONSOLATRICI GENTILLISSIME

DELLA DESOLATA.

INTRODUCTION

Frank Wentworth, the Perpetual Curate, was one of Mrs Oliphant's favourites. "I mean to bestow the very greatest care on him", she told her publisher, William Blackwood, as she set to work, with her usual rush of energy, to expand Frank's story from the glimpses we get of him in *The Rector* and *Salem Chapel*. In this third Chronicle, Carlingford is as respectable, slow-moving and opinionated as ever. Frank, on the other hand, is "throbbing . . . with wild life and trouble to the very finger-points". He is a dedicated priest, he is in love, and he is still (as he was in *The Rector*) too poor to marry, certainly too poor to marry Lucy Wodehouse, the young woman he loves.*

To be a perpetual curate, in the 1860s, meant exactly that. He was in charge of a church built, in the first place, to take the pressure of work off a large parish. To a great extent he was independent. But to rise higher he had (like any other curate) either to be preferred to a family living, or to be recommended by the Rector to his Bishop. If, however, he was "viewy" – meaning if he had views which his superiors didn't accept – the result was bound to be a high-spirited clash with the Rector, with which the chance of recommendation was likely to disappear.

Frank Wentworth is "viewy". He is a Ritualist. At his little church, St Roque's, built in hard stony Gothic by

*Frank's stipend isn't given, but in Trollope's *Framley Parsonage* (1861) the Rev. Josiah Crawley, Perpetual Curate of Hogglestock, earns £130 a year.

Gilbert Scott, there are candles, flowers, bells and a choir in white surplices. The worship there represents the later phase of the Tractarian movement whose effect was so disturbing that the Established Church had begun to take legal action against it. (One of the first of these cases, in fact, was brought against the Perpetual Curate of St James's, Brighton, who refused to give up hearing confessions.) Frank remains a good Anglican, and Mrs Oliphant never makes it very clear how extreme his opinions are, only that he holds them sincerely. And his Ritualism, of course, is not a matter of outward show, but of symbolising the truth to all comers. But the candles and flowers of St Roque's are a scandal to three-quarters of Carlingford.

Frank, however – and here he is in deeper trouble – doesn't confine himself to St Roque's. By the 1860s the Tractarian Movement had spread out from Oxford into missions to England's industrial slums. Frank's first Rector, old Mr Bury, had asked the energetic young man to help him, for the time being, in Wharfside, Carlingford's brick-working district down by the canals. Here his daily contact with extreme hardship, and the difficult lives and deaths of the poor, has brought out Frank's true vocation. In Wharfside he is respected and loved. His plain-spoken sermons fill the little tin chapel. But Wharfside is not in Frank's district. He has only come to think of it as his own. It is this that the new Rector, Mr Morgan, finds intolerable. Unquestionably the success of his ministry has gone to Frank's head. Morgan challenges him directly. He proposes to sweep away the tin chapel and build a new church in Wharfside. This is not power politics, it is a dispute over a "cure of souls", but still a dispute. And "next to happiness," as Mrs Oliphant puts it, "perhaps enmity is the most healthful stimulant of the human mind".

Since Frank cannot compromise on a matter of principle, he faces a future without advancement. This means the long-drawn-out waste of his love and Lucy's. Here is the central concern of the novel, and there are two minor episodes, comic and pathetic by turns, which stand as a kind of commentary on it. In the first place, the Morgans themselves have waited prudently through many years of genteel poverty. The appointment to Carlingford has been their first chance to marry. But by now Mrs Morgan is faded, her nose reddened by indigestion, while Morgan has the short temper of middle age. With a touching determination they brace themselves, after so many delays, to make the best of things. The railway for example, runs close behind the Rectory, the first house they have ever lived in together. The old gardener suggests that it won't show so much when the lime-trees have "growed a bit", but poor Mrs Morgan is "reluctant to await the slow processes of nature" – the processes, that is, which have tormented her for the past ten years. Then there is the terribly ugly, but perfectly good carpet left behind by the last Rector. Mrs Morgan detests this carpet. But she tells herself, with hard-won self-control, "It would not look like Christ's work . . . if we had it all our own way." She cannot afford to complain. Time has robbed her of the luxury of ingratitude. And in her heart she is afraid that it has narrowed her husband's mind, although this makes her more loyal to him than ever. "If only we had been less prudent!" Mrs Oliphant shows that, in spite of everything, the love between the Morgans goes deep, but Frank, passing them in Grange Lane, sees them as grotesque, and feels his own frustration as demon thoughts.

Secondly, there is the story of the elder Miss Wodehouse, the gentle, "dove-coloured", forty-year-old spinster who appears in the first of the Chronicles, *The Rector*. To all appearances she is resigned to a life without self, devoted to her pretty and much younger sister. But the Reverend Morley Proctor returns to Carlingford and offers her her "chance". True, he proposes disconcertingly with the words "You see we are neither of us young." But he allows Miss Wodehouse, for the first time, to set a value on herself, "a timid middle-aged confidence". She even has it in her power, for a while at least, to patronise Lucy. She will have a home of her own. When Lucy's happiness makes this unimportant, Miss Wodehouse has "a half-ludicrous, half-humiliating sense of being cast into the shade". A truly good-hearted woman, she cannot under-stand these new feelings. We have to recognise them for her.

Love, money, duty, passing time, the powerful inter-actions of the mid-Victorian novel, all bear down on the Perpetual Curate. But there is a possible way out. The Wentworths are a landed family and they have a living, with a good income, in their gift. The living is expected to fall vacant and Frank is the natural successor, unless – and the Wentworths have heard disturbing rumours of this – he has "gone over" to Ritualism. To investigate this, Frank's unmarried aunts, all firm Evangelicals, arrive in Carlingford. They are there to take stock of the flowers and candles, to hear whether their nephew preaches "the plain gospel", and to deliver their verdict accordingly. Although Mrs Oliphant objected to the fairy-tale element in Dickens, surely she is allowing herself to use it here. Three aunts – one gracious, one sentimental; one whose hair "wavered in weak-minded ringlets"; one stern and practical – install themselves in Grange Lane. From there they circulate through the town, at once menacing and ridiculous.

It is no surprise, however, in a novel by Mrs Oliphant, to find enterprise in the hands of the women. Frank's father, the Squire, is an attractive figure, but a bewildered one, with only "that glimmering of sense which keeps many a stupid man straight". He is shown, in fact, as acting largely on instinct. Outside his broad acres (where he is shrewd enough) he seems at a loss. From his three marriages there are numerous children with conflicting interests, and he hardly seems to know what to do with them either. And the family not only descends remorse-lessly on Frank but summons him home to deal with the problem of his stepbrother Gerald.

Gerald is the Rector of the parish of Wentworth itself.
But he has been struggling with doubts and has now been
converted – "perverted", the aunts call it – to the Roman
Catholic Church. The wound to his family and their sense
of betrayal leaves them almost helpless. "Rome, it's Antichrist," says the old Squire. "Every child in the village
school could tell you that." More monstrous still, Gerald
hopes to become a Catholic priest. And there there is a
very real obstacle: he is married. His wife, Louisa, is a
fool. While Gerald struggles to be "content to be nothing,
as the saints were", Louisa complains, through ready
tears, "We have always been used to the very best society!"
But she has the power of weak, silly women, a power
which fascinated Mrs Oliphant, herself an intelligent
woman who had to struggle to survive. Gerald, obsessed
with his wife's troubles and his own ordeal, is "like a man
whom sickness had reduced to the last stage of life".

Frank's generous heart aches for his brother. The whole
family relies on him to bring Gerald to his senses, and the
debate between the two of them is extended through the
central part of the novel. It begins at Wentworth Rectory,
where the solid green cedar tree on the lawn outside the
windows seems to stand for ancient certainties, and it
echoes the painful divisions in so many English families
after the turning-point of Newman's conversion in 1845.
Frank is aware that if Gerald resigns the Wentworth living
it will be there for himself and Lucy, but he hates himself
for remembering this. Indeed, all he has time for is the
distress of his brother's sacrifice.

Mrs Oliphant herself was no sectarian. The "warm Free
Churchism" of her early days was behind her, or rather it
had expanded, in the course of a hard life, into tolerance.
Forms of worship interested her very little. She knew
only, as she told one of her friends, that she was not afraid
of the loneliness of death because of "a silent companion,
God walking in the cool of the garden". Time and again
she relates religion to instinct and nature. This doesn't

mean that she treats Gerald and Frank's debate as unimportant, only that it follows its own lines. There is, for instance, nothing like Charlotte Brontë's romantic approach to the question in *Villette* (1853). The real point at issue is reached in Chapter XL when Gerald explains himself in terms of authority. He needs a Church which is "not a human institution", one which gives absolute certainty on all points. Although the steps by which he has reached this decision aren't given, there is a hint here of Charles Reding, the hero of Newman's *Loss and Gain* (1848).* Frank's answer is unexpected. He bases it, not upon freedom of conscience, but on the sufferings and inequalities of this life. How can the Catholic Church, which can no more explain these things than anyone else, claim that its authority is sufficient when it comes to doctrine? If trust in God is the only answer left to us for the pain of life, then, says Frank, "I am content to take my doctrines on the same terms."

Frank is to be seen here as the true priest, because he puts himself at the service of human suffering without pretending to be able to explain it. He understands, too, the relief from anxiety which Mrs Oliphant herself thought was "our highest sensation – higher than any positive enjoyment in this world. It used to sweep over me like a wave, sometimes when I opened a door, sometimes in a letter – in all simple ways." The complement of this is the sympathy for others which relief brings, "the compassion of happiness", and this, too, Frank feels at the last. But this is the same Frank Wentworth who has to restrain himself from whacking his aunt's horrible dog, and who lies awake maddened by the sound of the drainpipe – his landlady has "a passion for rain-water". Mrs Oliphant is determined to keep him human. Indeed, it is only on those terms that he can truly be a priest.

---

*Gerald's "Frank, it is salvation", suggests Reding's "The only motive which is sufficient to justify a move is the conviction that one's salvation depends on it."

After the success of *Salem Chapel*, Mrs Oliphant had asked for, and got, £1500 for the *The Perpetual Curate*. It was the highest payment she ever had from a publisher. John Blackwood's old clerk (she was told) turned pale at the idea of such a sum, and remonstrated with his master. The story began to run in *Blackwood's Magazine* in June, 1863, and was produced under even greater difficulties than usual. Mrs Oliphant wrote it only one or two instalments in advance – this at her own request, as the monthly deadline, she said, "kept her up". In the autumn she travelled, with her usual large party of friends and children, to Rome. There, in January, 1864, her only daughter fell sick, and died within a few weeks. Maggie was eleven, "the beloved companion", as Mrs Oliphant had been as a little girl, to her own mother. "It is hard to go out in the streets," she wrote, "to look out of the window and see the other women with their daughters. God knows it is an unworthy feeling, but it makes me shrink from going out."

In spite of this, "the roughest edge of grief", as she found it, she missed only one instalment for *Blackwood's*, for May 1864. Stress, perhaps, was responsible for a few mistakes (the church architect is called first Folgate, then Finial), and for the weakness of the sub-plot, involving Frank, as it does, in unlikely misunderstandings. Fourteen years earlier Mrs Oliphant had sent her first novel, *Margaret Maitland*, to the stout old critic Francis Jeffrey; he told her it was true and touching, but "sensibly injured by the indifferent matter which has been admitted to bring it up to the standard of three volumes". The difficulty remained, the standard length was still demanded in the 1860s by publishers and booksellers, and she set herself to meet it. Certainly the story, with its comings and goings from house to house, moves slowly at times. But Mrs Oliphant, I think, is able to persuade the reader to her own pace, so that we can truly say at the close that we know what it is like to have lived in Carlingford.

Whatever we may think of the turns of the plot, she is at

her shrewdest in this book, and at the same time at her most human. Her refusal to moralise is striking, even disconcerting. It is here in particular that she stands comparison with Trollope, whose titles *Can You Forgive Her?* and *He Knew He Was Right* challenge readers not so much to judge as to refer to their own conscience. In *The Perpetual Curate* the worthless do not repent. Jack Wentworth, the *bon viveur*, seems on the point of sacrificing his inheritance but the old Squire tells him sharply to do his duty. Everyone is fallible. Young Rosa, who causes so many complications, looks as though she is going to be a helpless victim of society. She turns out to be nothing of the sort. Miss Wodehouse becomes not gentler, but tougher. In Chapter XLIII she is treasuring up an incident which might be useful to her in arguments with her future husband. Lucy, because she had made up her mind to sacrifice herself and marry Frank, even though it means being a poor man's wife, can't rejoice whole-heartedly at his success; it lessens her, she feels "a certain sense of pain". And when Frank speaks of poetic justice, Miss Leonora says, "I don't approve of a man ending off neatly like a novel in this sort of ridiculous way."

Frank Wentworth's story returns to the problem of *The Rector* and *Salem Chapel* – what does it mean for a man to call himself a priest? and, closely related to this – what can he do without the partnership of a woman? "Partnership" is the right word here. Frank learns that "even in Eden itself, though the dew had not yet dried on the leaves, it would be highly incautious for any man to conclude that he was sure of having his own way". After *The Perpetual Curate*, Mrs Oliphant turns to the women of Carlingford. Their power from the start has been an unknown quantity, not recognised, or perhaps not admitted. In the last two volumes of the Chronicle they will become the centre of their own stories.

Penelope Fitzgerald, London, 1986

CHAPTER 1.

CARLINGFORD is, as is well known, essentially a quiet place. There is no trade in the town, properly so called. To be sure, there are two or three small counting-houses at the other end of George Street, in that ambitious pile called Gresham Chambers; but the owners of these places of business live, as a general rule, in villas, either detached or semi-detached, in the North-end, the new quarter, which, as everybody knows, is a region totally unrepresented in society. In Carlingford proper there is no trade, no manufactures, no anything in particular, except very pleasant parties and a superior class of people — a very superior class of people, indeed, to anything one expects to meet with in a country town, which is not even a county town, nor the seat of any particular interest. It is the boast of the place that it has no particular interest — not even a public school: for no reason in the world but because they like it, have so many nice people collected together in those pretty houses in Grange Lane — which is, of course, a very much higher tribute to the town than if any special inducement had led them there. But in every community some centre of life is necessary. This point, round which everything circles, is, in Carlingford, found in the clergy. They are the administrators of the commonwealth, the only people who have defined and compulsory duties to give a sharp outline to life. Somehow this touch of necessity and business seems needful even in the most refined society: a man who is obliged to be somewhere at a certain hour, to do something at a certain time, and whose public duties are not volunteer proceedings, but indispensable work, has a certain position of command among a leisurely and unoccupied community, not to say that it is a public boon to have some one whom everybody knows and can talk of. The minister in Salem Chapel was everything in his little world. That respectable connection would not have hung together half so closely but for this perpetual subject of discussion, criticism, and patronage; and, to compare great things with small, society in Carlingford recognised in some degree the same human want. An enterprising or non-enterprising rector made all the difference in the world in Grange Lane; and in the absence of a rector that counted for anything (and poor Mr Proctor was of no earthly use, as everybody knows), it followed, as a natural consequence, that a great deal of the interest and influence of the position fell into the hands of the Curate of St Roque's.

But that position was one full of difficulties, as any one acquainted with the real state of affairs must see in a moment. Mr Wentworth's circumstances were, on the whole, as delicate and critical as can be imagined, both as respected his standing in Carlingford and the place he held in his own family – not to speak of certain other personal matters which were still more troublesome and vexatious. These last of course were of his own bringing on; for if a young man chooses to fall in love when he has next to nothing to live upon, trouble is sure to follow. He had quite enough on his hands otherwise without that crowning complication. When Mr Wentworth first came to Carlingford, it was in the days of Mr Bury, the Evangelical rector – his last days, when he had no longer his old vigour, and was very glad of "assistance," as he said, in his public and parish work. Mr Bury had a friendship of old standing with the Miss Wentworths of Skelmersdale, Mr Francis Wentworth's aunts; and it was a long time before the old Rector's eyes were opened to the astounding fact, that the nephew of these precious and chosen women held "views" of the most dangerous complexion,

and indeed was as near Rome as a strong and lofty
conviction of the really superior catholicity of the Anglican
Church would permit him to be. Before he found this out,
Mr Bury, who had unlimited confidence in preaching and
improving talk, had done all he could to get the young
man to "work," as the good Rector called it, and had
voluntarily placed all that difficult district about the canal
under the charge of the Curate of St Roque's. It is said
that the horror with which, after having just written to
Miss Leonora Wentworth to inform her what "a great
work" his young friend was doing among the bargemen,
Mr Bury was seized upon entering St Roque's itself for the
first time after the consecration, when the young priest
had arranged everything his own way, had a very bad
effect on his health, and hastened his end. And it is indeed
a fact that he died soon after, before he had time to issue
the interdict he intended against Mr Wentworth's further
exertions in the parish of Carlingford. Then came Mr
Proctor, who came into the town as if he had dropped from
the skies, and knew no more about managing a parish than
a baby; and under his exceptional incumbency Mr Wentworth became more than ever necessary to the peace of
the community. Now a new *régime* had been inaugurated.
Mr Morgan, a man whom Miss Wodehouse described as
"in the prime of life," newly married, with a wife also in
the prime of life, who had waited for him ten years, and all
that time had been under training for her future duties –
two fresh, new, active, clergymanly intellects, entirely
open to the affairs of the town, and intent upon general
reformation and sound management – had just come into
possession. The new Rector was making a great stir all
about him, as was natural to a new man; and it seemed, on
the whole, a highly doubtful business whether he and Mr
Wentworth would find Carlingford big enough to hold
them both.

"We could not have expected to begin quite without
difficulties," said Mrs Morgan, as she and her husband

discussed the question in the drawing-room of the Rectory. It was a pretty drawing-room, though Mr Proctor's taste was not quite in accordance with the principles of the new incumbent's wife: however, as the furniture was all new, and as the former rector had no further need for it, it was of course, much the best and most economical arrangement to take it as it stood – though the bouquets on the carpet were a grievance which nothing but her high Christian principles could have carried Mrs Morgan through. She looked round as she spoke, and gave an almost imperceptible shake of her head: she, too, had her share of disagreeables. "It would not look like Christ's work, dear," said the clergyman's wife, "if we had it all our own way."

"My dear, I hope I am actuated by higher motives than a desire to have it all my own way," said the Rector. "I always felt sure that Proctor would make a mess of any parish he took in hand, but I did not imagine he would have left it to anybody who pleased to work it. You may imagine what my feelings were to-day, when I came upon a kind of impromptu chapel in that wretched district near the canal. I thought it a Little Bethel, you know, of course; but instead of that, I find young Wentworth goes there Wednesdays and Fridays to do duty, and that there is service on Sunday evening, and I can't tell what besides. It may be done from a good motive – but such a disregard of all constituted authority," said the Rector, with involuntary vehemence, "can never, in my opinion, be attended by good results."

"Mr Wentworth, did you say?" said Mrs Morgan, upon whose female soul the Perpetual Curate's good looks and good manners had not been without a certain softening effect. "I am so sorry. I don't wonder you are vexed; but don't you think there must be some mistake, William? Mr Wentworth is so gentlemanly and nice – and of very good family, too. I don't think he would choose to set himself in opposition to the Rector. I think there must be some mistake."

"It's a very aggravating mistake, at all events," said Mr Morgan, rising and going to the window. It was, as we have said, a very pretty drawing-room, and the windows opened upon as pretty a bit of lawn as you could see, with one handsome cedar sweeping its dark branches majestically over delicious greensward; but some people did think it was too near George Street and the railway. Just at that moment a puff of delicate white vapour appeared over the wall, and a sudden express-train, just released from the cover of the station, sprang with a snort and bound across the Rector's view, very imperfectly veiled by the lime-trees, which were thin in their foliage as yet. Mr Morgan groaned and retreated – out of his first exaltation he had descended all at once, as people will do after building all their hopes upon one grand event, into great depression and vexation, when he found that, after all, this event did not change the face of existence, but indeed brought new proofs of mortality in the shape of special annoyances belonging to itself in its train. "On the whole," said the Rector, who was subject to fits of disgust with things in general, "I am tempted to think it was a mistake coming to Carlingford; the drawbacks quite overbalance the advantages. I did hesitate, I remember – it must have been my better angel: that is, my dear," he continued, recollecting himself, "I would have hesitated had it not been for you."

Here there ensued a little pause. Mrs Morgan was not so young as she had been ten years ago, all which time she had waited patiently for the Fellow of All-Souls, and naturally these ten years and the patience had not improved her looks. There was a redness on her countenance nowadays which was not exactly bloom; and it stretched across her cheeks, and over the point of her nose, as she was painfully aware, poor lady. She was silent when she heard this, wondering with a passing pang whether he was sorry? But being a thoroughly sensible woman, and above indulging in those little appeals by which foolish ones confuse the calm of matrimonial friendship, she did not express the momentary feeling. "Yes, William," she said, sympathetically, casting her eyes again on the objectionable carpet, and feeling that there *were* drawbacks even to her happiness as the wife of the Rector of Carlingford; "but I suppose every place has its disadvantages; and then there is such good society; and a town like this is the very place for your talents; and when affairs are in your own hands—"

"It is very easy talking," said the vexed Rector. "Society and everybody would turn upon me if I interfered with Wentworth – there's the vexation. The fellow goes about it as if he had a right. Why, there's a Provident Society and all sorts of things going on, exactly as if it were his own parish. What led me to the place was seeing some ladies in grey cloaks – exactly such frights as you used to make yourself, my dear - flickering about. He has got up a sisterhood, I have no doubt; and to find all this in full operation in one's own parish, without so much as being informed of it! and you know I don't approve of sister-hoods – never did; they are founded on a mistake."

"Yes, dear. I know I gave up as soon as I knew your views on that subject," said Mrs Morgan. "I daresay so will the ladies here. Who were they? Did you speak to them? or perhaps they belonged to St Roque's."

"Nobody belongs to St Roque's," said the Rector, con-temptuously – "it has not even a district. They were the two Miss Wodehouses."

Mrs Morgan was moved to utter a little cry. "And their father is churchwarden!" said the indignant woman. "Really, William, this is too much – without even consul-ting you! But it is easy to see how *that* comes about. Lucy Wodehouse and young Wentworth are—; well, I don't know if they are engaged – but they are always together, walking and talking, and consulting with each other, and so forth – a great deal more than I could approve of; but that poor elder sister, you know, has no authority – nor indeed any experience, poor thing," said the Rector's wife; "that's how it is, no doubt."

"Engaged!" said the Rector. He gave a kindly glance at his wife, and melted a little. "Engaged, are they? Poor little thing! I hope she'll be as good as you have been, my dear; but a young man may be in love without interfering with another man's parish. I can't forgive that," said Mr Morgan, recovering himself; "he must be taught to know better; and it is very hard upon a clergyman," continued the spiritual ruler of Carlingford, "that he cannot move in a matter like this without incurring a storm of godless criticism. If I were sending Wentworth out of my parish, I shouldn't wonder if the 'Times' had an article upon it, denouncing me as an indolent priest and bigot, that would neither work myself nor let my betters work; that's how these fellows talk."

"But nobody could say such things of you," said Mrs Morgan, firing up.

"Of me! they'd say them of St Paul, if he had ever been in the circumstances," said the Rector; "and I should just like to know what he would have done in a parish like this, with the Dissenters on one side, and a Perpetual Curate without a district meddling on the other. Ah, my dear," continued Mr Morgan, "I daresay they had their troubles in those days; but facing a governor or so now and then, or even passing a night in the stocks, is a very different thing from a showing-up in the 'Times,' not to speak of the complications of duty. Let us go out and call at Folgate's, and see whether he thinks anything can be done to the church."

"Dear, you wouldn't mind the 'Times' if it were your duty?" said the Rector's wife, getting up promptly to prepare for the walk.

"No, I suppose not," said Mr Morgan, not without a thrill of importance; "nor the stake," he added, with a little laugh, for he was not without a sense of humour; and the two went out to the architect's to ascertain the result of his cogitations over the church. They passed that sacred edifice in their way, and went in to gaze at it with a disgust which only an unhappy priest of high culture and aesthetic tastes, doomed to officiate in a building of the eighteenth century, of the churchwarden period of architecture, could fully enter into. "Eugh!" said Mr Morgan, looking round upon the high pews and stifling galleries with an expressive contraction of his features – his wife looked on sympathetic; and it was at this unlucky moment that the subject of their late conference made his appearance cheerfully from behind the ugly pulpit, in close conference with Mr Folgate. The pulpit was a three-storeyed mass, with the reading-desk and the clerk's desk beneath – a terrible eyesore to the Rector and his wife.

"I can fancy the expediency of keeping the place in repair," said the Curate of St Roque's, happy in the consciousness of possessing a church which, though not old, had been built by Gilbert Scott, and cheerfully unconscious of the presence of his listeners; "but to beautify a wretched old barn like this is beyond the imagination of man. Money can't do everything," said the heedless young man as he came lounging down the middle aisle, tapping contemptuously with his cane upon the high pew-doors. "I wonder where the people expected to go to who built Carlingford Church? Curious," continued the young Anglican, stopping in mid career, "to think of bestowing *consecration* upon anything so hideous. What a pass the world must have come to, Folgate, when this erection was counted worthy to be the house of God! After all, perhaps it is wrong to feel so strongly about it. The walls *are* consecrated, though they are ugly; we can't revoke the blessing. But no wonder it was an unchristian age."

"We have our treasure in earthen vessels," said Mr Morgan, somewhat sternly, from where he stood, under shelter of the heavy gallery. Mr Wentworth was shortsighted, like most people nowadays. He put up his glass hastily, and then hurried forward, perhaps just a little abashed. When he had made his salutations, however, he returned undismayed to the charge.

"It's a great pity you have not something better to work upon," said the dauntless Curate; "but it is difficult to conceive what can be done with such an unhallowed type of construction. I was just saying to Folgate—"

"There is a great deal of cant abroad on this subject," said Mr Morgan, interrupting the young oracle. "I like good architecture, but I don't relish attributing moral qualities to bricks and mortar. The hallowing influence ought to be within. Mr Folgate, we were going to call at your office. Have you thought of the little suggestions I ventured to make? Oh, the drawings are here. Mr Wentworth does not approve of them, I suppose?" said the Rector, turning sternly round upon the unlucky Curate of St Roque's.

"I can only say I sympathise with you profoundly," said young Wentworth, with great seriousness. "Such a terrible church must be a great trial. I wish I had any advice worth offering; but it is my hour for a short service down at the canal, and I can't keep my poor bargees waiting. Good morning. I hope you'll come and give us your countenance, Mrs Morgan. There's no end of want and trouble at Wharfside."

"Is Mr Wentworth aware, I wonder, that Wharfside is in the parish of Carlingford?" said the Rector, with involuntary severity, as the young priest withdrew calmly to go to his "duty." Mr Folgate, who supposed himself to be addressed, smiled, and said, "Oh yes, of course," and unfolded his drawings, to which the clerical pair before him lent a disturbed attention. They were both in a high state of indignation by this time. It seemed indispensable that something should be done to bring to his senses an intruder so perfectly composed and at his ease.

CHAPTER II.

MEANWHILE Mr Wentworth, without much thought of his sins, went down George Street, meaning to turn off at the first narrow turning which led down behind the shops and traffic, behind the comfort and beauty of the little town, to that inevitable land of shadow which always dogs the sunshine. Carlingford proper knew little about it, except that it increased the poor-rates, and now and then produced a fever. The minister of Salem Chapel was in a state of complete ignorance on the subject. The late Rector had been equally uninformed. Mr Bury, who was Evangelical, had the credit of disinterring the buried creatures there about thirty years ago. It was an office to be expected of that much-preaching man; but what was a great deal more extraordinary, was to find that the only people now in Carlingford who knew anything about Wharfside, except overseers of the poor and guardians of the public peace, were the Perpetual Curate of St Roque's – who had nothing particular to do with it, and who was regarded by many sober-minded persons with suspicion as a dilettante Anglican, given over to floral ornaments and ecclesiastical upholstery – and some half-dozen people of the very *élite* of society, principally ladies residing in Grange Lane.

Mr Wentworth came to a hesitating pause at the head of the turning which would have led him to Wharfside. He looked at his watch and saw there was half an hour to spare. He gave a wistful lingering look down the long line of garden-walls, pausing upon one point where the blossomed boughs of an apple-tree overlooked that enclosure.

There was quite time to call and ask if the Miss Wodehouses were going down to the service this afternoon; but
was it duty? or, indeed, putting that question aside, was it
quite right to compound matters with his own heart's
desire and the work he was engaged in, in this undeniable
fashion? The young priest crossed the street very slowly,
swinging his cane and knitting his brows as he debated the
question. If it had been one of the bargemen bringing his
sweetheart, walking with her along the side of the canal to
which Spring and sweet Easter coming on, and Love,
perhaps, always helpful of illusions, might convey a certain greenness and sentiment of nature – and echoing her
soft responses to the afternoon prayers – perhaps the
Curate might have felt that such devotion was not entirely
pure and simple. But somehow, before he was aware of it,
his slow footstep had crossed the line, and he found
himself in Grange Lane, bending his steps towards Mr
Wodehouse's door. For one thing, to be sure, the Can-
ticles in the evening service could always be sung when
Lucy's sweet clear voice was there to lead the uncertain
melody; and it was good to see her singing the 'Magnificat'
with that serious sweet face, "full of grace," like Mary's
own. Thinking of that, Mr Wentworth made his way
without any further hesitation to the green door over
which hung the apple-blossoms, totally untroubled in his
mind as to what the reverend pair were thinking whom he
had left behind him in the ugly church; and unconscious
that his impromptu chapel at Wharfside, with its little
carved reading-desk, and the table behind, contrived so as
to look suspiciously like an altar, was a thorn in anybody's
side. Had his mind been in a fit condition at that moment
to cogitate trouble, his thoughts would have travelled in a
totally different direction, but in the mean time Mr Wentworth was very well able to put aside his perplexities. The
green door opened just as he reached it, and Lucy and her
elder sister came out in those grey cloaks which the Rector
had slandered. They were just going to Wharfside to the

service, and of course they were surprised to see Mr
Wentworth, who did not knock at that green door more
than a dozen times in a week, on the average. The Curate
walked between the sisters on their way towards their
favourite "district." Such a position would scarcely have
been otherwise than agreeable to any young man. Dear
old Miss Wodehouse was the gentlest of chaperones. Old
Miss Wodehouse people called her, not knowing why –
perhaps because that adjective was sweeter than the harsh
one of middle age which belonged to her; and then there
was such a difference between her and Lucy. Lucy was
twenty, and in her sweetest bloom. Many people thought
with Mr Wentworth that there were not other two such
eyes in Carlingford. Not that they were brilliant or penetrating, but as blue as heaven, and as serene and pure. So
many persons thought, and the Perpetual Curate among
them. The grey cloak fell in pretty folds around that light
elastic figure; and there was not an old woman in the town
so tender, so helpful, so handy as Lucy where trouble was,
as all the poor people knew. So the three went down
Prickett's Lane, which leads from George Street towards
the canal – not a pleasant part of the town by any means;
and if Mr Wentworth was conscious of a certain haze of
sunshine all round and about him, gliding over the poor
pavement, and here and there transfiguring some baby
bystander gazing open-mouthed at the pretty lady, could
any reasonable man be surprised?

"I hope your aunts were quite well, Mr Wentworth,
when you heard from them last," said Miss Wodehouse,
"and all your people at home. In such a small family as
ours, we should go out of our wits if we did not hear every
day; but I suppose it is different where there are so many.
Lucy, when she goes from home," said the tender elder
sister, glancing at her with a half-maternal admiration –
"and she might always be visiting about if she liked –
writes to me every day."

"I have nobody who cares for me enough to write every

week," said the Curate, with a look which was for Lucy's
benefit. "I am not so lucky as you. My aunts are quite
well, Miss Wodehouse, and they think I had better go up
to town in May for the meetings," added Mr Wentworth,
with a passing laugh; "and the rest of my people are very
indignant that I am not of their way of thinking. There is
Tom Burrows on the other side of the street; he is trying to
catch *your* eye," said the Curate, turning round upon
Lucy; for the young man had come to such a pass that he
could not address her in an ordinary and proper way like
other people, but, because he dared not yet call her by her
Christian name as if she belonged to him, had a strange
rude way of indicating when he was speaking to her, by
emphasis and action. It was singularly different from his
usual good-breeding; but Lucy somehow rather liked it
than otherwise. "He is not going to church for the sake of
the service. He is going to please *you*. He has never
forgotten what you did for that little boy of his; and,
indeed, if you continue to go on so," said Mr Wentworth,
lowering his voice, and more than ever bending his tall
head to one side, "I shall have to put a stop to it somehow,
for I am not prepared, whatever people say, to go in at
once for *public* worship of the saints."

"I am going in here to call," said Lucy. She looked up
very innocently in the Curate's face. "I promised the poor
sick woman in the back room to see her every day, and I
could not get out any sooner. I daresay I shall be at the
schoolroom before you begin. Good-bye just now," said
the young Sister of Mercy. She went off all at once on this
provoking but unexceptionable errand, looking with calm
eyes upon the dismay which overspread the expressive
countenance of her spiritual guide. Mr Wentworth stood
looking after her for a moment, stunned by the unexpected movement. When he went on, truth compels us to own
that a thrill of disgust had taken the place of that vague
general sense of beatitude which threw beauty even upon
Prickett's Lane. The Curate gave but a sulky nod to the

salutation of Tom Burrows, and walked on in a savage mood by the side of Miss Wodehouse, around whom no nimbus of ideal glory hovered.

"I am always afraid of its being too much for her, Mr Wentworth," said the anxious elder sister; "it upsets me directly; but then I never was like Lucy – I can't tell where all you young people have learned it; we never used to be taught so in my day; and though I am twice as old as she is, I know I am not half so much good in the world," said the kind soul, with a gentle sigh. "I should like to see you in a parish of your own, where you would have it all your own way. I hope Mr Morgan won't be meddling when he comes to have time for everything. I should almost think he would – though it seems unkind to say it – by his face."

"I am doing nothing more than my duty," said the Perpetual Curate, in morose tones. "This district was given into my hands by the late Rector. Mr Morgan's face does not matter to me."

"But I should like to see you in a parish of your own," said Miss Wodehouse, meaning to please him. "You know papa always says so. St Roque's is very nice, but—"

"If you wish me out of the way, Miss Wodehouse, I am sorry to say you are not likely to be gratified," said the Curate, "for I have no more expectation of any preferment than you have. Such chances don't come in everybody's way."

"But I thought your aunts, Mr Wentworth—" said poor Miss Wodehouse, who unluckily did not always know when to stop.

"My aunts don't approve of my principles," answered Mr Wentworth, who had his own reasons for speaking with a little asperity. "They are more likely to have me denounced at Exeter Hall. I will join you immediately. I must speak to these men across the street;" and the Curate accordingly walked into a knot of loungers opposite, with a decision of manner which Lucy's desertion had helped

him to. Miss Wodehouse, thus left alone, went on with
lingering and somewhat doubtful steps. She was not used
to being in "the district" by herself. It disturbed her mild,
middle-aged habits to be left straying about here alone
among all these poor people, whom she looked at half
wistfully, half alarmed, feeling for them in her kind heart,
but not at all knowing how to get at them as the young
people did. The unruly children and gossiping mothers at
the poor doors discomposed her sadly, and she was not
near so sure that her grey cloak defended her from all
rudeness as she pretended to be when assenting to the
enthusiasm of Mr Wentworth and Lucy. She made tremulous haste to get out of this scene, which she was not
adapted for, to the shelter of the schoolroom, where, at
least, she would be safe. "We never were taught so in my
day," she said to herself, with an unexpressed wonder
which was right; but when she had reached that haven of
shelter, was seized with a little panic for Lucy, and went
out again and watched for her at the corner of the street,
feeling very uncomfortable. It was a great relief to see her
young sister coming down alert and bright even before she
was joined by Mr Wentworth, who had carried his point
with the men he had been talking to. To see them coming
down together, smiling to all those people at the doors who
disturbed the gentle mind of Miss Wodehouse with
mingled sentiments of sympathy and repulsion, bestowing
nods of greeting here and there, pausing even to say a
word to a few favoured clients, was a wonderful sight to
the timid maiden lady at the corner of the street. Twenty
years ago some such companion might have been by Miss
Wodehouse's side, but never among the poor people in
Prickett's Lane. Even with Lucy before her she did not
understand it. As the two came towards her, other
thoughts united with these in her kind soul. "I wonder
whether anything will ever come of it?" she said to herself,
and with that wandered into anxious reflections what this
difference could be between Mr Wentworth and his aunts:

which cogitations, indeed, occupied her till the service began, and perhaps disturbed her due appreciation of it; for if Lucy and Mr Wentworth got attached, as seemed likely, and Mr Wentworth did not get a living, what was to come of it? The thought made this tender-hearted spectator sigh: perhaps she had some experience of her own to enlighten her on such a point. At least it troubled, with sympathetic human cares, the gentle soul which had lost the confidence of youth.

As for the two most immediately concerned, they thought nothing at all about aunts or livings. Whether it is the divine influence of youth, or whether the vague un-acknowledged love which makes two people happy in each other's presence carries with it a certain inspiration, this at least is certain, that there is an absolute warmth of devotion arrived at in such moments, which many a soul, no longer happy, would give all the world to reach. Such crowds and heaps of blessings fall to these young souls! They said their prayers with all their hearts, not aware of deriving anything of that profound sweet trust and happiness from each other, but expanding over all the rude but reverend worshippers around them, with an unlimited faith in their improvement, almost in their perfection. This was what the wondering looker-on, scarcely able to keep her anxieties out of her prayers, could not understand, having forgotten, though she did not think so, the exaltation of that time of youth, as people do. She thought it all their goodness that they were able to put away their own thoughts; she did not know it was in the very nature of those unexpressed emotions to add the confidence of happiness to their prayers.

And after a while they all separated and went away back into the world and the everyday hours. Young Wentworth and Lucy had not said a syllable to each other, except about the people in "the district," and the Provident Society; and how that sober and laudable conversation could be called love-making, it would be difficult

for the most ardent imagination to conceive. He was to
dine with them that evening; so it was for but a very brief
time that they parted when the Perpetual Curate left the
ladies at the green door, and went away to his room, to
attend to some other duties, before he arrayed himself for
the evening. As for the sisters, they went in quite comfortably, and had their cup of tea before they dressed for
dinner. Lucy was manager indoors as well as out. She was
good for a great deal more than Miss Wodehouse in every
practical matter. It was she who was responsible for the
dinner, and had all the cares of the house upon her head.
Notwithstanding, the elder sister took up her prerogative
as they sat together in two very cosy easy-chairs, in a little
room which communicated with both their bed-chambers
up-stairs – a very cosy little odd room, not a dressing-room
nor a boudoir, but something between the two, where the
sisters had their private talks upon occasion, and which
was consecrated by many a libation of fragrant tea.

"Lucy, my dear," said Miss Wodehouse, whose gentle
forehead was puckered with care, "I want to speak to you.
I have not been able to get you out of my mind since ever
we met Mr Wentworth at the green door."

"Was there any need for getting me out of your mind?"
said smiling Lucy. "I was a safe enough inmate, surely. I
wonder how often I am out of your mind, Mary dear,
night or day."

"That is true enough," said Miss Wodehouse, "but you
know that is not what I meant either. Lucy, are you quite
sure you're going on just as you ought—"

Here she made a troubled pause, and looked in the
laughing face opposite, intent upon her with its startled
eyes. "What have I done?" cried the younger sister. Miss
Wodehouse shook her head with a great deal of seriousness.

"It always begins with laughing," said the experienced
woman; "but if it ends without tears it will be something
new to me. It's about Mr Wentworth, Lucy. You're

always together, day after day; and, my dear, such things can't go on without coming to something – what is to come of it? I have looked at it from every point of view, and I am sure I don't know."

Lucy flushed intensely red, of course, at the Curate's name; perhaps she had not expected it just at that moment; but she kept her composure like a sensible girl as she was.

"I thought it was the other side that were questioned about their intentions," she said. "Am I doing anything amiss? Mr Wentworth is the Curate of St Roque's, and I am one of the district-visitors, and we can't help seeing a great deal of each other so long as this work goes on at Wharfside. You wouldn't like to stop a great work because we are obliged to see a good deal of – of one particular person?" said Lucy, with youthful virtue, looking at her sister's face; at which tone and look Miss Wodehouse immediately faltered, as the culprit knew she must.

"No – oh no, no – to be sure not," said the disturbed monitor. "When you say that, I don't know how to answer you. It must be right, I suppose. I am quite sure it is wonderful to see such young creatures as you, and how you can tell the right way to set about it. But things did not use to be so in my young days. Girls dare not have done such things twenty years ago – not in Carlingford. Lucy," said Miss Wodehouse; "and, dear, I think you ought to be a little careful, for poor Mr Wentworth's sake."

"I don't think Mr Wentworth is in any particular danger," said Lucy, putting down her cup, with a slight curve at the corners of her pretty mouth – "and it is quite time for you to begin dressing. You know you don't like to be hurried, dear;" with which speech the young house-keeper got up from her easy-chair, gave her sister a kiss as she passed, and went away, singing softly, to her toilette. Perhaps there was a little flutter in Lucy's heart as she bound it round with her favourite blue ribbons. Perhaps it was this that gave a certain startled gleam to her blue eyes, and made even her father remark them when she went down-stairs – "It seems to me as if this child were growing rather pretty, Molly, eh? I don't know what other people think," said Mr Wodehouse – and perhaps Mr Wentworth, who was just being ushered into the drawing-room at the moment, heard the speech, for he, too, looked as if he had never found it out before. Luckily there was a party, and no opportunity for sentiment. The party was in honour of the Rector and his wife; and Mr Wentworth could not but be conscious before the evening was over that he had done something to lose the favour of his clerical brother. There was a good deal of Church talk, as was natural, at the churchwarden's table, where three clergymen were dining – for Mr Morgan's curate was there as well; and the Curate of St Roque's, who was slightly hot-tempered, could not help feeling himself disapproved of. It was not, on the whole, a satisfactory evening. Mr Morgan talked rather big, when the ladies went away, of his plans for the reformation of Carlingford. He went into statistics about the poor, and the number of people who attended no church, without taking any notice of that "great work" which Mr Wentworth knew to be going on at Wharfside. The Rector even talked of Wharfside, and of the necessity of exertion on behalf of that wretched district, with a studious unconsciousness of Mr Wentworth; and all but declined to receive better information when Mr Wodehouse proffered it. Matters were scarcely better in the drawing-room, where Lucy was entertaining everybody, and had no leisure for the Perpetual Curate. He took his hat with a gloomy sentiment of satisfaction when it was time to go away; but when the green door was closed behind him, Mr Wentworth, with his first step into the dewy darkness, plunged headlong into a sea of thought. He had to walk down the whole length of Grange Lane to his lodging, which was in the last house of the row, a small house in a small garden, where Mrs Hadwin, the widow of a whilom curate, was permitted by public opinion, on the score of her own unexceptionable propriety,* to receive a lodger without loss of position thereby. It was moonlight, or rather it ought to have been moonlight, and no lamps were lighted in Grange Lane, according to the economical regulations of Carlingford; and as Mr Wentworth pursued his way down the dark line of garden-walls, in the face of a sudden April shower which happened to be falling, he had full scope and opportunity for his thoughts.

These thoughts were not the most agreeable in the world. In the first place it must be remembered that for nearly a year past Mr Wentworth had had things his own way in Carlingford. He had been more than rector, he had been archdeacon, or rather bishop, in Mr Proctor's time; for that good man was humble, and thankful for the advice and assistance of his young brother, who knew so much better than he did. Now, to be looked upon as an un-authorised workman, a kind of meddling, Dissenterish, missionising individual, was rather hard upon the young man. And then he thought of his aunts. The connection, imperceptible to an ignorant observer, which existed between the Miss Wentworths and Mr Morgan, and Lucy, and many other matters interesting to their nephew, was a sufficiently real connection when you came to know it. That parish of his own which Miss Wodehouse had wished him – which would free the young clergyman from all trammels so far as his work was concerned; and would enable him to marry, and do everything for him – it was in the power of the Miss Wentworths to bestow; but they were Evangelical women, very public-spirited, and thinking nothing of their nephew in comparison with their duty; and he was at that time of life, and of that disposi-tion, which, for fear of being supposed to wish to deceive them, would rather exaggerate and make a display of the

---

*She was the daughter of old Sir Jasper Shelton, a poor family, but very respectable, and connected with the Westerns.

difference of his own views. Not for freedom, not for
Lucy, would the Perpetual Curate temporise and manage
the matter; so the fact was that he stood at the present
moment in a very perilous predicament. But for this
family living, which was, with their mother's property, in
the hands of her co-heiresses, the three Miss Wentworths,
young Frank Wentworth had not a chance of preferment
in the world; for the respectable Squire his father had
indulged in three wives and three families, and such a
regiment of sons that all his influence had been fully taxed
to provide for them. Gerald, the clergyman of the first lot,
held the family living – not a very large one – which
belonged to the Wentworths; and Frank, who was of the
second, had been educated expressly with an eye to
Skelmersdale, which belonged to his aunts. How he came
at the end to differ so completely from these excellent
ladies in his religious views is not our business just at
present; but in the mean time matters were in a very
critical position. The old incumbent of Skelmersdale was
eighty, and had been ill all winter; and if the Miss Wentworths were not satisfied somehow, it was all over with
their nephew's hopes.

Such were the thoughts that occupied his mind as he
walked down Grange Lane in the dark, past the tedious,
unsympathetic line of garden-walls, with the rain in his
face. The evening's entertainment had stirred up a great
many dormant sentiments. His influence in Carlingford
had been ignored by this new-comer, who evidently
thought he could do what he liked without paying any
attention to the Curate of St Roque's; and, what was a
great deal worse, he had found Lucy unapproachable, and
had realised, if not for the first time, still with more
distinctness than ever before, that she did not belong to
him, and that he had no more right than any other
acquaintance to monopolise her society. This last discovery was bitter to the young man – it was this that made
him set his face to the rain, and his teeth, as if that could

do any good. He had been happy in her mere society
to-day, without entering into any of the terrible preliminaries of a closer connection. But now that was over. She
did not belong to him, and he could not bear the thought.
And how was she ever to belong to him? Not, certainly, if
he was to be a Perpetual Curate of St Roque's, or anywhere else. He felt, in the misery of the moment, as if he
could never go to that green door again, or walk by her
sweet side to that service in which they had joined so
lately. He wondered whether she cared, with a despairing
pang of anxiety, through which for an instant a celestial
gleam of consciousness leaped, making the darkness all
the greater afterwards. And to think that three old ladies,
of whom it was not in the nature of things that the young
man could be profoundly reverent, should hold in their
hands the absolute power of his life, and could determine
whether it was to be sweet with hope and love, or stern,
constrained, and impoverished, without Lucy or any other
immediate light! What a strange anomaly this was which
met him full in the face as he pursued his thoughts! If it
had been his bishop, or his college, or any fitting tribunal –
but his aunts! Mr Wentworth's ring at his own door was so
much more hasty than usual that Mrs Hadwin paused in
the hall, when she had lighted her candle, to see if
anything was the matter. The little neat old lady held up
her candle to look at him as he came in, glistening all over
with rain-drops.

"I hope you are not wet, Mr Wentworth," she said. "It
is only an April shower, and we want it so much in the
gardens. And I hope you have had a nice party and a
pleasant evening."

"Thank you – pretty well," said the Perpetual Curate,
with less suavity than usual, and a sigh that nearly blew
Mrs Hadwin's candle out. She saw he was discomposed,
and therefore, with a feminine instinct, found more to say
than usual before she made her peaceful way to bed. She
waited while Mr Wentworth lighted his candle too.

"Mr Wodehouse's parties are always pleasant," she said. "I never go out, you know; but I like to hear of people enjoying themselves. I insist upon you going up-stairs before me, Mr Wentworth. I have so little breath to spare, and I take such a long time going up, that you would be tired to death waiting for me. Now, don't be polite. I insist upon you going up first. Thank you. Now I can take my time."

And she took her time accordingly, keeping Mr Wentworth waiting on the landing to say good-night to her, much to his silent exasperation. When he got into the shelter of his own sitting-room, he threw himself upon a sofa, and continued his thoughts with many a troubled addition. A young man, feeling in a great measure the world before him, conscious of considerable powers, standing on the very threshold of so much possible good and happiness, – it was hideous to look up, in his excited imagination, and see the figures of these three old ladies, worse than Fates, standing across the prospect and barring the way.

And Lucy, meantime, was undoing her blue ribbons with a thrill of sweet agitation in her untroubled bosom. Perhaps Mary was right, and it was about coming to the time when this half-feared, half-hoped revelation could not be postponed much longer. For it will be perceived that Lucy was not in much doubt of young Wentworth's sentiments. And then she paused in the dark, after she had said her prayers, to give one timid thought to the sweet life that seemed to lie before her so close at hand – in which, perhaps, he and she were to go out together, she did not know where, for the help of the world and the comfort of the sorrowful; and not trusting herself to look much at that ideal, said another prayer, and went to sleep like one of God's beloved, with a tear too exquisite to be shed brimming under her long eyelashes. At this crisis of existence, perhaps for once in her life, the woman has the best of it; for very different from Lucy's were the thoughts with which the Curate sought his restless pillow, hearing the rain drip all the night, and trickle into Mrs Hadwin's reservoirs. The old lady had a passion for rain-water, and it was a gusty night.

CHAPTER III.

NEXT week was Passion Week, and full of occupation. Even if it had been consistent either with Mr Wentworth's principles or Lucy's to introduce secular affairs into so holy a season, they had not time or opportunity, as it happened, which was perhaps just as well; for otherwise the premonitory thrill of expectation which had disturbed Lucy's calm, and the bitter exasperation against himself and his fate with which Mr Wentworth had discovered that he dared not say anything, might have caused an estrangement between them. As it was, the air was thundery and ominous through all the solemn days of the Holy Week. A consciousness as of something about to happen overshadowed even the "district," and attracted the keen observation of the lively spectators at Wharfside. They were not greatly up in matters of doctrine, nor perhaps did they quite understand the eloquent little sermon which the Perpetual Curate gave them on Good Friday in the afternoon, between his own services, by way of impressing upon their minds the awful memories of the day; but they were as skilful in the variations of their young evangelist's looks, and as well qualified to decide upon the fact that there was "a something between" him and Miss Lucy Wodehouse, as any practised observer in the higher ranks of society. Whether the two had "'ad an unpleasantness," as, Wharfside was well aware, human

creatures under such circumstances are liable to have, the
interested community could not quite make out; but that
something more than ordinary was going on, and that the
prettiest of all the "Provident ladies" had a certain preoccupation in her blue eyes, was a fact perfectly apparent
to that intelligent society. And, indeed, one of the kinder
matrons in Prickett's Lane had even ventured so far as to
wish Miss Lucy "a 'appy weddin' when the time comes."
"And there's to be a sight o' weddings this Easter," had
added another, who was somewhat scandalised by the
flowers in the bonnet of one of the brides-elect, and
proceeded to say so in some detail. "But Miss Lucy won't
wear no bonnet; the quality goes in veils: and there never
was as full a church as there will be to see it, wishing you
your 'ealth and 'appiness, ma'am, as aint no more nor you
deserve, and you so good to us poor folks." All which
felicitations and inquiries had confused Lucy, though she
made her way out of them with a self-possession which
amazed her sister.

"You see what everybody thinks, dear," said that
gentle woman, when they had made their escape.

"Oh, Mary, how can you talk of such things at such a
time?" the young Sister of Mercy had answered once
more, turning those severe eyes of youthful devotion upon
her troubled elder sister, who, to tell the truth, not having
been brought up to it, as she said, felt much the same on
Easter Eve as at other times of her life; and thus once
more the matter concluded. As for Mr Wentworth, he was
much occupied on that last day of the Holy Week with a
great many important matters on hand. He had not seen
the Wodehouses since the Good Friday evening service,
which was an interval of about twenty hours, and had just
paused, before eating his bachelor's dinner, to ponder
whether it would be correct on that most sacred of vigils to
steal away for half an hour, just to ask Lucy if she thought
it necessary that he should see the sick woman at No. 10
Prickett's Lane before the morning. It was while he was

pondering this matter in his mind that Mr Wentworth's
heart jumped to his throat upon receipt, quite suddenly,
without preparation, of the following note:–

"MY DEAREST BOY, – Your aunts Cecilia, Leonora, and
I have just arrived at this excellent inn, the Blue Boar.
Old Mr Shirley at Skelmersdale is in a very bad way, poor
man, and I thought the *very best* thing I could do in my
dearest Frank's *best* interests, was to persuade them to
make you *quite* an *unexpected visit*, and see everything for
themselves. I am in a terrible fright now lest I should have
done wrong; but my dear, dear boy knows it is always his
interest that I have at heart; and Leonora is so intent on
having a *real gospel minister* at Skelmersdale, that she
never would have been content with anything less than
hearing you with her own ears. I hope and trust in
Providence that you don't intone like poor Gerald. And
oh, Frank, my dear boy, come directly and dine with us,
and don't fly in your aunt Leonora's face, and tell me I
haven't been imprudent. I thought it would be best to take
you unawares when you had everything prepared, and
when we should see you just as you always are; for I am
convinced Leonora and you only want to see more of each
other to understand each other perfectly. Come, my
dearest boy, and give a little comfort to your loving and
anxious

"AUNT DORA."

Mr Wentworth sat gazing blankly upon this horrible
missive for some minutes after he had read it, quite
unaware of the humble presence of the maid who stood
asking, Please was she to bring up dinner? When he came
to himself, the awful "No!" with which he answered that
alarmed handmaiden almost drove her into hysterics as
she escaped down-stairs. However, Mr Wentworth
immediately put his head out at the door and called after
her, "I can't wait for dinner, Sarah; I am suddenly called

out, and shall dine where I am going. Tell Cook," said the
young parson, suddenly recollecting Lucy's client, "to
send what she has prepared for me, if it is very nice, to
No. 10 Prickett's Lane. My boy will take it; and send him
off directly, please," with which last commission the
young man went up despairingly to his bedroom to prepare himself for this interview with his aunts. What was he
to do? Already before him, in dreadful prophetic vision,
he saw all three seated in one of the handsome open
benches in St Roque's, looking indescribable horrors at
the crown of spring lilies which Lucy's own fingers were to
weave for the cross above the altar, and listening to the
cadence of his own manly tenor as it rang through the
perfect little church of which he was so proud. Yes, there
was an end of Skelmersdale, without any doubt or
question now; whatever hope there might have been, aunt
Dora had settled the matter by this last move of hers – an
end to Skelmersdale, and an end of Lucy. Perhaps he had
better try not to see her any more; and the poor young
priest saw that his own face looked ghastly as he looked at
it in the glass. It gave him a little comfort to meet the boy
with a bundle pinned up in snowy napkins, from which a
grateful odour ascended, bending his steps to Prickett's
Lane, as he himself went out to meet his fate. It was a
last offering to that beloved "district" with which the
image of his love was blended; but he would have given
his dinner to Lucy's sick woman any day. To-night it was a
greater sacrifice that was to be required of him. He went
mournfully and slowly up Grange Lane, steeling himself
for the encounter, and trying to forgive aunt Dora in his
heart. It was not very easy. Things might have turned out
just the same without any interference – that was true; but
to have it all brought on in this wanton manner by a kind
foolish woman, who would wring her hands and gaze in
your face, and want to know, Oh! did you think it was
her fault? after she had precipitated the calamity, was
very hard; and it was with a very gloomy countenance,

accordingly, that the Curate of St Roque's presented
himself at the Blue Boar.

The Miss Wentworths were in the very best sitting-
room which the Blue Boar contained – the style in which
they travelled, with a man and two maids, was enough to
secure that; and the kitchen of that respectable establishment was doing its very best to send up a dinner worthy of
"a party as had their own man to wait." The three ladies
greeted their nephew with varying degrees of enthusiasm.
The eldest, Miss Wentworth, from whom he took his
second name Cecil, did not rise from her chair, but nevertheless kissed him in an affectionate dignified way when
he was brought to her. As for aunt Dora, she ran into her
dear Frank's arms, and in the very moment of that
embrace whispered in his ear the expression of her
anxiety, and the panic which always followed those rash
steps which she was in the habit of taking. "Oh, my dear, I
hope you don't think I'm to blame," she said, with her lips
at his ear, and gained but cold comfort from the Curate's
face. The alarming member of the party was Miss
Leonora. She rose and made two steps forward to meet the
unfortunate young man. She shook both his hands cor-
dially, and said she was very glad to see him, and hoped he
was well. She was the sensible sister of the three, and no
doubt required all the sense she had to manage her companions. Miss Wentworth, who had been very pretty in her
youth, was now a beautiful old lady, with snow-white hair
and the most charming smile; and Miss Dora, who was only
fifty, retained the natural colour of her own scanty light-
brown locks, which wavered in weak-minded ringlets over
her cheeks; but Miss Leonora was iron-grey, without any
complexion in particular, and altogether a harder type of
woman. It was she who held in her hands the fate of
Skelmersdale and of Frank Wentworth. Her terrible
glance it was which he had imagined gleaming fierce upon
his lilies – Lucy's lilies, his Easter decorations. It was by
her side the alarmed Curate was made to sit down. It was

she who took the foot of the table, and was the gentleman of the house. Her voice was of that class of voice which may be politely called a powerful contralto. Every way she was as alarming a critic as ever was encountered by a Perpetual Curate, or any other young man in trouble. Mr Wentworth said feebly that this was a very unexpected pleasure, as he met his aunt Leonora's eye.

"I hope it *is* a pleasure," said that penetrating observer. "To tell the truth, I did not expect it would be; but your aunt Dora thought so, and you know, when she sets her heart on anything, nobody can get any peace. Not that your aunt Cecilia and I would have come on that account, if we had not wished, for many reasons, to have some conversation with you, and see how you are getting on."

"Quite so, Leonora," said Miss Wentworth, smiling upon her nephew, and leaning back in her chair.

Then there was a little pause; for, after such a terrible address, it was not to be expected that the poor man, who understood every word of it, could repeat his common-place about the unlooked-for pleasure. Miss Dora of course seized the opportunity to rush in.

"We have been hearing such delightful things about you, my dear, from the people of the house. Leonora is so pleased to hear how you are labouring among the people, and doing your Master's work. We take all the happiness to ourselves, because, you know, you are *our* boy, Frank," said the anxious aunt, all her thin ringlets, poor lady, trembling with her eagerness to make everything comfortable for her favourite; "and we have come, you know, specially to hear you on Easter Sunday in your own church. I am looking forward to a great treat: to think I should never have heard you, though it is so long since you were ordained! None of us have ever heard you – not even Leonora; but it is such a pleasure to us all to know you are so much liked in Carlingford," cried the troubled woman, growing nervous at sight of the unresponsive quiet around her. Miss Leonora by no means replied to the covert appeals thus made to her. She left her nephew and her sister to keep up the conversation unassisted; and as for Miss Wentworth, conversation was not her forte.

"I'm afraid, aunt, you will not *hear* anything worth such a long journey," said Mr Wentworth, moved, like a rash young man as he was, to display his colours at once, and cry no surrender. "I don't think an Easter Sunday is a time for much preaching; and the Church has made such ample provision for the expression of our sentiments. I am more of a humble priest than an ambitious preacher," said the young man, with characteristic youthful pretence of the most transparent kind. He looked in Miss Leonora's face as he spoke. He knew the very name of priest was an offence in its way to that highly Evangelical woman; and if they were to come to single combat, better immediately than after intolerable suspense and delay.

"Perhaps, Dora, you will postpone your raptures about Frank's sermon – which may be a very indifferent sermon, as he says, for anything we can tell – till after dinner," said Miss Leonora. "We're all very glad to see him; and he need not think any little ill-tempered speeches he may make will disturb me. I daresay the poor boy would be glad to hear of some of the people belonging to him instead of all that nonsense. Come to dinner, Frank. Take the other side of the table, opposite Dora; and now that you've said grace, I give you full leave to forget that you're a clergyman for an hour at least. We were down at the old Hall a week ago, and saw your father and the rest. They are all well; and the last boy is rather like you, if you will think that any compliment. Mrs Wentworth is pleased, because you are one of the handsome ones, you know. Not much fear of the Wentworths dying out of the country yet awhile. Your father is getting at his wit's end, and does not know what to do with Cuthbert and Guy. Three sons are enough in the army, and two at sea; and I rather think it's as much as we can stand," continued Miss Leonora, not without a gleam of humour in her iron-grey eyes, "to have two in the Church."

"That is as it may happen," said the Perpetual Curate, with a little spirit. "If the boys are of my way of thinking, they will consider the Church the highest of professions; but Guy and Cuthbert must go to Australia, I suppose, like most other people, and take their chance – no harm in that."

"Not a bit of harm," said the rich aunt; "they're good boys enough, and I daresay they'll get on. As for Gerald, if you have any influence with your brother, I think he's in a bad way. I think he has a bad attack of Romishness coming on. If you are not in that way yourself," said Miss Leonora, with a sharp glance, "I think you should go and see after Gerald. He is the sort of man who would do anything foolish, you know. He doesn't understand what prudence means. Remember, I believe he is a good Christian all the same. It's very incomprehensible; but the fact is, a man may be a very good Christian, and have the least quality of sense that is compatible with existence. I've seen it over and over again. Gerald's notions are idiocy to me," said the sensible but candid woman, shrugging her shoulders; "but I can't deny that he's a good man, for all that."

"He is the best man I ever knew," said young Wentworth, with enthusiasm.

"Quite so, Frank," echoed aunt Cecilia, with her sweet smile: it was almost the only conversational effort Miss Wentworth ever made.

"But it is so sad to see how he's led away," said Miss Dora; "it is all owing to the bad advisers young men meet with at the universities; and how can it be otherwise as long as tutors and professors are chosen just for their learning, without any regard to their principles? What is Greek and Latin in comparison with a pious guide for the young? We would not have to feel frightened, as we do so often, about young men's principles," continued aunt Dora, fixing her eyes with warning significance on her nephew, and trying hard to open telegraphic communications with him, "if more attention was paid at the universities to give them sound guidance in their studies. So long as you are sound in your principles, there is no fear of you," said the timid diplomatist, trying to aid the warning look of her eyes by emphasis and inflection. Poor Miss Dora! it was her unlucky fate, by dint of her very exertions in smoothing matters, always to make things worse.

"He would be a bold man who would call those principles unsound which have made my brother Gerald what he is," said, with an affectionate admiration that became him, the Curate of St Roque's.

"It's a slavish system, notwithstanding Gerald," said Miss Leonora, with some heat; "and a false system, and leads to Antichrist at the end and nothing less. Eat your dinner, Frank – we are not going to argue just now. We expected to hear that another of the girls was engaged before we came away, but it has not occurred yet. I don't approve of young men dancing about a house for ever and ever, unless they mean something. Do you?"

Mr Wentworth faltered at this question; it disturbed his composure more than anything that had preceded it. "I – really I don't know," he said, after a pause, with a sickly smile – of which all three of his aunts took private notes, forming their own conclusions. It was, as may well be supposed, a very severe ordeal which the poor young man had to go through. When he was permitted to say goodnight, he went away with a sensation of fatigue more overpowering than if he had visited all the houses in Wharfside. When he passed the green door, over which the apple-tree rustled in the dark, it was a pang to his heart. How was he to continue to live – to come and go through that familiar road– to go through all the meetings and partings, when this last hopeless trial was over, and Lucy and he were swept apart as if by an earthquake? If his lips were sealed henceforward, and he never was at liberty to say what was in his heart, what would she think of him? He could not fly from his work because he lost Skelmersdale; and how was he to bear it? He went home

with a dull bitterness in his mind, trying, when he thought
of it, to quiet the aching pulses which throbbed all over
him, with what ought to have been the hallowed associations of the last Lenten vigil. But it was difficult, throbbing
as he was with wild life and trouble to the very finger-
points, to get himself into the shadow of that rock-hewn
grave, by which, according to his own theory, the Church
should be watching on this Easter Eve. It was hard just
then to be bound to that special remembrance. What he
wanted at this moment was no memory of one hour,
however memorable or glorious, not even though it contained the Redeemer's grave, but the sense of a living
Friend standing by him in the great struggle, which is the
essential and unfailing comfort of a Christian's life.

Next morning he went to church with a half-conscious,
youthful sense of martyrdom, of which in his heart he was
half ashamed. St Roque's was very fair to see that Easter
morning. Above the communion-table, with all its sacred
vessels, the carved oaken cross of the reredos was
wreathed tenderly with white fragrant festoons of spring
lilies, sweet Narcissus of the poets; and Mr Wentworth's
choristers made another white line, two deep, down each
side of the chancel. The young Anglican took in all the
details of the scene on his way to the reading-desk as the
white procession ranged itself in the oaken stalls. At that
moment — the worst moment for such a thought — it
suddenly flashed over him that, after all, a wreath of
spring flowers or a chorister's surplice was scarcely worth
suffering martyrdom for. This horrible suggestion, true
essence of an unheroic age, which will not suffer a man to
be absolutely sure of anything, disturbed his prayer as he
knelt down in silence to ask God's blessing. Easter, to be
sure, was lovely enough of itself without the garland, and
Mr Wentworth knew well enough that his white-robed
singers were no immaculate angel-band. It was Satan
himself, surely, and no inferior imp, who shot that sudden
arrow into the young man's heart as he tried to say his
private prayer; for the Curate of St Roque's was not only a

fervent Anglican, but also a young Englishman *sans reproche*, with all the sensitive, almost fantastic, delicacy of honour which belongs to that development of humanity; and not for a dozen worlds would he have sacrificed a lily or a surplice on this particular Easter, when all his worldly hopes hung in the balance. But to think at this crowning moment that a villanous doubt of the benefit of these surplices and lilies should seize his troubled heart! for just then the strains of the organ died away in lengthened whispers, and Miss Leonora Wentworth, severe and awful, swept up through the middle aisle. It was under these terrible circumstances that the Perpetual Curate, with his heart throbbing and his head aching, began to intone the morning service on that Easter Sunday, ever after a day so memorable in the records of St Roque's.

CHAPTER IV.

MR WENTWORTH's sermon on Easter Sunday was one which he himself long remembered, though it is doubtful whether any of his congregation had memories as faithful. To tell the truth, the young man put a black cross upon it with his blackest ink, a memorial of meaning unknown to anybody but himself. It was a curious little sermon, such as may still be heard in some Anglican pulpits. Though he had heart and mind enough to conceive something of those natural depths of divine significance and human interest, which are the very essence of the Easter festival, it was not into these that Mr Wentworth entered in his sermon. He spoke, in very choice little sentences, of the beneficence of the Church in appointing such a feast, and of all the beautiful arrangements she had made for the keeping of it. But even in the speaking, in the excited state of mind he was in, it occurred to the young man to see, by a sudden flash of illumination, how much higher, how much more catholic, after all, his teaching would have been, could he but have once ignored the Church, and gone direct, as Nature bade, to that empty grave in which all the hopes of humanity had been entombed. He saw it by gleams of that perverse light which seemed more Satanic than heavenly in the moments it chose for shining, while he was preaching his little sermon about the Church and her beautiful institution of Easter, just as he had seen the non-importance of his lily-wreath and surplices as he was about to suffer martyrdom for them. All these circumstances were hard upon the young man. Looking down straight into the severe iron-grey eyes of his aunt Leonora, he could not of course so much as modify a single sentence of the discourse he was uttering, no more than he could permit himself to slur over a single monotone of the service; but that sudden bewildering perception that he could have done so much better – that the loftiest High-Churchism of all might have been consistent enough with Skelmersdale, had he but gone into the heart of the matter – gave a bitterness to the deeper, unseen current of the Curate's thoughts.

Besides, it was terrible to feel that he could not abstract himself from personal concerns even in the most sacred duties. He was conscious that the two elder sisters went away, and that only poor aunt Dora, her weak-minded ringlets limp with tears, came tremulous to the altar rails. When the service was over, and the young priest was disrobing himself, she came to him and gave a spasmodic, sympathetic, half-reproachful pressure to his hand. "Oh, Frank, my dear, I did it for the best," said Miss Dora, with a doleful countenance; and the Perpetual Curate knew that his doom was sealed. He put the best face he could upon the matter, having sufficient doubts of his own wisdom to subdue the high temper of the Wentworths for that moment at least.

"What was it you did for the best?" said the Curate of St Roque's. "I suppose, after all, it was no such great matter *hearing* me as you thought; but I told you I was not an ambitious preacher. This is a day for worship, not for talk."

"Ah! yes," said Miss Dora; "but oh, Frank, my dear, it is hard upon me, after all my expectations. It would have been so nice to have had you at Skelmersdale. I hoped you would marry Julia Trench, and we should all have been so happy; and perhaps if I had not begged Leonora to come just now, thinking it would be so nice to take you just in your usual way – but she must have known sooner or later," said poor aunt Dora, looking wistfully in his face. "Oh, Frank, I hope you don't think I'm to blame."

"I never should have married Julia Trench," said the Curate, gloomily. He did not enter into the question of Miss Dora's guilt or innocence – he gave a glance at the lilies on the altar, and a sigh. The chances were he would never marry anybody, but loyalty to Lucy demanded instant repudiation of any other possible bride. "Where are you going, aunt Dora; back to the Blue Boar? or will you come with me?" he said, as they stood together at the door of St Roque's. Mr Wentworth felt as if he had caught the beginning threads of a good many different lines of thought, which he would be glad to be alone to work out.

"You'll come back with me to the inn to lunch?" said Miss Dora. "Oh, Frank, my dear, remember your Christian feelings, and don't make a breach in the family. It will be bad enough to face your poor dear father, after he knows what Leonora means to do; and I do so want to talk to you," said the poor woman, eagerly clinging to his arm. "You always were fond of your poor aunt Dora, Frank; when you were quite a little trot you used always to like me best; and in the holiday times, when you came down from Harrow, I used always to hear all your troubles. If you would only have confidence in me now!"

"But what if I have no troubles to confide?" said Mr Wentworth; "a man and a boy are very different things. Come, aunt Dora, I'll see you safe to your inn. What

should I have to grumble about? I have plenty to do, and
it is Easter; and few men can have everything their own
way."

"You won't acknowledge that you're vexed," said aunt
Dora, almost crying under her veil, "but I can see it all the
same. You always were such a true Wentworth; but if you
only would give in and say that you are disappointed and
angry with us all, I could bear it better, Frank. I would
not feel then that you thought it my fault! And oh, Frank,
dear, you don't consider how disappointed your poor dear
aunt Leonora was! It's just as hard upon us," she continued, pressing his arm in her eagerness, "as it is upon
you. We had all so set our hearts on having you at
Skelmersdale. Don't you think, if you were giving your
mind to it, you might see things in a different light?" with
another pressure of his arm. "Oh, Frank, what does it
matter, after all, if the heart is right, whether you read the
service in your natural voice, or give that little quaver at
the end? I am sure, for my part—"

"My dear aunt," said Mr Wentworth, naturally incensed by this manner of description, "I must be allowed to
say that my convictions are fixed, and not likely to be
altered. I am a priest, and you are – a woman." He
stopped short, with perhaps a little bitterness. It was very
true she was a woman, unqualified to teach, but yet she
and her sisters were absolute in Skelmersdale. He made a
little gulp of his momentary irritation, and walked on in
silence, with Miss Dora's kind wistful hand clinging to his arm.

"But, dear Frank among us Protestants, you know,
there is no sacerdotal caste," said Miss Dora, opportunely
recollecting some scrap of an Exeter Hall speech. "We are
all kings and priests to God. Oh, Frank, it is Gerald's
example that has led you away. I am sure, before you
went to Oxford you were never at all a ritualist – even
Leonora thought you such a pious boy; and I am sure your
good sense must teach you—" faltered aunt Dora, trying
her sister's grand tone.

"Hush, hush; I can't have you begin to argue with me;

you are not my aunt Leonora," said the Curate, half amused in spite of himself. This encouraged the anxious woman, and, clasping his arm closer than ever, she poured out all her heart.

"Oh, Frank, if you could only modify your views a little! It is not that there is any difference between your views and ours, except just in words, my dear. Flowers are very pretty decorations, and I know you look very nice in your surplice; and I am sure, for my part, I should not mind – but then that is not carrying the Word of God to the people, as Leonora says. If the heart is right, what does it matter about the altar?" said aunt Dora, unconsciously falling upon the very argument that had occurred to her nephew's perplexed mind in the pulpit. "Even though I was in such trouble, I can't tell you what a happiness it was to take the sacrament from your hands, my dear, dear boy; and but for these flowers and things that could do nobody any good, poor dear Leonora, who is very fond of you, though perhaps you don't think it, could have had that happiness too. Oh, Frank, don't you think you could give up these things that don't matter? If you were just to tell Leonora you have been thinking it over, and that you see you've made a mistake, and that in future—"

"You don't mean to insult me?" said the young man. "Hush – hush; you don't know what you are saying. Not to be made Archbishop of Canterbury, instead of Vicar of Skelmersdale. I don't understand how you could suggest such a thing to me."

Miss Dora's veil, which she had partly lifted, here fell over her face, as it had kept doing all the time she was speaking – but this time she did not put it back. She was no longer able to contain herself, but wept hot tears of distress and vexation, under the flimsy covering of lace. "No, of course, you will not do it – you will far rather be haughty, and say it is my fault," said poor Miss Dora. "We have all so much pride, we Wentworths – and you never think of our disappointment, and how we all calculated upon having you at Skelmersdale, and how

happy we were to be, and that you were to marry Julia
Trench—"

It was just at this moment that the two reached the corner
of Prickett's Lane. Lucy Wodehouse had been down there
seeing the sick woman. She had, indeed, been carrying
her dinner to that poor creature, and was just turning into
Grange Lane, with her blue ribbons hidden under the
grey cloak, and a little basket in her hand. They met full
in the face at this corner, and Miss Dora's words reached
Lucy's ears, and went through and through her with a
little nervous thrill. She had not time to think whether it
was pain or only surprise that moved her, and was not
even self-possessed enough to observe the tremulous pressure of the Curate's hand, as he shook hands with her, and
introduced his aunt. "I have just been to see the poor
woman at No. 10," said Lucy. "She is very ill to-day. If
you had time, it would be kind of you to see her. I think
she has something on her mind."

"I will go there before I go to Wharfside," said Mr
Wentworth. "Are you coming down to the service this
afternoon? I am afraid it will be a long service, for there
are all these little Burrowses, you know—"

"Yes, I am godmother," said Lucy, and smiled and
gave him her hand again as she passed him while aunt
Dora looked on with curious eyes. The poor Curate
heaved a mighty sigh as he looked after the grey cloak.
Not his the privilege now, to walk with her to the green
door, to take her basket from the soft hand of the merciful
Sister. On the contrary, he had to turn his back upon
Lucy, and walk on with aunt Dora to the inn – at this
moment a symbolical action which seemed to embody his
fate.

"Where is Wharfside? and who are the little Burrowses?
and what does the young lady mean by being godmother?"
said aunt Dora. "She looks very sweet and nice; but what is
the meaning of that grey cloak? Oh, Frank, I hope you
don't approve of nunneries, and that sort of thing. It is such
foolishness. My dear, the Christian life is very hard, as

your aunt Leonora always says. She says she can't bear to see people playing at Christianity—"

"People should not' speak of things they don't understand," said the Perpetual Curate. "Your Exeter-Hall men, aunt Dora, are like the old ascetics – they try to make a merit of Christianity by calling it hard and terrible; but there are some sweet souls in the world, to whom it comes natural as sunshine in May." And the young Anglican, with a glance behind him from the corner of his eye, followed the fair figure, which he believed he was never, with a clear conscience, to accompany any more. "Now, here is your inn," he said, after a little pause. "Wharfside is a district, where I am going presently to conduct service, and the little Burrowses are a set of little heathens, to whom I am to administer holy baptism this Easter Sunday. Good-bye just now."

"Oh, Frank, my dear, just come in for a moment, and tell Leonora – it will show her how wrong she is," said poor aunt Dora, clinging to his arm.

"Right or wrong, I am not going into any controversy. My aunt Leonora knows perfectly well what she is doing," said the Curate, with the best smile he could muster; and so shook hands with her resolutely, and walked back again all the way down Grange Lane, past the green door, to his own house. Nobody was about the green door at that particular moment to ask him in to luncheon, as sometimes happened. He walked down all the way to Mrs Hadwin's, with something of the sensations of a man who has just gone through a dreadful operation, and feels, with a kind of dull surprise after, that everything around him is just the same as before. He had come through a fiery trial, though nobody knew of it; and just at this moment, when he wanted all his strength, how strange to feel that haunting sense of an unnecessary sacrifice – that troubled new vein of thought which would be worked out, and which concerned matters more important than Skelmersdale, weighty as that was. He took his sermon out of his pocket when he got home, and marked a cross upon it, as we have

already said; but, being still a young man, he was thankful
to snatch a morsel of lunch, and hasten out again to his
duty, instead of staying to argue the question with himself. He went to No. 10 Prickett's Lane, and was a long
time with the sick woman, listening to all the woeful tale of
a troubled life, which the poor sick creature had been
contemplating for days and days, in her solitude, through
those strange exaggerated death-gleams which Miss
Leonora would have called "the light of eternity." She
remembered all sorts of sins, great and small, which filled
her with nervous terrors; and it was not till close upon the
hour for the Wharfside service, that the Curate could leave
his tremulous penitent. The schoolroom was particularly
full that day. Easter, perhaps, had touched the hearts – it
certainly had refreshed the toilettes – of the bargemen's
wives and daughters. Some of them felt an inward conviction that their new ribbons were undoubtedly owing to the
clergyman's influence, and that Tom and Jim would have
bestowed the money otherwise before the Church planted
her pickets in this corner of the enemy's camp; and the
conviction, though not of an elevated description, was a
great deal better than no conviction at all. Mr Wentworth's little sermon to them was a great improvement
upon his sermon at St Roque's. He told them about the
empty grave of Christ, and how He called the weeping
woman by her name, and showed her the earnest of the
end of all sorrows. There were some people who cried,
thinking of the dead who were still waiting for Easter,
which was more than anybody did when Mr Wentworth
discoursed upon the beautiful institutions of the Church's
year; and a great many of the congregation stayed to see
Tom Burrows's six children come up for baptism, preceded
by the new baby, whose infant claims to Christianity the
Curate had so strongly insisted upon, to the wakening of a
fatherly conscience in the honest bargeman. Lucy
Wodehouse, without her grey cloak, stood at the font,
holding that last tiny applicant for saving grace, while all
the other little heathens were signed with the sacred cross.

And strangely enough, when the young priest and the young woman stood so near each other, solemnly pledging, one after another, each little sun-browned, round-eyed pagan to be Christ's faithful servant and soldier, the cloud passed away from the firmament of both. Neither of them, perhaps, was of a very enlightened character of soul. They believed they were doing a great work for Tom Burrows's six children, calling God to His promise on their behalf, and setting the little feet straight for the gates of the eternal city; and in their young love and faith their hearts rose. Perhaps it was foolish of Mr Wentworth to suffer himself to walk home again thereafter, as of old, with the Miss Wodehouses – but it was so usual, and, after all, they were going the same way. But it was a very silent walk, to the wonder of the elder sister, who could not understand what it meant. "The Wharfside service always does me good," said Mr Wentworth, with a sigh. "And me, too," said Lucy; and then they talked a little about the poor woman in No. 10. But that Easter Sunday was not like other Sundays, though Miss Wodehouse could not tell why.

CHAPTER V.

NEXT day the Miss Wentworths made a solemn call at the Rectory, having known an aunt of Mrs Morgan at some period of their history, and being much disposed, besides, with natural curiosity, to ascertain all about their nephew's circumstances. Their entrance interrupted a consultation between the Rector and his wife. Mr Morgan was slightly heated, and had evidently been talking about something that excited him; while she, poor lady, looked just sufficiently sympathetic and indignant to withdraw her mind from that first idea which usually suggested itself on the entrance of visitors – which was, what could they possibly think of her if they supposed the carpet, &c., to be her own choice? Mrs Morgan cast her eye with a troubled look upon the big card which had been brought to her – Miss Wentworth, Miss Leonora Wentworth, Miss Dora Wentworth. "Sisters of his, I suppose, William," she said in an undertone; "now *do* be civil, dear." There was no time for anything more before the three ladies sailed in. Miss Leonora took the initiative, as was natural.

"You don't remember us, I daresay," she said, taking Mrs Morgan's hand; "we used to know your aunt Sidney, when she lived at the Hermitage. Don't you recollect the Miss Wentworths of Skelmersdale? Charley Sidney spent part of his furlough with us last summer, and Ada writes about you often. We could not be in Carlingford without coming to see the relation of such a dear friend."

"I am so glad to see anybody who knows my aunt Sidney," said Mrs Morgan, with modified enthusiasm. "Mr Morgan, Miss Wentworth. It was such a dear little house that Hermitage. I spent some very happy days there. Oh yes, I recollect Skelmersdale perfectly; but, to tell the truth, there is one of the clergy in Carlingford called Wentworth, and I thought it might be some relations of his coming to call."

"Just so," said Miss Wentworth, settling herself in the nearest easy-chair.

"And so it is," cried Miss Dora; "we are his aunts, dear boy – we are very fond of him. We came on purpose to see him. We are so glad to hear that he is liked in Carlingford."

"Oh – yes," said the Rector's wife, and nobody else took any notice of Miss Dora's little outburst. As for Mr Morgan, he addressed Miss Leonora as if she had done something particularly naughty, and he had a great mind to give her an imposition. "You have not been very long in Carlingford, I suppose," said the Rector, as if that were a sin.

"Only since Saturday," said Miss Leonora. "We came to see Mr Frank Wentworth, who is at St Roque's. I don't know what your bishop is about, to permit all those flowers and candlesticks. For my part, I never disguise my sentiments. I mean to tell my nephew plainly that his way of conducting the service is far from being to my mind."

"Leonora, dear, perhaps Mr Morgan would speak to Frank about it," interposed Miss Dora, anxiously; "he was always a dear boy, and advice was never lost upon him. From one that he respected so much as he must respect the Rector—"

"I beg your pardon. I quite decline interfering with Mr Wentworth; he is not at all under my jurisdiction. Indeed," said the Rector, with a smile of anger, "I might be more truly said to be under his, for he is good enough to help in my parish without consulting me; but that is not to the purpose. I would not for the world attempt to interfere with St Roque's."

"Dear, I am sure Mr Wentworth is very nice, and everything we have seen of him in private we have liked very much," said Mrs Morgan, with an anxious look at her husband. She was a good-natured woman, and the handsome Curate had impressed her favourably, notwithstanding his misdoings. "As for a little too much of the rubric, I think that is not a bad fault in a young man. It gets softened down with a little experience; and I do like proper solemnity in the services of the Church."

"I don't call intoning proper solemnity," said Miss Leonora. "The Church is a missionary institution, that is my idea. Unless you are really bringing in the perishing and saving souls, what is the good? and souls will never be saved by Easter decorations. I don't know what my nephew may have done to offend you, Mr Morgan; but it is very sad to us, who have very strong convictions on the subject, to see him wasting his time so. I daresay there is plenty of heathenism in Carlingford which might be attacked in the first place."

"I prefer not to discuss the subject," said the Rector. "So long as Mr Wentworth, or any other clergyman, keeps to his own sphere of duty, I should be the last in the world to interfere with him."

"You are offended with Frank," said Miss Leonora, fixing her iron-grey eyes upon Mr Morgan. "So am I; but I should be glad if you would tell me all about it. I have particular reasons for wishing to know. After all, he is only a young man," she continued, with that instinct of kindred which dislikes to hear censure from any lips but its own. "I don't think there can be anything more than inadvertence in it. I should be glad if you would tell me what you object to in him. I think it is probable that he may remain a long time in Carlingford," said Miss Leonora, with charming candour, "and it would be pleasant if we could help to set him right. Your advice and experience might be of so much use to him." She was not aware of the covert sarcasm of her speech. She did not know that the Rector's actual experience, though he was half as old again as her nephew, bore no comparison to that of the Perpetual Curate. She spoke in good faith and good nature, not moved in her own convictions of what must be done in respect to Skelmersdale, but very willing, if that were possible, to do a good turn to Frank.

"I am sure, dear, what we have seen of Mr Wentworth in private, we have liked very much," said the Rector's sensible wife, with a deprecating glance towards her husband. The Rector took no notice of the glance; he grew slightly red in his serious middle-aged face, and cleared his throat several times before he began to speak.

"The fact is, I have reason to be dissatisfied with Mr Wentworth, as regards my own parish," said Mr Morgan: "personally I have nothing to say against him – quite the reverse; probably, as you say, it arises from inadvertence, as he is still a very young man; but—"

"What has he done?" said Miss Leonora, pricking up her ears.

Once more Mr Morgan cleared his throat, but this time
it was to keep down the rising anger of which he was
unpleasantly sensible. "I don't generally enter into such
matters with people whom they don't concern," he said,
with a touch of his natural asperity; "but as you are Mr
Wentworth's relation—. He has taken a step perfectly
unjustifiable in every respect; he has at the present moment
a mission going on in my parish, in entire independence, I
will not say defiance, of me. My dear, it is unnecessary to
look at me so deprecatingly. I am indignant at having such
a liberty taken with me. I don't pretend not to be indignant.
Mr Wentworth is a very young man, and may not know
any better; but it is the most unwarrantable intrusion upon
a clergyman's rights. I beg your pardon, Miss Wentworth:
you have nothing to do with my grievances; but the fact is,
my wife and I were discussing this very unpleasant matter
when you came in."

"A mission in your parish?" said Miss Leonora, her iron-
grey eyes lighting up with a sparkle which did not look like
indignation; at this point it was necessary that Miss Dora
should throw herself into the breach.

"Oh, Mr Morgan, I am sure my dear Frank does not
mean it!" cried the unlucky peacemaker; "he would not
for the world do anything to wound anybody's feelings – it
must be a mistake."

"Mr Morgan would not have mentioned it if we had not
just been talking as you came in," said the Rector's wife,
by way of smoothing down his ruffled temper and giving
him time to recover. "I feel *sure* it is a mistake, and that
everything will come right as soon as they can talk it over
by themselves. The last Rector was not at all a working
clergyman – and perhaps Mr Wentworth felt it was his
duty – and now I daresay he forgets that it is not his own
parish. It will all come right after a time."

"But the mission is effective, I suppose, or you would
not object to it?" said Miss Leonora, who, though a very
religious woman, was not a peacemaker; and the Rector,

whose temper was hasty, swallowed the bait. He entered
into his grievances more fully than his wife thought
consistent with his dignity. She sat with her eyes fixed
upon the floor, tracing the objectionable pattern on the
carpet with her foot, but too much vexed for the moment
to think of those bouquets which were so severe a
cross to her on ordinary occasions. Perhaps she was
thinking secretly to herself how much better one knows a
man after being married to him three months than after
being engaged to him ten years; but the discovery that he
was merely a man after all, with very ordinary defects,
did not lessen her loyalty. She sat with her eyes bent upon
the carpet, feeling a little hot and uncomfortable as her
husband disclosed his weakness, and watching her opportunities to rush in and say a softening word now and then.
The chances were, perhaps, on the whole, that the wife
grew *more* loyal, if that were possible, as she perceived the
necessity of standing by him and backing him out. The
Rector went very fully into the subject, being drawn out
by Miss Leonora's questions, and betrayed an extent of
information strangely opposed to the utter ignorance
which he had displayed at Mr Wodehouse's party. He
knew the hours of Mr Wentworth's services, and the
number of people who attended, and even about Tom
Burrows's six children who had been baptised the day
before. Somehow Mr Morgan took this last particular as a
special offence; it was this which had roused him beyond
his usual self-control. Six little heathens brought into the
Christian fold in his own parish without the permission of
the Rector! It was indeed enough to try any clergyman's
temper. Through the entire narrative Miss Dora broke in
now and then with a little wail expressive of her general
dismay and grief, and certainty that her dear Frank did
not mean it. Mrs Morgan repeated apart to Miss Wentworth with a troubled brow the fact that all they had seen
of Mr Wentworth in private they had liked very much; to
which aunt Cecilia answered, "Quite so," with her beautiful

smile; while Miss Leonora sat and listened, putting artful questions, and fixing the heated Rector with that iron-grey eye, out of which the sparkle of incipient light had not faded. Mr Morgan naturally said a great deal more than he meant to say, and after it was said he was sorry; but he did not show the latter sentiment except by silence and an uneasy rustling about the room just before the Miss Wentworths rose to go – a sign apparent to his wife, though to nobody else. He gave Miss Wentworth his arm to the door with an embarrassed courtesy. "If you are going to stay any time at Carlingford, I trust we shall see more of you," said Mr Morgan: "I ought to beg your pardon for taking up so much time with my affairs;" and the Rector was much taken aback when Miss Wentworth answered, "Thank you, that is just what I was thinking." He went back to his troubled wife in great perplexity. What was it that was just what she was thinking? – that he would see more of them, or that he had spoken too much of his own affairs?

"You think I have been angry and made an idiot of myself," said Mr Morgan to his wife, who was standing looking from a safe distance through the curtains at the three ladies, who were holding a consultation with their servant out of the window of the solemn chariot provided by the Blue Boar, as to where they were to go next.

"Nonsense, dear; but I wish you had not said quite so much about Mr Wentworth," said the Rector's wife, seizing, with female art, on a cause for her annoyance which would not wound her Welshman's *amour propre*, "for I rather think he is dependent on his aunts. They have the living of Skelmersdale, I know; and I remember now that their nephew was to have had it. I hope this won't turn them against him, dear," said Mrs Morgan, who did not care the least in the world about Skelmersdale, looking anxiously in her husband's face.

This was the climax of the Rector's trouble. "Why did not you tell me that before?" he said, with conjugal injustice, and went off to his study with a disturbed mind, thinking that perhaps he had injured his own chances of getting rid of the Perpetual Curate. If Mrs Morgan had permitted herself to soliloquise after he was gone, the matter of her thoughts might have been interesting; but as neither ladies nor gentlemen in the nineteenth century are given to that useful medium of disclosing their sentiments, the veil of privacy must remain over the mind of the Rector's wife. She got her gardening gloves and scissors, and went out immediately after, and had an animated discussion with the gardener about the best means of clothing that bit of wall, over which every railway train was visible which left or entered Carlingford. That functionary was of opinion that when the lime-trees "growed a bit" all would be right: but Mrs Morgan was reluctant to await the slow processes of nature. She forgot her vexations about Mr Wentworth in consideration of the still more palpable inconvenience of the passing train.

CHAPTER VI.

Miss Dora Wentworth relapsed into suppressed sobbing when the three ladies were once more on their way. Between each little access a few broken words fell from the poor lady's lips. "I am sure dear Frank did not mean it," she said; it was all the plea his champion could find for him.

"He did not mean what? to do his duty and save souls?" said Miss Leonora – "is that what he didn't mean? It looks very much as if he did, though – as well as he knew how."

"Quite so, Leonora," said Miss Wentworth.

"But he could not mean to vex the Rector," said Miss

Dora –"my poor dear Frank: of course he meant it for the very best. I wonder you don't think so, Leonora – you who are so fond of missions. I told you what I heard him saying to the young lady – all about the sick people he was going to visit, and the children. He is a faithful shepherd, though you won't think so; and I am sure he means nothing but—"

"His duty, I think," said the iron-grey sister, resolutely indifferent to Miss Dora's little sniffs, and turning her gaze out of the window, unluckily just at the moment when the carriage was passing Masters's shop, where some engravings were hanging of a suspiciously devotional character. The name over the door, and the aspect of the shop-window, were terribly suggestive, and the fine profile of the Perpetual Curate was just visible within to the keen eyes of his aunt. Miss Dora, for her part, dried hers, and, beginning to see some daylight, addressed herself anxiously to the task of obscuring it, and damaging once more her favourite's chance.

"Ah, Leonora, if he had but a sphere of his own," cried Miss Dora, "where he would have other things to think of than the rubric, and decorations, and sisterhoods! I don't wish any harm to poor dear old Mr Shirley, I am sure; but when Frank is in the Rectory—"

"I thought you understood that Frank would not do for the Rectory," said Miss Leonora. "Sisterhoods!–look here, there's a young lady in a grey cloak, and I think she's going into *that* shop: if Frank carries on that sort of thing, I shall think him a greater fool than ever. Who is that girl?"

"I'm sure I don't know, dear," said Miss Dora, with unexpected wisdom. And she comforted her conscience that she did not know, for she had forgotten Lucy's name. So there was no tangible evidence to confirm Miss Leonora's doubts, and the carriage from the Blue Boar rattled down Prickett's Lane to the much amazement of that locality. When they got to the grimy canal-banks, Miss Leonora stopped the vehicle and got out. She declined the attendance of her trembling sister, and marched along the black pavement, dispersing with the great waves of her drapery the wondering children about, who swarmed as children will swarm in such localities. Arrived at the schoolroom, Miss Leonora found sundry written notices hung up in a little wooden frame inside the open door. All sorts of charitable businesses were carried on about the basement of the house; and a curt little notice about the Provident Society diversified the list of services which was hung up for the advantage of the ignorant. Clearly the Curate of St Roque's meant it. "As well as he knows how," his aunt allowed to herself, with a softening sentiment; but, pushing her inquiries further, was shown up to the schoolroom, and stood pondering by the side of the reading-desk, looking at the table which was contrived to be so like an altar. The Curate, who could not have dreamed of such a visit, and whose mind had been much occupied and indifferent to externals on the day before, had left various things lying about, which were carefully collected for him upon a bench. Among them was a little pocket copy of Thomas à Kempis, from which, when the jealous aunt opened it, certain little German prints, such as were to be had by the score at Masters's, dropped out, some of them unobjectionable enough. But if the Good Shepherd could not be found fault with, the feelings of Miss Leonora may be imagined when the meek face of a monkish saint, inscribed with some villanous Latin inscription, a legend which began with the terrible words *Ora pro nobis*, became suddenly visible to her troubled eyes. She put away the book as if it had stung her, and made a precipitate retreat. She shook her head as she descended the stair – she re-entered the carriage in gloomy silence. When it returned up Prickett's Lane, the three ladies again saw their nephew, this time entering the door of No. 10. He had his prayer-book under his arm, and Miss Leonora seized upon this professional symbol to wreak her wrath upon it. "I wonder if he can't pray by a sick woman without his prayer-book?" she cried. "I never was so

provoked in my life. How is it he doesn't know better? His
father is not pious, but he isn't a Puseyite, and old uncle
Wentworth was very sound – he was brought up under the
pure Gospel. How is that the boys are so foolish, Dora?"
said Miss Leonora, sharply; "it must be your doing. You
have told them tales and things, and put true piety out of
their head."

"My doing!" said Miss Dora, faintly; but she was too
much startled by the suddenness of the attack to make any
coherent remonstrance. Miss Leonora tossed back her
angry head, and pursued that inspiration, finding it a
relief in her perplexity.

"It must be *all* your doing," she said. "How can I tell
that you are not a Jesuit in disguise? one has read of such a
thing. The boys were as good, nice, pious boys as one
could wish to see; and there's Gerald on the point of
perversion, and Frank— I tell you, Dora, it must be your
fault."

"That was always my opinion," said Miss Cecilia; and
the accused, after a feeble attempt at speech, could find
nothing better to do than to drop her veil once more and
cry under it. It was very hard, but she was not quite
unaccustomed to it. However, the discoveries of the day
were important enough to prevent the immediate departure which Miss Leonora had intended. She wrote a note
with her own hands to her nephew, asking him to dinner.
"We meant to have gone away to-day, but should like to
see you first," she said in her note. "Come and dine – we
mayn't have anything pleasant to say, but I don't suppose
you expect that. It's a pity we don't see eye to eye." Such
was the intimation received by Mr Wentworth when he
got home, very tired, in the afternoon. He had been
asking himself whether, under the circumstances, it would
not be proper of him to return some books of Mr
Wodehouse's which he had in his possession, of course by
way of breaking off his too familiar, too frequent intercourse. He had been representing to himself that he would

make this call after their dinner would be over, at the hour
when Mr Wodehouse reposed in his easy-chair, and the
two sisters were generally to be found alone in the
drawing-room. Perhaps he might have an opportunity of
intimating the partial farewell he meant to take of them.
When he got Miss Leonora's note, the Curate's countenance clouded over. He said, "Another night lost," with
indignant candour. It was hard enough to give up his
worldly prospects, but he thought he had made up his
mind to that. However, refusal was impossible. It was still
daylight when he went up Grange Lane to the Blue Boar.
He was early, and went languidly along the well-known
road. Nobody was about at that hour. In those closed,
embowered houses, people were preparing for dinner, the
great event of the day, and Mr Wentworth was aware of
that. Perhaps he had expected to see somebody – Mr
Wodehouse going home, most likely, in order that he
might mention his own engagement, and account for his
failure in the chance evening call which had become so
much a part of his life. But no one appeared to bear his
message. He went lingering past the green door, and up
the silent deserted road. At the end of Grange Lane, just
in the little unsettled transition interval which interposed
between its aristocratic calm and the bustle of George
Street, on the side next Prickett's Lane, was a quaint little
shop, into which Mr Wentworth strayed to occupy the
time. This was Elsworthy's, who, as is well known, was
then clerk at St Roque's. Elsworthy himself was in his
shop that Easter Monday, and so was his wife and little
Rosa, who was a little beauty. Rosa and her aunt had just
returned from an excursion, and a prettier little apparition
could not be seen than that dimpled rosy creature, with
her radiant half-childish looks, her bright eyes, and soft
curls of dark-brown hair. Even Mr Wentworth gave a
second glance at her as he dropped languidly into a chair,
and asked Elsworthy if there was any news. Mrs
Elsworthy, who had been telling the adventures of the

holiday to her goodman, gathered up her basket of eggs and her nosegay, and made the clergyman a little curtsy as she hurried away; for the clerk's wife was a highly respectable woman, and knew her own place. But Rosa, who was only a kind of kitten, and had privileges, stayed. Mr Wentworth was by far the most magnificent figure she had ever seen in her little life. She looked at him with awe out of her bright eyes, and thought he looked like the prince in the fairy tales.

"Any news, sir? There aint much to call news, sir – not in a place like this," said Mr Elsworthy. "Your respected aunts, sir, 'as been down at the schoolroom. I haven't heard anything else as I could suppose you didn't know."

"My aunts!" cried the Curate; "how do you know any-thing about my aunts?" Mr Elsworthy smiled a com-placent and familiar smile.

"There's so many a-coming and a-going here that I know most persons as comes into Carlingford," said he; "and them three respected ladies is as good as a pictur. I saw them a-driving past and down Prickett's Lane. They was as anxious to know all about it as – as was to be expected in the circumstances," said Mr Elsworthy, fail-ing of a metaphor; "and I wish you your 'ealth and 'appiness, sir, if all as I hear is true."

"It's a good wish," said the Curate; "thank you, Elsworthy; but what you heard might not be true."

"Well, sir, it looks more than likely," said the clerk; "as far as I've seen in my experience, ladies don't go inquiring into a young gentleman's ways, not without some reason. If they was young ladies, and noways related, we know what we'd think, sir; but being old ladies, and aunts, it's equally as clear. For my part, Mr Wentworth, my worst wish is, that when you come into your fortune, it mayn't lead you away from St Roque's – not after everything is settled so beautiful, and not a thing wanted but some stained glass, as I hear a deal of people say, to make it as perfect a little church— "

"Yes, it is very true; a painted window is very much wanted," said Mr Wentworth, thoughtfully.

"Perhaps there's one o' the ladies, sir, as has some friend she'd like to put up a memorial to," said Mr Elsworthy, in insinuating tones. "A window is a deal cheerfuller a memorial than a tombstone, and it couldn't be described the improvement it would be to the church. I'm sorry to hear Mr Wodehouse aint quite so well as his usual to-night; a useful man like he is, would be a terrible loss to Carlingford; not as it's anything alarming, as far as I can hear, but being a stout man, it aint a safe thing his being took so sudden. I've heard the old doctor say, sir, as a man of a full 'abit might be took off at once, when a spare man would fight through. It would be a sad thing for his family, sir," said Mr Elsworthy, tying up a bundle of newspapers with a very serious face.

"Good heavens, Elsworthy, how you talk!" said the alarmed Curate. "What do you mean? – is Mr Wodehouse ill? – seriously ill?"

"Not serious, as I knows of," said the clerk, with solemnity; "but being a man of a full 'abit of body – I daresay as the town would enter into it by subscription if it was proposed as a memorial to *him*, for he's much respected in Carlingford is Mr Wodehouse. I see him a-going past, sir, at five o'clock, which is an hour earlier than common, and he was looking flabby, that's how he was looking. I don't know a man as would be a greater loss to his family; and they aint been without their troubles either, poor souls."

"I should be sorry to think that it was necessary to sacrifice Mr Wodehouse for the sake of our painted window," said the Curate, "as that seems what you mean. Send over this note for me please, as I have not time to call. No, certainly, don't send Rosa; that child is too young and too – too pretty to be out by herself at night. Send a boy. Haven't you got a boy? – there is a very nice little fellow that I could recommend to you," said Mr Wentworth, as

he hastily scribbled his note with a pencil, "whose mother
lives in Prickett's Lane."

"Thank *you*, sir, all the same; but I hope I don't need to
go into that neighbourhood for good service," said Mr
Elsworthy: "as for Rosa, I could trust her anywhere; and I
have a boy, sir, as is the best boy that ever lived – a real
English boy, that is. Sam, take this to Mr Wodehouse's
directly, and wait for an answer. No answer? – very well,
sir. You needn't wait for no answer, Sam. That's a boy,
sir, I could trust with untold gold. His mother's a Dissenter,
it is true, but the principles of that boy is beautiful. I hope
you haven't mentioned, sir, as I said Mr Wodehouse was
took bad? It was between ourselves, Mr Wentworth.
Persons don't like, especially when they've got to that
age, and are of a full 'abit of body, to have every little
attack made a talk about. You'll excuse me mentioning it,
sir, but it was as between ourselves."

"Perhaps you'd like me to show you my note," said the
Curate, with a smile; which, indeed, Elsworthy would
have very much liked, could he have ventured to say so.
Mr Wentworth was but too glad of an excuse to write and
explain his absence. The note was not to Lucy, however,
though various little epistles full of the business of the
district had passed between the two:–

"Dear Miss W., – I hear your father is not quite well. I
can't call just now, as I am going to dine with my aunts,
who are at the Blue Boar; but, if you will pardon the
lateness of the hour, I will call as I return to ask for him. –
Ever yours,

"F.C. Wentworth."

Such was the Curate's note. While he scribbled it, little
Rosa stood apart watching him with admiring eyes. He
had said she was too pretty to be sent across Grange Lane
by herself at this hour, though it was still no more than
twilight; and he looked up at her for an instant as he said
the words, – quite enough to set Rosa's poor little heart

beating with childish romantical excitement. If she could but have peeped into the note to see what he said! – for perhaps, after all, there might not be anything "between" him and Miss Lucy – and perhaps— The poor little thing stood watching, deaf to her aunt's call, looking at the strange ease with which that small epistle was written, and thinking it half divine to have such mastery of words and pen. Mr Wentworth threw it to Sam as if it were a trifle; but Rosa's lively imagination could already conceive the possibility of living upon such trifles and making existence out of them; so the child stood with her pretty curls about her ears, and her bright eyes gleaming dewy over the fair, flushed, rosebud cheeks, in a flutter of roused and innocent imagination anticipating her fate. As for Mr Wentworth, it is doubtful whether he saw Rosa, as he swung himself round upon the stool he was seated on, and turned his face towards the door. Somehow he was comforted in his mind by the conviction that it was his duty to call at Mr Wodehouse's as he came back. The evening brightened up and looked less dismal. The illness of the respected father of the house did not oppress the young man. He thought not of the sick-room, but of the low chair in one corner, beside the work-table where Lucy had always basketfuls of sewing in hand. He could fancy he saw the work drop on her knee, and the blue eyes raised. It was a pretty picture that he framed for himself as he looked out with a half smile into the blue twilight through the open door of Elsworthy's shop. And it was clearly his duty to call. He grew almost jocular in the exhilaration of his spirits.

"The Miss Wentworths don't approve of memorial windows, Elsworthy," he said; "and, indeed, if you think it necessary to cut off one of the chief people in Carlingford by way of supplying St Roque's with a little painted glass—"

"No, sir – no, no, sir; you're too hard upon me – there wasn't no such meaning in my mind; but I don't make no question the ladies were pleased with the church," said Elsworthy, with the satisfaction of a man who had helped to

produce an entirely triumphant effect. "I don't pretend to
be a judge myself of what you call 'igh art, Mr Wentworth;
but if I might venture an opinion, the altar was beautiful;
and we won't say nothing about the service, considering,
sir – if you won't be offended at putting them together, as
one is so far inferior – that both you and me—"

Mr Wentworth laughed and moved off his chair. "We
were not appreciated in this instance," he said, with an
odd comic look, and then went off into a burst of laughter,
which Mr Elsworthy saw no particular occasion for. Then
he took up his glove, which he had taken off to write the
note, and, nodding a kindly good-night to little Rosa, who
stood gazing after him with all her eyes, went away to the
Blue Boar. The idea, however, of his own joint performance
with Mr Elsworthy not only tickled the Curate, but gave
him a half-ashamed sense of the aspect in which he might
himself appear to the eyes of matter-of-fact people who
differed with him. The joke had a slight sting, which
brought his laughter to an end. He went up through the
lighted street to the inn, wishing the dinner over, and
himself on his way back again to call at Mr Wodehouse's.
For, to tell the truth, by this time he had almost exhausted
Skelmersdale, and, feeling in himself not much different
now from what he was when his hopes were still green,
had begun to look upon life itself with a less troubled eye,
and to believe in other chances which might make Lucy's
society practicable once more. It was in this altered state
of mind that he presented himself before his aunts. He
was less self-conscious, less watchful, more ready to amuse
them, if that might happen to be possible, and in reality
much more able to cope with Miss Leonora than when he
had been more anxious about her opinion. He had not
been two minutes in the room before all the three ladies
perceived this revolution, and each in her own mind
attempted to account for it. They were experienced women
in their way, and found a variety of reasons; but as none of
them were young, and as people *will* forget how youth

feels, not one of them divined the fact that there was no reason, but that this improvement of spirits arose solely from the fact that the Perpetual Curate had been for two whole days miserable about Skelmersdale, and had exhausted all his powers of misery – and that now youth had turned the tables, and he was still to see Lucy tonight.

CHAPTER VII.

"Your Rector is angry at some of your proceedings," said Miss Leonora. "I did not think a man of your views would have cared for missionary work. I should have supposed that you would think that vulgar, and Low-Church, and Evangelical. Indeed, I thought I heard you say you didn't believe in preaching, Frank? – neither do I, when a man preaches the Tracts for the Times. I was surprised to hear what you were doing at the place they call Wharfside."

"First let me correct you in two little inaccuracies," said Mr Wentworth, blandly, as he peeled his orange. "The Rector of Carlingford is not *my* rector, and I don't preach the Tracts for the Times. Let us always be particular, my dear aunt, as to points of fact."

"Exactly so," said Miss Leonora, grimly; "but, at the same time, as there seems no great likelihood of your leaving Carlingford, don't you think it would be wise to cultivate friendly relations with the Rector?" said the iron-grey inexorable aunt, looking full in his eyes as she spoke. So significant and plain a statement took for an instant the colour out of the Curate's cheeks – he pared his orange very carefully while he regained his composure, and it was at least half a minute before he found himself at leisure to reply. Miss Dora of course seized upon the opportunity, and, by way of softening matters, interposed in her unlucky person to make peace.

"But, my dear boy, I said I was sure you did not mean it," said Miss Dora; "I told Mr Morgan I felt convinced it could be explained. Nobody knows you so well as I do. You were always high-spirited from a child, and never would give in; but I know very well you never could mean it, Frank."

"Mean it?" said the Curate, with sparkling eyes: "what do you take me for, aunt Dora? Do you know what it is we are talking of? The question is, whether a whole lot of people, fathers and children, shall be left to live like beasts, without reverence for God or man, or shall be brought within the pale of the Church, and taught their duty? And you think I don't mean it? I mean it as much as my brother Charley meant it at the Redan," said young Wentworth, with a glow of suppressed enthusiasm, and that natural pride in Charley (who got the Cross for valour) which was common to all the Wentworths. But when he saw his aunt Leonora looking at him, the Perpetual Curate stood to his arms again. "I have still to learn that the Rector has anything to do with it," said the young Evangelist of Wharfside.

"It is in his parish, and he thinks he has," said Miss Leonora. "I wish you could see your duty more clearly, Frank. You seem to me, you know, to have a kind of zeal, but not according to knowledge. If you were carrying the real Gospel to the poor people, I shouldn't be disposed to blame you; for the limits of a parish are but poor things to pause for when souls are perishing; but to break the law for the sake of diffusing the rubric and propagating Tractarianism—"

"Oh, Leonora, how can you be so harsh and cruel?" cried Miss Dora; "only think what you are doing. I don't say anything about disappointing Frank, and perhaps injuring his prospects for life; for, to be sure, he is a true

Wentworth, and won't acknowledge that; but think of my poor dear brother, with so many sons as he has to provide for, and so much on his mind; and think of ourselves and all that we have planned so often. Only think what you have talked of over and over; how nice it would be when he was old enough to take the Rectory, and marry Julia Trench—"

"Aunt Dora," said the Curate, rising from the table. "I shall have to go away if you make such appeals on my behalf. And besides, it is only right to tell you that, whatever my circumstances were, I never could nor would marry Julia Trench. It is cruel and unjust to bring in her name. Don't let us hear any more of this, if you have any regard for me."

"Quite so, Frank," said Miss Wentworth; "that is exactly what I was thinking." Miss Cecilia was not in the habit of making demonstrations, but she put out her delicate old hand to point her nephew to his seat again, and gave a soft slight pressure to his as she touched it. Old Miss Wentworth was a kind of dumb lovely idol to her nephews; she rarely said anything to them, but they worshipped her all the same for her beauty and those languid tendernesses which she showed them once in ten years or so. The Perpetual Curate was much touched by this manifestation. He kissed his old aunt's beautiful hand as reverently as if it had been a saint's. "I knew you would understand me," he said, looking gratefully at her lovely old face; which exclamation, however, was a simple utterance of gratitude, and would not have borne investigation. When he had resumed his seat and his orange, Miss Leonora cleared her throat for a grand address.

"Frank might as well tell us he would not have Skelmersdale," she said. "Julia Trench has quite other prospects, I am glad to say, though Dora talks like a fool on this subject as well as on many others. Mr Shirley is not dead yet, and I don't think he means to die, for my part; and Julia would never leave her uncle. Besides, I don't think any inducement in the world would make her disguise herself like a Sister of Mercy. I hope she knows better. And it is a pity that Frank should learn to think of Skelmersdale as if it were a family living," continued Miss Leonora. "For my part, I think people detached from immediate ties as we are, are under all the greater responsibility. But as you are likely to stay in Carlingford, Frank, perhaps we could help you with the Rector," she concluded blandly, as she ate her biscuit. The Curate, who was also a Wentworth, had quite recovered himself ere this speech was over, and proved himself equal to the occasion.

"If the Rector objects to what I am doing, I daresay he will tell me of it," said Mr Wentworth, with indescribable suavity. "I had the consent of the two former rectors to my mission in their parish, and I don't mean to give up such a work without a cause. But I am equally obliged to you, my dear aunt, and I hope Mr Shirley will live for ever. How long are you going to stay in Carlingford? Some of the people would like to call on you, if you remain longer. There are some great friends of mine here; and as I have every prospect of being perpetually the Curate, as you kindly observe, perhaps it might be good for me if I was seen to have such unexceptionable relationships—"

"Satire is lost upon me," said Miss Leonora, "and we are going to-morrow. Here comes the coffee. I did not think it had been so late. We shall leave by an early train, and you can come and see us off, if you have time."

"I shall certainly find time," said the nephew, with equal politeness; "and now you will permit me to say good-night, for I have a – one of my sick people to visit. I heard he was ill only as I came here, and had not time to call," added the Curate, with unnecessary explanitoriness, and took leave of his aunt Cecilia, who softly put something into his hand as she bade him good-night. Miss Dora, for her part, went with him to the door, and lingered leaning on his arm, down the long passage, all unaware, poor lady, that his heart was beating with impatience to get away, and that the disappointment for which she wanted to console him had at the present moment not the slightest real hold upon his perverse heart. "Oh, my dear boy, I hope you don't think it's my fault," said Miss Dora, with tears. "It must have come to this, dear, sooner or later: you see, poor Leonora has such a sense of responsibility; but it is very hard upon us, Frank, who love you so much, that she should always take her own way."

"Then why don't you rebel?" said the Curate, who, in the thought of seeing Lucy, was exhilarated, and dared to jest even upon the awful power of his aunt. "You are two against one; why don't you take it into your own hands and rebel?"

Miss Dora repeated the words with an alarmed quiver. "Rebel! oh, Frank, dear, do you think we could? To be sure, we are co-heiresses, and have just as good a right as she has; and for your sake, my dear boy," said the troubled woman, "oh, Frank, I wish you would tell me what to do! I never should dare to contradict Leonora with no one to stand by me; and then, if anything happened, you would all think I had been to blame," said poor aunt Dora, clinging to his arm. She made him walk back and back again through the long passage, which was sacred to the chief suite of apartments at the Blue Boar. "We have it all to ourselves, and nobody can see us here; and oh, my dear boy, if you would only tell me what I ought to do?" she repeated, with wistful looks of appeal. Mr Wentworth was too good-hearted to show the impatience with which he was struggling. He satisfied her as well as he could, and said good-night half-a-dozen times. When he made his escape at last, and emerged into the clear blue air of the spring night, the Perpetual Curate had no such sense of disappointment and failure in his mind as the three ladies supposed. Miss Leonora's distinct intimation that Skelmersdale had passed out of the region of probabilities, had

indeed tingled through him at the moment it was uttered;
but just now he was going to see Lucy, anticipating with
impatience the moment of coming into her presence, and
nothing in the world could have dismayed him utterly. He
went down the road very rapidly, glad to find that it was
still so early, that the shopkeepers in George Street were
but just putting up their shutters, and that there was still
time for an hour's talk in that bright drawing-room. Little
Rosa was standing at the door of Elsworthy's shop, looking
out into the dark street as he passed; and he said, "A
lovely night, Rosa," as he went by. But the night was
nothing particular in itself, only lovely to Mr Wentworth,
as embellished with Lucy shining over it, like a distant
star. Perhaps he had never in his life felt so glad that he
was going to see her, so eager for her presence, as that
night which was the beginning of the time when it would
be no longer lawful for him to indulge in her society. He
heaved a big sigh as that thought occurred to him, but it
did not diminish the flush of conscious happiness; and in
this mood he went down Grange Lane, with light
resounding steps, to Mr Wodehouse's door.

But Mr Wentworth started with a very strange sensation when the door was stealthily, noiselessly opened to
him before he could ring. He could not see who it was that
called him in the darkness; but he felt that he had been
watched for, and that the door was thrown open very
hurriedly to prevent him from making his usual summons
at the bell. Such an incident was incomprehensible. He
went into the dark garden like a man in a dream, with a
horrible vision of Archimage and the false Una somehow
stealing upon his mind, he could not tell how. It was quite
dark inside, for the moon was late of rising that night, and
the faint stars threw no effectual lustre down upon the
trees. He had to grope before him to know where he was
going, asking in a troubled voice, "Who is there? What is
the matter?" and falling into more and more profound
bewilderment and uneasiness.

"Hush, hush, oh hush! – Oh, Mr Wentworth, it is I – I want to speak to you," said an agitated voice beside him. "Come this way – this way; I don't want any one to hear us." It was Miss Wodehouse who thus pitifully addressed the amazed Curate. She laid a tremulous hand on his arm, and drew him deeper into the shadows – into that walk where the limes and tall lilac-bushes grew so thickly. Here she came to a pause, and the sound of the terrified panting breath in the silence alarmed him more and more.

"Is Mr Wodehouse ill? What has happened?" said the astonished young man. The windows of the house were gleaming hospitably over the dark garden, without any appearance of gloom – the drawing-room windows especially, which he knew so well, brightly lighted, one of them open, and the sound of the piano and Lucy's voice stealing out like a celestial reality into the darkness. By the time he had become fully sensible of all these particulars his agitated companion had found her breath.

"Mr Wentworth, don't think me mad," said Miss Wodehouse; "I have come out to speak to you, for I am in great distress. I don't know what to do unless you will help me. Oh no, don't look at the house – nobody knows in the house; I would die rather than have them know. Hush, hush! don't make any noise. Is that some one looking out at the door?"

And just then the door was opened, and Mr Wodehouse's sole male servant looked out, and round the garden, as if he had heard something to excite his curiosity or surprise. Miss Wodehouse grasped the arm of the Perpetual Curate, and held him with an energy which was almost violence. "Hush, hush, hush," she said, with her voice almost at his ear. The excitement of this mild woman, the perfectly inexplicable mystery of the meeting, overwhelmed young Wentworth. He could think of nothing less than that she had lost her senses, and in his turn he took her hands and held her fast.

"What is the matter? I cannot tell you how anxious, how

distressed I am. What has happened?" said the young man, under his breath.

"My father has some suspicion," she answered, after a pause – "he came home early to-day looking ill. You heard of it, Mr Wentworth – it was your note that decided me. Oh, heaven help us! it is so hard to know what to do. I have never been used to act for myself, and I feel as helpless as a baby. The only comfort I have was that it happened on Easter Sunday," said the poor gentlewoman, incoherently; "and oh! if it should prove a rising from the dead! If you saw me, Mr Wentworth, you would see I look ten years older; and I can't tell you how it is, but I think my father has suspicions; – he looked so ill – oh, so ill – when he came home to-night. Hush! hush! did you hear anything? I daren't tell Lucy; not that I couldn't trust her, but it is cruel when a young creature is happy, to let her know such miseries. Oh, Mr Wentworth, I daresay I am not telling you what it is, after all. I don't know what I am saying – wait till I can think. It was on Easter Sunday, after we came home from Wharfside; you remember we all came home together, and both Lucy and you were so quiet. I could not understand how it was you were so quiet, but I was not thinking of any trouble – and then all at once there he was."

"Who?" said the Curate, forgetting caution in his bewilderment.

Once more the door opened, and John appeared on the steps, this time with a lantern and the watch-dog, a great brown mastiff, by his side, evidently with the intention of searching the garden for the owners of those furtive voices. Mr Wentworth drew the arm of his trembling companion within his own. "I don't know what you want of me, but whatever it is, trust to me like – like a brother," he said, with a sigh. "But now compose yourself; we must go into the house: it will not do for you to be found here." He led her up the gravel-walk into the light of the lantern, which the vigilant guardian of the house was flashing among the bushes as he set out upon his rounds. John fell back amazed but respectful when he saw his mistress and the familiar visitor. "Beg your pardon, ma'am, but I knew there was voices, and I didn't know as any of the family was in the garden," said the man, discomfited. It was all Mr Wentworth could do to hold up the trembling figure by his side. As John retreated, she gathered a little fortitude. Perhaps it was easier for her to tell her hurried tremulous story, as he guided *her* back to the house, than it would have been in uninterrupted leisure and quiet. The family tragedy fell in broken sentences from her lips, as the Curate bent down his astonished ear to listen. He was totally unprepared for the secret which only her helplessness and weakness and anxiety to serve her father could have drawn from Miss Wodehouse's lips; and it had to be told so hurriedly that Mr Wentworth scarcely knew what it was, except a terrible unsuspected shadow overhanging the powerful house, until he had time to think it all over. There was no such time at this moment. His trembling companion left him as soon as they reached the house, to "compose herself," as she said. When he saw her face in the light of the hall lamp it was ghastly, and quivering with agitation, looking not ten years, as she said, but a hundred years older than when, in the sweet precision of her Sunday dress and looks, old Miss Wodehouse had bidden him good-bye at the green door. He went up to the drawing-room, notwithstanding, with as calm a countenance as he himself could collect, to pay the visit which, in this few minutes, had so entirely changed in character. Mr Wentworth felt as if he saw everything exactly as he had pictured it to himself half an hour ago. Lucy, who had left the piano, was seated in her low chair again, not working, but talking to Mr Wodehouse, who lay on the sofa, looking a trifle less rosy than usual, like a man who had had a fright, or been startled by some possible shadow of a ghost. To walk into the room, into the bright household glow, and smile and shake hands with them, feeling all the time that he knew more about them than they themselves did, was the strangest sensation to the young man. He asked how Mr Wodehouse did, with a voice which, to himself, sounded hollow and unnatural, and sat down beside the invalid, almost turning his back upon Lucy in his bewilderment. It was indeed with a great effort that Mr Wentworth mastered himself, and was able to listen to what his companion said.

"We are all right," said Mr Wodehouse – "a trifle of a headache or so – nothing to make a talk about; but Molly has forsaken us, and we were just about getting bored with each other, Lucy and I; a third person was all we wanted to make us happy – eh? Well I thought you looked at the door very often – perhaps I was mistaken – but I could have sworn you were listening and looking for somebody. No wonder either – I don't think so. I should have done just the same at your age."

"Indeed, papa, you are quite mistaken," said Lucy. "I suppose that means that I cannot amuse you by myself, though I have been trying all the evening. Perhaps Mr Wentworth will be more fortunate." And, either for shame of being supposed to look for him, or in a little innocent pique, she moved away from where she was sitting, and rang for tea, and left the two gentlemen to talk to each other. That is to say, Mr Wodehouse talked, and the Perpetual Curate sat looking vaguely at the fair figure which flitted about the room, and wondering if he were awake, or the world still in its usual place. After a while Miss Wodehouse came in, very tremulous and pale, and dropped into the first chair she could find, and pretended to occupy herself over her knitting. She had a headache, Lucy said; and Mr Wentworth sat watching while the younger sister tended the elder, bringing her tea, kissing her, persuading her to go and lie down, taking all kinds of affectionate trouble to cheer the pale woman, who looked over Lucy's fair head with eyes full of meaning to the bewildered visitor, who was the only one there who understood what her trouble meant. When he got up to go away, she wrung his hand with a pitiful gaze which went to his heart. "Let me know!" she said in a whisper; and, not satisfied still, went to the door with him, and lingered upon the stair, following slowly. "Oh, Mr Wentworth! be sure you let me know," she repeated, again looking wistfully after him as he disappeared into the dark garden, going out. The stars were still shining, the spring dews lying sweet upon the plants and turf. It was a lovelier night now than when Mr Wentworth had said so to little Rosa Elsworthy an hour ago; but mists were rising from the earth, and clouds creeping over the sky, to the startled imagination of the Perpetual Curate. He had found out by practical experiments, almost for the first time, that there were more things in earth and heaven than are dreamt of in the philosophy of youth.

CHAPTER VIII.

IT was the next morning after this when Mrs Hadwin's strange lodger first appeared in the astonished house. He was the strangest lodger to be taken into a house of such perfect respectability, a house in Grange Lane; and it came to be currently reported in Carlingford after a time, when people knew more about it, that even the servants could not tell when or how he arrived, but had woke up one morning to find a pair of boots standing outside the closed door of the green room, which the good old lady kept for company, with sensations which it would be impossible to describe. Such a pair of boots they were too – muddy beyond expression, with old mud which had not been brushed off for days – worn shapeless, and patched at the sides; the strangest contrast to a handsome pair of Mr Wentworth's, which he, contrary to his usual neat habits, had kicked off in his sitting-room, and which Sarah, the housemaid, had brought and set down on the landing, close by these mysterious and unaccountable articles. When the bell of the green room rang an hour or two later, Sarah and the cook, who happened to be standing together, jumped three yards apart and stared at each other; the sound gave them both "a turn." But they soon got perfectly well used to that bell from the green room. It rung very often in the day, for "the gentleman" chose to sit there more than half his time; and if other people were private about him, it was a great deal more than he was about himself. He even sent the boots to be mended, to Sarah's shame and confusion. For the credit of the house, the girl invented a story about them to calm the cobbler's suspicions. "They was the easiest boots the gentleman had, being troubled with tender feet; and he wasn't a-going to give them up because they was shabby," said Sarah. He sent down his shabby clothes to be brushed, and wore Mr Wentworth's linen, to the indignation of the household. But he was not a man to be concealed in a corner. From where he sat in the green room, he whistled so beautifully that Mrs Hadwin's own pet canary paused astonished to listen, and the butcher's boy stole into the kitchen surreptitiously to try if he could learn the art: and while he whistled, he filled the tidy room with parings and cuttings of wood, and carved out all kinds of pretty articles with his knife. But though he rang his bell so often, and was so tiresome with his litter, and gave so much trouble, Sarah's heart, after a while, melted to "the gentleman." He made her a present of a needlecase, and was very civil-spoken – more so a great deal than the Curate of St Roque's; and such a subject of talk and curiosity had certainly not been in Carlingford for a hundred years.

As for Mrs Hadwin, she never gave any explanation at

all on the subject, but accepted the fact of a new inmate cheerfully, as if she knew all about it. Of course she could not ask any of her nieces to visit her while the green room was occupied; and as they were all rather large, interfering, managing women, perhaps the old lady was not very sorry. Mr Wentworth himself was still less explanatory. When Mr Wodehouse said to him, "What is this I hear about a brother of yours? – they tell me you've got a brother staying with you. Well, that's what I hear. Why don't you bring him up to dinner? Come to-morrow;" the Perpetual Curate calmly answered, "Thank you; but there's no brother of mine in Carlingford," and took no further notice. Naturally, however, this strange apparition was much discussed in Grange Lane; the servants first, and then the ladies, became curious about him. Sometimes, in the evenings, he might be seen coming out of Mrs Hadwin's garden-door – a shabby figure, walking softly in his patched boots. There never was light enough for any one to see him; but he had a great beard, and smoked a short little pipe, and had evidently no regard for appearances. It was a kind of thing which few people approved of. Mrs Hadwin ought not to permit it, some ladies said; and a still greater number were of the opinion that, rather than endure so strange a fellow-lodger, the Curate ought to withdraw, and find fresh lodgings. This was before the time when the public began to associate the stranger in a disagreeable way with Mr Wentworth. Before they came to that, the people in Grange Lane bethought themselves of all Mrs Hadwin's connections, to find out if there might not be some of them under hiding; and, of course, that excellent woman had a nephew or two whose conduct was not perfect; and then it came to be reported that it was Mr Wentworth's brother – that it was an unfortunate college chum of his – that it was somebody who had speculated, and whom the Curate had gone shares with: but, in the mean time, no real information could be obtained about this mysterious stranger. The butcher's boy, whose senses were quickened by mingled admiration and envy, heard him whistling all day long, sometimes hidden among the trees in the garden, sometimes from the open window of the green room, where, indeed, Lady Western's page was ready to take his oath he had once seen the audacious unknown leaning out in the twilight, smoking a pipe. But no trap of conversation, however ingenious – and many traps were laid for Mr Wentworth – ever elicited from the Perpetual Curate any acknowledgment of the other lodger's existence. The young Anglican opened his fine eyes a little wider than usual when he was asked sympathetically whether so many people in the house did not interfere with his quiet. "Mrs Hadwin's talk is very gentle," said the Curate; "she never disturbs me." And the mistress of the house was equally obtuse, and would not comprehend any allusion. The little household came to be very much talked of in Carlingford in consequence; and to meet that shabby figure in the evening, when one chanced to be out for a walk, made one's company sought after in the best circles of society: though the fact is, that people began to be remiss in calling upon Mrs Hadwin, and a great many only left their cards as soon as it became evident that she did not mean to give any explanation. To have the Curate to stay with her was possible, without infringing upon her position; but matters became very different when she showed herself willing to take "any one," even when in equivocal apparel and patched boots.

Probably the Curate had his own troubles during this period of his history. He was noticed to be a little quick and short in his temper for some time after Easter. For one thing, his aunts did not go away; they stayed in the Blue Boar, and sent for him to dinner, till the Curate's impatience grew almost beyond bearing. It was a discipline upon which he had not calculated, and which exceeded the bounds of endurance, especially as Miss Leonora questioned him incessantly about his "work," and still dangled before him, like an unattainable sweetmeat before a child, the comforts and advantages of

Skelmersdale, where poor old Mr Shirley had rallied for the fiftieth time. The situation altogether was very tempting to Miss Leonora; she could not make up her mind to go away and leave such a very pretty quarrel in progress; and there can be no doubt that it would have been highly gratifying to her vanity as an Evangelical woman to have had her nephew brought to task for missionary work carried on in another man's parish, even though that work was not conducted entirely on her own principles. She lingered, accordingly, with a great hankering after Wharfside, to which Mr Wentworth steadily declined to afford her any access. She went to the afternoon service sometimes, it is true, but only to be afflicted in her soul by the sight of Miss Wodehouse and Lucy in their grey cloaks, not to speak of the rubric to which the Curate was so faithful. It was a trying experience to his Evangelical aunt; but at the same time it was a "great work;" and she could not give up the hope of being able one time or other to appropriate the credit of it, and win him over to her own "views." If that consummation could but be attained, everything would become simple; and Miss Leonora was a true Wentworth, and wanted to see her nephew in Skelmersdale: so it may easily be understood that, under present circumstances, there were great attractions for her in Carlingford.

It was, accordingly, with a beating heart that Miss Dora, feeling a little as she might have been supposed to feel thirty years before, had she ever stolen forth from the well-protected enclosure of Skelmersdale Park to see a lover, put on her bonnet in the early twilight, and, escaping with difficulty the lively observations of her maid, went tremulously down Grange Lane to her nephew's house. She had never yet visited Frank, and this visit was unquestionably clandestine. But then the news with which her heart was beating were important enough to justify the step she was taking – at least so

she whispered to herself; though whether dear Frank
would be pleased, or whether he would still think it "my
fault," poor Miss Dora could not make up her mind.
Nothing happened in the quiet road, where there were
scarcely any passengers, and the poor lady arrived with
a trembling sense of escape from unknown perils at Mrs
Hadwin's garden-door. For Miss Dora was of opinion,
like some few other ladies, that to walk alone down the
quietest of streets was to lay herself open to unheard-of
dangers. She put out her trembling hand to ring the
bell, thinking her perils over – for of course Frank
would walk home with her – when the door suddenly
opened, and a terrible apparition, quite unconscious of
anybody standing there, marched straight out upon
Miss Dora, who gave a little scream, and staggered
backwards, thinking the worst horrors she had dreamed
of were about to be realised. They were so close
together that the terrified lady took in every detail of his
appearance. She saw the patched boots and that shabby
coat which Sarah the housemaid felt that she rather
demeaned herself by brushing. It looked too small for
him, as coats will do when they get shabby; and, to
complete the alarming appearance of the man, he had
no hat, but only a little travelling-cap surmounting the
redundancy of hair, mustache, and beard, which were
enough of themselves to strike any nervous woman with
terror. "Oh, I beg your pardon," cried poor Miss Dora,
hysterically; "I wanted to see Mr Wentworth:" and she
stood trembling and panting for breath, holding by the
wall, not quite sure that this apparition could be
appeased by any amount of apologies. It was a great
comfort to her when the monster took off its cap, and
when she perceived, by the undulations of the beard,
something like a smile upon its hidden lips. "I believe
Mr Wentworth is at church," said the new lodger: "may
I have the pleasure of seeing you safely across to St
Roque's?" At which speech Miss Dora trembled more

and more, and said, faintly, "No, thank you," – for who could tell what the man's intentions might be? The result was, however, that he only put on his cap again, and went off like any other human creature in the other direction, and that slowly; with tremulous steps Miss Dora pursued her way to her nephew's pretty church. She could not have described, as she herself said, what a relief it was after all this, to take Frank's arm, as she met him at the door of St Roque's. He was coming out, and the young lady with the grey cloak had been one of the congregation; and, to tell the truth, Miss Dora was an unwelcome addition just then to the party. Lucy's coming had been accidental, and it was very sweet to Mr Wentworth to be able to conclude that he was obliged to walk home with her. They were both coming out from their evening devotions into the tranquil spring twilight, very glad of the charmed quiet, and happy somehow to find themselves alone together. That had happened but seldom of late; and a certain expectation of something that might happen hovered over the heads of Lucy and the Curate. It did not matter that he dared not say to her what was in his heart. Mr Wentworth was only a young man after all, and the thrill of a possible revelation was upon him in that half-hour upon which he was entering with so profound a sense of happiness. And then it was an accidental meeting, and if anything did happen, they could not blame themselves as if they had sought this opportunity of being together. The circumstances were such that they might call it providential, if anything came of it. But just as the two had made their first step out of the church, where the organ was still murmuring low in the darkness, and where the music of the last Amen, in which he had recognised Lucy's voice, had not quite died from the Curate's ears, to meet Miss Dora, pale and fluttered, full of news and distress, with no other thought in her mind but to appropriate her dear Frank, and take his arm and gain his ear! It was very hard upon the Perpetual Curate. As for Lucy, she, of course, did not say anything, but merely arranged her veil and greeted Miss Wentworth sweetly. Lucy walked on the other side of the Curate, saying little as Miss Dora's eager shower of questions and remarks ran on. Perhaps she had a little insight into Mr Wentworth's feelings, and no doubt it was rather tantalising. When they came to Mrs Hadwin's door, the young Anglican made a spasmodic effort, which in his heart he felt to be unprincipled, and which, had it been successful, would have totally taken away the accidental and unpremeditated character of this walk with Lucy, which he could not find it in his heart to relinquish. He proposed that his aunt should go in and rest while he saw Miss Wodehouse safely home – he was sure she was tired, he said, eagerly. "No, my dear, not at all," said Miss Dora; "it is such a pleasant evening, and I know Miss Wodehouse's is not very far off. I should like the walk, and, besides, it is too late, you know, to see Mrs Hadwin, and I should not like to go in without calling on her; and besides—"

Mr Wentworth in his aggravation gave a momentary sudden glance at Lucy when she had no expectation of it. That glance of disappointment – of disgust – of love and longing, was no more intentional than their meeting; could he help it, if it revealed that heart which was in such a state of commotion and impatience? Anyhow, the look gave Lucy sufficient occupation to keep her very quiet on the other side while Miss Dora maundered on.

"I met the strangest man coming out when I was going to ring your bell. You will think it very foolish, Frank, but he frightened me," she said. "A man with a terrible beard, and a – a shabby man, my dear. Who could it be? Not a person to be seen coming out of a house where a clergyman lives. He could not be any friend of yours?"

"The other lodger, I suppose," said the Curate, briefly. "When are you going away?"

"Oh, my dear boy, we are not going away; I came to tell you. But, Frank, you don't mean to say that such a man as that lodges in Mrs Hadwin's house? I don't think it is safe for you – I don't think it is respectable. People might think he was a friend of yours. I wonder if Miss Wodehouse has ever seen him – a great man with a beard? To be sure, a man might have a beard and yet be respectable; but I am sure, if Miss Wodehouse saw him, she would agree with me in thinking— Frank, my dear boy, what is the matter? Have I said anything wrong?"

"Nothing that I know of," said the Curate, who had given her arm a little angry pressure to stop the stream of utterance – "only that I am not interested in the other lodger. Tell me about your going away."

"But I must appeal to Miss Wodehouse: it is for your own sake, my dear Frank," said aunt Dora – "a clergyman should be so careful. I don't know what your aunt Leonora would say. Don't you think to see a man like that coming out of Mr Wentworth's house is not as it should be? I assure you he frightened me."

"I don't think I have seen him," said Lucy. "But shouldn't a clergyman's house be like the church, open to good and bad? – for it is to the wicked and the miserable you are sent," said the Sister of Mercy, lowering her voice and glancing up at the Perpetual Curate. They could have clasped each other's hands at that moment, almost without being aware that it was any personal feeling which made their agreement so sweet. As for Miss Dora, she went on leaning on her nephew's arm, totally unconscious of the suppressed rapture and elevation in which the two were moving at the other side.

"That is very true. I am sure your aunt Leonora would approve of that, dear," said Miss Dora, with a little answering pressure on her nephew's arm – "but still I have a feeling that a clergyman should always take care to be respectable. Not that he should neglect the wicked," continued the poor aunt, apologetically, "for a poor sinner turning from the evil of his ways is the – the most interesting – sight in the world, even to the angels, you know; but to *live* with them in the same house, my dear – I am sure that is what I never could advise, nor Leonora either; and Mrs Hadwin ought to know better, and have him away. Don't you know who he is, Frank? I could not be content without finding out, if it was me."

"I have nothing to do with him," said the Curate, hurriedly: "it is a subject I don't want to discuss. Never mind him. What do you mean by saying you are not going away?"

"My dear, Leonora has been thinking it all over," said Miss Dora, "and we are so anxious about you. Leonora is very fond of you, though she does not show it; and you know the Meritons have just come home from India, and have not a house to go to. So you see we thought, as you are not quite so comfortable as we could wish to see you, Frank – and perhaps we might be of some use – and Mr Shirley is better again, and no immediate settlement has to be made about Skelmersdale; – that on the whole, if Leonora and you were to see more of each other – oh, my dear boy, don't be so hasty; it was all her own doing – it was not my fault."

"Fault! I am sorry to be the occasion of so many arrangements," said Mr Wentworth, with his stiff manner; "but, of course, if you like to stay in Carlingford I shall be very happy – though there is not much preaching here that will suit my aunt Leonora: as for Mr Shirley, I hope he'll live for ever. I was at No. 10 today," continued the Curate, turning his head to the other side, and changing his tone in a manner marvellous to Miss Dora. "I don't think she can live much longer. You have done a great deal to smooth her way in this last stage. Poor soul! she thinks she has been a great sinner," said the young man, with a kind of wondering pity. He had a great deal to vex him in his own person, and he knew of some skeletons very near at hand, but somehow at that moment it was hard to think of the extremities of mortal trouble, of death and anguish – those dark deeps of life by which Lucy and he sometimes stood together in their youth and happiness. A marvelling remorseful pity came to his heart. He could not believe in misery, with Lucy walking softly in the spring twilight by his side.

"But, Frank, you are not taking any notice of what I say," said Miss Dora, with something like a suppressed sob. "I don't doubt your sick people are very important, but I thought you would take *some* interest. I came down to tell you, all the way by myself."

"My sister would like to call on you, Miss Wentworth," said Lucy, interposing. "Gentlemen never understand what one says. Perhaps we could be of some use to you if you are going to settle in Carlingford. I think she has been a great deal better since she confessed," continued the charitable Sister, looking up to the Curate, and, like him, dropping her voice. "The absolution was such a comfort. Now she seems to feel as if she could die. And she has so little to live for!" said Lucy, with a sigh of sympathetic feeling, remorseful too. Somehow it seemed cruel to feel so young, so hopeful, so capable of happiness, with such desolation close at hand.

"Not even duty," said the Curate; "and to think that the Church should hesitate to remove the last barriers out of the way! I would not be a priest if I were debarred from the power of delivering such a poor soul."

"Oh, Frank," said Miss Dora, with a long breath of fright and horror, "*what* are you saying? Oh, my dear, don't say it over again, I don't want to hear it! I hope when we are dying we shall all feel what great great sinners we are," said the poor lady, who, between vexation and mortification, was ready to cry, "and not think that one is better than another. Oh, my dear, there is that man again! Do you think it is safe to meet him in such a

lonely road? If he comes across and speaks to me any
more I shall faint," cried poor Miss Dora, whose opinions
were not quite in accordance with her feelings. Mr Wentworth did not say anything to soothe her, but with his
unoccupied hand he made an involuntary movement
towards Lucy's cloak, and plucked at it to bring her
nearer, as the bearded stranger loomed dimly past,
looking at the group. Lucy felt the touch, and wondered
and looked up at him in the darkness. She could not
comprehend the Curate's face.

"Are *you* afraid of him?" she said, with a slight smile; "if
it is only his beard I am not alarmed; and here is papa
coming to meet me. I thought you would have come for
me sooner, papa. Has anything happened?" said Lucy,
taking Mr Wodehouse's arm, who had suddenly appeared
from underneath the lamp, still unlighted, at Dr
Marjoribanks's door. She clung to her father with unusual
eagerness, willing enough to escape from the darkness and
the Curate's side, and all the tremulous sensations of the
hour.

"What could happen?" said Mr Wodehouse, who still
looked "limp" from his recent illness, "though I hear there
are doubtful people about; so they tell me – but you ought
to know best, Wentworth. Who is that fellow in the beard
that went by on the other side? Not little Lake the drawing-
master? Fancied I had seen the build of the man before –
eh? – a stranger? Well, it's a mistake, perhaps. Can't be
sure of anything nowadays; – memory failing. Well, that's
what the doctor says. Come in and rest and see Molly; as
for me, I'm not good for much, but you won't get better
company than the girls, or else that's what folks tell me.
Who did you say that fellow was?" said the churchwarden,
leaning across his daughter to see Mr Wentworth's face.

"I don't know anything about him," said the Curate of
St Roque's.

And curiously enough silence fell upon the little party,
nobody could tell how; – for two minutes, which looked

like twenty, no one spoke. Then Lucy roused herself, apparently with a little effort. "We seem to talk of nothing but the man with the beard to-night," she said. "Mary knows everything that goes on in Carlingford – she will tell us about him; and if Miss Wentworth thinks it too late to come in, we will say good-night," she continued, with a little decision of tone, which was not incomprehensible to the Perpetual Curate. Perhaps she was a little provoked and troubled in her own person. To say so much in looks and so little in words, was a mode of procedure which puzzled Lucy. It fretted her, because it looked unworthy of her hero. She withdrew within the green door, holding her father's arm fast, and talking to him, while Mr Wentworth strained his ears after the voice, which he thought he could have singled out from a thousand voices. Perhaps Lucy talked to drown her thoughts; and the Curate went away dumb and abstracted, with his aunt leaning on his arm on the other side of the wall. He could not be interested, as Miss Dora expected him to be, in the Miss Wentworths' plans. He conducted her to the Blue Boar languidly, with an evident indifference to the fact that his aunt Leonora was about to become a permanent resident in Carlingford. He said "Good-night" kindly to little Rosa Elsworthy, looking out with bright eyes into the darkness at the door of her uncle's shop; but he said little to Miss Dora, who could not tell what to make of him, and swallowed her tears as quietly as possible under her veil. When he had deposited his aunt safely at the inn, the Perpetual Curate hastened down Grange Lane at a great pace. The first sound he heard on entering Mrs Hadwin's garden was the clear notes of the stranger's whistle among the trees; and with an impatient exclamation Mr Wentworth sought his fellow-lodger, who was smoking as usual, pacing up and down a shaded walk, where, even in daylight, he was pretty well concealed from observation. The Curate looked as if he had a little discontent and repugnance to get over before he could address the anonymous individual who whistled so cheerily under the trees. When he did speak it was an embarrassed and not very intelligible call.

"I say – are you there? I want to speak to you," said Mr Wentworth.

"Yes," said the stranger, turning sharply round. "I am here, a dog without a name. What have you got to say?"

"Only that you must be more careful," said Mr Wentworth again, with a little stiffness. "You will be recognised if you don't mind. I have just been asked who you were by – somebody who thought he had seen you before."

"By whom?"

"Well, by Mr Wodehouse," said the Curate. "I may as well tell you; if you mean to keep up this concealment you must take care."

"By Jove!" said the stranger, and then he whistled a few bars of the air which Mr Wentworth's arrival had interrupted. "What is a fellow to do?" he said, after an interjection. "I sometimes think I had better risk it all – eh! don't you think so? I can't shut myself up for ever here."

"That must be as you think best," said the Perpetual Curate, in whom there appeared no movement of sympathy; and he said no more, though the doubtful individual by his side lifted an undecided look to his face, and once more murmured in perplexed tones a troubled exclamation: "A man must have a little amusement somehow," the stranger said, with an aggrieved voice; and then abruptly left his unsociable companion, and went off to his room, where he summoned Sarah to bring lights, and tried to talk to her a little in utter dearth of society. Mr Wentworth stayed behind, pacing up and down the darkening walk. The Curate's thoughts were far from satisfactory. There was not much comfort anywhere, let him look where he pleased. When a man has no spot in all his horizon on which his eye can rest with comfort, there is something more discouraging in the prospect than a positive calamity. He could not take refuge even in the imaginations of his love, for it was clear enough that already a sentiment of surprise had risen in Lucy's mind, and her tranquillity was shaken. And perhaps he had done rashly to plunge into other people's troubles – he upon whom a curious committee of aunts were now to sit *en permanence*. He went in to write his sermon, far from being so assured of things in general as that discourse was when it was written, though it was a little relief to his mind to fall back upon an authority somewhere, and to refer, in terms which were perhaps too absolute to be altogether free of doubt, to the Church, which had arranged every-thing for her children in one department of their concerns at least. If it were only as easy to know what ought to be done in one's personal affairs as to decide what was the due state of mind expected by the Church on the second Sunday after Easter! But being under that guidance, at least he could not go wrong in his sermon, which was one point of ease amid the many tribulations of the Curate of St Roque's.

CHAPTER IX.

"IF they are going to stay in Carlingford, perhaps we could be of use to them? Yes, Lucy; and I am sure anything we could do for Mr Wentworth—"said Miss Wodehouse. "I wonder what house they will get. I am going to Elsworthy's about some paper, and we can ask him if he knows where they are going. That poor little Rosa should have some one to take care of her. I often wonder whether it would be kind to speak to Mrs Elsworthy about it, Lucy; she is a sensible woman. The little thing stands at the door in the evening, and talks to people who are passing, and I am afraid there are some people who are unprincipled, and tell her she is pretty, and say things to her," said Miss Wodehouse, shaking her head; "it is a great pity. Even Mr Wentworth is a great deal more civil to that little thing than he would be if she had not such a pretty face."

"I said you knew everything that went on in Carlingford," said Lucy, as they went out together from the green door, not in their grey cloaks this time; "but I forgot to ask you about one thing that puzzled us last night – who is the man in the beard who lives at Mrs Hadwin's? Mr Wentworth will not tell anybody about him, and I think he knows."

"Who is the man in the beard?" said Miss Wodehouse, with a gasp. She grew very pale, and turned away her head and shivered visibly. "How very cold it is!" she said, with her teeth chattering; "did you think it was so cold? I –I don't know any men with beards; and it is so strange of you to say I know everything that goes on in Carlingford. Don't stop to speak to that little girl just now. Did you say she came from Prickett's Lane? No. 10? It is very right to go to see the sick, but, indeed, I don't approve of your attendance upon that poor woman, Lucy. When I was a girl I dared not have gone away by myself as you do, and she might not be a proper person. There is a carriage that I don't know standing before Elsworthy's shop."

"But you have not told me yet about the man with the beard," said Lucy, whose curiosity was excited. She looked at her sister keenly with an investigating look, and poor Miss Wodehouse was fain to draw her shawl close round her, and complain again of the cold.

"I told you I did not know," she said, with a complaining tone in her voice. "It is strange you should think I knew; it looks as if you thought me a gossip, Lucy. I wonder who those people can be coming out of the carriage? My dear," said the elder sister, feeling within herself that an attack upon the enemy's country was the best means of meeting any sally – "I don't think you should go down to Prickett's Lane just now. I saw Mr Wentworth pass a little while ago, and people might say you went to meet each other. I can't keep people from talking, Lucy, and you are both so young; and you know I spoke to you before about your meeting so often. It will be a great deal better for you to come with me to call on his aunts."

"Only that my poor patient wants me," said Lucy. "Must I not do my duty to a poor woman who is dying, because Mr Wentworth is in Prickett's Lane? There is no reason why I should be afraid of meeting Mr Wentworth," said the young district-visitor, severely; and the elder sister saw that Lucy spoke in a different tone from that in which she had answered her before. She did not extinguish Miss Wodehouse by a reference to the great work. She treated the matter more as a personal one to-day; and a shadow – a very ghost of irritation – was in Lucy's voice. The two crossed the street silently after that to Elsworthy's, where a group of ladies were visible, who had come out of the strange carriage. One of them was seated in a chair by the counter, another was reading a list which Mr Elsworthy had just presented to her, and the third, who was not so tall as her sister, was pressing up to it on tiptoe, trying to read it too. "That is Miss Dora Wentworth," said Lucy, "and the other, I suppose, is Miss Leonora, who is so very Low-Church. I think I can see the Miss Hemmings coming down George Street. If I were to go in I should be in a dreadful minority; but you are Low-Church in your heart too."

"No, dear; only reasonable," said Miss Wodehouse, apologetically. "I don't go as far as you and Mr Wentworth do, but I like the service to be nicely done, and the – the authority of the Church respected too. As I have never met Miss Wentworth, you had better come in and introduce me. There is Rosa looking out of the front window, Lucy. I really must speak to Mrs Elsworthy

about that child. What a lovely old lady that is sitting by
the counter! Say I am your sister, and then if you are
resolved upon Prickett's Lane, you can go away."

"They are the two who wear the grey cloaks," said Miss
Leonora Wentworth to herself, as the introduction was
effected. "I am glad to make your acquaintance, Miss
Wodehouse. We are going to stay in Carlingford for a
time, and to know a few pious families will be a great
advantage. We don't go much into society, in the usual
sense of the word – but, I am sure, to make the acquaintance of ladies who help my nephew so much in his work,
is sure to be an advantage. I should like so much to hear
from you how he gets on, for he does not say a great deal
about it himself."

"He is so good and so nice," said kind Miss Wodehouse,
"he never makes a fuss about anything he does. I am sure,
to see such young creatures so pious and so devoted,
always goes to my heart. When we were young it used to
be so different – we took our own pleasure, and never
thought of our fellow-creatures. And the young people are
so good nowadays," said the gentle woman, falling instinctively into her favourite sentiment. Miss Leonora looked
at her with critical eyes.

"We are none of us good," said that iron-grey woman,
whose neutral tints were so different from the soft dove-
colour of her new acquaintance; "it does not become such
sinful creatures to talk of anybody being good. Good
works may only be beautiful sins, if they are not done in a
true spirit," said Miss Leonora, turning to her list of
furnished houses with a little contempt. But the Miss
Hemmings had come in while she was speaking, and it was
seldom that such edifying talk was heard in Carlingford.

"That is such a beautiful sentiment – oh, if we only bore
it always in mind!" murmured the eldest Miss Hemmings.
"Mr Elsworthy, I hope you have got the tracts I ordered.
They are so much wanted here. Poor dear Mr Bury would
not believe his eyes if he could see Carlingford now, given

up to Puseyism and Ritualism – but good men are taken away from the evil to come. I will pay for them now, please."

"If you wish it, ma'am," said Mr Elsworthy. "The town *is* changed; I don't say nothing different; but being in the ritual line as you say, you won't find no church as it's better done than in St Roque's. Mr Wentworth never spares no pains, ma'am, on anything as he takes up. I've heard a deal of clergymen in my day, but *his* reading is beautiful; I can't say as I ever heard reading as could equal it; – and them choristers, though they're hawful to manage, is trained as I never see boys trained in *my* life afore. There's one of them houses, ma'am," continued the optimist, turning to Miss Wentworth, "as is a beauty. Miss Wodehouse can tell you what it is; no lady in the land could desire a handsomer drawing-room; and as for the kitchings, – I don't pretend to be a judge up-stairs, but being brought up a blacksmith, I know what's what in a kitching-range. If you had all Grange Lane to dinner, there's a range as is equal to it," said Mr Elsworthy with enthusiasm – "and my wife will show you the 'ouse."

"I knew Mr Bury," said Miss Leonora; "he was a precious man. Perhaps you have heard him mention the Miss Wentworths? I am very sorry to hear that there is no real work going on in the town. It is very sad that there should be nobody able to enter into the labours of such a saint."

"Indeed," said Miss Wodehouse, who was excited, in spite of herself, by this conversation, "I think the Carling-ford people go quite as much to church as in Mr Bury's days. I don't think there is less religion than there used to be: there are not so many prayer meetings, perhaps; but—"

"There is nothing the carnal mind dislikes so much as prayer meetings," said Miss Hemmings. "There is a house in Grove Street, if Miss Wentworth is looking for a house. I don't know much about the kitchen-range, but I know it

belongs to a very pious family, and they wish so much to
let it. My sister and I would be so glad to take you there.
It is not in the gay world, like Grange Lane."

"But you might want to ask people to dinner; and then
we should be so near Frank," said Miss Dora, whispering
at her sister's elbow. As for the second Miss Hemmings,
she was dull of comprehension, and did not quite make out
who the strangers were.

"It is so sad to a feeling mind to see the mummeries that
go on at St Roque's," said this obtuse sister; "and I am
afraid poor Mr Wentworth must be in a bad way. They
say there is the strangest man in his house – some relation
of his – and he daren't be seen in the daylight; and people
begin to think there must be something wrong, and that
Mr Wentworth himself is involved; but what can you
expect when there is no true Christian principle?" asked
Miss Hemmings, triumphantly. It was a dreadful moment
for the bystanders; for Miss Leonora turned round upon
this new intelligence with keen eyes and attention; and
Miss Dora interposed, weeping; and Miss Wodehouse
grew so pale, that Mr Elsworthy rushed for cold water,
and thought she was going to faint. "Tell me all about
this," said Miss Leonora, with peremptory and command-
ing tones. "Oh, Leonora, I am sure my dear Frank has
nothing to do with it, if there is anything wrong," cried
Miss Dora. Even Miss Wentworth herself was moved out
of her habitual smile. She said, "He is my nephew" – an
observation which she had never been heard to make
before, and which covered the second Miss Hemmings
with confusion. As for Miss Wodehouse, she retreated
very fast to a seat behind Miss Cecilia, and said nothing.
The two who had arrived last slunk back upon each other
with fiery glances of mutual reproach. The former three
stood together in this emergency, full of curiosity, and
perhaps a little anxiety. In this position of affairs, Mr
Elsworthy, being the only impartial person present, took
the management of matters into his own hands.

"Miss Hemmings and ladies, if you'll allow *me*," said Mr Elsworthy, "it aint no more than a mistake. The new gentleman as is staying at Mrs Hadwin's may be an unfortunate gentleman for anything I can tell; but he aint no relation of our clergyman. There aint nobody belonging to Mr Wentworth," said the clerk of St Roque's, "but is a credit both to him and to Carlingford. There's his brother, the Rev. Mr Wentworth, as is the finest-spoken man, to be a clergyman, as I ever set eyes on; and there's respected ladies as needn't be named more particular. But the gentleman as is the subject of conversation is no more like Mr Wentworth than – asking pardon for the liberty – I am. I may say as I have opportunities for knowing more than most," said Mr Elsworthy, modestly, "me and Rosa; for if there's a thing Mr Wentworth is particular about, it's having his papers the first moment; and ladies as knows me knows I am one that never says more nor the truth. Not saying a word against the gentleman – as is a most respectable gentleman, for anything I know against him – he aint no connection of Mr Wentworth. He's Mrs Hadwin's lodger; and I wouldn't say as he isn't a relation there; but our clergyman has got no more to do with him than the babe unborn."

Mr Elsworthy wiped his forehead after he had made this speech, and looked round for the approbation which he was aware he had deserved; and Miss Leonora Wentworth threw a glance of disdainful observation upon the unhappy lady who had caused this disturbance. "If your wife will come with us, we will go and look at the house," she said, graciously. "I daresay if it is in Grange Lane it will suit us very well. My nephew is a very young man, Miss Wodehouse," said Miss Leonora, who had not passed over the agitation of that gentle woman without some secret comments; "he does not take advice in his work, though it might be of great assistance to him; but I hope he'll grow older and wiser, as indeed he cannot help doing if he lives. I hope you and your pretty sister will come to

see us when we're settled; – I don't see any sense, you
know, in your grey cloaks – I'm old, and you won't mind
me saying so; but I know what Frank Wentworth is," said
the indignant aunt, making a severe curtsy, accompanied
by lightning glances at the shrinking background of female
figures, as she went out of the shop.

"Oh, Leonora! I always said you were fond of him,
though you never would show it," cried poor Miss Dora.
"She is a great deal more affectionate than she will let
anybody believe; and my dear Frank means nothing but
good," cried the too zealous champion. Miss Leonora
turned back upon the threshold of the shop.

"You will please to let me know what Dissenting
chapels there are in the town, and what are the hours of
the services," she said. "There must surely be a Bethesda,
or Zion, or something – Salem? yes, to be sure; – perhaps
there's somebody there that preaches the gospel. Send me
word," said the peremptory woman; and poor Miss Dora
relapsed into her usual melancholy condition, and stole
into the carriage in a broken-hearted manner, weeping
under her veil.

After which Miss Wodehouse went home, not having
much heart for further visits. That is to say, she went all
the way down Grange Lane, somewhat tremulous and
uncertain in her steps, and went as far as Mrs Hadwin's,
and hesitated at the door as if she meant to call there; but,
thinking better of it, went on a little farther with very
lingering steps, as if she did not know what she wanted.
When she came back again, the door of Mrs Hadwin's
garden was open, and the butcher's boy stood blocking up
the way, listening with all his ears to the notes of the
whistle, soft and high and clear like the notes of a bird,
which come audibly from among the trees. Miss Wodehouse gave a little start when she heard it: again she
hesitated, and looked in with such a wistful face that
Sarah, the housemaid, who had been about to slam the
door hastily upon the too tender butcher, involuntarily

held it wide open for the expected visitor. "No, not to-day thank you," said Miss Wodehouse. "I hope your mistress is quite well; give her my love, and say I meant to come in, but I have a bad headache. No, thank you; not to-day." She went away after that with a wonderful expression of face, and reached home long before Lucy had come back from Prickett's Lane. Miss Wodehouse was not good for much in the house. She went to the little boudoir up-stairs, and lay down on the sofa, and had some tea brought her by an anxious maid. She was very nervous, trembling she could not say why, and took up a novel which was lying on the sofa, and read the most affecting scene, and cried over it; and then her sweet old face cleared, and she felt better. When Lucy came in she kissed her sister, and drew down the blinds, and brought her the third volume, and then went away herself to arrange the dessert, and see that everything was in order for one of Mr Wodehouse's little parties. These were their respective parts in the house; and surely a more peaceful, and orderly, and affectionate house, was not to be found that spring evening, either in England or Grange Lane.

CHAPTER X.

It may be easily supposed after this that Mr Wentworth and his proceedings were sufficiently overlooked and com- mented upon in Carlingford. The Miss Wentworths took old Major Brown's house for six months, which, as every- body knows, is next door to Dr Marjoribanks. It was just after Letty Brown's marriage, and the poor old Major was very glad to go away and pay a round of visits, and try to forget that his last daughter had gone the way of all the rest. There was a summer-house built in the corner of the garden, with a window in the outer wall looking on to Grange Lane, from which everything that happened could be inspected; and there was always somebody at that window when the Perpetual Curate passed by. Then he began to have a strange painful feeling that Lucy watched too, and was observing all his looks and ways, and what he did and said in these changed times. It was a strange difference from the sweet half-conscious bond between them which existed of old, when they walked home together from Wharfside, talking of the district and the people, in the tender union of unspoken love and fellow-ship. Not that they were altogether parted now; but Lucy contrived to leave the schoolroom most days before the young priest could manage to disrobe himself, and was seldom to be seen on the road lingering on her errands of kindness as she used to do. But still she knew all he was about, and watched, standing in doubt and wonder of him, which was at least a great deal better than indifference. On the whole, however, it was a cloudy world through which the Perpetual Curate passed as he went from his lodgings, where the whistle of the new lodger had become a great nuisance to him, past the long range of garden-walls, the sentinel window where Miss Dora looked out watching for him, and Mr Wodehouse's green door which he no longer entered every day. Over the young man's mind, as he went out to his labours, there used to come that sensation of having nobody to fall back upon, which is of all feelings the most desolate. Amid all those people who were watching him, there was no one upon whom he could rest, secure of understanding and sympathy. They were all critical – examining, with more or less compre-hension, what he did; and he could not think of anybody in the world just then who would be content with knowing that *he* did it, and take that as warranty for the act, unless, perhaps, his poor aunt Dora, whose opinion was not important to the young man. It was not a pleasant state of mind into which these feelings threw him; and the natural result was, that he grew more and more careful about the rubric, and confined his sermons, with increasing precision, to the beautiful arrangements of the Church. They were very clever little sermons, even within these limitations, and an indifferent spectator would probably have been surprised to find how much he could make out of them; but still it is undeniable that a man has less scope, not only for oratory, but for all that is worthy of regard in human speech, when, instead of the ever-lasting reciprocations between heaven and earth, he occupies himself only with a set of ecclesiastical arrangements, however perfect. The people who went to St Roque's found this out, and so did Mr Wentworth; but it did not alter the system pursued by the troubled Curate. Perhaps he gave himself some half-conscious credit for it, as being against his own interests; for there was no mistaking the countenance of Miss Leonora, when now and then, on rare occasions, she came to hear her nephew preach.

All this, however, was confined to St Roque's, where there was a somewhat select audience, people who agreed in Mr Wentworth's views; but things were entirely different at Wharfside, where the Perpetual Curate was not thinking about himself, but simply about his work, and how to do it best. The bargemen and their wives did not know much about the Christian year; but they understood the greater matters which lay beneath: and the women said to each other, sometimes with tears in their eyes, that there was nothing that the clergyman didn't make plain; and that if the men didn't do what was right, it was none o' Mr Wentworth's fault. The young priest indemnified himself in "the district" for much that vexed him elsewhere. There was no question of Skelmersdale, or of any moot point there, but only a quantity of primitive people under the original conditions of humanity, whose lives might be amended, and consoled, and elevated. That was a matter about which Mr Wentworth had no doubt. He put on his surplice with the conviction that in that white ephod the truest embodiment of Christian purity was brought within sight of the darkened world. He was not himself, but a Christian priest, with power to deliver and to bless, when he went to Wharfside.

Easter had been early that year, and Ascension Day was in the beginning of May, one of those sweet days of early summer which still occur now and then to prove that the poets were right in all they say of the tenderest month of the year. Mr Wentworth had done duty at St Roque's, and afterwards at Wharfside. The sweet day and the sweet season had moved his heart. He was young, and it was hard to live shut up within himself without any sympathy either from man or woman. He had watched the grey cloak gliding out as his rude congregation dispersed, and went away quicker than was his wont, with a stronger longing than usual to overtake Lucy, and recover his place beside her. But she was not to be seen when he got into Prickett's Lane. He looked up the weary length of the street, and saw nothing but the children playing on the pavement, and some slovenly mothers at the doors. It was a very disenchanting prospect. He went on again in a kind of gloomy discontent, displeased with everything. What was the good of it all? he said to himself – weariness, and toil, and trouble, and nothing ever to come of it. As for the little good he was doing in Wharfside, God did not need his poor exertions; and, to tell the truth, going on at St Roque's, however perfect the rubric and pretty the church, was, without any personal stimulant of happiness, no great prospect for the Perpetual Curate. Such was the tenor of his thoughts, when he saw a black figure suddenly emerge out of one of the houses, and stand at the door, throwing a long shadow over the pavement. It was the Rector who was standing there in Mr Wentworth's favourite district, talking to a shopkeeper who had always been on the opposition side. The young Anglican raised his drooping head instantly, and recovered his interest in the general world.

"Glad to see you, Mr Wentworth," said the Rector. "I have been speaking to this worthy man about the necessities of the district. The statistics are far from being satisfactory. Five thousand souls, and no provision for their spiritual wants; it is a very sad state of affairs. I mean to take steps immediately to remedy all that."

"A bit of a Methody chapel, that's all," said the opposition shopkeeper; "and the schoolroom, as Mr Wentworth—"

"Yes, I have heard of that," said the Rector, blandly; — somebody had advised Mr Morgan to change his tactics, and this was the first evidence of the new policy — "I hear you have been doing what little you could to mend matters. It is very laudable zeal in so young a man. But, of course, as you were without authority, and had so little in your power, it could only be a very temporary expedient. I am very much obliged to you for your good intentions."

"I beg your pardon," said the Perpetual Curate, rousing up as at the sound of the trumpet, "I don't care in the least about my good intentions; but you have been much deceived if you have not understood that there is a great work going on in Wharfside. I hope, Saunders, you have had no hand in deceiving Mr Morgan. I shall be glad to show you my statistics, which are more satisfactory than the town list," said Mr Wentworth. "The schoolroom is consecrated; and but that I thought we had better work slowly and steadily, there is many a district in worse condition which has its church and its incumbent. I shall be very happy to give you all possible information; it is best to go to the fountainhead."

"The fountainhead!" said the Rector, who began not unnaturally to lose his temper. "Are you aware, sir, that Wharfside is in my parish?"

"And so is St Roque's, I suppose," said the Curate, affably. "I have no district, but I have my cure of souls all the same. As for Wharfside, the Rector of Carlingford never had had anything to do with it. Mr Bury and Mr

Proctor made it over to me. I act upon their authority; but I should like to prove to you it is something more than a temporary expedient," said the young Anglican, with a smile. Mr Morgan was gradually getting very hot and flushed. His temper got the better of him; he could not tolerate to be thus bearded on his own ground.

"It appears to me the most extraordinary assumption," said the Rector. "I can't fancy that you are ignorant of the law. I repeat, Wharfside is in my parish; and on what ground you can possibly justify such an incredible intrusion—"

"Perhaps we might find a fitter place to discuss the matter," said the Curate, with great suavity. "If you care to go to the schoolroom, we could be quiet there."

"No, sir. I don't care to go to the schoolroom. I decline to have anything to do with such an unwarrantable attempt to interfere with my rights," said Mr Morgan. "I don't want to know what plausible arguments you may have to justify yourself. The fact remains, sir, that Wharfside is in my parish. If you have anything to say against that, I will listen to you," said the irascible Rector. His Welsh blood was up; he even raised his voice a little, with a kind of half-feminine excitement, common to the Celtic race; and the consquence was that Mr Wentworth, who stood perfectly calm to receive the storm, had all the advantage in the world over Mr Morgan. The Perpetual Curate bowed with immovable composure, and felt himself master of the field.

"In that case, it will perhaps be better not to say anything," he said; "but I think you will find difficulties in the way. Wharfside has some curious privileges, and pays no rates; but I have never taken up that ground. The two previous rectors made it over to me, and the work is too important to be ignored. I have had thoughts of applying to have it made into an ecclesiatical district," said the Curate, with candour, "not thinking that the Rector of Carlingford, with so much to occupy him, would care to interfere with my labours; but at all events, to begin another mission here would be folly – it would be copying the tactics of the Dissenters, if you will forgive me for saying so," said Mr Wentworth, looking calmly in the Rector's face.

It was all Mr Morgan could do to restrain himself. "I am not in the habit of being schooled by my – juniors," said the Rector, with suppressed fury. He meant to say inferiors, but the aspect of the Perpetual Curate checked him. Then the two stood gazing at each other for a minute in silence. "Anything further you may have to say, you will perhaps communicate to my solicitor," said the elder priest. "It is well known that some gentlemen of your views, Mr Wentworth, think it safe to do evil that good may come; – that is not my opinion; and I don't mean to permit any invasion of my rights. I have the pleasure of wishing you good morning."

Mr Morgan took off his hat, and gave it a little angry flourish in the air before he put it on again. He had challenged his young brother to the only duel permitted by their cloth, and he turned to the opposition tradesman with vehemence, and went in again to the dusty little shop, where a humble assortment of groceries were displayed for the consumption of Prickett's Lane. Mr Wentworth remained standing outside in much amazement, not to say amusement, and a general sense of awakening and recovery. Next to happiness, perhaps enmity is the most healthful stimulant of the human mind. The Perpetual Curate woke up and realised his position with a sense of exhilaration, if the truth must be told. He muttered something to himself, uncomplimentary to Mr Morgan's good sense, as he turned away; but it was astonishing to find how much more lively and interesting Prickett's Lane had become since that encounter. He went along cheerily, saying a word now and then to the people at the doors, every one of whom knew and recognised him, and acknowledged, in a lesser or greater degree, the sway of his

bishopric. The groups he addressed made remarks after
he had passed, which showed their sense of the improvement in his looks. "He's more like himsel' than he's bin
sin' Easter," said one woman, "and none o' that crossed
look, as if things had gone contrary; – Lord bless you, not
cross – he's a deal too good a man for that – but crossed-
looking; it might be crossed in love for what I can tell."
"Them as is handsome like that seldom gets crossed in
love," said another experienced observer; "but if it was
fortin, or whatever it was, there's ne'er a one in Wharfside
but wishes luck to the parson. It aint much matter for us
women. Them as won't strive to keep their children
decent out o' their own heads, they won't do much for a
clergyman; but, bless you, he can do a deal with the men,
and it's them as wants looking after." "I'd like to go to his
wedding," said another. "I'd give a deal to hear it was all
settled;" and amid these affectionate comments, Mr
Wentworth issued out of Prickett's Lane. He went direct
to Mr Wodehouse's green door, without making any
excuses to himself. For the first time for some weeks he
went in upon the sisters and told them all that had
happened as of old. Lucy was still in her grey cloak as she
had returned from the district, and it was with a feeling
more distinct than sympathy that she heard of this
threatened attack. "It is terrible to think that he could
interfere with such a work out of jealousy of *us*," said the
Sister of Charity, with a wonderful light in her blue eyes;
and she drew her low chair nearer, and listened with
eloquent looks, which were balm to the soul of the Perpetual Curate. "But we are not to give up?" she said,
giving him her hand, when he rose to go away. "Never!"
said Mr Wentworth; and if he held it more closely and
longer than there was any particular occasion for, Lucy
did not make any objection at that special moment. Then
it turned out that he had business at the other end of the
town, at the north end, where some trustee lived who had
to do with the Orphan Schools, and whom the curate was

obliged to see; and Miss Wodehouse gave him a timid invitation to come back to dinner. "But you are not to go home to dress; we shall be quite alone – and you must be so tired," said the elder sister, who for some reason or other was shy of Mr Wentworth, and kept away from him whenever he called. So he went in on his way back, and dined in happiness and his morning coat, with a sweet conscious return to the familiar intercourse which these few disturbed weeks had interrupted. He was a different man when he went back again down Grange Lane. Once more the darkness was fragrant and musical about him. When he was tired thinking of his affairs, he fell back upon the memories of the evening, and Lucy's looks and the "us" and "we," which were so sweet to his ears. To have somebody behind whom one can fall back upon to fill up the interstices of thought – *that* makes all the difference, as Mr Wentworth found out, between a bright and a heavy life.

When he opened the garden-door with his key, and went softly in in the darkness, the Perpetual Curate was much surprised to hear voices among the trees. He waited a little, wondering, to see who it was; and profound was his amazement when a minute after little Rosa Elsworthy, hastily tying her hat over her curls, came rapidly along the walk from under the big walnut-tree, and essayed, with rather a tremulous hand, to open the door. Mr Wentworth stepped forward suddenly and laid his hand on her arm. He was very angry and indignant, and no longer the benign superior being to whom Rosa was accustomed. "Whom have you been talking to?" said the Curate. "Why are you here alone so late? What does this mean?" He held the door close, and looked down upon her severely while he spoke. She made a frightened attempt to defend herself.

"Oh, please, I only came with the papers. I was talking to – Sarah," said the little girl, with a sob of shame and terror. "I will never do it again. Oh, please, *please*, let me go! Please, Mr Wentworth, let me go!"

"How long have you been talking to – Sarah?" said the Curate. "Did you ever do it before? No, Rosa; I am going to take you home. This must not happen any more."

"I will run all the way. Oh, don't tell my aunt, Mr Wentworth. I didn't mean any harm," said the frightened creature. "You are not really coming? Oh, Mr Wentworth, if you tell my aunt I shall die!" cried poor little Rosa. But she was hushed into awe and silence when the curate stalked forth, a grand, half-distinguished figure by her side, keeping pace with her hasty, tremulous steps. She even stopped crying, in the whirlwind of her feelings. What did he mean? Was he going to say anything to her? Was it possible that he could like her, and be jealous of her talk with – Sarah? Poor little foolish Rosa did not know what to think. She had read a great many novels, and knew that it was quite usual for gentlemen to fall in love with pretty little girls who were not of their own station; – why not with her? So she went on, half running, keeping up with Mr Wentworth, and sometimes stealing sly glances at him to see what intention was in his looks. But his looks were beyond Rosa's reading. He walked by her side without speaking, and gave a glance up at the window of the summer-house as they passed. And strange enough, that evening of all others, Miss Dora, who had been the victim of some of Miss Leonora's caustic criticisms, had strayed forth, in melancholy mood, to repose herself at her favourite window, and look out at the faint stars, and comfort herself with a feeble repetition of her favourite plea, that it was not "my fault." The poor lady was startled out of her own troubles by the sight of her nephew's tall unmistakable figure; and, as bad luck would have it, Rosa's hat, tied insecurely by her agitated fingers, blew off at that moment, so that Mr Wentworth's aunt became aware, to her inexpressible horror and astonishment, who his companion was. The unhappy Curate divined all the thoughts that would arise in her perturbed bosom, when he saw the indistinct figure at the window, and said

something to himself about *espionage*, which was barely
civil to Miss Dora, as he hurried along on his charitable
errand. He was out of one trouble into another, this
unlucky young man. He knocked sharply at Elsworthy's
closed door, and gave up his charge without speaking to
Rosa. "I brought her home because I thought it wrong to
let her go up Grange Lane by herself," said the Curate.
"Don't thank me; but if you have any regard for the child,
don't send her out at night again." He did not even bid
Rosa good-night, or look back at her, as she stood blushing
and sparkling in confused childish beauty, in the doorway;
but turned his back like any savage, and hastened home
again. Before he entered his own apartments, he knocked
at the door of the green room, and said something to the
inmate there which produced from that personage a growl
of restrained defiance. And after all these fatigues, it was
with a sense of relief that the Curate threw himself upon
his sofa, to think over the events of the afternoon, and to
take a little rest. He was very tired, and the consolation he
had experienced during the evening made him more disposed to yield to his fatigue. He threw hmself upon the
sofa, and stretched out his hand lazily for his letters, which
evidently did not excite any special expectations in his
mind. There was one from his sister, and one from an old
university friend, full of the news of the season. Last of
all, there was a neat little note, directed in a neat little
hand, which anybody who received it would naturally
have left to the last, as Mr Wentworth did. He opened it
quite deliberately, without any appearance of interest.
But as he read the first lines, the Curate gradually gathered
himself up off the sofa, and stretched out his hand for his
boots, which he had just taken off; and before he had
finished it, had walked across the room and laid hold of the
railway book in use at Carlingford, all the time reading
and re-reading the important little epistle. It was not so
neat inside as out, and blurred and blotted, and slightly
illegible; and this is what the letter said:–

"Oh, Frank, dear, I am so anxious and unhappy about Gerald. I can't tell what is the matter with him. Come directly, for heaven's sake, and tell me what you think, and try what you can do. Don't lose a train after you get this, but come directly – oh, come if you ever loved any of us. I don't know what he means, but he says the most awful things; and if he is not *mad*, as I sometimes hope, he has forgotten his duty to his family and to me, which is far worse. I can't explain more; but if there is any chance of anybody doing him good, it is you. I beg you, on my knees, come directly, dear Frank. I never was in such a state in my life. I shall be left so that nobody will be able to tell what I am; and my heart is bursting. Never mind business or anything; but come, come directly, whether it is night or day, to your broken-hearted sister,

"LOUISA."

"*P.S.* – In great haste, and *so* anxious to see you."

Half an hour after, Mr Wentworth, with a travelling-bag in his hand, was once more hastening up Grange Lane towards the railway station. His face was somewhat grey, as the lamps shone on it. He did not exactly know what he was anxious about, nor what might have happened at Wentworth Rectory before he could get there; but the express train felt slow to his anxious thoughts as it flashed out of the station. Mr Morgan and his wife were in their garden, talking about the encounter in Prickett's Lane, when the train plunged past, waking all the echoes; and Mrs Morgan, by way of making a diversion, appealed to the Rector about those creepers, with which she hoped in a year or two to shut out the sight of the railway. "The Virginian creeper would be the best," said the Rector's wife; and they went in to calculate the expenses of bringing Mr Wentworth before Dr Lushington. Miss Dora, at very nearly the same moment, was confiding to her sister Cecilia, under vows of secrecy, the terrible sight she had seen from the summer-house window. They went to bed with very sad hearts in consequence, both these good women. In the mean time, leaving all these gathering clouds behind him, leaving his reputation and his work to be discussed and quarrelled over as they might, the Perpetual Curate rushed through the night, his heart aching with trouble and anxiety, to help, if he could – and if not, at least to stand by – Gerald, in this unknown crisis of his brother's life.

CHAPTER XI.

Miss Dora Wentworth rose very unrefreshed next morning from her disturbed slumbers. It was hard to sit at breakfast with Leonora, and not betray to her the new anxiety; and the troubled sister ran into a countless number of digressions, which would have inevitably betrayed her had not Miss Leonora been at the moment otherwise occupied. She had her little budget of letters as usual, and some of them were more than ordinarily interesting. She too had a favourite district, which was in London, and where also a great work was going on; and her missionary, and her Scripture-readers, and her colporteur were all in a wonderful state of excitement about a new gin-palace which was being fitted out and decorated in the highest style of art on the borders of their especial domain. They were moving heaven and earth to prevent this temple of Satan from being licensed; and some of them were so very certain of the Divine acquiescence in their measures, that they announced the success of their exertions to be a test of the faithfulness of God; which Miss Leonora read out to her sisters as an instance of very touching and beautiful faith. Miss Wentworth, perhaps, was not so clear on that subject. During the course of her silent life, she had prayed for various things which it had not been God's pleasure to grant; and just now she, too, was very anxious about Frank, who seemed to be in a bad way; so she rather shook her head gently, though she did not contravene the statement, and concluded with sadness that the government of the earth might still go on as usual, and God's goodness remain as certain as ever, even though the public-house was licensed, or Frank did fall away. This was the teaching of experience; but aunt Cecilia did not utter it, for that was not her way. As for Miss Dora, she agreed in all the colporteur's sentiments, and thought them beautiful, as Leonora said, and was not much disturbed by any opinion of her own, expressed or unexpressed, but interspersed her breakfast with little sighing ejaculations of the temptations of the world, and how little one knew what was passing around one, and "let him that thinketh he standeth take heed lest he fall," which could not have failed to attract Miss Leonora's attention, and draw forth the whole story of her sister's suspicions, had not that quick-witted iron-grey woman been, as we have already mentioned, too deeply engaged. Perhaps her nephew's imaginary backsliding might have excited even Miss Leonora to an interest deeper than that which was awakened by the new gin-palace; but as it happened, it was the humbler intelligence alone which occupied itself with the supposed domestic calamity. Miss Dora's breakfast was affected by it in a way which did not appear in the morning meal of her sister; for somehow the most fervent love of souls seldom takes away the appetite, as the love of some unlucky individual occasionally does.

When breakfast was over, Miss Dora made a very elaborate excuse for going out by herself. She wanted to match some wool for a blanket she was making, "For Louisa's baby," the devoted aunt said, with a little tremor. "Poor Louisa! if Gerald were to go any further, you know, it would be so sad for her; and one would like to help to keep up her heart, poor dear, as much as one could."

"By means of a blanket for the bassinet in scarlet and white," said Miss Leonora; "but it's quite the kind of comfort for Louisa. I wonder if she ever had the smallest inkling what kind of a husband she has got. I don't think Frank is far wrong about Gerald, though I don't pin my faith to my nephew's judgment. I daresay he'll go mad or do worse with all those crotchets of his – but what he married Louisa for has always been a mystery to me."

"I suppose because he was very fond of her," suggested Miss Dora, with humility.

"But why was he fond of her? – a goose!" said the strong-minded sister, and so went about her letter-writing without further comment, leaving aunt Dora to pursue her independent career. It was with a feeling of relief, and yet of guilt, that this timid inquirer set forth on her mission, exchanging a sympathetic significant look with Miss Wentworth before she went out. If she should meet Frank at the door, looking dignified and virtuous, what could she possibly say to him? and yet, perhaps, he had only been imprudent, and did not mean anything. Miss Dora looked round her on both sides, up and down Grange Lane, as she went out into the lovely summer morning. Neither Frank nor any other soul, except some nurse-maids, was to be seen along the whole line of sunny road. She was relieved, yet she was disappointed at the same time, and went slowly up towards Elsworthy's shop, saying to herself that she was sure Frank could not mean anything. It must have been that forward little thing herself who had come up to him when he was out for his walk, or it must have been an accident. But then she remembered that she had heard the Curate call Rosa pretty; and Miss Dora wondered within herself what it mattered whether she was pretty or not, and what he had to do with it, and shook her head over the strange way men had of finding out such things.

For her own part, she was sure she never looked whether the girl was pretty or not; and the anxious aunt had just come round again, by a very circuitous and perplexing course, to her original sentiment, and strengthened herself in the thought that her dear Frank could not mean anything, when she reached Elsworthy's door.

That worthy trader was himself behind the counter, managing matters with his usual exactness. Berlin wool was one of the articles Mr Elsworthy dealt in, besides newspapers, and books when they were ordered. Miss Dora, who wore no crinoline, stumbled over her dress in her agitation as she went in, and saw, at the first glance, little Rosa, looking very blooming and pretty, tying up a parcel at the other end of the shop. The poor lady did not know how to enter upon so difficult a question. She offered her wool humbly to be matched, and listened to Mr Elsworthy's sentiments on the subject. He told her how he always had his wools from the best houses in London, and could match anything as was ever made in that line, and was proud to say as he always gave satisfaction. Miss Dora could not see any opening for the inquiries she hoped to make; for how was it possible to intimate the possibility of disapproval to an establishment so perfect in all its arrangements? The probabilities are, that she would have gone away without saying anything, had not Mr Elsworthy himself given her a chance.

"Miss Wodehouse has been my great help," said the shopkeeper; "she is the nicest lady, is Miss Wodehouse, in all Carlingford. I do respect them people; they've had their troubles, like most families, but there aint many as can lay their finger on the skeleton as is in their cupboard: they've kept things close, and there aint a many as knows; but Miss Wodehouse has spoke up for me, ma'am, right and left, and most persons as count for anything in Carlingford gets their fancy articles out o' my shop. Mr Wentworth, ma'am, our respected clergyman, gets all his papers of me – and partickler he is to a degree – and likes to have 'em first thing afore they're opened out o' the parcel. It's the way with gentlemen when they're young. Mostly people aint so partickler later in life – not as I could tell the reason why, unless it may be that folks gets used to most things, and stop looking for anything new. But there aint a many young gentlemen like our clergyman, though I say it as shouldn't," continued Mr Elsworthy, with a little effusion, as he succeeded in finding an exact match for the scarlet wool.

"And why shouldn't you say it, Mr Elsworthy?" said Miss Dora, a little tartly; "you are not in any way particularly connected with my nephew." Here she gave an angry glance at Rosa, who had drawn near to listen, having always in her vain little heart a certain palpitation at Mr Wentworth's name.

"I ask your pardon, ma'am; I'm clerk at St Roque's. It aint often as we have the pleasure of seeing you there – more's the pity," said the church official, "though I may say there aint a church as perfect, or where the duty is performed more beautiful, in all the country; and there never was a clergyman as had the people's good at heart like Mr Wentworth – not in my time. It aint no matter whether you're rich or poor, young or old, if there's a service as can be done to ever a one in his way, our clergyman is the man to do it. Why, no further gone than last night, ma'am, if you'll believe me, that little girl there—"

"Yes," said Miss Dora, eagerly, looking with what was intended to be a very stern and forbidding aspect in the little girl's face.

"She was a-coming up Grange Lane in the dark," said Mr Elsworthy – "not as there was any need, and me keeping two boys, but she likes a run out of an evening – when Mr Wentworth see her, and come up to her. It aint what many men would have done," said the admiring but unlucky adherent of the suspected Curate: "he come up, seeing as she was by herself, and walked by her, and gave

her a deal of good advice, and brought her home. Her
aunt and me was struck all of a heap to see the clergyman
a-standing at our door. 'I've brought Rosa home,' he said,
making believe a bit sharp. 'Don't send her out no more so
late at night,' and was off like a shot, not waiting for no
thanks. It's my opinion as there aint many such gentlemen. I can't call to mind as I ever met with his fellow
before."

"But a young creature like that ought not to have been
out so late," said Miss Dora, trying to harden herself into
severity. "I wonder very much that you like to walk up
Grange Lane in the dark. I should think it very unpleasant, for my part; and I am sure I would not allow it,
Mr Elsworthy," she said firmly, "if such a girl belonged to
me."

"But, please, I wasn't walking up Grange Lane," said
Rosa, with some haste. "I was at Mrs Hadwin's, where Mr
Wentworth lives. I am sure I did not want to trouble him,"
said the little beauty, recovering her natural spirit as she
went on, "but he insisted on walking with me; it was all his
own doing. I am sure I didn't want him;" and here Rosa
broke off abruptly, with a consciousness in her heart that
she was being lectured. She rushed to her defensive
weapons by natural instinct, and grew crimson all over her
pretty little face, and flashed lightning out of her eyes,
which at the same time were not disinclined to tears. All
this Miss Dora made note of with a sinking heart.

"Do you mean to say that you went to Mrs Hadwin's to
see Mr Wentworth?" asked that unlucky inquisitor, with a
world of horror in her face.

"I went with the papers," said Rosa, "and I – I met him
in the garden. I am sure it wasn't my fault," said the girl,
bursting into petulant tears. "Nobody has any occasion to
scold me. It was Mr Wentworth as would come;" and Rosa
sobbed, and lighted up gleams of defiance behind her
tears. Miss Dora sat looking at her with a very troubled,
pale face. She thought all her fears were true, and matters

worse than she imagined; and being quite unused to private inquisitions, of course she took all possible steps to create the scandal for which she had come to look.

"Did you ever meet him in the garden before?" asked Miss Dora, painfully, in a low voice. During this conversation Mr Elsworthy had been looking on, perplexed, not perceiving the drift of the examination. He roused himself up to answer now – a little alarmed, to tell the truth, by the new lights thrown on the subject, and vexed to see how unconsciously far both the women had gone.

"It aint easy to go into a house in Grange Lane without meeting of some one in the garden," said Mr Elsworthy; "not as I mean to say it was the right thing for Rosa to be going them errands after dark. My orders is against that, as she knows; and what's the good of keeping two boys if things isn't to be done at the right time? Mr Wentworth himself was a-reproving of me for sending out Rosa, as it might be the last time he was here; for she's one of them as sits in the chancel and helps in the singing, and he feels an interest in her, natural," said the apologetic clerk. Miss Dora gave him a troubled look, but took no further notice of his speech. She thought, with an instinctive contempt for the masculine spectator, that it was impossible he could know anything about it, and pursued her own wiser way.

"It is very wrong of you – a girl in your position," said Miss Dora, as severely as she could in her soft old voice, "to be seen walking about with a gentleman, even when he is your clergyman, and, of course, has nothing else in his head. Young men don't think anything of it," said the rash but timid preacher; "of course it was only to take care of you, and keep you out of harm's way. But then you ought to think what a trouble it was to Mr Wentworth, taking him away from his studies – and it is not nice for a young girl like you." Miss Dora paused to take breath, not feeling quite sure in her own mind whether this was the right thing to say. Perhaps it would have been better to have disbelieved the fact altogether, and declared it impossible. She was much troubled about it, as she stood looking into the flushed tearful face, with all that light of defiance behind the tears, and felt instinctively that little Rosa, still only a pretty, obstinate, vain, uneducated little girl, was more than a match for herself, with all her dearly-won experiences. The little thing was bristling with a hundred natural weapons and defences, against which Miss Dora's weak assault had no chance.

"If it was a trouble, he need not have come," said Rosa, more and more convinced that Mr Wentworth must certainly have meant something. "I am sure *I* did not want him. He insisted on coming, though I begged him not. I don't know why I should be spoke to like this," cried the little coquette, with tears, "for I never was one as looked at a gentleman; it's them," with a sob, "as comes after me."

"Rosa," said Mr Elsworthy, much alarmed, "your aunt is sure to be looking out for you, and I don't want you here, not now; nor I don't want you again for errands, and don't you forget. If it hadn't been that Mr Wentworth thought you a silly little thing, and had a kind feeling for my missis and me, you don't think he'd have took that charge of you? – and I won't have my clergyman, as has always been good to me and mine, made a talk of. You'll excuse me, ma'am," he said, in an under tone, as Rosa reluctantly went away – not to her aunt, however, but again to her parcel at the other end of the shop – "she aint used to being talked to. She's but a child, and don't know no better: and after all," said Rosa's uncle, with a little pride, "she is a tender-hearted little thing – she don't know no better, ma'am; she's led away by a kind word – for nobody can say but she's wonderful pretty, as is very plain to see."

"Is she?" said Miss Dora, following the little culprit to the back-counter with disenchanted eyes. "Then you had better take all the better care of her, Mr Elsworthy," she

said, with again a little asperity. The fact was, that Miss
Dora had behaved very injudiciously, and was partly
aware of it; and then this prettiness of little Rosa's, even
though it shone at the present moment before her, was not
so plain to her old-maidenly eyes. She did not make out
why everybody was so sure of it, nor what it mattered; and
very probably, if she could have had her own way, would
have liked to give the little insignificant thing a good
shake, and asked her how she dared to attract the eye of
the Perpetual Curate. As she could not do this, however,
Miss Dora gathered up her wool, and refused to permit Mr
Elsworthy to send it home for her. "I can carry it quite
well myself," said the indignant little woman. "I am sure
you must have a great deal too much for your boys to do,
or you would not send your niece about with the things.
But if you will take my advice, Mr Elsworthy," said Miss
Dora, "you will take care of that poor little thing; she will
be getting ridiculous notions into her head;" and aunt
Dora went out of the shop with great solemnity, quite
unaware that she had done more to put ridiculous notions
into Rosa's head than could have got there by means of a
dozen darkling walks by the side of the majestic Curate,
who never paid her any compliments. Miss Dora went
away more than ever convinced in her mind that Frank
had forgotten himself and his position, and everything
that was fit and seemly. She jumped to a hundred horrible
conclusions as she went sadly across Grange Lane with her
scarlet wool in her hand. What Leonora would say to such
an irremediable folly? – and how the Squire would receive
his son after such a *mésalliance?* "He might change his
views," said poor Miss Dora to herself, "but he could not
change his wife;" and it was poor comfort to call Rosa a
designing little wretch, and to reflect that Frank at first
could not have meant anything. The poor lady had a bad
headache, and was in a terribly depressed condition all
day. When she saw from the window of her summer-house
the pretty figure of Lucy Wodehouse in her grey cloak

pass by, she sank into tears and melancholy reflections. But then Lucy Wodehouse's views were highly objectionable, and she bethought herself of Julia Trench, who had long ago been selected by the sisters as the clergyman's wife of Skelmersdale. Miss Dora shook her head over the blanket she was knitting for Louisa's baby, thinking of clergymen's wives in general, and the way in which marriages came about. Who had the ordering of these inexplicable accidents? It was surely not Providence, but some tricky imp or other who loved confusion; and then Miss Dora paused with compunction, and hoped she would be forgiven for entertaining, even for one passing moment, such a wicked, wicked thought.

CHAPTER XII.

On the afternoon of the same day Mr Morgan went home late, and frightened his wife out of her propriety by the excitement and trouble in his face. He could do nothing but groan as he sat down in the drawing-room, where she had just been gathering her work together, and putting stray matters in order, before she went up-stairs to make herself tidy for dinner. The Rector paid no attention to the fact that the dinner-hour was approaching, and only shook his head and repeated his groan when she asked him anxiously what was the matter. The good man was too much flushed and heated and put out, to be able at first to answer her questions.

"Very bad, very bad," he said, when he had recovered sufficient composure – "far worse than I feared. My dear, I am afraid the beginning of my work in Carlingford will be for ever associated with pain to us both. I am discouraged and distressed beyond measure by what I have heard to-day."

"Dear William, tell me what it is," said the Rector's wife.

"I feared it was a bad business from the first," said the disturbed Rector. "I confess I feared, when I saw a young man so regardless of lawful authority, that his moral principles must be defective, but I was not prepared for what I have heard to-day. My dear, I am sorry to grieve you with such a story; but as you are sure to hear it, perhaps it is better that you should have the facts from me."

"It must be about Mr Wentworth," said Mrs Morgan. She was sorry; for though she had given in to her husband's vehemence, she herself in her own person had always been prepossessed in favour of the Perpetual Curate; but she was also sensible of a feeling of relief to know that the misfortune concerned Mr Wentworth, and was not specially connected with themselves.

"Yes, it's about Mr Wentworth," said the Rector. He wiped his face, which was red with haste and exhaustion, and shook his head. He was sincerely shocked and grieved, to do him justice; but underneath there was also a certain satisfaction in the thought that he had foreseen it, and that his suspicions were verified. "My dear, I am very glad he had not become intimate in our house," said Mr Morgan; "that would have complicated matters sadly. I rejoice that your womanly instincts prevented that inconvenience;" and as the Rector began to recover himself, he looked more severe than ever.

"Yes," said Mrs Morgan, with hesitation; for the truth was, that her womanly instincts had pronounced rather distinctly in favour of the Curate of St Roque's. "I hope he has not done anything very wrong, William. I should be very sorry; for I think he has very good qualities," said the Rector's wife. "We must not let our personal objections prejudice us in respect to his conduct otherwise. I am sure you are the last to do that."

"I have never known an insubordinate man who was a perfect moral character," said the Rector. "It is very discouraging altogether; and you thought he was engaged to Wodehouse's pretty daughter, didn't you? I hope not – I sincerely hope not. That would make things doubly bad; but, to be sure, when a man is faithless to his most sacred engagements, there is very little dependence to be placed on him in other respects."

"But you have not told me what it is," said the Rector's wife, with some anxiety; and she spoke the more hastily as she saw the shadow of a curate – Mr Morgan's own curate, who must inevitably be invited to stop to dinner – crossing the lawn as she spoke. She got up and went a little nearer the window to make sure. "There is Mr Leeson," she said, with some vexation. "I must run up-stairs and get ready for dinner. Tell me what it is!"

Upon which the Rector, with some circumlocution, described the appalling occurrence of the previous night, – how Mr Wentworth had walked home with little Rosa Elsworthy from his own house to hers, as had, of course, been seen by various people. The tale had been told with variations, which did credit to the ingenuity of Carlingford; and Mr Morgan's version was that they had walked arm in arm, in the closest conversation, and at an hour which was quite unseemly for such a little person as Rosa to be abroad. The excellent Rector gave the story with strong expressions of disapproval; for he was aware of having raised his wife's expectations, and had a feeling, as he related them, that the circumstances, after all, were scarcely sufficiently horrifying to justify his preamble. Mrs Morgan listened with one ear towards the door, on the watch for Mr Leeson's knock.

"Was that all?" said the sensible woman. "I think it very likely it might be explained. I suppose Mr Leeson must have stopped to look at my ferns; he is very tiresome with his botany. That was all! Dear, I think it might be explained. I can't fancy Mr Wentworth is a man to

commit himself in that way – if that is all!" said Mrs
Morgan; but I must run up-stairs to change my dress."

"That was not all," said the Rector, following her to the
door. "It is said that this sort of thing has been habitual,
my dear. He takes the 'Evening Mail,' you know, all to
himself, instead of having the 'Times' like other people,
and she carries it down to his house, and I hear of
meetings in the garden, and a great deal that is very
objectionable," said Mr Morgan, speaking very fast in
order to deliver himself before the advent of Mr Leeson.
"I'm afraid it is a very bad business. I don't know what to
do about it. I suppose I must ask Leeson to stay to dinner?
It is absurd of him to come at six o'clock."

"Meetings in the garden?" said Mrs Morgan, aghast. "I
don't feel as if I could believe it. There is that tiresome
man at last. Do as you like, dear, about asking him to stay;
but I must make my escape," and the Rector's wife
hastened up-stairs, divided between vexation about Mr
Leeson and regret at the news she had just heard. She put
on her dress rather hastily, and was conscious of a little ill-
temper, for which she was angry with herself; and the
haste of her toilette, and the excitement under which she
laboured, aggravated unbecomingly that redness of which
Mrs Morgan was painfully sensible. She was not at all
pleased with her own appearance as she looked in the
glass. Perhaps that sense of looking not so well as usual
brought back to her mind a troublesome and painful idea,
which recurred to her not unfrequently when she was in
any trouble. The real Rector to whom she was married
was so different from the ideal one who courted her; could
it be possible, if they had married in their youth instead of
now, that her husband would have been less open to the
ill-natured suggestions of the gossips in Carlingford, and
less jealous of the interferences of his young neighbour? It
was hard to think that all the self-denial and patience of
the past had done more harm than good; but though she
was conscious of his defects, she was very loyal to him,

and resolute to stand by him whatever he might do or say; though Mrs Morgan's "womanly instincts," which the Rector had quoted, were all on Mr Wentworth's side, and convinced her of his innocence to start with. On the whole, she was annoyed and uncomfortable; what with Mr Leeson's intrusion (which had occurred three or four times before, and which Mrs Morgan felt it her duty to check) and the Rector's uncharitableness, and her own insufficient time to dress, and the disagreeable heightening of her complexion, the Rector's wife felt in rather an unchristian frame of mind. She did not look well, and she did not feel better. She was terribly civil to the Curate when she went down-stairs, and snubbed him in the most unqualified way when he too began to speak about Mr Wentworth. "It does not seem to me to be at all a likely story," she said, courageously, and took away Mr Leeson's breath.

"But I hear a very unfavourable general account," said the Rector, who was almost equally surprised. "I hear he has been playing fast and loose with that very pretty person, Miss Wodehouse, and that her friends begin to be indignant. It is said that he has not been nearly so much there lately, but, on the contrary, always going to Elsworthy's, and has partly educated this little thing. My dear, one false step leads to another. I am not so incredulous as you are. Perhaps I have studied human nature a little more closely, and I know that error is always fruitful; – that is my experience," said Mr Morgan. His wife did not say anything in answer to this deliverance, but she lay in wait for the Curate, as was natural, and had her revenge upon him as soon as his ill fate prompted him to back the Rector out.

"I am afraid Mr Wentworth had always too much confidence in himself," said the unlucky individual who was destined to be scapegoat on this occasion; "and as you very justly observe, one wrong act leads to another. He has thrown himself among the bargemen on such an equal footing that I daresay he has got to like that kind of society. I shouldn't be surprised to find that Rosa Elsworthy suited him better than a lady with refined tastes."

"Mr Wentworth is a gentleman," said the Rector's wife, with emphasis, coming down upon the unhappy Leeson in full battle array. "I don't think he would go into the poorest house, if it were even a bargeman's, without the same respect of the privacy of the family as is customary among – persons of our own class, Mr Leeson. I can't tell how wrong or how foolish he may have been, of course – but that he couldn't behave to anybody in a disrespectful manner, or show himself intrusive, or forget the usages of good society," said Mrs Morgan, who was looking all the time at the unfortunate Curate, "I am perfectly convinced."

It was this speech which made Mr Morgan "speak seriously," as he called it, later the same night, to his wife, about her manner to poor Leeson, who was totally extinguished, as was to be expected. Mrs Morgan busied herself among her flowers all the evening, and could not be caught to be admonished until it was time for prayers: so that it was in the sacred retirement of her own chamber that the remonstrance was delivered at last. The Rector said he was very sorry to find that she still gave way to temper in a manner that was unbecoming in a clergyman's wife; he was surprised, after all her experience, and the way in which they had both been schooled in patience, to find she had still to learn that lesson: upon which Mrs Morgan, who had been thinking much on the subject, broke forth upon her husband in a manner totally unprecedented, and which took the amazed Rector altogether by surprise.

"Oh, William, if we had only forestalled the lesson, and been *less* prudent!" she cried in a womanish way, which struck the Rector dumb with astonishment; "if we hadn't been afraid to marry ten years ago, but gone into life when

we were young, and fought through it like so many
people, don't you think it would have been better for us?
Neither you nor I would have minded what gossips said, or
listened to a pack of stories when we were five-and-
twenty. I think I was better then than I am now," said the
Rector's wife. Though she filled that elevated position,
she was only a woman, subject to outbreaks of sudden
passion, and liable to tears like the rest. Mr Morgan
looked very blank at her as she sat there crying, sobbing
with the force of a sentiment which was probably untrans-
latable to the surprised, middle-aged man. He thought it
must be her nerves which were in fault somehow, and
though much startled, did not inquire farther into it,
having a secret feeling in his heart that the less that was
said the better on that subject. So he did what his good
angel suggested to him, kissed his wife, and said he was
well aware what heavy calls he had made upon her
patience, and soothed her the best way that occurred to
him. "But you were very hard upon poor Leeson, my
dear," said the Rector, with his puzzled look, when she
had regained her composure. Perhaps she was disappointed that she had not been able to convey her real meaning
to her husband's matter-of-fact bosom; at all events, Mrs
Morgan recovered herself immediately, and flashed forth
with all the lively freshness of a temper in its first youth.

"He deserved a great deal more than I said to him,"
said the Rector's wife. "It might be an advantage to take
the furniture, as it was all new, though it is a perpetual
vexation to me, and worries me out of my life; but there
was no need to take the curate, that I can see. What right
has he to come day after day at your dinner-hour? he
knows we dine at six as well as we do ourselves; and I do
believe he knows what we have for dinner," exclaimed the
incensed mistress of the house; "for he always makes his
appearance when we have anything he likes. I hope I
know my duty, and can put up with what cannot be
mended," continued Mrs Morgan, with a sigh, and a

mental reference to the carpet in the drawing-room; "but there are some things really that would disturb the temper of an angel. I don't know anybody that could endure the sight of a man always coming unasked to dinner; – and he to speak of Mr Wentworth, who, if he were the greatest sinner in the world, is *always* a gentleman!" Mrs Morgan broke off with a sparkle in her eye, which showed that she had neither exhausted the subject, nor was ashamed of herself; and the Rector wisely retired from the controversy. He went to bed, and slept, good man, and dreamt that Sir Charles Grandison had come to be his curate in place of Mr Leeson; and when he woke, concluded quietly that Mrs Morgan had "experienced a little attack on the nerves," as he explained afterwards to Dr Marjoribanks. Her compunctions, her longings after the lost life they might have lived together, her wistful womanish sense of the impoverished existence, deprived of so many experiences, on which they had entered in the dry maturity of their middle age, remained for ever a mystery to her faithful husband. He was very fond of her, and had a high respect for her character; but if she had spoken Sanscrit, he could not have had less understanding of the meaning her words were intended to convey.

Notwithstanding, a vague idea that his wife was disposed to side with Mr Wentworth had penetrated the brain of the Rector, and was not without its results. He told her next morning, in his curt way, that he thought it would be best to wait a little before taking any steps in the Wharfside business. "If all I hear is true, we may have to proceed in a different way against the unhappy young man," said Mr Morgan, solemnly; and he took care to ascertain that Mr Leeson had an invitation somewhere else to dinner, which was doing the duty of a tender husband, as everybody will allow.

CHAPTER XIII.

"I want to know what all this means about young Wentworth," said Mr Wodehouse. "He's gone off, it appears, in a hurry, nobody knows where. Well, so they say. To his brother's, is it? *I* couldn't know that; but look here – that's not all, nor nearly all – they say he meets that little Rosa at Elsworthy's every night, and walks home with her, and all that sort of thing. I tell you I don't know – that's what people say. You ought to understand all the rights of it, you two girls. I confess I thought it was Lucy he was after, for my part – and a very bad match, too, and one I should never have given my consent to. And then there is another fine talk about some fellow he's got at his house. What's the matter, Molly? – she looks as if she was going to faint."

"Oh no," said Miss Wodehouse, faintly; "and I don't believe a word about Rosa Elsworthy," she said, with sudden impetuosity, a minute after. "I am sure Mr Wentworth could vindicate himself whenever he likes. I daresay the one story is just as true as the other; but then," said the gentle elder sister, turning with anxious looks towards Lucy, "he is proud, as is natural; and I shouldn't think he would enter into explanations if he thought people did not trust him without them."

"That is all stuff," said Mr Wodehouse; "why should people trust him? I don't understand trusting a man in all sorts of equivocal circumstances, because he's got dark eyes, &c., and a handsome face – which seems *your* code of morality; but I thought he was after Lucy – that was my belief – and I want to know if it's all off."

"It never was on, papa," said Lucy, in her clearest voice. "I have been a great deal in the district, you know, and Mr Wentworth and I could not help meeting each other; that is all about it: but people must always have something to talk about in Carlingford. I hope you don't think I and Rosa Elsworthy could go together," she went on, turning round to him with a smile. "I don't think that would be much of a compliment;" and, saying this, Lucy went to get her work out of its usual corner, and sat down opposite to her father, with a wonderfully composed face. She was so composed, indeed, that any interested beholder might have been justified in thinking that the work suffered in consequence, for it seemed to take nearly all Lucy's strength and leisure to keep up that look.

"Oh!" said Mr Wodehouse, "that's how it was? Then I wonder why that confounded puppy came here so constantly? I don't like that sort of behaviour. Don't you go into the district any more and meet him – that's all I've got to say."

"Because of Rosa Elsworthy?" said Lucy, with a little smile, which did not flicker naturally, but was apt to get fixed at the corners of her pretty mouth. "That would never do, papa. Mr Wentworth's private concerns are nothing to us; but, you know, there is a great work going on in the district, and *that* can't be interfered with," said the young Sister of Mercy, looking up at him with a decision which Mr Wodehouse was aware he could make no stand against. And when she stopped speaking, Lucy did a little work, which was for the district too. All this time she was admitting to herself that she had been much startled by this news about Rosa Elsworthy, – much startled. To be sure, it was not like Mr Wentworth, and very likely it would impair his influence; and it was natural that any friend taking an interest in him and the district, should be taken a little aback by such news. Accordingly, Lucy sat a little more upright than usual, and was conscious that when she smiled, as she had just done,

the smile did not glide off again in a natural way, but
settled down into the lines of her face with a kind of
spasmodic tenacity. She could do a great deal in the way
of self-control, but she could not quite command these
refractory muscles. Mr Wodehouse, who was not particularly penetrating, could not quite make her out; he saw
there was something a little different from her ordinary
look about his favourite child, but he had not insight
enough to enable him to comprehend what it was.

"And about his man who is staying at Mrs Hadwin's?"
said the perplexed churchwarden; "does any one know
who the fellow is? I don't understand how Wentworth has
got into all this hot water in a moment. Here's the Rector
in a state of fury, – and his aunts, – and now here's this
little bit of scandal to crown all; – and who is this fellow in
his house?"

"It must be somebody he has taken in out of charity,"
said Miss Wodehouse, with tears in her eyes; "I am sure it
is somebody whom he has opened his doors to out of
Christian charity and the goodness of his heart. I don't
understand how you can all desert him at the first word.
All the years he has been here, you know there never was
a whisper against him; and is it in reason to think he would
go so far wrong all in a moment?" cried the faithful
advocate of the Perpetual Curate. Her words were
addressed to Mr Wodehouse, but her eyes sought Lucy,
who was sitting very upright doing her work, without any
leisure to look round. Lucy had quite enough to occupy
her within herself at that emergency, and the tearful
appeal of her elder sister had no effect upon her. As for Mr
Wodehouse, he was more and more puzzled how to interpret these tears in his daughter's eyes.

"I don't make it out at all," said the perplexed father,
getting up to leave the room. "I hope *you* weren't in love
with him, Molly? you ought to have too much sense for
that. A pretty mess he'll find when he comes home; but he
must get out of it the best way he can, for *I* can't help him,

at least. I don't mean to have him asked here any more – you understand, Lucy," he said, turning round at the door, with an emphatic creak of his boots. But Lucy had no mind to be seduced into any such confession of weakness.

"You are always having everybody in Carlingford to dinner," said the young housekeeper, "and all the clergymen, even *that* Mr Leeson; and I don't see why you should except Mr Wentworth, papa; he has done nothing wicked, so far as we know. I daresay he won't want to bring Rosa Elsworthy with him; and why shouldn't he be asked here?" said Lucy, looking full in his face with her bright eyes. Mr Wodehouse was entirely discomfited, and did not know what to say. "I wonder if you know what you mean yourselves, you women," he muttered; and then, with a shrug of his shoulders, and a hasty "settle it as you please," the churchwarden's boots creaked hastily out of the room, and out of the house.

After this a dead silence fell upon the drawing-room and its two occupants. They did not burst forth into mutual comment upon this last piece of Carlingford news, as they would have done under any other circumstances; on the contrary, they bent over their several occupations with quite an unusual devotion, not exchanging so much as a look. Lucy, over her needlework, was the steadiest of the two; she was still at the same point in her thoughts, owning to herself that she was startled, and indeed shocked, by what she had heard – that it was a great pity for Mr Wentworth; perhaps that it was not quite what might have been expected of him, – and then she checked herself, and went back again to her original acknowledgment. To tell the truth, though she assured herself that she had nothing to do with it, a strange sense of having just passed through an unexpected illness, lay underneath Lucy's composure. It was none of her business, to be sure, but she could not help feeling as if she had just had a fever, or some other sudden unlooked-for attack, and that nobody knew of it,

and that she must get well as best she could, without any
help from without.

It was quite half an hour before Miss Wodehouse got up
from the knitting which she had spoiled utterly, trying to
take up the dropped stitches with her trembling fingers,
and dropping others by every effort she made. The poor
lady went wistfully about the room, wandering from
corner to corner, as if in search of something; at last she
took courage to speak, when she found herself behind her
young sister. "Dear, I am sure it is not true," said Miss
Wodehouse, suddenly, with a little sob; and then she came
close to Lucy's chair, and put her hand timidly upon her
sister's shoulder. "Think how many good things you two
have done together, dear; and is it likely you are to be
parted like this?" said the injudicious comforter. It felt
rather like another attack of fever to Lucy, as unexpected
as the last.

"Don't speak so, please," said the poor girl, with a
momentary shiver. "It is about Mr Wentworth you
mean?" she went on, after a little, without turning her
head. "I – am sorry, of course. I am afraid it will do him –
harm," and then she made a pause, and stumbled over her
sewing with fingers which felt feeble and powerless to the
very tips – all on account of this fever she had had. "But I
don't know any reason why you and I should discuss it,
Mary," she said, getting up in her turn, not quite sure
whether she could stand at this early period of her con-
valescence, but resolved to try. "We are both Mr Wentworth's friends – and we need not say any harm of him. I
have to get something out of the storeroom for to-night."

"But, Lucy," said the tender, trembling sister, who did
not know how to be wise and silent, "*I* trust him, and *you*
don't. Oh, my dear, it will break my heart. I know some
part of it is not true. I know one thing in which he is quite
– quite innocent. Oh, Lucy, my darling, if you distrust him
it will be returning evil for good!" cried poor Miss Wodehouse, with tears. As for Lucy, she did not quite know what

her sister said. She only felt that it was cruel to stop her, and look at her, and talk to her; and there woke up in her mind a fierce sudden spark of resistance to the intolerable.

"Why do you hold me? I may have been ill, but I can stand well enough by myself," cried Lucy, to her sister's utter bewilderment. "That is, I – I mean, I have other things to attend to," she cried, breaking into a few hot tears of mortification over this self-betrayal; and so went away in a strange glow and tremble of sudden passion, such as had never been seen before in that quiet house. She went direct to the storeroom, as she had said, and got out what was wanted; and only after that was done permitted herself to go up to her own room, and turn the key in her door. Though she was a Sister of Mercy, and much beloved in Prickett's Lane, she was still but one of Eve's poor petulant women-children, and had it in her to fly at an intruder on her suffering, like any other wounded creature. But she did not make any wild demonstration of her pain, even when shut up thus in her fortress. She sat down on the sofa, in a kind of dull heaviness, looking into vacancy. She was not positively thinking of Mr Wentworth, or of any one thing in particular. She was only conscious of a terrible difference somehow in everything about her – in the air which choked her breathing, and the light which blinded her eyes. When she came to herself a little, she said over and over, half-aloud, that everything was just the same as it had always been, and that to her at least nothing had happened; but that declaration, though made with vehemence, did not alter matters. The world altogether had sustained a change. The light that was in it was darkened, and the heart stilled. All at once, instead of a sweet spontaneous career, providing for its own wants day by day, life came to look like something which required such an amount of courage and patience and endurance as Lucy had not at hand to support her in the way; and her heart failed her at the moment when she found this out.

Notwithstanding, the people who dined at Mr Wodehouse's that night thought it a very agreeable little party,
and more than once repeated the remark, so familiar to
most persons in society in Carlingford – that Wodehouse's
parties were the pleasantest going, though he himself was
humdrum enough. Two or three of the people present had
heard the gossip about Mr Wentworth, and discussed it, as
was natural, taking different views of the subject; and
poor Miss Wodehouse took up his defence so warmly, and
with such tearful vehemence, that there were smiles to be
seen on several faces. As for Lucy, she made only a very
simple remark on the subject. She said: "Mr Wentworth is
a great friend of ours, and I think I would rather not hear
any gossip about him." Of course there were one or two
keen observers who put a subtle meaning to this, and
knew what was signified by her looks and her ways all the
evening; but, most likely, they were altogether mistaken
in their suppositions, for nobody could possibly watch her
so closely as did Miss Wodehouse, who know no more than
the man in the moon, at the close of the evening, whether
her young sister was very wretched or totally indifferent.
The truth was certainly not to be discovered, for that night
at least, in Lucy's looks.

CHAPTER XIV.

THE next afternoon there were signs of a considerable
commotion in Mr Elsworthy's shop. Rosa had disappeared
altogether, and Mrs Elsworthy, with an ominous redness
on her cheeks, had taken the place generally held by that
more agreeable little figure. All the symptoms of having
been engaged in an affray from which she had retired not

altogether victorious were in Mrs Elsworthy's face, and
the errand-boys vanished from her neighbourhood with
inconceivable rapidity, and found out little parcels to
deliver which would have eluded their most anxious
search in other circumstances. Mr Elsworthy himself
occupied his usual place in the foreground, without the
usual marks of universal content and satisfaction with all
his surroundings which generally distinguished him. An
indescribable appearance of having been recently
snubbed hung about the excellent man, and his glances
towards the back-shop, and the glances directed from the
back-shop to him, told with sufficient significance the
quarter from which his humiliation had proceeded. It had
done him good, as such painful discipline generally does;
for he was clearing out some drawers in which sundry
quires of paper had broken loose and run into confusion,
with the air of a man who ought to have done it weeks ago.
As for the partner of his bosom, she was standing in the
obscure distance behind the counter knitting a blue
stocking, which was evidently intended for no foot but his.
There was a chair close by, but Mrs Elsworthy disdained
to sit down. She stood with her knitting in conscious
power, now and then suffering a confession of her faith to
escape her. "There's nothing as don't go contrary in this
world," said the discontented wife, "when a man's a fool."
It was hard upon Mr Elsworthy that his ears were sharp,
and that he knew exactly what this agreeable murmur
was. But he was wise in his generation, and made no
reply.

Things were in this condition when, of all persons in
Carlingford, it occurred to Miss Leonora Wentworth to
enter Mr Elsworthy's shop. Not that she was alone, or
bent upon any errand of inquiry; for Miss Leonora seldom
moved about unattended by her sisters, whom she felt it
her duty to take out for exercise; and wonderfully enough,
she had not found out yet what was the source of Miss
Dora's mysteries and depression, having been still

occupied meantime by her own "great work" in her London district, and the affair of the gin-palace, which was still undecided. She had been talking a great deal about this gin-palace for the last twenty-four hours; and to hear Miss Leonora, you might have supposed that all the powers of heaven must fail and be discomfited before this potent instrument of evil, and that, after all, Bibles and missionaries were much less effective than the stoppage of the licence, upon which all her agents were bent. At all events, such an object of interest had swept out from her thoughts the vague figure of her nephew Frank, and aunt Dora's mysterious anxieties on his account. When the three ladies approached Elsworthy's, the first thing that attracted their attention was Rosa, the little Rosa who had been banished from the shop, and whom Mrs Elsworthy believed to be expiating her sins in a back room, in tears and darkness; instead of which the little girl was looking out of her favourite window, and amusing herself much with all that was going on in Grange Lane. Though she was fluttered by the scolding she had received, Rosa only looked prettier than usual with her flushed cheeks; and so many things had been put into her nonsensical little head during the last two days, especially by her aunt's denunciations, that her sense of self-importance was very much heightened in consequence. She looked at the Miss Wentworths with a throb of mingled pride and alarm, wondering whether perhaps she might know more of them some day, if Mr Wentworth was really fond of her, as people said – which thought gave Rosa a wonderful sensation of awe and delighted vanity. Meanwhile the three Miss Wentworths looked at her with very diverse feelings. "I must speak to these people about that little girl, if nobody else has sense enough to do it," said Miss Leonora; "she is evidently going wrong as fast as she can, the little fool;" and the iron-grey sister went into Mr Elsworthy's in this perfectly composed and ordinary frame of mind, with her head full of the application which was to be made to the licensing magistrates today, in the parish of St Michael, and totally unaware that anybody belonging to herself could ever be connected with the incautious little coquette at the window. Miss Dora's feelings were very different. It was much against her will that she was going at all into this obnoxious shop, and the eyes which she hastily uplifted to the window and withdrew again with lively disgust and dislike, were both angry and tearful; "Little forward shameless thing," Miss Dora said to herself, with a little toss of her head. As for Miss Wentworth, it was not her custom to say anything – but she, too, looked up, and saw the pretty face at the window, and secretly concluded that it might all be quite true, and that she had known a young man make a fool of himself before now for such another. So they all went in, unwitting that they came at the end of a domestic hurricane, and that the waters were still in a state of disturbance. Miss Wentworth took the only chair, as was natural, and sat down sweetly to wait for Leonora, and Miss Dora lingered behind while her sister made her purchases. Miss Leonora wanted some books—

"And I came here," she said, with engaging candour, "because I see no other shop in this part of the town except Masters's, which, of course, I would not enter. It is easy enough to do without books, but I can't afford to compromise my principles, Mr Elsworthy;" to which Mr Elsworthy had replied, "No, ma'am, of course not – such a thing aint to be expected;" with one eye upon his customer, and one upon his belligerent wife.

"And, by the by, if you will permit me to speak about what does not concern me," said Miss Leonora cheerfully, " I think you should look after that little girl of yours more carefully; – recollect I don't mean any offence; but she's very pretty, you know, and very young, and vain, as a matter of course. I saw her the other evening going down Grange Lane, a great deal too late for such a creature to be out; and though I don't doubt, you are very particular where she goes—"

It was at this conjuncture that Mrs Elsworthy, who could not keep silence any longer, broke in ardently, with all her knitting-needles in front of her, disposed like a kind of porcupine mail—

"I'm well known in Carlingford – better known than most," said Mrs Elsworthy, with a sob; "such a thing as not being particular was never named to me. I strive and I toil from morning to night, as all things should be respectable and kep' in good order; but what's the good? Here's my heart broken, that's all; and Elsworthy standing gaping like a gaby as he is. There aint nothing as don't go contrary, when folks is tied to a set of fools!" cried the indignant matron. "As for pretty, I don't know nothing about it; I've got too much to do minding my own business. Them as has nothing to think of but stand in the shop and twiddle their thumbs, ought to look to that; but, ma'am, if you'll believe me, it aint no fault of mine. It aint my will to throw her in any young gentleman's way; not to say a clergyman as we're bound to respect. Whatever you does, ladies, – and I shouldn't wonder at your taking away your custom, nor nothing else as was a punishment – don't blame me!"

"But you forget, Mrs Elsworthy, that we have nothing to do with it, – nothing at all; my nephew knows very well what he is about," said Miss Dora, in injudicious haste. "Mr Wentworth is not at all likely to forget himself," continued that poor lady, getting confused as her sister turned round and stared at her. "Of course it was all out of kindness; – I – I know Frank did not mean anything," cried the unfortunate aunt. Leonora's look, as she turned round and fixed her eyes upon her, took away what little breath Miss Dora had.

"Mr Wentworth?" asked Miss Leonora; "I should be glad to know, if anybody would inform me, what Mr Wentworth can possibly have to do with it? I daresay you misunderstood me; I said you were to look after that little girl – your niece, or whatever she is; I did not say anything about Mr Wentworth," said the strong-minded sister, looking round upon them all. For the moment she forgot all about the licence, and turned upon Mr Elsworthy with an emphasis which almost drive that troubled citizen to his knees.

"That was how I understood it," said the clerk of St Roque's, humbly; "there wasn't nothing said about Mr Wentworth – nor there couldn't be as I know of, but what was in his favour, for there aint many young men like our clergyman left in the Church. It aint because I'm speaking to respected ladies as is his relations; folks may talk," said Mr Elsworthy, with a slight faltering, "but I never see his equal; and as for an act of kindness to an orphan child—"

"The orphan child is neither here not there," said his angry wife, who had taken up her post by his side; "a dozen fathers and mothers couldn't have done better by her than we've done; and to go and lay out her snares for them as is so far above her, if you'll believe me, ma'am, it's nigh broken my heart. She's neither flesh nor blood o' mine," cried the aggrieved woman; "there would have been a different tale to tell if she had belonged to me. I'd have – murdered her, ma'am, though it aint proper to say so, afore we'd have gone and raised a talk like this; it aint my blame, if it was my dying word," cried Mrs Elsworthy, relapsing into angry tears: "I'm one as has always shown her a good example, and never gone flirting about, nor cast my eyes to one side or another for the best man as ever walked; and to think as a respectable family should be brought to shame through her doings, and a gentleman as is a clergyman got himself talked about – it's gone nigh to kill me, that's what it's done," sobbed the virtuous matron; "and I don't see as nobody cares."

Miss Leonora had been woke up suddenly out of her abstract occupations; she penetrated to the heart of the matter while all this talk was going on. She transfixed her sister Dora, who seemed much inclined to cry like Mrs Elsworthy, with a look which overwhelmed that trembling woman; then she addressed herself with great suavity to the matter in hand.

"I suppose it is this poor little foolish child who has been getting herself talked about?" said Miss Leonora. "It's a pity, to be sure, but I daresay it's not so bad as you think. As for her laying snares for people above her, I wouldn't be afraid of that. Poor little thing! It's not so easy as you think laying snares. Perhaps it's the new minister at Salem Chapel who has been paying attention to her? I would not take any notice of it if I were you. Don't let her loll about at the window as she's doing, and don't let her go out so late, and give her plenty of work to do. My maid wants some one to help in her needlework. Perhaps this child would do, Cecilia?" said Miss Leonora. "As for her snares, poor thing, I don't feel much afraid of them. I daresay if Mr Wentworth had Sunday classes for the young people as I wished him to have, and took pains to give them proper instruction, such things would not happen. If you send her to my maid, I flatter myself she will soon come to her senses. Good morning; and you will please to send me the books – there are some others I want you to get for me next week," said Mr Elsworthy's patroness. "I will follow you, Dora, please," and Miss Leonora swept her sisters out before her, and went upon her way with indescribable grandeur. Even little Rosa felt the change, where she sat at the window looking out. The little vain creature no longer felt it possible to believe, as she looked after them, that she ever could be anything to the Miss Wentworths except a little girl in a shop. It shook her confidence in what people said; and it was as well for her that she withdrew from the window at that conjuncture, and so had an opportunity of hearing her aunt come up-stairs, and of darting back again to the penitential darkness of her own chamber at the back of the house – which saved Rosa some angry words at least.

As for Miss Leonora Wentworth, she said nothing to her sisters on this new subject. She saw them safely home to their own apartments, and went out again without explaining her movements. When she was gone, Miss

Wentworth listened to Miss Dora's doubts and tears with her usual patience, but did not go into the matter much. "It doesn't matter whether it is your fault or not," said aunt Cecilia, with a larger amount of words than usual, and a sharpness very uncommon with her; "but I daresay Leonora will set it all right." After all, the confidence which the elder sister had in Leonora was justified. She did not entirely agree with her about the "great work," nor was disposed to connect the non-licensing of the gin-palace in any way with the faithfulness of God: but she comprehended in her gentle heart that there were other matters of which Leonora was capable. As for Miss Dora, she went to the summer-house at last, and, seating herself at the window, cried under her breath till she had a very bad headache, and was of no use for any purpose under heaven. She thought nothing less than that Leonora had gone abroad to denounce poor Frank, and tell everybody how wicked he was; and she was so sure her poor dear boy did not mean anything! She sat with her head growing heavier and heavier, watching for her sister's return, and calculating within herself how many places Leonora must have called at, and how utterly gone by this time must be the character of the Perpetual Curate. At last, in utter despair, with her thin curls all limp about her poor cheeks, Miss Dora had to go to bed and have the room darkened, and swallow cups of green tea and other nauseous compounds, at the will and pleasure of her maid, who was learned in headache. The poor lady sobbed herself to sleep after a time, and saw, in a hideous dream, her sister Leonora marching from house to house of poor Frank's friends, and closing door after door with all sorts of clang and dash upon the returning prodigal. "But oh, it was not my fault – oh, my dear, she found it out herself. You do not think *I* was to blame?" sobbed poor aunt Dora in her troubled slumber; and her headache did not get any better notwithstanding the green tea.

Miss Dora's visions were partly realised, for it was quite

true that her iron-grey sister was making a round of calls upon Frank's friends. Miss Leonora Wentworth went out in great state that day. She had her handsomest dress on, and the bonnet which her maid had calculated upon as her own property, because it was much too nice for Miss Leonora. In this impossible attire she went to see Mrs Hadwin, and was very gracious to that unsuspecting woman, and learned a few things of which she had not the least conception previously. Then she went to the Miss Wodehouses, and made the elder sister there mighty uncomfortable by her keen looks and questions; and what Miss Leonora did after that was not distinctly known to any one. She got into Prickett's Lane somehow, and stumbled upon No. 10, much to the surprise of the inhabitants; and before she returned home she had given Mrs Morgan her advice about the Virginian creeper which was intended to conceal the continual passage of the railway trains. "But I would not trust to trellis-work. I would build up the wall a few feet higher, and then you will have some satisfaction in your work," said Miss Leonora, and left the Rector's wife to consider the matter in rather an agreeable state of mind, for that had been Mrs Morgan's opinion all along. After this last visit the active aunt returned home, going leisurely along George Street, and down Grange Lane, with meditative steps. Miss Leonora, of course, would not for kingdoms have confessed that any new light had come into her mind, or that some very ordinary people in Carlingford, no one of whom she could have confidently affirmed to be a converted person, had left a certain vivid and novel impression upon her thoughts. She went along much more slowly than usual in this new mood of reflectiveness. She was not thinking of the licensing magistrates of St Michael's nor the beautiful faith of the colporteur. Other ideas filled her mind at the moment. Whether perhaps, after all, a man who did his duty by rich and poor, and could encounter all things for love and duty's sake, was not about the best man for a parish priest,

even though he did have choristers in white surplices, and
lilies on the Easter altar? Whether it might not be a
comfort to know that in the pretty parsonage at Skelmersdale there was some one ready to start at a moment's
notice for the help of a friend or the succour of a soul –
brother to Charley who won the Cross for valour, and not
unworthy of the race? Some strange moisture came into
the corners of Miss Leonora's eyes. There was Gerald too,
whom the Perpetual Curate had declared to be the best
man he ever knew; and the Evangelical woman, with all
her prejudices, could not in her heart deny it. Various
other thoughts of a similar description, but too shadowy to
bear expression, came in spite of herself through Miss
Leonora's mind. "We know that God heareth not sinners;
but if any man be a worshipper of God and doeth His will,
him He heareth;" and it occurred to her vaguely, for the
first time, that she was harder to please than her Master.
Not that such an idea could get possession of a mind so
well fortified, at the first assault; but it was strange how
often the thought came back to her that the man who had
thrilled through all those people about Prickett's Lane a
kind of vague sense that they were Christians, and not
hopeless wretches, forgotten of God; and who had taken
in the mysterious lodger at Mrs Hadwin's, bearing the
penalty of suspicion without complaint, would be true at
his post wherever he might be, and was a priest of God's
appointing. Such were the strangely novel ideas which
went flashing through Miss Leonora's mind as she went
home to dinner, ejecting summarily the new gin-palaces
and her favourite colporteur. If anybody had stated them
in words, she would have indignantly scouted such lati-
tudinarian stuff; but they kept flickering in the strangest
fluctuations, coming and going, bringing in native
Wentworth prejudices and natural affections to overcome
all other prepossessions, in the most inveterate, unexplainable way. For it will be apparent that Miss Leonora,
being a woman of sense, utterly scorned the Rosa

Elsworthy hypothesis, and comprehended as nearly how it happened as it was possible for any one unaware of the facts to do.

Such were the good and bad angels who fought over the Curate's fate while he was away. He might have been anxious if he had known anything about them, or had been capable of imagining any such clouds as those which overshadowed his good name in the lively imagination of Carlingford. But Rosa Elsworthy never could have occurred to the unconscious young man as a special danger, any more than the relenting in the heart of his aunt Leonora could have dawned upon him as a possible happiness. To tell the truth, he had left home, so far as he himself was concerned, in rather a happy state of mind than otherwise, with healthful impulses of opposition to the Rector, and confidence in the sympathy of Lucy. To hear that Lucy had given him up, and that Miss Leonora and Mrs Morgan were the only people who believed in him, would have gone pretty far at this moment to make an end of the Perpetual Curate. But fortunately he knew nothing about it; and while Lucy held her head high with pain, and walked over the burning coals a conscious martyr, and Miss Dora sobbed herself asleep in her darkened room, all on his account, there was plenty of trouble, perplexity, and distress in Wentworth Rectory to occupy to the full all the thoughts and powers of the Curate of St Roque's.

CHAPTER XV.

It was mid-day, and more than twelve hours after he had left Carlingford, before Mr Wentworth reached the Rectory. He had snatched a few hours' sleep in London, where he was obliged to pause because of the trains, which did not correspond; and accordingly, though he was very anxious about Gerald, it was with a mien and gait very much like his usual appearance that he jumped out of the railway carriage at the little station which was on his father's property, and where everybody knew the Squire's son. Left in entire uncertainty as he was in respect to the trouble which has overtaken his brother, it was a little comfort to the Curate to find that everybody looked surprised to see him, and that nobody seemed to know of any cause demanding his presence. All was well at the Hall, so far as the station-master knew; and as for the Rector, he had no special place in the local report which the handiest porter supplied "Mr Frank" – a blessed neglect, which was very consolatory to the heart of the anxious brother, to whom it became evident that nothing had happened, and who began to hope that Gerald's wife, who never was very wise, had been seized with some merely fantastic terror. With this hope he walked on briskly upon the familiar road to his brother's house, recovering his courage, and falling back upon his own thoughts, and at last taking pleasure in the idea of telling all his troubles to Gerald, and getting strength and enlightenment from his advice. He had come quite into this view of the subject when he arrived at the Rectory, and saw the pretty old-fashioned house, with its high ivied garden-walls, and the famous cedar on the lawn, standing all secure and sweet in the early sunshine, like something too steadfast to be moved, as if sorrow or conflict could never enter there. Unconsciously to himself, the perfect tranquillity of everything altered the entire scope of Frank Wentworth's thoughts. He was no longer in anxiety about his brother. He was going to ask Gerald's advice upon his own troubles, and lay the difficulties and dangers of his position before the clear and lucid eyes of the best man he ever knew.

It shook him a little out of his position, however, to find himself admitted with a kind of scared expectation by Mrs Gerald Wentworth's maid, who made no exclamation of wonder at the sight of him, but opened the door in a troubled, stealthy way, strangely unlike the usual customs of the place. "Is my brother at home?" said the Curate, going in with a step that rang on the hall, and a voice that sounded into the house. He would have proceeded straight, as usual, to Gerald's study after this question, which was one of form merely, but for the disturbed looks of the woman, who put up her hand imploringly. "Oh hush! Mr Frank; hush! My mistress wants to see you first. She said I was to show you into her sitting-room," said the maid, half in a whisper, and led him hastily down a side-passage to a little out-of-the-way room, which he knew was where Louisa was wont to retire when she had her headaches, as was well known to all the house of Wentworth. The Curate went in with some impatience and some alarm to this retired apartment. His eyes, dazzled by the sunshine, could not penetrate at first the shadowy greenness of the room, which, what with the trees without and the Venetian blind within, was lost in a kind of twilight, grateful enough after a while, but bewildering at the first moment. Out of this darkness somebody rose as he entered, and walked into his arms with trembling eagerness. "Oh Frank, I am so thankful you are come! now perhaps something may be done; for *you* always understood," said his little sister-in-law, reaching up to kiss him. She was a tiny little woman, with soft eyes and a tender little blooming face, which he had never before seen obscured by any cloud, or indeed moved by any particular sentiment. Now the firmament was all overcast, and Louisa, it was evident, had been sitting in the shade of her drawn blinds, having a quiet cry, and going into all her grievances. To see such a serene creature all clouded over and full of tears, gave the Curate a distinct shock of alarm and anxiety. He led her back to her sofa, seeing clearer and clearer, as he watched her face, the plaintive lines of complaint, the heavy burden of trouble which she was about to cast on his shoulders. He grew more and more afraid as he looked at her. "Is Gerald ill?" he said, with a thrill of terror; but even this could scarcely account for the woeful look of all the accessories to the picture.

"Oh, Frank, I am so glad you are come!" said Louisa through her tears. "I felt sure you would come when you got my letter. Your father thinks I make a fuss about nothing, and Cuthbert and Guy do nothing but laugh at me, as if they could possibly know; but you always understand me, Frank. I knew it was just as good as sending for a brother of my own; indeed better," said Mrs Wentworth, wiping her eyes; "for though Gerald is using me so badly, I would not expose him out of his own family, or have people making remarks – oh, not for the world!"

"Expose him!" said the Curate, with unutterable astonishment. "You don't mean to say you have any complaint to make about Gerald?" The idea was so preposterous that Frank Wentworth laughed; but it was not a laugh pleasant to hear.

"Oh, Frank, if you but knew all," said Louisa; "what I have had to put up with for months – all my best feelings outraged, and so many things to endure that were dreadful to think of. And I that was always brought up so differently; but now," cried the poor little woman, bursting into renewed tears, "it's come to such a pass that

it can't be concealed any longer. I think it will break my
heart; people will be sure to say I have been to blame; and
how I am ever to hold up my head in society, and what is
to be my name, and whether I am to be considered a
widow—"

"A widow!" cried the Perpetual Curate, in utter consternation.

"Or worse," sobbed Gerald's poor little wife: "it feels
like being divorced – as if one had done something wrong;
and I am sure I never did anything to deserve it; but when
your husband is a Romish priest," cried the afflicted
woman, pressing her handkerchief to her eyes, "I would
just ask anybody what are you? You can't be his wife,
because he is not allowed to have any wife; and you can't
go back to your maiden name, because of the children;
and how can you have any place in society? Oh, Frank, I
think I shall go distracted," said poor Louisa; "it will feel
as if one had done something wicked, and been put out of
the pale. How can I be called Mrs Wentworth any more
when my husband has left me? and even if he is a priest,
and can't have any wife, still he will be alive, and I shall
not have the satisfaction of being a widow even. I am sure
I don't know what I say," she concluded, with a fresh
outburst; "for to be a widow would be a poor satisfaction,
and I don't know how I could ever, ever live without
Gerald; but to feel as if you were an improper person, and
all the children's prospects in life! – Oh, Frank!" cried the
weeping Louisa, burying her face in her handkerchief, "I
think I shall go distracted, and my heart will break."

To all this strange and unexpected revelation the
startled Curate listened like a man in a dream. Possibly
his sister-in-law's representation of this danger, as seen
entirely from her own point of view, had a more alarming
effect upon him that any other statement of the case. He
could have gone into Gerald's difficulties with so much
sympathy and fellow-feeling that the shock would have
been trifling in comparison; and between Rome and the

highest level of Anglicanism there was no such difference
as to frighten the accustomed mind of the Curate of St
Roque's. But, seen from Louisa's side, matters appeared
very different: here the foundations of the earth were
shaking, and life itself going to pieces; even the absurdity
of her distress made the whole business more real; and the
poor little woman, whose trouble was that she herself
would neither be a wife nor a widow, had enough of truth
on her side to unfold a miserable picture to the eyes of the
anxious spectator. He did not know what answer to make
her; and perhaps it was a greater consolation to poor
Louisa to be permitted to run on—

"And you know it never needed to have come to this if
Gerald had been like other people," she said, drying her
tears, and with a tone of remonstrance. "Of course it is a
family living, and it is not likely his own father would have
made any disturbance; and there is no other family in the
parish but the Skipwiths, and they are great friends, and
never would have said a word. He might have preached in
six surplices if he had liked," cried poor Louisa – "who
would have minded? And as for confession, and all that, I
don't believe there is anybody in the world who had done
any wrong that could have helped confessing to Gerald; he
is so good – oh, Frank, you know he is so good!" said the
exasperated little wife, overcome with fondness and
admiration and impatience, "and there is nobody in the
parish that I ever heard of that does not worship him; but
when I tell him so, he never pays the least attention. And
then Edward Plumstead and he go on talking about subscription, and signing articles, and nonsense, till they
make my head swim. Nobody, I am sure, wants Gerald to
subscribe or sign articles. I am sure I would subscribe any
amount," cried the poor little woman, once more falling
into tears – "a thousand pounds if I had it, Frank – only to
make him hear reason; for why should he leave Wentworth, where he can do what he likes, and nobody will
interfere with him? The Bishop is an old friend of my

father's, and I am sure he never would say anything; and
as for candles and crosses and – anything he pleases,
Frank—"

Here poor Louisa paused, and put her hand on his arm,
and looked up wistfully into his face. She wanted to
convince herself that she was right, and that the faltering
dread she had behind all this, of something more mysterious than candles or crosses – something which she did
not attempt to understand – was no real spectre after all.
"Oh, Frank, I am sure I never would oppose him, nor
your father, nor anybody; and why should he go and take
some dreadful step, and upset everything?" said Mrs
Wentworth. "Oh, Frank! we will not even have enough to
live upon; and as for me, if Gerald leaves me, how shall I
ever hold up my head again, or how will anybody know
how to behave to me? I can't call myself Miss Leighton
again, after being married so long; and if I am not his wife,
what shall I be?" Her crying became hysterical as she
came back to this point; and Mr Wentworth sat by her
trying to soothe her, as wretched as herself.

"But I must see Gerald, Louisa," said the Curate; "he
has never written to me about this. Perhaps things have
not gone so far as you think; but as for the crosses and the
candles, you know, and not being interfered with—"

"I would promise to do anything he likes," cried the
weeping woman. "I never would worry him any more
about anything. After aunt Leonora was here, perhaps I
said things I should not have said; but, oh Frank, whatever he likes to do I am sure I will give in to it. I don't
really mind seeing him preach in his surplice, only you
know poor papa was so *very* Low-Church; and as for the
candles, what are they to pleasing one's husband? Oh,
Frank, if you would only tell him – I can't argue about
things like a man – tell him nobody will ever interfere, and
he shall do whatever he pleases. I trust to you to say
everything," said the poor wife. "You can reason with him
and explain things. Nobody understands Gerald like you.

You will not forsake me in my trouble, Frank? I thought immediately of you. I knew you could help us, if anybody could. You will tell him all I have said," she continued, rising as Mr Wentworth rose, and going after him to the door, to impress once more upon him the necessities of the case. "Oh, Frank, remember how much depends upon it! – everything in the world for me, and all the children's prospects in life; and he would be miserable himself if he were to leave us. You know he would?" said Louisa, looking anxiously into his face, and putting her hand on his arm. "Oh, Frank, you don't think Gerald could be happy without the children – and me?"

The terrible thought silenced her. She stopped crying, and a kind of tearless horror and dread came over her face. She was not very wise, but her heart was tender and full of love in its way. What if perhaps this life, which had gone so smoothly over her unthinking head without any complications, should turn out to be a lie, and her happiness a mere delusion? She could not have put her thoughts into words, but the doubt suddenly came over her, putting a stop to all her lamentations. If perhaps Gerald *could* be happy without the children and herself, what dreadful fiction had all her joy been built upon! Such an inarticulate terror seemed to stop the very beating of her heart. It was not a great calamity only but an overthrowal of all confidence in life; and she shivered before it like a dumb creature piteously beholding an approaching agony which it could not comprehend. The utterance of her distress was arrested upon her lips, – she looked up to her brother with an entreating look, so suddenly intensified and grown desperate that he was startled by it. It alarmed him so much that he turned again to lead her back to her sofa, wondering what momentary passion it could be which had woke such a sudden world of confused meaning in Louisa's eyes.

"You may be sure he could not," said the Curate, warmly. "Not happy, certainly; but to men like Gerald there are things in the world dearer than happiness," he said, after a little pause, with a sigh, wondering to himself whether, if Lucy Wodehouse were his, his dearest duty could make him consent to part with her. "If he thinks of such a step, he must think of it as of martyrdom – is that a comfort to you?" he continued, bending, in his pity and wonder, over the trembling wife, who burst forth into fresh tears as he spoke, and forgot her momentary horror.

"Oh, Frank, go and speak to him, and tell him how miserable I am, and what a dreadful thing it would be; tell him everything, Frank. Oh, don't leave him till you have persuaded him. Go, go; never mind me," cried Mrs Wentworth; and then she went to the door after him once more – "Don't say I sent for you. He – he might not be pleased," she said, in her faltering, eager voice; "and oh, Frank, consider how much hangs upon what you say." When he left her, Louisa stood at the door watching him as he went along the passage towards her husband's room. It was a forlorn-hope; but still the unreasoning, uncomprehending heart took a little comfort from it. She watched his figure disappearing along the narrow passage with a thrill of mingled anxiety and hope; arguing with Gerald, though it was so ineffectual when she tried it, might still be of some avail in stronger hands. His brother understood him, and could talk to him better than anybody else could; and though she had never convinced anybody of anything all her life, Mrs Wentworth had an inalienable confidence in the effect of "being talked to." In the momentary stimulus she went back to her darkened room and drew up the blind, and went to work in a tremulous way; but as the slow time went on, and Frank did not return, poor Louisa's courage failed her; her fingers refused their office, and she began to imagine all sorts of things that might be going on in Gerald's study. Perhaps the argument might be going the wrong way; perhaps Gerald might be angry at his brother's interference; perhaps they might come to words – they who had been such good friends – and it would be her fault. She jumped up with her heart beating loud when she heard a door opened somewhere; but when nobody came, grew sick and faint, and hid her face, in the impatience of her misery. Then the feeling grew upon her that those precious moments were decisive, and that she must make one last appeal, or her heart would burst. She tried to resist the impulse in a feeble way, but it was not her custom to resist impulses, and it got the better of her; and this was why poor Louisa rushed into the library, just as Frank thought he had made a little advance in his pleading, and scattered his eloquence to the winds with a set of dreadful arguments which were all her own.

CHAPTER XVI.

THE Curate of St Roque's found his brother in his library, looking very much as he always looked at first glance. But Gerald was not reading nor writing nor doing anything. He was seated in his usual chair, by his usual table, with all the ordinary things around. Some manuscript – lying loosely about, and looking as if he had thrown down his pen in disgust, and pushed it away from him in the middle of a sentence – was on the table, and an open book in his other hand; but neither the book nor the manuscript occupied him; he was sitting leaning his head in his hands, gazing blankly out through the window, as it appeared, at the cedar, which flung its serene shadow over the lawn outside. He jumped up at the sound of his brother's voice, but seemed to recall himself with a little difficulty even for that, and did not look much surprised to see him. In short, Frank read in Gerald's eyes that he would not at that moment have been surprised to see any one, and that, in his own consciousness, the emergency was great enough to justify any unlooked-for appearance, though it might be from heaven or from the grave.

"I am glad you have come," he said, after they had greeted each other, his mouth relaxing ever so slightly into the ghost of his old smile; "you and I always understood each other, and it appears I want interpretation now. And one interpretation supposes many," he said with a gleam, half of pathos half of amusement, lighting up his face for a moment; "there is no such thing as accepting a simple version even of one man's thoughts. You have come at a very fit time, Frank— that is, for me."

"I am glad you think so," said the other brother; and then there was a pause, neither liking to enter upon the grand subject which stood between them.

"Have you seen Louisa?" said Gerald. He spoke like a man who was ill, in a preoccupied interrupted way. Like a sick man, he was occupied with himself, with the train of thought which was always going on in his mind whatever he might be doing, whether he was working or resting, alone or in company. For months back he had carried it with him everywhere. The cedar-tree outside, upon which his thoughtful eyes fell as he looked straight before him out of the library window, was all garlanded with the reasonings and questionings of this painful spring. To Frank's eyes, Gerald's attention was fixed upon the fluttering of a certain twig at the extremity of one of those broad solemn immovable branches. Gerald, however, saw not the twig, but one of his hardest difficulties which was twined and twined in the most inextricable way round that little sombre cluster of spikes; and so kept looking out, not at the cedar, but at the whole confused yet distinct array of his own troubled thoughts.

"If you have seen Louisa, she has been talking to you, no doubt," he said, after another little pause, with again the glimmer of a smile. "We have fallen upon troubles,

and we don't understand each other, Frank. That's all
very natural; she does not see things from my point of view:
I could not expect she should. If I could see from hers, it
might be easier for us all; but that is still less to be
expected; and it is hard upon her, Frank – very hard,"
said Gerald, turning round in his old ingenuous way, with
that faculty for seeing other people's difficulties which was
so strong a point in his character. "She is called upon to
make, after all, perhaps, the greater sacrifice of the two;
and she does not see any duty in it – the reverse, indeed.
She thinks it a sin. It is a strange view of life, to look at it
from Louisa's point. Here will be an unwilling, unintentional martyrdom; and it is hard to think I should take all
the merit, and leave my poor little wife the suffering
without any compensation!" He began to walk up and
down the room with uneasy steps, as if the thought was
painful, and had to be got rid of by some sudden movement. "It must be that God reckons with women for what
they have endured, as with men for what they have done,"
said Gerald. He spoke with a kind of grieved certainty,
which made his brother feel, to start with, the hopeless-
ness of all argument.

"But must this be? Is it necessary to take such a final,
such a terrible step?" said the Perpetual Curate.

"I think so." Gerald went to the window, to resume his
contemplation of the cedar, and stood there with his back
turned to Frank, and his eyes going slowly over all the
long processes of his self-argument, laid up as they were
upon those solemn levels of shadow. "Yes – you have gone
so far with me; but I don't want to take you any farther,
Frank. Perhaps, when I have reached the perfect peace to
which I am looking forward, I may try to induce you to
share it, but at present there are so many pricks of the
flesh. You did not come to argue with me, did you?" and
again the half-humorous gleam of old came over Gerald's
face as he looked round. "Louisa believes in arguing," he
said, as he came back to the table and took his seat again;

"not that she has ever gained much by it, so far as I am aware. Poor girl! she talks and talks, and fancies she is persuading me; and all the time my heart is bleeding for her. There it is!" he exclaimed, suddenly hiding his face in his hands. "This is what crushes one to think of. The rest is hard enough, Heaven knows – separation from my friends, giving up my own people, wounding and grieving, as I know I shall, everybody who loves me. I could bear that; but Louisa and her children – God help me, there's the sting!"

They were both men, and strong men, not likely to fall into any sentimental weakness; but something between a groan and a sob, wrung out of the heart of the elder brother at the thought of the terrible sacrifice before him, echoed with a hard sound of anguish into the quiet. It was very different from his wife's trembling, weeping, hoping agony; but it reduced the Curate more than ever to that position of spectator which he felt was so very far from the active part which his poor sister expected of him.

"I don't know by what steps you have reached this conclusion," said Frank Wentworth; "but even if you feel it your duty to give up the Anglican Church (in which, of course, I think you totally wrong," added the High Churchman in a parenthesis), "I cannot see why you are bound to abandon all duties whatever. I have not come to argue with you; I daresay poor Louisa may expect it of me, but I can't, and you know very well I can't. I should like to know how it has come about all the same; but one thing only, Gerald – a man may be a Christian without being a priest. Louisa—"

"Hush, I am a priest, or nothing. I can't relinquish my life!" cried the elder brother, lifting his hands suddenly, as if to thrust away something which threatened him. Then he rose up again and went towards the window and his cedar, which stood dark in the sunshine, slightly fluttered at its extremities by the light summer-wind, but throwing glorious level lines of shadow, which the wind could not

disturb, upon the grass. The limes near, and that one
delicate feathery birch which was Mrs Wentworth's pride,
had all some interest of their own on hand, and went
on waving, rustling, coquetting with the breezes and the
sunshine in a way which precluded any arbitrary line of
shade. But the cedar stood immovable, like a verdant
monument, sweeping its long level branches over the
lawn, passive under the light, and indifferent, except at its
very tops and edges, to the breeze. If there had been any
human sentiment in that spectator of the ways of man,
how it must have groaned and trembled under the pitiless
weight of thoughts, the sad lines of discussion and argument and doubt, which were entangled in its branches!
Gerald Wentworth went to his window to refer to it, as if it
were a book in which all his contests had been recorded.
The thrill of the air in it tingled through him as he stood
looking out; and there, without looking at Frank, except
now and then for a moment when he got excited with his
subject, he went into the history of his struggle – a history
not unprecedented or unparalleled, such as has been told
to the world before now by men who have gone through it,
in various shapes, with various amounts of sophistry and
simplicity. But it is a different thing reading of such a
conflict in a book, and hearing it from lips pallid with the
meaning of the words they uttered, and a heart which was
about to prove its sincerity by voluntary pangs more hard
than death. Frank Wentworth listened to his brother with
a great deal of agreement in what he said, and again with
an acute perception of mistakes on Gerald's part, and
vehement impulses of contradiction, to which, at the same
time, it was impossible to give utterance; for there was
something very solemn in the account he was giving of
himself, as he stood with his face half turned to the
anxious listener, leaning on the window, looking into the
cedar. Gerald did not leave any room for argument or
remonstrance; he told his brother how he had been led
from one step to another, without any lingering touch of

possibility in the narrative that he might be induced to
retrace again that painful way. It was a path, once trod,
never to be returned upon; and already he stood steadfast
at the end, looking back mournfully, yet with a strange
composure. It would be impossible to describe the mixture
of love, admiration, impatience – even intolerance –
which swelled through the mind of the spectator as he
looked on at this wonderful sight, nor how hard he found it
to restrain the interruptions which rushed to his lips, the
eager arguments which came upon him in a flood, all his
own favourite fences against the overflow of the tide which
ran in lawful bounds in his own mind, but which had
inundated his brother's. But though it was next to impossible to keep silence, it was altogether impossible to break
in upon Gerald's history of this great battle through which
he had just come. He *had* come through it, it was plain; the
warfare was accomplished, the weapons hung up, the
conflict over; and nothing could be more apparent than
that he had no intention of entering the battle-field again.
When he had ended, there was another pause.

"I am not going to argue with you," said Frank
Wentworth; "I don't even need to tell you that I am
grieved to the heart. It isn't so very many years ago," said
the younger brother, almost too much touched by the
recollection to preserve his composure, "since I took all
my opinions from you; and since the time came for
independent action, I too have gone over all this ground.
My conclusions have been very different from yours,
Gerald. I see you are convinced, and I can say nothing;
but they do not convince me – you do not convince me,
nor the sight of your faith, though that is the most touching
of all arguments. Will you go back and go over it again?"
said the Curate, spurred, by a thought of poor Louisa, to
contradict himself, while the words were still on his lips.

"No," said Gerald; "it would be of no use, Frank. We
should only grieve each other more."

"Then I give up that subject," said the younger brother:

"but there is one matter which I must go back to. You may go to Rome, and cease to be a priest of the Anglican Church, but you cannot cease to be a man, to bear the weight of your natural duties. Don't turn away, but hear me. Gerald, Louisa—"

"Don't say any more. Do you imagine I have not thought of that?" said Gerald, once more, with a gesture of pain, and something like terror; "I have put my hand to the plough and I cannot go back. If I am not a priest, I am nothing." But when he came to that point, his cedar-tree no longer gave him any assistance; he came back to his chair, and covered his face with his hands.

"Louisa is your wife; you are not like a man free from the bonds of nature," said the Curate of St Roque's. "It is not for me to speak of the love between you; but I hold it, as the Scripture says, for a holy mystery, like the love of Christ for his Church – the most sacred of all bonds," said the young man, with a certain touch of awe and emotion, as became a young man and a true lover. He made a little pause to regain command of himself before he continued, "And she is dependent on you – outwardly, for all the comfort of her life – and in her heart, for everything, Gerald. I do not comprehend what that duty is which could make you leave her, all helpless and tender, as you know her to be, upon the mercies of the world. She herself says" – and poor Louisa's complaint grew into pathos under the subliming force of her advocate's sympathy – "that she would be like a widow, and worse than a widow. I am not the man to bid you suppress your convictions because they will be your ruin, in the common sense of the word; but, Gerald – your wife—"

Gerald had bent his head down upon his clasped hands; sometimes a great heave of his frame showed the last struggle that was going on within him – a struggle more painful, more profound, than anything that had gone before. And the voice of the Curate, who, like his brother, was nothing if not a priest, was choked, and painful with the force of his emotion. He drew his breath hard between his words: it was not an argument, but an admonition; an appeal, not from a brother only, but from one who spoke with authority, as feeling himself accredited from God. He drew closer towards the voluntary martyr beside him, the humbleness of his reverential love for his elder brother mingling in that voice of the priest, which was natural to him, and which he did not scruple to adopt. "Gerald, – your wife," he said, in softened but firm tones, laying his hand on his brother's arm. And it was at this moment, when in his heart he felt that his influence might be of some avail, and when all the powers of his mind were gathering to bear upon this last experiment, that the door opened suddenly, and poor Louisa, all flushed and tearful, in womanish hot impatience and misery that knew no prudence, burst, without any warning, into the room.

"I can't bear it any longer," cried the poor wife. "I knew you were talking it all over, and deciding what it was to be; and when one's life is hanging on a chance, how can one keep quiet and not interfere? Oh, Gerald, Gerald! I have been a true wife to you. I know I am not clever; but I would have died to do you any good. You are not going to forsake me!" cried poor Louisa, going up to him and putting her arms round him. "I said Frank was to tell you everything, but a man can never tell what is in a woman's heart. Oh, Gerald, why should you go and kill me! I will never oppose you any more; whatever you want, I will give in to it as freely as if it were my own way. I will make *that* my own way, Gerald, if you will only listen to me. Whatever changes you please, oh Gerald, I will never say a word, nor your father, nor any one! If the Bishop should interfere, we would all stand up for you. There is not a soul in Wentworth to oppose – you know there is not. Put anything you please in the church – preach how you please – light the candles or anything. Gerald, you know it is true I am saying— I am not trying to deceive you!" cried the poor soul, bewildered in her folly and her grief.

"No, Louisa, no – only you don't understand," said her husband, with a groan: he had raised his head, and was looking at her with a hopeless gleam of impatience in the pity and anguish of his eyes. He took her little hand and held it between his own, which were trembling with all this strain – her little tender helpless woman's hand, formed only for soft occupations and softer caresses; it was not a hand which could help a man in such an emergency; it was without any grasp in it to take hold upon him, or force of love to part – a clinging impotent hand, such as holds down, but cannot raise up. He held it in a close tremulous pressure, as she stood looking down upon him, questioning him with eager hopeful eyes, and taking comfort in her ignorance from his silence, and the way in which he held her. Poor Louisa concluded she was yet to win the day.

"I will turn Puseyite too," she said with a strange little touch of attempted laughter. "I don't want to have any opinions different from my husband's; and you don't think your father is likely to do anything to drive you out of the church? You have only given us a terrible fright, dear," she continued, beginning to tremble again, as he shook his head and turned away from her. "You did not really mean such a dreadful thing as sending *me* away. You could not do without me, Gerald – you know you could not." Her breath was getting short, her heart quickening in its throbs – the smile that was quivering on her face got no response from her husband's downcast eyes. And then poor Louisa lost all her courage; she threw herself down at his feet, kneeling to him. "Oh, Gerald, it is not because you want to get rid of me? You are not doing it for that? If you don't stay in the Rectory, we shall be ruined – we shall not have enough to eat! and the Rectory will go to Frank, and your children will be cast upon the world – and what, oh what is it for, unless it is to get rid of me?" cried Mrs Wentworth. "You could have as much freedom as you like here at your own living – nobody would ever interfere or say what are you doing? and the Bishop is papa's old friend. Oh, Gerald, be wise in time, and don't throw away all our happiness for a fancy. If it was anything that could not be arranged, I would not mind so much; but if we all promise to give in to you, and that you shall do what you please, and nobody will interfere, how can you have the heart to make us all so wretched? We will not even be respectable," said the weeping woman; "a family without any father, and a wife without her husband – and he living all the time! Oh, Gerald, though I think I surely might be considered as much as candles, have the altar covered with lights if you wish it; and if you never took off your surplice any more, I would never say a word. You can do all that and stay in the Rectory. You have not the heart – surely – surely you have not the heart – all for an idea of your own, to bring this terrible distress upon the children and me?"

"God help us all!" said Gerald, with a sigh of despair, as he lifted her up sobbing in a hysterical fit, and laid her on the sofa. He had to stand by her side for a long time holding her hand, and soothing her, with deeper and deeper shadows growing over his face. As for Frank, after pacing the room in great agitation for some time, after trying to interpose, and failing, he went away in a fever of impatience and distress into the garden, wondering whether he could ever find means to take up the broken thread, and urge again upon his brother the argument which, but for this fatal interruption, he thought might have moved him. But gathering thoughts came thick upon the Perpetual Curate. He did not go back to make another attempt, even when he knew by the sounds through the open windows that Louisa had been led to her own room up-stairs. He stood outside and looked at the troubled house, which seemed to stand so serene and secure in the sunshine. Who could have supposed that it was torn asunder in such a hopeless fashion? And Louisa's suggestion came into his mind, and drove him wild with a sense

of horror and involuntary guilt, as though he had been
conspiring against them. "The Rectory will go to Frank."
Was it his fault that at that moment a vision of Lucy
Wodehouse, sweet and strong and steadfast – a delicate,
firm figure, on which a man could lean in his trouble –
suddenly rose up before the Curate's eyes? Fair as the
vision was, he would have banished it if he could, and
hated himself for being capable of conjuring it up at such a
time. Was it for him to profit by the great calamity which
would make his brother's house desolate? He could not
endure the thought, nor himself for finding it possible; and
he was ashamed to look in Gerald's face with even the
shadow of such an imagination on his own. He tapped at
the library window after a while, and told his brother that
he was going up to the Hall. Louisa had gone up-stairs, and
her husband sat once more, vacant yet occupied, by his
writing-table. "I will follow you presently," said Gerald.
"Speak to my father without any hesitation, Frank; it is
better to have it over while we are all together – for it must
be concluded now." And the Curate saw in the shadow of
the dim apartment that his brother lifted from the table the
grand emblem of all anguish and victory, and pressed
upon it his pale lips. The young man turned away with the
shadow of that cross standing black between him and the
sunshine. His heart ached at the sight of the symbol most
sacred and most dear in the world. In an agony of grief
and impatience, he went away sadly through the familiar
road to his father's house. Here had he to stand by and see
this sacrifice accomplished. This was all that had come of
his mission of consolation and help.

CHAPTER XVII.

THE Curate of St Roque's went sadly along the road he knew so well from Wentworth Rectory to the Hall. There was scarcely a tree nor the turning of a hedgerow which had not its own individual memories to the son of the soil. Here he had come to meet Gerald returning from Eton – coming back from the university in later days. Here he had rushed down to the old Rector, his childless uncle, with the copy of the prize-list when his brother took his first-class. Gerald, and the family pride in him, was interwoven with the very path, and now— The young man pressed on to the Hall with a certain bitter moisture stealing to the corner of his eye. He felt indignant and aggrieved in his love, not at Gerald, but at the causes which were conspiring to detach him from his natural sphere and duties. When he recollected how he had himself dallied with the same thoughts, he grew angry with his brother's nobleness and purity, which never could see less than its highest ideal soul in anything, and with a certain fierce fit of truth, glanced back at his own Easter lilies and choristers, feeling involuntarily that he would like to tear off the flowers and surplices and tread them under his feet. Why was it that he, an inferior man, should be able to confine himself to the mere accessories which pleased his fancy, and could judge and reject the dangerous principles beneath; while Gerald, the loftier, purer intelligence, should get so hopelessly lost in mazes of sophistry and false argument, to the peril of his work, his life, and all that he could ever know of happiness? Such were the thoughts that passed through the mind of the

Perpetual Curate as he went rapidly through the winding country-road going "home." Perhaps he was wrong in thinking that Gerald was thus superior to himself; but the error was a generous one, and the Curate held it in simplicity and with all his heart.

Before he reached the house he saw his father walking under the lime-trees, which formed a kind of lateral aisle to the great avenue, which was one of the boasts of the Wentworths. The Squire was like most squires of no particular character; a hale, ruddy, clear-complexioned, well-preserved man, looking his full age, but retaining all the vigour of his youth. He was not a man of any intellect to speak of, nor did he pretend to it; but he had that glimmering of sense which keeps many a stupid man straight, and a certain amount of natural sensibility and consideration for other people's feelings which made persons who knew no better give Mr Wentworth credit for tact, a quality unknown to him. He was walking slowly in a perplexed manner under the lime-trees. They were all in glorious blossom, filling the air with that mingling sense of fragrance and music which is the soul of the murmurous tree: but the short figure of the Squire, in his morning-coat, with his perplexed looks, was not at all an accessory in keeping with the scene. He was taking his walk in a subdued way, pondering something – and it puzzled him sorely in his straightforward, unprofound understanding. He shook his head sometimes as he went along, sad and perplexed and unsatisfactory, among his limes. He had got a note from Gerald that morning; and how his son could intend to give up living and station, and wife and children, for anything in heaven or earth, was more than the Squire could understand. He started very much when he heard Frank's voice calling to him. Frank, indeed, was said to be, if any one was, the Squire's weakness in the family; he was as clever as Gerald, and he had the practical sense which Mr Wentworth prized as knowing himself to possess it. If he could have wished for any one in the present emergency, it would have been Frank – and he turned round overjoyed.

"Frank, my boy, you're heartily welcome home!" he said, holding out his hand to him as became a British parent – "always welcome, but particularly just now. Where did you come from? how did you come? have you eaten anything this morning? it's close upon lunch, and we'll go in directly; but, my dear boy, wait here a moment, if you're not particularly hungry; I can't tell you how glad I am you're come. I'd rather see you than a hundred pound!"

When Frank had thanked him, and returned his greetings, and answered his questions (which the Squire had forgotten), and made his own inquiries, to which Mr Wentworth replied only by a hasty nod, and an "Oh yes, thank you, all well – all well," the two came to a momentary pause: they had nothing particular to add about their happiness in seeing each other; and as Frank wrote to his sisters pretty regularly, there was nothing to tell. They were quite free to plunge at once, as is to British relatives under the trying circumstances of a meeting a blessed possibility, into the first great subject which happened to be at hand.

"Have you heard anything about Gerald?" said Mr Wentworth, abruptly; "perhaps you called there on your way from the station? Gerald has got into a nice mess. He wrote to tell me about it, and I can't make head nor tail of it. Do you think he's a little touched here?" and the Squire tapped his own round forehead, with a troubled look: "there's no other explanation possible that I can see: a good living, a nice house, a wife that just suits him (and it's not everybody that would suit Gerald), and a lot of fine children – and he talks to me of giving up everything; as if a man could give up everything! It's all very well talking of self-renunciation, and so forth; and if it meant simply considering other people, and doing anything disagreeable for anybody's sake, I don't know a man more likely than my son Gerald. Your brother's a fine fellow, Frank – a noble sort of fellow, though he has his crotchets," said the father, with a touch of involuntary pathos; "but you don't mean to tell me that my son, a man like Gerald Wentworth, has a mind to throw away his position, and give up all the duties of his life? He can't do it, sir! I tell you it's impossible, and I won't believe it." Mr Wentworth drew up his shirt-collar, and kicked away a fallen branch with his foot, and looked insulted and angry. It was a dereliction of which he would not suppose the possibility of a Wentworth being guilty. It did not strike him as a conflict between belief and non-belief; but on the question of a man abandoning his post, whatever it might be, the head of the house held strong views.

"I agree it's impossible; but it looks as if it were true," said the Curate. "I don't understand it any more than you do; but I am afraid we shall have to address ourselves to the reality all the same. Gerald has made up his mind that the Church of Rome is the only true Church, and therefore he is in a false position in the Church of England: he can't remain a priest of the Anglican communion with such views, any more than a man could fight against his country, or in a wrong quarrel—"

"But, good heavens, sir!" said the Squire, interrupting him, "is it a time to inquire into the quarrel when you're on the ground? Will you tell me, sir, that my son Charley should have gone into the question between Russia and England when he was before Sebastopol – and deserted," said Mr Wentworth, with a snort of infinite scorn, "if he found the Czar had right on his side? God bless my soul! that's striking at the root of everything. As for the Church of Rome, it's Antichrist – why, every child in the village school could tell you that; and if Gerald entertains any such absurd ideas, the thing for him to do is to read up all that's been written on the subject, and get rid of his doubts as soon as possible. The short and the long of it is," said the troubled Squire, who found it much the easiest way to be angry, "that you ask me to believe that your brother

Gerald is a fool and a coward; and I won't believe it, Frank, if you should preach to me for a year."

"And for my part, I would stake my life on his wisdom and his courage," said the Curate, with a little heat; "but that is not the question – he believes that truth and honour require him to leave his post. There is something more involved which we might yet prevent. I have been trying, but Louisa interrupted me – I don't know if you realise fully what he intends. Gerald cannot cease to be a priest – he will become a Catholic priest when he ceases to be Rector of Wentworth – and that implies—"

"God bless my soul!" cried the bewildered Squire – he was silent for a long time after he had uttered that bene-diction. He took out Gerald's letter and read it over while the two walked on in silence under the lime-trees, and the paper shook in his hands, notwithstanding all his steadiness. When he spoke again, it was only after two or three efforts to clear his voice. "I can't make out that he says *that*, Frank – I don't see that *that's* what he means," said Mr Wentworth, in a fainter tone than usual; and then he continued, with more agitation, "Louisa is a dear good soul, you know; but she's a bit of a fool, like most women. She always takes the worst view – if she can get a good cry out of anything, she will. It's she that's put this fancy into your head, eh? You don't say you had it from Gerald himself? You don't mean to tell me that? By Jove, sir! – by heaven, sir!" cried the excited Squire, blazing up suddenly in a burst of passion, "he can't be any son of mine— For any damnable Papistical madness to give up his wife! Why, God bless us, he was a man, wasn't he, before he became a priest? A priest! He's not a priest – he's a clergyman, and the Rector of Wentworth. I can't believe it – I won't believe it!" said the head of the house, with vehemence. "Tell me one of my sons is a sneak and a traitor! – and if you weren't another of my sons, sir, I'd knock you down for your pains." In the excitement of the moment Mr Wentworth came full force against a projecting branch which he did not see, as he spoke these words; but though the sudden blow half stunned him, he did not stop in his vehement contradiction. "It can't be. I tell you it can't – it shan't be, Frank!" cried the Squire. He would not pay any attention to the Curate's anxieties, or accept the arm Frank offered, though he could not deny feeling faint and giddy after the blow. It took away all the colour from his ruddy face, and left him pale, with a red welt across his forehead, and wonderfully unlike himself. "Confound it! I told Miles to look after that tree weeks ago. If he thinks I'll stand his carelessness, he's mistaken," said Mr Wentworth, by way of relieving himself. He was a man who always eased his mind by being angry with somebody when anything happened to put him out.

"My dear father," said the Curate as soon as it was practicable, "I want you to listen to me and help me; there's only one thing to be done that I can see. Gerald is in a state of high excitement, fit for any martyrdom. We can't keep him back from one sacrifice, but by all the force we can gather we must detain him from the other. He must be shown that he can't abandon his natural duties. He was a man before he was a priest, as you say; he can no more give up his duty to Louisa than he can give up his own life. It is going on a false idea altogether; but falsehood in anything except in argument could never be named or dreamed of in connection with Gerald," said his brother, with some emotion; "we all know that."

There was another pause of a few minutes, during which they walked on side by side without even the heart to look at each other. "If it had been Huxtable or Plumstead, or any other fool," burst forth the Squire, after that interval, "but Gerald!" Huxtable was the husband of the eldest Miss Wentworth, and Plumstead was the Squire's sister's son, so the comparison was all in the family. "I suppose your aunt Leonora would say such a thing was sent to bring down my pride and keep me low," said Mr Wentworth, bitterly. "Jack being what he is, was it anything but natural that I should be proud of Gerald? There never was any evil in him, that I could see, from a child; but crotchety, always crotchety, Frank. I can see it now. It must have been their mother," said the Squire, meditatively; "she died very young, poor girl! her character was not formed. As for *your* dear mother, my boy, she was always equal to an emergency; she would have given us the best of advice, had she been spared to us this day. Mrs Wentworth is absorbed in her nursery, as is natural, and I should not care to consult her much on such a subject. But, Frank, whatever you can do or say, trust to me to back you out," said the anxious father of three families. "Your mother was the most sensible woman I ever knew," he continued, with a patriarchal composure. "Nobody could ever manage Jack and Gerald as she did. She'd have seen at a glance what to do now. As for Jack, he is not assistance to anybody; but I consider you very like your mother, Frank. If anybody can help Gerald, it will be you. He has got into some ridiculous complications, you know – that must be the explanation of it. You have only to talk to him, and clear up the whole affair," said the Squire, recovering himself a little. He believed in "talking to," like Louisa, and like most people who are utterly incapable of talking to any purpose. He took some courage from the thought, and recovered his colour a little. "There is the bell for luncheon, and I am very glad of it," he said; "a glass of sherry will set me all right. Don't say anything to alarm Mrs Wentworth. When Gerald comes we'll retire to the library, and go into the matter calmly, and between us we will surely be able to convince him. I'll humour him, for my part, as far as my conscience will allow me. We must not give in to him, Frank. He will give it up if we show a very firm front and yield nothing," said the Squire, looking with an unusually anxious eye in his son's face.

"For my part, I will not enter into the controversy between the Churches," said the Curate; "it is mere waste of time. I must confine myself to the one point. If he must forsake us, he must, and I can't stop him: but he must not forsake his wife."

"Tut – it's impossible!" said the Squire; "it's not to be thought of for a moment. You must have given undue importance to something that was said. Things will turn out better than you think." They were very nearly at the great entrance when these words were said, and Mr Wentworth took out his handkerchief and held it to his forehead to veil the mark, until he could explain it, from the anxious eye of his wife. "If the worst should come to the worst, as you seem to think," he said, with a kind of sigh, "I should at least be able to provide for you, Frank. Of course, the Rectory would go to you; and you don't seem to have much chance of Skelmersdale, so far as I can learn. Leonora's a very difficult person to deal with. God bless my soul!" exclaimed the Squire – "depend upon it, she has had something to do with this business of Gerald's. She's goaded him into it, with her Low-Church ways. She's put poor Louisa up to worrying him; there's where it is. I did not see how your brother could possibly have fallen into such a blunder of his own accord. But come to luncheon; you must be hungry. You will think the boys grown, Frank; and I must ask you what you think, when you have a little leisure, of Cuthbert and Guy."

So saying, the Squire led the way into the house; he had been much appalled by the first hint of this threatened calamity, and was seriously distressed and anxious still; but he was the father of many sons, and the misfortunes or blunders of one could not occupy all his heart. And even the Curate, as he followed his father into the house, felt that Louisa's words, so calmly repeated, "Of course, the Rectory will go to you," went tingling to his heart like an arrow, painfully recalling him, in the midst of his anxiety, to a sense of his own interests and cares. Gerald was coming up the avenue at the moment slowly, with all the feelings of a man going to the stake. He was looking at everything round as a dying man might, not knowing what

terrible revolution of life might have happened before he
saw them again –

> "He looked on hill, and sea, and shore,
>   As he might never see them more."

Life was darkened over to his preoccupied eyes, and the
composure of nature jarred upon him, as though it were
carelessness and indifference to the fate which he felt to be
coming in the air. He thought nothing less than that his
father and brother were discussing him with hearts as
heavy and clouded as his own; for even he, in all his
tolerance and impartiality, did not make due account of the
fact, that every man has his own concerns next to him,
close enough to ameliorate and lighten the weight of his
anxieties for others. The prospect was all gloom to Gerald,
who was the sufferer; but the others found gleams of
comfort in their own horizon, which threw reflected lights
upon his; for perfect sympathy is not, except in dreams.
There was quite a joyful little commotion at the luncheon
table when Frank's arrival was discovered; and his sisters
were kissing him, and his young brothers shaking his hand
off, while Gerald came slowly up, with preoccupied,
lingering steps, underneath the murmurous limes. All
kinds of strange miseries were appearing to him as he
pursued his way. Glimpses of scenes to come – a dark
phantasmagoria of anticipated pain. He saw his wife and
his children going away out of their happy house; he saw
himself severed from all human ties, among alien faces
and customs, working out a hard novitiate. What could he
do? His heart, so long on the rack, was aching with dull
throbs of anguish, but he did not see any way of escape.
He was a priest by all the training, all the habits of his life;
how could he give up that service to which he was called
before everything, the most momentous work on earth?
For ease, for happiness, for even sacred love, could he
defraud God of the service he had vowed, and go back to

secular work just at the moment when the true meaning of ecclesiastical work seemed dawning upon him? He had decided that question before, but it came back and back. His eyes were heavy with thought and conflict as he went up to his father's house. All this was wearing out his strength, and sapping his very life. The sooner it was over the better would it be for all.

CHAPTER XVIII.

VERY little came, as was natural, of the talk in the library, to which the entire afternoon was devoted. The Squire, in his way, was as great an interruption to the arguments of the Curate as was poor Louisa in hers; and Gerald sat patiently to listen to his father's indignant monologue, broken as it was by Frank's more serious attacks. He was prepared for all they could say to him, and listened to it, sometimes with a kind of wondering smile, knowing well how much more strongly, backed by all his prejudices and interests, he had put the same arguments to himself. All this time nobody discussed the practicability of the matter much, nor what steps he meant to take: what immediately occupied both his father and brother was his determination itself, and the reasons which had led him to it, which the Squire, like Louisa, could not understand.

"If I had made myself disagreeable," said Mr Wentworth; "if I had remonstrated with him, as Leonora urged me to do; if I had put a stop to the surplice and so forth, and interfered with his decorations or his saints' days, or anything, it might have been comprehensible. But I never said a syllable on the subject. I give you my

word, I never did. Why couldn't he have sent down for
Louisa now, and dined at the Hall, as usual, when any of
my sons come home? I suppose a man may change his
religion, sir, without getting rid of his natural affections,"
said the Squire, gazing out with puzzled looks to watch
Gerald going slowly down the avenue. "A man who talks
of leaving his wife, and declines to dine at his father's
house with his brothers and sisters, is a mystery I can't
understand."

"I don't suppose he cares for a lively party like ours at
this moment," said the Curate: "I don't take it as any sign
of a want of affection for me."

The Squire puffed forth a large sigh of trouble and
vexation as he came from the window. "If *I* were to give in
to trouble when it appears, what would become of our
lively party, I wonder?" he said. "I'm getting an old man,
Frank; but there's not a young man in Christendom has
more need to take care of himself, and preserve his
health, than I have. I am very well, thank God, though I
have had a touch of our Wentworth complaint – just one
touch. My father had it ten years earlier in life, and lived
to eighty, all the same; but that is an age I shall never see.
Such worries as I have would kill any man. I've not
spoken to anybody about it," said the Squire, hastily, "but
Jack is going a terrible pace just now. I've had a good deal
of bother about bills and things. He gets worse every year;
and what would become of the girls and the little children
if the estate were to come into Jack's hands, is a thought I
don't like to dwell upon, Frank. I suppose he never writes
to you?"

"Not for years past," said the Curate – "not since I was
at Oxford. Where is he now?"

"Somewhere about town, I suppose," said the aggrieved
father, "or wherever the greatest scamps collect when
they go out of town – that's where he is. I could show you a
little document or two, Frank – but now," said the Squire,
shutting up a drawer which he had unlocked and partly

opened, "I won't; you've enough on your mind with
Gerald, and I told you I should be glad of your advice
about Cuthbert and Guy."

Upon which the father and son plunged into family
affairs. Cuthbert and Guy were the youngest of the
Squire's middle family – a "lot" which included Frank and
Charley and the three sisters, one of whom was married.
The domestic relations of the Wentworths were complicated in this generation. Jack and Gerald were of the first
marriage, a period in his history which Mr Wentworth
himself had partly forgotten; and the troop of children at
present in the Hall nursery were quite beyond the powers
of any grown-up brother to recognise or identify. It was
vaguely understood that "the girls" knew all the small fry
by head and name, but even the Squire himself was apt to
get puzzled. With such a household, and with an heir
impending over his head like Jack, it may be supposed
that Mr Wentworth's anxiety to get his younger boys
disposed of was great. Cuthbert and Guy were arrows in
the hand of the giant, but he had his quiver so full that the
best thing he could do was to draw his bow and shoot them
away into as distant and as fresh a sphere as possible.
They were sworn companions and allies, but they were
not clever, Mr Wentworth believed, and he was very glad
to consult over New Zealand and Australia, and which was
best, with their brother Frank.

"They are good boys," said their father, "but they have
not any brains to speak of – not like Gerald and you; –
though, after all, I begin to be doubtful what's the good of
brains," added the Squire, disconsolately, "if this is all
that comes of them. After building so much on Gerald for
years, and feeling that one might live to see him a bishop –
but, however, there's still *you* left; you're all right, Frank?"

"Oh yes, I am all right," said the Curate, with a sigh;
"but neither Gerald nor I are the stuff that bishops are
made of," he added, laughing. "I hope you don't dream of
any such honour for me."

But the Squire was too troubled in his mind for laughter. "Jack was always clever, too," he said, dolefully, "and little good has come of that. I hope he won't disgrace the family any more than he has done, in my time, Frank. You young fellows have all your life before you; but when a man comes to my age, and expects a little comfort, it's hard to be dragged into the mire after his children. I did my duty by Jack too – I can say that for myself. He had the same training as Gerald had – the same tutor at the university – everything just the same. How do you account for that, sir, you that are a philosopher?" said Mr Wentworth again, with a touch of irritation. "Own brothers both by father and mother; brought up in the same house, same school and college and everything; and all the time as different from each other as light and darkness. How do you account for that? Though, to be sure, here's Gerald taken to bad ways too. It must have been some weakness by their mother's side. Poor girl! she died too young to show it herself; but it's come out in her children," said the vexed Squire. "Though it's a poor sort of thing to blame them that are gone," he added, with penitence; and he got up and paced uneasily about the room. Who was there else to blame? Not himself, for he had done his duty by his boys. Mr Wentworth never was disturbed in mind, without, as his family were well aware, becoming excited in temper too; and the unexpected nature of the new trouble had somehow added a keener touch of exasperation to his perennial dissatisfaction with his heir. "If Jack had been the man he ought to have been, his advice might have done some good – for a clergyman naturally sees things in a different light from a man of the world," said the troubled father; and Frank perceived that he too shared in his father's displeasure, because he was not Jack, nor a man of the world; notwithstanding that, being Frank and a clergyman, he was acknowledged by public opinion to be the Squire's favourite in the family. Things continued in this uncom-

fortable state up to the dinner-hour, so that the Curate,
even had his own feelings permitted it, had but little
comfort in his home visit. At dinner Mr Wentworth did not
eat, and awoke the anxiety of his wife, who drove the old
gentleman into a state of desperation by inquiries after his
health.

"Indeed, I wish you would remonstrate with your papa,
Frank," said his stepmother, who was not a great deal
older than the Curate. "After his attack he ought to be
more careful. But he never takes the least trouble about
himself, no more than if he were five-and-twenty. After
getting such a knock on the forehead too; and you see he
eats nothing. I shall be miserable if the doctor is not sent
for to-night."

"Stuff!" cried the Squire, testily. "Perhaps you will
speak to the cook about these messes she insists on
sending up to disgust one, and leave me to take care of my
own health. Don't touch that dish, Frank; it's poison. I am
glad Gerald is not here: he'd think we never had a dinner
without that confounded mixture. And then the wonder is
that one can't eat!" said Mr Wentworth, in a tone which
spread consternation round the table. Mrs Wentworth
secretly put her handkerchief to her eyes behind the great
cover, which had not yet been removed; and one of the
girls dashed in violently to the rescue, of course making
everything worse.

"Why did not Gerald and Louisa come to dinner?" cried
the ignorant sister. "Surely, when they knew Frank had
come, they would have liked to be here. How very odd it
was of you not to ask them, papa! they always do come
when anybody has arrived. Why aren't they here
to-night?"

"Because they don't choose to come," said the Squire,
abruptly. "If Gerald has reasons for staying away from his
father's house, what is that to you? Butterflies," said Mr
Wentworth, looking at them in their pretty dresses, as
they sat regarding him with dismay. "that don't

understand any reason for doing anything except liking it or not liking it. I daresay by this time your sister knows better."

"My sister is married, papa," said Letty, with her saucy look.

"I advise you to get married too, and learn what life is like," said the savage Squire; and conversation visibly flagged after this effort. When the ladies got safely into the drawing-room, they gathered into a corner to consult over it. They were all naturally anxious about him after his "attack."

"Don't you remember he was just like this before it came on?" said Mrs Wentworth, nervously; "so cross, and finding fault with the made dishes. Don't you think I might send over a message to Dr Small – not to come on purpose, you know, but just as if it were a call in passing?"

But the girls both agreed this would make matters worse.

"It must be something about Jack," they both said in a breath, in a kind of awe of their elder brother, of whom they had a very imperfect knowledge. "And it seems we never are to have a chance of a word with Frank!" cried Letty, who was indignant and exasperated. But at least it was a consolation that "the boys" were no better off. All next day Cuthbert and Guy hung about in the vain hope of securing the company and attention of the visitor. He was at the Rectory the whole morning, sometimes with Gerald, sometimes with Louisa, as the scouts of the family, consisting of a variety of brothers, little and big, informed the anxious girls. And Louisa was seen to cry on one of these occasions; and Gerald looked cross, said one little spy, whereupon he had his ears boxed, and was dismissed from the service. "As if Gerald ever looked anything but a saint!" said the younger sister, who was an advanced Anglican. Letty, however, holding other views, confuted this opinion strongly: "When one thinks of a saint, it is aunt Leonora one thinks of," said this profane young woman. "I'll tell you what Gerald looks like – something just half-way between a conqueror and a martyr. I think, of all the men I ever saw, he is my hero," said Letty, meditatively. The youngest Miss Wentworth was not exactly of this latter opinion, but she did not contradict her sister. They were kept in a state of watchfulness all day, but Frank's mission remained a mystery which they could not penetrate; and in the evening Gerald alone made his appearance at the hall to dinner, explaining that Louisa had a headache. Now Louisa's headaches were not unfrequent, but they were known to improve in the prospect of going out to dinner. On the whole, the matter was wrapt in obscurity, and the Wentworth household could not explain it. The sisters sat up brushing their hair, and looking very pretty in their dressing-gowns, with their bright locks (for the Wentworth hair was golden-brown of a Titian hue) over their shoulders, discussing the matter till it was long past midnight; but they could make nothing of it, and the only conclusion they came to was, that their two clergymen brothers were occupied in negotiating with the Squire about some secret not known to the rest of the family, but most probably concerning Jack. Jack was almost unknown to his sisters, and awoke no very warm anxiety in their minds; so they went to sleep at last in tolerable quiet, concluding that whatever mystery there was concerned only the first-born and least loved of the house.

While the girls pursued these innocent deliberations, and reasoned themselves into conviction, the Squire too sat late – much later than usual. He had gone with Frank to the library, and sat there in half-stupefied quietness, which the Curate could not see without alarm, and from which he roused himself up now and then to wander off into talk, which always began with Gerald, and always came back to his own anxieties and his disappointed hopes in his eldest son. "If Jack had been the man he ought to have been, I'd have telegraphed for him, and he'd have managed it all," said the Squire, and then relapsed once more into silence. "For neither you nor I are men of the world, Frank," he would resume again, after a pause of half an hour, revealing pitifully how his mind laboured under the weight of this absorbing thought. The Curate sat up with him in the dimly-lighted library, feeling the silence and the darkness to his heart. He could not assist his father in those dim ranges of painful meditation. Grieved as he was, he could not venture to compare his own distress with the bitterness of the Squire, disappointed in all his hopes and in the pride of his heart; and then the young man saw compensations and heroisms in Gerald's case which were invisible to the unheroic eyes of Mr Wentworth, who looked at it entirely from a practical point of view, and regarded with keen mortification an event which would lay all the affairs of the Wentworths open to general discussion, and invite the eye of the world to a renewed examination of his domestic skeletons. Everything had been hushed and shut up in the Hall for at least an hour, when the Squire got up at last and lighted his candle, and held out his hand to his son – "This isn't a very cheerful visit for you, Frank," he said; "but we'll try again to-morrow, and have one other talk with Gerald. Couldn't you read up some books on the subject, or think of something new to say to him? God bless my soul! if I were as young and as much accustomed to talking as you are, I'd surely find out some argument," said the Squire, with a momentary spark of temper, which made his son feel more comfortable about him. "It's your business to convince a man when he's wrong. We'll try Gerald once more, and perhaps something may come of it; and as for Jack—" Here the Squire paused, and shook his head, and let go his son's hand. "I suppose it's sitting up so late that makes one feel so cold and wretched, and as if one saw ghosts," said Mr Wentworth. "Don't stay here any longer, and take care of the candles. I ought to have been in bed two hours ago. Good-night."

And as he walked away, the Curate could not but observe what an aged figure it looked, moving with a certain caution to the door. The great library was so dim that the light of the candle which the Squire carried in his hand was necessary to reveal his figure clearly, and there was no mistaking his air of age and feebleness. The Curate's thoughts were not very agreeable when he was left by himself in the half-lighted room. His imagination jumped to a picture very possible, but grievous to think of – Jack seated in his father's place, and "the girls" and the little children turned out upon the world. In such a case, who would be their protector and natural guardian? Not Gerald, who was about to divest himself of ties still closer and more sacred. The Curate lit his candle too, and went hastily to his room when that thought came upon him. There might be circumstances still more hopeless and appalling than the opposition of a rector or the want of a benefice. He preferred to return to his anxiety about Gerald, and to put away that thought, as he went hurriedly up-stairs.

CHAPTER XIX.

"The sum of it all is, that you won't hear any reason, Gerald," said the Squire. "What your brother says, and what I say, are nothing; your poor wife is nothing; and all a man's duties, sir, in life – all your responsibilities, everything that is considered most sacred—"

"You may say what you will to me, father," said Gerald. "I can't expect you should speak differently. But you may imagine I have looked at it in every possible light before I came to this resolution. A man does not decide easily

when everything he prizes on earth is at stake. I cannot
see with Frank's eyes, or with yours; according to the light
God has given me, I must see with my own."

"But, God bless my soul! what do you mean by seeing
with your own eyes?" said the Squire. "Don't you know
that is a Protestant doctrine, sir? Do you think they'll let
you see with any eyes but theirs when you get among a set
of Papists? Instead of an easy-going bishop, and friendly
fellows for brother clergymen, and parishioners that think
everything that's good of you, how do you suppose you'll
feel as an Englishman when you get into a dead French-
ified system, with everything going by rule and measure,
and bound to believe just as you're told? It'll kill you, sir –
that's what will be the end of it. If you are in your grave
within the year, it will be no wonder to me."

"Amen!" said Gerald, softly. "If that is to be all, we will
not quarrel with the result;" and he got up and went to the
window, as if to look for his cedar, which was not there.
Perhaps the absence of his silent referee gave him a kind of
comfort, though at the same time it disappointed him in
some fantastical way, for he turned with a curious look of
relief and vexation to his brother. "We need not be always
thinking of it, even if this were to be the end," he said.
"Come down the avenue with me, Frank, and let us talk
of something else. The girls will grumble, but they can
have you later: come, I want to hear about yourself."

Unfortunately the Squire got up when his sons did,
which was by no means their intention; but Mr Wentworth
was vexed and restless, and was not willing to let Gerald
off so easily. If he were mad, at least he ought to be made
duly wretched in his madness, Mr Wentworth thought;
and he went out with them, and arrested the words on
their lips. Somehow everything seemed to concur in hin-
dering any appeal on the part of the Curate. And Gerald,
like most imaginative men, had a power of dismissing his
troubles after they had taken their will of him. It was he
who took the conversation on himself when they went out

of doors. Finding Frank slow in his report, Gerald went into all the country news for the instruction of his brother. He had been down to the very depths during the two previous days, and now he had come aloft again; for a man cannot be miserable every moment of his life, however heavy his burden may be. The "girls," whose anxieties had been much stimulated by the renewed conference held with closed doors in the library, stood watching them from one of the drawing-room windows. The boldest of the two had, indeed, got her hat to follow them, not comprehending why Frank should be monopolised for days together by anybody but herself, his favourite sister; but something in the aspect of the three men, when they first appeared under the lime-trees, had awed even the lively Letty out of her usual courage. "But Gerald is talking and laughing just as usual," she said, as she stood at the window dangling her hat in her hand — "more than usual, for he has been very glum all this spring. Poor fellow! I daresay Louisa worries him out of his life;" and with this easy conclusion the elder brother was dismissed by the girls. "Perhaps Frank is going to be married," said the other sister, who, under the lively spur of this idea, came back to the window to gaze at him again, and find out whether any intimation of this alarming possibility could be gathered from the fit of his long clerical coat, or his manner of walk, as he sauntered along under the limes. "As if a Perpetual Curate could marry!" said Letty, with scorn, who knew the world. As for little Janet, who was a tender-hearted little soul, she folded her two hands together, and looked at her brother's back with a great increase of interest. "If one loved him, one would not mind what he was," said the little maiden, who had been in some trouble herself, and understood about such matters. So the girls talked at their window, Mrs Wentworth being, as usual, occupied with her nursery, and nobody else at hand to teach them wisdom, and soon branched off into speculations about the post-bag, which was "due," and

which, perhaps, was almoşt more interesting, to one of
them at least, than even a brother who was going to be
married.

In the mean time Gerald was talking of Huxtable and
Plumstead, the brother-in-law and cousin, who were both
clergymen in the same district, and about the people in
the village whom they had known when they were boys,
and who never grew any older. "There is old Kilweed, for
example, who was Methuselah in those days – he's not
eighty yet," he said, with a smile and a sigh; "it is we who
grow older and come nearer to the winter and the sunset.
My father even has come down a long way off the awful
eminence on which I used to behold him: every year that
falls on my head seems to take one off his: if we both live
long enough, we shall feel like contemporaries by-and-
by," said Gerald: "just now the advantage of years is all on
my side; and you are my junior, sir." He was switching
down the weeds among the grass with his cane as he
spoke, like any schoolboy; the air, and perhaps a little
excitement, had roused the blood to his cheek. He did
not look the same man as the pale martyr in the library –
not that he had any reason for appearing different, but
only that inalienable poetic waywardness which kept him
up through his trouble. As for Mr Wentworth, he resented
the momentary brightening, which he took for levity.

"I thought we came out here to prolong our discussion,"
said the Squire. "I don't understand this light way of
talking. If you mean what you have said, sir, I should
never expect to see you smile more."

"The smiling makes little difference," said Gerald; but
he stopped short in his talk, and there was a pause among
them till the postboy came up to them with his bag, which
Mr Wentworth, with much importance, paused to open.
The young men, who had no special interest in its contents,
went on. Perhaps the absence of their father was a relief to
them. They were nearer to each other, understood each
other better than he could do; and they quickened their

pace insensibly as they began to talk. It is easy to imagine what kind of talk it was – entire sympathy, yet disagreement wide as the poles – here for a few steps side by side, there darting off at the most opposite tangent; but they had begun to warm to it, and to forget everything else, when a succession of lusty hollos from the Squire brought them suddenly to themselves, and to a dead stop. When they looked round, he was making up to them with choleric strides. "What the deuce do you mean, sir, by having telegrams sent here?" cried Mr Wentworth, pitching at his son Frank an ominous ugly envelope, in blue and red, such as the unsophisticated mind naturally trembles at. "Beg your pardon, Gerald; but I never can keep my temper when I see a telegraph. I daresay it's something about Charley," said the old man, in a slightly husky voice – "to make up to us for inventing troubles." The Squire was a good deal disturbed by the sight of that ill-omened message; and it was the better way, as he knew by experience, to throw his excitement into the shape of anger rather than that of grief.

"It's nothing about Charley," said Frank; and Mr Wentworth blew his nose violently and drew a long breath. "I don't understand it," said the Curate, who looked scared and pale; "it seems to be from Jack; though why *he* is in Carlingford, or what he has to do—"

"He's ill, sir, I suppose – dying; nothing else was to be looked for," said the Squire, and held out his hand, which trembled, for the telegram. "Stuff! why shouldn't I be able to bear it? Has he been any comfort to me? Can't you read it, one of you?" cried the old man.

"'John Wentworth to the Reverend—'"

"God bless my soul! can't you come to what he says?"

"'Come back directly – you are wanted here; I am in trouble, as usual; and T.W.—'"

Here the Squire took a step backwards, and set himself against a tree. "The sun comes in one's eyes," he said, rather feebly. "There's something poisonous in the air

today. Here's Gerald going out of the Church; and here's
Frank in Jack's secrets. God forgive him! Lads, it seems
you think I've had enough of this world's good. My heir's
a swindling villain, and you know it; and here's Frank
going the same road too."

The Squire did not hear the words that both the brothers
addressed to him; he was unconscious of the Curate's
disclaimer and eager explanation that he knew nothing
about Jack, and could not understand his presence in
Carlingford. The blow he had got the previous day had
confused his brain outside, and these accumulated vexations
had bewildered it within. "And I could have sworn by
Frank!" said the old man, piteously, to himself, as he put
up his hand unawares and tugged at the dainty starched
cravat which was his pride. If they had not held him in
their arms, he would have slid down at the foot of the tree,
against which he had instinctively propped himself. The
attack was less alarming to Gerald, who had seen it
before, than to Frank, who had only heard of it; but the
postboy was still within call, by good fortune, and was sent
off for assistance. They carried him to the Hall, gasping
for breath, and in a state of partial unconsciousness, but
still feebly repeating those words which went to the
Curate's heart – "I could have sworn by Frank!" The
house was in a great fright and tumult, naturally, before
they reached it, Mrs Wentworth fainting, the girls looking
on in dismay, and the whole household moved to awe and
alarm, knowing that one time or other Death would come
so. As for the Curate of St Roque's, he had already made
up his mind, with unexpected anguish, not only that his
father was dying, but that his father would die under a
fatal misconception about himself; and between this overwhelming thought, and the anxiety which nobody understood or could sympathise with respecting Jack's message,
the young man was almost beside himself. He went away in
utter despair from the anxious consultations of the family
after the doctor had come, and kept walking up and down

before the house, waiting to hear the worst, as he thought;
but yet unable, even while his father lay dying, to keep
from thinking what miserable chance, what folly or crime,
had taken Jack to Carlingford, and what his brother could
have to do with the owner of the initials named in his
telegram. He was lost in this twofold trouble when Gerald
came out to him with brightened looks.

"He is coming round, and the doctor says there is no
immediate danger," said Gerald; "and it is only immediate
danger one is afraid of. He was as well as ever last time in
a day or two. It is the complaint of the Wentworths, you
know – we all die of it; but, Frank, tell me what is this
about Jack?"

"I know no more than you do," said the Curate, when
he had recovered himself a little. "I must go back, not
having done much good here, to see."

"And T.W.?" said Gerald. The elder brother looked at
the younger suspiciously, as if he were afraid for him; and
it was scarcely in human nature not to feel a momentary
flash of resentment.

"I tell you I know nothing about it," said Frank, "except
what is evident to any one, that Jack has gone to Carlingford in my absence, being in trouble somehow. I suppose
he always is in trouble. I have not heard from him since I
went there; but as it don't seem I can be of any use here,
as soon as my father is safe, I will go back. Louisa
imagined, you know—; but she was wrong."

"Yes," said Gerald, quietly. That subject was concluded,
and there was no more to say.

The same evening, as the Squire continued to improve,
and had been able to understand his energetic explanation
that he was entirely ignorant of Jack's secrets, Frank
Wentworth went back again with a very disturbed mind.
He went into the Rectory as he passed down to the station,
to say good-bye to Louisa, who was sitting in the drawing-
room with her children round her, and her trouble considerably lightened, though there was no particular cause

for it. Dressing for dinner had of itself a beneficial effect upon Louisa: she could not understand how a life could ever be changed which was so clearly ordained of Heaven; for if Gerald was not with her, what inducement could she possibly have to dress for dinner? and then what would be the good of all the pretty wardrobe with which Providence had endowed her? Must not Providence take care that its gifts were not thus wasted? So the world was once more set fast on its foundations, and the pillars of earth remained unshaken, when Frank glanced in on his way to the station to say good-bye.

"Don't be afraid, Louisa; I don't believe he would be allowed to do it," said the Curate in her ear. "The Church of Rome does not go in the face of nature. She will not take him away from you. Keep your heart at ease as much as you can. Good-bye."

"You mean about Gerald. Oh, you don't *really* think he could ever have had the heart?" said Mrs Wentworth. "I am so sorry you are going away without any dinner or anything comfortable; and it was so good of you to come, and I feel so much better. I shall always be grateful to you, dear Frank, for showing Gerald his mistake; and tell dear aunt Dora I am so much obliged to her for thinking of the blanket for the bassinet. I am sure it will be lovely. Must you go? Good-bye. I am sure you have always been like my own brother – Frank, dear, good-bye. Come and kiss your dear uncle, children, and say good-bye."

This was how Louisa dismissed him after all his efforts on her behalf. The girls were waiting for him on the road, still full of anxiety to know why he had come so suddenly, and was going away so soon. "We have not had half a peep of you," said Letty; "and it is wicked of you not to tell us; as if anybody could sympathise like your sisters – your very own sisters, Frank," said the young lady, with a pressure on his arm. In such a mixed family the words meant something.

"We had made up our minds you had come to tell

papa," said Janet, with her pretty shy look; "that was my
guess – you might tell us her name, Frank."

"Whose name?" said the unfortunate Curate; and the
dazzling vision of Lucy Wodehouse's face, which came
upon him at the moment, was such, that the reluctant
blood rose high in his cheeks – which, of course, the girls
were quick enough to perceive.

"It *is* about some girl, after all," said Letty; "oh me! I did
not think you had been like all the rest. I thought you had
other things to think of. Janet may say what she likes – but I
do think it's contemptible always to find out, when a man,
who can do lots of things, is in trouble, that it's about some
girl or other like one's self! I did not expect it of you, Frank
– but all the same, tell us who she is?" said the favourite
sister, clasping his arm confidentially, and dropping her voice.

"There is the train. Good-bye, girls, and be sure you
write to me to-morrow how my father is," said the Curate.
He had taken his seat before they could ask further
questions, and in a minute or two more was dashing out of
the little station, catching their smiles and adieus as he
went, and turning back last of all for another look at
Gerald, who stood leaning on his stick, looking after the
train, with the mist of preoccupation gathering again over
his smiling eyes. The Curate went back to his corner after
that, and lost himself in thoughts and anxieties still more
painful. What had Jack to do in Carlingford? what connection had he with those initials, or how did he know their
owner? All sorts of horrible fears came over the Curate of
St Roque's. He had not seen his elder brother for years,
and Jack's career was not one for the family to be proud
of. Had he done something too terrible to be hidden – too
clamorous to let his name drop out of remembrance, as
was to be desired for the credit of the Wentworths? This
speculation wiled the night away but drearily, as the
Perpetual Curate went back to the unknown tide of cares
which had surged in his absence into his momentarily
abandoned place.

CHAPTER XX.

MR WENTWORTH got back to Carlingford by a happy concurrence of trains before the town had gone to sleep. It was summer, when the days are at the longest, and the twilight was just falling into night as he took his way though George Street. He went along the familiar street with a certain terror of looking into people's faces whom he met, and of asking questions, such as was natural to a man who did not know whether something of public note might not have happened in his absence to call attention to his name. He imagined, indeed, that he did see a strange expression in the looks of the townsfolk he encountered on his way. He thought they looked at him askance as they made their salutations, and said something to each other after they passed, which, indeed, in several cases was true enough, though the cause was totally different from anything suspected by Mr Wentworth. Anxious to know, and yet unwilling to ask, it was with a certain relief that the Curate saw the light gleaming out from the open door of Elsworthy's shop as he approached. He went in and tossed down his travelling-bag on the counter, and threw himself on the solitary chair which stood outside for the accommodation of customers, with a suppressed excitement, which made his question sound abrupt and significant to the ears of Elsworthy. "Has anything happened since I went away?" said Mr Wentworth, throwing a glance round the shop which alarmed his faithful retainer. Somehow, though nothing was farther from his mind than little Rosa, or any thought of her, the Curate missed the pretty little figure at the first glance.

"Well – no, sir; not much as I've heard of," said Elsworthy, with a little confusion. He was tying up his newspapers as usual, but it did not require the touch of suspicion and anxiety which gave sharpness to the Curate's eyes to make it apparent that the cord was trembling in Mr Elsworthy's hand. "I hope you've had a pleasant journey, sir, and a comfortable visit – it's been but short – but we always miss you in Carlingford, Mr Wentworth, if it was only for a day."

"I'll take my paper," said the young man, who was not satisfied – "so there's no news, isn't there? – all well, and everything going on as usual?" And the look which the suspicious Curate bent upon Mr Elsworthy made that virtuous individual, as he himself described it, "shake in his shoes."

"Much as usual, sir," said the frightened clerk, – "nothing new as I hear of but gossip, and that aint a thing to interest a clergyman. There's always one report or another flying about, but them follies aint for your hearing. Nothing more," continued Mr Elsworthy, conscious of guilt, and presenting a very tremulous countenance to the inspection of his suspicious auditor, "not if it was my last word – nothing but gossip, as you wouldn't care to hear."

"I might possibly care to hear if it concerned myself," said the Curate, – "or anybody I am interested in," he added, after a little pause, with rather a forced smile – which convinced Mr Elsworthy that his clergyman had heard all about Rosa, and that the days of his incumbency as clerk of St Roque's were numbered.

"Well, sir, if you did hear, it aint no blame of mine," said the injured bookseller; "such a notion would never have come into my mind – no man, I make bold to say, is more particular about keeping to his own rank of life nor me. What you did, sir, you did out of the kindness of your heart, and I'd sooner sell up and go off to the end of the world than impose upon a gentleman. Her aunt's took her away," continued Mr Elsworthy, lowering his voice, and cautiously pointing to the back of the shop – "She'll not bother you no more."

"She! – who?" cried the Perpetual Curate, in sudden consternation. He was utterly bewildered by the introduction of a female actor into the little drama, and immediately ran over in his mind all the women he could think of who could, by any possibility, be involved in mysterious relations with his brother Jack.

"She's but a child," said Elsworthy, pathetically; "she don't know nothing about the ways o' the world. If she was a bit proud o' being noticed, there wasn't no harm in that. But seeing as there's nothing in this world that folks won't make a talk of when they've started, her aunt, as is very partic'lar, has took her away. Not as I'm meaning no reproach to you, Mr Wentworth; but she's a loss to us, is Rosa. She was a cheerful little thing, say the worst of her," said Mr Elsworthy;"going a-singing and a-chirping out and in the shop; and I won't deny as the place looks desolate, now she's away. But that aint neither here nor there. It was for her good, as my missis says. Most things as is unpleasant *is* sent for good, they tell me; and I wouldn't – not for any comfort to myself– have a talk got up about the clergyman—"

By this time Mr Wentworth had awakened to a sense of the real meaning of Elsworthy's talk. He sat upright on his chair, and looked into the face of the worthy shopkeeper until the poor man trembled. "A talk about the clergyman?" said the Curate. "About me, do you mean? and what has little Rosa to do with me? Have you gone crazy in Carlingford – what is the meaning of it all?" He sat with his elbows on the counter, looking at his trembling adherent – looking through and through him, as Elsworthy said. "I should be glad of an explanation; what does it mean?" said Mr Wentworth, with a look which there was no evading; and the clerk of St Roque's cast an anxious glance round him for help. He would have accepted it from any quarter at that overwhelming moment; but there

was not even an errand-boy to divert from him the Curate's
terrible eyes.

"I – I don't know – I – can't tell how it got up," said the
unhappy man, who had not even his "missis" in the
parlour as a moral support. "One thing as I know is, it
wasn't no blame o' mine. I as good as went down on my
knees to them three respected ladies when they come to
inquire. I said as it was kindness in you a-seeing of the
child home, and didn't mean nothing more. I ask you, sir,
what could I do?" cried Mr Elsworthy. "Folks in Carlingford will talk o' two straws if they're a-seen a-blowing up
Grange Lane on the same breath o' wind. I couldn't do no
more nor contradict it," cried Rosa's guardian, getting
excited in his self-defence; "and to save your feelings, Mr
Wentworth, and put it out o' folks's power to talk, the
missis has been and took her away."

"To save my feelings!" said the Curate, with a laugh of
contempt and vexation and impatience which it was not
pleasant to hear. At another moment an accusation so
ridiculous would have troubled him very little; but just now,
with a sudden gleam of insight, he saw all the complications which might spring out of it to confuse further the
path which he already felt to be so burdened. "I'll tell you
what, Elsworthy," said Mr Wentworth; "if you don't want
to make me your enemy instead of your friend, you'll send
for this child instantly, without a day's delay. Tell your
wife that my orders are that she should come back directly.
My feelings! do the people in Carlingford think me an
idiot, I wonder?" said the Curate, walking up and down to
relieve his mind.

"I don't know, sir, I'm sure," said Elsworthy, who
thought some answer was required of him. To tell the
truth, Rosa's uncle felt a little spiteful. He did not see
matters in exactly the same light as Mr Wentworth did. At
the bottom of his heart, after all, lay a thrill of awakened
ambition. Kings and princes had been known to marry far
out of their degree for the sake of a beautiful face; and why

a Perpetual Curate should be so much more lofty in his sentiments, puzzled and irritated the clerk of St Roque's. "There aint a worm but will turn when he's trod upon," said Mr Elsworthy to himself; and when his temper was roused, he became impertinent, according to the manner of his kind.

Mr Wentworth gave him a quick look, struck by the changed tone, but unable to make out whether it might not be stupidity. "You understand what I mean, Elsworthy," he said, with his loftiest air. "If Rosa does not return instantly, I shall be seriously offended. How you and your friends could be such utter idiots as to get up this ridiculous fiction, I can't conceive; but the sooner it's over the better. I expect to see her back to-morrow," said the Curate, taking up his bag and looking with an absolute despotism, which exasperated the man, in Elsworthy's face.

"You may be sure, sir, if she knows as you want to see her, she'll come," said the worm which had been trampled on; "and them as asks me why, am I to say it was the clergyman's orders?" said Elsworthy, looking up in his turn with a consciousness of power. "That means a deal, does that. I wouldn't take it upon me to say as much, not of myself; but if them's your orders, Mr Wentworth—"

"It appears to me, Elsworthy," said the Curate, who was inwardly in a towering passion, though outwardly calm enough, "either that you've been drinking or that you mean to be impertinent – which is it?"

"Me! – drinking, sir?" cried the shopkeeper. "If I had been one as was given that way, I wouldn't have attended to your interests not as I have done. There aint another man in Carlingford as has stood up for his clergyman as I have; and as for little Rosa, sir, most folks as had right notions would have inquired into that; but being as I trusted in you, I wasn't the one to make any talk. I've said to everybody as has asked me that there wasn't nothing in it but kindness. I don't say as I hadn't my own thoughts –

for gentlemen don't go walking up Grange Lane with a
pretty little creature like that all for nothing; but instead o'
making anything of that, or leading of you on, or putting it
in the child's head to give you encouragement, what was it
I did but send her away afore you came home, that you
mightn't be led into temptation! And instead of feelin'
grateful, you say I've been drinking! It's a thing as I scorn
to answer," said Mr Elsworthy; "there aint no need to
make any reply – all Carlingford knows *me*; but as for
Rosa, if it is understood plain between us that it's your
wish, I aint the man to interfere," continued Rosa's guardian, with a smile which drove the Curate frantic; "but she
hasn't got no father, poor thing, and it's my business to
look after her; and I'll not bring her back, Mr Wentworth,
unless it's understood between us plain."

Strong language, forcible, but unclerical, was on the
Curate's lips, and it was only with an effort that he
restrained himself. "Look here, Elsworthy," he said; "it
will be better for you not to exasperate me. You understand perfectly what I mean. I repeat, Rosa must come
back, and that instantly. It is quite unnecessary to explain
to you why I insist upon this, for you comprehend it.
Pshaw! don't let us have any more of this absurdity," he
exclaimed, impatiently. "No more, I tell you. Your wife is
not such a fool. Let anybody who inquires about me
understand that I have come back, and am quite able to
account for all my actions," said the Curate, shouldering
his bag. He was just about leaving the shop when Elsworthy
rushed after him in an access of alarm and repentance.

"One moment, sir," cried the shopkeeper; "there aint
no offence, Mr Wentworth? I am sure there aint nobody in
Carlingford as means better, or would do as much for his
clergyman. One moment, sir; there was one thing I forgot
to mention. Mr Wodehouse, sir, has been took bad. There
was a message up a couple of hours ago to know when you
was expected home. He's had a stroke, and they don't
think as he'll get over it – being a man of a full 'abit of

body," said Mr Elsworthy in haste, lest the Curate should break in on his unfinished speech, "makes it dangerous. I've had my fears this long time past."

"A stroke," said the Curate – "a fit, do you mean? When, and how? and, good heavens! to think that you have been wasting my time with rubbish, and knew this!" Mr Wentworth tossed down his travelling-bag again, and wiped his forehead nervously. He had forgotten his real anxiety in the irritation of the moment. Now it returned upon him with double force. "How did it come on?" he asked, "and when?" and stood waiting for the answer, with a world of other questions, which he could not put to Elsworthy, hanging on his lips.

"I have a deal of respect for that family, sir," said Elsworthy; "they have had troubles as few folks in Carlingford know of. How close they have kep' things, to be sure! – but not so close as them that has good memories, and can put two and two together, couldn't call to mind. My opinion, sir, if you believe me," said the clerk of St Roque's, approaching close to the Curate's ear, "is, that it's something concerning the son."

"The son!" said Mr Wentworth, with a troubled look. Then, after a pause, he added, as if his exclamation had been an oversight, "What son? has Mr Wodehouse a son?"

"To think as they should have been so close with the clergyman!" said Elsworthy, innocently; "though he aint no credit that they should talk of him. He's been gone out o' Carlingford nigh upon twenty year; but he aint dead for all that; and I'm told as he's been seen about Grange Lane this last spring. I am one as hears all the talk that's a-going on, being, as you might say, in a public position of life. Such a thing mightn't maybe come to your ears, sir?" he continued, looking inquisitively in Mr Wentworth's face; "but wherever he is, you may be sure it's something about him as has brought on this attack on the old man. It was last night as he was took so bad, and a couple of hours ago a message came up. Miss Wodehouse (as is the nicest lady

in Grange Lane, and a great friend to me) had took a
panic, and she was a-crying for you, the man said, and
wouldn't take no denial. If I had known where you was to
be found, I'd have sent word."

"Send down my bag to my house," said the Curate,
hastily interrupting him. "Good-night – don't forget what I
said about the other matter." Mr Wentworth went out of
the shop with a disagreeable impression that Elsworthy
had been examining his face like an inquisitor, and was
already forming conclusions from what he had seen there.
He went away hurriedly, with a great many vague fears in
his mind. Mr Wodehouse's sudden illness seemed to him a
kind of repetition and echo of the Squire's, and in the
troubled and uncertain state of his thoughts, he got to
confusing them together in the centre of this whirl of
unknown disaster and perplexity. Perhaps even thus it
was not all bitterness to the young man to feel his family
united with that of Lucy Wodehouse. He went down
Grange Lane in the summer darkness under the faint
stars, full of anxiety and alarm, yet not without a thrill in
his heart, a sweeter under-current of conscious agitation in
the knowledge that he was hastening to her presence.
Sudden breaks in his thoughts revealed her, as if behind a
curtain, rising to receive him, giving him her hand, meeting
his look with a smile; so that, on the whole, neither Gerald's
distress, nor Jack's alarming call, nor his father's attack,
nor Mr Wodehouse's illness, nor the general atmosphere
of vexation and trouble surrounding his way, could succeed
in making the young man totally wretched. He had this
little stronghold of his own to retire into. The world could
not fall to pieces so long as he continued with eager steps
to devour the road which led to Mr Wodehouse's garden-
door.

Before he had reached that goal, however, he met a
group who were evidently returning from some little dinner
in Grange Lane. Mr Wentworth took off his hat hastily in
recognition of Mrs Morgan, who was walking by her

husband's side, with a bright-coloured hood over her head
instead of a bonnet. The Curate, who was a man of taste,
could not help observing, even in the darkness, and amid
all his preoccupations, how utterly the cherry-coloured
trimmings of her head-dress were out of accordance with
the serious countenance of the Rector's wife, who was a
little heated with her walk. She was a good woman, but
she was not fair to look upon; and it occurred to Mr
Wentworth to wonder, if Lucy were to wait ten years for
him, would the youthful grace dry and wither out of her
like this! And then all at once another idea flashed upon
his mind, without any wish of his. Like the unhappy lover
in the ballad, he was suddenly aware of a temptation –

> "How there looked him in the face
>   An angel beautiful and bright,
>   And how he knew it was a fiend."

"Of course the Rectory will go to Frank." He could not
tell why at that moment the words rang into his ear with
such a penetrating sound. That he hated himself for being
able to think of such a possibility made no difference. It
came darting and tingling into his mind like one of those
suggestions of blasphemy which the devils whispered in
Christian's ear as he went through the Valley of the
Shadow of Death. He went on faster than ever to escape
from it, scarcely observing that Mrs Morgan, instead of
simply acknowledging his bow as she passed, stopped to
shake hands, and to say how glad she was he had come
back again. He thought of it afterwards with wonder and a
strange gratitude. The Rector's wife was not like the
conventional type of a pitying angel; and even had she
been so, he had not time to recognise her at that moment
as he went struggling with his demons to Mr Wodehouse's
green door.

CHAPTER XXI.

WHEN the green door was opened, Mr Wentworth saw at a glance that there was agitation and trouble in the house. Lights were twinkling irregularly in the windows here and there, but the family apartment, the cheerful drawing-room, which generally threw its steady, cheerful blaze over the dark garden, shone but faintly with half-extinguished lights and undrawn curtains. It was evident at a glance that the room was deserted, and its usual occupants engaged elsewhere. "Master's very bad, sir," said the servant who opened the door; "the young ladies is both with him, and a hired nurse come in besides. The doctor don't seem to have no great hopes, but it will be a comfort to know as you have come back. Miss Wodehouse wanted you very bad an hour or two ago, for they thought as master was reviving, and could understand. I'll go and let them know you are here."

"Don't disturb them, unless I can be of use," said Mr Wentworth. The look of the house, and the atmosphere of distress and anxiety about it, chilled him suddenly. His visions and hopes seemed guilty and selfish as he went slowly up those familiar steps and into the house, over which the shadow of death seemed already lying. He went by himself into the forsaken drawing-room, where two neglected candles were burning feebly in a corner, and the wistful sky looking in as if to ask why the domestic temple was thus left open and uncared for. After the first moment he went hastily to the windows, and drew down the blinds in a kind of tender impatience. He could not bear that anything in the world, even her father's danger, should discompose the sweet, good order of the place where Lucy's image dwelt. There was a chair and her basket of work, and on the little table a book marked with pencil-marks, such as youthful readers love to make; and by degrees that breath of Lucy lingering in the silent room overcame its dreariness, and the painful sense of desertion which had struck him at first. He hovered about that corner where her usual place was, feeling in his heart that Lucy in trouble was dearer, if possible, than Lucy in happiness, and hung over her chair, with a mixture of reverence and tenderness and yearning, which could never be expressed in words. It was the divinest phase of love which was in his mind at the moment; for he was not thinking of himself, but of her, and of how he could succour and comfort her, and interpose his own true heart and life between her and all trouble. It was at this moment that Lucy herself entered the room; she came in softly, and surprised him in the overflowing of his heart. She held out her hand to him as usual, and smiled, perhaps less brightly, but that of course arose from the circumstances of the house; and her voice was very measured and steady when she spoke, less variable than of old. What was it she said? Mr Wentworth unconsciously left the neighbourhood of that chair over which he had been bending, which, to tell the truth, he had leaned his head upon, lover-like, and perhaps even kissed for her sake, five minutes before, and grew red and grew pale with a strange revulsion and tumult of feeling. He could not tell what the difference was, or what it meant. He only felt in an instant, with a sense of the change that chilled him to the heart, as if somehow a wall of ice had risen between them. He could see her through the transparent veil, and hear her speak, and perceive the smile which cast no warmth of reflection on him; but in a moment, in the twinkling of an eye, everything in heaven and earth was changed. Lucy herself, to her own consciousness, trembled and faltered, and felt as if her voice and her looks must betray an amount of emotion which she would have died rather than show; but then Lucy had rehearsed this scene before, and knew all she intended by it; whereas upon the Curate, in his little flush and overflow of tenderness, it fell like a sudden earthquake, rending his fair edifice of happiness asunder, and casting him out into unexpected darkness. Sudden confusion, mortification, even a sense of injury and bitterness, came swelling over his heart as he set a chair for her as far away as possible from the corner in which he had been indulging such vain and unwarrantable dreams.

"It happened yesterday," said Lucy; "we have not been quite able to make out what was the cause; at least I have not been able to find it out. The clerks at the office say it was something about – but that does not matter," she went on, with her sweet politeness: "you don't care for the details. I sometimes fancy Mary knows more than she tells me, and I think you are in her confidence, Mr Wentworth. But I am not going to ask you any questions. The doctors say he is not suffering so much as he seems to be. It is terrible to see him lie there not knowing any of us," said Lucy, with a tremble in her voice.

"But you thought him better some time ago?" said the Curate, whose words choked him, and who could not endure to speak.

"Yes, about six o'clock," said Lucy, "he tried to speak, and put Mary in a great fright, I cannot tell why. Would you be good enough, Mr Wentworth," she went on hastily, with a strange mixture of earnestness and coldness, "if you know of anything she is keeping secret, to bid her tell me? I am able to bear anything there may be to bear – surely as well as she is, who has had no trouble," said Lucy, softly; and for a moment she wavered in her fixed composure, and the wall of ice moved as if it might fall.

"Nor you?" said the Curate, bending anxiously forward to look into her eyes. He was inexpressibly moved and agitated by the inference, which perhaps no listener less intensely concerned would have drawn from what Lucy said. He could not bear that she should have any trouble which he might not do something to relieve her of.

"Oh, no, nor I," said Lucy, quickly, and in that moment the softening of tone disappeared entirely. "Mary will be pleased to see you, Mr Wentworth. I will go and relieve her presently. Papa is asleep just now, and I was downstairs giving some directions when you came in. I wanted to ask you to look after that poor woman at No. 10. She still keeps living on, and I have not been able to see her today. She misses me when I don't go," said Lucy, with a very little unconscious sigh. "Would you see her, please, to-morrow, if you have time?"

"Yes, certainly," said the Curate; and then there was a pause. "Is there nothing but this that you will let me do for you?" he asked, trusting to his looks to show the heart, which at this moment he was so much tempted to disclose to her, but dared not. And even in all her trouble Lucy was too much of a woman to neglect an opportunity so tempting.

"Thank you," she said. "Yes, there are those poor little Bertrams I was to have seen today – if you would be so very good as to send some one to them." Lucy lifted her eyes only as she ended this little speech. She had meant it cruelly, to be sure, and the arrow had gone home; but when she met the look that was fixed on her after her little shaft was fired, Lucy's resolution faltered. The tears came rushing to her eyes so hot and rapid that she could not restrain them. Some trouble of her own gave poignancy to that outbreak of filial grief. "Papa is so very ill!" she said, with a sob, as a scalding drop fell upon her hand; and then got up suddenly, afraid of the consequences. But the Curate, mortified, wounded, and disheartened as he was, had no comprehension either of the bitterness or the relenting that was in Lucy's thoughts. Rosa Elsworthy did not so much as occur to him in all his confused wonderings.

He went after her to the door, too much perplexed and distressed to be indignant, as his first impulse was. She turned half round, with a tremulous little inclination of her head, which was all the good-night she could venture on. But the young man was too much disturbed to permit this.

"You will give me your hand, surely," he said, taking it, and holding it fast – a hand so different from that weak woman's hand that clung to Gerald without any force to hold him, in Wentworth Rectory. Those reluctant fingers, so firm and so soft, which scorned any struggle to withdraw themselves, but remained passive in his with a more effectual protest still against his grasp, wrung the very heart of the Perpetual Curate. He let them go with a sigh of vexation and disappointment. "Since that is all I can do, I will do it," he said – "that or anything else." She had left him almost before the words were said; and it was in a very disconsolate mood that he turned back into the deserted drawing-room. To tell the truth, he forgot everything else for the moment, asking himself what it could mean; and walked about stumbling over the chairs, feeling all his little edifice of personal consolation falling to the winds, and not caring much though everything else should follow. He was in this state of mind when Miss Wodehouse came to him, moving with noiseless steps, as everybody did in the stricken house.

"Oh, Mr Wentworth, I am so glad you have come," said that mild woman, holding out both her hands to him. She was too much agitated to say anything more. She was not equal to the emergency, or any emergency, but sank down on a chair, and relieved herself by tears, while the Curate stood anxiously by, waiting for what she had to say to him. "My father is very ill," she said, like Lucy, through her crying; "I don't know what good anybody can do; but thank God you've come home – now I shall feel I have somebody to apply to, whatever happens," said poor Miss Wodehouse, drying the eyes that were suffused again the next moment. Her helpless distress did not overwhelm the spectator, like Lucy's restrained trouble, but that was natural enough.

"Tell me about it," said Mr Wentworth; "the cause – can I guess at the cause? it is something about your—"

"Oh hush! don't say his name," cried Miss Wodehouse. "Yes, yes, what else could it be? Oh, Mr Wentworth, will you close the door, please, and see that there's no one about. I dare not speak to you till I am sure there's no one listening; not that I suspect anybody of listening," said the distressed woman; "but one never knows. I am afraid it is all my fault," she continued, getting up suddenly to see that the windows were closed. "I ought to have sent him away, instead of putting my trouble upon you; and now he is in greater danger than ever. Oh, Mr Wentworth, I meant it for the best; and now, unless you can help us, I don't know what I am to do."

"I cannot help you unless you tell me what is wrong," said the Curate, making her sit down, and drawing a chair close to her. He took her hand, by way of compelling her attention – a fair, soft hand, too, in its restless, anxious way. He held it in a brotherly grasp, trying to restore her to coherence, and induce her to speak.

"I don't know enough about business to tell you," she said. "He was in danger when I threw him upon your charity; and oh, Mr Wentworth, thank you, thank you a thousand times, for taking him in like a brother. If Lucy only knew! But I don't feel as if I dared to tell her – and yet I sometimes think I ought, for your – I mean for all our sakes. Yes, I will try to explain it if I can; but I can't – indeed I don't understand," cried the poor lady, in despair. "It is something about a bill – it was something about a bill before; and I thought I could soften papa, and persuade him to be merciful; but it has all turned to greater wretchedness and misery. The first one was paid, you know, and I thought papa might relent; – but – don't cast us off, Mr Wentworth – don't go and denounce him; you might, but you will not. It would be justice, I acknowledge," cried the weeping woman; "but there is something higher than justice even in this world. You are younger than I am, and so is Lucy; but you are better than me, you young people, and you must be more merciful too. I have seen you going among the poor people and among the sick, and I could not have done it; and you won't forsake me – oh, Mr Wentworth, you won't forsake me, when you know that my trouble is greater than I can bear!"

"I will not forsake you," said the Curate; "but tell me what it is. I have been summoned to Carlingford by my brother, and I am bewildered and disturbed beyond what I can tell you—"

"By your brother?" said Miss Wodehouse, with her unfailing instinct of interest in other people. "I hope there is no trouble in your own family, Mr Wentworth. One gets so selfish when one is in great distress. I hope he is not ill. It sounds as if there was comfort in the very name of a brother," said the gentle woman, drying her tears, "and I hope it is so with you; but it isn't always so. I hope you will find he is better when you get home. I am very, very sorry to hear that you are in trouble too."

Mr Wentworth got up from his chair with a sigh of impatience. "Will nobody tell me what is the matter?" he said. "Mr Wodehouse is ill, and there is some mysterious cause for it; and you are miserable, and there is a cause for that too; and I am to do something to set things right without knowing what is wrong. Will you not tell me? What is it? Has your—"

"Oh, Mr Wentworth, don't say anybody's name – don't speak so loud. There may be a servant in the staircase or something," cried Miss Wodehouse. "I hear somebody coming now." She got up to listen, her face growing white with panic, and went a few steps towards the door, and then tottered into another chair, unable to command herself. A certain sick thrill of apprehension came over the Curate, too, as he hastened forward. He could not tell what he was afraid of, or whether it was only the accumulated agitation of the day that made him weak. Somebody was coming up the stairs, and towards the room, with a footstep more careless than those stealthy steps with which all the servants were stealing about the house. Whoever he was, he stopped at the door a moment, and then looked cautiously in. When he saw the figure of the Curate in the imperfect light, he withdrew his head again as if deliberating with himself, and then, with a sudden rush, came in, and shut the door after him. "Confound these servants, they're always prowling about the house," said the new-comer. He was an alarming apparition in his great beard and his shabbiness, and the fugitive look he had. "I couldn't help it," he broke forth, with a spontaneous burst of apology and self-defence. "I heard he was ill, and I couldn't keep quiet. How is he? You don't mean to say *that's* my fault. Molly, can't you speak to me? How could I tell I should find you and the parson alone here, and all safe? I might have been risking my – my – freedom – everything I care for; but when I heard he was ill, I couldn't stay quiet. Is he dying? – what's the matter? Molly, can't you speak?"

"Oh, Mr Wentworth, somebody will see him," cried Miss Wodehouse, wringing her hands. "Oh Tom, Tom, how could you do it? Suppose somebody was to come in – John or somebody. If you care for your own life, oh, go away, go away!"

"They can't touch my life," said the stranger, sullenly. "I daresay she doesn't know that. Nor the parson need not look superior – there are more people concerned than I; but if I've risked everything to hear, you may surely tell me how the old man is."

"If it was love that brought you," said poor Miss Wodehouse; "but oh, Tom, you know I can't believe that. He is very, very ill; and it is you that have done it," cried the mild woman, in a little gush of passion – "you whom he has forgiven and forgiven till his heart is sick. Go away. I tell you, go away from the house that you have shamed.

Oh, Mr Wentworth, take him away," she cried, turning to
the Curate with clasped hands – "tell him to hide – to fly –
or he'll be taken: he will not be forgiven this time; and if
my father – if my dear father dies—" But when she got so
far her agitation interrupted her. She kept her eyes upon
the door with a wild look of terror, and waved her helpless
hands to warn the intruder away.

"If he dies, matters will be altered," said the stranger:
"you and I might change places then, for that matter. I'm
going away from Carlingford. I can't stay in such a
wretched hole any longer. It's gout or something?" said
the man, with a tone of nature breaking through his
bravado – "it's not anything that has happened? Say so,
and I'll never trouble you more."

"Oh, if Lucy were to see him!" said poor Miss Wodehouse. The words came unawares out of her heart without
any thought; but the next thing of which she was conscious
was that the Perpetual Curate had laid his hand on the
stranger's arm, and was leading him reluctantly away. "I
will tell you all you want to know," said Mr Wentworth,
"but not here;" and with his hand upon the other's arm,
moved him somehow with an irresistible command, half
physical, half mental, to the door. Before Miss Wodehouse could say anything they were gone; before she could
venture to draw that long sighing breath of relief, she
heard the door below close, and the retreating footsteps in
the garden. But the sound, thankful though she was,
moved her to another burst of bitter tears. "To think I
should have to tell a stranger to take him away," she
sobbed, out of the anguish of her heart; and sat weeping
over him with a relenting that wrung her tender spirit,
without power to move till the servant came up with
alarmed looks to ask if any one had come in in his absence.
"Oh, no; it was only Mr Wentworth – and a – gentleman
who came to fetch him," said Miss Wodehouse. And she
got up, trembling as she was, and told John he had better
shut up the house and go to bed. "For I hope papa will

have a better night, and we must not waste our strength,"
she said, with a kind of woeful smile, which was a wonder
to John. He said Miss Wodehouse was a tender-hearted
one, to be sure, when he went down-stairs; but that was no
very novel piece of information to anybody there.

Meantime the Curate went down Grange Lane with that
strange lodger of Mrs Hadwin's, who had broken thus into
Miss Wodehouse's solitude. They did not say much to
each other as they went sullenly side by side down the
silent road; for the stranger, whose feelings were not
complicated by any very lively sense of gratitude, looked
upon his companion as a kind of jailer, and had an
unspeakable grudge against the man who exercised so
calm an ascendancy over him; though to be sure it might
have been difficult to resist the moral force of the Curate
of St Roque's, who was three inches taller than himself,
and had the unbroken vigour of youth and health to back
him. As for Mr Wentworth, he went on without speaking,
with a bitterness in his heart not to be expressed. His own
personal stronghold of happiness and consolation had shat-
tered in pieces in that evening's interview; and as he went
to his own house he asked himself what he should find in it?
This wretched man, with whose sins he had been hitherto
but partially acquainted; and Jack, with whom the other
had heaven knew what horrible connection. Should he
find a den of thieves where he had left only high thoughts
and lofty intentions? It was thus, after his three days'
absence, that he returned home.

CHAPTER XXII.

WHEN Mr Wentworth entered Mrs Hadwin's garden in the dark, his first glance up at the house showed him that a certain change had passed on it also. The decorous little house had been turned inside out. The windows of his own sitting-room were open, the blind drawn up to the top, and in addition to his usual lamp some candles were flaring wildly in the draught. He could see into the room as he paused at the garden-door, and was able to distinguish that the table was still covered as for dinner, and to catch the purple gleam of the light in the claret-jug which occupied the place of honour; but nobody was visible in the room. That wildly-illuminated and open apartment stood in strange contrast with the rest of the house, where everything was dark, save in Mrs Hadwin's own chamber. The Curate proceeded on his way, after that moment's pause, with hasty and impatient steps. On the way up he encountered Sarah the housemaid, who stopped in the middle of the stairs to make a frightened little curtsy, and utter an alarmed "La!" of recognition and surprise. But Sarah turned round as soon as she had recovered herself, to say that her missis wanted very bad to see Mr Wentworth as soon as he came home; but she was gone up to bed now, and didn't he think it would be a pity to wake her up? The Curate gave her only a little nod of general acquiescence, as he hurried on; but felt, notwithstanding, that this prompt request, ready prepared for his arrival, was a tacit protest against his guests, and expression of disapproval. Mrs Hadwin was only his landlady, an old woman, and not a particularly wise one, but her disapproval vexed the Perpetual Curate. It was a kind of sign of the times – those times in which it appeared that everybody was ready to turn upon him and embarrass his path. He had forgotten all about his companion as he hurried into the familiar room which was so little like itself, but yet was somehow conscious with annoyance that the stranger followed him through its half-shut door. The scene within was one which was never effaced from Mr Wentworth's memory. There were several bottles upon the table, which the poor Curate knew by sight, and which had been collected in his little cellar more for the benefit of Wharfside than of himself. Removed out of the current of air which was playing freely through the apartment, was some one lying on a sofa, with candles burning on a table beside him. He was in a dressing-gown, with his shirt open at the throat, and his languid frame extended in perfect repose to catch the refreshment of the breeze. Clouds of languid smoke, which were too far out of the way to feel the draught between the windows, curled over him: he had a cigar in one hand, which he had just taken from his lips, and with which he was faintly waving off a big nightmoth which had been attracted by the lights; and a French novel, unmistakable in its paper cover, had closed upon the other. Altogether a more languid figure never lay at rest in undisturbed possession of the most legitimate retirement. He had the Wentworth hair, the golden-brown, which, like all their other family features, even down to their illnesses, the race was proud of, and a handsome silky beard. He had lived a hard life of pleasure and punishment; but though he had reached middle age, there was not a hair on the handsome reprobate's head which had changed out of its original colour. He looked languidly up when the door opened, but did not stop the delicate fence which he was carrying on against the moth, nor the polyglot oaths which he was swearing at it softly half under his breath.

"Frank, I suppose," he said, calmly, as the Curate

came hastily forward. "How d'ye do? I am very glad you've come back. The country was very charming the first day, but that's a charm that doesn't last. I suppose you've dined: or will you ring and order something?" he said, turning slowly round on his sofa. "Accidcntc! thc thing will kill itself after all. Would you mind catching it in your handkerchief before you sit down? But don't take away the candles. It's too late to make any exertion," said the elegant prodigal, leaning back languidly on his sofa; "but I assure you that light is half my life."

The Curate was tired, heated, and indignant. He lifted the candles away from the table, and then put them back again, too much excited to think of the moth. "Your arrival must have been very sudden," he said, throwing himself into the nearest chair. "I was very much surprised by your message. It looks inhospitable, but I see you make yourself quite at home—"

"Perfectly," said the elder brother, resuming his cigar. "I always do. It is much more agreeable for all parties. But I don't know how it is that a man's younger brothers are always so rapid and unreasonable in their movements. Instead of saving that unhappy insect, you have precipitated its fate. Poor thing – and it had no soul," said the intruder, with a tone of pathos. The scene altogether was a curious one. Snugly sheltered from the draught, but enjoying the coolness of the atmosphere which it produced, lay the figure on the sofa at perfect ease and leisure, with the light shed brightly upon him, on his shining beard, the white cool expanse of linen at his breast, and the bright hues of his dressing-gown. Near him, fatigued, dusty, indignant, and perplexed, sat the Curate, with the night air playing upon him, and moving his disordered hair on his forehead; while at the other end of the room hovered the stranger who had followed Mr Wentworth – a broad, shabby, indistinct figure, who stood with his back to the others, looking vaguely out of the window into the darkness. Over these two the night air blew with no small force between the open windows, making the candles on the centre table flare wildly, and flapping the white tablecloth. An occasional puff from the cigar floated now and then across the room. It was a pause before the storm.

"I was about to say," said the Perpetual Curate, "that though it might seem inhospitable, the first thing I had to ask was, What brought you here – and why did you send for me?"

"Don't be abrupt, pray," said Jack, taking his cigar from his mouth, and slightly waving the hand that held it. "Don't let us plunge into business all at once. You bring a sense of fatigue into the room with you, and the atmosphere was delightful a little while ago. I flatter myself I know how to enjoy the cool of the evening. Suppose you were to – ah – refresh yourself a little," he said, with a disapproving glance at his brother's dusty boots, "before we begin to talk of our affairs."

The Curate of St Roque's got up from his chair, feeling that he had an unchristian inclination to kick the heir of the Wentworths. As he could not do that, he shut the window behind him emphatically, and extinguished the flaring candles on the centre table. "I detest a draught," said the Perpetual Curate, which, unfortunately, was not a statement entirely founded on fact, though so far true in the present instance that he hated anything originated by the intruder. "I have hurried home in reply to your message, and I should be glad to know what it means, now that I am here – what you are in trouble about – and why you come to me – and what you have to do with him?"

"But you need not have deranged the temperature," said Jack. "Impetuosity always distresses me. All these are questions which it will take some time to answer. Let me persuade you, in the first place, to make yourself comfortable. Don't mind me; I am at the crisis of my novel, which is very interesting. I have just been thinking how it might be adapted for the stage – there's a character that Fechter could make anything of. Now, my dear fellow, don't stand on ceremony. Take a bath and change your dress, and in the mean time there will be time to cook something – the cookery here is not bad for the country. After that we'll discuss all our news. I daresay our friend there is in no hurry," said the elder brother, opening his book and puffing slowly towards the Curate the languid smoke of his cigar.

"But, by Jove, I *am* in a hurry, though," said that nameless individual, coming forward. "It's all very well for you: you put a man up to everything that's dangerous, and then you leave him in the lurch, and say it don't matter. I daresay it don't matter to you. All that you've done has been to share the profit – you've nothing to do with the danger; but I'm savage to-night, and I don't mean to stand it any more," said the stranger, his great chest expanding with a panting breath. He, too, looked as if he would have liked to seize the languid spectator in his teeth and shake some human feeling into him. Jack Wentworth raised his eyebrows and looked at him, as he might have looked at a wild beast in a rage.

"Sit down, savage, and be quiet," he said. "Why should I trouble myself about you? – any fool could get into your scrape. I am not in the habit of interfering in a case of common crime. What I do, I do out of pity," he continued, with an air of superiority, quite different from his tone to his brother. But this look, which had answered before, was not successful to-night.

"By Jove, I *am* savage!" said the other, setting his teeth, "and I know enough of your ways to teach you different behaviour. The parson has treated me like a gentleman – like what I used to be, though he don't like me; but you!— By Jove! It was only my own name I signed, after all," he continued, after a pause, lowering his voice; "but you, you blackleg—"

"Stop a little," said the Curate, rising up. "Though you seem both to have forgotten it, this is my room. I don't mean to have any altercations here. I have taken you in for the sake of your – family," said Mr Wentworth, with a momentary gasp, "and you have come because you are my brother. I don't deny any natural claims upon me; but I am master of my own house and my own leisure. Get up, Jack, and tell me what you want. When I understand what it is, you can lounge at your will; but in the mean time get up and explain: and as for you, Wodehouse—"

Jack Wentworth faced round on his sofa, and then, with a kind of involuntary motion, slid his feet to the ground. He looked at his brother with extreme amazement as he closed his novel and tossed away the end of his cigar. "It's much better not to mention names," he said, in a half-apologetic way. "Our friend here is under a temporary cloud. His name, in fact, is – Smith, I think." But as he spoke he sat upright, a little startled to find that Frank, whom he remembered only as a lad, was no longer to be coerced and concussed. As for the other, he came forward with the alacrity of a man who began to see some hope.

"By Jove, my name *is* Wodehouse, though," he said, in the argumentative tone which seemed habitual to him; his voice came low and grumbling through his beard. He was not of the class of triumphant sinners, whatever wickedness he might be capable of. To tell the truth, he had long, long ago fallen out of the butterfly stage of dissipation, and had now to be the doer of dirty work, despised and hustled about by such men as Jack Wentworth. The wages of sin had long been bitter enough, though he had neither any hope of freeing himself, nor any wish to do so; but he took up a grumbling tone of self-assertion as soon as he had an opening. "The parson treats me like a gentleman – like what I used to be," he repeated, coming into the light, and drawing a chair towards the table. "My name is Wodehouse – it's my own name that I have signed after all, by Jove!" said the unlucky prodigal. It seemed to give him a little comfort to say that over again, as if to convince himself.

"As for Wodehouse, I partly understand what he has done," said the Curate. "It appears likely that he has killed his father, by the way; but I suppose you don't count that. It is forgery in the mean time; I understand as much."

"It's my name as well as his, by Jove!" interrupted, hastily, the stranger, under his breath.

"Such strong terms are unnecessary," said Jack; "everybody knows that bills are drawn to be renewed, and nursed, and taken care of. We've had a great failure in luck as it happens, and these ones have come down to this deuced place; and the old fellow, instead of paying them like a gentleman, has made a row, and dropped down dead, or something. I suppose you don't know any more than the women have told you. The old man made a row in the office, and went off in fire and flame, and gave up our friend here to his partner's tender mercies. I sent for you, as you've taken charge of him. I suppose you have your reasons. This is an unlikely corner to find him in, and I suppose he couldn't be safer anywhere. That's about the state of the case. I came down to look after him, out of kind feeling," said the heir of the Wentworths. "If you don't mean to eat any dinner, have a cigar."

"And what have you to do with each other? what is the connection between you?" said the Curate of St Roque's. "I have my reasons, as you say, for taking an interest in him – but you—"

"I am only your elder brother," said Jack, shrugging his shoulders and resuming his place on the sofa. "We understand that difference. Business connection – that's all," he said, leisurely selecting another cigar from his case. When he had lighted it, he turned round and fixed his eyes upon the stranger. "We don't want any harm to happen to him," he said, with a little emphasis. "I have come here to protect him. If he keeps quiet and doesn't show, it will blow over. The keenest spy in the place could scarcely suspect him to be here. I have come entirely on his account – much to my own disgust – and yours," said the exquisite, with another shrug. He laid back his head and looked up at the ceiling, contemplating the fragrant wreaths of smoke with the air of a man perfectly at his ease. "We don't mean him to come to any harm," said Jack Wentworth, and stretched out his elegant limbs on the sofa, like a potentate satisfied that his protection was enough to make any man secure.

"I'm too much in their secrets, by Jove!" said poor Wodehouse, in his beard. "I *do* know their secrets, though they talk so big. It's not any consideration for me. It's to save themselves, by Jove, that's what it is!" cried the indignant drudge, of whom his superior deigned to take no notice. As for Mr Wentworth, he rose from his seat in a state of suppressed indignation, which could not express itself merely in words.

"May I ask what share I am expected to play in the drama?" he asked, pushing his chair aside in his excitement. The elder brother turned instinctively, and once more slid his feet to the ground. They looked at each other for a moment; the Curate, pale with a passion which he could not conceal, had something in his eyes which brought shame even to Jack Wentworth's face.

"You can betray him if you like," he said, sulkily. "I have no – particular interest in the matter; but in that case he had better make the best of his time and get away. You hear?" said the master-spirit, making a sign to Wodehouse. He had roused himself up, and looked now like a feline creature preparing for a spring – his eyes were cast down, but under the eyelids he followed his brother's movements with vigilant observation. "If you like, you can betray him," he repeated, slowly, understanding, as bad men so often do, the generosities of the nature to which his own was so much opposed.

And perhaps there was an undue degree of exasperation in the indignant feelings which moved Mr Wentworth. He kicked off his dusty boots with an indecorum quite unusual to him, and hunted up his slippers out of the adjoining room with perhaps an unnecessary amount of noise and haste. Then he went and looked out of the window into the serene summer darkness and the dewy garden, getting a little fresh air upon his heated face. Last of all he came back, peremptory and decided. "I shall not betray him," said the Perpetual Curate; "but I will have no further schemes concocted nor villany carried on in my house. If I consent to shield him, and, if possible, save him from the law, it is neither for his sake – nor yours," said the indignant young man. "I suppose it is no use saying anything about your life; but both of you have fathers very like to die of this—"

"My dear fellow," said Jack Wentworth, "we have gone through that phase ages ago. Don't be so much after date. I have brought down my father's grey hairs, &c., a hundred times; and, I daresay, so has he. Don't treat us as if we were in the nursery – a parson of advanced views like you should have something a little more novel to say."

"And so I have," said Mr Wentworth, with a heightened colour. "There are capital rooms at the Blue Boar, which you will find very comfortable, I am sure. I don't remember that we have ever been more than acquaintances; and to take possession of a man's house in his absence argues a high degree of friendship, as you are aware. It will be with difficulty that I shall find room for myself to-night; but to-morrow, I trust, if business requires you to remain in Carlingford, you will be able to find accommodation at the Blue Boar."

The elder brother grew very red all over his face. "I will go at once," he said, with a little start; and then he took a second thought. "It is a poor sort of way of winning a victory," he said, in contemptuous tones, after he had overcome his first impulse; "but if you choose that, it is no matter to me. I'll go to-morrow, as you say – to pack up to-night is too much for my energies. In the mean time it won't disturb you, I hope, if I go on with my novel. I don't suppose any further civilities are necessary between you and me," said Jack, once more putting up his feet on the sofa. He arranged himself with an indifference which was too genuine for bravado, opening his book, and puffing his cigar with great coolness. He did all but turn his back upon the others, and drew the little table nearer to him, in utter disregard of the fact that the Curate was leaning his arm on it. In short, he retired from the contest with a kind of grandeur, with his cigar and his novel, and the candles which lighted him up placidly, and made him look like the master of the house and the situation. There was a pause for some minutes, during which the others looked on – Mr Wentworth with a perfectly unreasonable sense of defeat, and poor Wodehouse with that strange kind of admiration which an unsuccessful good-for-nothing naturally feels for a triumphant rascal. They were in the shade looking on, and he in the light enjoying himself calmly in his way. The sight put an end to various twinges of repentance in the bosom of the inferior sinner. Jack Wentworth, lying on the sofa in superb indifference, victorious over all sense of right, did more to confirm his humble admirer in the life which he had almost made up his mind to abandon, than even his own inclination towards forbidden pleasure. He was dazzled by the success of his principal; and in comparison with that instructive sight, his father's probable deathbed, his sisters' tears, and even his own present discomfort, faded into insignificance. What Jack Wentworth was, Tom Wodehouse could never be; but at least he could follow his great model humbly and afar off. These sentiments made him receive but sulkily the admonitions of the Curate, when he led the way out of the preoccupied sitting-room; for Mr Wentworth was certainly not the victor in this passage of arms.

"I will do what I can to help you out of this," said the Curate, pausing within the door of Wodehouse's room, "for the sake of your – friends. But look here, Wodehouse; I have not preached to you hitherto, and I don't mean to do so now. When a man has done a crime, he is generally past preaching. The law will punish you for forging your father's name—"

"It's *my* name as well as his, by Jove!" interrupted the culprit, sullenly; "I've a right to sign it wherever I please."

"But the law," said Mr Wentworth, with emphasis, "has nothing to do with the breaking of your father's heart. If he dies, think whether the recollection will be a comfortable one. I will save you, if I can, and there is time, though I am compromised already, and it may do me serious injury. If you get free and are cleared from this, will you go away and break off your connection with – yes, you are quite right – I mean with my brother, whatever the connection may be? I will only exert myself for you on condition that you promise. You will go away somehow, and break off your old habits, and try if it is possible to begin anew?"

Wodehouse paused before he answered. The vision of Jack in the Curate's sitting-room still dazzled him. "You daren't say as much to your brother as you say to me," he replied, after a while, in his sulky way; "but I'm a gentleman, by Jove, as well as he is." And he threw himself down in a chair, and bit his nails, and grumbled into his beard. "It's hard to ask a fellow to give up his liberty," he said, without lifting his eyes. Mr Wentworth, perhaps, was a little contemptuous of the sullen wretch who already had involved him in so much annoyance and trouble.

"You can take your choice," he said; "the law will respect your liberty less than I shall;" and all the Curate's self-control could not conceal a certain amount of disdain.

"By Jove!" said Wodehouse, lifting up his eyes, "if the old man should die, you'd change your tone;" and then he stopped short and looked suspiciously at the Curate. "There's no will, and I'm the heir," he said, with sullen braggadocio. Mr Wentworth was still young, and this look made him sick with disgust and indignation.

"Then you can take your chance," he said, impatiently, making a hasty step to the door. He would not return, though his ungrateful guest called him back, but went away, much excited and disgusted, to see if the fresh air outside would restore his composure. On his way downstairs, he again met Sarah, who was hovering about in a restless state of curiosity. "I've made a bed for you, please, sir, in the little dressing-room," said Sarah; "and, please, Cook wants to know, wouldn't you have anything to eat?" The question reminded Mr Wentworth that he had eaten nothing since luncheon, which he took in his father's house. Human nature, which can bear great blows with elasticity so wonderful, is apt to be put out, as everybody knows, by their most trifling accessories, and a man naturally feels miserable when he had had no dinner, and has not a place to shelter him while he snatches a necessary mouthful. "Never mind; all the rooms are occupied to-night," said the Perpetual Curate, feeling thoroughly wretched. But Cook and Sarah had arranged all that, being naturally indignant that their favourite clergyman should be put "upon" by his disorderly and unexpected guests.

"I have set your tray, sir, in missis's parlour," said Sarah, opening the door to that sanctuary; and it is impossible to describe the sense of relief with which the Perpetual Curate flung himself down on Mrs Hadwin's sofa, deranging a quantity of cushions and elaborate crochet-work draperies without knowing it. Here at least he was safe from intrusion. But his reflections were far from being agreeable as he ate his beef-steak. Here he was, without any fault of his own, plunged into the midst of a complication of disgrace and vice. Perhaps already the name of Lucy Wodehouse was branded with her brother's shame; perhaps still more overwhelming infamy might overtake, through that means, the heir and the name of the Wentworths. And for himself, what he had to do was to attempt with all his powers to defeat justice, and save from punishment a criminal for whom it was impossible to feel either sympathy or hope. When he thought of Jack up-stairs on the sofa over his French novel, the heart of the Curate burned within him with indignation and resentment; and his disgust at his other guest was, if less intense, an equally painful sensation. It was hard to waste his strength, and perhaps compromise his character, for such men as these; but on the other hand he saw his father, with that malady of the Wentworths hanging over his head, doing his best to live and last, like a courageous English gentleman as he was, for the sake of "the girls" and the little children, who had so little to expect from Jack; and poor stupid Mr Wodehouse dying of the crime which assailed his own credit as well as his son's safety. The Curate of St Roque's drew a long breath, and raised himself up unconsciously to his full height as he rose to go up-stairs. It was he against the world at the moment, as it appeared. He set himself to his uncongenial work with a heart that revolted against the evil cause of which he was about to constitute himself the champion. But for the Squire, who had misjudged him – for Lucy who had received him with such icy smiles, and closed up her heart against his entrance; – sometimes there is a kind of bitter sweetness in the thought of spending love and life in one lavish and prodigal outburst upon those to whom our hearts are bound, but whose affections make us no return.

CHAPTER XXIII.

THE Curate went to breakfast next morning with a little curiosity and a great deal of painful feeling. He had been inhospitable to his brother, and a revulsion had happened such as happens invariably when a generous man is forced by external circumstances to show himself churlish. Though his good sense and his pride alike prevented him from changing his resolution of the previous night, still his heart had relented toward Jack, and he felt sorry and half ashamed to meet the brother to whom he had shown so much temper and so little kindness. It was much later than usual when he came down-stairs, and Jack was just coming out of the comfortable chamber which belonged of right to his brother, when the Curate entered the sitting-room. Jack was in his dressing-gown, as on the previous night, and came forth humming an air out of the 'Trovatore,' and looking as wholesomely fresh and clean and dainty as the most honest gentleman in England. He gave his brother a good-humoured nod, and wished him good morning. "I am glad to see you don't keep distressingly early hours," he said, between the bars of the air he was humming. He was a man of perfect digestion, like all the Wentworths, and got up accordingly, in a good temper, not disposed to make too much of any little incivility that might have taken place. On the contrary, he helped himself to his brother's favourite omelet with the most engaging cheerfulness, and entered into such conversation as might be supposed to suit a Perpetual Curate in a little country town.

"I daresay you have a good many nice people about here," said Jack. "I've done nothing but walk about since I came – and it does a man good to see those fresh little women with their pink cheeks. There's one, a sister of our friend's, I believe," he continued, with a nod towards the door to indicate Wodehouse – "an uncommonly pretty girl, I can tell you; and there's a little rosebud of a creature at that shop, whom, they tell me, you're interested in. Your living is not worth much, I suppose? It's unlucky having two clergymen in a family; but, to be sure, you're going in for Skelmersdale. By the way, that reminds me – how are the aunts? I have not heard anything of them for ages. Female relations of that description generally cling to the parsons of the race. I suppose they are all living – all three? Some people never seem to die."

"They are here," said the Curate, succinctly, "living in Carlingford. I wonder nobody has told you."

A sudden bright spark lighted in the prodigal's eyes. "Ah, they are here, are they?" he said, after a momentary pause; "so much the better for you; but in justice you ought to be content with the living. I say so as your elder brother. Gerald has the best right to what they've got to leave. By the by, how are Gerald and the rest? you've just been there. I suppose our respected parent goes on multiplying. To think of so many odious little wretches calling themselves Wentworth is enough to make one disgusted with the name."

"My father was very ill when I left; he has had another attack," said the Curate. "He does not seem able to bear any agitation. Your telegram upset him altogether. I don't know what you've been about – he did not tell me," continued the younger brother, with a little emotion, "but he is very uneasy about you."

"Ah, I daresay," said Jack; "that's natural; but he's wonderfully tough for such an old fellow. I should say it would take twenty attacks to finish him; and this is the second, isn't it? I wonder how long an interval there was between the two; it would be a pretty calculation for a *post-obit*. Wodehouse seems to have brought his ancestor down at the first shot almost; but then there's no entail in his case, and the old fellow may have made a will. I beg your pardon; you don't like this sort of talk. I forgot you were a clergyman. I rather like this town of yours, do you know. Sweet situation, and good for the health, I should say. I'll take your advice, I think, about the – how did you call it? – Black Boar. Unless, indeed, some charitable family would take me in," said the elder brother, with a glance from under his eyelids. His real meaning did not in the least degree suggest itself to the Curate, who was thinking more of what was past than of what was to come.

"You seem to take a great interest in Wodehouse?" said Mr Wentworth.

"Yes; and so do you," said Jack, with a keen glance of curiosity – "I can't tell why. My interest in him is easily explained. If the affair came to a trial, it might involve other people who are of retiring dispositions and dislike publicity. I don't mind saying," continued the heir of the Wentworths, laying down his knife and fork, and looking across at his brother with smiling candour, "that I might myself be brought before the world in a way which would wound my modesty; so it must not be permitted to go any further, you perceive. The partner has got a warrant out, but has not put it into execution as yet. That's why I sent for you. You are the only man, so far as I can see, that can be of any use."

"I don't know what you mean," said the Curate, hastily, "nor what connection you can possibly have with Wodehouse; perhaps it is better not to inquire. I mean to do my best for him, independent of you."

"Do," said Jack Wentworth, with a slight yawn; "it is much better not to inquire. A clergyman runs the risk of hearing things that may shock him when he enters into worldly business; but the position of mediator is thoroughly professional. Now for the Black Boar. I'll send for my traps when I get settled," he said, rising in his languid way. He had made a very good breakfast, and he was not at all disposed to make himself uncomfortable by quarrelling with his brother. Besides, he had a new idea in his mind. So he gave the Curate another little good-humoured nod, and disappeared into the sleeping-room, from which he emerged a few minutes after with a coat replacing the dressing-gown, ready to go out. "I daresay I shall see you again before I leave Carlingford," he said, and left the room with the utmost suavity. As for Mr Wentworth, it is probable that his brother's serenity had quite the reverse of a soothing effect upon his mind and temper. He rose from the table as soon as Jack was gone, and for a long time paced about the room composing himself, and planning what he was to do – so long, indeed, that Sarah, after coming up softly to inspect, had cleared the table and put everything straight in the room before the Curate discovered her presence. It was only when she came up to him at last, with her little rustical curtsy, to say that, please, her missis would like to see him for a moment in the parlour, that Mr Wentworth found out that she was there. This interruption roused him out of his manifold and complicated thoughts. "I am too busy just now, but I will see Mrs Hadwin to-night," he said; "and you can tell her that my brother has gone to get rooms at the Blue Boar." After he had thus satisfied the sympathetic handmaiden, the Curate crossed over to the closed door of Wodehouse's room and knocked. The inmate there was still in bed, as was his custom, and answered Mr Wentworth through his beard in a recumbent voice, less sulky and more uncertain than on the previous night. Poor Wodehouse had neither the nerve nor the digestion of his more splendid associate. He had no strength of evil in himself when he was out of the way of it; and the consequence of a restless night was a natural amount of penitence and shame in the morning. He met the Curate with a depressed countenance, and answered all his questions readily enough, even giving him the particulars of the forged bills, in respect to which Thomas Wodehouse the younger could not, somehow, feel so guilty as if it had been a name different from his own which he had affixed to those fatal bits of paper; and he did not hesitate much to promise that he would go abroad and try to make a new beginning if this matter could be settled. Mr Wentworth went out with some satisfaction after the interview, believing in his heart that his own remonstrances had had their due effect, as it is so natural to believe – for he did not know, having slept very soundly, that it had rained a good deal during the night, and that Mrs Hadwin's biggest tub (for the old lady had a passion for rain-water) was immediately under poor Wodehouse's window, and kept him awake as it filled and ran over all through the summer darkness. The recollection of Jack Wentworth, even in his hour of success, was insufficient to fortify the simple soul of his humble admirer against that ominous sound of the unseen rain, and against the flashes of sudden lightning that seemed to blaze into his heart. He could not help thinking of his father's sick-bed in those midnight hours, and of all the melancholy array of lost years which had made him no longer "a gentleman, as he used to be," but a skulking vagabond in his native place; and his penitence lasted till after he had had his breakfast and Mr Wentworth was gone. Then perhaps the other side of the question recurred to his mind, and he began to think that if his father died there might be no need for his banishment; but Mr Wentworth knew nothing of this change in his *protégé's* sentiments, as he went quickly up Grange Lane. Wharfside and all the district had lain neglected for three long days, as the Curate was aware, and he had promised to call at No. 10 Prickett's Lane, and to look after the little orphan children whom Lucy had taken charge of. His occupations, in short, both public and private, were overpowering, and he could not tell how he was to get through them; for, in addition to everything else, it was Friday, and there was a litany service at twelve o'clock at St Roque's. So the young priest had little time to lose as he hurried up once again to Mr Wodehouse's green door.

It was Miss Wodehouse who came to meet the Curate as soon as his presence was known in the house – Miss Wodehouse, and not Lucy, who made way for her sister to pass her, and took no notice of Mr Wentworth's name. The elder sister entered very hurriedly the little parlour down-stairs, and shut the door fast, and came up to him with an anxious inquiring face. She told him her father was just the same, in faltering tones. "And oh, Mr Wentworth, has anything happened?" she exclaimed, with endless unspeakable questions in her eyes. It was so hard for the gentle woman to keep her secret – the very sight of somebody who knew it was a relief to her heart.

"I want you to give me full authority to act for you," said the Curate. "I must go to Mr Wodehouse's partner and discuss the whole matter."

Here Miss Wodehouse gave a little cry, and stopped him suddenly. "Oh, Mr Wentworth, it would kill papa to know you had spoken to any one. You must send him away," she said, breathless with anxiety and terror. "To think of discussing it with any one when even Lucy does not know—!" She spoke with so much haste and fright that it was scarcely possible to make out her last words.

"Nevertheless I must speak to Mr Waters," said the Curate; "I am going there now. He knows all about it already, and has a warrant for *his* apprehension; but we must stop that. I will undertake that it shall be paid, and you must give me full authority to act for you." When Miss Wodehouse met the steady look he gave her, she veered immediately from her fright at the thought of having it spoken of, to gratitude to him who was thus ready to take her burden into his hands.

"Oh, Mr Wentworth, it is so good of you – it is like a brother!" said the trembling woman; and then she made a pause. "I say a brother," she said, drawing an involuntary moral, "though we have never had any good of ours; and oh, if Lucy only knew—!"

The Curate turned away hastily, and wrung her hand without being aware of it. "No," he said, with a touch of bitterness, "don't let her know. I don't want to appeal to her gratitude;" and with that he became silent, and fell to listening, standing in the middle of the room, if perhaps he might catch any sound of footsteps coming down-stairs.

"She will know better some day," said Miss Wodehouse, wiping her eyes; "and oh, Mr Wentworth, if papa ever gets better—!" Here the poor lady broke down into inarticulate weeping. "But I know you will stand by us," she said, amid her tears; "it is all the comfort I have – and Lucy—"

There was no sound of any footstep on the stair –

nothing but the ticking of the timepiece on the mantelshelf, and the rustling of the curtains in the soft morning breeze which came through the open window, and Miss Wodehouse's crying. The Curate had not expected to see Lucy, and knew in his heart that it was better they should not meet just at this moment; but, notwithstanding this, it was strange how bitter and disappointed he felt, and what an impatient longing he had for one look of her, even though it should be a look which would drive him frantic with mortified love and disappointed expectation. To know that she was under the same roof, and that she knew he was here, but kept away, and did not care to see him, was gall to his excited mind. He went away hastily, pressing poor Miss Wodehouse's hand with a kind of silent rage. "Don't talk about Lucy," he said, half to himself, his heart swelling and throbbing at the sound of the name. It was the first time he had spoken it aloud to any ear but his own, and he left the house tingling with an indignation and mortification and bitter fondness which could not be expressed in words. What he was about to do was for her sake, and he thought to himself, with a forlorn pride, that she would never know it, and it did not matter. He could not tell that Lucy was glancing out furtively over the blind, ashamed of herself in her wounded heart for doing so, and wondering whether even now he was occupied with that unworthy love which had made an everlasting separation between them. If it had been any one worthy, it would have been different, poor Lucy thought, as she pressed back the tears into her eyes, and looked out wistfully at him over the blind. She above-stairs in the sick-room, and he in the fresh garden hastening out to his work, were both thinking in their hearts how perverse life was, and how hard it was not to be happy – as indeed they well might in a general way; though perhaps one glance of the Curate's eyes upward, one meeting of looks, might have resulted quite reasonably in a more felicitous train of thinking, at least for that day.

CHAPTER XXIV.

WHEN Mr Wentworth arrived in the little vestry at St
Roque's to robe himself for the approaching service, it was
after a long and tough contest with Mr Wodehouse's
partner, which had to a great extent exhausted his
energies. Mr Wodehouse was the leading attorney in
Carlingford, the chief family solicitor in the county, a man
looked upon with favourable eyes even by the great
people as being himself a cadet of a county family. His
partner, Mr Waters, was altogether a different description
of man. He was much more clever, and a good deal more
like a gentleman, but he had not a connection in the
world, and had fought his way up to prosperity through
many a narrow, and perhaps, if people spoke true, many a
dirty avenue to fortune. He was very glad of the chance
which brought his partner's reputation and credit thus
under his power, and he was by no means disposed to deal
gently with the prodigal son. That is to say, he was quite
disinclined to let the family out of his clutches easily, or to
consent to be silent and "frustrate the ends of justice" for
anything else than an important equivalent. Mr Wentworth
had much ado to restrain his temper while the wily attorney
talked about his conscience; for the Curate was clear-
sighted enough to perceive at the first glance that Mr
Waters had no real intention of proceeding to extremities.
The lawyer would not pledge himself to anything, notwithstanding all Mr Wentworth's arguments. "Wodehouse
himself was of the opinion that the law should take its
course," he said; but out of respect for his partner he
might wait a few days to see what turn his illness would

take. "I confess that I am not adapted for my profession, Mr Wentworth. My feelings overcome me a great deal too often," said the sharp man of business, looking full into the Curate's eyes, "and while the father is dying I have not the heart to proceed against the son; but I pledge myself to nothing – recollect, to nothing." And with this and a very indignant mind Mr Wentworth had been forced to come away. His thoughts were occupied with the contrarieties of the world as he hastened along to St Roque's – how one man had to bear another's burdens in every station and capacity of life, and how another man triumphed and came to success by means of the misfortunes of his friends. It was hard to tell what made the difference, or how humankind got divided into these two great classes, for possibly enough the sharp attorney was as just in his way as the Curate; but Mr Wentworth got no more satisfaction in thinking of it than the speculatists generally have when they investigate this strange, wayward, fantastical humanity which is never to be calculated upon. He came into the little vestry of St Roque's, which was a stony little room with a groined roof and windows too severely English in their character to admit any great amount of light, with a sensation of fatigue and discouragement very natural to a man who had been interfering in other people's affairs. There was some comfort in the litany which he was just going to say, but not much comfort in any of the human individuals who would come into Mr Wentworth's mind as he paused in the midst of the suffrage for "sick persons" and for those who "had erred and were deceived," that the worshippers might whisper into God's ear the names for which their hearts were most concerned. The young priest sighed heavily as he put on his surplice, pondering all the obstinate selfishness and strange contradictions of men; and it was only when he heard a rather loud echo to his breath of weariness that he looked up and saw Elsworthy, who was contemplating him with a very curious expression of face. The clerk started a little on being discovered, and began to look over all the choristers' books and set them in readiness, though, indeed, there were no choristers on Fridays, but only the ladies, who chanted the responses a great deal more sweetly, and wore no surplices. Thinking of that, it occurred to Mr Wentworth how much he would miss the round full notes which always betrayed Lucy's presence to him even when he did not see her; and he forgot Elsworthy, and sighed again without thinking of any comment which might be made upon the sound.

"I'm sorry to see, sir, as you aint in your usual good spirits?" said that observant spectator, coming closer up to "his clergyman." Elsworthy's eyes were full of meanings which Mr Wentworth could not, and had no wish to, decipher.

"I am perfectly well, thank you," said the Perpetual Curate, with his coldest tone. He had become suspicious of the man, he could scarcely tell why.

"There's a deal of people in church this morning," said the clerk; and then he came closer still, and spoke in a kind of whisper. "About that little matter as we was speaking of, Mr Wentworth – that's all straight, sir, and there aint no occasion to be vexed. She came back this morning," said Elsworthy, under his breath.

"Who came back this morning?" asked the Curate, with a little surprise. His thoughts had been so much with Lucy that no one else occurred to him at the moment; and even while he asked the question, his busy fancy began to wonder where she could have been, and what motive could have taken her away?

"I couldn't mean nobody but Rosa, as I talked to you about last night," said Elsworthy. "She's come back, sir, as you wished; and I *have* heard as she was in Carlingford last night just afore you come, Mr Wentworth, when I thought as she was far enough off; which you'll allow, sir, whoever it was she come to see, it wasn't the right thing, nor what her aunt and me had reason to expect."

The Curate of St Roque's said "Pshaw!" carelessly to himself. He was not at all interested in Rosa Elsworthy. Instead of making any answer, he drew on the scarlet band of his hood, and marched away gravely into the reading-desk, leaving the vestry-door open behind him for the clerk to follow. The little dangers that harassed his personal footsteps had not yet awakened so much as an anxiety in his mind. Things much more serious preoccupied his thoughts. He opened his prayer-book with a conscious-ness of the good of it which comes to men only now and then. At Oxford, in his day, Mr Wentworth had entertained his doubts like others, and like most people was aware that there were a great many things in heaven and earth totally unexplainable by any philosophy. But he had always been more of a man than a thinker, even before he became a high Anglican; and being still much in earnest about most things he had to do with, he found great comfort just at this moment, amid all his perplexities, in the litany he was saying. He was so absorbed in it, and so full of that appeal out of all troubles and miseries to the God who cannot be indifferent to His creatures, that he was almost at the last Amen before he distinguished that voice, which of all voices was most dear to him. The heart of the young man swelled, when he heard it, with a mingled thrill of sym-pathy and wounded feeling. She had not left her father's sick-bed to see *him*, but she *had* found time to run down the sunny road to St Roque's to pray for the sick and the poor. When he knelt down in the reading-desk at the end of the service, was it wrong, instead of more abstract supplications, that the young priest said over and over, "God bless her," in an outburst of pity and tenderness? And he did not try to overtake her on the road, as he might have done had his heart been less deeply touched, but went off with abstracted looks to Wharfside, where all the poor people were very glad to see him, and where his absence was spoken of as if he had been three months instead of three days away. It was like going back a

century or two into primitive life, to go into "the district,"
where civilisation did not prevail to any very distressing
extent, and where people in general spoke their minds
freely. But even when he came out of No. 10, where the
poor woman still kept on living, Mr Wentworth was made
aware of his private troubles; for on the opposite side of
the way, where there was a little bit of vacant ground, the
Rector was standing with some of the schismatics of
Wharfside, planning how to place the iron church which, it
was said, he meant to establish in the very heart of the
"district." Mr Morgan took off his hat very stiffly to the
Perpetual Curate, who returned up Prickett's Lane with a
heightened colour and quickened pulse. A man must be an
angel indeed who can see his work taken out of his hands
and betray no human emotion. Mr Wentworth went into
Elsworthy's, as he went back, to write a forcible little note
to the Rector on the subject before he returned home. It
was Rosa who handed him the paper he wanted, and he
gave her a little nod without looking at her. But when he
had closed his note, and laid it on the counter to be
delivered, the Curate found her still standing near, and
looked at the little blushing creature with some natural
admiration. "So you have come back," he said; "but mind
you don't go into Grange Lane any more after dark, little
Rosa." When he had left the shop and finished this little
matter, he bethought himself of his aunts, whom he had
not seen since he returned. Aunt Dora was not at her usual
sentinel window when he crossed Grange Lane towards
their garden-door; and the door itself was open, and some
one from the Blue Boar was carrying in a large port-
manteau. Mr Wentworth's curiosity was strangely excited
by the sight. He said, "Who has come, Lewis?" to Miss
Wentworth's man, who stood in the hall superintending
the arrival, but ran up-stairs without waiting for any
answer. He felt by instinct that the visitor was some one
likely to increase the confusion of affairs, and perplex
matters more and more to himself.

But even this presentiment did not prepare him for the astonishing sight which met his eyes when he entered the drawing-room. There the three ladies were all assembled, regarding with different developments of interest the new-comer, who had thrown himself, half-reclining, on a sofa. Aunt Dora was sitting by him with a bottle of eau-de-Cologne in her hand, for this meeting had evidently gone to the heart of the returned prodigal. Aunt Dora was ready to have sacrificed all the veal in the country in honour of Jack's repentance; and the Curate stood outside upon the threshold, looking at the scene with the strangest half-angry, half-comical realisation of the state of mind of the elder brother in the parable. He had himself been rather found fault with, excused, and tolerated, among his relations; but Jack had at once become master of the position, and taken possession of all their sympathies. Mr Wentworth stood gazing at them, half-amused, and yet more angry than amused – feeling, with a little indignation, as was natural, that the pretended penitence of the clever sinner was far more effective and interesting than his own spotless loyalty and truth. To be sure, they were only three old ladies – three old aunts – and he smiled at the sight; but though he smiled, he did not like it, and perhaps was more abrupt than usual in his salutations. Miss Leonora was seated at her writing-table, busy with her correspondence. The question of the new gin-palace was not yet decided, and she had been in the middle of a letter of encouragement to her agents on the subject, reminding them that, even though the licence was granted, the world would still go on all the same, and that the worst possi-bilities must be encountered, when Jack the prodigal made his appearance, with all the tokens of reformation and repentance about him, to throw himself upon the Christian charity of his relations. A penitent sinner was too tempting a bait for even Miss Leonora's good sense to withstand, and she had postponed her letter-writing to hear his explanations. But Jack had told his story by this time, and had explained how much he wanted to withdraw out of the world in which he had been led astray, and how sick he was of all its whirl of temptations and disappointment; and Miss Leonora had returned to her letter when her younger nephew arrived. As for Miss Wentworth, she was seated placidly in her usual easy-chair, smiling with equable smiles upon both the young men, and lifting her beautiful old cheek for Frank to kiss, just as she had lifted it to Jack. It was Miss Dora who was most shaken out of her allegiance; she who had always made Frank her special charge. Though she had wept herself into a day's headache on his behalf so short a time ago, aunt Dora for a moment had allowed the more effusive prodigal to supersede Frank. Instead of taking him into her arms as usual, and clinging to him, she only put the hand that held the eau-de-Cologne over his shoulder as she kissed him. Jack, who had been so dreadfully, inexpressibly wicked, and who had come back to his aunts to be converted and restored to his right mind, was more interesting than many curates. She sat down again by her penitent as soon as she had saluted his brother; and even Miss Leonora, when she paused in her letter, turned her eyes towards Jack.

"So Gerald is actually going over to Rome," said the strong-minded aunt. "I never expected anything else. I had a letter from Louisa yesterday, asking me to use my influence: as if I had any influence over your brother! If a silly wife was any justification for a man making an idiot of himself, Gerald might be excused; but I suppose the next thing we shall hear of will be that you have followed him, Frank. Did you hear anything further about Janet and that lover of hers? In a large family like ours there is always something troublesome going on," said Miss Leonora. "I am not surprised to hear of your father's attack. *My* father had a great many attacks, and lived to eighty; but he had few difficulties with the female part of his household," she continued, with a grim little smile – for Miss Leonora rather piqued herself upon her exemption from any known sentimental episode, even in her youth.

"Dear Jack's return will make up for a great deal," said aunt Dora. "Oh, Frank, my dear, your brother has made us all so happy. He has just been telling us that he means to give up all his racing and betting and wickedness; and when he has been with us a little, and learned to appreciate a domestic circle—" said poor Miss Dora, putting her handkerchief to her eyes. She was so much overcome that she could not finish the sentence. But she put her disengaged hand upon Jack's arm and patted it, and in her heart concluded that as soon as the blanket was done for Louisa's bassinet, she would work him a pair of slippers, which should endear more and more to him the domestic circle, and stimulate the new-born virtue in his repentant heart.

"I don't know what Jack's return may do," said Mr Wentworth, "but I hope you don't imagine it was Gerald who caused my father's illness. *You* know better, at least," said the indignant Curate, looking at the hero on the sofa. That interesting reprobate lifted his eyes with a covert gleam of humour to the unresponsive countenance of his brother, and then he stroked his silky beard and sighed.

"My dear aunt, Frank is right," said Jack, with a melancholy voice. "I have not concealed from you that my father has great reason to be offended with me. I have done very much the reverse of what I ought to have done. I see even Frank can't forgive me; and I don't wonder at it," said the prodigal, "though I have done him no harm that I know of;" and again the heir of the Wentworths sighed, and covered his face for a moment with his hand.

"Oh, Frank," cried Miss Dora, with streaming eyes – "oh, my dear boy! – isn't there joy in heaven over one sinner that repenteth? You're not going to be the wicked elder brother that grudged the prodigal his welcome – you're not going to give way to jealousy, Frank?"

"Hold your tongue, Dora," said the iron-grey sister; "I daresay Frank knows a great deal better than you do; but

I want to know about Gerald, and what is to be done. If he goes to Rome, of course you will take Wentworth Rectory; so it will not be an unmingled evil," said Miss Leonora, biting her pen, and throwing a keen glance at the Curate of St Roque's, "especially as you and we differ so entirely in our views. I could not consent to appoint anybody to Skelmersdale, even if poor Mr Shirley were to die, who did not preach the Gospel; and it would be sad for you to spend all your life in a Perpetual Curacy, where you could have no income, nor ever hope to be able to marry," she continued steadily, with her eyes fixed upon her nephew. "Of course, if you had entered the Church for the love of the work, it would be a different matter," said the strong-minded aunt. "But that sort of thing seems to have gone out of fashion. I am sorry about Gerald – very sorry; but after what I saw of him, I am not surprised; and it is a comfort to one's mind to think that you will be provided for, Frank." Miss Leonora wrote a few words of the letter as she finished this speech. What she was saying in that epistle was (in reference to the gin-palace) that all discouragements were sent by God, and that, no doubt, His meaning was, that we should work all the harder to make way against them. After putting down which encouraging sentiment, she raised her eyes again, and planted her spear in her nephew's bosom with the greatest composure in the world.

"My Perpetual Curacy suits me very well," said Mr Wentworth, with a little pride; "and there is a good deal to do in Carlingford. However, I did not come here to talk about that. The Rector is going to put up an iron church in my district," said the young man, who was rather glad of a subject which permitted a little of his indignation to escape. "It is very easy to interfere with other people's work." And then he paused, not choosing to grumble to an unsympathetic audience. To feel that nobody cares about your feelings, is better than all the rules of self-control. The Perpetual Curate stopped instinctively with a dignified restraint, which would have been impossible to him under other circumstances. It was no merit of his, but he reaped the advantage of it all the same.

"But oh, my dear," said Miss Dora, "what a comfort to think of what St Paul says – 'Whether it be for the right motive or not, Christ is still preached.' And one never knows what chance word may touch a heart," said the poor little woman, shaking her limp curls away from her cheeks. "It was you being offended with him that made dear Jack think of coming to us; and what a happiness it is to think that he sees the error of his ways!" cried poor Miss Dora, drying her tears. "And oh, Frank, my dear boy, I trust you will take warning by your brother, and not run into temptation," continued the anxious aunt, remembering all her troubles. "If you were to go wrong, it would take away all the pleasure of life."

"That is just what I was thinking," said aunt Cecilia from her easy-chair.

"For, oh, Frank, my dear," said Miss Dora, much emboldened by this support, "you must consider that you are a clergyman, and there are a great many things that are wrong in a clergyman that would not matter in another man. Oh, Leonora, if you would speak to him, he would mind you," cried the poor lady; "for you know a clergyman is quite different;" and Miss Dora again stopped short, and the three aunts looked at the bewildered Curate, who, for his part, sat gazing at them without an idea what they could mean.

"What have I been doing that would be right in another man?" he said, with a smile which was slightly forced; and then he turned to Jack, who was laughing softly under his breath, and stroking his silky beard. The elder brother was highly amused by the situation altogether, but Frank, as was natural, did not see it in the same light. "What have you been saying?" said the indignant Curate; and his eyes gave forth a sudden light which frightened Miss Dora, and brought her in to the rescue.

"Oh, Frank, he has not been saying anything," cried that troubled woman; "it is only what we have heard everywhere. Oh, my dear boy, it is only for your good I ever thought of speaking. There is nobody in the world to whom your welfare is so precious," said poor Miss Dora. "Oh, Frank, if you and your brother were to have any difference, I should think it all my fault – and I always said you did not mean anything," she said, putting herself and her eau-de-Cologne between the two, and looking as if she were about to throw herself into the Curate's arms. "Oh, Frank, dear, don't blame any one else – it is my fault!" cried aunt Dora, with tears; and the tender-hearted foolish creature kept between them, ready to rush in if any conflict should occur, which was a supposition much resented by the Curate of St Roque's.

"Jack and I have no intention of fighting, I daresay," he said, drawing his chair away with some impatience; and Jack lay back on the sofa and stroked his beard, and looked on with the greatest composure while poor Miss Dora exhausted her alarm. "It is all my fault," sobbed aunt Dora; "but, oh, my dear boy, it was only for your good; and I always said you did not mean anything," said the discomfited peacemaker. All this, though it was highly amusing to the prodigal, was gall and bitterness to the Perpetual Curate. It moved him far more deeply than he could have imagined it possible for anything spoken by his aunt Dora to move him. Perhaps there is something in human nature which demands to be comprehended, even where it is aware that comprehension is impossible; and it wounded him in the most unreasonable way to have it supposed that he was likely to get into any quarrel with his brother, and to see Jack thus preferred to himself.

"Don't be a fool," said Miss Leonora, sharply: "I wish you would confine yourself to Louisa's bassinet, and talk of things you can understand. I hope Frank knows what he is doing better than a set of old women. At the same time, Frank," said Miss Leonora, rising and leading the way to the door, "I want to say a word to you. Don't think you are above misconception. Most people believe a lie more readily than the truth. Dora is a fool," said the elder sister, pausing, when she had led her nephew outside the drawing-room door, "but so are most people; and I advise you to be careful, and not to give occasion for any gossip; otherwise, I don't say *I* disapprove of your conduct." She had her pen in one hand, and held out the other to him, dismissing him; and even this added to the painful feeling in the Curate's heart.

"I should hope not," he said, somewhat stiffly; "good-bye – my conduct is not likely to be affected by any gossip, and I don't see any need for taking precautions against imaginary danger." Miss Leonora thought her nephew looked very ungracious as he went away. She said to herself that Frank had a great deal of temper, and resembled his mother's family more than the Wentworths, as she went back to her writing-table; and though she could not disapprove of him, she felt vexed somehow at his rectitude and his impatience of advice; whereas, Jack, poor fellow! who had been a great sinner, was, according to all appearance, a great penitent also, and a true Wentworth, with all the family features. Such were Miss Leonora's thoughts as she went back to finish her letters, and to encourage her agents in her London district to carry on the good work.

"God moves in a mysterious way, His wonders to perform," she wrote apropos of the gin-palace, and set very distinctly before her spiritual retainers all that Providence might intend by this unexpected hindrance; and so quite contented herself about her nephew, whose views on this and many other subjects were so different from her own.

Meanwhile Mr Wentworth went about the rest of the day's work in a not unusual, but far from pleasant, frame of mind. When one suddenly feels that the sympathy upon which one calculated most surely has been withdrawn, the shock is naturally considerable. It might not be anything

very great while it lasted, but still one feels the difference
when it is taken away. Lucy had fallen off from him; and
even aunt Dora had ceased to feel his concerns the first in the
world. He smiled at himself for the wound he felt; but that
did not remove the sting of it. After the occupations of the
day were over, when at last he was going home, and when
his work and the sense of fatigue which accompanied it
had dulled his mind a little, the Curate felt himself still
dwelling on the same matter, contemplating it in a half-
comic point of view, as proud men are not unapt to
contemplate anything that mortifies them. He began to
realise, in a humorous way, his own sensations as he stood
at the drawing-room door and recognised the prodigal on
the sofa; and then a smile dawned upon his lip as he
thought once more of the prodigal's elder brother, who
regarded that business with unsympathetic eyes and
grudged the supper. And from that he went into a half-
professional line of thought, and imagined to himself, half
smiling, how, if he had been Dr Cumming or the minister
of Salem Chapel, he might have written a series of sermons
on the unappreciated characters of Scripture, beginning
with that virtuous uninteresting elder brother; from which
suggestion, though he was not the minister of Salem nor
Dr Cumming, it occurred to the Perpetual Curate to
follow out the idea, and to think of such generous careless
souls as Esau, and such noble unfortunates as the peasant-
king, the mournful magnificent Saul – people not generally
approved of, or enrolled among the martyrs or saints. He
was pursuing this kind of half-reverie, half-thought, when
he reached his own house. It was again late and dark, for
he had dined in the mean time, and was going home now
to write his sermon, in which, no doubt, some of these
very ideas were destined to reappear. He opened the
garden-gate with his latch-key, and paused, with an
involuntary sense of the beauty and freshness of the night,
as soon as he got within the sheltering walls. The stars
were shining faint and sweet in the summer blue, and all

the shrubs and the grass breathing forth that subdued
breath of fragrance and conscious invisible life which gives
so much sweetness to the night. He thought he heard
whispering voices, as he paused glancing up at the sky;
and then from the side-walk he saw a little figure run, and
heard a light little footstep fluttering towards the door
which he had just closed. Mr Wentworth started and went
after this little flying figure with some anxiety. Two or
three of his long strides brought him up with the escaping
visitor, as she fumbled in her agitation over the handle of
the door. "You have come again, notwithstanding what I
said to you? but you must not repeat it, Rosa," said the
Curate; "no good can come of these meetings. I will tell
your uncle, if I ever find you here again."

"Oh no, no, please don't," cried the girl; "but, after all,
I don't mind," she said, with more confidence: "he would
think it was something very different;" and Rosa raised
her eyes to the Curate's face with a coquettish inquiry.
She could not divest herself of the thought that Mr
Wentworth was jealous, and did not like to have her come
there for anybody but himself.

"If you were not such a child, I should be very angry,"
said the Curate; "as it is, I *am* very angry with the person
who deludes you into coming. Go home, child," he said,
opening the door to her, "and remember I will not allow
you on any pretext to come here again."

His words were low, and perhaps Rosa did not care
much to listen; but there was quite light enough to show
them both very plainly, as he stood at the door and she
went out. Just then the Miss Hemmings were going up
Grange Lane from a little tea-party with their favourite
maid, and all their eyes about them. They looked very full
in Mr Wentworth's face, and said How d'ye do? as they
passed the door; and when they had passed it, they looked
at each other with eyes which spoke volumes. Mr
Wentworth shut the door violently with irrepressible
vexation and annoyance when he encountered that glance.

He made no farewells, nor did he think of taking care of Rosa on the way home as he had done before. He was intensely annoyed and vexed, he could not tell how. And this was how it happened that the last time she was seen in Carlingford, Rosa Elsworthy was left standing by herself in the dark at Mr Wentworth's door.

CHAPTER XXV.

THE Curate got up very early next morning. He had his sermon to write and it was Saturday, and all the events of the week had naturally enough unsettled his mind, and indisposed him for sermon-writing. When the events of life come fast upon a man, it is seldom that he finds much pleasure in abstract literary composition, and the style of the Curate of St Roque's was not of that hortatory and impassioned character which sometimes gives as much relief to the speaker as excitement to the audience. So he got up in the early sweetness of the summer morning, when nobody but himself was astir in the house, with the sense of entering upon a task, and taking up work which wa far from agreeable to him. When he came into the little room which he used as a study, and threw the window open, and breathed the delicious air of the morning, which was all thrilling and trembling with the songs of birds, Mr Wentworth's thoughts were far from being concentrated upon any one subject. He sat down at his writing-table and arranged his pens and paper, and wrote down the text he had selected; and when he had done so much, and could feel that he had made a beginning, he leaned back in his chair, and poised the idle pen on his finger, and abandoned himself to his thoughts. He had so much to think about.

There was Wodehouse under the same roof, with whom he had felt himself constrained to remonstrate very sharply on the previous night. There was Jack, so near, and certainly come to Carlingford on no good errand. There was Gerald, in his great perplexity and distress, and the household at home in their anxiety; and last, but worst of all, his fancy would go fluttering about the doors of the sick chamber in Grange Lane, longing and wondering. He asked himself what it could be which had raised that impalpable wall between Lucy and himself – that barrier too strong to be overthrown, too ethereal to be complained of; and wondered over and over again what her thoughts were towards him – whether she thought of him at all, whether she was offended, or simply indifferent? – a question which any one else who had observed Lucy as closely could have solved without any difficulty, but which, to the modest and true love of the Perpetual Curate, was at present the grand doubt of all the doubts in the universe. With this matter to settle, and with the consciousness that it was still only five o'clock, and that he was at least one hour beforehand with the world, it is easy to understand why Mr Wentworth mused and loitered over his work, and how, when it was nearly six o'clock, and Sarah and the cook were beginning to stir from their sleep, there still remained only the text written upon the sermon-paper, which was so nicely arranged before him on the table. "When the wicked man turneth away from the evil of his ways, and doeth that which is lawful and right." – This was the text; but sitting at the open window, looking out into the garden, where the birds, exempt, as they seemed to think, for once from the vulgar scrutiny of man, were singing at the pitch of all their voices as they prepared for breakfast; and where the sweet air of the morning breathed into his mind a freshness and hopefulness which youth can never resist, and seduced his thoughts away from all the harder problems of his life to dwell upon the sweeter trouble of that doubt about Lucy, – was not the best means of getting on with his work. He sat thus leaning back

– sometimes dipping his pen in the ink, and hovering over
the paper for two or three seconds at a time, sometimes
reading over the words, and making a faint effort to recall
his own attention to them; for, on the whole, perhaps, it is
not of much use getting up very early in the morning when
the chief consequence of it is, that a man feels he has an hour
to spare, and a little time to play before he begins.

Mr Wentworth was still lingering in this peaceful pause,
when he heard, in the stillness, hasty steps coming down
Grange Lane. No doubt it was some workmen going to their
work, and he felt it must be nearly six o'clock, and dipped
his pen once more in the ink; but, the next moment, paused
again to listen, feeling in his heart a strange conviction that
the steps would stop at his door, and that something was
going to happen. He was sure of it, and yet somehow the
sound tingled upon his heart when he heard the bell ring,
waking up echoes in the silent house. Cook and Sarah had
not yet given any signs of coming down-stairs, and nobody
stirred even at the sound of the bell. Mr Wentworth put
down his pen altogether, and listened with an anxiety which
he could scarcely account for – knowing, as he said to
himself, that it must be the milk, or the baker, or somebody.
But neither the milk nor the baker would have dared to
knock, and shake, and kick the door as the new arrivals
were doing. Mr Wentworth sat still as long as he could, then
he added to the din they were making outside by an
indignant ring of his own bell; and finally getting anxious, as
was natural, and bethinking himself of his father's attack
and Mr Wodehouse's illness, the Curate took the matter into
his own hands, and hastened down-stairs to open the door.
Mrs Hadwin called to him as he passed her room, thinking it
was Sarah, and begging for goodness gracious sake to know
directly what was the matter; and he felt himself growing
agitated as he drew back the complicated bolts, and turned
the key in the door, which was elaborately defended, as was
natural. When he hurried out into the garden, the songs of
the birds and the morning air seemed to have changed their

character. He thought he was about to be summoned to the deathbed of one or other of the old men upon whom their sons had brought such misery. He was but little acquainted with the fastenings of the garden-door, and fumbled a little over them in his anxiety. "Wait a moment and you shall be admitted," he called out to those outside, who still continued to knock; and he fancied, even in the haste and confusion of the moment, that his voice caused some little commotion among them. Mr Wentworth opened the door, looking anxiously out for some boy with a telegram, or other such mournful messenger; but to his utter amazement was nearly knocked down by the sudden plunge of Elsworthy, who entered with a spring like that of a wild animal, and whose face looked white and haggard as he rushed in. He came against the Curate so roughly as to drive him a step or two farther into the garden, and naturally aroused somewhat sharply the temper of the young man, who had already begun to regard him with disagreeable sensations as a kind of spy against himself.

"What in the world do you want at such an early hour in the morning?" cried Mr Wentworth – "and what do you mean by making such a noise? Is Mr Wodehouse worse? or what has happened?" for, to tell the truth, he was a little relieved to find that the two people outside both belonged to Carlingford, and that nowhere was there any visible apparition of a telegraph boy.

"Don't trifle with me, Mr Wentworth," said Elsworthy. "I'm a poor man; but a worm as is trodden on turns. I want my child, sir! – give me my child. I'll find her out if it was at the end of the world. I've only brought down my neighbour with me as I can trust," he continued, hoarsely – "to save both your characters. I don't want to make no talk; if you do what is right by Rosa, neither me or him will ever say a word. I want Rosa, Mr Wentworth. Where's Rosa? If I had known as it was for this you wanted her home! But I'll take my oath not to make no talk," cried the clerk, with passion and earnestness, which confounded Mr Wentworth – "if you'll promise to do what's right by her, and let me take her home."

"Elsworthy, are you mad?" cried the Curate – "is he out of his senses? Has anything happened to Rosa? For heaven's sake, Hayles, don't stand there like a man of wood, but tell me if the man's crazy, or what he means."

"I'll come in, sir, if you've no objection, and shut the door, not to make a talk," said Elsworthy's companion, Peter Hayles, the druggist. "If it can be managed without any gossip, it'll be best for all parties," said this worthy, shutting the door softly after him. "The thing is, where's Rosa, Mr Wentworth? I can't think as you've got her here."

"She's all the same as my own child!" cried Elsworthy, who was greatly excited. "I've had her and loved her since she was a baby. I don't mean to say as I'd put myself forward to hurt her prospects if she was married in a superior line o' life; but them as harms Rosa has me to reckon with," he said, with a kind of fury which sat strangely on the man. "Mr Wentworth, where's the child? God forgive you both, you've given me a night o' weeping; but if you'll do what's right by Rosa, and send her home in the mean time—"

"Be silent, sir!" cried the Curate. "I know nothing in the world about Rosa. How dare you venture to come on such an errand to me? I don't understand how it is," said the young man, growing red and angry, "that you try so persistently to connect this child with me. I have never had anything to do with her, and I will not submit to any such impertinent suspicion. Leave my house, sir, immediately, and don't insult me by making such inquiries here."

Mr Wentworth was very angry in the first flush of his wrath. He did not think what misery was involved in the question which had been addressed to him, nor did he see for the moment the terrible calamity to Rosa which was suggested by this search for her. He thought only of himself, as was natural, at the first shock – of the injurious and insulting suspicion with which he seemed to be pursued, and of the annoyance which she and her friends were causing him. "What do you mean by rousing a whole household at this hour in the morning?" cried Mr Wentworth, as he saw with vexation, Sarah, very startled and sleepy, come stealing round by the kitchen door.

"You don't look as if you had wanted any rousing," said Elsworthy, who was too much in earnest to own the Curate's authority. "She was seen at your door the last thing last night, and you're in your clothes, as bright as day, and a-waiting for us afore six o'clock in the morning. Do you think as I've shut my eyes because it's my clergyman?" cried the injured man, passionately. "I want my little girl – my little Rosa – as is flesh of my flesh and bone of my bone. If Mr Wentworth didn't know nothing about it, as he says," cried Elsworthy, with sudden insight, "he has a feelin' heart, and he'd be grieved about the child; but he aint grieved, nor concerned, nor nothing in the world but angry; and will you tell me there aint nothing to be drawn from that? But it's far from my intention to raise a talk," said the clerk, drawing closer and touching the arm of the Perpetual Curate; "let her come back, and if you're a man of your word, and behave honourable by her, there shan't be nothing said in Carlingford. I'll stand up for you, sir, against the world."

Mr Wentworth shook off his assailant's hand with a mingled sense of exasperation and sympathy. "I tell you, upon my honour, I know nothing about her," he said. "But it is true enough I have been thinking only of myself," he continued, addressing the other. "How about the girl? When was she lost? and can't you think of any place she can have gone to? Elsworthy, hear reason," cried the Curate anxiously. "I assure you, on my word, that I have never seen her since I closed this garden-gate upon her last night."

"And I would ask you, sir, what had Rosa to do at your garden-gate?" cried the clerk of St Roque's. "He aint denying it, Hayles; you can see as he aint a-denying of it. What was it as she came here for but you? Mr Wentworth,

I've always had a great respect for you," said Elsworthy. "I've respected you as my clergyman, sir, as well as for other things; but you're a young man, and human nature is frail. I say again as you needn't have no fear of me. I aint one as likes to make a talk, and no more is Hayles. Give up the girl, and give me your promise, and there aint a man living as will be the wiser; Mr Wentworth—"

"Hold your tongue, sir!" cried the Curate, furious with indignation and resentment. "Leave this place instantly! If you don't want me to pitch you into the middle of the road, hold your tongue and go away. The man is mad!" said Mr Wentworth, turning towards the spectator, Hayles, and pausing to take breath. But it was evident that this third person was by no means on the Curate's side.

"I don't know, sir, I'm sure," said Hayles, with a blank countenance. "It appears to me, sir, as it's an awkward business for all parties. Here's the girl gone, and no one knows where. When a girl don't come back to her own 'ome all night, things look serious, sir; and it has been said as the last place she was seen was at your door."

"Who says so?" cried Mr Wentworth.

"Well – it was – a party, sir – a highly respectable party – as I have good reason to believe," said Hayles, "being a constant customer – one as there's every confidence to be put in. It's better not to name no names, being at this period of the affair."

And at that moment, unluckily for Mr Wentworth, there suddenly floated across his mind the clearest recollection of the Miss Hemmings, and the look they gave him in passing. He felt a hot flush rush over his face as he recalled it. They, then, were his accusers in the first place; and for the first time he began to realise how the tide of accusation would surge through Carlingford, and how circumstances would be patched together, and very plausible evidence concocted out of the few facts which were capable of an inference totally opposed to the truth. The blood rushed to his face in an overpowering glow, and then he felt the warm tide going back upon his heart, and realised the position in which he stood for the first time in its true light.

"And if you'll let me say it, sir," said the judicious Hayles, "though a man may be in a bit of a passion, and speak more strong that is called for, it aint unnatural in the circumstances; things may be better than they appear," said the druggist, mildly; "I don't say nothing against that; it may be as you've took her away, sir (if so be as you have took her away), for to give her a bit of education, or suchlike, before making her your wife; but folks in general aint expected to know that; and when a young girl is kep' out of her 'ome for a whole night, it aint wonderful if her friends take fright. It's a sad thing for Rosa whoever's taken her away, and wherever she is."

Now, Mr Wentworth, notwithstanding the indignant state of mind which he was in, was emphatically of the tolerant temper which is so curiously characteristic of his generation. He could not be unreasonable even in his own cause; he was not partisan enough, even in his own behalf, to forget that there was another side to the question, nor to see how hard and how sad was that other side. He was moved in spite of himself to grieve over Rosa Elsworthy's great misfortune.

"Poor little deluded child," he said, sadly; "I acknowledge it is very dreadful for her and for her friends. I can excuse a man who is mad with grief and wretchedness and anxiety, and doesn't know what he is saying. As for any man in his senses imagining," said the Curate again, with a flush of sudden colour, "that I could possibly be concerned in anything so base, that is simply absurd. When Elsworthy returns to reason, and acknowledges the folly of what he has said, I will do anything in the world to help him. It is unnecessary for you to wait," said Mr Wentworth, turning to Sarah, who had stolen up behind, and caught some of the conversation, and who was staring with round eyes of wonder, partly guessing, partly

inquiring, what had happened – "these people want me;
go indoors and never mind."

"La, sir! Missis is a-ringing all the bells down to know
what 'as 'appened," said Sarah, holding her ground.

This was how it was to be – the name of the Curate of St
Roque's was to be linked to that of Rosa Elsworthy, let the
truth be what it might, in the mouths of every maid and
every mistress in Carlingford. He was seized with a
sudden apprehension of this aspect of the matter, and it
was not wonderful if Mr Wentworth drew his breath hard
and set his teeth, as he ordered the woman away, in a tone
which could not be disobeyed.

"I don't want to make no talk," said Elsworthy, who
during this time had made many efforts to speak; "I've
sait it before, and I say it again – it's Mr Wentworth's fault
if there's any talk. She was seen here last night," he went
on rapidly, "and afore six o'clock this blessed morning,
you, as are never known to be stirring early, meets us at
the door, all shaved and dressed; and it aint very difficult
to see, to them as watches the clergyman's countenance,"
said Elsworthy, turning from one to another, "as everything isn't as straight as it ought to be; but I aint going to
make no talk, Mr Wentworth," he went on, drawing
closer, and speaking with conciliatory softness; "me and
her aunt, sir, loves her dearly, but we're not the folks to
stand in her way, if a gentleman was to take a fancy to
Rosa. If you'll give me your word to make her your wife
honourable, and tell me where she is, tortures wouldn't
draw no complaints from me. One moment, sir; it aint only
that she's pretty, but she's good as well – she won't do you
no discredit, Mr Wentworth. Put her to school, or what
you please, sir," said Rosa's uncle; "me and my wife will
never interfere, so be as you make her your wife honourable; but I aint a worm to be trampled on," cried
Elsworthy, as the Curate, finding him approach very
closely, thrust him away with vehement indignation; "I
aint a slave to be pushed about. Them as brings Rosa to

shame shall come to shame by me; I'll ruin the man as ruins that child. You may turn me out," he cried, as the Curate laid his powerful hand upon his shoulder and forced him towards the door, "but I'll come back, and I'll bring all Carlingford. There shan't be a soul in the town as doesn't know. Oh, you young viper, as I thought was a pious clergyman! you aint got rid of me. My child – where's my child?" cried the infuriated clerk, as he found himself ejected into the road outside, and the door suddenly closed upon him. He turned round to beat upon it in blind fury, and kept calling upon Rosa, and wasting his threats and arguments upon the calm air outside. Some of the maid-servants in the other houses came out, broom in hand, to the green doors, to see what was the matter, but they were not near enough to hear distinctly, and no early wayfarers had as yet invaded the morning quiet of Grange Lane.

Mr Wentworth, white with excitement, and terribly calm and self-possessed, turned to the amazed and trembling druggist, who still stood inside. "Look here, Hayles," said the Curate; "I have never seen Rosa Elsworthy since I closed this door upon her last night. What had brought her here I don't know – at least she came with no intention of seeing me – and I reproved her sharply for being out so late. This is all I know about the affair, and all I intend to say to any one. If that idiot outside intends to make a disturbance, he must do it; I shall take no further trouble to clear myself of such an insane accusation. I think it right to say as much to you, because you seem to have your senses about you," said the Curate, pausing, out of breath. He was perfectly calm, but it was impossible to ignore the effect of such a scene upon ordinary flesh and blood. His heart was beating loudly, and his breath came short and quick. He turned away and walked up to the house-door, and then came back again. "You understand me, I suppose?" he said; "and if Elsworthy is not mad, you had better suggest to him not to lose his only chance of recovering Rosa by vain bluster with me, who know nothing about her. I shan't be idle in the mean time," said Mr Wentworth. All this time Elsworthy was beating against the door, and shouting his threats into the quiet of the morning; and Mrs Hadwin had thrown up her window, and stood there visibly in her nightcap, trying to find out what the noise was about, and trembling for the respectability of her house – all which the Curate apprehended with that extraordinary swiftness and breadth of perception which comes to men at the eventful moments of life.

"I'll do my best, sir," said Hayles, who felt that his honour was appealed to; "but it's an awkward business for all parties, that's what it is;" and the druggist backed out in a state of great bewilderment, having a little struggle at the door with Elsworthy to prevent his re-entrance. "There aint nothing to be got out of *him*," said Mr Hayles, as he succeeded at last in leading his friend away. Such was the conclusion of Mr Wentworth's morning studies, and the sermon which was to have been half written before breakfast upon that eventful Saturday. He went back to the house, as was natural, with very different thoughts in his mind.

CHAPTER XXVI.

The first thing Mr Wentworth did was to hasten up-stairs to Wodehouse's room. Sarah had gone before him, and was by this time talking to her mistress, who had left the window, and stood, still in her nightcap, at the door of her own chamber. "It's something about Rosa Elsworthy, ma'am," said Sarah; "she's gone off with some one, which nothing else was to be expected; and her uncle's been a-raving and a-raging at Mr Wentworth, which proves as a gentleman should never take no notice of them shop-girls. I always heard as she was a bad lot."

"Oh, Mr Wentworth – if you would excuse my nightcap," said Mrs Hadwin– "I am so shaken and all of a tremble with that noise; I couldn't help thinking it must be a murder at the least," said the little old lady; "but I never could believe that there was anything between you and—Sarah, you may go away; I should like to talk to Mr Wentworth by himself," said Mrs Hadwin, suddenly remembering that Mr Wentworth's character must not be discussed in the presence of even her favourite maid.

"Presently," said the unhappy Curate, with mingled impatience and resignation; and, after a hasty knock at the door, he went into Wodehouse's room, which was opposite, so full of a furious anxiety to question him that he had burst into speech before he perceived that the room was empty. "Answer me this instant," he had cried, "where is Rosa Elsworthy?" and then he paused, utterly taken aback. It had not occurred to him that the culprit would be gone. He had parted with him late on the previous night, leaving him, according to appearances, in a state of sulky half-penitence; and now the first impulse of his consternation was to look in all the corners for the fugitive. The room had evidently been occupied that night; part of the Curate's own wardrobe, which he had bestowed upon his guest, lay about on the chairs, and on a little table were his tools and the bits of wood with which he did his carving. The window was open, letting in the fresh air, and altogether the apartment looked so exactly like what it might have done had the occupant gone out for a virtuous morning walk, that Mr Wentworth stopped short in blank amazement. It was a relief to him to hear the curious Sarah still rustling in the passage outside. He came out upon her so hastily that Sarah was startled. Perhaps she had been so far excited out of her usual propriety as to think of the keyhole as a medium of information.

"Where is Wode— Mr Smith?" cried the Curate; "he is not in his room – he does not generally get up so early. Where is he? Did he go out last night?"

"Not as I knows of, sir," said Sarah, who grew a little pale, and gave a second glance at the open door. "Isn't the gentleman in his room? He do take a walk in the morning, now and again," and Sarah cast an alarmed look behind to see if her mistress was still within hearing; but Mrs Hadwin, intent on questioning Mr Wentworth himself, had fortunately retired to put on her cap, and closed her door.

"Where is he?" said the Curate, firmly.

"Oh, please sir, I don't know," said Sarah, who was very near crying. "He's gone out for a walk, that's all. Oh, Mr Wentworth, don't look at me so dreadfully, and I'll tell you hall," cried the frightened girl, "*hall* – as true as if I was on my oath. He 'as a taking way with him," said poor Sarah, to whom the sulky and shabby rascal was radiant still with the fascinating though faded glory of "a gentleman" – "and he aint one as has been used to regular hours; and seeing as he was a friend of yours, I knew as hall was safe, Mr Wentworth; and oh, sir, if you'll not tell missis, as might be angry. I didn't mean no harm; and knowing as he was a friend of yours, I let him have the key of the little door."

Here Sarah put her apron to her eyes; she did not cry much into it, or wet it with her tears – but under its cover she peeped at Mr Wentworth, and, encouraged by his looks, which did not seem to promise any immediate catastrophe, went on with her explanation.

"He's been and took a walk often in the morning," said Sarah, with little gasps which interrupted her voice, "and come in as steady as steady, and nothing happened. He's gone for a walk now, poor gentleman. Them as goes out first thing in the morning, can't mean no harm, Mr

Wentworth. If it was at night, it would be different," said the apologetic Sarah. "He'll be in afore we've done our breakfast in the kitchen; that's his hour, for I always brings him a cup of coffee. If you hadn't been up not till *your* hour, sir, you'd never have known nothing about it;" and here even Mrs Hadwin's housemaid looked sharply in the Curate's face. "I never knew you so early, sir, not since I've been here," said Sarah; and though she was a partisan of Mr Wentworth, it occurred even to Sarah that perhaps, after all, Elsworthy might be right.

"If he comes in let me know immediately," said the Curate; and he went to his study and shut himself in, to think it all over with a sense of being baited and baffled on every side. As for Sarah, she went off in great excitement to discuss the whole business with the cook, tossing her head as she went. "Rosa Elsworthy, indeed!" said Sarah to herself, thinking her own claims to admiration quite as well worth considering – and Mr Wentworth had already lost one humble follower in Grange Lane.

The Curate sat down at his table as before, and gazed with a kind of exasperation at the paper and the text out of which his sermon was to have come. "When the wicked man turneth away from the evil of his ways" – he began to wonder bitterly whether that ever happened, or if it was any good trying to bring it about. If it were really the case that Wodehouse, whom he had been labouring to save from the consequences of one crime, had, at the very crisis of his fate, perpetrated another of the basest kind, what was the good of wasting strength in behalf of a wretch so abandoned? Why should such a man be permitted to live to bring shame and misery on everybody connected with him? and why, when noxious vermin of every other description were hunted down and exterminated, should the vile human creature be spared to suck the blood of his friends? Mr Wentworth grew sanguinary in his thoughts as he leaned back in his chair, and tried to return to the train of reflection which Elsworthy's arrival had banished. That was totally impossible, but another train of ideas came fast enough to fill up the vacant space. The Curate saw himself hemmed in on every side without any way of escape. If he could not extract any information from Wodehouse, or if Wodehouse denied any knowledge of Rosa, what could he do to clear himself from an imputation so terrible? and if, on the other hand, Wodehouse did not come back, and so pleaded guilty, how could he pursue and put the law upon the track of the man whom he had just been labouring to save from justice, and over whose head a criminal prosecution was impending? Mr Wentworth saw nothing but misery, let him turn where he would – nothing but disgrace, misapprehension, unjust blame. He divined with the instinct of a man in deadly peril, that Elsworthy, who was a mean enough man in common circumstances, had been inspired by the supposed injury he had sustained into a relentless demon; and he saw distinctly how strong the chain of evidence was against him, and how little he could do to clear himself. As his miseries grew upon him, he got up, as was natural, and began to walk about the room to walk down his impatience, if he could, and acquire sufficient composure to enable him to wait for the time when Wodehouse might be expected to arrive. Mr Wentworth had forgotten at the moment that Mrs Hadwin's room was next to his study, and that, as she stood putting on her cap, his footsteps vibrated along the flooring, which thrilled under her feet almost as much as under his own. Mrs Hadwin, as she stood before her glass smoothing her thin little braids of white hair, and putting on her cap, could not but wonder to herself what could make Mr Wentworth walk about the room in such an agitated way. It was not by any means the custom of the Perpetual Curate, who, up to the time of his aunts' arrival in Carlingford, had known no special disturbances in his individual career. And then the old lady thought of that report about little Rosa Elsworthy, which she had never believed, and grew troubled, as old ladies are not unapt to

do under such circumstances, with all that lively faith in
the seductions of "an artful girl," and all that contemptuous pity for a "poor young man," which seems to come
natural to a woman. All the old ladies in Carlingford, male
and female, were but too likely to entertain the same
sentiments, which at least, if they did nothing else,
showed a wonderful faith in the power of love and folly
common to human nature. It did not occur to Mrs Hadwin
any more than it did to Miss Dora, that Mr Wentworth's
good sense and pride, and superior cultivation, were sufficient defences against little Rosa's dimpled cheeks and
bright eyes; and with some few exceptions, such was likely
to be the opinion of the little world of Carlingford. Mrs
Hadwin grew more and more anxious about the business
as she felt the boards thrill under her feet, and heard the
impatient movements in the next room; and as soon as she
had settled her cap to her satisfaction, she left her own
chamber and went to knock, as was to be expected, at Mr
Wentworth's door.

It was just at this moment that Mr Wentworth saw
Wodehouse's shabby figure entering at the garden-gate;
he turned round suddenly without hearing Mrs Hadwin's
knock, and all but ran over the old lady in his haste and
eagerness – "Pardon me; I am in a great hurry," said the
Curate, darting past her. Just at the moment when she
expected her curiosity to be satisfied, it was rather hard
upon Mrs Hadwin to be dismissed so summarily. She went
down-stairs in a state of great dignity, with her lace mittens
on, and her hands crossed before her. She felt she had
more and more reason for doubting human nature in
general, and for believing that the Curate of St Roque's in
particular could not bear any close examination into his
conduct. Mrs Hadwin sat down to her breakfast accordingly
with a sense of pitying virtue which was sweet to her
spirit, notwithstanding that she was, as she would have
frankly acknowledged, very fond of Mr Wentworth; she
said, "Poor young man," to herself, and shook her head

over him as she poured out her solitary cup of tea. She had never been a beauty herself, nor had she exercised any overwhelming influence that she could remember over any one in the days of her distant youth: but being a true woman, Mrs Hadwin believed in Rosa Elsworthy, and pitied, not without a certain half-conscious female disdain, the weakness of the inevitable victim. He did not dare to stop to explain to *her* what it meant. He rushed out of her way as soon as he saw she meant to question him. That designing girl had got him entirely under her sway, the poor young man!

Meanwhile the Curate, without a single thought for his landlady, made a rush to Wodehouse's room. He did not wait for any answer to his knock, but went in, not as a matter of policy, but because his eagerness carried him on in spite of himself. To Mr Wentworth's great amazement Wodehouse was undressing, intending, apparently, to return to bed. The shabby fugitive, looking broad and brawny in his shirt-sleeves, turned round when he heard the voice with an angry exclamation. His face grew black as he saw the Curate at the door. "What the deuce have you to do in my room at this hour?" he growled into his beard. "Is a man never to have a little peace?" and with that threw down his coat, which he still had in his hand, and faced round towards the intruder with sullen looks. It was his nature to stand always on the defensive, and he had got so much accustomed to being regarded as a culprit, that he naturally took up the part, whether there might be just occasion or not.

"Where have you been?" exclaimed the Curate; "answer me truly — I can't submit to any evasion. I know it all, Wodehouse. Where is she? where have you hid her? If you do not give her up, I must give you up to justice. Do you hear me? where is Rosa Elsworthy? This is a matter that touches my honour, and I must know the truth."

Mr Wentworth was so full of the subject that it did not occur to him how much time he was giving his antagonist to prepare his answer. Though Wodehouse was not clever, he had the instinct of a baited animal driven to bay; and resistance and denial came natural to a man who had been accused and condemned all his life.

"Rosa Elsworthy?" said the vagabond, "what have I to do with Rosa Elsworthy? A pretty man I should be to run away with a girl; all that I have in the world is a shilling or two, and, by Jove, it's an expensive business, that is. You should ask your brother," he continued, giving a furtive glance at the Curate – "it's more in his way, by Jove, than mine."

Mr Wentworth was recalled to himself by this reply. "Where is she?" he said, sternly, – "no trifling. I did not ask if you had taken her away. I ask, where is she?" He had shut the door behind him, and stood in the middle of the room facing Wodehouse, and overawing him by his superior stature, force, and virtue. Before the Curate's look the eyes of the other fell; but he had fallen by chance on a reasonable defence enough, and so long as he held by that felt himself tolerably safe.

"I don't know anything about her," he repeated; "how should I know anything about her? I aint a fool, by Jove, whatever I may be: a man may talk to a pretty girl without any harm. I mayn't be as good as a parson, but, by Jove, I aint a fool," he muttered through his beard. He had begun to speak with a kind of sulky self-confidence; but his voice sunk lower as he proceeded. Jack Wentworth's elegant levity was a terrible failure in the hands of the coarser rascal. He fell back by degrees upon the only natural quality which enabled him to offer any resistance. "By Jove, I aint an idiot," he repeated with dull obstinacy, and upon that statement made a stand in his dogged, argumentative way.

"Would you like it better if I said you were a villain?" asked the exasperated Curate. "I don't want to discuss your character with you. Where is Rosa Elsworthy? She is scarcely more than a child," said Mr Wentworth, "and a fool, if you like. But where is she? I warn you that unless you tell me you shall have no more assistance from me."

"And I tell you that I don't know," said Wodehouse; and the two men stood facing each other, one glowing with youthful indignation, the other enveloped in a cloud of sullen resistance. Just then there came a soft knock at the door, and Sarah peeped in with a coquettish air, which at no other time in her existence had been visible in the sedate demeanour of Mrs Hadwin's favourite handmaid. The stranger lodger was "a gentleman," notwithstanding his shabbiness, and he was a very civil-spoken gentleman, without a bit of pride; and Sarah was still a woman, though she was plain and a housemaid. "Please, sir, I've brought you your coffee," said Sarah, and she carried in her tray, which contained all the materials for a plentiful breakfast. When she saw Mr Wentworth standing in the room, and Wodehouse in his shirt sleeves, Sarah said, "La!" and set down her tray hastily and vanished; but the episode, short as it was, had not been without its use to the culprit who was standing on his defence.

"I'm not staying here on my own account," said Wodehouse, – "it's no pleasure to me to be here. I'm staying for your brother's sake and – other people's; it's no pleasure to me, by Jove! I'd go to-morrow if I had my way – but I aint a fool," continued the sulky defendant: "it's of no use asking me such questions. By Jove, I've other things to think of than girls; and you knew pretty well how much money I've got," he continued, taking out an old purse and emptying out the few shillings it contained into his hand. When he had thrown them about, out and in, for nearly a minute, he turned once more upon the Curate. "I'd like to have a little more pocket-money before I ran away with any one," said Wodehouse, and tossed the shillings back contemptuously. As for Mr Wentworth, his reasonableness once more came greatly in his way. He began to ask himself whether this penniless vagabond, who seemed to have no dash or daring in his character, could have been the man to carry little Rosa away; and, perplexed by this idea, Mr Wentworth put himself unawares into the position of his opponent, and in that character made an appeal to his imaginary generosity and truth.

"Wodehouse," he said, seriously, "look here. I am likely to be much annoyed about this, and perhaps injured. I entreat you to tell me, if you know, where the girl is. I've been at some little trouble for you; be frank with me for once," said the Curate of St Roque's. Nothing in existence could have prevented himself from responding to such an appeal, and he made it with a kind of absurd confidence that there must be some kindred depths even in the meaner nature with which he had to deal, which would have been to Jack Wentworth, had he seen it, a source of inextinguishable laughter. Even Wodehouse was taken by surprise. He did not understand Mr Wentworth, but a certain vague idea that the Curate was addressing him as if he still were "a gentleman as he used to be" – though it did not alter his resolution in any way – brought a vague flush of shame to his unaccustomed cheek.

"I aint a fool," he repeated rather hastily, and turned away not to meet the Curate's eyes. "I've got no money – how should *I* know anything about her? If I had, do you think I should have been here?" he continued, with a sidelong look of inquiry: then he paused and put on his coat, and in that garb felt himself more of a match for his opponent. "I'll tell you one thing you'll thank me for," he said, – "the old man is dying, they think. They'll be sending for you presently. That's more important than a talk about a girl. I've been talked to till I'm sick," said Wodehouse, with a little burst of irrepressible nature, "but things may change before you all know where you are." When he had said so much, the fear in his heart awoke again, and he cast another look of inquiry and anxiety at the Curate's face. But Mr Wentworth was disgusted, and had no more to say.

"Everything changes – except the heart of the churl, which can never be made bountiful," said the indignant young priest. It was not a fit sentiment, perhaps, for a preacher who had just written that text about the wicked man turning from the evil of his ways. Mr Wentworth went away in a glow of indignation and excitement, and left his guest to Sarah's bountiful provision of hot coffee and new-laid eggs, to which Wodehouse addressed himself with a perfectly good appetite, notwithstanding all the events of the morning, and all the mystery of the night.

CHAPTER XXVII.

Mr Wentworth retired to his own quarters with enough to think about for one morning. He could not make up his mind about Wodehouse – whether he was guilty or not guilty. It seemed incredible that, penniless as he was, he could have succeeded in carrying off a girl so well known in Carlingford as Rosa Elsworthy; and, if he had taken her away, how did it happen that he himself had come back again? The Curate saw clearly enough that his only chance for exculpating himself in the sight of the multitude was by bringing home the guilt to somebody else; and in proportion to the utter scorn with which he had treated Elsworthy's insinuations at first, was his serious apprehension now of the danger which surrounded him. He divined all that slander would make of it with the quickened intelligence of a man whose entire life, and reputation dearer than life, were at stake. If it could not be cleared up – if even any investigation which he might be able to demand was not perfectly successful – Mr Wentworth was quite well aware that the character of a clergyman was almost as susceptible as that of a woman, and that the vague stigma might haunt and overshadow him all his life. The thought was overwhelming at this moment, when his first hopes of finding a speedy solution of the mystery had come to nothing. If he had but lived a century earlier, the chances are that no doubt of Wodehouse's guilt would have entered his mind; but Mr Wentworth was a man of the present age – reasonable to a fault, and apt to consider other people as much as possible from their own point of view. He did not see, looking at the circumstances, how Wodehouse *could* be guilty; and the Curate would not permit the strong instinctive certainty that he *was* guilty, to move his own mind from what he imagined to be its better judgment. He was thinking it over very gloomily when his breakfast was brought to him and his letters, feeling that he could be sure of nobody in such an emergency, and dreading more the doubt of his friends than the clamour of the general world. He could bear (he imagined) to be hooted at in the streets, if it ever came to that; but to see the faces of those who loved him troubled with a torturing doubt of his truth was a terrible thought to the Perpetual Curate. And Lucy? But here the young man got up indignant and threw off his fears. He doubted her regard with a doubt which threw darkness over the whole universe; but that she should be able for a moment to doubt his entire devotion to her, seemed a blindness incredible. No; let who would believe ill of him in this respect, to Lucy such an accusation must look as monstrous as it was untrue. *She*, at least, knew otherwise; and, taking this false comfort to his heart, Mr Wentworth took up his letters, and presently was deep in the anxieties of his brother Gerald, who wrote to him as to a man at leisure, and without any overwhelming perplexities of his own. It requires a very high amount of unselfishness in the person thus addressed to prevent a degree of irritation which is much opposed to sympathy; and Mr Wentworth, though he was very impartial and reasonable, was not, being still young and meaning to be happy, unselfish to any inhuman degree. He put down Gerald's letter, after he had read through half of it, with an exclamation of impatience which he could not restrain, and then poured out his coffee, which had got cold in the mean time, and gulped it down with a sense of half-comforting disgust – for there are moments when the mortification of the flesh is a relief to the spirit; and then it occurred to him to remember Wodehouse's tray, which was a kind of love-offering to the shabby vagabond, and the perfect good order in which *he* had his breakfast; and Mr Wentworth laughed at himself with a whimsical perception of all that was absurd in his own position which did him good, and broke the spell of his solitary musings. When he took up Gerald's letter again, he read it through. A man more sympathetic, open-hearted, and unselfish than Gerald Wentworth did not exist in the world, as his brother well knew; but nevertheless, Gerald's mind was so entirely preoccupied that he passed over the Curate's cares with the lightest reference imaginable. "I hope you found all right when you got back, and nothing seriously amiss with Jack," the elder brother wrote, and then went on to his own affairs. All right! nothing seriously amiss! To a man who felt himself standing on the edge of possible ruin, such expressions seemed strange indeed.

The Rector of Wentworth, however, had enough in his mind to excuse him for a momentary forgetfulness of others. Things had taken a different turn with him since his brother left. He had been so busy with his change of faith and sentiment, that the practical possibilities of the step which he contemplated had not disturbed Gerald. He had taken it calmly for granted that he *could* do what he wanted to do. But a new light had burst upon him in that respect, and changed the character of his thoughts. Notwithstanding the conviction into which he had reasoned himself, the Rector of Wentworth had not contemplated the idea of becoming simply a Catholic layman. He was

nothing if not a priest, he had said, passionately. He could
have made a martyr of himself — have suffered tortures
and deaths with the steadiest endurance; but he could not
face the idea of taking all meaning and significance out of
his life, by giving up the profession which he felt to be laid
upon him by orders indelible, beyond the power of
circumstances to revoke. Such was the new complication
to which Gerald had come. He was terribly staggered in
his previous resolution by this new doubt, and he wrote to
pour his difficulties into the ear of his brother. It had been
Frank's question which first awoke in his mind a doubt as
to the practicability of the step he contemplated; and one
of Louisa's relations, appealed to by her in her next access
of terror, had brought this aspect of the matter still more
distinctly before the Rector of Wentworth. Gerald had
been studying Canon law, but his English intelligence did
not make very much of it; and the bare idea of a dispen-
sation making that right which in itself was wrong, touched
the high-minded gentleman to the quick, and brought him
to a sudden standstill. He who was nothing if not a priest,
stood sorrowfully looking at his contemplated martyrdom
— like Brother Domenico of St Mark's sighing on the edge
of the fiery ordeal into which the Church herself would not
let him plunge. If it was so, he no longer knew what to do.
He would have wrapped the vestment of the new priesthood about him, though it was a garment of fire; but to
stand aside in irksome leisure was a harder trial, at which
he trembled. This was the new complication in which
Gerald asked his brother's sympathy and counsel. It was a
long letter, curiously introspective, and full of self-argument; and it was hard work, with a mind so occupied as
was that of the Perpetual Curate, to give it due attention.
He put it away when he had done with his cold breakfast,
and deferred the consideration of the subject, with a kind
of vague hope that the family firmament might possibly
brighten in that quarter at least; but the far-off and
indistinct interest with which he viewed, across his own

gloomy surroundings, this matter which had engrossed him so completely a few days before, was wonderful to see.

And then he paused to think what he was to do. To go out and face the slander which must already have crept forth on its way – to see Elsworthy and ascertain whether he had come to his senses, and try if anything could be done for Rosa's discovery – to exert himself somehow, in short, and get rid of the feverish activity which he felt consuming him, – that was what he longed to do. But, on the other hand, it was Saturday, and Mr Wentworth was conscious that it would be more dignified, and in better taste altogether, if he went on writing his sermon and took no notice of this occurrence, with which, in reality, he had nothing to do. It was difficult, but no doubt it was the best; and he tried it accordingly – putting down a great many sentences which had to be scratched out again, and spoiling altogether the appearance of the sermon-paper. When a message came from Mr Wodehouse's about eleven o'clock, bringing the news that he was much worse and not expected to live, and begging Mr Wentworth's immediate presence, the Curate was as nearly glad as it was possible for a man to be under the circumstances. He had "a feeling heart," as even Elsworthy allowed, but in such a moment of excitement any kind of great and terrible event seemed to come natural. He hastened out into the fresh morning sunshine, which still seemed thrilling with life and joy, and went up Grange Lane with a certain sense of curiosity, wondering whether everybody was already aware of what had happened. A long way off a figure which much resembled that of the Rector was visible crossing over to Dr Marjoribanks's door; and it occurred to the Curate that Mr Morgan was crossing to avoid him, which brought a smile of anger and involuntary dislike to his face, and nerved him for any other encounter. The green door at Mr Wodehouse's – a homely sign of the trouble in the house – had been left unlatched, and was swinging ajar with the wind when the Curate came up; and as he went in (closing it carefully after him, for that forlorn little touch of carelessness went to his heart), he encountered in the garden Dr Marjoribanks and Dr Rider, who were coming out together with very grave looks. They did not stop for much conversation, only pausing to tell him that the case was hopeless, and that the patient could not possibly live beyond a day or two at most; but even in the few words that were spoken Mr Wentworth perceived, or thought he perceived, that something had occurred to lessen him in the esteem of the shrewd old Scotch doctor, who contemplated him and his prayer-book with critical eyes. "I confess, after all, that there are cases in which written prayers are a kind of security," Dr Marjoribanks said in an irrelevant manner to Dr Rider when Mr Wentworth had passed them – an observation at which, in ordinary cases, the Curate would have smiled; but to-day the colour rose to his face, and he understood that Dr Marjoribanks did not think him qualified to carry comfort or instruction to a sick-bed. Perhaps the old doctor had no such idea in his mind – perhaps it was simply a relic of his national Presbyterianism, to which the old Scotchman kept up a kind of visionary allegiance. But whether he meant it or not, Mr Wentworth understood it as a reproach to himself, and went on with a bitter feeling of mortification to the sick-room. He had gone with his whole heart into his priestly office, and had been noted for his ministrations to the sick and poor; but now his feelings were much too personal for the atmosphere into which he was just about to enter. He stopped at the door to tell John that he would take a stroll round the garden before he came in, as he had a headache, and went on through the walks which were sacred to Lucy, not thinking of her, but wondering bitterly whether anybody would stand by him, or whether an utterly baseless slander would outweigh all the five years of his life which he had spent among the people of Carlingford. Meanwhile John stood at the door and watched him, and of course thought it was very "queer." "It aint as if he'd a-been sitting up all night, like our young ladies," said John to himself, and unconsciously noted the circumstance down in his memory against the Curate.

When Mr Wentworth entered the sick-room, he found all very silent and still in that darkened chamber. Lucy was seated by the bedside, wrapped in a loose dressing-gown, and looked as if she had not slept for several nights; while Miss Wodehouse, who, notwithstanding all her anxiety to be of use, was far more helpless than Lucy, stood on the side next the door, with her eyes fixed on her sister, watching with pathetic unserviceableness for the moment when she could be of some use. As for the patient himself, he lay in a kind of stupor, from which he scarcely ever could be roused, and showed no tokens at the moment of hearing or seeing anybody. The scene was doubly sad, but it was without the excitement which so often breathes in the atmosphere of death. There was no eager listening for the last word, no last outbreaks of tenderness. The daughters were both hushed into utter silence; and Lucy, who was more reasonable than her sister, had even given up those wistful beseeching looks at the patient, with which Miss Wodehouse still regarded him, as if perhaps he might be thus persuaded to speak. The nurse whom Dr Marjoribanks had sent to assist them was visible through an open door, sleeping very comfortably in the adjoining room. Mr Wentworth came into the silent chamber with all his anxieties throbbing in his heart, bringing life at its very height of agitation and tumult into the presence of death. He went forward to the bed, and tried for an instant to call up any spark of intelligence that might yet exist within the mind of the dying man; but Mr Wodehouse was beyond the voice of any priest. The Curate said the prayers for the dying at the bedside, suddenly filled with a great pity for the man who was thus taking leave unawares of all this mournful splendid world. Though the young man knew many an ordinary sentiment about the vanity of life, and

had given utterance to that effect freely in the way of his
duty, he was still too fresh in his heart to conceive actually
that any one could leave the world without poignant
regrets; and when his prayer was finished, he stood looking
at the patient with inexpressible compassion. Mr Wodehouse had scarcely reached old age; he was well off, and
only a week ago seemed to have so much to enjoy; now,
here he lay stupefied, on the edge of the grave, unable to
respond even by a look to the love that surrounded him.
Once more there rose in the heart of the young priest a
natural impulse of resentment and indignation; and when
he thought of the cause of this change, he remembered
Wodehouse's threat, and roused himself from his contemplation of the dying to think of the probable fate of those
who must live.

"Has he made his will?" said Mr Wentworth, suddenly.
He forgot that it was Lucy who was standing by him; and it
was only when he caught a glance of reproach and horror
from her eyes that he recollected how abrupt his question
was. "Pardon me," he said; "you think me heartless to
speak of it at such a time; but tell me, if you know: Miss
Wodehouse, has he made his will?"

"Oh, Mr Wentworth, I don't know anything about
business," said the elder sister. "He said he would; but we
have had other things to think of – more important things,"
said poor Miss Wodehouse, wringing her hands, and
looking at Mr Wentworth with eyes full of warning and
meaning, beseeching him not to betray her secret. She
came nearer to the side of the bed on which Lucy and the
Curate were standing, and plucked at his sleeve in her
anxiety. "We have had very different things to think of.
Oh, Mr Wentworth, what does it matter?" said the poor
lady, interposing her anxious looks, which suggested every
kind of misfortune, between the two.

"It matters everything in the world," said Mr Wentworth.
"Pardon me if I wound you – I must speak; if it is possible
to rouse him, an effort must be made. Send for Mr

Waters. He must not be allowed to go out of the world and leave your interests in the hands of—"

"Oh, hush, Mr Wentworth, hush! – oh, hush, hush! Don't say any more," cried Miss Wodehouse, grasping his arm in her terror.

Lucy rose from where she had been sitting at the bedside. She had grown paler than before, and looked almost stern in her youthful gravity. "I will not permit my father to be disturbed," she said. "I don't know what you mean, or what you are talking of; but he is not to be disturbed. Do you think I will let him be vexed in his last hours about money or anybody's interest? " she said, turning upon the Curate a momentary glance of scorn. Then she sat down again, with a pang of disappointment added to her grief. She could not keep her heart so much apart from him, as not to expect a little comfort from his presence. And there had been comfort in his prayers and his looks; but to hear him speak of wills and worldly affairs by her father's deathbed, as any man might have done, went to Lucy's heart. She sat down again, putting her hand softly upon the edge of the pillow, to guard the peace of those last moments which were ebbing away so rapidly. What if all the comfort of the world hung upon it? Could she let her kind father be troubled in his end for anything so miserable? Lucy turned her indignant eyes upon the others with silent resolution. It was she who was *his* protector now.

"But it must be done," said Mr Wentworth. "You will understand me hereafter. Miss Wodehouse, you must send for Mr Waters, and in the mean time I will do what I can to rouse him. It is no such cruelty as you think," said the Curate, with humility; "it is not for money or interest only – it concerns all the comfort of your life."

This he said to Lucy, who sat defending her father. She, for her part, looked up at him with eyes that broke his heart. At that moment of all others, the unfortunate Curate perceived, by a sudden flash of insight, that nothing less than love could look at him with such force of disappointment and reproach and wounded feeling. He replied to the look by a gesture of mingled entreaty and despair. "What can I do?" he cried – "you have no one else to care for you. I cannot even explain to you all that is at stake. I must act as I ought, even though you hate me for it. Let us send for Mr Waters; – if there is a will—"

Mr Wentworth had raised his voice a little in the excitement of the moment, and the word caught the dull ear of the dying man. The Curate saw instantly that there was comprehension in the flicker of the eyelash and the tremulous movement of the hand upon the bed. It was a new and unaccustomed part which he had now to play; he went hurriedly to the other side and leaned over the pillow to make out the stammering words which began to be audible. Lucy had risen up also and stood looking at her father still with her look of defence. As the feeble lips babbled forth unintelligible words, Lucy's face grew sterner and sterner. As for Miss Wodehouse, she stood behind, crying and trembling. "Oh, Mr Wentworth, do you think it is returning life – do you think he is better?" she cried, looking wistfully at the Curate; and between the two young people, who were leaning with looks and feelings so different over his bed, the patient lay struggling with those terrible bonds of weakness, labouring to find expression for something which wrought him into a fever of excitement. While Mr Wentworth bent his ear closer and closer, trying to make some sense of the inarticulate torrent of sound, Lucy, inspired by grief and horror and indignation, leaned over her father on the other side, doing everything possible to calm him. "Oh, papa, don't say any more – don't say any more; we understand you," she cried, and put her soft hands upon his flushed forehead, and her cheek to his. "No more, no more!" cried the girl in the dulled ear which could not hear. "We will do everything you wish – we understand all," said Lucy. Mr Wentworth withdrew vanquished in that strange struggle

– he stood looking on while she caressed and calmed and
subdued into silence the dying passion which he would
have given anything in the world to stimulate into clearer
utterance. She had baffled his efforts, made him helpless
to serve her, perhaps injured herself cruelly; but all the
more the Curate loved her for it, as she expanded over her
dying father, with the white sleeves hanging loose about
her arms like the white wings of an angel, as he thought.
Gradually the agony of utterance got subdued, and then
Lucy resumed her position by the bed. "He shall not be
disturbed," she said again, through lips that were parched
with emotion; and so sat watchful over him, a guardian
immovable, ready to defy all the world in defence of his
peace.

Mr Wentworth turned away with his heart full. He
would have liked to go and kiss her hand or her sleeve or
anything belonging to her; and yet he was impatient
beyond expression, and felt that she had baffled and
vanquished him. Miss Wodehouse stood behind, still
looking on with a half perception of what had happened;
but the mind of the elder sister was occupied with vain
hopes and fears, such as inexperienced people are subject
to in the presence of death.

"He heard what you said," said Miss Wodehouse; "don't
you think that was a good sign? Oh, Mr Wentworth,
sometimes I think he looks a little better," said the poor
lady, looking wistfully into the Curate's face. Mr Wentworth could only shake his head as he hurried away.

"I must go and consult Mr Waters," he said, as he
passed her. "I shall come back presently;" and then Miss
Wodehouse followed him to the door, to beg him not to
speak to Mr Waters of *anything particular* – "For papa has
no confidence in him," she said, anxiously. The Curate
was nearly driven to his wits' end as he hastened out. He
forgot the clouds that surrounded him in his anxiety about
this sad household; for it seemed but too evident that Mr
Wodehouse had made no special provision for his

daughters; and to think of Lucy under the power of her unknown brother, made Mr Wentworth's blood boil.

The shutters were all put up that afternoon in the prettiest house in Grange Lane. The event took Carlingford altogether by surprise; but other events just then were moving the town into the wildest excitement; for nothing could be heard, far or near, of poor little Rosa Elsworthy, and everybody was aware that the last time she was seen in Carlingford she was standing by herself in the dark, at Mr Wentworth's garden-door.

CHAPTER XXVIII.

MRS MORGAN was in the garden watering her favourite ferns when her husband returned home to dinner on the day of Mr Wodehouse's death. The Rector was late, and she had already changed her dress, and was removing the withered leaves from her prettiest plant of maidenhair, and thinking, with some concern, of the fish, when she heard his step on the gravel; for the cook at the Rectory was rather hasty in her temper, and was apt to be provoking to her mistress next morning when the Rector chose to be late. It was a very hot day, and Mr Morgan was flushed and uncomfortable. To see his wife looking so cool and tranquil in her muslin dress rather aggravated him than otherwise, for she did not betray her anxiety about the trout, but welcomed him with a smile, as she felt it her duty to do, even when he was late for dinner. The Rector looked as if all the anxieties of the world were on his shoulders, as he came hurriedly along the gravel; and Mrs Morgan's curiosity was sufficiently excited by his looks to have overcome any consideration but that of the trout, which, however, was too serious to be trifled with; so, instead of asking questions, she thought it wiser simply to remind her husband that it was past six o'clock. "Dinner is waiting," she said, in her composed way; and the Rector went up-stairs to wash his hands, half disposed to be angry with his wife. He found her already seated at the head of the table when he came down after his rapid ablutions; and though he was not particularly quick of perception, Mr Morgan perceived, by the looks of the servant as well as the mistress, that he was generally disapproved of throughout the household for being half an hour too late. As for Thomas, he was at no pains to conceal his sentiments, but conducted himself with distant politeness towards his master, expressing the feelings of the household with all the greater freedom that he had been in possession of the Rectory since Mr Bury's time, and felt himself more secure in his tenure than any incumbent, as was natural to a man who had already outlived two of these temporary tenants. Mr Morgan was disposed to be conciliatory when he saw the strength of the opposite side.

"I am a little late today," said the politic Rector. "Mr Leeson was with me, and I did not want to bring him home to dinner. It was only on Wednesday he dined with us, and I know you don't care for chance guests."

"I think it shows a great want of sense in Mr Leeson to think of such a thing," said Mrs Morgan, responding by a little flush of anger to the unlucky Curate's name. "He might understand that people like to be by themselves now and then. I am surprised that you give in to him so much as you do, William. Good-nature must stop somewhere, and I think it is always best to draw a line."

"I wish it were possible for everybody to draw a line," said the Rector, mysteriously, with a sigh. "I have heard something that has grieved me very much to-day. I will tell you about it afterwards." When he had said this, Mr Morgan addressed himself sadly to his dinner, sighing over it, as if that had something to do with his distress.

"Perhaps, ma'am," suggested Thomas, who was scarcely on speaking terms with his master, "the Rector mayn't have heard as Mr Wodehouse has been took very bad again, and aint expected to see out the night."

"I am very sorry," said the Rector. "Poor ladies! it will come very hard upon them. My dear, I think you should call and ask if you can do anything. Troubles never come singly, it is said. I am very sorry for that poor young creature; though, perhaps, things have not gone so far as one imagined." The Rector sighed again, and looked as though his secret, whatever it might be, was almost too much for him. The consequence, of course, was, that Thomas prolonged his services to the last possibility, by way of hearing what had happened; as for Mrs Morgan, she sat on thorns, though her sense of propriety was too great to permit her to hurry over the dinner. The pudding, though it was the Rector's favourite pudding, prepared from a receipt only known at All-Souls, in which the late respected Head of that learned community had concentrated all his genius, was eaten in uneasy silence, broken only by the most transparent attempts on both sides to make a little conversation. Thomas hovered sternly over his master and mistress all the time, exacting with inexorable severity every usage of the table. He would not let them off the very smallest detail, but insisted on handing round the peaches, notwithstanding Mrs Morgan's protest. "They are the first out of the new orchard-house," said the Rector's wife. "I want your opinion of them. That will do, Thomas; we have got everything now, I think." Mrs Morgan was a little anxious about the peaches, having made a great many changes on her own responsibility in the gardening department; but the Rector took the downy fruit as if it had been a turnip, and notwithstanding her interest in the long-delayed news, his wife could not but find it very provoking that he took so little notice of her exertions.

"Roberts stood out against the new flue as long as he

could," said Mrs Morgan. "Mr Proctor took no interest in the garden, and everything had gone to ruin; though I must say it was very odd that anybody from *your* college, William, should be careless about such a vital matter," said the Rector's wife, with a little asperity. "I suppose there must be something in the air of Carlingford which makes people indifferent." Naturally, it was very provoking, after all the trouble she had taken, to see her husband slicing that juicy pulp as if it had been any ordinary market fruit.

"I beg your pardon, my dear," said Mr Morgan; "I was thinking of this story about Mr Wentworth. One is always making new discoveries of the corruption of human nature. He had behaved very badly to me; but it is very sad to see a young man sacrifice all his prospects for the indulgence of his passions; though that is a very secular way of looking at the subject," said the Rector, shaking his head mournfully. "If it is bad in a worldly point of view, what is it in a spiritual? and in this age, too, when it is so important to keep up the character of the clergy!" Mr Morgan sighed again more heavily than ever as he poured out the single glass of port, in which his wife joined him after dinner. "Such an occurrence throws a stigma upon the whole Church, as Mr Leeson very justly remarked."

"I thought Mr Leeson must have something to do with it," said the Rector's wife. "What has Mr Wentworth been doing? When you keep a Low-Church Curate, you never can tell what he may say. If he had known of the All-Souls pudding he would have come to dinner, and we should have had it at first-hand," said Mrs Morgan, severely. She put away her peach in her resentment, and went to a side-table for her work, which she always kept handy for emergencies. Like her husband, Mrs Morgan had acquired some little "ways" in the long ten years of their engagement, one of which was a confirmed habit of needlework at all kinds of unnecessary moments, which much disturbed the Rector when he had anything particular to say.

"My dear, I am very sorry to see you so much the victim of prejudice," said Mr Morgan. "I had hoped that all our long experiences—" and here the Rector stopped short, troubled to see the rising colour in his wife's face. "I don't mean to blame you, my dear," said the perplexed man; "I know you were always very patient;" and he paused, not knowing what more to say, comforting himself with the thought that women were incomprehensible creatures, as so many men have done before.

"I am not patient," said the Rector's wife; "it never was my nature. I can't help thinking sometimes that our long experiences have done us more harm than good; but I hope nothing will ever make me put up with a Curate who tells tales about other people, and flatters one's self, and comes to dinner without being asked. Perhaps Mr Wentworth is very sinful, but at least he is a gentleman," said Mrs Morgan; and she bent her head over her work, and drove her needle so fast through the muslin she was at work upon, that it glimmered and sparkled like summer lightning before the spectator's dazzled eyes.

"I am sorry you are so prejudiced," said the Rector. "It is a very unbecoming spirit, my dear, though I am grieved to say so much to you. Mr Leeson is a very good young man, and he has nothing to do with this terrible story about Mr Wentworth. I don't wish to shock your feelings – but there are a great many things in the world that one can't explain to ladies. He has got himself into a most distressing position, and a public inquiry will be necessary One can't help seeing the hand of Providence in it," said the Rector, playing reflectively with the peach on his plate.

It was at this moment that Thomas appeared at the door to announce Mr Leeson, who had come to talk over the topic of the day with the Rector – being comfortably obtuse in his perceptions, and quite disposed to ignore Mrs Morgan's general demeanour towards himself. "I am sure she has a bad temper," he would say to his confidants in the parish; "you can see it by the redness in her face: but I never take any notice when she says rude things to me." The redness was alarming in Mrs Morgan's face as the unlucky man became visible at the door. She said audibly, "I knew we should be interrupted!" and got up from her chair. "As Mr Leeson is here, you will not want me, William," she added, in her precisest tones. "If anything has happened since you came in, he will be able to tell you about it; and perhaps I had better send you your coffee here, for I have a great many things to do." Mr Morgan gave a little groan in his spirit as his wife went away. To do him justice, he had a great deal of confidence in her, and was unconsciously guided by her judgment in many matters. Talking it over with Mr Leeson was a totally different thing; for whatever might be said in his defence, there could not be any doubt that the Curate professed Low-Church principles, and had been known to drink tea with Mr Beecher, the new minister of Salem Chapel. "Not that I object to Mr Beecher because he is a Dissenter," Mr Morgan said, "but because, my dear, you know, it is a totally different class of society." When the Rector was left alone to discuss parish matters with this doubtful subordinate, instead of going into the subject with his wife, the good man felt a pang of disappointment; for though he professed to be reluctant to shock her, he had been longing all the time to enter into the story, which was certainly the most exciting which had occurred in Carlingford since the beginning of his incumbency. Mrs Morgan, for her part, went up-stairs to the drawing-room with so much indignation about this personal grievance that she almost forgot her curiosity. Mr Leeson hung like a cloud over all the advantages of Carlingford; he put out that new flue in the greenhouse, upon which she was rather disposed to pique herself, and withered her ferns, which everybody allowed to be the finest collection within a ten miles' circuit. This sense of disgust increased upon her as she went into the drawing-room, where her eye naturally caught that carpet which had been the first cross of her married life. When she had laid down her work, she began to plan how the offensive bouquets might be covered with a pinafore of linen, which looked very cool and nice in summer-time. And then the Rector's wife reflected that in winter a floor covered with white looked chilly, and that a woollen drugget of an appropriate small pattern would be better on the whole; but no such thing was to be had without going to London for it, which brought her mind back again to Mr Leeson and all the disadvantages of Carlingford. These subjects occupied Mrs Morgan to the exclusion of external matters, as was natural; and when she heard the gentlemen stir down-stairs as if with ideas of joining her in the drawing-room, the Rector's wife suddenly recollected that she had promised some tea to a poor woman in Grove Street, and that she could not do better this beautiful evening than take it in her own person. She was very active in her district at all times, and had proved herself an admirable clergywoman; but perhaps it would not have occurred to her to go out upon a charitable errand that particular evening had it not been for the presence of Mr Leeson down-stairs.

It was such a very lovely night, that Mrs Morgan was tempted to go further than she intended. She called on two or three of her favourites in Grove Street, and was almost as friendly with them as Lucy Wodehouse was with the people in Prickett's Lane; but being neither pretty and young, like Lucy, nor yet a mother with a nursery, qualified to talk about the measles, her reception was not quite as enthusiastic as it might have been. Somehow it would appear as though our poor neighbours loved most the ministrations of youth, which is superior to all ranks in the matter of possibility and expectation, and inferior to all ranks in the matter of experience; and so holds a kind of balance and poise of nature between the small and the great. Mrs Morgan was vaguely sensible of her disadvantages in this respect as well as in others. She never could help imagining what she might have been had she married ten years

before at the natural period. "And even then not a girl,"
she said to herself in her sensible way, as she carried this
habitual thread of thought with her along the street, past
the little front gardens, where there were so many mothers
with their children. On the other side of the way the
genteel houses frowned darkly with their staircase windows
upon the humility of Grove Street; and Mrs Morgan began
to think within herself of the Miss Hemmings and other
spinsters, and how they got along upon this path of life,
which, after all, is never lightsome to behold, except in the
future or the past. It was dead present with the Rector's
wife just then, and many speculations were in her mind, as
was natural. "Not that I could not have lived unmarried,"
she continued within herself, with a woman's pride; "but
things looked so different at five-and-twenty!" and in her
heart she grudged the cares she had lost, and sighed over
this wasting of her years.

It was just then that the youngest Miss Hemmings saw
Mrs Morgan, and crossed over to speak to her. Miss
Hemmings had left five-and-thirty behind a long time ago,
and thought the Rector's wife a happy woman in the
bloom of youth. When she had discovered conclusively
that Mrs Morgan would not go in to have a cup of tea, Miss
Hemmings volunteered to walk with her to the corner; and
it is not necessary to say that she immediately plunged
into the topic which at that moment engaged all minds in
Carlingford. "If I had not seen it with my own eyes, I
should not have believed it," said Miss Hemmings. "I
should have thought it a got-up story; not that I ever could
have thought it *impossible*, as you say – for, alas! I know
well that without grace every wickedness is more than
possible – but I saw them with my own eyes, my dear Mrs
Morgan; she standing outside, the bold little thing, and he at
the door – as if it was right for a clergyman to open the door
like a man-servant – and from that moment to this she has
not been seen by any living creature in Carlingford: who can
tell what may have been done with her?" cried the horrified eyewitness. "She has never been seen from that hour!"

"But that was only twenty-four hours ago," said Mrs Morgan; "she may have gone off to visit some of her friends."

"Ah, my dear Mrs Morgan, twenty-four hours is a long time for a girl to disappear out of her own home," said Miss Hemmings; "and all her friends have been sent to, and no word can be heard of her. I am afraid it will go very hard with Mr Wentworth; and I am sure it looks like a judgment upon him for all his candlesticks and flowers and things," she continued, out of breath with the impetuosity of her tale.

"Do you think, then, that God makes people sin in order to punish them?" said Mrs Morgan, with some fire, which shocked Miss Hemmings, who did not quite know how to reply.

"I do so wish you would come in for a few minutes and taste our tea; my sister Sophia was just making it when I came out. We get it from our brother in Assam, and we think a great deal of it," said Miss Hemmings; "it can't possibly be adulterated, you know, for it comes direct from his plantation. If you can't come in just now, I will send you some to the Rectory, and you shall tell us how you like it. We are quite proud of our tea. My brother has a large plantation, and he hopes—"

"Thank you," said Mrs Morgan, "but the Rector will be waiting for me, and I must go. It must be very nice to have your tea direct from the plantation; and I hope you will change your mind about Mr Wentworth," she continued, without much regard for punctuation, as she shook hands at the corner. Mrs Morgan went down a narrow street which led to Grange Lane, after this interview, with some commotion in her mind. She took Mr Wentworth's part instinctively, without asking any proofs of his innocence. The sun was just setting, and St Roque's stood out dark and picturesque against all the glory of the western sky as the Rector's wife went past. She could not help thinking of him, in his youth and the opening of his career, with a kind of wistful interest. If he had married Lucy Wodehouse, and confined himself to his own district (but then he had no district), Mrs Morgan would have contemplated the two, not, indeed, without a certain half-resentful self-reference and contrast, but with natural sympathy. And now, to think of this dark and ugly blot on his fair beginning disturbed her much. When Mrs Morgan recollected that she had left her husband and his Curate consulting over this matter, she grew very hot and angry, and felt humiliated by the thought. Was it her William, her hero, whom she had magnified for all these ten years, though not without occasional twinges of enlightenment, into something great, who was thus sitting upon his young brother with so little human feeling and so much middle-aged jealousy? It hurt her to think of it, though not for Mr Wentworth's sake. Poor Mrs Morgan, though not at all a sentimental person, had hoarded up her ideal so much after the ordinary date, that it came all the harder upon her when everything thus merged into the light of common day. She walked very fast up Grange Lane, which was another habit of her maidenhood not quite in accord with the habit of sauntering acquired during the same period by the Fellow of All-Souls. When Mrs Morgan was opposite Mr Wodehouse's, she looked across with some interest, thinking of Lucy; and it shocked her greatly to see the closed shutters, which told of the presence of death. Then, a little farther up, she could see Elsworthy in front of his shop, which was already closed, talking vehemently to a little group round the door. The Rector's wife crossed the street, to avoid coming into contact with this excited party; and, as she went swiftly along under the garden-walls, came direct, without perceiving it, upon Mr Wentworth, who was going the opposite way. They were both absorbed in their own thoughts, the Perpetual Curate only perceiving Mrs Morgan in time to take off his hat to her as he passed; and, to tell the truth, having no desire for any further intercourse. Mrs Morgan, however, was of a different mind. She stopped instantly, as soon as she perceived him. "Mr Wentworth, it is getting late – will you walk with me as far as the Rectory?" she said, to the Curate's great astonishment. He could not help looking at her with curiosity as he turned to accompany her. Mrs Morgan was still wearing her wedding things, which were not now in their first freshness - not to say that the redness, of which she was so painfully sensible, was rather out of accordance with the orange blossoms. Then she was rather flurried and disturbed in her mind; and, on the whole, Mr Wentworth ungratefully concluded the Rector's wife to be looking her plainest, as he turned with very languid interest to see her safely home.

"A great many things seem to be happening just now," said Mrs Morgan, with a good deal of embarrassment; "I suppose the people in Carlingford are grateful to anybody who gives them something to talk about."

"I don't know about the gratitude," said the Perpetual Curate; "it is a sentiment I don't believe in."

"You ought to believe in everything as long as you are young," said Mrs Morgan. "I want very much to speak to you, Mr Wentworth; but then I don't know how you will receive what I am going to say."

"I can't tell until I know what it is," said the Curate, shutting himself up. He had an expressive face generally, and Mrs Morgan saw the shutters put up, and the jealous blinds drawn over the young man's countenance as clearly as if they had been tangible articles. He did not look at her, but kept swinging his cane in his hand, and regarding the pavement with downcast eyes; and if the Rector's wife had formed any expectations of finding in the Perpetual Curate an ingenuous young heart, open to sympathy and criticism, she now discovered her mistake.

"If I run the risk, perhaps you will forgive me," said Mrs Morgan. "I have just been hearing a dreadful story about you; and I don't believe it in the least, Mr Wentworth," she continued, with a little effusion; for though she was very sensible, she was only a woman, and did not realise the possibility of having her sympathy rejected, and her favourable judgment received with indifference.

"I am much flattered by your good opinion. What was the dreadful story?" asked Mr Wentworth, looking at her with careless eyes. They were just opposite Elsworthy's shop, and could almost hear what he was saying, as he stood in the midst of his little group of listeners, talking loud and vehemently. The Perpetual Curate looked calmly at him across the road, and turned again to Mrs Morgan, repeating his question, "What was the dreadful story? – one gets used to romances," he said, with a composure too elaborate to be real; but Mrs Morgan did not think of that.

"If you don't care about it, I need not say anything," said the Rector's wife, who could not help feeling affronted. "But I am so sorry that Mr Morgan and you don't get on," she continued, after a little pause. "I have no right to speak; but I take an interest in everything that belongs to the parish. If you would put a little confidence in my husband, things might go on better; but, in the mean time, I thought I might say to you, on my own account, that I had heard this scandal, and that I don't believe in it. If you do not understand my motive I can't help it," said the Rector's wife, who was now equally ready for friendship or for battle.

"Thanks; I understand what you mean," said Mr Wentworth, who had come to himself. "But will you tell me what it is you don't believe in?" he asked, with a smile which Mrs Morgan did not quite comprehend.

"I will tell you," she said, with a little quiet exasperation. "I don't think you would risk your prospects, and get yourself into trouble, and damage your entire life, for the sake of any girl, however pretty she might be. Men don't do such things for women nowadays, even when it is a worthy object," said the disappointed optimist. "And I believe you are a great deal more sensible, Mr Wentworth." There was just that tone of mingled approval and contempt in this speech which a woman knows how to deliver herself of without any appearance of feeling; and which no young man, however *blasé*, can hear with composure.

"Perhaps not," he said, with a little heat and a rising colour. "I am glad you think me so sensible." And then there ensued a pause, upon the issue of which depended the question of peace or war between these two. Mr Wentworth's good angel, perhaps, dropped softly through the dusky air at that moment, and jogged his perverse charge with the tip of a celestial wing. "And yet there might be women in the world for whom—" said the Curate; and stopped again. "I daresay you are not anxious to know my sentiments on the subject," he continued, with a little laugh. "I am sorry you think so badly – I mean so well of me."

"I don't think badly of you," said Mrs Morgan, hastily. "Thank you for walking with me; and whatever happens, remember that I for one don't believe a word of it," she said, holding out her hand. After this little declaration of friendship, the Rector's wife returned to the Rectory, where her husband was waiting for her, more than ever prepared to stand up for Mr Wentworth. She went back to the drawing-room, forgetting all about the carpet, and poured out the tea with satisfaction, and made herself very agreeable to Mr Finial, the architect, who had come to talk over the restorations. In that moment of stimulation she forgot all her experience of her husband's puzzled looks, of the half-comprehension with which he looked at her, and the depths of stubborn determination which were far beyond the reach of her hastier and more generous spirit, and so went on with more satisfaction and gaiety than she had felt possible for a long time, beating her drums and blowing her trumpets, to the encounter in which her female forces were so confident of victory.

CHAPTER XXIX.

Mr Wentworth went upon his way, after he had parted from Mrs Morgan, with a moment's gratitude; but he had not gone half-a-dozen steps before that amiable sentiment yielded to a sense of soreness and vexation. He had almost acknowledged that he was conscious of the slander against which he had made up his mind to present a blank front of unconsciousness and passive resistance, and he was angry with himself for his susceptibility to this unexpected voice of kindness. He was going home, but he did not care for going home. Poor Mrs Hadwin's anxious looks of suspicion had added to the distaste with which he thought of encountering again the sullen shabby rascal to whom he had given shelter. It was Saturday night, and he had still his sermon to prepare for the next day; but the young man was in a state of disgust with all the circumstances of his lot, and could not make up his mind to go in and address himself to his work as he ought to have done. Such a sense of injustice and cruelty as possessed him was not likely to promote composition, especially as the pulpit addresses of the Curate of St Roque's were not of a declamatory kind. To think that so many years' work could be neutralised in a day by a sudden breath of scandal, made him not humble or patient, but fierce and resentful. He had been in Wharfside that afternoon, and felt convinced that even the dying woman at No. 10 Prickett's Lane had heard of Rosa Elsworthy; and he saw, or imagined he saw, many a distrustful inquiring glance thrown at him by people to whom he had been a kind of secondary Providence. Naturally the mere thought of the failing allegiance of the "district" went to Mr Wentworth's heart. When he turned round suddenly from listening to a long account of one poor family's distresses, and saw Tom Burrows, the gigantic bargeman, whose six children the Curate had baptised in a lump, and whose baby had been held at the font by Lucy Wodehouse herself, looking at him wistfully with rude affection, and something that looked very much like pity, it is impossible to describe the bitterness that welled up in the mind of the Perpetual Curate. Instead of leaving Wharfside comforted as he usually did, he came away wounded and angry, feeling to its full extent the fickleness of popular sympathy. And when he came into Grange Lane and saw the shutters closed, and Mr Wodehouse's green door shut fast, as if never more to open, all sources of consolation seemed to be shut against him. Even the habit he had of going into Elsworthy's to get his newspaper, and to hear what talk might be current in Carlingford, contributed to the sense of utter discomfort and wretchedness which overwhelmed him. Men in other positions have generally to consult the opinion of their equals only; but all sorts of small people can plant thorns in the path of a priest who has given himself with fervour to the duties of his office. True enough, such clouds blow by, and sometimes leave behind a sky clearer than before; but that result is doubtful, and Mr Wentworth was not of the temper to comfort himself with philosophy. He felt ingratitude keenly, as men do at eight-and-twenty, even when they have made up their minds that gratitude is a delusion; and still more keenly, with deep resentment and indignation, he felt the horrible doubt which had diffused itself around him, and seemed to be looking at him out of everybody's eyes. In such a state of mind one bethinks one's self of one's relations – those friends not always congenial, but whom one looks to instinctively, when one is young, in the crisis of life. He knocked at his aunts' door almost without knowing it, as he went down Grange Lane, after leaving Mrs Morgan, with vague sentences of his sermon floating in his mind through all the imbroglio of other thoughts. Even aunt Dora's foolish affection might have been a little comfort at the moment, and he could not but be a little curious to know whether they had heard Elsworthy's story, and what the patronesses of Skelmersdale thought of the matter. Somehow, just then, in the midst of his distresses, a vision of Skelmersdale burst upon the Perpetual Curate like a glimpse of a better world. If he could but escape there out of all this sickening misconception and ingratitude – if he could but take Lucy into his protecting arms, and carry her away far from the clouds that were gathering over her path as well as his own. The thought found vent in an impatient long-drawn sigh, and was then expelled contemptuously from the young man's bosom. If a hundred Skelmersdales were in his power, here, where his honour had been attacked, it was necessary to remain, in the face of all obstacles, till it was cleared.

The Miss Wentworths had just come up to the drawing-room after dinner when their nephew entered. As for Miss Dora, she had seated herself by the window, which was open, and, with her light little curls fluttering upon her cheek, was watching a tiny puff of smoke by the side of the great laurel, which indicated the spot occupied at this moment by Jack and his cigar. "Dear fellow, he does enjoy the quiet," she said, with a suppressed little sniff of emotion. "To think we should be in such a misery about poor dear Frank, and have Jack, about whom we have all been so unbelieving, sent to us for a consolation. My poor brother will be so happy," said Miss Dora, almost crying at the thought. She was under the influence of this sentiment when the Curate entered. It was perhaps impossible for Mr Wentworth to present himself before his three aunts at the present crisis without a certain consciousness in his looks; and it was well that it was twilight, and he could not read distinctly all that was written in their countenances. Miss Cecilia held out her lovely old hand to him first of all. She said, "How do you do, Frank?" which was not very original, but yet counted for a good deal in the silence. When he came up to her, she offered him her sweet old cheek with a look of pity which touched, and yet affronted, the Perpetual Curate. He thought it was the wisest way to accept the challenge at once.

"It is very good of you, but you need not be sorry for me," he said, as he sat down by her. And then there was a little pause – an awful pause; for Miss Wentworth had no further observations to offer, and Miss Dora, who had risen up hastily, dropped into her chair again in a disconsolate condition, when she saw that her nephew did not take any notice of her. The poor little woman sat down with miserable sensations, and did not find the comfort she hoped for in contemplation of the smoke of Jack's cigar. After all, it was Frank who was the original owner of Miss Dora's affections. When she saw him, as she thought, in a state of guilt and trouble, received with grim silence by the dreaded Leonora, the poor lady began to waver greatly, divided between a longing to return to her old allegiance, and a certain pride in the new bonds which bound her to so great a sinner as Jack. She could not help feeling the distinction of having such a reprobate in her hands. But the sight of Frank brought back old habits, and Miss Dora felt at her wits' end, and could not tell what to do.

At length Miss Leonora's voice, which was decided contralto, broke the silence. "I am very glad to see you, Frank," said the strong-minded aunt. "From something we heard, I supposed you had gone away for a time, and we were rather anxious about your movements. There are so many things going on in the family just now, that one does not know what to think. I am glad to see you are still in Carlingford."

"I never had the least intention of going away," said Mr

Wentworth. "I can't imagine who could tell you so."

"Nobody told us," said Miss Leonora; "we drew that conclusion from other things we heard. Dora, give Frank the newspaper with that paragraph about Gerald. I have prophesied from the very first which way Gerald was tending. It is very shocking of him, and I don't know what they are to do, for Louisa is an expensive little fool; and if he leaves the Rectory, they can't have enough to live on. If you knew what your brother was going to do, why didn't you advise him otherwise? Besides, he will be wretched," said the discriminating woman. "I never approved of his ways, but I could not say anything against his sincerity. I believe his heart was in his work; a man may be very zealous, and yet very erroneous," said Miss Leonora, like an oracle, out of the shadows.

"I don't know if he is erroneous or not – but I know I should like to punch this man's head," said the Curate, who had taken the paper to the window, where there was just light enough to make out the paragraph. He stood looming over Miss Dora, a great black shadow against the fading light. "All the mischief in the world comes of these villanous papers," said Mr Wentworth. "Though I did not think anybody nowadays believed in the 'Chronicle.' Gerald has not gone over to Rome, and I don't think he means to go. I daresay you have agitated yourselves unnecessarily about more than one supposed event in the family," he continued, throwing the paper on the table. "I don't know anything very alarming that has happened as yet, except, perhaps, the prodigal's return," said the Perpetual Curate, with a slight touch of bitterness. His eye had just lighted on Jack sauntering through the garden with his cigar; and Mr Wentworth was human, and could not entirely refrain from the expression of his sentiments.

"But oh, Frank, my dear, you are not angry about poor Jack?" said Miss Dora. "He has not known what it was to be at home for years and years. A stepmother is so different from an own mother, and he never has had any

opportunities; and oh, Frank, don't you remember that
there is joy in heaven?" cried the anxious aunt – "not to
say that he is the eldest son. And it is such a thing for the
family to see him changing his ways in such a beautiful
spirit!" said Miss Dora. The room was almost dark by this
time, and she did not see that her penitent had entered
while she spoke.

"It is very consoling to gain your approval, aunt Dora,"
said Jack. "My brother Frank doesn't know me. If the
Squire *will* make a nursery of his house, what can a man
do? But a fellow can't be quite ruined as long as he has—"
aunts, the reprobate was about to say, with an inflection of
laughter intended for Frank's ear only in his voice; but he
fortunately remembered in time that Miss Leonora had an
acute intelligence, and was not to be trifled with – "As long
as he has female relations," said Jack, in his most feeling
tone. "Men never sympathise with men." He seemed to
be apologising for Frank's indifference, as well as for his
own sins. He had just had a very good dinner – for the
Miss Wentworths' cook was the best in Carlingford – and
Jack, whose digestion was perfect, was disposed to please
everybody, and had, in particular, no disposition to
quarrel with Frank.

"Oh, my dear, you see how humble and forgiving he
is," said Miss Dora, rising on tiptoe to whisper into the
Curate's ear; "and always takes your part whenever you
are mentioned," said the injudicious aunt. Meantime the
other sisters were very silent, sitting each in the midst of
her own group of shadows. Then Miss Leonora rose with a
sudden rustling of all her draperies, and with her own
energetic hand rang the bell.

"Now the lamp is coming," said Jack, in a tone of
despair, "a bright, blank, pitiless globe like the world; and
instead of this delicious darkness, where one can see
nothing distinctly, my heart will be torn asunder for the
rest of the evening by the sight of suicide. Why do we ever
have lights?" said the exquisite, laying himself down softly

on a sofa. When the lamp was brought in, Jack became visible stretched out in an attitude of perfect repose and tranquillity, with a quiet conscience written in every fold of his scrupulous apparel. As for Frank, on the contrary, he was still in morning dress, and was biting his nails, and had a cloud upon his brow which the sudden light disclosed like a traitor before he was prepared for it. Between the two brothers such a contrast was visible that it was not surprising if Miss Dora, still wavering in her allegiance, went back with relief to the calm countenance of her penitent, and owned to herself with trembling that the Curate looked preoccupied and guilty. Perhaps Miss Leonora came to a similar conclusion. She seated herself at her writing-table with her usual air of business, and made a pen to a hard point by the light of the candles, which were sacred to her particular use.

"I heard some news this morning which pleased me very much," said Miss Leonora. "I daresay you remember Julia Trench? You two used to be a great deal together at one time. She is going to be married to Mr Shirley's excellent curate, who is a young man of the highest character. He did very well at the university, I believe," said the patroness of Skelmersdale; "but I confess I don't care much for academical honours. He is an excellent clergyman, which is a great deal more to the purpose, and I thoroughly agree with his views. So, knowing the interest we take in Julia, you may think how pleased we were," said Miss Leonora, looking full into her nephew's face. He knew what she meant as distinctly as if she had put it in words.

"When is old Shirley going to die?" said Jack from the sofa. "It's rather hard upon Frank, keeping him out of the living so long; and if I were you, I'd be jealous of this model curate," said the fine gentleman, with a slight civil yawn. "I don't approve of model curates upon family livings. People are apt to make comparisons," said Jack, and then he raised his head with a little energy – "Ah, there it is," said the Sybarite, "the first moth. Don't be precipitate, my dear fellow. Aunt Dora, pray sit quietly where you are, and don't disturb our operations. It is only a moth, to be sure; but don't let us cut short the moments of a creature that has no hereafter," said Jack, solemnly. He disturbed them all by this eccentric manifestation of benevolence, and flapped his handkerchief round Miss Dora, upon whose white cap the unlucky moth, frightened by its benefactor's vehemence, was fluttering wildly. Jack even forgot himself so far as to swear softly in French at the frightened insect as it flew wildly off at a tangent, not to the open window, but to Miss Leonora's candles, where it came to an immediate end. Miss Leonora sat rather grimly looking on at all this byplay. When her elegant nephew threw himself back once more upon his sofa, she glanced from him to his brother with a comparison which perhaps was not so much to the disadvantage of the Perpetual Curate. But even Miss Leonora, though so sensible, had her weaknesses; and she was very evangelical, and could put up with a great deal from the sinner who had placed himself for conversion in her hands.

"We have too great a sense of our responsibility to treat Skelmersdale simply as a family living," she said. "Besides, Frank of course is to have Wentworth Rectory. Gerald's perversion is a great blow; but still, if it *is* to be, Frank will be provided for at least. As for our parish—"

"I beg your pardon," said the Curate; "I have not the least intention of leaving Carlingford. At the present moment neither Skelmersdale nor Wentworth would tempt me. I am in no doubt as to where my work lies, and there is enough of it to satisfy any man." He could not help thinking, as he spoke, of ungrateful Wharfside, for which he had done so much, and the recollection brought a little flush of indignant colour to his cheek.

"Oh, Frank, my dear," said Miss Dora in a whisper, stealing up to him, "if it is not true, you must not mind. Oh, my dear boy, nobody will mind it if it is not true." She put her hand timidly upon his arm as she reached up to his ear, and at the same time the poor little woman, who was trying all she could to serve two masters, kept one eye upon Jack, lest her momentary return to his brother might have a disastrous effect upon the moral reformation which she was nursing with so much care. As for the Curate, he gave her a hasty glance, which very nearly made an end of Miss Dora. She retired to her seat with no more courage to say anything, unable to make out whether it was virtuous reproach or angry guilt which looked at her so sternly. She felt her headache coming on as she sank again upon her chair. If she could but have stolen away to her own room, and had a good comforting cry in the dark, it might have kept off the headache; but then she had to be faithful to her post, and to look after the reformation of Jack.

"I have no doubt that a great work might be done in Carlingford," said Miss Leonora, "if you would take my advice and organise matters properly, and make due provision for the lay element. As for Sisters of Mercy, I never had any belief in them. They only get young clergymen into mischief," said the strong-minded aunt. "We are going to have tea, Frank, if you will have some. Poor Mr Shirley has got matters into very bad order at Skelmersdale, but things will be different under the new incumbent, I hope," said Miss Leonora, shooting a side-glance of keen inspection at the Curate, who bore it steadily.

"I hope he will conduct himself to your satisfaction," said Mr Wentworth, with a bland but somewhat grim aspect, from the window; "but I can't wait for tea. I have still got some of my work to do for to-morrow; so good-night."

"I'll walk with you, Frank," said his elder brother. "My dear aunts, don't look alarmed; nothing can happen to me. There are few temptations in Grange Lane; and, besides, I shall come back directly. *I* cannot do without my tea," said Jack, by way of consoling poor Miss Dora, who had

started with consternation at the proposal. And the two
brothers went out into the fresh evening air together, their
aunt Dora watching them from the window with
inexpressible anxiety; for perhaps it was not quite right for
a clergyman to saunter out of doors in the evening with
such a doubtful member of society as Jack; and perhaps
Frank, having himself fallen into evil ways, might hinder
or throw obstacles in the way of his brother's re-establish-
ment in the practice of all the virtues. Miss Dora, who had
to carry them both upon her shoulders, and who got no
sympathy in the present case from her hard-hearted
sisters, was fain at last to throw a shawl over her head and
steal out to that summer-house which was built into the
garden-wall, and commanded Grange Lane from its little
window. There she established herself in the darkness, an
affectionate spy. There ought to have been a moon that
night, and accordingly the lamps were not lighted at that
end of Grange Lane, for the authorities in Carlingford
bore a frugal mind. But the sky had become cloudy, and
the moon shone only at intervals, which gave a certain
character of mystery and secrecy to the night. Through
this uncertain light the anxious woman saw her two
nephews coming and going under the window, apparently
in the most eager conversation. Miss Dora's anxiety grew
to such a height that she opened softly a chink of the
window in hopes of being able to hear as well as to see, but
that attempt was altogether unsuccessful. Then, when
they had walked about for half an hour, which looked like
two hours to Miss Dora, who was rapidly taking one of her
bad colds at the half-open window, they were joined by
another figure which she did not think she had ever seen
before. The excitement was growing tremendous, and the
aspect of the three conspirators more and more alarming,
when the poor lady started with a little scream at a noise
behind her, and turning round, saw her maid, severe as a
pursuing Fate, standing at the door. "After giving me your
word as you wouldn't come no more?" said the reproachful

despot who swayed Miss Dora's soul. After that she had to make the best of her way indoors, thankful not to be carried to her room and put into hot water, which was the original intention of Collins. But it would be impossible to describe the emotions of Miss Dora's mind after this glimpse into the heart of the volcano on which her innocent feet were standing. Unless it were murder or high treason, what could they have to plot about? or was the mysterious stranger a disguised Jesuit, and the whole business some terrible Papist conspiracy? Jack, who had been so much abroad, and Gerald, who was going over to Rome, and Frank, who was in trouble of every description, got entangled together in Miss Dora's disturbed imagination. No reality could be so frightful as the fancies with which she distracted herself after that peep from the summer-house; and it would be impossible to describe the indignation of Collins, who knew that her mistress would kill herself some day, and was aware that she, in her own person, would get little rest that night.

CHAPTER XXX.

"I don't know what is the exact connection between tea and reformation," said Jack Wentworth, with a wonderful yawn. "When I consider that this is all on account of that stupid beast Wodehouse, I feel disposed to eat him. By the way, they have got a capital cook; I did not think such a *cuisine* was the sort of thing to be found in the bosom of one's family, which has meant boiled mutton up to this moment, to my uninstructed imagination. But the old ladies are in a state of excitement which, I presume, is unusual to them. It appears you have been getting into scrapes like other people, though you are a parson. As your elder brother, my dear Frank—"

"Look here," said the Perpetual Curate; "you want to ask about Wodehouse. I will answer your questions, since you seem to have some interest in him; but I don't speak of my private affairs to any but my intimate friends," said Mr Wentworth, who was not in a humour to be trifled with.

The elder brother shrugged his shoulders. "It is curious to remark the progress of the younger members of one's family," he said, reflectively. "When you were a little boy, you took your drubbings dutifully; but never mind, we've another subject in hand. I take an interest in Wodehouse, and so do you – I can't tell for what reason. Perhaps he is one of the intimate friends with whom you discuss your private affairs? but that is a matter quite apart from the subject. The thing is that he has to be taken care of – not for his own sake, as I don't need to explain to you," said Jack. "I hear the old fellow died today, which was the best thing he could have done, upon the whole. Perhaps you can tell me how much he had, and how he has left it? We may have to take different sides, and the fellow himself is a snob; but I should like to understand exactly the state of affairs between you and me as gentlemen," said the heir of the Wentworths. Either a passing spasm of compunction passed over him as he said the word, or it was the moon, which had just flung aside the last fold of cloud and burst out upon them as they turned back facing her. "When we know how the affair stands, we can either negotiate or fight," he added, puffing a volume of smoke from his cigar. "Really a very fine effect – that little church of yours comes well against that bit of sky. It looks like a Constable, or rather it would look like a Constable, thrusting up that bit of spire into the blue, if it happened to be daylight," said Jack, making a tube of his hand, and regarding the picture with great interest. Miss Dora at her window beheld the movement with secret horror and apprehension, and took it for some mysterious sign.

"I know nothing about Mr Wodehouse's property," said
the Curate: "I wish I knew enough law to understand it.
He has left no will, I believe;" and Mr Wentworth watched
his brother's face with no small interest as he spoke.

"Very like a Constable," said Jack, still with his hands
to his eyes. "These clouds to the right are not a bad
imitation of some effects of his. I beg your pardon, but
Constable is my passion. And so old Wodehouse has left
no will? What *has* he left? some daughters? Excuse my
curiosity," said the elder brother. "I am a man of the
world, you know. If you like this other girl well enough to
compromise yourself on her account (which, mind you, I
think a great mistake), you can't mean to go in at the same
time for that pretty sister, eh? It's a sort of sport I don't
attempt myself – though it may be the correct thing for a
clergyman, for anything I can tell to the contrary," said
the tolerant critic.

Mr Wentworth had swallowed down the interruptions
that rushed to his lips, and heard his brother out with
unusual patience. After all, perhaps Jack was the only
man in the world whom he could ask to advise him in such
an emergency. "I take it for granted that you don't mean
to insult either me or my profession," he said, gravely;
"and, to tell the truth, here is one point upon which I
should be glad of your help. I am convinced that it is
Wodehouse who has carried away this unfortunate girl.
She is a little fool, and he has imposed upon her. If you
can get him to confess this, and to restore her to her
friends, you will lay me under the deepest obligation,"
said the Perpetual Curate, with unusual energy. "I don't
mind telling you that such a slander disables me, and goes
to my heart." When he had once begun to speak on the
subject, he could not help expressing himself fully; and
Jack, who had grown out of acquaintance with the nobler
sentiments, woke up with a slight start through all his
moral being to recognise the thrill of subdued passion and
scorn and grief which was in his brother's voice. Innocent

Miss Dora, who knew no evil, had scarcely a doubt in *her* mind that Frank was guilty; but Jack, who scarcely knew what goodness was, acquitted his brother instantaneously, and required no other proof. Perhaps if he had been capable of any impression beyond an intellectual one, this little incident might, in Miss Dora's own language, have "done him good."

"So you have nothing to do with it?" he said, with a smile. "Wodehouse! but then the fellow hasn't a penny. I see some one skulking along under the walls that looks like him. Hist! Smith – Tom – what do they call you? We want you here," said Jack, upon whom the moon was shining full. When he stood in his evening coat and spotless breadth of linen, the heir of the Wentworths was ready to meet the eye of all the world. His shabby subordinate stopped short, with a kind of sullen admiration, to look at him. Wodehouse knew the nature of Jack Wentworth's pursuits a great deal better than his brother did, and that some of them would not bear much investigation; but when he saw him stand triumphant in gorgeous apparel, fearing no man, the poor rascal, whom everybody kicked at, rose superior to his own misfortunes. He had not made much of it in his own person, but that life was not altogether a failure which had produced Jack Wentworth. He obeyed his superior's call with instinctive fidelity, proud, in spite of himself, to be living the same life and sharing the same perils. When he emerged into the moonlight, his shaggy countenance looked excited and haggard. Notwithstanding all his experiences, he was not of a constitution which could deny nature. He had inflicted every kind of torture upon his father while living; but, notwithstanding, the fact of the death affected him. His eyes looked wilder than usual, and his face older and more worn, and he looked round him with a kind of clandestine skulking instinct as he came out of the shadow into the light.

This was the terrible conjunction which Miss Dora saw from her window. The anxious woman did not wait long

enough to be aware that the Curate left the other two to
such consultations as were inevitable between them, and
went away very hastily to his own house, and to the work
which still awaited him – "When the wicked man turneth
away from the evil of his ways, and doeth that which is
lawful and right." Mr Wentworth, when he came back to
it, sat for about an hour over his text before he wrote a
single syllable. His heart had been wrung that day by the
sharpest pangs which can be inflicted upon a proud and
generous spirit. He was disposed to be bitter against all
the world – against the dull eyes that would not see, the
dull ears that could shut themselves against all suggestions
either of gratitude or justice. It appeared to him, on the
whole, that the wicked man was every way the best off in
this world, besides being wooed and besought to accept
the blessings of the other. And the Curate was conscious of
an irrepressible inclination to exterminate the human
vermin who made the earth such an imbroglio of distress
and misery; and was sore and wounded in his heart to feel
how his own toils and honest purposes availed him nothing,
and how all the interest and sympathy of bystanders went
to the pretender. These sentiments naturally complicated
his thoughts, and made composition difficult; not to say
that they added a thrill of human feeling warmer than
usual to the short and succinct sermon. It was not an
emotional sermon, in the ordinary sense of the word; but it
was so for Mr Wentworth, who carried to an extreme point
the Anglican dislike for pulpit exaggeration in all forms.
The Perpetual Curate was not a natural orator. He had
very little of the eloquence which gave Mr Vincent so
much success in the Dissenting connection during his short
stay in Carlingford, which was a kind of popularity not
much to the taste of the Churchman. But Mr Wentworth
had a certain faculty of concentrating his thoughts into the
tersest expression, and of uttering in a very few words, as
if they did not mean anything particular, ideas which were
always individual, and often of distinct originality – a kind

of utterance which is very dear to the English mind. As was natural, there were but a limited amount of people able to find him out; but those who did so were rather fond of talking about the "restrained power" of the Curate of St Roque's.

Next morning was a glorious summer Sunday – one of those days of peace on which this tired old earth takes back her look of innocence, and deludes herself with thoughts of Eden. To be sure, there were tumults enough going on over her surface – vulgar merry-makings and noises, French drums beating, all kinds of discordant sounds going on here and there, by land and sea, under that tranquil impartial sun. But the air was very still in Carlingford, where you could hear the bees in the lime-blossoms as you went to church in the sunshine. All that world of soft air in which the embowered houses of Grange Lane lay beatified, was breathing sweet of the limes; but notwithstanding the radiance of the day, people were talking of other subjects as they came down under the shadow of the garden-walls to St Roque's. There was a great stream of people – greater than usual; for Carlingford was naturally anxious to see how Mr Wentworth would conduct himself in such an emergency. On one side of the way Mr Wodehouse's hospitable house, shut up closely, and turning all its shuttered windows to the light, which shone serenely indifferent upon the blank frames, stood silent, dumbly contributing its great moral to the human holiday; and on the other, Elsworthy's closed shop, with the blinds drawn over the cheerful windows above, where little Rosa once amused herself watching the passengers, interposed a still more dreadful discordance. The Carlingford people talked of both occurrences with composure as they went to St Roque's. They were sorry, and shocked, and very curious; but that wonderful moral atmosphere of human indifference and self-regard which surrounds every individual soul, kept their feelings quite within bounds. Most people wondered much what Mr Wentworth would

say; whether he would really venture to face the Carlingford world; whether he would take refuge in a funeral
sermon for Mr Wodehouse; or how it was possible for him
to conduct himself under such circumstances. When the
greater part of the congregation was seated, Miss Leonora
Wentworth, all by herself, in her iron-grey silk, which
rustled like a breeze along the narrow passage, although
she wore no crinoline, went up to a seat immediately in
front, close to Mr Wentworth's choristers, who just then
came trooping in in their white surplices, looking like
angels of unequal height and equivocal reputation. Miss
Leonora placed herself in the front row of a little group of
benches arranged at the side, just where the Curate's wife
would have been placed, had he possessed such an
appendage. She looked down blandly upon the many lines
of faces turned towards her, accepting their inspection
with perfect composure. Though her principles were
Evangelical, Miss Leonora was still a Wentworth, and a
woman. She had not shown any sympathy for her nephew
on the previous night; but she had made up her mind to
stand by him, without saying anything about her determination. This incident made a great impression on the
mind of Carlingford. Most likely it interfered with the
private devotions, from which a few heads popped up
abruptly as she passed; but she was very devout and
exemplary in her own person, and set a good example, as
became the clergyman's aunt.

Excitement rose very high in St Roque's when Mr
Wentworth came into the reading-desk, and Elsworthy,
black as a cloud, became visible underneath. The clerk
had not ventured to absent himself, nor to send a substitute
in his place. Never, in the days when he was most devoted
to Mr Wentworth, had Elsworthy been more determined
to accompany him through every particular of the service.
They had stood together in the little vestry, going through
all the usual preliminaries, the Curate trying hard to talk
as if nothing had happened, the clerk going through all his

duties in total silence. Perhaps there never was a church
service in Carlingford which was followed with such intense
interest by all the eyes and ears of the congregation.
When the sermon came, it took Mr Wentworth's admirers
by surprise, though they could not at the moment make
out what it was that puzzled them. Somehow the perverse
manner in which for once the Curate treated that wicked
man who is generally made so much of in sermons, made
his hearers slightly ashamed of themselves. As for Miss
Leonora, though she could not approve of his sentiments,
the thought occurred to her that Frank was not nearly so
like his mother's family as she had supposed him to be.
When the service was over, she kept her place, steadily
watching all the worshippers out, who thronged out a great
deal more hastily than usual to compare notes, and ask
each other what they thought. "I can't fancy he looks
guilty," an eager voice here and there kept saying over
and over. But on the whole, after they had got over the
momentary impression made by his presence and aspect,
the opinion of Carlingford remained unchanged; which
was – that, notwithstanding all the evidence of his previous
life, it was quite believable that Mr Wentworth was a
seducer and a villain, and ought to be brought to condign
punishment; but that in the mean time it was very
interesting to watch the progress of this startling little
drama; and that he himself, instead of merely being the
Curate of St Roque's, had become a most captivating
enigma, and had made chuch-going itself half as good as a
play.

As for Miss Leonora, she waited for her nephew, and,
when he was ready, took his arm and walked with him up
Grange Lane to her own door, where they encountered
Miss Wentworth and Miss Dora returning from church,
and overwhelmed them with astonishment. But it was not
about his own affairs that they talked. Miss Leonora did
not say a word to her nephew about himself. She was
talking of Gerald most of the time, and inquiring into all

the particulars of the Squire's late "attack." And she
would very fain have found out what Jack's motive was in
coming to Carlingford; but as for Rosa Elsworthy and her
concerns, the strong-minded woman ignored them completely. Mr Wentworth even went with her to lunch, on
her urgent invitation; and it was from his aunts' house that
he took his way to Wharfside, pausing at the green door to
ask after the Miss Wodehouses, who were, John said,
with solemnity, as well as could be expected. They were
alone, and they did not feel equal to seeing anybody —
even Mr Wentworth; and the Perpetual Curate, who
would have given all he had in the world for permission to
soothe Lucy in her sorrow, went away sadly from the
hospitable door, which was now for the first time closed to
him. He could not go to Wharfside, to the "district"
through which they had so often gone together, about
which they had talked, when all the little details discussed
were sweet with the love which they did not name,
without going deeper and deeper into that sweet shadow
of Lucy which was upon his way wherever he went. He
could not help missing her voice when the little choir,
which was so feeble without her, sang the 'Magnificat,'
which, somehow, Mr Wentworth always associated with
her image. He read the same sermon to the Wharfside
people which he had preached in St Roque's, and saw,
with a little surprise, that it drew tears from the eyes of his
more open-hearted hearers, who did not think of the
proprieties. He could see their hands stealing up to their
faces, and a great deal of persistent winking on the part of
the stronger members of the congregation. At the close of
the service Tom Burrows came up to the Curate with a
downcast countenance. "Please, sir, if I've done ye
injustice in my own mind, as went sore against the grain,
and wouldn't have happened but for the women, I axes
your pardon," said the honest bargeman, which was balm
and consolation to Mr Wentworth. There was much talk in
Prickett's Lane on the subject as he went to see the sick

woman in No. 10. "There aint no doubt as he sets our duty before us clear," said one family mother; "he don't leave the men no excuse for their goings-on. He all but named the Bargeman's Arms out plain, as it was the place all mischief comes from." "If he'd have married Miss Lucy, like other folks, at Easter," said one of the brides whom Mr Wentworth had blessed, "such wicked stories couldn't never have been made up." "A story may be made up, or it mayn't be made up," said a more experienced matron; "but it can't be put out of the world unbeknowst no more nor a babby. I don't believe in stories getting up that aint true. I don't say as he don't do his duty; but things was different in Mr Bury's time, as was the real Rector; and, as I was a-saying, a tale's like a babby – it may come when it didn't ought to come, or when it aint wanted, but you can't do away with it, anyhow as you like to try." Mr Wentworth did not hear this dreary prediction as he went back again into the upper world. He was in much better spirits, on the whole. He had calmed his own mind and moved the hearts of others, which is to every man a gratification, even though nothing higher should be involved. And he had regained the moral countenance of Tom Burrows, which most of all was a comfort to him. More than ever he longed to go and tell Lucy as he passed by the green door. Tom Burrows's repentant face recalled Mr Wentworth's mind to the fact that a great work was doing in Wharfside, which, after all, was more worth thinking of than any tantalising vision of an impossible benefice. But this very thought, so consoling in itself, reminded him of all his vexations, of the public inquiry into his conduct which was hanging over him, and of his want of power to offer to Lucy the support and protection of which she might so soon stand in need; and having thus drawn upon his head once more his whole burden of troubles, Mr Wentworth went in to eat his dinner with what appetite he could.

The Perpetual Curate sat up late that night, as indeed

was his custom. He sat late, hearing, as everybody does
who sits up alone in a hushed and sleeping household, a
hundred fantastic creaks and sounds which did not mean
anything, and of which he took no notice. Once, indeed,
when it was nearly midnight, he fancied he heard the
garden-gate close hurriedly, but explained it to himself as
people do when they prefer not to give themselves trouble.
About one o'clock in the morning, however, Mr Wentworth
could no longer be in any doubt that some stealthy step
was passing his door and moving about the house. He was
not alarmed, for Mrs Hadwin had occasional "attacks,"
like most people of her age; but he put down his pen and
listened. No other sound was to be heard except this
stealthy step, no opening of doors, nor whisper of voices,
nor commotion of any kind; and after a while Mr Wentworth's curiosity was fully awakened. When he heard it
again, he opened his door suddenly, and threw a light
upon the staircase and little corridor into which his room
opened. The figure he saw there startled him more than if
it had been a midnight robber. It was only Sarah, the
housemaid, white and shivering with terror, who fell down
upon her knees before him. "Oh, Mr Wentworth, it aint
my fault!" cried Sarah. The poor girl was only partially
dressed, and trembled pitifully. "They'll say it was my
fault; and oh, sir, it's my character I'm a-thinking of," said
Sarah, with a sob; and the Curate saw behind her the door
of Wodehouse's room standing open, and the moonlight
streaming into the empty apartment. "I daren't go down-
stairs to see if he's took anything," cried poor Sarah,
under her breath; "there might be more of them about the
place. But oh, Mr Wentworth, if Missis finds out as I gave
him the key, what will become of me?" Naturally, it was
her own danger which had most effect upon Sarah. Her full,
good-humoured face was all wet and stained with crying,
her lips quivering, her eyes dilated. Perhaps a thrill of
private disappointment mingled with her dread of losing
her character. "He used to tell me all as he was a-going to

do," said Sarah; "but, oh, sir, he's been and gone away,
and I daren't go down-stairs to look at the plate, and I'll
never more sleep in quiet, if I was to live a century. It aint
as I care for *him*, but it's the key and my character as I'm
a-thinking of," cried the poor girl, bursting into audible
sobs that could be restrained no longer. Mr Wentworth
took a candle and went into Wodehouse's empty room,
leaving her to recover her composure. Everything was
cleared and packed up in that apartment. The little
personal property he had, the shabby boots and worn
habiliments, had disappeared totally; even the rubbish of
wood-carving on his table was cleared away. Not a trace
that he had been there a few hours ago remained in the
place. The Curate came out of the room with an anxious
countenance, not knowing what to make of it. And by this
time Sarah's sobs had roused Mrs Hadwin, who stood,
severe and indignant, at her own door in her nightcap, to
know what was the matter. Mr Wentworth retired into his
own apartments after a word of explanation, leaving the
mistress and maid to fight it out. He himself was more
disturbed and excited than he could have described. He
could not tell what this new step meant, but felt instinctively that it denoted some new development in the
tangled web of his own fortunes. Some hidden danger
seemed to him to be gathering in the air over the house of
mourning, of which he had constituted himself a kind of
guardian. He could not sleep all night, but kept starting at
every sound, thinking now that the skulking rascal, who
was Lucy's brother, was coming back, and now that his
departure was only a dream. Mr Wentworth's restlessness
was not soothed by hearing all the night through, in the
silence of the house, suppressed sobs and sounds of
weeping proceeding from the attic overhead, which poor
Sarah shared with her fellow-servant. Perhaps the civilities
of "the gentleman" had dazzled Sarah, and been too much
for her peace of mind; perhaps it was only her character,
as the poor girl said. But as often as the Curate started

from his uneasy and broken snatches of sleep, he heard the murmur of crying and consoling up-stairs. Outside the night was spreading forth those sweetest unseen glories of the starlight and the moonlight and the silence, which Nature reserves for her own enjoyment, when the weary human creatures are out of the way and at rest; – and Jack Wentworth slept the sleep of the righteous, uttering delicate little indications of the depth of his slumber, which it would have been profane to call by any vulgar name. *He* slept sweetly while his brother watched and longed for daylight, impatient for the morrow which must bring forth something new. The moonlight streamed full into the empty room, and made mysterious combinations of the furniture, and chased the darkness into corners which each held their secret. This was how Mrs Hadwin's strange lodger, whom nobody could ever make out, disappeared as suddenly as he had come, without any explanations; and only a very few people could ever come to understand what he had to do with the after-events which struck Grange Lane dumb, and turned into utter confusion all the ideas and conclusions of society in Carlingford.

CHAPTER XXXI.

"I will do what I can for you," said Mr Morgan; "yours is a very hard case, as you say. Of course it would not do for me to give any opinion – but such a thing shall not occur in Carlingford, while I am here, without being looked into," said the Rector, with dignity; "of that you may be sure."

"I don't want no more nor justice," said Elsworthy – "no more nor justice. I'm a man as has always been respected, and never interfered with nobody as didn't interfere with me. The things I've stood from my clergyman, I wouldn't have stood from no man living. The way as he'd talk, sir, of them as was a deal better than himself! We was a happy family afore Mr Wentworth came nigh of us. Most folks in Carlingford knows me. There wasn't a more industrious family in Carlingford, though I say it as shouldn't, nor one as was more content, or took things more agreeable, afore Mr Wentworth come to put all wrong."

"Mr Wentworth has been here for five years," said the Rector's wife, who was present at this interview; "have things been going wrong for all that time?"

"I couldn't describe to nobody what I've put up with," said the clerk of St Roque's, evading the question. "He hadn't the ways of such clergymen as I've been used to. Twice the pay wouldn't have made up for what I've suffered in my feelings; and I ask you, sir, is this how it's all to end? My little girl's gone," cried Elsworthy, rising into hoarse earnestness – "my little girl as was so sweet, and as everybody took notice on. She's gone, and I don't know as I'll ever see her again; and I can't get no satis-faction one way or another; and I ask you, sir, is a villain as could do such a thing to hold up his head in the town, and go on the same as ever? I aint a man as is contrary, or as goes agin' my superiors; but it's driving me mad, that's what it's doing," said Elsworthy, wiping the moisture from his forehead. The man was trembling and haggard, changed even in his looks – his eyes were red with passion and watching, and looked like the eyes of a wild beast lying in wait for its prey. "I can't say as I've ever slept an hour since it happened," he cried; "and as for my missis, it's a-killing of her. We aint shut up, because we've got to live all the same; and because, if the poor thing come back, there's always an open door. But I'll have justice, if I was to die for it!" cried Elsworthy. "I don't ask no more than justice. If it aint to be had one way, I'll have it another. I'll set the police on him – I will. When a man's drove wild, he aint answerable for what he's a-doing; and to see him a-walking about Carlingford, and a-holding up his head, is a thing as I won't stand no longer, not if it was to be my ruin. I'm as good as ruined now, and I don't care." He broke off short with these words, and sat down abruptly on the chair Thomas had placed for him in front of the Rector's table. Up to this moment he had been standing, in his vehemence and agitation, without taking advantage of the courtesy accorded to his misfortune; now the poor man sat down by way of emphasis, and began to polish his hat round and round with his trembling hands.

As for Mr Morgan, he, on the contrary, got up and walked instinctively to the fireplace, and stood there with his back to the empty grate, contemplating the world in general with a troubled countenance, as was usual. Not to speak of his prejudice against Mr Wentworth, the Rector was moved by the sight of Elsworthy's distress; but then his wife, who unluckily had brought her needlework into the library on this particular morning, and who was in the interest of the Curate of St Roque's, was seated watchful by the window, occasionally looking up, and entirely cognisant, as Mr Morgan was aware, of everything that happened. The Rector was much embarrassed to feel himself thus standing between the two parties. "Yours is a very hard case – but it is necessary to proceed with caution, for, after all, there is not much proof," he said, faltering a little. "My dear, it is a pity to detain you from your walk," Mr Morgan continued, after a momentary pause, and looked with a flush of consciousness at his wife, whose absence would have been such a relief to him. Mrs Morgan looked up with a gracious smile.

"You are not detaining me, William – I am very much interested," said the designing woman, and immediately began to arrange and put in order what the Rector knew by experience to be a long piece of work, likely to last her an hour at least. Mr Morgan uttered a long breath, which sounded like a little snort of despair.

"It is very difficult to know what to do," said the

Rector, shifting uneasily upon the hearthrug, and plunging his hands into the depths of his pockets. "If you could name anybody you would like to refer it to – but being a brother clergyman—"

"A man as conducts himself like that, didn't ought to be a clergyman, sir," cried Elsworthy. "I'm one as listened to him preaching on Sunday, and could have jumped up and dragged him out of the pulpit, to hear him a-discoursing as if he wasn't a bigger sinner nor any there. I aint safe to stand it another Sunday. I'd do something as I should be sorry for after. I'm asking justice, and no more." With these words Elsworthy got up again, still turning round in his hands the unlucky hat, and turned his person, though not his eyes, towards Mrs Morgan. "No man could be more partial to his clergyman nor I was," he said hoarsely. "There was never a time as I wasn't glad to see him. He came in and out as if it belonged to him, and I had no more thought as he was meaning any harm than the babe unborn; but a man as meddles with an innocent girl aint nothing but a black-hearted villain!" cried Elsworthy, with a gleam out of his red eyes; "and I don't believe as anybody would take his part as knew all. I put my confidence in the Rector, as is responsible for the parish," he went on, facing round again: "not to say but what it's natural for them as are Mr Wentworth's friends to take his part – but I'll have justice, wherever it comes from. It's hard work to go again' any lady as I've a great respect for, and wouldn't cross for the world; but it aint in reason that I should be asked to bear it and not say nothing; and I'll have justice, if I should die for it," said Elsworthy. He turned from one to another as he spoke, but kept his eyes upon his hat, which he smoothed and smoothed as if his life depended on it. But for the reality of his excitement, his red eyes, and hoarse voice, he would have been a ludicrous figure, standing as he did in the middle of Mr Morgan's library, veering round, first to one side and then to the other, with his stooping head and ungainly person.

As for the Rector, he too kept looking at his wife with a very troubled face.

"It is difficult for me to act against a brother clergyman," said Mr Morgan; "but I am very sorry for you, Elsworthy – very sorry; if you could name, say, half-a-dozen gentlemen—"

"But don't you think," said the Rector's wife, interposing, "that you should inquire first whether there is any evidence? It would make you all look very ridiculous if you got up an inquiry and found no proof against Mr Wentworth. Is it likely he would do such a thing all at once without showing any signs of wickedness beforehand – is it possible? To be sorry is quite a different thing, but I don't see—"

"Ladies don't understand such matters," said the Rector, who had been kept at bay so long that he began to get desperate. "I beg your pardon, my dear, but it is not a matter for you to discuss. We shall take good care that there is plenty of evidence," said the perplexed man – "I mean, before we proceed to do anything," he added, growing very red and confused. When Mr Morgan caught his wife's eye, he got as nearly into a passion as was possible for so good a man. "You know what I mean," he said, in his peremptory way; "and, my dear, you will forgive me for saying this is not a matter to be discussed before a lady." When he had uttered this bold speech, the Rector took a few little walks up and down the room, not caring, however, to look at his wife. He was ashamed of the feeling he had that her absence would set him much more at ease with Elsworthy, but still could not help being conscious that it was so. He did not say anything more, but he walked up and down the room with sharp short steps, and betrayed his impatience very manifestly. As for Mrs Morgan, who was a sensible woman, she saw that the time had come for her to retire from the field.

"I think the first thing to be done is to try every possible means of finding the girl," she said, getting up from her seat; "but I have no doubt what you decide upon will be the best. You will find me in the drawing-room when you want me, William." Perhaps her absence for the first moment was not such a relief to her husband as he had expected. The mildness of her parting words made it very apparent that she did not mean to take offence; and he perceived suddenly, at a glance, that he would have to tell her all he was going to do, and encounter her criticism single-handed, which was rather an appalling prospect to the Rector. Mrs Morgan, for her part, went up-stairs not without a little vexation, certainly, but with a comforting sense of the opportunity which awaited her. She felt that, in his unprotected position, as soon as she left him, the Rector would conduct himself rashly, and that her time was still to come.

The Rector went back to the hearthrug when his wife left the room, but in the heat of his own personal reflections he did not say anything to Elsworthy, who still stood smoothing his hat in his hand. On the whole, Mr Morgan was rather aggravated for the moment by the unlucky cause of this little encounter, and was not half so well disposed towards Mr Wentworth's enemy as half an hour before, when he recognised his wife as the champion of the Curate, and felt controlled by her presence; for the human and even the clerical mind has its impulses of perversity. He began to get very impatient of Elsworthy's hat, and the persistent way in which he worked at it with his hands.

"I suppose you would not be so certain about it if you had not satisfactory evidence?" he said, turning abruptly, and even a little angrily, upon the supplicant; for Mr Morgan naturally resented his own temper and the little semi-quarrel he had got into upon the third person who was the cause of all.

"Sir," said Elsworthy, with eagerness, "it aint no wonder to me as the lady takes Mr Wentworth's part. A poor man don't stand no chance against a young gentleman as has had every advantage. It's a thing as I'm prepared for, and it don't have no effect upon me. A lady as is so respected and thought a deal of both in town and country—"

"I was not speaking of my wife," said the Rector, hastily. "don't you think you had better put down your hat? I think you said it was on Friday it occurred. It will be necessary to take down the facts in a business-like way," said Mr Morgan, drawing his chair towards the table and taking up his pen. This was how the Rector was occupied when Thomas announced the most unexpected of all possible visitors, Mr Proctor, who had been Mr Morgan's predecessor in Carlingford. Thomas announced his old master with great solemnity as "the late Rector" — a title which struck the present incumbent with a sense of awe not unnatural in the circumstances. He jumped up from his chair and let his pen fall out of his startled fingers when his old friend came in. They had eaten many a good dinner together in the revered hall of All-Souls, and as the familiar countenance met his eyes, perhaps a regretful thought of that Elysium stole across the mind of the late Fellow, who had been so glad to leave the sacred brother-hood, and marry, and become as other men. He gave but a few hurried words of surprise and welcome to his visitor, and then, with a curious counterpoise of sentiment, sent him up-stairs to see "my wife," feeling, even while half envious of him, a kind of superiority and half contempt for the man who was not a Rector and married, but had given up both these possibilities. When he sent him up-stairs to see "my wife," Mr Morgan looked after the elderly celi-bate with a certain pity. One always feels more inclined to take the simple view of any matter — to stand up for injured innocence, and to right the wronged — when one feels one's self better off than one's neighbours. A reverse position is apt to detract from the simplicity of one's conceptions, and to suggest two sides to the picture. When Mr Proctor was gone, the Rector addressed himself with great devotion to Elsworthy and his evidence. It could not be doubted, at least, that the man was in earnest, and believed what he said; and things unquestionably looked rather ugly for Mr Wentworth. Mr Morgan took down all about the Curate's untimely visit to Elsworthy on the night when he took Rosa home; and when he came to the evidence of the Miss Hemmings, who had seen the Curate talking to the unfortunate little girl at his own door the last time she was seen in Carlingford, the Rector shook his head with a prolonged movement, half of satisfaction, half of regret; for, to be sure, he had made up his mind beforehand who the culprit was, and it was to a certain extent satisfactory to have his opinion confirmed.

"This looks very bad, very bad, I am sorry to say," said Mr Morgan; "for the unhappy young man's own sake, an investigation is absolutely necessary. As for you, Elsworthy, everybody must be sorry for you. Have you no idea where he could have taken the poor girl? – that is," said the uncautious Rector, "supposing that he is guilty – of which I am afraid there does not seem much doubt."

"There aint no doubt," said Elsworthy; "there aint nobody else as could have done it. Just afore my little girl was took away, sir, Mr Wentworth went off of a sudden, and it was said as he was a-going home to the Hall. I was a-thinking of sending a letter anonymous, to ask if it was known what he was after. I read in the papers the other day as his brother was a-going over to Rome. There don't seem to be none o' them the right sort; which it's terrible for two clergymen. I was thinking of dropping a bit of a note anonymous—"

"No – no – no," said the Rector, "that would never do; nothing of that sort, Elsworthy. If you thought it likely she was there, the proper thing would be to go and inquire; nothing anonymous – no, no; that is a thing I could not possibly countenance," said Mr Morgan. He pushed away his pen and paper, and got very red and uncomfortable. If either of the critics up-stairs, his wife, or his predecessor in the Rectory, could but know that he was having an

anonymous letter suggested to him – that anybody ventured to think him capable of being an accomplice in such
proceedings! The presence of these two in the house,
though they were most probably at the moment engaged
in the calmest abstract conversation, and totally unaware
of what was going on in the library, had a great effect upon
the Rector. He felt insulted that any man could venture to
confide such an intention to him almost within the hearing
of his wife. "If I am to take up your case, everything must
be open and straightforward," said Mr Morgan; while
Elsworthy, who saw that he had said something amiss,
without precisely understanding what, took up his hat as a
resource, and once more began to polish it round and
round in his hands.

"I didn't mean no harm, sir, I'm sure," he said; "I don't
seem to see no other way o' finding out; for I aint like a
rich man as can go and come as he pleases; but I won't say
no more, since it's displeasing to you. If you'd give me the
list of names, sir, as you have decided on to be the
committee, I wouldn't trouble you no longer, seeing as
you've got visitors. Perhaps, if the late Rector aint going
away directly, he would take it kind to be put on the
committee; and he's a gentleman as I've a great respect
for, though he wasn't not to say the man for Carlingford,"
said Elsworthy, with a sidelong look. He began to feel the
importance of his own position as the originator of a
committee, and at the head of the most exciting movement which had been for a long time in Carlingford, and
could not help being sensible, notwithstanding his afflic-
tion, that he had a distinction to offer which even the late
Rector might be pleased to accept.

"I don't think Mr Proctor will stay," said Mr Morgan;
"and if he does stay, I believe he is a friend of Mr
Wentworth's." It was only after he had said this that the
Rector perceived the meaning of the words he had
uttered; then, in his confusion and vexation, he got up
hastily from the table, and upset the inkstand in all the

embarrassment of the moment. "Of course that is all the
greater reason for having his assistance," said Mr Morgan,
in his perplexity; "we are all friends of Mr Wentworth.
Will you have the goodness to ring the bell? There are few
things more painful than to take steps against a brother
clergyman, if one did not hope it would be for his benefit
in the end. Oh, never mind the table. Be so good as to ring
the bell again – louder, please."

"There aint nothing equal to blotting-paper, sir," said
Elsworthy, eagerly. "With a bit o' blotting-paper I'd
undertake to rub out ink-stains out o' the finest carpet – if
you'll permit me. It aint but a small speck, and it'll be
gone afore you could look round. It's twenty times better
nor lemon-juice, or them poisonous salts as you're always
nervous of leaving about. Look you here, sir, if it aint a-
sopping up beautiful. There aint no harm done as your
respected lady could be put out about; and I'll take the list
with me, if you please, to show to my wife, as is a-
breaking her heart at home, and can't believe as we'll
ever get justice. She says as how the quality always takes
a gentleman's part against us poor folks, but that aint been
my experience. Don't you touch the carpet, Thomas –
there aint a speck to be seen when the blotting-paper's
cleared away. I'll go home, not to detain you no more, sir,
and cheer up the poor heart as is a-breaking," said
Elsworthy, getting up from his knees where he had been
operating upon the carpet. He had got in his hand the list
of names which Mr Morgan had put down as referees in
this painful business, and it dawned faintly upon the
Rector for the moment that he himself was taking rather
an undignified position as Elsworthy's partisan.

"I have no objection to your showing it to your wife,"
said Mr Morgan; "but I shall be much displeased if I hear
any talk about it, Elsworthy; and I hope it is not revenge
you are thinking of, which is a very unchristian sentiment,"
said the Rector, severely, "and not likely to afford comfort
either to her or to you."

"No, sir, nothing but justice," said Elsworthy, hoarsely, as he backed out of the room. Notwithstanding this statement, it was with very unsatisfactory sensations that Mr Morgan went up-stairs. He felt somehow as if the justice which Elsworthy demanded, and which he himself had solemnly declared to be pursuing the Curate of St Roque's, was wonderfully like revenge. "All punishment must be more or less vindictive," he said to himself as he went up-stairs; but that fact did not make him more comfortable as he went into his wife's drawing-room, where he felt more like a conspirator and assassin than an English Rector in broad daylight, without a mystery near him, had any right to feel. This sensation confused Mr Morgan much, and made him more peremptory in his manner than ever. As for Mr Proctor, who was only a spectator, and felt himself on a certain critical eminence, the suggestion that occurred to his mind was, that he had come in at the end of a quarrel, and that the conjugal firmament was still in a state of disturbance: which idea acted upon some private projects in the hidden mind of the Fellow of All-Souls, and produced a state of feeling little more satisfactory than that of the Rector of Carlingford.

"I hope Mr Proctor is going to stay with us for a day or two," said Mrs Morgan. "I was just saying it must look like coming home to come to the house he used to live in, and which was even furnished to his own taste," said the Rector's wife, shooting a little arrow at the late Rector, of which that good man was serenely unconscious. All this time, while they had been talking, Mrs Morgan had scarcely been able to keep from asking who could possibly have suggested such a carpet. Mr Proctor's chair was placed on the top of one of the big bouquets, which expanded its large foliage round him with more than Eastern prodigality – but he was so little conscious of any culpability of his own in the matter, that he had referred his indignant hostess to one of the leaves as an illustration of the kind of diaper introduced into the new window which had lately been put up in the chapel of All-Souls. "A naturalistic treatment, you know," said Mr Proctor, with the utmost serenity; "and some people objected to it," added the unsuspicious man.

"I should have objected very strongly," said Mrs Morgan, with a little flush. "If you call that naturalistic treatment, I consider it perfectly out of place in decoration – of every kind—" Mr Proctor happened to be looking at her at the moment, and it suddenly occurred to him that Miss Wodehouse never got red in that uncomfortable way, which was the only conclusion he drew from the circumstance, having long ago forgotten that any connection had ever existed between himself and the carpet on the drawing-room in Carlingford Rectory. He addressed his next observation to Mr Morgan, who had just come in.

"I saw Mr Wodehouse's death in the 'Times,'" said Mr Proctor, "and I thought the poor young ladies might feel – at least they might think it a respect – or, at all events, it would be a satisfaction to one's self," said the late Rector, who had got into a mire of explanation. "Though he was far from being a young man, yet having a young daughter like Miss Lucy—"

"Poor Lucy!" said Mr Morgan. "I hope that wretched fellow, young Wentworth" – and here the Rector came to a dead stop, and felt that he had brought the subject most to be avoided head and shoulders into the conversation, as was natural to an embarrassed man. The consequence was that he got angry, as might have been expected. "My dear, you must not look at me as you do. I have just been hearing all the evidence. No unbiassed mind could possibly come to any other decision," said Mr Morgan, with exasperation. Now that he had committed himself, he thought it was much the best thing to go in for it wholly, without half measures, which was certainly the most straightforward way.

"What has happened to Wentworth?" said Mr Proctor. "He is a young man for whom I have a great regard.

Though he is so much younger than I am, he taught me some lessons while I was in Carlingford which I shall never forget. If he is in any trouble that I can help him in, I shall be very glad to do it, both for his sake and for—" Mr Proctor slurred over the end of his sentence a little, and the others were occupied with their own difficulties, and did not take very much notice – for it was difficult to state fully the nature and extent of Mr Wentworth's enormities after such a declaration of friendship. "I met him on my way here," said the Fellow of All-Souls, "not looking quite as he used to do. I supposed it might be Mr Wodehouse's death, perhaps." All Mr Proctor's thoughts ran in that channel of Mr Wodehouse's death, which, after all, though sad enough, was not so great an event to the community in general as the late Rector seemed to suppose.

It was Mrs Morgan at length who took heart to explain to Mr Proctor the real state of affairs. "He has been a very good clergyman for five years," said Mrs Morgan; "he might behave foolishly, you know, about Wharfside, but then that was not his fault so much as the fault of the Rector's predecessors. I am sure I beg your pardon, Mr Proctor – I did not mean that you were to blame," said the Rector's wife; "but, notwithstanding all the work he has done, and the consistent life he has led, there is nobody in Carlingford who is not quite ready to believe that he has run away with Rosa Elsworthy – a common little girl without any education, or a single idea in her head. I suppose she is what you would call pretty," said the indignant woman. "Everybody is just as ready to believe that he is guilty as if he were a stranger or a bad character." Mrs Morgan stopped in an abrupt manner, because her quick eyes perceived a glance exchanged between the two gentlemen. Mr Proctor had seen a good deal of the world in his day, as he was fond of saying now and then to his intimate friends: and he had learned at the university and other places that a girl who is "what you would call pretty," counts for a great deal in the history of a young

man, whether she has any ideas in her head or not. He did
not, any more than the people of Carlingford, pronounce
at once on *a priori* evidence that Mr Wentworth must be
innocent. The Curate's "consistent life" did not go for
much in the opinion of the middle-aged Fellow of All-
Souls, any more than of the less dignified populace. He
said, "Dear me, dear me!" in a most perplexed and
distressed tone, while Mrs Morgan kept looking at him;
and looked very much as if he were tempted to break forth
into lamentations over human nature, as Mr Morgan
himself had done.

"I wonder what the Miss Wodehouses think of it," he
said at last. "One would do a great deal to keep them from
hearing such a thing; but I wonder how they are feeling
about it," said Mr Proctor – and clearly declined to discuss
the matter with Mrs Morgan, who was counsel for the
defence. When the Rector's wife went to her own room to
dress for dinner, it is very true that she had a good cry
over her cup of tea. She was not only disappointed, but
exasperated, in that impatient feminine nature of hers.
Perhaps if she had been less sensitive, she would have had
less of that redness in her face which was so great a trouble
to Mrs Morgan. These two slow middle-aged men, without
any intuitions, who were coming lumbering after her
through all kind of muddles of evidence and argument,
exasperated the more rapid woman. To be sure, they
understood Greek plays a great deal better than she did;
but she was penetrated with the liveliest impatience of
their dulness all the same. Mrs Morgan, however, like
most people who are in advance of their age, felt her utter
impotence against that blank wall of dull resistance. She
could not make them see into the heart of things as she
did. She had to wait until they had attacked the question
in the orthodox way of siege, and made gradual entrance
by dint of hard labour. All she could do to console herself
was, to shed certain hot tears of indignation and annoyance
over her tea, which, however, was excellent tea, and did

her good. Perhaps it was to show her sense of superiority, and that she did not feel herself vanquished, that, after that, she put on her new dress, which was very much too nice to be wasted upon Mr Proctor. As for Mr Leeson, who came in as usual just in time for dinner, having heard of Mr Proctor's arrival, she treated him with a blandness which alarmed the Curate. "I quite expected you, for we have the All-Souls pudding to-day," said the Rector's wife, and she smiled a smile which would have struck awe into the soul of any curate that ever was known in Carlingford.

CHAPTER XXXII.

I⊤ was the afternoon of the same day on which Mr Proctor arrived in Carlingford that Mr Wentworth received the little note from Miss Wodehouse which was so great a consolation to the Perpetual Curate. By that time he had begun to experience humiliations more hard to bear than anything he had yet known. He had received constrained greetings from several of his most cordial friends; his people in the district, all but Tom Burrows, looked askance upon him; and Dr Marjoribanks, who had never taken kindly to the young Anglican, had met him with satirical remarks in his dry Scotch fashion, which were intolerable to the Curate. In these circumstances, it was balm to his soul to have his sympathy once more appealed to, and by those who were nearest to his heart. The next day was that appointed for Mr Wodehouse's funeral, to which Mr Wentworth had been looking forward with a little excite-ment – wondering, with indignant misery, whether the covert insults he was getting used to would be repeated even over his old friend's grave. It was while this was in

his mind that he received Miss Wodehouse's little note. It
was very hurriedly written, on the terrible black-edged
paper which, to such a simple soul as Miss Wodehouse, it
was a kind of comfort to use in the moment of calamity.
"Dear Mr Wentworth," it said, "I am in great difficulty,
and don't know what to do: come, I beg of you, and tell me
what is best. My dear Lucy insists upon going to-morrow,
and I can't cross her when her heart is breaking, and I
don't know what to do. Please to come, if it were only for a
moment. Dear, dear papa, and all of us, have always had
such confidence in you!" Mr Wentworth was seated, very
disconsolate, in his study when this appeal came to him:
he was rather sick of the world and most things in it; a
sense of wrong eclipsed the sunshine for the moment, and
obscured the skies; but it was comforting to be appealed to
— to have his assistance and his protection sought once
more. He took his hat immediately and went up the sunny
road, on which there was scarcely a passenger visible, to
the closed-up house, which stood so gloomy and irrespon-
sive in the sunshine. Mr Wodehouse had not been a man
likely to attract any profound love in his lifetime, or sense
of loss when he was gone; but yet it was possible to think,
with the kindly, half-conscious delusion of nature, that
had *he* been living, he would have known better; and the
Curate went into the darkened drawing-room, where all
the shutters were closed, except those of the little window
in the corner, where Lucy's work-table stood, and where a
little muffled sunshine stole in through the blind. Everything was in terribly good order in the room. The two
sisters had been living in their own apartments, taking
their forlorn meals in the little parlour which communicated
with their sleeping chambers, during this week of darkness;
and nobody had come into the drawing-room except the
stealthy housemaid, who contemplated herself and her
new mourning for an hour at a stretch in the great mirror
without any interruption, while she made "tidy" the furniture which nobody now disturbed. Into this sombre apart-

ment Miss Wodehouse came gliding, like a gentle ghost, in
her black gown. She too, like John and the housemaid and
everybody about, walked and talked under her breath.
There was now no man in the house entitled to disturb
those proprieties with which a female household naturally
hedges round all the great incidents of life; and the affairs
of the family were all carried on in a whisper, in accordance
with the solemnity of the occasion – a circumstance
which had naturally called the ghost of a smile to the
Curate's countenance as he followed John up-stairs. Miss
Wodehouse herself, though she was pale, and spent half
her time, poor soul! in weeping, and had, besides, living
encumbrances to trouble her helpless path, did not look
amiss in her black gown. She came in gliding without any
noise, but with a little expectation in her gentle countenance. She was one of the people whom experience
never makes any wiser; and she could not help hoping to
be delivered from her troubles this time, as so often
before, as soon as she should have transferred them to
somebody else's shoulders, and taken "advice."

"Lucy has made up her mind that we are to go to-
morrow," said Miss Wodehouse, drying her tears. "It was
not the custom in my young days, Mr Wentworth, and I
am sure I don't know what to say; but I can't bear to cross
her, now that she has nobody but me. She was always the
best child in the world," said the poor lady – "far more
comfort to poor dear papa than I ever could be; but to hear
her talk you would think that she had never done anything.
And oh, Mr Wentworth, if that was all I should not mind;
but we have always kept things a secret from her; and now
I have had a letter, and I don't know what it is possible to
do."

"A letter from your brother?" asked Mr Wentworth,
eagerly.

"From Tom," said the elder sister; "poor, poor Tom! I
am sure papa forgave him at the last, though he did not
say anything. Oh, Mr Wentworth, he was such a nice boy

once; and if Lucy only knew, and I could summon up the courage to tell her, and he would change his ways, as he promised – don't think me fickle or changeable, or look as if I didn't know my own mind," cried poor Miss Wodehouse, with a fresh flow of tears; "but oh, Mr Wentworth, if he only would change his ways, as he promised, think what a comfort it would be to us to have him at home!"

"Yes," said the Curate, with a little bitterness. Here was another instance of the impunities of wickedness. "I think it very likely indeed that you will have him at home," said Mr Wentworth – "almost certain; the wonder is that he went away. Will you tell me where he dates his letter from? I have a curiosity to know."

"You are angry," said the anxious sister. "Oh, Mr Wentworth, I know he does not deserve anything else, but you have always been so kind. I put his letter in my pocket to show you – at least, I am sure I intended to put it in my pocket. We have scarcely been in this room since – since—" and here Miss Wodehouse broke down, and had to take a little time to recover. "I will go and get the letter," she said, as at last she regained her voice, and hurried away through the partial darkness with her noise-less step, and the long black garments which swept noiselessly over the carpet. Mr Wentworth for his part went to the one window which was only veiled by a blind, and comforted himself a little in the sunshine. The death atmosphere weighed upon the young man and took away his courage. If he was only wanted to pave the way for the reception of the rascally brother for whose sins he felt convinced he was himself suffering, the consolation of being appealed to would be sensibly lessened, and it was hard to have no other way of clearing himself than by criminating Lucy's brother, and bringing dishonour upon her name. While he waited for Miss Wodehouse's return, he stood by Lucy's table, with very little of the feeling which had once prompted him to fold his arms so caressing-ly with an impulse of tenderness upon the chair which stood

beside it. He was so much absorbed in his own thoughts
that he did not hear at first the sound of a hesitating hand
upon the door, which at length, when repeated, went to
the Curate's heart. He turned round rapidly, and saw
Lucy standing on the threshold in her profound mourning.
She was very pale, and her blue eyes looked large and full
beyond their natural appearance, dilated with tears and
watching; and when they met those of Mr Wentworth,
they filled full like flower-cups with dew; but besides this
Lucy made no demonstration of her grief. After that
momentary hesitation at the door, she came in and gave
the Curate her hand. Perhaps it was a kind of defiance,
perhaps a natural yearning, which drew her out of her
chamber when she heard of his presence; both sentiments
sprang out of the same feeling; and the Curate, when he
looked at her, bethought himself of the only moment when
he had been able to imagine that Lucy loved him; that
moment by her father's bedside, of which the impression
had been dulled since then by a crowd of events, when she
looked with such reproach and disappointment and indignation into his face.

"I heard you were here," said Lucy, "and I thought you
might think it strange not to see us both." And then she
paused, perhaps finding it less easy than she thought to
explain why she had come. "We ought to thank you, Mr
Wentworth, for your kindness, though I—"

"You were angry with me," said the Curate. "I know
you thought me heartless; but a man must bear to be
misconceived when he has duty to do," the young clergyman added, with a swelling heart. Lucy did not know the
fuller significance of his words; and there was a loftiness in
them which partly affronted her, and set all her sensitive
woman-pride in arms against him.

"I beg your pardon," she said, faltering, and then the
two stood beside each other in silence, with a sense of
estrangement. As for Lucy, all the story about Rosa
Elsworthy, of which she had not yet heard the last chapter,

rushed back upon her mind. Was it to see little Rosa's lover that she had come out of the darkness of her room, with a natural longing for sympathy which it was impossible to restrain? The tenderness of the instinctive feeling which had moved her, went back upon her heart in bitterness. That he must have divined why she had come, and scorned her for it, was the mildest supposition in Lucy's mind. She could almost have imagined that he had come on purpose to elicit this vain exhibition of regard, and triumph over it; all this, too, when she was in such great trouble and sorrow, and wanted a little compassion, a little kindness, so much. This was the state of mind to which Lucy had come, in five minutes after she entered the room, when Miss Wodehouse came back with the letter. The elder sister was almost as much astonished at Lucy's presence as if she had been the dead inhabitant who kept such state in the darkened house. She was so startled that she went back a step or two when she perceived her, and hastily put the letter in her pocket, and exclaimed her sister's name in a tone most unlike Miss Wodehouse's natural voice.

"I came down-stairs because – I mean they told me Mr Wentworth was here," said Lucy, who had never felt so weak and so miserable in her life, "and I wanted to thank him for all his kindness." It was here for the first time that Lucy broke down. Her sorrow was so great, her longing for a word of kindness had been so natural, and her shame and self-condemnation at the very thought that she was able to think of anything but her father, were so bitter, that the poor girl's forces, weakened by watching, were not able to withstand them. She sank into the chair that stood nearest, and covered her face with her hands, and cried as people cry only at twenty. And as for Mr Wentworth, he had no right to take her in his arms and comfort her, nor to throw himself at her feet and entreat her to take courage. All he could do was to stand half a yard, yet a whole world, apart looking at her, his heart beating with all the remorseful half-angry tenderness of love. Since it was not his to console her, he was almost impatient of her tears.

"Dear, I have been telling Mr Wentworth about to-morrow," said Miss Wodehouse, weeping too, as was natural, "and he thinks – he thinks – oh, my darling! and so do I – that it will be too much for you. When I was young it never was the custom; and oh, Lucy, remember that ladies are not to be expected to have such command over their feelings," said poor Miss Wodehouse, dropping on her knees by Lucy's chair. Mr Wentworth stood looking on in a kind of despair. He had nothing to say, and no right to say anything; even his presence was a kind of intrusion. But to be referred to thus as an authority against Lucy's wishes, vexed him in the most unreasonable way.

"Mr Wentworth does not know me," said Lucy, under her breath, wiping away her tears with a trembling, indignant hand. "If we had had a brother, it might have been different; but there must be somebody there that loves him," said the poor girl, with a sob, getting up hastily from her chair. She could not bear to stay any longer in the room, which she had entered with a vague sense of possible consolation. As for the Curate, he made haste to open the door for her, feeling the restraint of his position almost intolerable. "*I* shall be there," he said, stopping at the door to look into the fair, pallid face which Lucy would scarcely raise to listen. "Could you not trust *me*?" It looked like giving him a pledge of something sacred and precious to put her hand into his, which was held out for it so eagerly. But Lucy could not resist the softening of nature; and not even Miss Wodehouse, looking anxiously after them, heard what further words they were that Mr Wentworth said in her ear. "I am for your service, however and wherever you want me," said the Curate, with a young man's absolutism. Heaven knows he had enough to do with his own troubles; but he remembered no obstacle which could prevent him from dedicating all his time and life to her as he spoke.

When Lucy reached her own room, she threw herself upon the sofa, and wept like a woman inconsolable; but it was somehow because this consolation, subtle and secret, had stolen into her heart that her tears flowed so freely. And Mr Wentworth returned to her sister relieved, he could not have told why. At all events, come what might, the two had drawn together again in their mutual need.

"Oh, Mr Wentworth, how can I cross her?" said Miss Wodehouse, wringing her hands. "If we had a brother – did you hear what she said? Here is his letter, and I hope you will tell me candidly what you think. If we could trust him – if we could but trust him! I daresay you think me very changeable and foolish; but now we are alone," said the poor lady, "think what a comfort it would be if he only would change his ways as he promised! Lucy is a great deal more use than I am, and understands things; but still we are only two women," said the elder sister. "If you think we could put any dependence upon him, Mr Wentworth, I would never hesitate. He might live with us, and have his little allowance." Miss Wodehouse paused, and raised her anxious face to the Curate, pondering the particulars of the liberality she intended. "He is not a boy," she went on. "I daresay now he must feel the want of the little comforts he once was used to; and though he is not like what he used to be, neither in his looks nor his manners, people would be kind to him for our sakes. Oh, Mr Wentworth, don't you think we might trust him?" said the anxious woman, looking in the Curate's face.

All this time Mr Wentworth, with an impatience of her simplicity which it was difficult to restrain, was reading the letter, in which he perceived a very different intention from any divined by Miss Wodehouse. The billet was disreputable enough, written in pencil, and without any date.

"MARY, – I mean to come to my father's funeral," wrote Mr Wodehouse's disowned son. "Things are changed now,

as I said they would be. I and a friend of mine have set
everything straight with Waters, and I mean to come in
my own name, and take the place I have a right to. How it
is to be after this depends on how you behave; but things
are changed between you and me, as I told you they
would be; and I expect you won't do anything to make 'em
worse by doing or saying what's unpleasant. I add no
more, because I hope you'll have sense to see what I
mean, and to act accordingly. – Your brother,
"THOMAS WODEHOUSE."

"You see he thinks I will reproach him," said Miss
Wodehouse, anxiously; perhaps it had just glanced across
her own mind that something more important still might
have dictated language so decided. "He has a great deal
more feeling than you would suppose, poor fellow! It is
very touching in him to say, 'the place he has a right to' –
don't you think so, Mr Wentworth? Poor Tom! if we could
but trust him, and he would change his ways as he
promised! Oh, Mr Wentworth, don't you think I might
speak of it to him to-morrow? If we could – bury – everything – in dear papa's grave," cried the poor lady, once
more breaking down. Mr Wentworth took no notice of
Miss Wodehouse's tears. They moved him with sentiments
entirely different from those with which he regarded
Lucy's. He read the note over again without any attempt
to console her, till she had struggled back into composure;
but even then there was nothing sympathetic in the
Curate's voice.

"And I think you told me you did not know anything
about the will?" he said, with some abruptness, making no
account whatever of the suggestion she had made.

No," said Miss Wodehouse; "but my dear father was a
business man, Mr Wentworth, and I feel quite sure –
quite —"

"Yes," said the Perpetual Curate; "nor of the nature of
his property, perhaps?" added the worldly-minded young

man whom poor Miss Wodehouse had chosen for her adviser. It was more than the gentle woman could bear.

"Oh, Mr Wentworth, you know I am not one to understand," cried the poor lady. "You ask me questions, but you never tell me what you think I should do. If it were only for myself, I would not mind, but I have to act for Lucy," said the elder sister, suddenly sitting upright and drying her tears. "Papa, I am sure, did what was best for us," she said, with a little gentle dignity, which brought the Curate back to his senses; "but oh, Mr Wentworth, look at the letter, and tell me, for my sister's sake, what am I to do?"

The Curate went to the window, from which the sunshine was stealing away, to consider the subject; but he did not seem to derive much additional wisdom from that sacred spot, where Lucy's work-table stood idle. "We must wait and see," he said to himself. When he came back to Miss Wodehouse, and saw the question still in her eyes, it only brought back his impatience. "My dear Miss Wodehouse, instead of speculating about what is to happen, it would be much better to prepare your sister for the discovery she must make to-morrow," said Mr Wentworth; "I cannot give any other advice, for my part. I think it is a great pity that you have kept it concealed so long. I beg your pardon for speaking so abruptly, but I am afraid you don't know all the trouble that is before you. We are all in a great deal of trouble," said the Perpetual Curate, with a little unconscious solemnity. "I can't say I see my way through it; but you ought to prepare her – to see – her brother." He said the words with a degree of repugnance which he could not conceal, and which wounded his companion's tender heart.

"He was so different when he was young," said Miss Wodehouse, with a suppressed sob – "he was a favourite everywhere. You would not have looked so if you had known him then. Oh, Mr Wentworth, promise me that you will not turn your back upon him if he comes home,

after all your kindness. I will tell Lucy how much you
have done for him," said Miss Wodehouse. She was only
half-conscious of her own gentle artifice. She took the
Curate's hand in both her own before he left her, and said
it was such a comfort to have his advice to rely upon; and
she believed what she said, though Mr Wentworth himself
knew better. The poor lady sat down in Lucy's chair, and
had a cry at her ease after he went away. She was to tell
Lucy – but how? and she sat pondering this hard question
till all the light had faded out of the room, and the little
window which was not shuttered dispersed only a grey
twilight through the empty place. The lamp, meantime,
had been lighted in the little parlour where Lucy sat, very
sad, in her black dress, with 'In Memoriam' on the table
by her, carrying on a similar strain in her heart. She was
thinking of the past, so many broken scenes of which kept
flashing up before her, all bright with indulgent love and
tenderness – and she was thinking of the next day, when
she was to see all that remained of her good father laid in
his grave. He was not very wise nor remarkable among
men, but he had been the tenderest father to the child of
his old age; and in her heart she was praying for him still,
pausing now and then to think whether it was right. The
tears were heavy in her young eyes, but they were natural
tears, and Lucy had no more thought that there was in the
world anything sadder than sorrow, or that any complications lay in her individual lot, than the merest child in
Prickett's Lane. She thought of going back to the district,
all robed and invested in the sanctity of her grief – she
thought it was to last for ever, as one has the privilege of
thinking when one is young; and it was to this young saint,
tender towards all the world, ready to pity everybody, and
to save a whole race, if that had been possible, that Miss
Wodehouse went in, heavy and burdened, with her tale of
miserable vice, unkindness, estrangement. How was it possible to begin? Instead of beginning, poor Miss Wodehouse,
overpowered by her anxieties and responsibilities, was

taken ill and fainted, and had to be carried to bed. Lucy
would not let her talk when she came to herself; and so
the only moment of possible preparation passed away,
and the event itself, which one of them knew nothing
of, and the other did not understand, came in its own
person, without any *avant-couriers*, to open Lucy's eyes
once for all.

CHAPTER XXXIII.

MR WENTWORTH had to go into Carlingford on some
business when he left Miss Wodehouse; and as he went
home again, having his head full of so many matters, he
forgot for the moment what most immediately concerned
himself, and was close upon Elsworthy's shop, looking into
the window, before he thought of it. Elsworthy himself
was standing behind the counter, with a paper in his hand,
from which he was expounding something to various
people in the shop. It was getting late, and the gas was
lighted, which threw the interior into very bright relief
to Mr Wentworth outside. The Curate was still only a
young man, though he was a clergyman, and his movements were not always guided by reason or sound sense.
He walked into the shop, almost before he was aware what
he was doing. The people were inconsiderable people
enough – cronies of Elsworthy – but they were people who
had been accustomed to look up very reverentially to the
Curate of St Roque's and Mr Wentworth was far from
being superior to their disapproval. There was a very
visible stir among them as he entered, and Elsworthy
came to an abrupt stop in his elucidations, and thrust the
paper he had been reading into a drawer. Dead and

sudden silence followed the entrance of the Curate. Peter Hayles, the druggist, who was one of the auditors, stole to the door with intentions of escape, and the women, of whom there were two or three, looked alarmed, not knowing what might come of it. As for Mr Wentworth, there was only one thing possible for him to say. "Have you heard anything of Rosa, Elsworthy?" he asked, with great gravity, fixing his eyes upon the man's face. The question seemed to ring into all the corners. Whether it was innocence or utter abandonment nobody could tell, and the spectators held their breath for the answer. Elsworthy, for his part, was as much taken by surprise as his neighbours. He grew very pale and livid in his sudden excitement, and lost his voice, and stood staring at the Curate like a man struck dumb. Perhaps Mr Wentworth got bolder when he saw the effect he had produced. He repeated the question, looking towards poor Mrs Elsworthy, who had jumped from her husband's side when he came in. The whole party looked like startled conspirators to Mr Wentworth's eyes, though he had not the least idea what they had been doing. "Have you heard anything of Rosa?" he asked again; and everybody looked at Elsworthy, as if he were the guilty man, and had suborned the rest; which, indeed, in one sense, was not far from being the case.

When Elsworthy came to himself, he gave Mr Wentworth a sidelong dangerous look. "No, sir – nothing," said Rosa's uncle. "Them as has hidden her has hidden her well. I didn't expect to hear not yet," said Elsworthy. Though Mr Wentworth did not know what he meant, his little audience in the shop did, and showed, by the slightest murmur in the world, their conviction that the arrow had gone home, which naturally acted like a spur upon the Curate, who was not the wisest man in the world.

"I am very sorry to see you in so much distress," said the young man, looking at Mrs Elsworthy's red eyes, "but I trust things will turn out much better than you imagine.

If I can do anything to help you, let me know," said Mr
Wentworth. Perhaps it was foolish to say so much,
knowing what he did, but unfortunately prudence was not
the ruling principle at that moment in the Curate's soul.

"I was a-thinking of letting you know, sir," said the
clerk of St Roque's, with deadly meaning; "leastways not
me, but them as has taken me by the hand. There's every
prospect as it'll all be known afore long," said Elsworthy,
pushing his wife aside and following Mr Wentworth, with
a ghastly caricature of his old obsequiousness, to the door.
"There's inquiries a-being made as was never known to
fail. For one thing, I've written to them as knows a deal
about the movements of a party as is suspected – not to
say as I've got good friends," said Rosa's guardian,
standing upon the step of his own door, and watching the
Curate out into the darkness. Mr Wentworth could not
altogether restrain a slight thrill of unpleasant emotion, for
Elsworthy, standing at his door with the light gleaming
over him from behind, and his face invisible, had an
unpleasant resemblance to a wild beast waiting for his prey.

"I am glad to think you are likely to be so successful.
Send me word as soon as you know," said the Curate, and
he pursued his way home afterwards, with feelings far
from pleasant. He saw something was about to come of
this more than he had thought likely, and the crisis was
approaching. As he walked rapidly home, he concluded
within himself to have a conversation with the Rector
next day after Mr Wodehouse's funeral, and to ask for an
investigation into the whole matter. When he had come to
this conclusion, he dismissed the subject from his mind as
far as was possible, and took to thinking of the other
matters which disturbed his repose, in which, indeed, it
was very easy to get perplexed and bewildered to his
heart's content. Anyhow, one way and another, the day of
poor Mr Wodehouse's funeral must necessarily be an
exciting and momentous day.

Mr Wentworth had, however, no idea that its interest

was to begin so early. When he was seated at breakfast reading his letters, a note was brought to him, which, coming in the midst of a lively chronicle of home news from his sister Letty, almost stopped for the moment the beating of the Curate's heart. It took him so utterly by surprise, that more violent sentiments were lost for the moment in mere wonder. He read it over twice before he could make it out. It was from the Rector, and notwithstanding his wife's remonstrances, and his own qualms of doubt and uncertainty, this was what Mr Morgan said:–

"Dear Sir, – It is my painful duty to let you know that certain rumours have reached my ears very prejudicial to your character as a clergyman, and which I understand to be very generally current in Carlingford. Such a scandal, if not properly dealt with, is certain to have an unfavourable effect upon the popular mind, and injure the clergy in the general estimation – while it is, as I need not point out to you, quite destructive of your own usefulness. Under the circumstances, I have thought it my duty, as Rector of the parish, to take steps for investigating these reports. Of course I do not pretend to any authority over you, nor can I enforce in any way your participation in the inquiry or consent to it; but I beg to urge upon you strongly, as a friend, the advantage of assenting freely, that your innocence (if possible) may be made apparent, and your character cleared. I enclose the names of the gentlemen whose assistance I intend to request for this painful duty, in case you should object to any of them; and would again urge you, *for your own sake*, the expediency of concurrence. I regret to say that, though I would not willingly prejudge any man, much less a brother clergyman, I do not feel that it would be seemly on my part, under the circumstances, to avail myself of your assistance today in the burial-service for the late Mr Wodehouse. – Believe me, very sincerely yours,

"W. Morgan."

When Mr Wentworth looked up from this letter, he caught sight of his face in the mirror opposite, and gazed into his own eyes like a man stupefied. He had not been without vexations in eight-and-twenty years of a not uneventful life, but he had never known anything like the misery of that moment. It was nearly four hours later when he walked slowly up Grange Lane to the house, which before night might own so different a master, but he had found as yet no time to spare for the Wodehouses – even for Lucy – in the thoughts which were all occupied by the unlooked-for blow. Nobody could tell, not even himself, the mental discipline he had gone through before he emerged, rather stern, but perfectly calm, in the sunshine in front of the closed-up house. If it was not his to meet the solemn passenger at the gates with words of hope, at least he could do a man's part to the helpless who had still to live; but the blow was cruel, and all the force of his nature was necessary to sustain it. All Carlingford knew, by the evidence of its senses, that Mr Wentworth had been a daily visitor of the dead, and one of his most intimate friends, and nobody had doubted for a moment that to him would be assigned as great a portion of the service as his feelings permitted him to undertake. When the bystanders saw him join the procession, a thrill of surprise ran through the crowd; but nobody – not even the man who walked beside him – ventured to trifle with the Curate's face so far as to ask why. The Grand Inquisitor himself, if such a mythical personage exists any longer, could not have invented a more delicate torture than that which the respectable and kind-hearted Rector of Carlingford inflicted calmly, without knowing it, upon the Curate of St Roque's. How was Mr Morgan to know that the sting would go to his heart? A Perpetual Curate without a district has nothing to do with a heart so sensitive. The Rector put on his own robes with a peaceful mind, feeling that he had done his duty, and, with Mr Leeson behind him, came to the church door with great solemnity to meet the procession. He read the words which are so sweet and so terrible with his usual reading-desk voice as he read the invitations every Sunday. He was a good man, but he was middle-aged, and not accessible to impression from the mere aspect of death; and he did not know Mr Wodehouse, nor care much for anything in the matter, except his own virtue in excluding the Perpetual Curate from any share in the service. Such was the Rector's feeling in respect to this funeral, which made so much commotion in Carlingford. He felt that he was vindicating the purity of his profession as he threaded his way through the pathetic hillocks, where the nameless people were lying, to poor Mr Wodehouse's grave.

This, however, was not the only thing which aroused the wonder and interest of the townspeople when the two shrinking, hooded female figures, all black and unrecognisable, rose up trembling to follow their dead from the church to the grave. Everybody saw with wonder that their place was contested, and that somebody else, a man whom no one knew, thrust himself before them, and walked alone in the chief mourner's place. As for Lucy, who, through her veil and her tears, saw nothing distinctly, this figure, which she did not know, struck her only with a vague astonishment. If she thought of it at all, she thought it a mistake, simple enough, though a little startling, and went on, doing all she could to support her sister, saying broken prayers in her heart, and far too much absorbed in the duty she was performing to think who was looking on, or to be conscious of any of the attending circumstances, except Mr Morgan's voice, which was not the voice she had expected to hear. Miss Wodehouse was a great deal more agitated than Lucy. She knew very well who it was that placed himself before her, asserting his own right without offering any help to his sisters; and vague apprehensions, which she herself could not understand, came over her just at the moment when she required her strength most. As there were no other relations present, the place

of honour next to the two ladies had been tacitly conceded
to Mr Proctor and Mr Wentworth; and it was thus that the
Curate rendered the last service to his old friend. It was a
strange procession, and concentrated in itself all that was
most exciting in Carlingford at the moment. Everybody
observed and commented upon the strange man, who, all
remarkable and unknown, with his great beard and sullen
countenance, walked by himself as chief mourner. Who
was he? and whispers arose and ran through the outskirts
of the crowd of the most incredible description. Some said
he was an illegitimate son whom Mr Wodehouse had left
all his property to, but whom the ladies knew nothing of;
some that it was a strange cousin, whom Lucy was to be
compelled to marry or lose her share; and after a while
people compared notes, and went back upon their recollections, and began to ask each other if it was true that
Tom Wodehouse died twenty years ago in the West
Indies? Then behind the two ladies – poor ladies, whose
fate was hanging in the balance, though they did not know
it – came Mr Wentworth in his cap and gown, pale and
stern as nobody ever had seen him before in Carlingford,
excluded from all share in the service, which Mr Leeson,
in a flutter of surplice and solemnity, was giving his
valuable assistance in. The churchyard at Carlingford had
not lost its semi-rural air though the town had increased so
much, for the district was very healthy, as everybody
knows, and people did not die before their time, as in
places less favoured. The townspeople, who knew Mr
Wodehouse so well, lingered all about among the graves,
looking with neighbourly, calm regret, but the liveliest
curiosity. Most of the shopkeepers at that end of George
Street had closed their shops on the mournful occasion,
and felt themselves repaid. As for Elsworthy, he stood
with a group of supporters round him, as near as possible
to the funeral procession; and farther off in the distance,
under the trees, was a much more elegant spectator – an
unlikely man enough to assist at such a spectacle, being no

less a person than Jack Wentworth, in the perfection of an
English gentleman's morning apparel, perfectly at his ease
and indifferent, yet listening with close attention to all the
scraps of talk that came in his way. The centre of all this
wondering, curious crowd, where so many passions and
emotions and schemes and purposes were in full tide, and
life was beating so strong and vehement, was the harmless
dead, under the heavy pall which did not veil him so
entirely from the living as did the hopes and fears and
curious speculations which had already sprung up over
him, filling up his place. Among the whole assembly there
was not one heart really occupied by thoughts of him,
except that of poor Lucy, who knew nothing of all the
absorbing anxieties and terrors that occupied the others.
She had still a moment's leisure for her natural grief. It
was all she could do to keep upright and support her sister,
who had burdens to bear which Lucy knew nothing of; but
still, concealed under her hood and veil, seeing nothing
but the grave before her, hearing nothing but the sacred
words and the terrible sound of "dust to dust," the young
creature stood steadfast, and gave the dead man who had
loved her his due — last offering of nature and love,
sweeter to anticipate than any honours. Nobody but his
child offered to poor Mr Wodehouse that last right of
humanity, or made his grave sacred with natural
tears.

When they went back sadly out of all that blinding
sunshine into the darkened house, it was not all over, as
poor Lucy had supposed. She had begun to come to
herself and understand once more the looks of the people
about her, when the old maid, who had been the attendant
of the sisters during all Lucy's life, undid her wrappings,
and in her agitation of the moment kissed her white cheek,
and held her in her arms. "Oh, Miss Lucy, darling, don't
take on no more than you can help. I'm sore, sore afeared
that there's a deal of trouble afore you yet," said the
weeping woman. Though Lucy had not the smallest

possible clue to her meaning, and was almost too much worn out to be curious, she could not help a vague thrill of alarm. "What is it, Alland?" she said, rising up from the sofa on which she had thrown herself. But Alland could do nothing but cry over her nursling and console her. "Oh, my poor dear! oh, my darling! as he never would have let the wind of heaven to blow rough upon her!" cried the old servant. And it was just then that Miss Wodehouse, who was trembling all over hysterically, came into the room.

"We have to go down-stairs," said the elder sister. "Oh Lucy, my darling, it was not my fault at first. I should have told you last night to prepare you, and I had not the heart. Mr Wentworth has told me so often—"

"Mr Wentworth?" said Lucy. She rose up, not quite knowing where she was; aware of nothing, except that some sudden calamity, under which she was expected to faint altogether, was coming to her by means of Mr Wentworth. Her mind jumped at the only dim possibility that seemed to glimmer through the darkness. He must be married, she supposed, or about to be married; and it was this they insulted her by thinking that she could not bear. There was not a particle of colour in her face before, but the blood rushed into it with a bitterness of shame and rage which she had never known till now. "I will go down with you if it is necessary," said Lucy; "but surely this is a strange time to talk of Mr Wentworth's affairs." There was no time to explain anything farther, for just then old Mrs Western, who was a distant cousin, knocked at the door. "God help you, my poor dear children!" said the old lady; "they are all waiting for you down-stairs," and it was with this delusion in her mind, embittering every thought, that Lucy went into the drawing-room where they were all assembled. The madness of the idea did not strike her somehow, even when she saw the grave assembly, which it was strange to think could have been brought together to listen to any explanation from the Perpetual Curate. He was standing there prominent enough among them, with a

certain air of suppressed passion in his face, which Lucy
divined almost without seeing it. For her own part, she
went in with perfect firmness, supporting her sister, whose
trembling was painful to see. There was no other lady in the
room except old Mrs Western, who would not sit down,
but hovered behind the chairs which had been placed for
the sisters near the table at which Mr Waters was standing.
By the side of Mr Waters was the man who had been at
the funeral, and whom nobody knew, and a few gentlemen who were friends of the family were in the room – the
Rector, by virtue of his office, and Mr Proctor and Dr
Marjoribanks; and any one whose attention was sufficiently
disengaged to note the details of the scene might have
perceived John, who had been fifteen years with Mr
Wodehouse, and the old cook in her black gown, who was
of older standing in the family than Alland herself, peeping
in, whenever it was opened, through the door.

"Now that the Miss Wodehouses are here, we may
proceed to business," said Mr Waters. "Some of the party
are already aware that I have an important communication
to make. I am very sorry if it comes abruptly upon
anybody specially interested. My late partner, much respected though he has always been, was a man of peculiar
views in many respects. Dr Marjoribanks will bear me out
in what I say. I had been his partner for ten years before I
found this out, highly important as it will be seen to be;
and I believe Mr Wentworth, though an intimate friend of
the family, obtained the information by a kind of accident—"

The stranger muttered something in his beard which
nobody could hear, and the Perpetual Curate interposed
audibly. "Would it not be best to make the explanations
afterwards?" said Mr Wentworth – and he changed his
own position and went over beside old Mrs Western, who
was leaning upon Lucy's chair. He put his own hand on
the back of the chair with an involuntary impulse. As for
Lucy, her first thrill of nervous strength had failed her:
she began to get confused and bewildered; but whatever it

was, no insult, no wound to her pride or affections, was
coming to her from that hand which she knew was on her
chair. She leaned back a little, with a long sigh. Her
imagination could not conceive anything important enough
for such a solemn intimation, and her attention began to
flag in spite of herself. No doubt it was something about
that money which people thought so interesting. Meanwhile Mr Waters went on steadily with what he had to say,
not sparing them a word of the preamble; and it was not
till ten minutes later that Lucy started up with a sudden
cry of incredulity and wonder, and repeated his last
words. "His son! – whose son?" cried Lucy. She looked all
round her, not knowing whom to appeal to in her sudden
consternation. "We never had a brother," said the child of
Mr Wodehouse's old age; "it must be some mistake."
There was a dead pause after these words. When she
looked round again, a sickening conviction came to Lucy's
heart that it was no mistake. She rose up without knowing
it, and looked round upon all the people, who were
watching her with various looks of pity and curiosity and
spectator-interest. Mr Waters had stopped speaking, and
the terrible stranger made a step forward with an air that
identified him. It was at him that Mr Proctor was staring,
who cleared his voice a great many times, and came
forward to the middle of the room and looked as if he
meant to speak; and upon him every eye was fixed except
Mr Wentworth's, who was watching Lucy, and Miss
Wodehouse's, which were hidden in her hands. "We
never had a brother," she repeated, faltering; and then, in
the extremity of her wonder and excitement, Lucy turned
round, without knowing it, to the man whom her heart
instinctively appealed to. "Is it true?" she said. She held
out her hands to him with a kind of entreaty not to say so.
Mr Wentworth made no reply to her question. He said
only, "Let me take you away – it is too much for you,"
bending down over her, without thinking what he did, and
drawing her hand through his arm. "She is not able for any

more," said the Curate, hurriedly; "afterwards we can explain to her." If he could have remembered anything about himself at the moment, it is probable that he would have denied himself the comfort of supporting Lucy – he, a man under ban; but he was thinking only of her, as he stood facing them all with her arm drawn through his; upon which conjunction the Rector and the late Rector looked with a grim aspect, disposed to interfere, but not knowing how.

"All this may be very interesting to you," said the stranger out of his beard; "if Lucy don't know her brother, it is no fault of mine. Mr Waters has only said half he has got to say; and as for the rest, to sum it up in half-a-dozen words, I'm very glad to see you in my house, gentlemen, and I hope you will make yourselves at home. Where nobody understands, a man has to speak plain. I've been turned out all my life and, by Jove! I don't mean to stand it any longer. The girls can have what their father's left them," said the vagabond, in his moment of triumph. "They aint my business no more than I was theirs. The property is freehold, and Waters is aware that I'm the heir."

Saying this, Wodehouse drew a chair to the table, and sat down with emphasis. He was the only man seated in the room, and he kept his place in his sullen way amid the excited group which gathered round him. As for Miss Wodehouse, some sense of what had happened penetrated even her mind. She too rose up and wiped her tears from her face, and looked round, pale and scared, to the Curate. "I was thinking – of speaking to Lucy. I meant to ask her – to take you back, Tom," said the elder sister. "Oh, Mr Wentworth, tell me, for heaven's sake, what does it mean?"

"If I had only been permitted to explain," said Mr Waters; "my worthy partner died intestate – his son is his natural heir. Perhaps we need not detain the ladies longer, now that they understand it. All the rest can be better arranged with their representative. I am very sorry to add to their sufferings today," said the polite lawyer, opening the door; "everything else can be made the subject of an arrangement." He held the door open with a kind of civil coercion compelling their departure. The familiar room they were in no longer belonged to the Miss Wodehouses. Lucy drew her arm out of Mr Wentworth's, and took her sister's hand.

"You will be our representative," she said to him, out of the fulness of her heart. When the door closed, the Perpetual Curate took up his position, facing them all with looks more lofty than belonged even to his Wentworth blood. They had kept him from exercising his office at his friend's grave, but nobody could take from him the still nobler duty of defending the oppressed.

CHAPTER XXXIV.

When the door closed upon Lucy and her sister, Mr Wentworth stood by himself, facing the other people assembled. The majority of them were more surprised, more shocked, than he was; but they were huddled together in their wonder at the opposite end of the table, and had somehow a confused, half-conscious air of being on the other side.

"It's a very extraordinary revelation that has just been made to us," said Dr Marjoribanks. "I am throwing no doubt upon it, for my part; but my conviction was, that Tom Wodehouse died in the West Indies. He was just the kind of man to die in the West Indies. If it's you," said the Doctor, with a growl of natural indignation, "you have the constitution of an elephant. You should have been dead ten years ago, at the very least; and it appears to me there would be some difficulty in proving identity, if anybody would take up that view of the question." As he spoke, Dr Marjoribanks walked round the new-comer, looking at him with medical criticism. The Doctor's eyes shot out fiery hazel gleams as he contemplated the heavy figure. "More appearance than reality," he muttered to himself, with a kind of grim satisfaction, poising a forefinger in air, as if to prove the unwholesome flesh; and then he went round to the other elbow of the unexpected heir. "The thing is now, what you mean to do for them, to repair your father's neglect," he said, tapping peremptorily on Wodehouse's arm.

There is something else to be said in the mean time," said Mr Wentworth. "I must know precisely how it is that a state of affairs so different from anything Mr Wodehouse could have intended has come about. The mere absence of a will does not seem to me to explain it. I should like to have Mr Brown's advice – for my own satisfaction, if nothing else."

"The parson has got nothing to do with it, that I can see," said Wodehouse, "unless he was looking for a legacy, or that sort of thing. As for the girls, I don't see what right I have to be troubled; they took deuced little trouble with me. Perhaps they'd have taken me in as a sort of footman without pay – you heard what they said, Waters? By Jove! I'll serve Miss Mary out for that," said the vagabond. Then he paused a little, and, looking round him, moderated his tone. "I've been badly used all my life," said the prodigal son. "They would never give me a hearing. They say I did heaps of things I never dreamt of. Mary aint above thinking of her own interest—"

Here Mr Proctor came forward from the middle of the room where he had been standing in a perplexed manner since the ladies went away. "Hold – hold your tongue, sir!" said the late Rector; "haven't you done enough injury already—" When he had said so much, he stopped as abruptly as he had begun, and seemed to recollect all at once that he had no title to interfere.

"By Jove!" said Wodehouse, "you don't seem to think I know what belongs to me, or who belongs to me. Hold *your* tongue, Waters; I can speak for myself. I've been long enough snubbed by everybody that had a mind. I don't mean to put up with this sort of thing any longer. Any man who pleases can consult John Brown. I recollect John Brown as well as anybody in Carlingford. It don't matter to me what he says, or what anybody says. The girls are a parcel of girls, and I am my father's son, as it happens. I should have thought the parson had enough on his hands for one while," said the new heir, in the insolence of triumph. "He tried patronising me, but that wouldn't answer. Why, there's his brother, Jack Wentworth, his elder brother, come down here purposely to manage matters for me. He's the eldest son, by Jove! and one of the greatest swells going. He has come down here on purpose to do the friendly thing by me. We're great friends, by Jove! Jack Wentworth and I; and yet here's a beggarly younger brother, that hasn't a penny—"

"Wodehouse," said Mr Wentworth, with some contempt, "sit down and be quiet. You and I have some things to talk of which had better not be discussed in public. Leave Jack Wentworth's name alone, if you are wise, and don't imagine that I am going to bear your punishment. Be silent, sir!" cried the Curate, sternly; "do you suppose I ask any explanations from you? Mr Waters, I want to hear how this has come about? When I saw you in this man's interest some time ago, you were not so friendly to him. Tell me how it happens that he is now your client, and that you set him forth as the heir!"

"By Jove, the parson has nothing to do with it! Let him find it out," muttered Wodehouse in his beard; but the words were only half audible, and the vagabond's shabby soul was cowed in spite of himself. He gave the lawyer a furtive thrust in the arm as he spoke, and looked at him a little anxiously; for the position of a man standing lawfully on his natural rights was new to Wodehouse; and all his certainty of the facts did not save him from a sensation of habit which suggested that close examination was alarming, and that something might still be found out. As for Mr Waters, he looked with placid contempt at the man, who was not respectable, and still had the instincts of a vagabond in his heart.

"I am perfectly ready to explain," said the irreproachable solicitor, who was quite secure in his position. "The tone of the request, however, might be modified a little; and as I don't, any more than Mr Wodehouse, see exactly what right Mr Wentworth has to demand—"

"I ask an explanation, not on my own behalf, but for the Miss Wodehouses, who have made me their deputy," said the Curate, "for their satisfaction, and that I may consult Mr Brown. You seem to forget that all *he* gains they lose; which surely justifies their representative in asking how did it come about?"

It was at this point that all the other gentlemen present pressed closer, and evinced an intention to take part. Dr Marjoribanks was the first to speak. He took a pinch of snuff, and while he consumed it looked from under his grizzled sandy eyebrows with a perplexing mixture of doubt and respect at the Perpetual Curate. He was a man of some discrimination in his way, and the young man's lofty looks impressed him a little in spite of himself.

"Not to interrupt the explanation," said Dr Marjoribanks, "which we'll all be glad to hear – but Mr Wentworth's a young man, not possessed, so far as I am aware, of any particular right; – except that he has been very generous and prompt in offering his services," said the Doctor, moved to the admission by a fiery glance from the Curate's eye, which somehow did not look like the eye of a guilty man. "I was thinking, an old man, and an old friend, like myself, might maybe be a better guardian for the ladies' interests—"

Mr Proctor, who had been listening very anxiously, was seized with a cough at this moment, which drowned out the Doctor's words. It was a preparatory cough, and out of it the late Rector rushed into speech. "I have come from – from Oxford to be of use," said the new champion. "My time is entirely at my own – at Miss Wodehouse's – at the Miss Wodehouses' disposal. I am most desirous to be of use," said Mr Proctor, anxiously. And he advanced close to the table to prefer his claim.

Such a discussion seems quite unnecessary," said Mr Wentworth, with some haughtiness. "I shall certainly do in the mean time what has been intrusted to me. At present we are simply losing time."

"But—" said the Rector. The word was not of importance nor uttered with much resolution, but it arrested Mr Wentworth more surely than the shout of a multitude. He turned sharp round upon his adversary, and said "Well?" with an air of exasperation; while Wodehouse, who had been lounging about the room in a discomfited condition, drew near to listen.

"I am comparatively a stranger to the Miss Wodehouses," said Mr Morgan; "still I am their clergyman; and I think with Dr Marjoribanks, that a young man like Mr Wentworth, especially a man so seriously compromised—"

"Oh, stop! I do think you are all a great deal too hard upon Mr Wentworth," said the lawyer, with a laugh of toleration, which Wodehouse echoed behind him with a sense of temerity that made his laughter all the louder. He was frightened, but he was glad to make himself offensive, according to his nature. Mr Wentworth stood alone, for his part, and had to put up with the laugh as he best could.

"If any one here wishes to injure me with the Miss Wodehouses, an opportunity may easily be found," said the Curate, with as much composure as he could muster; "and I am ready to relinquish my charge when they call on me to do so. In the mean time, this is not the place to investigate my conduct. Sit down, sir, and let us be free of your interference for this moment at least," he said, fiercely, turning to the new heir. "I warn you again, you

have nothing but justice to expect at my hands. Mr
Waters, we wait your explanations." He was the tallest
man in the room, which perhaps had something to do with
it; the youngest, best born, and best endowed. That he
would have carried the day triumphantly in the opinion of
any popular audience, there could be no kind of doubt.
Even in this middle-aged unimpressionable assembly, his
indignant self-control had a certain influence. When he
drew a chair towards the table and seated himself, the
others sat down unawares, and the lawyer began his story
without any further interruption. The explanation of all
was, that Mr Wodehouse, like so many men, had an
ambition to end his days as a country gentleman. He had
set his heart for years on an estate in the neighbourhood of
Carlingford, and had just completed his long-contemplated
purchase at the moment of his last seizure. Nobody knew,
except the Curate and the lawyer, what the cause of that
seizure was. They exchanged looks without being aware of
it, and Wodehouse, still more deeply conscious, uttered,
poor wretch! a kind of gasp, which sounded like a laugh to
the other horrified spectators. After all, it was his crime
which had brought him his good fortune, for there had
been an early will relating to property which existed no
longer – property which had been altogether absorbed in
the newly-acquired estate. "I have no doubt my late
excellent partner would have made a settlement had the
time been permitted him," said Mr Waters. "I have not
the slightest doubt as to his intentions; but the end was
very unexpected at the last. I suppose death always is
unexpected when it comes," said the lawyer, with a little
solemnity, recollecting that three of his auditors were
clergymen. "The result is painful in many respects; but
law is law, and such accidents cannot be entirely avoided.
With the exception of a few trifling personal matters, and
the furniture, and a little money at the bank, there is
nothing but freehold property, and of course the son takes
that. I can have no possible objection to your consulting

Mr Brown; but Mr Brown can give you no further information." If there had been any little hope of possible
redress lingering in the mind of the perplexed assembly,
this brought it to a conclusion. The heir, who had been
keeping behind with an impulse of natural shame, came
back to the table when his rights were so clearly established.
He did not know how to behave himself with a good grace,
but he was disposed to be conciliatory, as far as he could,
especially as it began to be disagreeably apparent that the
possession of his father's property might not make any
particular difference in the world's opinion of himself.

"It aint my fault, gentlemen," said Wodehouse. "Of
course, I expected the governor to take care of the girls.
I've been kept out of it for twenty years, and that's a long
time. By Jove! I've never known what it was to be a rich
man's son since I was a lad. I don't say I won't do
something for the girls if they behave to me as they ought;
and as for you, gentlemen, who were friends of the family,
I'll always be glad to see you in my house," he said, with
an attempt at a friendly smile. But nobody took any notice
of the overtures of the new heir.

"Then they have nothing to depend upon," said Mr
Proctor, whose agitated looks were the most inexplicable
feature of the whole – "no shelter even; no near relations I
ever heard of – and nobody to take care of Lucy if—"
Here he stopped short and went to the window, and stood
looking out in a state of great bewilderment. The late
Rector was so buried in his own thoughts, whatever they
might be, that he did not pay any attention to the further
conversation which went on behind him – of which, however, there was very little – and only came to himself
when he saw Mr Wentworth go rapidly through the garden.
Mr Proctor rushed after the Perpetual Curate. He might
be seriously compromised, as Mr Morgan said; but he was
more sympathetic than anybody else in Carlingford under
present circumstances; and Mr Proctor, in his middle-aged
uncertainty, could not help having a certain confidence in

the young man's promptitude and vigour. He made up to him out of breath when he was just entering George Street. Carlingford had paid what respect it could to Mr Wodehouse's memory; and now the shutters were being taken off the shop-windows, and people in general were very willing to reward themselves for their self-denial by taking what amusement they could out of the reports which already began to be circulated about the way in which the Miss Wodehouses were "left." When the late Rector came up with the Perpetual Curate opposite Masters's shop there was quite a group of people there who noted the conjunction. What could it mean? Was there going to be a compromise? Was Carlingford to be shamefully cheated out of the "investigation," and all the details about Rosa Elsworthy, for which it hungered? Mr Proctor put his arm through that of the Curate of St Roque's, and permitted himself to be swept along by the greater impetus of the young man's rapid steps, for at this moment, being occupied with more important matters, the late Rector had altogether forgotten Mr Wentworth's peculiar position, and the cloud that hung over him.

"What a very extraordinary thing!" said Mr Proctor. "What could have betrayed old Wodehouse into such a blunder! He must have known well enough. This son – this fellow – has been living all the time, of course. It is quite inexplicable to me," said the aggrieved man. "Do you know if there are any aunts or uncles – any people whom poor little Lucy might live with, for instance, if—" And here Mr Proctor once more came to a dead stop. Mr Wentworth, for his part, was so far from thinking of her as "poor little Lucy," that he was much offended by the unnecessary commiseration.

"The sisters will naturally remain together," he said; "and, of course, there are many people who would be but too glad to receive them. Miss Wodehouse is old enough to protect her sister – though, of course, the balance of character is on the other side," said the inconsiderate young man; at which Mr Proctor winced, but made no definite reply.

"So you think there are people she could go to?" said the late Rector, after a pause. "The thing altogether is so unexpected, you know. My idea was—"

"I beg your pardon," said the Curate; "I must see Mr Brown, and this is about the best time to find him at home. Circumstances make it rather awkward for me to call at the Rectory just now," he continued, with a smile – "circumstances over which I have no control, as people say; but perhaps you will stay long enough to see me put on my trial. Good-bye now."

"Stop a moment," said Mr Proctor; "about this trial. Don't be affronted – I have nothing to do with it, you know; and Morgan means very well, though he's stupid enough. I should like to stand your friend, Wentworth; you know I would. I wish you'd yield to tell me all about it. If I were to call on you to-night after dinner – for perhaps it would put Mrs Hadwin out to give me a chop?"

The Curate laughed in spite of himself. "Fellows of All-Souls don't dine on chops," he said, unable to repress a gleam of amusement; "but come at six, and you shall have something to eat, as good as I can give you. As for telling you all about it," said Mr Wentworth, "all the world is welcome to know as much as I know."

Mr Proctor laid his hand on the young man's arm, by way of soothing him. "We'll talk it all over," he said, confidentially; "both this affair, and – and the other. We have a good deal in common, if I am not much mistaken, and I trust we shall always be good friends," said the inexplicable man. His complexion heightened considerably after he had made this speech, which conveyed nothing but amazement to the mind of the Curate; and then he shook hands hastily, and hurried back again towards Grange Lane. If there had been either room or leisure in Frank Wentworth's mind for other thoughts, he might have laughed or puzzled over the palpable mystery; but as it was, he had dismissed the late Rector entirely from his mind before he reached the door of Mr Brown's room, where the lawyer was seated alone. John Brown, who was altogether a different type of man from Mr Waters, held out his hand to his visitor, and did not look at all surprised to see him. "I have expected a call from you," he said, "now that your old friend is gone, from whom you would naturally have sought advice in the circumstances. Tell me what I can do for you;" and it became apparent to Mr Wentworth that it was his own affairs which were supposed to be the cause of his application. It may be supposed after this that the Curate stated his real object very curtly and clearly without any unnecessary words, to the unbounded amazement of the lawyer, who, being a busy man, and not a friend of the Wodehouses, had as yet heard nothing of the matter. Mr Brown, however, could only confirm what had been already said. "If it is really freehold property, and no settlement made, there cannot be any question about it," he said; "but I will see Waters to-morrow and make all sure, if you wish it; though he dares not mislead you on such a point. I am very sorry for the ladies, but I don't see what can be done for them," said Mr Brown; "and about yourself, Mr Wentworth?" Perhaps it was because of a certain look of genuine confidence and solicitude in John Brown's honest face that the Curate's heart was moved. For the first time he condescended to discuss the matter – to tell the lawyer, with whom indeed he had but a very slight acquaintance (for John Brown lived at the other end of Carlingford, and could not be said to be in society), all he knew about Rosa Elsworthy, and something of his suspicions. Mr Brown, for his part, knew little of the Perpetual Curate in his social capacity, but he knew about Wharfside, which was more to the purpose; and having himself been truly in love once in his life, commonplace as he looked, this honest man did not believe it possible that Lucy Wodehouse's representative could be Rosa Elsworthy's seducer – the

two things looked incompatible to the straightforward
vision of John Brown.

"I'll attend at their investigation," he said, with a smile,
"which, if you were not particularly interested, you'd find
not bad fun, Mr Wentworth. These private attempts at
law are generally very amusing. I'll attend and look after
your interests; but you had better see that this Tom
Wodehouse, – I remember the scamp – he used to be bad
enough for anything, – don't give you the slip and get out
of the way. Find out if you can where he has been living
these two days. I'll attend to the other matter, too," the
lawyer said, cheerfully, shaking hands with his new client;
and the Curate went away with a vague feeling that
matters were about to come right somehow, at which he
smiled when he came to think of it, and saw how little
foundation he had for such a hope. But his hands were full
of business, and he had no time to consider his own affairs
at this particular moment. It seemed to him a kind of
profanity to permit Lucy to remain under the same roof
with Wodehouse, even though he was her brother; and Mr
Proctor's inquiries had stimulated his own feeling. There
was a certain pleasure, besides, in postponing himself and
his own business, however important, to her and her
concerns; and it was with this idea that he proceeded to
the house of his aunts, and was conducted to a little
private sitting-room appropriated to the sole use of Miss
Leonora, for whom he had asked. As he passed the door of
the drawing-room, which was ajar, he glanced in, and saw
his aunt Dora bending over somebody who wept, and
heard a familiar voice pouring out complaints, the general
sound of which was equally familiar, though he could not
make out a word of the special subject. Frank was startled,
notwithstanding his preoccupations, for it was the same
voice which had summoned him to Wentworth Rectory
which now poured out its lamentations in the Miss
Wentworths' drawing-room in Carlingford. Evidently
some new complication had arisen in the affairs of the

family. Miss Leonora was in her room, busy with the books of a Ladies' Association, of which she was treasurer. She had a letter before her from the missionary employed by the society, which was a very interesting letter, and likely to make a considerable sensation when read before the next meeting. Miss Leonora was taking the cream off this piece of correspondence, enjoying at once itself and the impression it would make. She was slightly annoyed when her nephew came in to disturb her. "The others are in the drawing-room, as usual," she said. "I can't imagine what Lewis could be thinking of, to bring you here. Louisa's coming can make no difference to you."

"So Louisa has come? I thought I heard her voice. What has happened to bring Louisa here?" said the Curate, who was not sorry to begin with an indifferent subject. Miss Leonora shook her head and took up her letter.

"She is in the drawing-room," said the strong-minded aunt. "If you have no particular business with me, Frank, you had better ask herself: of course, if you want me, I am at your service – but otherwise I am busy, you see."

"And so am I," said Mr Wentworth, "as busy as a man can be whose character is at stake. Do you know I am to be tried to-morrow? But that is not what I came to ask you about."

"I wish you would *tell* me about it," said Miss Leonora. She got up from her writing-table and from the missionary's letter, and abandoned herself to the impulses of nature. "I have heard disagreeable rumours. I don't object to your reserve, Frank, but things seem to be getting serious. What does it mean?"

The Curate had been much braced in his inner man by his short interview with John Brown; that, and the representative position he held, had made a wonderful change in his feelings: besides, a matter which was about to become so public could not be ignored. "It means only that a good many people in Carlingford think me a villain," said Mr Wentworth: "it is not a flattering idea; and it seems to me, I must say, an illogical induction from the facts of my life. Still it is true that some people think so – and I am to be tried to-morrow. But in the mean time, something else has happened. I know you are a good woman, aunt Leonora. We don't agree in many things, but that does not matter. There are two ladies in Carlingford who up to this day have been rich, well off, well cared for, and who have suddenly lost all their means, their protector, even their home. They have no relations that I know of. One of them is good for any exertion that may be necessary," said the Curate, his voice softening with a far-off masculine suggestion as of tears; "but she is young – too young to contend with the world – and she is now suffering her first grief. The other is old enough, but not good for much—"

"You mean the two Miss Wodehouses?" said Miss Leonora. "Their father has turned out to be – bankrupt? – or something?—"

"Worse than bankrupt," said the Curate: "there is a brother who takes everything. Will you stand by them – offer them shelter? – I mean for a time. I don't know anybody I should care to apply to but you."

Miss Leonora paused and looked at her nephew. "First tell me what you have to do with them," she asked. "If there is a brother, he is their natural protector – certainly not you – unless there is something I don't know of. Frank, you know you can't marry," said Miss Leonora, with a little vehemence, once more looking in her nephew's face.

"No," said Frank, with momentary bitterness; "I am not likely to make any mistake about that – at present, at least. The brother is a reprobate of whom they know nothing. I have no right to consider myself their protector – but I am their friend at least," said the Curate, breaking off with again that softening in his voice. "They may have a great many friends, for anything I know; but I have confidence in you, aunt Leonora: you are not perhaps particularly sympathetic," he went on, with a laugh; "you

don't condole with Louisa, for instance; but I could trust
you with—"

"Lucy Wodehouse!" said Miss Leonora; "I don't dislike
her at all, if she would not wear that ridiculous grey cloak;
but young men don't take such an interest in young
women without some reason for it. What are we to do for
you, Frank?" said the strong-minded woman, looking at
him with a little softness. Miss Leonora, perhaps, was not
used to be taken into anybody's confidence. It moved her
more than might have been expected from so self-possessed
a woman. Perhaps no other act on the part of her nephew
could have had so much effect, had he been able to pursue
his advantage, upon the still undecided fate of Skelmersdale.

"Nothing," said the Curate. He met her eye very
steadily, but she was too clear-sighted to believe that he
felt as calmly as he looked. "Nothing," he repeated again
– "I told you as much before. I have been slandered here,
and here I must remain. There are no parsonages or
paradises for me."

With which speech Mr Wentworth shook hands with his
aunt and went away. He left Miss Leonora as he had left
her on various occasions – considerably confused in her
ideas. She could not enjoy any longer the cream of the
missionary's letter. When she tried to resume her reading,
her attention flagged over it. After a while she put on her
bonnet and went out, after a little consultation with her
maid, who assisted her in the housekeeping department.
The house was tolerably full at the present moment, but it
was elastic. She was met at the green door of Mr
Wodehouse's garden by the new proprietor, who stared
excessively, and did not know what to make of such an
apparition. "Jack Wentworth's aunt, by Jove!" he said to
himself, and took off his hat, meaning to show her "a little
civility." Miss Leonora thought him one of the attendants
at the recent ceremonial, and passed him without any
ceremony. She was quite intent upon her charitable mission.
Mr Wentworth's confidence was justified.

CHAPTER XXXV.

MR WENTWORTH'S day had been closely occupied up to this point. He had gone through a great many emotions, and transacted a good deal of business, and he went home with the comparative ease of a man whose anxieties are relieved, not by any real deliverance, but by the soothing influence of fatigue and the sense of something accomplished. He was not in reality in a better position than when he left his house in the morning, bitterly mortified, injured, and wounded at the tenderest point. Things were very much the same as they had been, but a change had come over the feelings of the Perpetual Curate. He remembered with a smile, as he went down Grange Lane, that Mr Proctor was to dine with him, and that he had rashly undertaken to have something better than a chop. It was a very foolish engagement under the circumstances. Mr Wentworth was cogitating within himself whether he could make an appeal to the sympathies of his aunt's cook for something worthy of the sensitive palate of a Fellow of All-Souls, when all such thoughts were suddenly driven out of his mind by the apparition of his brother Gerald – perhaps the last man in the world whom he could have expected to see in Carlingford. Gerald was coming up Grange Lane in his meditative way from Mrs Hadwin's door. To look at him was enough to reveal to any clear-sighted spectator the presence of some perpetual argument in his mind. Though he had come out to look for Frank, his eyes were continually forsaking his intention, catching spots of lichen on the wall and clumps of herbage on the roadside. The

long discussion had become so familiar to him, that even
now, when his mind was made up, he could not relinquish
the habit which possessed him. When he perceived Frank,
he quickened his steps. They met with only such a
modified expression of surprise on the part of the younger
brother as was natural to a meeting of English kinsfolk. "I
heard Louisa's voice in my aunt's drawing-room," said
Frank; "but, oddly enough, it never occurred to me that
you might have come with her;" and then Gerald turned
with the Curate. When the ordinary family questions
were asked and answered, a silence ensued between the
two. As for Frank, in the multiplicity of his own cares, he
had all but forgotten his brother; and Gerald's mind,
though full of anxiety, had something of the calm which
might be supposed to subdue the senses of a dying man.
He was on the eve of a change, which appeared to him
almost as great as death; and the knowledge of that gave
him a curious stillness of composure – almost a reluctance
to speak. Strangely enough, each brother at this critical
moment felt it necessary to occupy himself with the affairs
of the other, and to postpone the consideration of his own.

"I hope you have changed your mind a little since we
last met," said Frank; "your last letter—"

"We'll talk of that presently," said the elder brother;
"in the mean time I want to know about *you*. What is all
this? My father is in a great state of anxiety. He does not
seem to have got rid of his fancy that you were somehow
involved with Jack – and Jack is here," said Gerald, with
a look which betokened some anxiety on his own part. "I
wish you would give me your confidence. Right or wrong,
I have come to stand by you, Frank," said the Rector of
Wentworth, rather mournfully. He had been waiting at
Mrs Hadwin's for the last two hours. He had seen that
worthy woman's discomposed looks, and felt that she did
not shake her head for nothing. Jack had been the
bugbear of the family for a long time past. Gerald was
conscious of adding heavily at the present moment to the

Squire's troubles. Charley was at Malta, in indifferent health; all the others were boys. There was only Frank to give the father a little consolation; and now Frank, it appeared, was most deeply compromised of all; no wonder Gerald was sad. And then he drew forth the anonymous letter which had startled all the Wentworths on the previous night. "This is written by somebody who hates you," said the elder brother; "but I suppose there must be some meaning in it. I wish you would be frank with me, and tell me what it is."

This appeal had brought them to Mrs Hadwin's door, which the Curate opened with his key before he answered his brother. The old lady herself was walking in the garden in a state of great agitation, with a shawl thrown over the best cap, which she had put on in honour of the stranger. Mrs Hadwin's feelings were too much for her at that moment. Her head was nodding with the excitement of age, and injured virtue trembled in every line of her face. "Mr Wentworth, I cannot put up with it any longer; it is a thing I never was used to," she cried, as soon as the Curate came within hearing. "I have shut my eyes to a great deal, but I cannot bear it any longer. If I had been a common lodging-house keeper, I could not have been treated with less respect; but to be outraged – to be insulted—"

"What is the matter, Mrs Hadwin?" said Mr Wentworth, in dismay.

"Sir," said the old lady, who was trembling with passion, "you may think it no matter to turn a house upside down as mine has been since Easter; to bring all sorts of disreputable people about – persons whom a gentlewoman in my position ought never to have heard of. I received your brother into my house," cried Mrs Hadwin, turning to Gerald, "because he was a clergyman and I knew his family, and hoped to find him one whose principles I could approve of. I have put up with a great deal, Mr Wentworth, more than I could tell to anybody. I took in his friend when he asked me, and gave him the spare room, though it was against my judgment. I suffered a man with a beard to be seen stealing in and out of my house in the evening, as if he was afraid to be seen. You gentlemen may not think much of that, but it was a terrible thing for a lady in my position, unprotected, and not so well off as I once was. It made my house like a lodging-house, and so my friends told me; but I was so infatuated I put up with it all for Mr Frank's sake. But there *is* a limit," said the aggrieved woman. "I would not have believed it – I *could* not have believed it of you – not whatever people might say: to think of that abandoned disgraceful girl coming openly to my door—"

"Good heavens!" cried the Curate: he seized Mrs Hadwin's hand, evidently forgetting everything else she had said. "What girl? – whom do you mean? For heaven's sake compose yourself and answer me. Who was it? Rosa Elsworthy? This is a matter of life and death for me," cried the young man. "Speak quickly: when was it? – where is she? For heaven's sake, Mrs Hadwin, speak—"

"Let me go, sir!" cried the indignant old lady; "let me go this instant – this is insult upon insult. I appeal to you, Mr Gerald – to think I should ever be supposed capable of encouraging such a horrid shameless— ! How dare you – how dare you name such a creature to me?" exclaimed Mrs Hadwin, with hysterical sobs. "If it were not for your family, you should never enter my house again. Oh, thank you, Mr Gerald Wentworth – indeed I am not able to walk. I am sure I don't want to grieve you about your brother – I tried not to believe it – I tried as long as I could not to believe it – but you hear how he speaks. Do you think, sir, I would for a moment permit such a creature to enter my door?" she cried again, turning to Frank Wentworth as she leaned upon his brother's arm.

"I don't know what kind of a creature the poor girl is," said the Curate; "but I know that if you had taken her in, it would have saved me much pain and trouble. Tell me, at least, when she came, and who saw her – or if she left any message? Perhaps Sarah will tell me," he said, with a sigh of despair, as he saw that handmaiden hovering behind. Sarah had been a little shy of Mr Wentworth since the night Wodehouse disappeared. She had betrayed herself to the Curate, and did not like to remember the fact. Now she came up with a little toss of her head and a sense of equality, primed and ready with her reply.

"I hope I think more of myself than to take notice of any sich," said Sarah; but her instincts were more vivid than those of her mistress, and she could not refrain from particulars. "Them as saw her now, wouldn't see much in her; I never see such a changed creature," said Sarah; "not as I ever thought anything of her looks! a bit of a shawl dragged around her, and her eyes as if they would jump out of her head. Laws! she didn't get no satisfaction here," said the housemaid, with a little triumph.

"Silence, Sarah!" said Mrs Hadwin; "that is not a way to speak to your clergyman. I'll go in, Mr Wentworth, please – I am not equal to so much agitation. If Mr Frank will come indoors, I should be glad to have an explanation – for this sort of thing cannot go on," said the old lady. As for the Curate he did not pay the least attention either to the disapproval or the impertinence.

"At what time did she come? – which way did she go? – did she leave any message?" he repeated; "a moment's common-sense will be of more use than all this indignation. It is of the greatest importance to me to see Rosa Elsworthy. Here's how it is, Gerald," said the Curate, driven to his wit's end; "a word from the girl is all I want to make an end of all this – this disgusting folly – and you see how I am thwarted. Perhaps they will answer *you*. When did she come? – did she say anything?" he cried, turning sharply upon Sarah, who, frightened by Mr Wentworth's look, and dismayed to see her mistress moving away, and to feel herself alone opposed to him, burst at last into an alarmed statement.

"Please, sir, it aint no fault of mine," said Sarah; "it was Missis as saw her. She aint been gone not half an hour. It's all happened since your brother left. She come to the side-door; Missis wouldn't hear nothing she had got to say, nor let her speak. Oh, Mr Wentworth, don't you go after her!" cried the girl, following him to the side-door, to which he rushed immediately. Not half an hour gone! Mr Wentworth burst into the lane which led up to Grove Street, and where there was not a soul to be seen. He went back to Grange Lane, and inspected every corner where she could have hid herself. Then, after a pause, he walked impetuously up the quiet road, and into Elsworthy's shop. Mrs Elsworthy was there alone, occupying her husband's place, who had gone as usual to the railway for the evening papers. She jumped up from the high stool she was seated on when the Curate entered. "Good gracious, Mr Wentworth!" cried the frightened woman, and instinctively called the errand-boy, who was the only other individual within hearing. She was unprotected, and quite unable to defend herself if he meant anything; and it was impossible to doubt that there was meaning of the most serious and energetic kind in Mr Wentworth's face.

"Has Rosa come back?" he asked. "Is she here? Don't stare at me, but speak. Has she come back? I have just heard that she was at my house half an hour ago: have you got her safe?"

It was at this moment that Wodehouse came lounging in, with his cigar appearing in the midst of his beard, and a curious look of self-exhibition and demonstration in his general aspect. When the Curate, hearing the steps, turned round upon him, he fell back for a moment, not expecting such an encounter. Then the vagabond recovered himself, and came forward with the swagger which was his only alternative.

"I thought you weren't on good terms here," said Wodehouse; "who are you asking after? It's a fine evening, and they don't seem up to much in my house. I have asked Jack Wentworth to the Blue Boar at seven – will you come? I don't want to bear any grudge. I don't know if they can cook anything fit to be eaten in my house. It wasn't me you were asking after?" The fellow came and stood close, shoulder to shoulder, by the Perpetual Curate. "By Jove, sir! I've as good a right here as you – or anywhere," he muttered, as Mr Wentworth withdrew from him. He had to say it aloud to convince himself of the fact; for it was hard, after being clandestine for half a lifetime, to move about freely in the daylight. As for Mr Wentworth, he fixed his eyes full on the new-comer's face.

"I want to know if Rosa has come home," he repeated, in the clearest tones of his clear voice. "I am told she called at Mrs Hadwin's half an hour ago. Has she come back?"

He scarcely noticed Mrs Elsworthy's answer, for, in the mean time, the cigar dropped out of Wodehouse's beard, out of his fingers. He made an involuntary step back out of the Curate's way. "By Jove!" he exclaimed to himself – the news was more important to him than to either of the others. After a minute he turned his back upon them, and kicked the cigar which he had dropped out into the street with much blundering and unnecessary violence – but turned round and stopped short in this occupation as soon as he heard Mrs Elsworthy's voice.

"She hasn't come here," said that virtuous woman, sharply. "I've give in to Elsworthy a deal, but I never said I'd give in to take her back. She's been and disgraced us all; and she's not a drop's blood to me," said Mrs Elsworthy. "Them as has brought her to this pass had best look after her; I've washed my hands of Rosa, and all belonging to her. She knows better than to come here."

"Who's speaking of Rosa?" said Elsworthy, who just then came in with his bundle of newspapers from the railway. "I might have know'd as it was Mr Wentworth. Matters is going to be cleared, sir, between me and you. If you was going to make a proposal, I aint revengeful; and

I'm open to any arrangement as is honourable, to save things coming afore the public. I've been expecting of it. You may speak free, sir. You needn't be afraid of me."

"Fool!" said the Curate, hotly, "your niece has been seen in Carlingford; she came to my door, I am told, about an hour ago. Give up this folly, and let us make an effort to find her. I tell you she came to my house—"

"In course, sir," said Elsworthy; "it was the most naturalest place for her to go. Don't you stand upon it no longer, as if you could deceive folks. It will be your ruin, Mr Wentworth – you know that as well as I do. I aint no fool but I'm open to a honourable proposal, I am. It'll ruin you – ay, and I'll ruin you," cried Rosa's uncle, hoarsely – "if you don't change your mind afore to-morrow. It's your last chance, if you care for your character, is to-night."

Mr Wentworth did not condescend to make any answer. He followed Wodehouse, who had shuffled out after his cigar, and stopped him on the step. "I wonder if it is any use appealing to your honour," he said. "I suppose you were a gentleman once, and had the feelings of—"

"By Jove! I'm as good a gentleman as you are," cried the new heir. "I could buy you up – you and all that belongs to you, by Jove! I'm giving Jack Wentworth a dinner at the Blue Boar to-night. I'm not a man to be cross-questioned. It appears to me you have got enough to do if you mind your own business," said Wodehouse, with a sneer. "You're in a nice mess, though you are the parson. I told Jack Wentworth so last night."

The Curate stood on the step of Elsworthy's shop with his enemy behind, and the ungrateful vagabond whom he had rescued and guarded, standing in front of him, with that sneer on his lips. It was hard to refrain from the natural impulse which prompted him to pitch the vagabond out of his way. "Look here," he said, sharply, "you have not much character to lose; but a scamp is a different thing from a criminal. I will make the principal people in Carlingford aware what were the precise circumstances under which you came here at Easter if you do not immediately restore this unhappy girl to her friends. Do you understand me? If it is not done at once I will make use of my information – and you know what that means. You can defy me if you please; but in that case you had better make up your mind to the consequences; you will have to take your place as a—"

"Stop!" cried Wodehouse, with a shiver. "We're not by ourselves – we're in the public street. What do you mean by talking like that here? Come to my house, Wentworth – there's a good fellow – I've ordered a dinner—"

"Be silent, sir!" said the Curate. "I give you till noon to-morrow; after that I will spare you no longer. You understand what I mean. I have been too merciful already. To-morrow, if everything is not arranged to my satisfaction here—"

"It was my own name," said Wodehouse, sullenly; "nobody can say it wasn't my own name. You couldn't do me any harm – you know you wouldn't, either, for the sake of the girls; I'll – I'll give them a thousand pounds or so, if I find I can afford it. Come, you don't mean that sort of thing, you know," said the conscious criminal; "you wouldn't do me any harm."

"If I have to fight for my own reputation I shall not spare you," cried the Curate. "Mind what I say! You are safe till twelve o'clock to-morrow; but after that I will have no mercy – not for your sisters' sake, not for any inducement in the world. If you want to be known as a—"

"Oh Lord, don't speak so loud! – what do you mean? Wentworth, I say, hist! Mr Wentworth! By Jove, he won't listen to me!" cried Wodehouse, in an agony. When he found that the Curate was already out of hearing, the vagabond looked round him on every side with his natural instinct of suspicion. If he had known that Mr Wentworth was thinking only of disgrace and the stern sentence of public opinion, Wodehouse could have put up with it; but he himself, in his guilty imagination, jumped at the bar and the prison which had haunted him for long. Somehow it felt natural that such a Nemesis should come to him after the morning's triumph. He stood looking after the Curate, guilty and horror-stricken, till it occurred to him that he might be remarked; and then he made a circuit past Elsworthy's shop-window as far as the end of Prickett's Lane, where he ventured to cross over so as to get to his own house. His own house! – the wretched thrill of terror that went through him was a very sufficient offset against his momentary triumph; and this was succeeded by a flush of rage as he thought of the Curate's other information. What was to be done? Every moment was precious; but he felt an instinctive horror of venturing out again in the daylight. When it approached the hour at which he had ordered that dinner at the Blue Boar, the humbled hero wrapped himself in an old overcoat which he found in the hall, and slunk into the inn like the clandestine wretch he was. He had no confidence in himself, but he had confidence in Jack Wentworth. He might still be able to help his unlucky associate out.

When Mr Wentworth reached his rooms, he found that his guest had arrived before him, and consequently the threatened explanation with Mrs Hadwin was forestalled for that night. Mr Proctor and Gerald were sitting together, not at all knowing what to talk about; for the late Rector was aware that Frank Wentworth's brother was on the verge of Rome, and was confused, and could not help feeling that his position between a man on the point of perversion in an ecclesiastical point of view, and another whose morals were suspected and whose character was compromised, was, to say the least, a very odd position for a clergyman of unblemished orthodoxy and respectability; besides, it was embarrassing, when he had come for a very private consultation, to find a stranger there before him. The Curate went in very full of what had just occurred. The events of the last two or three hours had worked a total change in his feelings. He was no longer the injured, insulted, silent object of a petty but virulent persecution. The contemptuous silence with which he had treated the scandal at first, and the still more obstinate sense of wrong which latterly had shut his lips and his heart, had given way to-day to warmer and more generous emotions. What would have seemed to him in the morning only the indignant reserve of a man unjustly suspected, appeared now a foolish and unfriendly reticence. The only thing which restrained him was a still lingering inclination to screen Wodehouse, if possible, from a public exposure, which would throw shame upon his sisters as well as himself. If any generosity, if any gentlemanly feeling, were still left in the vagabond's soul, it was possible he might answer the Curate's appeal; and Mr Wentworth felt himself bound to offer no public explanation of the facts of the case until this last chance of escape had been left for the criminal. But, so far as regarded himself, his heart was opened, his wounded pride mollified, and he was ready enough to talk of what had just happened, and to explain the whole business to his anxious companions. When he joined them, indeed, he was so full of it as almost to forget that he himself was still believed the hero of the tale. "This unfortunate little girl has been here, and I have missed her," he said, without in the least concealing his vexation, and the excitement which his rapid walk had not subdued; to the great horror of Mr Proctor, who tried all he could, by telegraphic glances, to recall the young man to a sense of that fact that Sarah was in the room.

"I must say I think it is imprudent – highly imprudent," said the late Rector: "they will call these women to prove that she has been here again; and what conclusion but one can possibly be drawn from such a fact? I am very sorry to see you so unguarded." He said this, seizing the moment after Sarah had removed the salmon, which was very good, and was served with a sauce which pleased Mr Proctor all the more that he had not expected much from an impromptu dinner furnished by a Perpetual Curate;

but the fact was, that Gerald's arrival had awakened Mrs Hadwin to a proper regard for her own credit, which was at stake.

When Sarah withdrew finally, and they were left alone, Frank Wentworth gave the fullest explanation he was able to his surprised auditors. He told them that it was Wodehouse, and not himself, whom Rosa had met in the garden, and whom she had no doubt come to seek at this crisis of their fortunes. There was not the least doubt in his own mind that Wodehouse had carried her away, and hidden her somewhere close at hand; and when he had given them all his reasons for thinking so, his hearers were of the same opinion; but Mr Proctor continued very doubtful and perplexed, clear though the story was. He sat silent, brooding over the new mystery, while the brothers discussed the original questions.

"I cannot think why you did not go to the Rector at once and tell him all this," said Gerald. "It is always best to put a stop to gossip. At least you will see him to-morrow, or let me see him—"

"The Rector is deeply prejudiced against me," said the Perpetual Curate, "for a very unworthy reason, if he has any reason at all. He has never asked me to explain. I shall not interfere with his investigation," said the young man, haughtily; "let it go on. I have been working here for five years, and the Carlingford people ought to know better. As for the Rector, I will make no explanations to him."

"It is not for the Rector, it is for yourself," said Gerald; "and this fellow Wodehouse surely has no claim—"

But at the sound of this name, Mr Proctor roused himself from his pause of bewilderment, and took the words out of Mr Wentworth's mouth.

"He has been here since Easter; but why?" said the late Rector. "I cannot fancy why Mr Wodehouse's son should come to you when his father's house was so near. In hiding? why was he in hiding? He is evidently a scamp," said Mr Proctor, growing red; "but that is not so unusual. I don't understand – I am bound to say I don't understand it. He may be the culprit, as you say; but what was he doing here?"

"I took him in at Miss Wodehouse's request. I cannot explain why – *she* will tell you," said the Curate. "As for Wodehouse, I have given him another chance till twelve o'clock to-morrow: if he does not make his appearance then—"

Mr Proctor had listened only to the first words; he kept moving uneasily in his seat while the Curate spoke. Then he broke in, "It appears I cannot see Miss Wodehouse," he said, with an injured tone; "she does not see any one. I cannot ask for any explanation; but it seems to me most extraordinary. It is three months since Easter. If he had been living with you all the time, there must have been some occasion for it. I don't know what to think, for my part; and yet I always imagined that I was considered a friend of the family," said the late Rector, with an aggrieved look. He took his glass of claret very slowly, looking at it as if expecting to see in the purple reflection some explanation of the mystery. As for Gerald Wentworth, he relapsed into silence when he found that his arguments did not alter Frank's decision; he too was disappointed not to find his brother alone. He sat with his eyes cast down, and a singular look of abstraction on his face. He had got into a new atmosphere – a different world. When his anxieties about Frank were satisfied, Gerald withdrew himself altogether from the little party. He sat there, it is true, not unaware of what was going on, and even from time to time joining in the conversation; but already a subtle change had come over Gerald. He might have been repeating an "office," or carrying on a course of private devotions, from his looks. Rome had established her dualism in his mind. He had no longer the unity of an Englishman trained to do one thing at a time, and to do it with his might. He sat in a kind of languor, carrying on

within himself a thread of thought, to which his external occupation gave no clue; yet at the same time suffering no indication to escape him of the real condition of his mind. The three were consequently far from being good company. Mr Proctor, who was more puzzled than ever as to the true state of the case, could not unburden himself of his own intentions as he had hoped to do; and after a while the Curate, too, was silent, finding his statements received, as he thought, but coldly. It was a great relief to him when he was called out by Sarah to speak to some one, though his absence made conversation still more difficult for the two who were left behind. Mr Proctor, from the other side of the table, regarded Gerald with a mixture of wonder and pity. He did not feel quite sure that it was not his duty to speak to him – to expound the superior catholicity of the Church of England, and call his attention to the schismatic peculiarities of the Church of Rome. "It might do him good to read Burgon's book," Mr Proctor said to himself; and by way of introducing that subject, he began to talk of Italy, which was not a bad device, and did credit to his invention. Meanwhile the Curate had gone to his study, wondering a little who could want him, and, to his utter bewilderment, found his aunt Dora, veiled, and wrapped up in a great shawl.

"Oh, Frank, my dear, don't be angry! I couldn't help coming," cried Miss Dora. "Come and sit down by me here. I slipped out and did not even put on my bonnet, that nobody might know. Oh, Frank, I don't know what to say. I am so afraid you have been wicked. I have just seen that – that girl. I saw her out of my window. Frank! don't jump up like that. I can't go on telling you if you don't stay quiet here."

"Aunt, let me understand you," cried the Curate. "You saw whom? Rosa Elsworthy? Don't drive me desperate, as all the others do with their stupidity. You saw her? when? – where?"

"Oh Frank, Frank! to think it should put you in such a

way – such a girl as that! Oh, my dear boy, if I had thought you cared so much, I never would have come to tell you. It wasn't to encourage you – it wasn't. Oh, Frank, Frank! that it should come to this!" cried Miss Dora, shrinking back from him with fright and horror in her face.

"Come, we have no time to lose," said the Curate, who was desperate. He picked up her shawl, which had fallen on the floor, and bundled her up in it in the most summary way. "Come, aunt Dora," said the impetuous young man; "you know you were always my kindest friend. Nobody else can help me at this moment. I feel that you are going to be my deliverer. Come, aunt Dora – we must go and find her, you and I. There is not a moment to lose."

He had his arm round her, holding on her shawl. He raised her up from her chair, and supported her, looking at her as he had not done before since he was a boy at school, Miss Dora thought. She was too frightened, too excited, to cry, as she would have liked to do; but the proposal was so terrible and unprecedented that she leaned back trembling on her nephew's arm, and could not move either to obey or to resist him. "Oh, Frank, I never went after any improper person in my life," gasped aunt Dora. "Oh, my dear, don't make me do anything that is wrong; they will say it is my fault!" cried the poor lady, gradually feeling herself obliged to stand on her feet and collect her forces. The shawl fell back from her shoulders as the Curate withdrew his arm. "You have lost my large pin," cried aunt Dora, in despair; "and I have no bonnet. And oh! what will Leonora say? I never, never would have come to tell you if I had thought of this. I only came to warn you, Frank. I only intended—"

"Yes," said the Curate. The emergency was momentous, and he dared not lose patience. He found her large pin even, while she stood trembling, and stuck it into her shawl as if it had been a skewer. "You never would have come if you had not been my guardian angel," said the deceitful young man, whose heart was beating high with anxiety and hope. "Nobody else would do for me what you are going to do – but I have always had confidence in my aunt Dora. Come, come! We have not a moment to lose."

This was how he overcame Miss Dora's scruples. Before she knew what had happened she was being hurried through the clear summer night past the long garden-walls of Grange Lane. The stars were shining overhead, the leaves rustling on all sides in the soft wind – not a soul to be seen in the long line of darkling road. Miss Dora had no breath to speak, however much disposed she might have been. She could not remonstrate, having full occasion for all her forces to keep her feet and her breath. When Mr Wentworth paused for an instant to ask "which way did she go?" it was all Miss Dora could do to indicate with her finger the dark depths of Prickett's Lane. Thither she was immediately carried as by a whirlwind. With a shawl over her head, fastened together wildly by the big pin – with nothing but little satin slippers, quite unfit for the exertion required of them – with an agonised protest in her heart that she had never, never in her life gone after any improper person before – and, crowning misfortune of all, with a horrible consciousness that she had left the garden-door open, hoping to return in a few minutes, Miss Dora Wentworth, single woman as she was, and ignorant of evil, was whirled off in pursuit of the unfortunate Rosa into the dark abysses of Prickett's Lane.

While this terrible Hegira was taking place, Mr Proctor sat opposite Gerald Wentworth, sipping his claret and talking of Italy. "Perhaps you have not read Burgon's book," said the late Rector. "There is a good deal of valuable information in it about the Catacombs, and he enters at some length into the question between the Roman Church and our own. If you are interested in that, you should read it," said Mr Proctor; "it is a very important question."

"Yes," said Gerald; and then there followed a pause.

Mr Proctor did not know what to make of the faint passing
smile, the abstracted look, which he had vaguely observed
all the evening; and he looked so inquiringly across the
table that Gerald's new-born dualism came immediately
into play, to the great amazement of his companion. Mr
Wentworth talked, and talked well; but his eyes were still
abstracted, his mind was still otherwise occupied; and Mr
Proctor, whose own intelligence was in a state of unusual
excitement, perceived the fact without being at all able to
explain it. An hour passed, and both the gentlemen looked
at their watches. The Curate had left them abruptly
enough, with little apology; and as neither of them had
much interest in the other, nor in the conversation, it was
natural that the host's return should be looked for with
some anxiety. When the two gentlemen had said all they
could say about Italy – when Mr Proctor had given a little
sketch of his own experiences in Rome, to which his
companion did not make the usual response of narrating
his – the two came to a dead pause. They had now been
sitting for more than two hours over that bottle of Lafitte,
many thoughts having in the mean time crossed Mr
Proctor's mind concerning the coffee and the Curate.
Where could he have gone? and why was there not somebody in the house with sense enough to clear away the
remains of dessert, and refresh the wearied interlocutors
with the black and fragrant cup which cheers all students?
Both of the gentlemen had become seriously uneasy by
this time; the late Rector got up from the table when he
could bear it no longer. "Your brother must have been
called away by something important," said Mr Proctor,
stiffly. "Perhaps you will kindly make my excuses. Mr
Morgan keeps very regular hours, and I should not like to
be late—"

"It is very extraordinary. I can't fancy what can be the
reason – it must be somebody sick," said Gerald, rising
too, but not looking by any means sure that Frank's
absence had such a laudable excuse.

"Very likely," said the late Rector, more stiffly than ever. "You are living here, I suppose?"

"No; I am at Miss Wentworth's – my aunt's," said Gerald. "I will walk with you;" and they went out together with minds considerably excited. Both looked up and down the road when they got outside the garden-gate: both had a vague idea that the Curate might be visible somewhere in conversation with somebody disreputable; and one being his friend and the other his brother, they were almost equally disturbed about the unfortunate young man. Mr Proctor's thoughts, however, were mingled with a little offence. He had meant to be confidential and brotherly, and the occasion had been lost; and how was it possible to explain the rudeness with which Mr Wentworth had treated him? Gerald was still more seriously troubled. When Mr Proctor left him, he walked up and down Grange Lane in the quiet of the summer night, watching for his brother. Jack came home smoking his cigar, dropping Wodehouse, whom the heir of the Wentworths declined to call his friend, before he reached his aunts' door, and as much surprised as it was possible for him to be, to find Gerald lingering, meditating, along the silent road; but still Frank did not come. By-and-by a hurried light gleamed in the window of the summer-house, and sounds of commotion were audible in the orderly dwelling of the Miss Wentworths; and the next thing that happened was the appearance of Miss Leonora, also with a shawl over her head, at the garden-door. Just then, when they were all going to bed, Collins, Miss Dora's maid, had come to the drawing-room in search of her mistress. She was not to be found anywhere, though her bonnets and all her outdoor gear were safe in their place. For the first time in her life the entire family were startled into anxiety on Miss Dora's account. As for Mrs Gerald Wentworth, she jumped at once to the conclusion that the poor lady was murdered, and that Frank must have something to do with it, and filled the house with lamentations. Nobody went to bed, not even aunt Cecilia, who had not been out of her room at eleven o'clock for centuries. Collins had gone into the summer-house and was turning over everything there as if she expected to find her mistress's body in the cupboard or under the sofa; Lewis, the butler, was hunting through the garden with a lantern, looking under all the bushes. No incident so utterly unaccountable had occurred before in Miss Dora Wentworth's life.

CHAPTER XXXVI.

THE first investigation into the character of the Rev. F. C. Wentworth, Curate of St Roque's was fixed to take place in the vestry of the parish church, at eleven o'clock on the morning of the day which followed this anxious night. Most people in Carlingford were aware that the Perpetual Curate was to be put upon his trial on that sunny July morning; and there was naturally a good deal of curiosity among the intelligent townsfolk to see how he looked, and what was the aspect of the witnesses who were to bear testimony for or against him. It is always interesting to the crowd to see how a man looks at a great crisis of his life – or a woman either, for that matter; and if a human creature, at the height of joy, or in the depths of sorrow, is a spectacle to draw everybody's eyes, there is a still greater dramatic interest in the sight when hope and fear are both in action, and the alternative hangs between life or death. It was life or death to Mr Wentworth, though the tribunal was one which could inflict no penalties. If he should be found guilty, death would be a light doom to the downfall and moral extinction which would make an end of the unfaithful priest; and, consequently, Carlingford had reason for its curiosity. There was a crowd about the back entrance which led to the shabby little sacristy where Mr Morgan and Mr Leeson were accustomed to robe themselves; and scores of people strayed into the church itself, and hung about, pretending to look at the improvements which the Rector called restorations. Mrs Morgan herself, looking very pale, was in and out half-a-dozen times in the hour, talking with terrible science and technicalism to Mr Finial's clerk of works, who could not make her see that she was talking Gothic – a language which had nothing to do with Carlingford Church, that building being of the Revolution or churchwarden epoch. She was a great deal too much agitated at that moment to be aware of the distinction. As for Mr Wentworth, it was universally agreed that, though he looked a little flushed and excited, there was no particular discouragement visible in his face. He went in to the vestry with some eagerness, not much like a culprit on his trial. The Rector, indeed, who was heated and embarrassed and doubtful of himself, looked more like a criminal than the real hero. There were six of the amateur judges, of whom one had felt his heart fail him at the last moment. The five who were steadfast were Mr Morgan, Dr Marjoribanks, old Mr Western (who was a distant cousin of the Wodehouses, and brother-in-law, though old enough to be her grandfather, of the beautiful Lady Western, who once lived in Grange Lane), and with them Mr Centum, the banker, and old Colonel Chiley. Mr Proctor, who was very uneasy in his mind, and much afraid lest he should be called upon to give an account of the Curate's behaviour on the previous night, had added himself as a kind of auxiliary to this judicial bench. Mr Waters had volunteered his services as counsellor, perhaps with the intention of looking after the interests of a very different client; and to this imposing assembly John Brown had walked in, with his hands in his pockets, rather disturbing the composure of the company in general, who were aware what kind of criticism his was. While the bed of justice was being arranged, a very odd little group collected in the outer room, where Elsworthy, in a feverish state of excitement, was revolving about the place from the door to the window, and where the Miss Hemmings sat up against the wall, with their drapery drawn up about them, to show that they were of different clay from Mrs Elsworthy, who, respectful but sullen, sat on the same bench. The anxious public peered in at the door whenever it had a chance, and took peeps through the window when the other privilege was impossible. Besides the Miss Hemmings and the Elsworthys there was Peter Hayles, who also had seen something, and the wife of another shopkeeper at the end of George Street; and there was the Miss Hemmings' maid, who had escorted them on that eventful night of Rosa's disappearance. Not one of the witnesses had the smallest doubt as to the statement he or she was about to make ; they were entirely convinced of the righteousness of their own cause, and the justice of the accusation, which naturally gave a wonderful moral force to their testimony. Besides – but that was quite a different matter – they all had their little grudges against Mr Wentworth, each in his secret heart.

When Elsworthy was called in to the inner room it caused a little commotion amid this company outside. The Miss Hemmings looked at each other, not with an agreeable expression of face. "They might have had the politeness to call us first," Miss Sophia said to her sister; and Miss Hemmings shook her head and sighed, and said, "Dear Mr Bury!" an observation which meant a great deal, though it did not seem perfectly relevant. "Laws! I'll forget everything when I'm took in there," said the shopkeeper's wife to Miss Hemmings' maid; and the ladies drew still closer up, superior to curiosity, while the others stretched their necks to get a peep into the terrible inner room.

It was indeed a formidable tribunal. The room was

small, so that the unfortunate witness was within the closest range of six pairs of judicial eyes, not to speak of the vigilant orbs of the two lawyers, and those of the accused and his supporters. Mr Morgan, by right of his position, sat at the end of the table, and looked very severely at the first witness as he came in – which Elsworthy did, carrying his hat before him like a kind of shield, and polishing it carefully round and round. The Rector was far from having any intention of discouraging the witness, who was indeed his mainstay; but the anxiety of his peculiar position, as being at once counsel for the prosecution, and chief magistrate of the bed of justice, gave an unusual sternness to his face.

"Your name is George Elsworthy," said the Rector, filling his pen with ink, and looking penetratingly in the witness's face.

"George Appleby Elsworthy," said Rosa's uncle, a little alarmed; "not as I often signs in full; for you see, sir, it's a long name, and life's short, and it aint necessary in the way of business—"

"Stationer and newsmonger in Carlingford," interrupted the Rector; "I should say in Upper Grange Lane, Carlingford; aged—?"

"But it doesn't appear to me that newsmonger is a correct expression," said old Mr Western, who was very conversational; "newsmonger means a gossip, not a tradesman; not that there is any reason why a tradesman should not be a gossip, but—"

"Aged?" said Mr Morgan, holding his pen suspended in the air. "I will say newsvendor if that will be better – one cannot be too particular – Aged—?"

"He is come to years of discretion," said Dr Marjoribanks, "that's all we need; don't keep us all day waiting, man, but tell your story about this elopement of your niece. When did it take place, and what are the facts? Never mind your hat, but say out what you have got to say."

"You are much too summary, Doctor," said Mr Morgan, with a little offence; but the sense of the assembly was clearly with Dr Marjoribanks – so that the Rector dashed in 45 as the probable age of the witness, and waited his further statement.

After this there was silence, and Elsworthy began his story. He narrated all the facts of Rosa's disappearance, with an intention and bias which made his true tale a wonderful tacit accusation. Rage, revenge, a sense of wrong, worked what in an indifferent narrator only the highest skill could have wrought. He did not mention the Curate's name, but arranged all his facts in lines like so many trains of artillery. How Rosa was in the habit of going to Mrs Hadwin's (it was contrary to Elsworthy's instinct to bring in at this moment any reference to Mr Wentworth) every night with the newspaper – "not as I sent her of errands for common – keeping two boys for the purpose," said the injured man; "but, right or wrong, there's where she'd go as certain as the night come. I've seen her with my own eyes go into Mrs Hadwin's garden-door, which she hadn't no need to go in but for being encouraged; and it would be half an hour at the least afore she came out."

"But, bless me! that was very imprudent of you," cried Mr Proctor, who up to this time had not uttered a word.

"There was nobody there but the old lady and her maids – except the clergyman," said Elsworthy. "It wasn't my part to think as she could get any harm from the clergyman. She wouldn't hear no remonstrances from me; she *would* go as regular as the evening come."

"Yes, yes," said Mr Waters, who saw John Brown's humorous eye gleaming round upon the little assembly; "but let us come to the immediate matter in hand. Your niece disappeared from Carlingford on the—?"

"Yes, yes," said Mr Western, "we must not sink into conversation; that's the danger of all unofficial investigations. It seems natural to let him tell his story as he likes: but here we have got somebody to keep us in order. It's natural, but it aint law − is it, Brown?"

"I don't see that law has anything to do with it," said John Brown, with a smile.

"Order! order!" said the Rector, who was much goaded and aggravated by this remark. "I request that there may be no conversation. The witness will proceed with what he has to say. Your niece disappeared on the 15th. What were the circumstances of her going away?"

"She went down as usual with the newspaper," said Elsworthy; "it had got to be a custom as regular as regular. She stopped out later nor common, and my wife and me was put out. I don't mind saying, gentlemen," said the witness, with candour, "as my missis and I wasn't altogether of the same mind about Rosa. She was late, but I can't say as I was anxious. It wasn't above a week afore that Mr Wentworth himself brought her home safe, and it was well known as he didn't like her to be out at night; so I was easy in my mind, like. But when eleven o'clock came, and there was no denying of its being past hours, I began to get a little fidgety. I stepped out to the door, and I looked up and down, and saw nobody; so I took up my hat and took a turn down the road—"

At this moment there was a little disturbance outside. A voice at which the Curate started was audible, asking entrance. "I must see Mr Wentworth immediately," this voice said, as the door was partially opened; and then, while his sons both rose to their feet, the Squire himself suddenly entered the room. He looked round upon the assembled company with a glance of shame and grief that went to the Curate's heart. Then he bowed to the judges, who were looking at him with an uncomfortable sense of his identity, and walked across the room to the bench on which Gerald and Frank were seated together. "I beg your pardon, gentlemen," said the Squire, "if I interrupt your proceedings; but I have only this moment arrived in Carlingford, and heard what was going on, and I trust I may be allowed to remain, as my son's honour is concerned." Mr Wentworth scarcely waited for the assent which everybody united in murmuring, but seated himself heavily on the bench, as if glad to sit down anywhere. He suffered Frank to grasp his hand, but scarcely gave it; nor, indeed, did he look, except once, with a bitter momentary glance at the brothers. They were sons a father might well have been proud of, so far as external appearances went; but the Squire's soul was bitter within him. One was about to abandon all that made life valuable in the eyes of the sober-minded country gentleman. The other— "And I could have sworn by Frank," the mortified father was saying in his heart. He sat down with a dull dogged composure. He meant to hear it all, and have it proved to him that his favourite son was a villain. No wonder that he was disinclined to respond to any courtesies. He set himself down almost with impatience that the sound of his entrance should have interrupted the narrative, and looked straight in front of him, fixing his eyes on Elsworthy, and taking no notice of the anxious glances of the possible culprit at his side.

"I hadn't gone above a step or two when I see Mr Hayles at his door. I said to him, 'It's a fine evening,' – as so it was, and the stars shining. 'My Rosa aint been about your place, has she?' I says; and he says, 'No.' But, gentlemen, I see by the look of his eye as he had more to say. 'Aint she come home yet?' says Mr Hayles—"

"Stop a moment," said John Brown. "Peter Hayles is outside, I think. If the Rector wishes to preserve any sort of legal form in this inquiry, may I suggest that a conversation repeated is not evidence? Let Elsworthy tell what he knows, and the other can speak for himself."

"It is essential we should hear the conversation," said the Rector, "since I believe it was of importance. I believe it is an imporant link in the evidence – I believe—"

"Mr Morgan apparently has heard the evidence before," said the inexorable John Brown.

Here a little commotion arose in the bed of justice.
"Hush, hush," said Dr Marjoribanks; "the question is,
What has the witness got to say of his own knowledge? Go
on, Elsworthy; we can't possibly spend the whole day
here. Never mind what Hayles said, unless he
communicated something about the girl."

"He told me as the Miss Hemmings had seen Rosa," said
Elsworthy, slowly; "had seen her at nine, or half after nine
– I won't be sure which – at Mrs Hadwin's gate."

"The Miss Hemmings are outside. Let the Miss
Hemmings be called," said Mr Proctor, who had a great
respect for Mr Brown's opinion.

But here Mr Waters interposed. "The Miss Hemmings
will be called presently," he said; "in the mean time let
this witness be heard out; afterwards his evidence will be
corroborated. Go on, Elsworthy."

"The Miss Hemmings had seen my Rosa at Mrs
Hadwin's gate," repeated Elsworthy, "a-standing outside,
and Mr Wentworth a-standing inside; there aint more
respectable parties in all Carlingford. It was them as saw
it, not me. Gentlemen, I went back home. I went out
again. I went over all the town a-looking for her. Six
o'clock in the morning come, and I had never closed an
eye, nor took off my clothes, nor even sat down upon a
chair. When it was an hour as I could go to a gentleman's
house and no offence, I went to the place as she was last
seen. Me and Mr Hayles, we went together. The shutters
was all shut but on one window, which was Mr
Wentworth's study. We knocked at the garden-door, and
I aint pretending that we didn't make a noise; and,
gentlemen, it wasn't none of the servants – it was Mr
Wentworth hisself as opened the door."

There was here a visible sensation among the judges. It
was a point that told. As for the Squire, he set his stick
firmly before him, and leaned his clasped hands upon it to
steady himself. His healthful, ruddy countenance was
paling gradually. If it had been an apostle who spoke, he

could not have taken in more entirely the bitter tale.

"It was Mr Wentworth hisself, gentlemen," said the triumphant witness; "not like a man roused out of his sleep, but dressed and shaved, and his hair brushed, as if it had been ten instead o'six. It's well known in Carlingford as he aint an early man; and gentlemen here knows it as well as me. I don't pretend as I could keep my temper. I give him my mind, gentlemen, being an injured man; but I said as – if he do his duty by her—"

"Softly a moment," said Mr Brown. "What had Mr Wentworth's aspect at six o'clock in the morning to do with Rosa Elsworthy's disappearance at nine on the previous night?"

"I don't see that the question is called for at the present moment," said Mr Waters. "Let us hear what reasons you have for attributing to Mr Wentworth an unusual degree of interest in your niece."

"Sir," said Elsworthy, "he come into my shop as regular as the day; he never come but he asked after Rosa, or spoke to her if she was there. One night he walked all the way up Grange Lane and knocked at my door and brought her in all of a glow, and said I wasn't to send her out late no more. My missis, being a woman as is very particular, was struck, and thought as harm might come of it; and, not to be talked of, we sent Rosa away. And what does Mr Wentworth do, but the moment he hears of it comes right off to my shop! He had been at his own home, sir, a-visiting his respected family," said Elsworthy, turning slightly towards the side of the room where the father and sons sat together. "He came to my shop with his carpet-bag as he come off the railway, and he gave me my orders as I was to bring Rosa back. What he said was, 'Directly,' that very day. I never had no thought but what his meaning was honourable – being a clergyman," said the witness, with a heavy sigh; and then there ensued a little pause.

"The Miss Hemmings had better be called now," said Mr Waters. "Elsworthy, you can retire; but we may require you again, so you had better not go away. Request Miss Hemmings to do us the favour of coming here."

The Squire lifted his heavy eyes when the next witness entered. She made a very solemn curtsy to the gentlemen, and sat down on the chair which somebody placed for her. Being unsupported, a lady – not to say an unmarried lady profoundly conscious of the fact – among a number of men, Miss Hemmings was naturally much agitated. She was the eldest and the softest-hearted; and it occurred to her for the first time, as she gave a frightened look towards the Curate, that he was like her favourite younger brother, who had died ever so many years ago – a thought which, for the first time, made her doubtful of her testimony, and disposed to break down in her evidence.

"You were in Grange Lane on the evening of the 15th ultimo," said Mr Morgan, after he had carefully written down her name, "about nine o'clock?"

"Oh yes, Mr Morgan," said the poor lady; "we were at St Roque's Cottage drinking tea with Mrs Bland, who was lodging with Mrs Smith in the same rooms Mrs Rider used to have. I put the note of invitation in my pocket in case there should be any doubt; but, indeed, poor Mrs Bland was taken very ill on the 16th, and Dr Marjoribanks was called, and he knows it could not be any other evening – and besides—"

"About nine o'clock," said Mr Waters; "did I understand you, it was about nine o'clock?"

"She was such an invalid, poor dear," said Miss Hemmings, apologetically; "and it is such a privilege to have real Christian conversation. We dined early on purpose, and we were asked for half-past six. I think it must have been a little after nine; but Mary is here, and she knows what hour she came for us. Shall I call Mary, please?"

"Presently," said the counsel for the prosecution. "Don't

be agitated; one or two questions will do. You passed Mrs Hadwin's door coming up. Will you kindly tell the gentlemen what you saw there?"

"Oh!" cried Miss Hemmings. She looked round at the Curate again, and he was more than ever like Willie who died. "I–I don't take much notice of what I see in the streets," she said, faltering; "and there are always so many poor people going to see Mr Wentworth." Here the poor lady stopped short. She had never considered before what harm her evidence might do. Now her heart smote her for the young man who was like Willie. "He is so very kind to all the poor people," continued the unwilling witness, looking doubtfully round into all the faces near her; "and he's such a young man," she added, in her tremulous way. It was Miss Sophia who was strongminded; all the poor women in Back Grove Street were perfectly aware that their chances were doubled when they found Miss Jane.

"But you must tell us what you saw all the same," said Dr Marjoribanks. "I daresay Mr Wentworth wishes it as much as we do."

The Curate got up and came forward with one of his impulses. "I wish it a great deal more," he said. "My dear Miss Hemmings, thank you for your reluctance to say anything to harm me; but the truth can't possibly harm me: tell them exactly what you saw."

Miss Hemmings looked from one to another, and trembled more and more. "I am sure I never meant to injure Mr Wentworth," she said; "I only said I thought it was imprudent of him – that was all I meant. Oh, I am sure, if I had thought of this, I would rather have done anything than say it. And whatever Sophia might have imagined, I assure you, gentlemen, *I* never, never for a moment thought Mr Wentworth meant any harm."

"Never mind Mr Wentworth," said Mr Brown, who now took the matter in hand. "When you were passing Mrs Hadwin's house about nine o'clock on the evening of

the 15th, you saw some one standing at the door. Mr
Wentworth particularly wishes you to say who it was."

"Oh, Mr Brown – oh, Mr Morgan," cried the poor lady;
"it was little Rosa Elsworthy. She was a designing little
artful thing. When she was in my Sunday class, she was
always thinking of her vanities. Mr Wentworth was talking
to her at the garden-door. I daresay he was giving her
good advice; and oh, gentlemen, if you were to question
me for ever and ever, that is all I have got to say."

"Did you not hear what they were talking about?" said
Mr Proctor. "If it was good advice –" The late Rector
stopped short, and grew red, and felt that his supposition
was that of a simpleton. "You heard what they were
talking about? What did they say?" he concluded,
peremptorily, in a tone which frightened the reluctant
witness more and more.

"I did not hear a single word," she cried – "not a word.
That is all I know about it. Oh, please, let me go away. I
feel very faint. I should like a little cold water, please. I
did not hear a word – not a word. I have told you
everything I have got to say."

Everybody looked more serious when Miss Hemmings
stumbled from her chair. She was so frightened at her own
testimony, and so unwilling to give it, that its importance
was doubled in the eyes of the inexperienced judges. The
Squire gave a low groan under his breath, and turned his
eyes, which had been fixed upon her, on the ground
instead; but raised them immediately, with a gleam of
anxiety as his son again rose from his side. All that the
Curate meant to do was to give the trembling lady his
arm, and lead her out; but the entire assembly, with the
exception of John Brown, started and stared as if he had
been about to take instant revenge upon the frightened
woman. Miss Hemmings burst into tears when Mr Wentworth set a chair for her by the door, and brought her a
glass of water, in the outer room; and just then somebody
knocked and gave him a note, with which he returned to

the presence of the awful tribunal. Miss Sophia Hemmings was corroborating her sister's statement when the Perpetual Curate re-entered. He stood behind her quite quietly, until she had finished, with a slight smile upon his lips, and the note in his hand. Dr Marjoribanks was not partial to Miss Sophia Hemmings. She was never ill herself, and rarely permitted even her sister to enjoy the gentle satisfaction of a day's sickness. The old Doctor looked instead at the Perpetual Curate. When Miss Hemmings withdrew, Dr Marjoribanks interposed. "It appears to me that Mr Wentworth has something to say," said the Doctor. "It is quite necessary that he should have a hearing as well as the rest of us. Let Peter Hayles wait a moment, till we hear what Mr Wentworth has to say."

"It is not yet time for us to receive Mr Wentworth's statement," said the Rector. "He shall certainly be heard in his own defence at the proper time. Mr Waters, call Peter Hayles."

"One moment," said the Curate. "I have no statement to make, and I can wait till you have heard what everybody has to say, if the Rector wishes it; but it might save time and trouble to hear me. I have another witness whom, up to this moment, I have been reluctant to bring forward – a witness all-important for me, whom I cannot produce in so public a place, or at an hour when everybody is abroad. If you will do me the favour to adjourn this inquiry till the evening, and to meet then in a private house – in my own, or Miss Wentworth's, or wherever you may appoint – I think I can undertake to make this whole business perfectly clear."

"Bless me!" said Mr Proctor, suddenly. This unexpected and irrelevant benediction was the first sound distinctly audible in the little stir of surprise, expectation, and excitement which followed the Curate's speech. The Squire let his stick fall out of his hands, and groped after it to pick it up again. Hope had suddenly all at once come into possession of the old man's breast. As for the Rector, he was too much annoyed at the moment to speak.

"You should have thought of this before," said Dr Marjoribanks. "It would have been just as easy to fix this meeting for the evening, and in a private house, and would have saved time. You are very welcome to my dining-room, if you please; but I don't understand why it could not have been settled so at once, and saved our time," said the Doctor; to which sentiment there were several murmurs of assent.

"Gentlemen," said the Curate, whose eyes were sparkling with excitement, "you must all know in your hearts that this trial ought never to have taken place. I have lived among you for five years, and you ought to have known me by this time. I have never been asked for an explanation, neither could any explanation which it was possible for me to make have convinced a mind prejudiced against me," he said, after a moment's pause, with a meaning which everybody understood. "It is only now that I feel myself able to clear up the whole matter, and it is for this reason alone that I ask you to put off your inquiry till to-night."

"I don't feel inclined to consent to any adjournment," said Mr Morgan; "it looks like an attempt to defeat the ends of justice." The Rector was very much annoyed — more than he dared confess to himself. He believed in his heart that young Wentworth was guilty, and he felt equally convinced that here was some unexpected loophole through which he would escape. But public opinion was strong in Grange Lane — stronger than a new Rector. The Banker and the Doctor and the Indian Colonel, not to speak of old Mr Western, were disposed to grant the request of the Curate; and when even Mr Proctor forsook his side, the Rector himself yielded. "Though it is against my judgment," he said, "and I see no advantage to be gained by it, the meeting had better be held in the Rectory, this evening at seven o'clock."

"Most of us dine at seven o'clock," said Dr Marjoribanks.

"This evening at eight o'clock," said the Rector, severely. "I will request all the witnesses to be in attendance, and we must hope to find Mr Wentworth's witness of sufficient importance to justify the change. At eight o'clock this evening, in my house, gentlemen," said the Rector. He collected his notes and went outside, and began talking to his witnesses, while the others collected together round the table to consult over this new phase of the affair. The three Mr Wentworths went out together, the father between his two tall sons. The Squire's strength was much shaken, both in mind and body. When they were out of the shadow of the church, he looked up in Frank's face.

"I hope you consider me entitled to an immediate explanation," said Mr Wentworth. "When I read that anonymous letter, it went a long way towards breaking my heart, sir; I can tell you it did. Jack here too, and your brother making up his mind as he has done, Frank. I am not a man to complain. If it were all over with me to-morrow, I shouldn't be sorry, so far as I am concerned, if it weren't for the girls and the little children. But I always thought I could have sworn by Frank," said the old man, mournfully. He was ever so much older since he had said these words before in the long lime avenue at Wentworth Hall.

CHAPTER XXXVII.

THE little assembly which met in the vestry of Carlingford Church to inquire into the conduct of the Perpetual Curate, had so many different interests in hands when it

dispersed, and so much to do, that it is difficult for the
narrator of this history to decide which thread should be
taken up first. Of all the interlocutors, however, perhaps
Mr Proctor was the one who had least succeeded in his
efforts to explain himself, and accordingly demands in the
first place the attention of an impartial historian. The
excellent man was still labouring under much perplexity
when the bed of justice was broken up. He began to
recollect that Mr Wentworth's explanation on the previous
night had convinced him of his innocence, and to see that
it was indeed altogether inconceivable that the Curate
should be guilty; but then, other matters still more disagreeable to contemplate than Mr Wentworth's guilt came
in to darken the picture. This vagabond Wodehouse,
whom the Curate had taken in at his sister's request –
what was the meaning of that mystery? Mr Proctor had
never been anyhow connected with mysteries; he was
himself an only son, and had lived a straightforward
peaceable life. Neither he nor his estimable parents, so far
as the late Rector was aware, had ever done anything to
be ashamed of; and he winced a little at the thought of
connecting himself with concealment and secrecy. And
then the Curate's sudden disappearance on the previous
evening perplexed and troubled him. He imagined all
kinds of reasons for it as he walked down Grange Lane.
Perhaps Miss Wodehouse, who would not receive himself,
had sent for Mr Wentworth; perhaps the vagabond brother
was in some other scrape, out of which he had to be
extricated by the Curate's assistance. Mr Proctor was
perfectly honest, and indeed determined, in his
"intentions;" but everybody will allow that for a middle-
aged lover of fifty or thereabouts, contemplating a
sensible match with a lady of suitable years and means, to
find suddenly that the object of his affections was not only
a penniless woman, but the natural guardian of an equally
penniless sister, was startling, to say the least of it. He was
a true man, and it did not occur to him to decline the

responsibility altogether; on the contrary, he was perhaps more eager than he would have been otherwise, seeing that his elderly love had far more need of his devotion than he had ever expected her to have; but, notwithstanding, he was disturbed by such an unlooked-for change of circumstances, as was natural, and did not quite know what was to be done with Lucy. He was full of thoughts on this subject as he proceeded towards the house, to the interview which, to use sentimental language, was to decide his fate. But, to tell the truth, Mr Proctor was not in a state of very deep anxiety about his fate. The idea of being refused was too unreasonable an idea to gain much ground in his mind. He was going to offer his personal support, affection, and sympathy to Miss Wodehouse at the least fortunate moment in her life; and if there was anything consolatory in marriage at all, the late Rector sensibly concluded that it must be doubly comforting under such circumstances, and that the offer of an honest man's hand and house and income was not a likely thing to be rejected by a woman of Miss Wodehouse's experience and good sense – not to speak of his heart, which was very honest and true and affectionate, though it had outlived the fervours of youth. Such was Mr Proctor's view of the matter; and the chances were strong that Miss Wodehouse entirely agreed with him – so, but for a certain shyness which made him rather nervous, it would not be correct to say that the late Rector was in a state of special anxiety about the answer he was likely to receive. He was, however, anxious about Lucy. His bachelor mind was familiar with all the ordinary traditions about the inexpediency of being surrounded by a wife's family; and he had a little of the primitive male sentiment, shared one way or other by most husbands, that the old system of buying a woman right out, and carrying her off for his own sole and private satisfaction, was, after all, the correct way of managing such matters. To be sure, a pretty, young, unmarried sister, was perhaps the least objectionable encumbrance a woman could have; but, notwithstanding, Mr Proctor would have been glad could he have seen any feasible way of disposing of Lucy. It was utterly out of the question to think of her going out as a governess; and it was quite evident that Mr Wentworth, even were he perfectly cleared of every imputation, having himself nothing to live upon, could scarcely offer to share his poverty with poor Mr Wodehouse's cherished pet and darling. "I daresay she has been used to live expensively," Mr Proctor said to himself, wincing a little in his own mind at the thought. It was about one o'clock when he reached the green door – an hour at which, during the few months of his incumbency at Carlingford, he had often presented himself at that hospitable house. Poor Mr Wodehouse! Mr Proctor could not help wondering at that moment how he was getting on in a world where, according to ordinary ideas, there are no lunch nor dinner parties, no old port nor savoury side-dishes. Somehow it was impossible to realise Mr Wodehouse with other surroundings than those of good-living and creature-comfort. Mr Proctor sighed, half for the departed, half at thought of the strangeness of that unknown life for which he himself did not feel much more fitted than Mr Wodehouse. In the garden he saw the new heir sulkily marching about among the flower-beds smoking, and looking almost as much out of place in the sweet tranquillity of the English garden, as a church-warden of Carlingford or a Fellow of All-Souls could look, to carry out Mr Proctor's previous imagination, in the vague beatitude of a disembodied heaven. Wodehouse was so sick of his own company that he came hastily forward at the sight of a visitor, but shrank a little when he saw who it was.

"I suppose you have brought some news," he said, in his sullen way. "I suppose he has been making his statements, has he? Much I care! He may tell what lies he pleases; he can't do me any harm. I never did anything but sign my own name, by Jove! Jack Wentworth himself

says so. I don't care *that* for the parson and his threats,"
said Wodehouse, snapping his fingers in Mr Proctor's face.
The late Rector drew back a little, with a shudder of
disgust and resentment. He could not help thinking that
this fellow would most likely be his brother-in-law presently,
and the horror he felt made itself visible in his face.

"I am quite unaware what you can mean," said Mr
Proctor. "I am a parson, but I never made any threats
that I know of. I wish to see Miss Wodehouse. I–I think
she expects me at this hour," he said, with a little
embarrassment, turning to John, who, for his part, had been
standing by in a way which became his position as a respectable and faithful servant, waiting any opportunity that
might come handy to show his disgust for the new *régime*.

"Yes, sir," said John, promptly, and with emphasis.
"My mistress expects you, sir. She's come down to the
drawing-room for the first time. Miss Lucy keeps her
room, sir, still; she's dreadfully cut up, poor dear young
lady. My mistress will be glad to see you, sir," said John.
This repetition of a title which Miss Wodehouse had not
been in the habit of receiving was intended for the special
advantage of the new master, whom John had no intention
of recognising in that capacity. "If you should know of any
one, sir, as is in want of a steady servant," the man
continued, as he led the way into the house, with a shrewd
glance at Mr Proctor, whose "intentions" were legible
enough to John's experienced eyes – "not as I'm afeared
of getting suited, being well known in Carlingford; but it
would come natural to be with a friend of the family.
There aint a servant in the house, sir, as will stay when
the ladies go, and I think as Miss Wodehouse would speak
for me," said John, with natural astuteness. This address
made Mr Proctor a little uneasy. It recalled to him the
unpleasant side of the important transaction in which he
was about to engage. He was not rich, and did not see his
way now to any near prospect of requiring the services of
"a steady servant," and the thought made him sigh.

"We'll see," he said, with a troubled look. To persevere honourably in his "intentions" was one thing, but to be insensible to the loss of much he had looked forward to was quite another. It was accordingly with a grave and somewhat disturbed expression that he went to the interview which was "to decide his fate." Miss Wodehouse was seated in the drawing-room, looking slightly flushed and excited. Though she knew it was very wrong to be thus roused into a new interest the day after her father's funeral, the events altogether had been of so startling a description that the usual decorum of an afflicted household had already been ruthlessly broken. And on the whole, notwithstanding her watching and grief, Mr Proctor thought he had never seen the object of his affections looking so well as she did now in the long black dress, which suited her better than the faint dove colours in which she arrayed herself by preference. She was not, it is true, quite sure what Mr Proctor wanted in this interview he had solicited, but a certain feminine instinct instructed her in its probable eventualities. So she sat in a subdued flutter, with a little colour fluctuating on her cheek, a tear in her eyes, and some wonder and expectation in her heart. Perhaps in her youth Miss Wodehouse might have come to such a feminine crisis before; but if so, it was long ago, and the gentle woman had never been given to matrimonial speculations, and was as fresh and inexperienced as any girl. The black frame in which she was set made her soft colour look fresher and less faded. Her plaintive voice, the general softness of her demeanour, looked harmonious and suitable to her circumstances. Mr Proctor, who had by no means fallen in love with her on account of any remnants of beauty she might possess, had never admired her so much as he did now; he felt confused, good man, as he stood before her, and, seeing her so much younger and fairer than his former idea, began to grow alarmed, and wonder at his serenity. What if she thought him an old fogey? what if she refused him? This supposition brought a crimson colour to Mr Proctor's middle-aged countenance, and was far from restoring his courage. It was a wonderful relief to him when she, with the instinct of a timid woman, rushed into hasty talk.

"It was very kind of you to come yesterday," she said; "Lucy and I were very grateful. We have not many relatives, and my dear father—"

"Yes," said the late Rector, again embarrassed by the tears which choked her voice, "he was very much respected: that must be a consolation to you. And he had a long life – and – and I suppose, on the whole, a happy one," said Mr Proctor, "with you and your sister—"

"Oh, Mr Proctor, he had a great deal to put up with," said Miss Wentworth, through her tears. She had, like most simple people, an instinctive disinclination to admit that anybody was or had been happy. It looked like an admission of inferiority. "Mamma's death, and poor Tom," said the elder sister. As she wiped her eyes, she almost forgot her own little feminine flutter of expectancy in respect to Mr Proctor himself. Perhaps it was not going to happen this time, and as she was pretty well assured that it would happen one day or another, she was not anxious about it. "If I only knew what to do about Tom," she continued, with a vague appeal in her voice.

Mr Proctor got up from his chair and walked to the window. When he had looked out he came back, rather surprising Miss Wodehouse by his unlooked-for movements. "I wanted very much to have a little conversation with you," he said, growing again very red. "I daresay you will be surprised – but I have accepted another living, Miss Wodehouse;" and here the good man stopped short in a terrible state of embarrassment, not knowing what next to say.

"Yes?" said Miss Wodehouse, interrogatively. Her heart began to beat quicker, but perhaps he was only going to tell her about the new work he had undertaken; and then she was a woman, and had some knowledge, which came

by nature, how to conduct herself on an occasion such as
this.

"I don't know whether you recollect," said Mr Proctor –
"I shall never forget it – one time when we all met in a
house where a woman was dying, – I mean your sister and
young Wentworth, and you and I; – and neither you nor I
knew anything about it," said the late Rector, in a strange
voice. It was not a complimentary way of opening his
subject, and the occurrence had not made so strong an
impression upon Miss Wodehouse as upon her companion.
She looked a little puzzled, and, as he made a pause, gave
only a murmur of something like assent, and waited to
hear what more he might have to say.

"We neither of us knew anything about it," said Mr
Proctor – "neither you how to manage her, nor I what to
say to her, though the young people did. I have always
thought of you from that time. I have thought I should like
to try whether I was good for anything now – if you would
help me," said the middle-aged lover. When he had said
this he walked to the window, and once more looked out,
and came back redder than ever. "You see we are neither
of us young," said Mr Proctor; and he stood by the table
turning over the books nervously, without looking at her,
which was certainly an odd commencement for a wooing.

"That is quite true," said Miss Wodehouse, rather
primly. She had never disputed that fact by word or deed,
but still it was not pleasant to have the statement thus
thrust upon her without any apparent provocation. It was
not the sort of thing which a woman expects to have said to
her under such circumstances. "I am sure I hope you will
do better – I mean be more comfortable – this time," she
continued, after a pause, sitting very erect on her seat.

"If you will help me," said Mr Proctor, taking up one of
the books and reading the name on it, which was lucky for
him, for it was Miss Wodehouse's name, which he either
had forgotten or never had known.

And here they came to a dead stop. What was she to

say? She was a little affronted, to tell the truth, that he should remember more distinctly than anything else her age, and her unlucky failure on that one occasion. "You have just said that I could not manage," said the mild woman, not without a little vigour of her own; "and how then could I help you, Mr Proctor? Lucy knows a great deal more about parish work than I do," she went on in a lower tone; and for one half of a second there arose in the mind of the elder sister a kind of wistful half envy of Lucy, who *was* young, and knew how to manage – a feeling which died in unspeakable remorse and compunction as soon as it had birth.

"But Lucy would not have me," said the late Rector; "and indeed I should not know what to do with her if she would have me; – but you— It is a small parish, but it's not a bad living. I should do all I could to make you comfortable. At least we might try," said Mr Proctor, in his most insinuating tone. "Don't you think we might try? at least it would do— " He was going to say "no harm," but on second thoughts rejected that expression. "At least I should be very glad if you would," said the excellent man, with renewed confusion. "It's a nice little rectory, with a pretty garden, and all that sort of thing; and – and perhaps – it might help you to settle about going away – and – and I daresay there would be room for Lucy. Don't you think you would try?" cried Mr Proctor, volunteering, in spite of himself, the very hospitality which he had thought it hard might be required of him; but somehow his suit seemed to want backing at the actual moment when it was being made.

As for Miss Wodehouse, she sat and listened to him till he began to falter, and then her composure gave way all at once. "But as for trying," she gasped, in broken mouthfuls of speech, "that would never – never do, Mr Proctor. It has to be done – done for good and all – if – if it is done at all," sobbed the poor lady, whose voice came somewhat muffled through her handkerchief and her tears.

"Then it shall be for good and all!" cried Mr Proctor, with a sudden impulse of energy. This was how it came about that Miss Wodehouse and the late Rector were engaged. He had an idea that he might be expected to kiss her, and certainly ought to call her Mary after this; and hovered for another minute near her seat, not at all disinclined for the former operation. But his courage failed him, and he only drew a chair a little closer and sat down, hoping she would soon stop crying. And indeed, by the time that he produced out of his pocket-book the little photograph of the new rectory, which he had had made for her by a rural artist, Miss Wodehouse had emerged out of her handkerchief, and was perhaps in her heart as happy in a quiet way as she had ever been in her life. She who had never been good for much, was now, in the time of their need, endowed with a home which she could offer Lucy. It was she, the helpless one of the family, who was to be her young sister's deliverer. Let it be forgiven to her if, in the tumult of the moment, this was the thought that came first.

When Miss Wodehouse went up-stairs after this agitating but satisfactory interview, she found Lucy engaged in putting together some books and personal trifles of her own which were scattered about the little sitting-room. She had been reading 'In Memoriam' until it vexed her to feel how inevitably good sense came in and interfered with the enthusiasm of her grief, making her sensible that to apply to her fond old father all the lofty lauds which were appropriate to the poet's hero would be folly indeed. He had been a good tender father to her, but he was not "the sweetest soul that ever looked with human eyes;" and Lucy could not but stop in her reading with a kind of pang and self-reproach as this consciousness came upon her. Miss Wodehouse looked rather aghast when she found her sister thus occupied. "Did you think of accepting Miss Wentworth's invitation, after all?" said Miss Wodehouse; "but, dear, I am afraid it would be awkward; and oh,

Lucy, my darling, I have so many things to tell you," said
the anxious sister, who was shy of communicating her own
particular news. Before many minutes had passed, Lucy
had thrown aside all the books, and was sitting by her
sister's side in half-pleased, disconcerted amazement to
hear her story. Only half-pleased – for Lucy, like most
other girls of her age, thought love and marriage were things
which belonged only to her own level of existence, and
was a little vexed and disappointed to find that her elder
sister could condescend to such youthful matters. On the
whole, she rather blushed for Mary, and felt sadly as if she
had come down from an imaginary pedestal. And then Mr
Proctor, so old and so ordinary, whom it was impossible to
think of as a bridegroom, and still less as a brother. "I
shall get used to it presently," said Lucy, with a burning
flush on her cheek, and a half feeling that she had reason
to be ashamed; "but it is so strange to think of you in that
way, Mary. I always thought you were too – too sensible
for that sort of thing," which was a reproach that went to
Miss Wodehouse's heart.

"Oh, Lucy, dear," said that mild woman, who in this
view of the matter became as much ashamed of herself as
Lucy could desire, "what could I do? I know what you
mean, at my time of life; but I could not let you be
dependent on Tom, my darling," said Miss Wodehouse,
with a deprecating appealing look.

"No indeed," said Lucy; "that would be impossible
under any circumstances: nor on you either, Mary dear. I
can do something to make a living, and I should like it. I
have always been fond of work. I will not permit you to
sacrifice yourself for me," said the younger sister, with
some dignity. "I see how it has been. I felt sure it was not
of your own accord."

Miss Wodehouse wrung her hands with dismay and
perplexity. What was she to do if Lucy stood out and
refused her consent? She could not humble herself so far
as to confess that she rather liked Mr Proctor, and was, on

the whole, not displeased to be married; for the feeling
that Lucy expected her to be too sensible for that sort of
thing overawed the poor lady. "But, Lucy, I have given
him my promise," said poor Miss Wodehouse. "It – it
would make him very unhappy. I can't use him badly,
Lucy dear."

"I will speak to him, and explain if it is necessary.
Whatever happens, I can't let you sacrifice yourself for
me," said Lucy. All the answer Miss Wodehouse could
make was expressed in the tears of vexation and
mortification which rushed to her eyes. She repelled her
young sister's ministrations for the first time in her life
with hasty impatience. Her troubles had not been few for
the last twenty-four hours. She had been questioned
about Tom till she had altogether lost her head, and
scarcely knew what she was saying; and Lucy had not
applauded that notable expedient of throwing the shame
of the family upon Mr Wentworth, to be concealed and
taken care of, which had brought so many vexations to the
Perpetual Curate. Miss Wodehouse at last was driven to
bay. She had done all for the best, but nobody gave her
any credit for it; and now this last step, by which she had
meant to provide a home for Lucy, was about to be
contradicted and put a stop to altogether. She put away
Lucy's arm, and rejected her consolations. "What is the
use of pretending to be fond of me if I am always to be
wrong, and never to have my – my own way in anything?"
cried the poor lady, who, beginning with steadiness, broke
down before she reached the end of her little speech. The
words made Lucy open her blue eyes with wonder; and
after that there followed a fuller explanation, which greatly
changed the ideas of the younger sister. After her
"consent" had been at last extracted from her, and when
Miss Wodehouse regained her composure, she reported to
Lucy the greater part of the conversation which had taken
place in the drawing-room, of which Mr Proctor's proposal
constituted only a part, and which touched upon matters

still more interesting to her hearer. The two sisters, pre-occupied by their father's illness and death, had up to this time but a vague knowledge of the difficulties which surrounded the Perpetual Curate. His trial, which Mr Proctor had reported to his newly-betrothed, had been unsuspected by either of them; and they were not even aware of the event which had given rise to it – the disappearance of Rosa Elsworthy. Miss Wodehouse told the story with faltering lips, not being able to divest herself of the idea that, having been publicly accused, Mr Wentworth must be more or less guilty; while, at the same time, a sense that her brother must have had something to do with it, and a great reluctance to name his name, complicated the narrative. She had already got into trouble with Lucy about this unlucky brother, and unconsciously, in her story, she took an air of defence. "I should have thought better of Mr Wentworth if he had not tried to throw the guilt on another," said the perplexed woman. "Oh, Lucy dear, between two people it is so hard to know what to do."

"I know what I shall do," said Lucy, promptly; but she would not further explain herself. She was, however, quite roused up out of 'In Memoriam.' She went to her desk and drew out some of the paper deeply edged with black, which announced before words its tale of grief to all her correspondents. It was with some alarm that Miss Wodehouse awaited this letter, which was placed before her as soon as finished. This was what, as soon as she knew the story, Lucy's prompt and generous spirit said: –

"DEAR MR WENTWORTH, – We have just heard of the vexations you have been suffering, to our great indignation and distress. Some people may think it is a matter with which I have no business to interfere; but I cannot have you think for a moment, that we, to whom you have been so kind, could put the slightest faith in any such accusations against you. We are not of much consequence, but we are

two women, to whom any such evil would be a horror. If it
is any one connected with us who has brought you into this
painful position, it gives us the more reason to be indignant
and angry. I know now what you meant about the will. If
it was to do over again, I should do just the same; but for
all that, I understand now what you meant. I understand,
also, how much we owe to you, of which, up to yesterday,
I was totally unaware. You ought never to have been
asked to take our burden upon your shoulders. I suppose
you ought not to have done it; but all the same, thank you
with all my heart. I don't suppose we ever can do anything
for you to show our gratitude; and indeed I do not believe
in paying back. But in the mean time, thank you – and
don't, from any consideration for us, suffer a stain which
belongs to another to rest upon yourself. You are a clergyman, and your reputation must be clear. Pardon me for
saying so, as if I were qualified to advise you; but it would
be terrible to think that you were suffering such an injury
out of consideration for us. – Gratefully and truly yours,

"LUCY WODEHOUSE."

The conclusion of this letter gave Lucy a good deal of
trouble. Her honest heart was so moved with gratitude
and admiration that she had nearly called herself
"affectionately" Mr Wentworth's. Why should not she?
"He has acted like a brother to us," Lucy said to herself;
and then she paused to inquire whether his conduct had
indeed arisen from brotherly motives solely. Then, when
she had begun to write "faithfully" instead, a further
difficulty occurred to her. Not thus lightly and unsolicited
could she call herself "faithful," for did not the word mean
everything that words could convey in any human
relationship? When she had concluded it at last, and
satisfied her scruples by the formula above, she laid the
letter before her sister. This event terminated the active
operations of the day in the dwelling of the Wodehouses.
Their brother had not asked to see them, had not

interrupted them as yet in their retreat up-stairs, where they were sedulously waited upon by the entire household. When Miss Wodehouse's agitation was over, she too began to collect together her books and personalities, and they ended by a long consultation where they were to go and what they were to do, during the course of which the elder sister exhibited with a certain shy pride that little photograph of the new rectory, in which there was one window embowered in foliage, which the bride had already concluded was to be Lucy's room. Lucy yielded during this sisterly conference to sympathetic thoughts even of Mr Proctor. The two women were alone in the world. They were still so near the grave and the deathbed that chance words spoken without thought from time to time awakened in both the ready tears. Now and then they each paused to consider with a sob what *he* would have liked best. They knew very little of what was going on outside at the moment when they were occupied with those simple calculations. What was to become of them, as people say – what money they were to have, or means of living – neither was much occupied in thinking of. They had each other; they had, besides, one a novel and timid middle-aged confidence, the other an illimitable youthful faith in one man in the world. Even Lucy, whose mind and thoughts were more individual than her sister's, wanted little else at that moment to make her happy with a tender tremulous consolation in the midst of her grief.

CHAPTER XXXVIII.

WHILE matters were thus arranging themselves in the ideas at least of the two sisters whose prospects had been so suddenly changed, explanations of a very varied kind were going on in the house of the Miss Wentworths. It was a very full house by this time, having been invaded and taken possession of by the "family" in a way which entirely obliterated the calmer interests and occupations of the habitual inhabitants. The three ladies had reached the stage of life which knows no personal events except those of illness and death; and the presence of Jack Wentworth, of Frank and Gerald, and even of Louisa, reduced them altogether to the rank of spectators, the audience, or at the utmost the chorus, of the drama; though this was scarcely the case with Miss Dora, who kept her own room, where she lay on the sofa, and received visits, and told the story of her extraordinary adventure, the only adventure of her life. The interest of the household centred chiefly, however, in the dining-room, which, as being the least habitable apartment in the house, was considered to be most adapted for anything in the shape of business. On the way from the church to Miss Wentworth's house the Curate had given his father a brief account of all the events which had led to his present position; but though much eased in his mind, and partly satisfied, the Squire was not yet clear how it all came about. His countenance was far from having regained that composure, which indeed the recent course of events in the family had pretty nearly driven out of his life. His fresh light-coloured morning dress, with all its little niceties, and the fresh colour which even anxiety could not drive away from his cheeks, were somehow contradicted in their sentiment of cheerfulness by the puckers in his forehead and the harassed look of his face. He sat down in the big leathern chair by the fireplace, and looked round him with a sigh, and the air of a man who wonders what will be the next vexation. "I'd like to hear it over again, Frank," said the Squire. "My mind is not what it used to be: I don't say I ever was clever, like you young fellows, but I used to understand what was said to me. Now I seem to require to hear everything twice over; perhaps it is because I have had myself to say the same things over again a great many times lately," he added, with a sigh of weariness. Most likely his eye fell on Gerald as he said so; at all events, the Rector of Wentworth moved sadly from where he was standing and went to the window, where he was out of his father's range of vision. Gerald's looks, his movements, every action of his, seemed somehow to bear a symbolic meaning at this crisis in his life. He was no longer in any doubt; he had made up his mind. He looked like a martyr walking to his execution, as he crossed the room; and the Squire looked after him, and once more breathed out of his impatient breast a heavy short sigh. Louisa, who had placed herself in the other great chair at the other side of the forlorn fireplace, from which, this summer afternoon, there came no cheerful light, put up her handkerchief to her eyes and began to cry with half-audible sobs – which circumstances surrounding him were far from being encouraging to Frank as he entered anew into his own story – a story which he told with many interruptions. The Squire, who had once "sworn by Frank," had now a terrible shadow of distrust in his mind. Jack was here on the spot, of whom the unfortunate father knew more harm than he had ever told, and the secret dread that he had somehow corrupted his younger brother came like a cold shadow over Mr Wentworth's mind. He could not slur over any part of the narrative, but cross-examined his son to the extent of his ability, with an anxious inquisition into all the particulars. He was too deeply concerned to take anything for granted. He sat up in his chair with those puckers in his forehead, with that harassed look in his eyes, making an anxious, vigilant, suspicious investigation, which was pathetic to behold. If the defendant, who was thus being examined on his honour, had been guilty, the heart of the judge would have broken; but that was all the more reason for searching into it with jealous particularity, and with a suspicion which kept always gleaming out of his troubled eyes in sudden anxious glances, saying, "You are guilty? Are you guilty?" with mingled accusations and appeals. The accused, being innocent, felt this suspicion more hard to bear than if he had been a hundred times guilty.

"I understand a little about this fellow Wodehouse," said the Squire; "but what I want to know is, why you took him in? What did you take him in for, sir, at first? Perhaps I could understand the rest if you would satisfy me of that."

"I took him in," said the Curate, rather slowly, "because his sister asked me. She threw him upon my charity – she told me the danger he was in—"

"What danger was he in?" asked the Squire.

The Curate made a pause, and as he paused Mr Wentworth leaned forward in his chair, with another pucker in his forehead and a still sharper gleam of suspicion in his eyes. "His father had been offended time after time in the most serious way. This time he had threatened to give him up to justice. I can't tell you what he had done, because it would be breaking my trust – but he had made himself obnoxious to the law," said Frank Wentworth. "To save him from the chance of being arrested, his sister brought him to me."

The Squire's hand shook a good deal as he took out his handkerchief and wiped his forehead. "Perhaps it would be the best way if one had not too much regard for the honour of the family," he said, tremulously, like a man under a sudden temptation; "but the sister, sir, why did she bring him to you?" he added, immediately after, with renewed energy. Mr Wentworth was not aware that, while he was speaking, his eldest son had come into the room. He had his back to the door, and he did not see Jack, who stood rather doubtfully on the threshold, with a certain shade of embarrassment upon his ordinary composure. "It is not everybody that a woman would confide her brother's life to," said the Squire. "Who is the sister? Is she – is there any – any entanglement that I don't know of? It will be better for all of us if you tell me plainly," said the old man, with a querulous sound in his voice. He forgot the relationship of his own girls to Jack, and groaned within himself at what appeared almost certain evidence that the sister of a criminal like Wodehouse had got possession of Frank.

"Miss Wodehouse is about the same age as my aunt Dora," said the Curate. It was an exaggeration which would have gone to the poor lady's heart, but Frank Wentworth, in the unconscious insolence of his youth, was quite unaware and careless of the difference. Then he paused for a moment with an involuntary smile. "But I am a clergyman, sir," he continued, seriously. "If a man in my position is good for anything, it is his business to help the helpless. I could do no good in any other way – I took him into my house."

"Frank," said the Squire, "I beg your pardon. I believe in my heart you're true and honest. If I were not driven out of my senses by one thing and another," said Mr Wentworth, with bitterness. "They make me unjust to you, sir – unjust to you! But never mind; go on. Why didn't you tell these fellows what you've told me? That would have settled the business at once, without any more ado."

"Mr Morgan is a great deal too much prejudiced against me to believe anything I said. I thought it better to let him prove to himself his own injustice; and another still more powerful reason—" said the Curate.

"Stop, sir, stop; I can't follow you to more than one thing at a time. Why is Mr Morgan prejudiced against you?" said the Squire, once more sitting upright and recommencing his examination.

Frank Wentworth laughed in spite of himself, though he was far from being amused. "I know no reason, except that I have worked in his parish without his permission," he answered, briefly enough, "for which he threatened to have me up before somebody or other – Dr Lushington, I suppose, who is the new Council of Trent, and settles all our matters for us nowadays," said the Curate, not without a little natural scorn, at which, however, his father groaned.

"There is nothing to laugh at in Dr Lushington," said the Squire. "He gives you justice, at all events, which you parsons never give each other, you know. You ought not to have worked in the Rector's parish, sir, without his permission. It's like shooting in another man's grounds. However, that's not my business; – and the other reason, sir?" said Mr Wentworth, with his anxious look.

"My dear father," said the Curate, touched by the anxiety in the Squire's face, and sitting down by him with a sudden impulse, "I have done nothing which either you or I need be ashamed of. I am grieved that you should think it necessary to examine me so closely. Wodehouse is a rascal, but I had taken charge of him; and as long as it was possible to shield him, I felt bound to do so. I made an appeal to his honour, if he had any, and to his fears, which are more to be depended on, and gave him until noon to-day to consider it. Here is his note, which was given me in the vestry; and now you know the whole business, and how it is that I postponed the conclusion till to-night."

The Squire put on his spectacles with a tremulous hand to read the note which his son gave him. The room was very still while he read it, no sound interrupting him except an occasional sniff from Louisa, who was in a permanent state of whimpering, and, besides, had ceased to be interested in Frank's affairs. Jack Wentworth, standing in the background behind the Squire's chair, had the whole party before him, and studied them keenly with thoughts which nobody guessed at. Gerald was still standing by the window, leaning on it with his face only half turned to the others. Was he thinking of the others? was he still one of them? or was he saying his office from some invisible breviary abstracted into another life? That supposition looked the most like truth. Near him was his wife, who had thrown herself, a heap of bright fluttering muslin, into the great chair, and kept her handkerchief to her red eyes. She had enough troubles of her own to occupy her, poor soul! Just at that moment it occurred to her to think of the laburnum berries in the shrubbery at the Rectory, which, it was suddenly borne in upon her, would prove fatal to one or other of the children in her absence; – the dear Rectory which she had to leave so soon! "And Frank will have it, of course," Louisa said to herself, "and marry somebody;" and then she thought of the laburnum berries in connection with his problematical children, not without a movement of satisfaction. Opposite to her was the Squire, holding Wodehouse's epistle in a hand which shook a little, and reading aloud slowly as he could make it out. The note was short and insolent enough. While it was being read, Jack Wentworth, who was not easily discomposed, grew red and restless. He had not dictated it certainly, nor even suggested the wording of the epistle; but it was he who, half in scorn and half in pity of the vagabond's terrors, had reassured Wodehouse, and convinced him that it was only the punishments of public opinion which the Curate could bring upon him. Hardened as Jack was, he could not but be conscious that thus to stand in his brother's way was a shabby business enough, and to feel that he himself and his protégé cut a very poor figure in presence of the manful old Squire with all his burdens, and of Frank, who had, after all, nothing to explain which was not to his honour. Notwithstanding that he was at the present moment his brother's adversary, actually working against him and prolonging his difficulties, an odd kind of contempt and indignation against the fools who could doubt Frank's honour possessed the prodigal at the moment. "A parcel of asses," he said to himself; and so stood and listened to Wodehouse's little note of defiance, which, but for his prompting, the sullen vagabond would never have dared to send to his former protector. The letter itself was as follows: –

"I have consulted my friends about what you said to-day, and they tell me it is d—d nonsense. You can't do me any harm; and I don't mean to get myself into any scrape for you. You can do what you like – I shan't take any notice. Your love affairs are no business of mine. – Yours truly,

"T. WODEHOUSE."

Mr Wentworth threw the miserable scrawl on the table. "The fellow is a scoundrel," said the Squire; "he does not seem to have a spark of gratitude. You've done a deal too much for him already; and if the sister is as old as Dora—" he continued, after a long pause, with a half-humorous relaxation of his features. He was too much worn out to smile.

"Yes," said the Curate. The young man was sensible of a sudden flush and heat, but did not feel any inclination to smile. Matters were very serious just then with Frank Wentworth. He was about to shake himself free of one vexation, no doubt; but at this moment, when Lucy Wodehouse was homeless and helpless, he had nothing to offer her, nor any prospects even which he dared ask her to share with him. This was no time to speak of the other sister, who was not as old as Miss Dora. He was more than ever the Perpetual Curate now. Perhaps, being a clergyman, he ought not to have been swayed by such merely

human emotions; but honour and pride alike demanded
that he should remain in Carlingford, and he had no
shelter to offer Lucy in the time of her need.

After this there followed a pause, which was far from
being cheerful. Frank could not but be disconsolate enough
over his prospects when the excitement died away; and
there was another big, terrible event looming darkly in the
midst of the family, which they had not courage to name
to each other. The long, uneasy pause was at length
broken by Louisa, whose voice sounded in the unnatural
silence like the burst of impatient rain which precedes a
thunderstorm.

"Now that you have done with Frank's affairs, if you
have done with them," said Louisa, "perhaps somebody
will speak to Gerald. I don't mean in the way of arguing.
If some one would only speak *sense* to him. You all know
as well as I do how many children we've got, and – and –
an – other coming," sobbed the poor lady, "if something
doesn't happen to me, which I am sure is more than likely,
and might be expected. I don't blame dear grandpapa, for
he has said everything, and so have I; but I do think his
brothers ought to take a little more interest. Oh, Frank,
you know it doesn't matter for you. You are a young man,
you can go anywhere; but when there are five children
and – and – an – other— And how are we to live? You
know what a little bit of money I had when Gerald
married me. Everybody knows Gerald never cared for
money. If I had had a good fortune it would have been
quite different," cried poor Louisa, with a little flow of
tears and a querulous sob, as though that too was Gerald's
fault. "He has not sent off his letter yet, Frank," said the
injured wife; "if you would but speak to him. He does not
mind me or grandpapa, but he might mind you. Tell him
we shall have nothing to live on; tell him—"

"Hush," said Gerald. He came forward to the table,
very pale and patient, as became a man at the point of
legal death. "I *have* sent away my letter. By this time I

am no longer Rector of Wentworth. Do not break my heart. Do you think there is any particular in the whole matter which I have not considered – the children, yourself, everything? Hush; there is nothing now to be said."

The Squire rose, almost as pale as his son, from his chair. "I think I'll go out into the air a little," said Mr Wentworth. "There's always something new happening. Here is a son of my own," said the old man, rising into a flush of energy, "who has not only deserted his post, but deserted it secretly, Frank. God bless my soul! don't speak to me, sir; I tell you he's gone over to the enemy as much as Charley would have done if he had deserted at the Alma – and done it when nobody knew or was thinking. I used to be thought a man of honour in my day," said Mr Wentworth, bitterly; "and it's a mean thing to say it came by their mother's side. There's Jack—"

The eldest son roused himself up at the mention of his own name. Notwithstanding all his faults, he was not a man to stand behind backs and listen to what was said of him. He came forward with his usual ease, though a close observer might have detected a flush on his face. "I am here, sir," said the heir. "I cannot flatter myself you will have much pleasure in seeing me; but I suppose I have still a right to be considered one of the family." The Squire, who had risen to his feet, and was standing leaning against the table when Jack advanced, returned to his chair and sat down as his eldest son confronted him. They had not met for years, and the shock was great. Mr Wentworth put his hand to his cravat and pulled at it with an instinctive movement. The old man was still feeble from his late illness, and apprehensive of a return of the disease of the Wentworths. He restrained himself, however, with force so passionate that Jack did not guess at the meaning of the gasp which, before the Squire was able to speak to him, convulsed his throat, and made Frank start forward to offer assistance which his father impatiently rejected. The Squire made, indeed, a great effort to speak with dignity. He looked from one to another of his tall sons as he propped himself up by the arms of his chair.

"You are the most important member of the family," said Mr Wentworth; "it is long since you have been among us, but that is not our fault. If things had been different, I should have been glad of your advice as a man of the world. Anyhow, I can't wish you to be estranged from your brothers," said the Squire. It was all any one could say. The heir of Wentworth was not to be denounced or insulted among his kindred, but he could not be taken to their bosom. Perhaps the reception thus given him was more galling than any other could have been to Jack Wentworth's pride. He stood at the table by himself before his father, feeling that there existed no living relations between himself and any one present. He had keen intellectual perceptions, and could recognise the beauty of honour and worth as well as most people; and the contrast between himself and the others who surrounded him presented itself in a very forcible light to Jack. Instead of Gerald and Frank, Wodehouse was *his* allotted companion. For that once he was bitter, notwithstanding his habitual good-humour.

"Yes," he said; "it would be a pity to estrange me from my brothers. We are, on the whole, a lucky trio. I, whom my relations are civil to; and Frank, who is not acquitted yet, though he seems so confident; and Gerald, who has made the greatest mistake of all—"

"Jack," said the Curate, "nobody wants to quarrel with you. You've dealt shabbily by me, but I do not mind. Only talk of things you understand – don't talk of Gerald."

For a moment Jack Wentworth was roused almost to passion. "What is Gerald that I should not understand him?" said Jack; "he and I are the original brood. You are all a set of interlopers, the rest of you. What is Gerald that I should not talk of him? In the world, my dear Frank," continued the heir, superciliously, "as the Squire himself will testify, a man is not generally exempted from criticism because he is a parson. Gerald is—"

"I am a simple Catholic layman, nothing more," said Gerald; "not worth criticism, having done nothing. I am aware I am as good as dead. There is no reason why Jack should not talk if it pleases him. It will make no difference to me."

"And yet," said Frank, "it is only the other day that you told us you were nothing if not a priest."

Gerald turned upon him with a look of melancholy reproach that went to the Curate's heart. "It is true I said so," he replied, and then he made a pause, and the light died out of his pale face. "Don't bring up the ghosts of my dead battles, Frank. I said so only the other day. But it is the glory of the true Church," said the convert, with a sudden glow which restored colour for a moment to his face, "to restrain and subdue the last enemy, the will of man. I am content to be nothing, as the saints were. The fight has been hard enough, but I am not ashamed of the victory. When the law of the Church and the obedience of the saints ordain me to be nothing, I consent to it. There is nothing more to say."

"And this is how it is to be!" cried Louisa. "He knows what is coming, and he does not care – and none of you will interfere or speak to him! It is not as if he did not know what would happen. He tells you himself that he will be nothing; and even if *he* can put up with it after being a man of such consideration in the county, how am *I* to put up with it? We have always been used to the very best society," said poor Louisa, with tears. "The Duke himself was not more thought of; and now he tells you he is to be nothing!" Mrs Wentworth stopped to dry her eyes with tremulous haste. "*He* may not mind," said Louisa, "for at least he is having his own way. It is all very well for a man, who can do as he pleases; but it is his poor wife who will have to suffer. I don't know who will visit me after it's all over, and people will give over asking us if we don't ask them again; and how can we ever have anybody, with five children – or more – and only a few hundreds a-year? Oh, Frank, it kills me to think of it. Don't you think you might speak to him again?" she whispered, stretching up to his ear, when Gerald, with a sigh, had gone back to his window. The Squire, too, cast an appealing glance at his younger son.

"It is all true enough that she says," said Mr Wentworth. "She mayn't understand *him*, Frank, but she's right enough in what she's saying. If things were different between your brother and me, I'd ask his advice," said the Squire, with a sigh. He gave a longing look at his eldest son, who stood with his usual ease before the fireplace. Matters had gone a great deal too far between the father and son to admit of the usual displeasure of an aggrieved parent – all that was over long ago; and Mr Wentworth could not restrain a certain melting of the heart towards his first-born. "He's not what I could wish, but he's a man of the world, and might give us some practical advice," said the Squire, with his anxious looks. Of what possible advantage advice, practical or otherwise, could have been in the circumstances, it was difficult to see; but the Squire was a man of simple mind, and still believed in the suggestions of wisdom. He still sat in the easy-chair, looking wistfully at Jack, and with a certain faith that matters might even yet be mended, if the counsel of his eldest son, as a man of the world, could be had and could be trusted; when Frank, who had an afternoon service at Wharfside, had to leave the family committee. Gerald, who roused up when his younger brother mentioned the business he was going upon, looked at Frank almost as wistfully as his father looked at Jack. "It may be the last time," he said to himself: "if you'll let me, I'll go with you, Frank;" and so the little conclave was broken up. The people in Prickett's Lane were greatly impressed by the aspect of Gerald Wentworth, as he went, silent and pale, by his brother's side, down the crowded pavement. They thought it must be a bishop at least who accompanied the Curate of St Roque's; and the women gathered at a little distance and made their comments, as he stood waiting for his brother after the service. "He don't look weakly nor sickly no more nor the clergyman," said one; "but he smiles at the little uns for all the world like my man smiled the night he was took away." "Smilin' or not smilin'," said another, "I don't see as it makes no matter; but I'd give a deal to know what Elsworthy and them as stands by Elsworthy can say after that." "Maybe, then, he'd give the poor fatherless children a blessing afore he'd go," suggested a poor Irish widow, who, having been much under Mr Wentworth's hands "in her trouble," was not quite sure now what faith she professed, or at least which Church she belonged to. Such was the universal sentiment of Prickett's Lane. Meanwhile Gerald stood silent, and looked with pathetic, speechless eyes at the little crowd. He was no priest now — he was shorn of the profession which had been his life. His hope of being able to resign all things for Christ's sake had failed him. Too wary and politic to maintain in a critical age and country the old licence of the ages of Faith, even his wife's consent, could he have obtained it, would not have opened to the convert the way into the priesthood. A greater trial had been required of him; he was nothing, a man whose career was over. He stood idly, in a kind of languor, looking on while the Curate performed the duties of his office — feeling like a man whom sickness had reduced to the last stage of life, and for whom no earthly business remained; while, at the same time, his aspect struck awe, as that of a bishop at the least, to the imagination of Prickett's Lane.

CHAPTER XXXIX.

MR MORGAN did not go home direct from the investigation of the morning; on the contrary, he paid various visits, and got through a considerable amount of parish business, before he turned his face towards the Rectory. On the whole, his feelings were far from being comfortable. He did not know, certainly, who Mr Wentworth's witness was, but he had an unpleasant conviction that it was somebody who would clear the Curate. "Of course I shall be very glad," the Rector said to himself; but it is a fact, that in reality he was far from being glad, and that a secret conviction of this sentiment, stealing into his mind, made matters still more uncomfortable. This private sense of wishing evil to another man, of being unwilling and vexed to think well of his neighbour, was in itself enough to disturb the Rector's tranquillity; and when to this was added the aggravation that his wife had always been on the other side, and had warned him against proceeding, and might, if she pleased, say, "I told you so," it will be apparent that Mr Morgan's uneasiness was not without foundation. Instead of going home direct to acquaint his wife with the circumstances, about which he knew she must be curious, it was late in the afternoon before the Rector opened his own gate. Even then he went through the garden with a reluctant step, feeling it still more difficult to meet her now than it would have been at first, although his delay had arisen from the thought that it would be easier to encounter her keen looks after an interval. There was, however, no keen look to be dreaded at this moment. Mrs Morgan was busy with her ferns, and

she did not look up as her husband approached. She went
on with her occupation, examining carefully what withered
fronds there might be about her favourite maidenhair,
even when he stopped by her side. Though her husband's
shadow fell across the plants she was tending, Mrs
Morgan, for the first time in her married life, did not look
up to welcome the Rector. She made no demonstration,
said no word of displeasure, but only showed herself
utterly absorbed in, and devoted to, her ferns. There was,
to be sure, no such lover of ferns in the neighbourhood of
Carlingford as the Rector's wife.

As for Mr Morgan, he stood by her side in a state of
great discomfort and dicomfiture. The good man's perceptions were not very clear, but he saw that she had heard
from some one the issue of the morning's inquiry, and that
she was deeply offended by his delay, and that, in short,
they had arrived at a serious difference, the first quarrel
since their marriage. Feeling himself in the wrong, Mr
Morgan naturally grew angry too.

"I should like to have dinner earlier to-day," he said,
with the usual indiscretion of an aggrieved husband.
"Perhaps you will tell the cook, my dear. I think I should
like to have it at five, if possible. It can't make much
difference for one day."

Mrs Morgan raised herself up from her ferns, and no
doubt it was a relief to her to find herself provided with so
just a cause of displeasure. "Much difference!" cried the
Rector's wife; "it is half-past four now. I wonder how you
could think of such a thing, William. There is some lamb,
which of course is not put down to roast yet, and the
ducks. If you wish the cook to give warning immediately,
you may send such a message. It is just like a man to think
it would make no difference! But I must say, to do them
justice," said the Rector's wife, "it is not like a man of
your college!" When she had fired this double arrow, she
took off her gardening gloves and lifted her basket. "I
suppose you told Mr Proctor that you wished to dine

early?" said Mrs Morgan, with severity, pausing on the
threshold. "Of course it is quite impossible to have dinner
at five unless he knows."

"Indeed I – I forgot all about Proctor," said the Rector,
who now saw the inexpediency of his proposal. "On second
thoughts, I see it does not matter much. But after dinner I
expect some people about Mr Wentworth's business. It
was not settled this morning, as I expected."

"So I heard," said Mrs Morgan. "I will tell Thomas to
show them into the library," and she went indoors, carrying
her basket. As for the Rector, he stood silent, looking after
her, and feeling wonderfully discomfited. Had she found
fault with him for his delay – had she even said "I told you
so!" it would have been less overwhelming than this
indifference. They had never had a quarrel before, and
the effect was proportionately increased. After standing
bewildered at the door for a few minutes, he retired into
his study, where the change in his wife's demeanour
haunted him, and obscured Mr Wentworth. Mrs Morgan
sat at the head of the table at dinner with an equal want of
curiosity. Even when the subject was discussed between
the Rector and Mr Proctor, she asked no questions – a
course of procedure very puzzling and trying to Mr
Morgan, who could not make it out.

It was after eight o'clock before the tribunal of the
morning was reconstituted at the Rectory. Most of the
gentlemen came late, and the little assembly brought with
it a flavour of port, which modified the serious atmosphere.
When the bed of justice was again formed, Mr Wentworth
entered with the bodyguard of Wentworths, which
numbered half as many as his judges. Half from curiosity,
half from a reluctant inclination to please his father, Jack
had joined the others, and they came in together, all of
them noticeable men, profoundly different, yet identified
as belonging to each other by the touching bond of family
resemblance. After the four gentlemen had taken possession
of their corner, Mr Waters made a somewhat hurried

entry, bringing after him the sullen reluctant figure of Wodehouse, who made an awkward bow to the assembled potentates, and looked ashamed and vigilant, and very ill at ease. Mr Waters made a hasty explanation to the Rector before he sat down by the side of his unlucky client. "I thought it possible there might be some attempt made to shift the blame upon him, therefore I thought it best to bring him," said the lawyer. Mr Morgan gave him a dry little nod without answering. To tell the truth, the Rector felt anything but comfortable; when he glanced up at the stranger, who was looking askance at the people in the room as if they had been so many policemen in disguise, a disagreeable sudden conviction that this sullen rascal looked a great deal more like the guilty man than Mr Wentworth did, came into Mr Morgan's mind, and made him sick with annoyance and embarrassment. If it should turn out so! if it should become apparent that he, for private prejudices of his own, had been persecuting his brother! This thought produced an actual physical effect for the moment upon the Rector, but its immediate visible consequence was simply to make him look more severe, almost spiteful, in a kind of unconscious self-vindication. Last of all, Elsworthy, who began to be frightened too, but whose fears were mingled with no compunction nor blame of himself, stole in and found an uncomfortable seat on a stool near the door, where scarcely any one saw him, by favour of Thomas, and screened by the high back of the Rector's easy-chair. When all were assembled Mr Morgan spoke.

"We are met this evening, gentlemen, to complete, if there is sufficient time, the investigation we began this morning," said the Rector. "I have no doubt I express the sentiments of every one present when I say I shall be glad – *unfeignedly* glad," said Mr Morgan, with a defiant emphasis, which was meant to convince himself, "to find that Mr Wentworth's witness is of sufficient importance to justify the delay. As we were interrupted this morning solely on his account, I presume it will be most satisfactory that this witness should be called at once."

"I should like to say something in the first place," said the Curate. Mr Morgan made an abrupt nod indicative of his consent, and, instead of looking at the defendant, shaded his eyes with his hand, and made figures with his pen upon the blotting-paper. A conviction, against which it was impossible to strive, had taken possession of the Rector's soul. He listened to Frank Wentworth's address with a kind of impatient annoyance and resistance. "What is the good of saying any more about it?" Mr Morgan was saying in his soul. "For heaven's sake let us bury it and be done with it, and forget that we ever made such asses of ourselves." But at the same time the Rector knew this was quite impossible; and as he sat leaning over his blotting-book, writing down millions after millions with his unconscious pen, he looked a very model of an unwilling listener – a prejudiced judge – a man whom no arguments could convince; which was the aspect under which he appeared to the Curate of St Roque's.

"I should like to say something first," said the Perpetual Curate. "I could not believe it possible that I, being tolerably well known in Carlingford as I have always supposed, could be suspected by any rational being of such an insane piece of wickedness as has been laid to my charge; and consequently it did not occur to me to vindicate myself, as I perhaps ought to have done, at the beginning. I have been careless all along of vindicating myself. I had an idea," said the young man, with involuntary disdain, "that I might trust, if not to the regard, at least to the common-sense of my friends—"

Here John Brown, who was near his unwary client, plucked at the Curate's coat, and brought him to a momentary half-angry pause. "Softly, softly," said Dr Marjoribanks; "common-sense has nothing to do with facts; we're inquiring into facts at this moment; and, besides, it's a very foolish and unjustifiable confidence to trust to any man's common-sense," said the old Doctor, with a humorous glance from under his shaggy eyebrows at his fellow-judges; upon which there ensued a laugh, not very agreeable in its tone, which brought the Rector to a white heat of impatience and secret rage.

"It appears to me that the witness ought to be called at once," said Mr Morgan, "if this is not a mere expedient to gain time, and if it is intended to make any progress to-night."

"My explanations shall be very brief," said Frank Wentworth, facing instantly to his natural enemy. "I have suspected from the beginning of this business who was the culprit, and have made every possible attempt to induce him to confess, and, so far as he could, amend the wrong that he had done. I have failed; and now the confession, the *amende*, must be made in public. I will now call my witness," said the Curate. But this time a commotion rose in another part of the room. It was Wodehouse, who struggled to rise, and to get free from the detaining grasp of his companion.

"By Jove! I aint going to sit here and listen to a parcel of lies!" cried the vagabond. "If I am to be tried, at least I'll have the real thing, by Jove!" He had risen up, and was endeavouring to pass Mr Waters and get out, casting a suspicious defiant look round the room. The noise he made turned all eyes upon him, and the scrutiny he had brought upon himself redoubled his anxiety to get away. "I'll not stand it, by Jove! Waters, let me go," said the craven, whose confused imagination had mixed up all his evil doings together, and who already felt himself being carried off to prison. It was at this moment that Jack Wentworth rose from his place in his easy careless way, and went forward to the table to adjust the lamp, which was flaring a little. Wodehouse dropped back into a chair as soon as he caught the eye of this master of his fate. His big beard moved with a subterranean gasp like the panting of a hunted creature, and all the colour that had

remained died away out of his haggard, frightened face.
As for Jack Wentworth, he took no apparent notice of the
shabby rascal whom he held in awe. "Rather warm this
room for a court of justice. I hope Frank's witness is not
fat," said Jack, putting himself up against the wall, and
lifting languidly his glass to his eye – which byplay was
somewhat startling, but totally incomprehensible, to the
amateur judges, who looked upon him with angry eyes.

"I must request that the proceedings may not be
interrupted," said Mr Morgan; and then everybody looked
towards the open door: the sight they saw there was
enough to startle the calmest spectator. Elsworthy, who
was seated close by, sprang from his stool with a low
resounding howl of amazement, upsetting his lowly seat,
and staggering back against the wall, in the excess of his
wonder and consternation. The judges themselves forgot
their decorum, and crowded round upon each other to
stare – old Mr Western putting his arm round the Rector's
neck in his curiosity, as if they had been two boys at a
peep-show. It was Miss Leonora Wentworth's erect iron-
grey figure that appeared in the doorway, half leading in,
half pushing before her, the unfortunate cause of all the
commotion – Rosa Elsworthy herself. A change had passed
upon the little girl's rosy, dewy, April beauty. Her pretty
dark eyes were enlarged and anxious, and full of tears; her
cheeks had paled out of their sweet colour, her red lips
were pressed tightly together. Passion and shame had set
their marks upon the child's forehead – lightly, it is true,
but still the traces were there; but beyond all other sentiments, anxiety, restless, breathless, palpitating, had
possession of Mr Wentworth's all-important witness. It
was very clear that, whatever might be the opinion of her
judges, Rosa's case was anything but hopeless in her own
eyes. She came in drooping, shrinking, and abashed, as
was natural; but her shame was secondary in Rosa's mind,
even in the moment of her humiliation. She came to a
dead stop when she had made a few steps into the room,

and cast furtive glances at the dread tribunal, and began to cry. She was trembling with nervous eagerness, with petulance and impatience. Almost all her judges, except the Rector and Mr Proctor, had been known to Rosa from her earliest years. She was not afraid of them, nor cast down by any sense of overwhelming transgression – on the contrary, she cast an appealing look round her, which implied that they could still set everything right if they would exert themselves; and then she began to cry.

"Gentlemen, before you ask any questions," said Miss Leonora Wentworth, "I should like to explain why I am here. I came not because I approve of *her*, but because it is right that my nephew should have a respectable woman to take charge of the witness. She was brought to my house last night, and has been in my charge ever since; – and I come with her now, not because I approve of her, but because she ought to be in charge of some woman," said Miss Leonora, sitting down abruptly in the chair some one had placed for her. The chair was placed close by the spot where Rosa stood crying. Poor, pretty, forsaken child! Perhaps Miss Leonora, who sat beside her, and occupied the position of her protector, was of all the people present the only one who had not already forgiven Rosa, the only one who would have still been disposed to punish her, and did not pardon the weeping creature in her heart.

"Now that you're here, Rosa," said Dr Marjoribanks, "the only sensible thing you can do is to dry your eyes and answer the questions that have to be put to you. Nobody will harm you if you speak the truth. Don't be frightened, but dry your eyes, and let us hear what you have to say."

"Poor little thing," said old Mr Western; "of course she has done very wrong. I don't mean to defend her – but, after all, she is but a child. Poor little thing! Her mother died, you know, when she was a baby. She had nobody to tell her how to behave. – I don't mean to defend her, for she has done very wrong, poor little—"

"We are falling into mere conversation," said the Rector, severely. "Rosa Elsworthy, come to the table. The only thing you can do to make up for all the misery you have caused to your friends, is to tell the truth about everything. You are aged – how much? eighteen years?"

"Please, sir, only seventeen," said Rosa; "and oh, please, sir, I didn't mean no harm. I wouldn't never have gone, no, not a step, if he hadn't a-promised that we was to be married. Oh, please, sir—"

"Softly a little," said John Brown, interfering. "It is not you who are on your trial, Rosa. We are not going to question you about your foolishness; all that the Rector wants you to tell him is the name of the man who persuaded you to go away."

At which question Rosa cried more and more. "I don't think he meant no harm either," cried the poor little girl. "Oh, if somebody would please speak to him! We couldn't be married then, but now if anybody would take a little trouble! I told him Mr Wentworth would, if I was to ask him; but then I thought perhaps as Mr Wentworth mightn't like to be the one as married me," said Rosa, with a momentary gleam of vanity through her tears. The little simper with which the girl spoke, the coquettish looks askance at the Perpetual Curate, who stood grave and unmoved at a distance, the movement of unconscious self-deception and girlish vanity which for a moment distracted Rosa, had a great effect upon the spectators. The judges looked at each other across the table, and Dr Marjoribanks made a commentary of meditative nods upon that little exhibition. "Just so," said the Doctor; "maybe Mr Wentworth might have objected. If you tell me the man's name, I'll speak to him, Rosa," said the old Scotsman, grimly. As for the Rector, he had put down his pen altogether, and looked very much as if he were the culprit. Certainly his shame and confusion and self-disgust were greater than that of any one else in the room.

"Oh, Doctor, please don't be angry. Oh, if somebody

would only speak to him!" cried poor Rosa. "Oh, please, it wasn't my fault – I haven't got no – nobody to speak for me!" At this moment she got a glimpse of her uncle's face, dark and angry, looming behind the Rector's chair. Rosa shrank back with a frightened movement, and caught fast hold of Miss Leonora's dress. "Oh, please, don't let him kill me!" cried the terrified girl. She sank down at Miss Wentworth's feet, and held tightly by her unwilling protectress. She was a frightened child, afraid of being whipped and punished; she was not an outraged woman, forsaken and miserable. Nobody knew what to do with her as she crouched down, panting with fright and anxiety, by Miss Leonora's side.

"We must know who this man is," said John Brown. "Look here, Rosa; if anybody is to do you good, it is necessary to know the man. Rise up and look round, and tell me if you can see him here."

After a moment's interval Rosa obeyed. She stood up trembling, resting her hand to support herself on Miss Leonora's chair – almost, she trembled so, on Miss Leonora's shoulder. Up to this moment the ignorant little creature had scarcely felt the shame of her position; she had felt only the necessity of appealing to the kindness of people who knew her – people who were powerful enough to do very nearly what they pleased in Carlingford; for it was in this light that Rosa, who knew no better, regarded the Doctor and her other judges. This time her eye passed quickly over those protectors. The tears were still hanging on her eyelashes; her childish bosom was still palpitating with sobs. Beyond the little circle of light round the table, the room was comparatively in shadow. She stood by herself, her pretty face and anxious eyes appearing over Miss Wentworth's head, her fright and her anxiety both forgotten for the moment in the sudden hope of seeing her betrayer. There was not a sound in the room to disturb the impartiality of her search. Every man kept still, as if by chance he might be the offender. Rosa's eyes, bright with anxiety, with eagerness, with a feverish hope, went searching into the shadow, gleaming harmless over the Wentworth brothers, who were opposite. Then there was a start and a loud cry. She was not ashamed to be led before the old men, who were sorry for her, and who could protect her; but now at last the instinct of her womanhood seized upon the unfortunate creature. She had made an involuntary rush towards him when she saw him first. Then she stopped short, and looked all round her with a bewildered sudden consciousness. The blood rushed to her face, scorching and burning; she uttered a sudden cry of anguish and shame. "Oh, don't forsake me! – don't forsake me! – listen to the gentlemen!" cried poor Rosa, and fell down in a sudden agony of self-comprehension at Wodehouse's feet.

For a few minutes after there was nothing but confusion in the room. Elsworthy had been standing behind backs, with a half-fiendish look of rage and disappointment on his commonplace features. "Let them help her as likes; I washes my hands of her," he cried bitterly, when he saw her fall; and then rushed into the midst of the room, thrusting the others out of his way. The man was beside himself with mortification, with disgust, and fury, and at the same time with a savage natural affection for the creature who had baffled and disgraced him, yet still was his own. "Let alone – let alone, I tell you! There's nobody as belongs to her but me!" cried Elsworthy, pushing up against the Doctor, who had lifted her from the ground. As for Wodehouse, he was standing scowling down upon the pretty figure at his feet: not that the vagabond was utterly heartless, or could look at his victim without emotion; on the contrary, he was pale with terror, thinking he had killed her, wondering in his miserable heart if they would secure him at once, and furtively watching the door to see if he had a chance of escape. When Mr Waters seized his arm, Wodehouse gave a hoarse outcry of horror. "I'll marry her – oh, Lord, I'll marry her! I never meant

anything else," the wretched man cried, as he sank back
again into his chair. He thought she was dead, as she lay
with her upturned face on the carpet, and in his terror and
remorse and cowardice his heart seemed to stop beating.
If he could have had a chance of escaping, he would not
have hesitated to dash the old Doctor out of his way, and
rush over the body of the unhappy girl whom he thought
he had murdered. But Waters held him fast; and he sank
back, panting and horrified, on his seat. "I never touched
her; nobody can say I touched her," muttered the poor
wretch to himself; and watched with fascinated eyes and
the distinct apprehension of terror every movement and
change of position, calculating how he might dart out
when the window was opened – having forgotten for the
moment that Jack Wentworth, as well as the companion
who kept immediate watch over him, was in the room.

"She'll come to herself presently," said Dr Marjoribanks.
"We'll carry her up-stairs. Yes, I know you don't approve
of her, Miss Wentworth; nobody said you were to approve
of her. Not that I think she's a responsible moral agent
myself," said the Doctor, lifting her up in his vigorous
arms; "but in the mean time she has to be brought to life.
Keep out of my way, Elsworthy; you should have looked
better after the little fool. If she's not accountable for her
actions, *you* are," he went on with a growl, thrusting away
with his vigorous shoulder the badly-hung frame of Rosa's
uncle, who was no match for the Doctor. Thus the poor
little girl was carried away in a kind of procession, Miss
Leonora going first. "Not that I think her worth all this
fuss, the vain little fool," said Miss Leonora; "she'll come
to herself, no fear of her;" but, notwithstanding her
protest, the strong-minded woman led the way. When the
room was cleared, the gentlemen who remained took their
seats mechanically, and stared at each other. In the shame
and confusion of the moment nobody could find anything
to say, and the Curate was magnanimous, and did not take
advantage of his triumph. The silence was broken by the

Rector, who rose up solemnly from his chair to speak. Probably no one in the room had suffered so acutely as Mr Morgan; his face was crimson, his eyes suffused and angry. Frank Wentworth rose involuntarily at the same moment, expecting, he could not tell why, to be addressed, but sat down again in a little confusion when he found that the Rector had turned his eyes in a totally different direction. Mr Morgan put the lamp out of the way, that he might be able to transfix with the full glow of his angry eyes the real offender, who sat only half conscious, absorbed with his own terror, by the lawyer's side.

"Sir!" said the Rector, in a tone which, severe as his voice was by nature, nobody had ever heard from his lips before, "you have put us all in a most ridiculous and painful position to-night. I don't know whether you are capable of feeling the vileness of your own misconduct as regards the unhappy girl who has just been carried out of the room, but you certainly shall not leave the house without hearing—"

Wodehouse gave such a start at these words that Mr Morgan paused a moment. The Rector was quite unaware of the relief, the sense of safety, which he had inadvertently conveyed to the mind of the shabby rascal whom he was addressing. He was then to be allowed to leave the house? "I'll leave the d—d place to-night, by Jove!" he muttered in his beard, and immediately sat up upon his chair, and turned round with a kind of sullen vivacity to listen to the remainder of Mr Morgan's speech.

"You shall not leave this house," said the Rector, more peremptorily still, "without hearing what must be the opinion of every gentleman, of every honest man. You have been the occasion of bringing an utterly unfounded accusation against a – a young clergyman," said Mr Morgan, with a succession of gasps, "of – of the very highest character. You have, as I understand, sir, abused his hospitality, and – and done your utmost to injure him when you owed him gratitude. Not content with that, sir," continued the Rector, "you have kept your – your very existence concealed, until the moment when you could injure your sisters. You may perhaps be able to make a miserable amends for the wrong you have done to the unfortunate girl up-stairs, but you can never make amends to me, sir, for betraying me into a ridiculous position, and leading me to do – an – an absurd and – and incredible injustice – to a – to my – to Mr Frank Wentworth. Sir, you are a scoundrel!" cried Mr Morgan, breaking down abruptly in an access of sudden fury. When the Rector had recovered himself, he turned with great severity to the rest of the company: "Gentlemen, my wife will be glad to see you up-stairs," said Mr Morgan. The sound of this hospitable invitation was as if he had ordered the entire assembly to the door; but nevertheless most of the company followed him as he rose, and, without condescending to look round again, marched out of the library. The Squire rose with the rest, and took the hand of his son Frank and grasped it closely. Somehow, though he believed Frank before, Mr Wentworth was easier in his mind after the Rector's speech.

"I think I will go up-stairs and shake hands with him," said the Squire, "and you had better come too, Frank. No doubt he will expect it. He spoke up very well at the last, and I entirely agree with the Rector," he said, looking sternly, but with a little curiosity, at the vagabond, who stood recovering himself, and ready to resume his hopeless swagger. It was well for Mr Wentworth that he left the room at once, and went cheerfully up-stairs to pay his respects to Mrs Morgan. The Squire said, "Thank God!" quietly to himself when he got out of the library. "Things are mending, surely – even Jack – even Jack," Mr Wentworth said, under his breath; and the simple gentleman said over a part of the general thanksgiving, as he went slowly, with an unusual gladness, up the stair. He might not have entered Mrs Morgan's drawing-room with such a relieved and brightened countenance had he stayed ten minutes longer in the library, and listened to the further conversation there.

CHAPTER XL.

"Now, Mr Wodehouse," said Jack Wentworth, "it appears that you and I have a word to say to each other." They had all risen when the other gentlemen followed Mr Morgan out of the room, and those who remained stood in a group surrounding the unhappy culprit, and renewing his impression of personal danger. When he heard himself thus addressed, he backed against the wall, and instinctively took one of the chairs and placed it before him. His furtive eye sought the door and the window, investigating the chances of escape. When he saw that there was none, he withdrew still a step further back, and stood at bay.

"By Jove! I aint going to stand all this," said Wodehouse; "as if every fellow had a right to bully me – it's more than flesh and blood can put up with. I don't care for that old fogey that's gone up-stairs; but, by Jove! I won't stand any more from men that eat my dinners, and win my money, and—"

Jack Wentworth made half a step forward with a superb smile – "My good fellow, you should never reproach a man with his good actions," he said; "but at the same time, having eaten your dinners, as you describe, I have a certain claim on your gratitude. We have had some – a – business connection – for some years. I don't say you have reason to be actually grateful for that; but, at least, it brought you now and then into the society of gentlemen. A man who robs a set of women, and leaves the poor creature he has ruined destitute, is a sort of cur we have nothing to say to," said the heir of the Wentworths, contemptuously. "We do not pretend to be saints, but we are not blackguards; that is to say," said Jack, with a perfectly calm and harmonious smile, "not in theory, nor in our own opinion. The fact accordingly is, my friend, that you must choose between *us* and those respectable meannesses of yours. By Jove! the fellow ought to have been a shopkeeper, and as honest as – Diogenes," said Jack. He stood looking at his wretched associate with the overwhelming impertinence of a perfectly well-bred man, no way concealing the contemptuous inspection with which his cool eyes travelled over the disconcerted figure from top to toe, seeing and exaggerating all its tremors and clumsy guiltiness. The chances are, had Jack Wentworth been in Wodehouse's place, he would have been master of the position as much as now. He was not shocked nor indignant like his brothers. He was simply contemptuous, disdainful, not so much of the wickedness as of the clumsy and shabby fashion in which it had been accomplished. As for the offender, who had been defiant in his sulky fashion up to this moment, his courage oozed out at his finger-ends under Jack Wentworth's eye.

"I am my own master," he stammered, "nowadays. I aint to be dictated to – and I shan't be, by Jove! As for Jack Wentworth, he's well known to be neither more nor less—"

"Than what, Mr Wodehouse?" said the serene and splendid Jack. "Don't interest yourself on my account, Frank. This is my business at present. If you have any prayer-meetings in hand, we can spare you – and don't forget our respectable friend in your supplications. Favour us with your definition of Jack Wentworth, Mr Wodehouse. He is neither more nor less— ?"

"By Jove! I aint going to stand it," cried Wodehouse; "if a fellow's to be driven mad, and insulted, and have his money won from him, and made game of – not to say tossed about as I've been among 'em, and made a drudge of, and set to do the dirty work," said the unfortunate subordinate, with a touch of pathos in his hoarse voice; — "I don't mean to say I've been what I ought; but, by Jove! to be put upon as I've been, and knocked about; and at the last they haven't the pluck to stand by a fellow, by Jove!" muttered Mr Wodehouse's unlucky heir. What further exasperation his smiling superior intended to heap upon him nobody could tell; for just as Jack Wentworth was about to speak, and just as Wodehouse had again faced towards him, half-cowed, half-resisting, Gerald, who had been looking on in silence, came forward out of the shadow. He had seen all and heard all, from that moral deathbed of his, where no personal cares could again disturb him; and though he had resigned his office, he could not belie his nature. He came in by instinct to cherish the dawn of compunction which appeared, as he thought, in the sinner's words.

"The best thing that can happen to you," said Gerald, at the sound of whose voice everybody started, "is to find out that the wages of sin are bitter. Don't expect any sympathy or consolation from those who have helped you to do wrong. My brother tries to induce you to do a right act from an unworthy motive. He says your former associates will not acknowledge you. My advice to you is to forsake your former associates. My brother," said Gerald, turning aside to look at him, "would do himself honour if he forsook them also — but for you, here is your opportunity. You have no temptation of poverty now. Take the first step, and forsake them. I have no motive in advising you — except, indeed, that I am Jack Wentworth's brother. He and you are different," said Gerald, involuntarily glancing from one to the other. "And at present you have the means of escape. Go now and leave them," said the man who was a priest by nature. The light returned to his eye while he spoke; he was no longer passive, contemplating his own moral death; his natural office had come back to him unawares. He stretched his arm towards the

door, thinking of nothing but the escape of the sinner.
"Go," said Gerald. "Refuse their approbation; shun their
society. For Christ's sake, and not for theirs, make amends
to those you have wronged. Jack, I command you to let him
go."

Jack, who had been startled at first, had recovered
himself long before his brother ceased to speak. "Let him
go, by all means," he said, and stood superbly indifferent
by Gerald's side, whistling under his breath a tripping
lively air. "No occasion for solemnity. The sooner he goes
the better," said Jack. "In short, I see no reason why any
of us should stay, now the business is accomplished. I
wonder would his reverence ever forgive me if I lighted
my cigar?" He took out his case as he spoke, and began to
look over its contents. There was one in the room, however,
who was better acquainted with the indications of Jack
Wentworth's face than either of his brothers. This
unfortunate, who was hanging in an agony of uncertainty
over the chair he had placed before him, watched every
movement of his leader's face with the anxious gaze of a
lover, hoping to see a little corresponding anxiety in it, but
watched in vain. Wodehouse had been going through a
fever of doubt and divided impulses. The shabby fellow
was open to good impressions, though he was not much in
the way of practising them; and Gerald's address, which,
in the first place, filled him with awe, moved him afterwards with passing thrills of compunction, mingled with a
kind of delight at the idea of getting free. When his
admonitor said "Go," Wodehouse made a step towards
the door, and for an instant felt the exhilaration of
enfranchisement. But the next moment his eye sought
Jack Wentworth's face, which was so superbly careless, so
indifferent to him and his intentions, and the vagabond's
soul succumbed with a canine fidelity to his master. Had
Jack shown any interest, any excitement in the matter, his
sway might have been doubtful; but in proportion to
the sense of his own insignificance and unimportance

Wodehouse's allegiance confirmed itself. He looked wistfully towards the hero of his imagination, as that skilful personage selected his cigar. He would rather have been kicked again than left alone, and left to himself. After all, it was very true what Jack Wentworth said. They might be a bad lot, but they were gentlemen (according to Wodehouse's understanding of the word) with whom he had been associated; and beatific visions of peers and baronets and honourables, amongst whom his own shabby person had figured, without feeling much below the common level, crossed his mind with all the sweetness which belongs to a past state of affairs. Yet it was still in his power to recall these vanishing glories. Now that he was rich, and could "cut a figure" among the objects of his admiration, was that brilliant world to be closed upon him for ever by his own obstinacy? As these thoughts rushed through his mind, little Rosa's beauty and natural grace came suddenly to his recollection. Nobody need know how he had got his pretty wife, and a pretty wife she would be – a creature whom nobody could help admiring. Wodehouse looked wistfully at Jack Wentworth, who took no notice of him as he chose his cigar. Jack was not only the ideal of the clumsy rogue, but he was the doorkeeper of that paradise of disreputable nobles and ruined gentlemen which was Wodehouse's idea of good society; and from all this was he about to be banished? Jack Wentworth selected his cigar with as much care as if his happiness depended on it, and took no notice of the stealthy glances thrown at him. "I'll get a light in the hall," said Jack; "good evening to you," and he was actually going away.

"Look here," said Wodehouse, hastily, in his beard; "I aint a man to forsake old friends. If Jack Wentworth does not mean anything unreasonable, or against a fellow's honour— Hold your tongue, Waters; by Jove! I know my friends. I know you would never have been one of them but for Jack Wentworth. He's not the common sort, I can tell you. He's the greatest swell going, by Jove!" cried

Jack's admiring follower, "and through thick and thin he's stood by me. I aint going to forsake him now – that is, if he don't want anything that goes against a fellow's honour," said the repentant prodigal, again sinking the voice which he had raised for a moment. As he spoke he looked more wistfully than ever towards his leader, who said "Pshaw!" with an impatient gesture, and put back his cigar.

"This room is too hot for anything," said Jack; "but don't open the window, I entreat of you. I hate to assist at the suicide of a set of insane insects. For heaven's sake, Frank, mind what you're doing. As for Mr Wodehouse's remark," said Jack, lightly, "I trust I never could suggest anything which would wound his keen sense of honour. I advise you to marry and settle, as I am in the habit of advising young men; and if I were to add that it would be seemly to make some provision for your sisters—"

"Stop there!" said the Curate, who had taken no part in the scene up to this moment. He had stood behind rather contemptuously, determined to have nothing to do with his ungrateful and ungenerous protégé. But now an unreasonable impulse forced him into the discussion. "The less that is said on that part of the subject the better," he said, with some natural heat. "I object to the mixing up of names which – which no one here has any right to bandy about—"

"That is very true," said Mr Proctor; "but still they have their rights," the late Rector added after a pause. "We have no right to stand in the way of their – their interest, you know." It occurred to Mr Proctor, indeed, that the suggestion was on the whole a sensible one. "Even if they were to – to marry, you know, they might still be left unprovided for," said the late Rector. "I think it is quite just that some provision should be made for that."

And then there was a pause. Frank Wentworth was sufficiently aware after his first start of indignation that he had no right to interfere, as Mr Proctor said, between the

Miss Wodehouses and their interest. He had no means of providing for them, of setting them above the chances of fortune. He reflected bitterly that it was not in his power to offer a home to Lucy, and through her to her sister. What he had to do was to stand by silently, to suffer other people to discuss what was to be done for the woman whom he loved, and whose name was sacred to him. This was a stretch of patience of which he was not capable. "I can only say again," said the Curate, "that I think this discussion has gone far enough. Whatever matters of business there may be that require arrangement had better be settled between Mr Brown and Mr Waters. So far as private feeling goes—"

"Never fear, I'll manage it," said Jack Wentworth, "as well as a dozen lawyers. Private feeling has nothing to do with it. Have a cigar, Wodehouse? We'll talk it over as we walk home," said the condescending potentate. These words dispersed the assembly, which no longer had any object. As Jack Wentworth sauntered out, his faithful follower pressed through the others to join him. Wodehouse was himself again. He gave a sulky nod to the Curate, and said, "Good-night, parson, I don't owe much to you," and hastened out close upon the heels of his patron and leader. All the authorities of Carlingford, the virtuous people who conferred station and respectability by a look, sank into utter insignificance in presence of Jack. His admiring follower went after him with a swell of pride. He was a poor enough rogue himself, hustled and abused by everybody, an unsuccessful and shabby vagabond, notwithstanding his new fortune; but Jack was the glorified impersonation of cleverness and wickedness and triumph to Wodehouse. He grew insolent when he was permitted to put his arm through that of his hero, and went off with him trying to copy, in swagger and insolence, his careless step and well-bred ease. Perhaps Jack Wentworth felt a little ashamed of himself as he emerged from the gate of the Rectory with his shabby and disreputable companion.

He shrugged his shoulders slightly as he looked back and saw Gerald and Frank coming slowly out together. "*Coraggio!*" said Jack to himself, "it is I who am the true philanthropist. Let us do evil that good may come." Notwithstanding, he was very thankful not to be seen by his father, who had wished to consult him as a man of the world, and had shown certain yearnings towards him, which, to Jack's infinite surprise, awakened responsive feelings in his own unaccustomed bosom. He was half ashamed of this secret movement of natural affection, which, certainly, nobody else suspected; but it was with a sensation of relief that he closed the Rectory gate behind him, without having encountered the keen inquiring suspicious glances of the Squire. The others dispersed according to their pleasure – Mr Waters joining the party up-stairs, while Mr Proctor followed Jack Wentworth and Wodehouse to the door with naïve natural curiosity. When the excellent man recollected that he was listening to private conversation, and met Wodehouse's look of sulky insolence, he turned back again, much fluttered and disturbed. He had an interest in the matter, though the two in whose hands it now lay were the last whom he would have chosen as confidants; and to do him justice, he was thinking of Lucy only in his desire to hear what they decided upon. "Something might happen to me," he said to himself; "and, even if all was well, she would be happier not to be wholly dependent upon her sister;" with which self-exculpatory reflection, Mr Proctor slowly followed the others into the drawing-room. Gerald and Frank, who were neither of them disposed for society, went away together. They had enough to think of, without much need of conversation, and they had walked half-way down Grange Lane before either spoke. Then it was Frank who broke the silence abruptly with a question which had nothing to do with the business in which they had been engaged.

"And what do you mean to do?" said Frank, suddenly.

It was just as they came in sight of the graceful spire of St Roque's; and perhaps it was the sight of his own church which roused the Perpetual Curate to think of the henceforth aimless life of his brother. "I don't understand how you are to give up your work. To-night even——"

"I did not forget myself," said Gerald; "every man who can distinguish good from evil has a right to advise his fellow-creature. I have not given up that common privilege – don't hope it, Frank," said the martyr, with a momentary smile.

"If I could but understand why it is that you make this terrible sacrifice!" said the Curate – "No, I don't want to argue – of course, you are convinced. I can understand the wish that our unfortunate division had never taken place; but I can't understand the sacrifice of a man's life and work. Nothing is perfect in this world; but at least to do something in it – to be good for something – and with your faculties, Gerald!" cried the admiring and regretful brother. "Can abstract right in an institution, if that is what you aim at, be worth the sacrifice of your existence – your power of influencing your fellow-creatures?" This Mr Wentworth said, being specially moved by the circumstances in which he found himself – for, under any other conditions, such sentiments would have produced the warmest opposition in his Anglican bosom. But he was so far sympathetic that he could be tolerant to his brother who had gone to Rome.

"I know what you mean," said Gerald; "it is the prevailing theory in England that all human institutions are imperfect. My dear Frank, I want a Church which is not a human institution. In England it seems to be the rule of faith that every man may believe as he pleases. There is no authority either to decide or to punish. If you can foresee what that may lead us to, I cannot. I take refuge in the true Church, where alone there is certainty – where," said the convert, with a heightened colour and a long-drawn breath, "there is authority clear and decisive. In

England you believe what you will, and the result will be one that I at least fear to contemplate; in Rome we believe what – we must," said Gerald. He said the words slowly, bowing his head more than once with determined submission, as if bending under the yoke. "Frank, it is salvation!" said the new Catholic, with the emphasis of a despairing hope. And for the first time Frank Wentworth perceived what it was which had driven his brother to Rome.

"I understand you now," said the Perpetual Curate; "it is because there is no room for our conflicting doctrines and latitude of belief. Instead of a Church happily so far imperfect, that a man can put his life to the best account in it, without absolutely delivering up his intellect to a set of doctrines, you seek a perfect Church, in which, for a symmetrical system of doctrine, you lose the use of your existence!" Mr Wentworth uttered this opinion with all the more vehemence, that it was in direct opposition to his own habitual ideas; but even his veneration for his "Mother" yielded for the moment to his strong sense of his brother's mistake.

"It is a hard thing to say," said Gerald, "but it is true. If you but knew the consolation, after years of struggling among the problems of faith, to find one's self at last upon a rock of authority, of certainty – one holds in one's hand at last the interpretation of the enigma," said Gerald. He looked up to the sky as he spoke, and breathed into the serene air a wistful lingering sigh. If it was certainty that echoed in that breath of unsatisfied nature, the sound was sadly out of concord with the sentiment. His soul, notwithstanding that expression of serenity, was still as wistful as the night.

"Have you the interpretation?" said his brother; and Frank, too, looked up into the pure sky above, with its stars which stretched over them serene and silent, arching over the town that lay behind, and of which nobody knew better than he the human mysteries and wonderful unanswerable questions. The heart of the Curate ached to think how many problems lay in the darkness, over which that sky stretched silent, making no sign. There were the sorrowful of the earth, enduring their afflictions, lifting up pitiful hands, demanding of God in their bereavements and in their miseries the reason why. There were all the inequalities of life, side by side, evermore echoing dumbly the same awful question; and over all shone the calm sky which gave no answer. "Have you the interpretation?" he said. "Perhaps you can reconcile freewill and predestination – the need of a universal atonement and the existence of individual virtue? But these are not to me the most difficult questions. Can your Church explain why one man is happy and another miserable? – why one has everything and abounds, and the other loses all that is most precious in life? My sister Mary, for example," said the Curate, "she seems to bear the cross for our family. Her children die and yours live. Can you explain to her why? I have heard her cry out to God to know the reason, and He made no answer. Tell me, have you the interpretation?" cried the young man, on whom the hardness of his own position was pressing at the moment. They went on together in silence for a few minutes, without any attempt on Gerald's part to answer. "You accept the explanation of the Church in respect to doctrines," said the Curate, after that pause, "and consent that her authority is sufficient, and that your perplexity is over – that is well enough, so far as it goes: but outside lies a world in which every event is an enigma, where nothing that comes offers any explanation of itself; where God does not show Himself always kind, but by times awful, terrible – a God who smites and does not spare. It is easy to make a harmonious balance of doctrine; but where is the interpretation of life?" The young priest looked back on his memory, and recalled, as if they had been in a book, the daily problems with which he was so well acquainted. As for Gerald, he bowed his head a little, with a kind of reverence, as if he had been bowing before the shrine of a saint.

"I have had a happy life," said the elder brother. "I have not been driven to ask such questions for myself. To these the Church has but one advice to offer: Trust God."

"We say so in England," said Frank Wentworth; "it is the grand scope of our teaching. Trust God. He will not explain Himself, nor can we attempt it. When it is certain that I must be content with this answer for all the sorrows of life, I am content to take my doctrines on the same terms," said the Perpetual Curate; and by this time they had come to Miss Wentworth's door. After all, perhaps it was not Gerald, except so far as he was carried by a wonderful force of human sympathy and purity of soul, who was the predestined priest of the family. As he went up to his own room, a momentary spasm of doubt came upon the new convert — whether, perhaps, he was making a sacrifice of his life for a mistake. He hushed the thought forcibly as it rose; such impulses were no longer to be listened to. The same authority which made faith certain, decided every doubt to be sin.

CHAPTER XLI.

NEXT morning the Curate got up with anticipations which were far from cheerful, and a weary sense of the monotony and dulness of life. He had won his little battle, it was true; but the very victory had removed that excitement which answered in the absence of happier stimulations to keep up his heart and courage. After a struggle like that in which he had been engaged, it was hard to come again into the peaceable routine without any particular hope to

enliven or happiness to cheer it, which was all he had at
present to look for in his life; and it was harder still to feel
the necessity of being silent, of standing apart from Lucy
in her need, of shutting up in his own heart the longing he
had towards her, and refraining himself from the desperate
thought of uniting his genteel beggary to hers. That was
the one thing which must not be thought of, and he
subdued himself with an impatient sigh, and could not but
wonder, as he went down-stairs, whether, if Gerald had
been less smoothly guided through the perplexing paths of
life, he would have found time for all the difficulties which
had driven him to take refuge in Rome. It was with this
sense of hopeless restraint and incapacity, which is perhaps
of all sensations the most humbling, that he went down-
stairs, and found lying on his breakfast table, the first
thing that met his eye, the note which Lucy Wodehouse
had written to him on the previous night. As he read it, the
earth somehow turned to the sun; the dubious light brightened in the skies. Unawares, he had been wondering
never to receive any token of sympathy, any word of
encouragement, from those for whom he had made so
many exertions. When he had read Lucy's letter, the
aspect of affairs changed considerably. To be sure, nothing
that she had said or could say made any difference in the
facts of the case; but the Curate was young, and still liable
to those changes of atmosphere which do more for an
imaginative mind than real revolutions. He read the letter
several times over as he lingered through his breakfast,
making on the whole an agreeable meal, and finding
himself repossessed of his ordinary healthful appetite. He
even canvassed the signature as much in reading as Lucy
had done in writing it – balancing in his mind the maidenly
"truly yours" of that subscription with as many ingenious
renderings of its possible meaning as if Lucy's letter had
been articles of faith. "Truly mine," he said to himself,
with a smile; which indeed meant all a lover could require;
and then paused, as if he had been Dr Lushington or Lord

Westbury, to inquire into the real force of the phrase. For after all, it is not only when signing the Articles that the bond and pledge of subscription means more than is intended. When Mr Wentworth was able to tear himself from the agreeable casuistry of this self-discussion, he got up in much better spirits to go about his daily business. First of all, he had to see his father, and ascertain what were the Squire's intentions, and how long he meant to stay in Carlingford; and then— It occurred to the Perpetual Curate that after that, politeness demanded that he should call on the Miss Wodehouses, who had, or at least one of them, expressed so frankly their confidence in him. He could not but call to thank her, to inquire into their plans, perhaps to back aunt Leonora's invitation, which he was aware had been gratefully declined. With these ideas in his mind he went down-stairs, after brushing his hat very carefully and casting one solicitous glance in the mirror as he passed – which presented to him a very creditable reflection, an eidolon in perfect clerical apparel, without any rusty suggestions of a Perpetual Curacy. Yet a Perpetual Curacy it was which was his sole benefice or hope in his present circumstances, for he knew very well that, were all other objections at an end, neither Skelmersdale nor Wentworth could be kept open for him; and that beyond these two he had not a hope of advancement – and at the same time he was pledged to remain in Carlingford. All this, however, though discouraging enough, did not succeed in discouraging Mr Wentworth after he had read Lucy's letter. He went down-stairs so lightly that Mrs Hadwin, who was waiting in the parlour in her best cap, to ask if he would pardon her for making such a mistake, did not hear him pass, and sat waiting for an hour, forgetting, or rather neglecting to give any response, when the butcher came for orders – which was an unprecedented accident. Mr Wentworth went cheerfully up Grange Lane, meeting, by a singular chance, ever so many people, who stopped to shake hands with him, or at least bowed their good wishes and friendly acknowledgments. He smiled in himself at these evidences of popular penitence, but was not the less pleased to find himself reinstated in his place in the affections and respect of Carlingford. "After all, it was not an unnatural mistake," he said to himself, and smiled benignly upon the excellent people who had found out the error of their own ways. Carlingford, indeed, seemed altogether in a more cheerful state than usual, and Mr Wentworth could not but think that the community in general was glad to find that it had been deceived, and so went upon his way, pleasing himself with those maxims about the ultimate prevalence of justice and truth, which make it apparent that goodness is always victorious, and wickedness punished, in the end. Somehow even a popular fallacy has an aspect of truth when it suits one's own case. The Perpetual Curate went through his aunts' garden with a conscious smile, feeling once more master of himself and his concerns. There was, to tell the truth, even a slight shade of self-content and approbation upon his handsome countenance. In the present changed state of public opinion and private feeling, he began to take some pleasure in his sacrifice. To be sure, a Perpetual Curate could not marry; but perhaps Lucy – in short, there was no telling what might happen; and it was accordingly with that delicious sense of goodness which generally attends an act of self-sacrifice, mingled with an equally delicious feeling that the act, when accomplished, might turn out no such great sacrifice after all – which it is to be feared is the most usual way in which the sacrifices of youth are made – that the Curate walked into the hall, passing his aunt Dora's toy terrier without that violent inclination to give it a whack with his cane in passing which was his usual state of feeling. To tell the truth, Lucy's letter had made him at peace with all the world.

When, however, he entered the dining-room, where the family were still at breakfast, Frank's serenity was unexpectedly disturbed. The first thing that met his eyes was his aunt Leonora, towering over her tea-urn at the upper end of the table, holding in her hand a letter which she had just opened. The envelope had fallen in the midst of the immaculate breakfast "things," and indeed lay, with its broad black edge on the top of the snow-white lumps, in Miss Leonora's own sugar-basin; and the news had been sufficiently interesting to suspend the operations of tea-making, and to bring the strong-minded woman to her feet. The first words which were audible to Frank revealed to him the nature of the intelligence which had produced such startling effects.

"He was always a contradictory man," said Miss Leonora; "since the first hour he was in Skelmersdale, he has made a practice of doing things at the wrong time. I don't mean to reproach the poor man now he's gone; but when he has been so long of going, what good could it do him to choose this particular moment, for no other reason that I can see, except that it was specially uncomfortable to us? What my brother has just been saying makes it all the worse," said Miss Leonora, with a look of annoyance. She had turned her head away from the door, which was at the side of the room, and had not perceived the entrance of the Curate. "As long as we could imagine that Frank was to succeed to the Rectory, the thing looked comparatively easy. I beg your pardon, Gerald. Of course, you know how grieved I am – in short, that we all feel the deepest distress and vexation; but, to be sure, since you have given it up, somebody must succeed you – there can be no doubt of that."

"Not the least, my dear aunt," said Gerald.

"I am glad you grant so much. It is well to be sure of something," said the incisive and peremptory speaker. "It would have been a painful thing for us at any time to place another person in Skelmersdale while Frank was unprovided for; but, of course," said Miss Leonora, sitting down suddenly, "nobody who knows me could suppose for a minute that I would let my feelings stand in the way of my public duty. Still it is very awkward just at this moment when Frank, on the whole, has been behaving very properly, and one can't help so far approving of him—"

"I am much obliged to you, aunt Leonora," said the Curate.

"Oh, you are there, Frank," said his sensible aunt; and strong-minded though she was, a slight shade of additional colour appeared for a moment on Miss Leonora's face. She paused a little, evidently diverted from the line of discourse which she had contemplated, and wavered like a vessel disturbed in its course. "The fact is, I have just had a letter announcing Mr Shirley's death," she continued, facing round towards her nephew, and setting off abruptly, in face of all consequences, on the new tack.

"I am very sorry," said Frank Wentworth; "though I have an old grudge at him on account of his long sermons; but as you have expected it for a year or two, I can't imagine your grief to be overwhelming," said the Curate, with a touch of natural impertinence to be expected under the circumstances. Skelmersdale had been so long thought interesting to him, that now, when it was not in the least interesting, he got impatient of the name.

"I quite agree with you, Frank," said Miss Wentworth. Aunt Cecilia had not been able for a long time to agree with anybody. She had been, on the contrary, shaking her head and shedding a few gentle tears over Gerald's silent submission and Louisa's noisy lamentations. Everything was somehow going wrong; and she who had no power to mend, at least could not assent, and broke through her old use and wont to shake her head, which was a thing very alarming to the family. The entire party was moved by a sensation of pleasure to hear Miss Cecilia say, "I quite agree with you, Frank."

"You are looking better this morning, my dear aunt," said Gerald. They had a great respect for each other these two; but when Miss Cecilia turned to hear what her elder nephew was saying, her face lost the momentary look of approval it had worn, and she again, though very softly, almost imperceptibly, began to shake her head.

"We were not asking for your sympathy," said Miss Leonora, sharply. "Don't talk like a saucy boy. We were talking of our own embarrassment. There is a very excellent young man, the curate of the parish, whom Julia Trench is to be married to. By the way, of course, this must put it off; but I was about to say, when you interrupted me, that to give it away from you at this moment, just as you had been doing well – doing – your duty," said Miss Leonora, with unusual hesitation, "was certainly very uncomfortable, to say the least, to us."

"Don't let that have the slightest influence on you, I beg," cried the Perpetual Curate, with all the pride of his years. "I hope I have been doing my duty all along," the young man added, more softly, a moment after; upon which the Squire gave a little nod, partly of satisfaction and encouragement to his son – partly of remonstrance and protest to his sister.

"Yes, I suppose so – with the flowers at Easter, for example," said Miss Leonora, with a slight sneer. "I consider that I have stood by you through all this business, Frank – but, of course, in so important a matter as a cure of souls, neither relationship, nor, to a certain extent, approval," said Miss Leonora, with again some hesitation, "can be allowed to stand against public duty. We have the responsibility of providing a good gospel minister—"

"I beg your pardon for interrupting you, Leonora," said the Squire, "but I can't help thinking that you make a mistake. I think it's a man's bounden duty, when there is a living in the family, to educate one of his sons for it. In my opinion, it's one of the duties of property. You have no right to live off your estate, and spend your money elsewhere; and no more have you any right to give less than – than your own flesh and blood to the people you have the charge of. You've got the charge of them to – to a certain extent – soul and body, sir," said the Squire, growing warm, as he put down his 'Times,' and forgetting that he addressed a lady. "I'd never have any peace of mind if I filled up a family living with a stranger – unless, of course," Mr Wentworth added in a parenthesis – an unlikely sort of contingency which had not occurred to him at first – "you should happen to have no second son. – The eldest the squire, the second the rector. That's my idea, Leonora, of Church and State."

Miss Leonora smiled a little at her brother's semi-feudal, semi-pagan ideas. "I have long known that we were not of the same way of thinking," said the strong-minded aunt, who, though cleverer than her brother, was too wise in her own conceit to perceive at the first glance the noble, simple conception of his own duties and position, which was implied in the honest gentleman's words. "Your second son might be either a fool or a knave, or even, although neither, might be quite unfit to be intrusted with the eternal interests of his fellow-creatures. In my opinion, the duty of choosing a clergyman is one not to be exercised without the gravest deliberation. A conscientious man would make his selection dependent, at least, upon the character of his second son – if he had one. We, however—"

"But then his character is *so* satisfactory, Leonora," cried Miss Dora, feeling emboldened by the shadow of visitors under whose shield she could always retire. "Everybody knows what a good clergyman he is – I am sure it would be like a new world in Skelmersdale if you were there, Frank, my dear – and he preaches such beautiful sermons!" said the unlucky little woman, upon whom her sister immediately descended, swift and sudden, like a storm at sea.

"We are generally perfectly of accord in our conclusions," said Miss Leonora; "as for Dora, she comes to the same end by a roundabout way. After what my brother has been saying—"

"Yes," said the Squire, with uncomfortable looks, "I was saying to your aunt, Frank, what I said to you about poor Mary. Since Gerald *will* go, and since you don't want to come, the best thing to do would be to have Huxtable. He's a very good fellow on the whole, and it might cheer her up, poor soul, to be near her sisters. Life has been hard work to her, poor girl – very hard work, sir," said the Squire, with a sigh. The idea was troublesome and uncomfortable, and always disturbed his mind when it occurred to him. It was indeed a secret humiliation to the Squire, that his eldest daughter possessed so little the characteristic health and prosperity of the Wentworths. He was very sorry for her, but yet half angry and half ashamed, as if she could have helped it; but, however, he had been obliged to admit, in his private deliberations on the subject, that, failing Frank, Mary's husband had the next best right to Wentworth Rectory – an arrangement of which Miss Leonora did not approve.

"I was about to say that we have no second son," she said, taking up the thread of her discourse where it had been interrupted. "Our duty is solely towards the Christian people. I do not pretend to be infallible," said Miss Leonora, with a meek air of self-contradiction; "but I should be a very poor creature indeed, if, at my age, I did not know what I believed, and was not perfectly convinced that I am right. Consequently (though, I repeat, Mr Shirley has chosen the most inconvenient moment possible for dying), it can't be expected of me that I should appoint my nephew, whose opinions in most points are exactly the opposite of mine."

"I wish, at least, you would believe what I say," interrupted the Curate, impatiently. "There might have been some sense in all this three months ago; but if Skelmersdale were the high-road to everything desirable in the Church, you are all quite aware that I could not accept it. Stop, Gerald; I am not so disinterested as you think," said Frank; "if I left Carlingford now, people would remember against me that my character had been called in question here. I can remain a perpetual curate," said the young man, with a smile, "but I can't tolerate any shadow upon my honour. I am sorry I came in at such an awkward moment. Good morning, aunt Leonora. I hope Julia Trench, when she has the Rectory, will always keep of your way of thinking. She used to incline a little to mine," he said, mischievously, as he went away.

"Come back, Frank, presently," said the Squire, whose attention had been distracted from his 'Times.' Mr Wentworth began to be tired of such a succession of exciting discussions. He thought if he had Frank quietly to himself he could settle matters much more agreeably; but the 'Times' was certainly an accompaniment more tranquillising so far as a comfortable meal was concerned.

"He can't come back presently," said aunt Leonora. "You speak as if he had nothing to do; when, on the contrary, he has everything to do – that is worth doing," said that contradictory authority. "Come back to lunch, Frank; and I wish you would eat your breakfast, Dora, and not stare at me."

Miss Dora had come down to breakfast as an invalid, in a pretty little cap, with a shawl over her dressing-gown. She had not yet got over her adventure and the excitement of Rosa's capture. That unusual accident, and all the applauses of her courage which had been addressed to her since, had roused the timid woman. She did not withdraw her eyes from her sister, though commanded to do so; on the contrary, her look grew more and more emphatic. She meant to have made a solemn address, throwing off Leonora's yoke, and declaring her intention, in this grave crisis of her nephew's fortunes, of acting for herself; but her feelings were too much for Miss Dora. The tears came creeping to the corners of her eyes, and she could not keep them back; and her attempt at dignity broke down. "I am never consulted," she said, with a gasp. "I don't mean to pretend to know better than Leonora; but – but I think it is

very hard that Frank should be disappointed about
Skelmersdale. You may call me as foolish as you please,"
said Miss Dora, with rising tears, "I know everybody will
say it is my fault; but I must say I think it is very hard that
Frank should be disappointed. He was always brought up
for it, as everybody knows; and to disappoint him, who is
so good and so nice, for a fat young man, buttered all over
like – like – a pudding-basin," cried poor Miss Dora,
severely adhering to the unity of her desperate metaphor.
"I don't know what Julia Trench can be thinking of; I – I
don't know what Leonora means."

"I am of the same way of thinking," said aunt Cecilia,
setting down, with a little gentle emphasis, her cup of tea.

Here was rebellion, open and uncompromised. Miss
Leonora was so much taken by surprise, that she lifted the
tea-urn out of the way, and stared at her interlocutors with
genuine amazement. But she proved herself, as usual,
equal to the occasion.

"It's unfortunate that we never see eye to eye just at
once," she said, with a look which expressed more distinctly
than words could have done the preliminary flourish of his
whip by means of which a skilful charioteer gets his team
under hand without touching them; "but it is very lucky
that we always come to agree in the end," she added,
more significantly still. It was well to crush insubordination
in the bud. Not that she did not share the sentiment of
her sisters; but then they were guided like ordinary women
by their feelings; whereas Miss Leonora had the rights of
property before her, and the approval of Exeter Hall.

"And he wants to marry, poor dear boy," said Miss
Dora, pale with fright, yet persevering; "and she is a dear
good girl – the very person for a clergyman's wife; and
what is he to do if he is always to be Curate of St Roque's?
You may say it is my fault, but I cannot help it. He always
used to come to me in all his little troubles; and when he
wants anything very particular, he knows there is nothing
I would not do for him," sobbed the proud aunt, who could

not help recollecting how much use she had been to Frank. She wiped her eyes at the thought, and held up her head with a thrill of pride and satisfaction. Nobody could blame her in that particular at least. "He knew he had only to tell me what he wanted," said Miss Dora, swelling out her innocent plumes. Jack, who was sitting opposite, and who had been listening with admiration, thought it time to come in on his own part.

"I hope you don't mean to forsake *me*, aunt Dora," he said. "If a poor fellow cannot have faith in his aunt, whom can he have faith in? I thought it was too good to last," said the neglected prodigal. "You have left the poor sheep in the wilderness and gone back to the ninety-and-nine righteous men who need no repentance." He put up his handkerchief to this eyes as he spoke, and so far forgot himself as to look with laughter in his face at his brother Gerald. As for the Squire, he was startled to hear his eldest son quoting Scripture, and laid aside his paper once more to know what it meant.

"I am sure I beg your pardon, Jack," said aunt Dora, suddenly stopping short, and feeling guilty. "I never meant to neglect you. Poor dear boy, he never was properly tried with female society and the comforts of home; but then you were dining out that night," said the simple woman, eagerly. "I should have stayed with you, Jack, *of course,* had you been at home."

From this little scene Miss Leonora turned away hastily, with an exclamation of impatience. She made an abrupt end of her tea-making, and went off to her little business-room with a grim smile upon her iron-grey countenance. She too had been taken in a little by Jack's pleasant farce of the Sinner Repentant; and it occurred to her to feel a little ashamed of herself as she went up-stairs. After all, the ninety-and-nine just men of Jack's irreverent quotation were worth considering now and then; and Miss Leonora could not but think with a little humiliation of the contrast between her nephew Frank and the comfortable young

Curate who was going to marry Julia Trench. He *was* fat, it could not be denied; and she remembered his chubby looks, and his sermons about self-denial and mortification of the flesh, much as a pious Catholic might think of the Lenten oratory of a fat friar. But then he was perfectly sound in his doctrines, and it was undeniable that the people liked him, and that the appointment was one which even a Scotch ecclesiastical community full of popular rights could scarcely have objected to. According to her own principles, the strong-minded woman could not do otherwise. She threw herself into her arm-chair with unnecessary force, and read over the letter which Miss Trench herself had written. "It is difficult to think of any consolation in such a bereavement," wrote Mr Shirley's niece; "but still it is a little comfort to feel that I can throw myself on your sympathy, my dear and kind friend." "Little calculating thing!" Miss Leonora said to herself as she threw down the mournful epistle; and then she could not help thinking again of Frank. To be sure, he was not of her way of thinking; but when she remembered the "investigation" and its result, and the secret romance involved in it, her Wentworth blood sent a thrill of pride and pleasure through her veins. Miss Leonora, though she was strong-minded, was still woman enough to perceive her nephew's motives in his benevolence to Wodehouse; but these motives, which were strong enough to make him endure so much annoyance, were not strong enough to tempt him from Carlingford and his Perpetual Curacy, where his honour and reputation, in the face of love and ambition, demanded that he should remain. "It would be a pity to balk him in his self-sacrifice," she said to herself, with again a somewhat grim smile, and a comparison not much to the advantage of Julia Trench and *her* curate. She shut herself up among her papers till luncheon, and only emerged with a stormy front when that meal was on the table; during the progress of which she snubbed everybody who ventured to speak to her, and spoke to her nephew

Frank as if he might have been suspected of designs upon the plate-chest. Such were the unpleasant consequences of the struggle between duty and inclination in the bosom of Miss Leonora; and, save for other unforeseen events which decided the matter for her, it is not by any means so certain as, judging from her character, it ought to have been, that duty would have won the day.

CHAPTER XLII.

FRANK WENTWORTH once more went up Grange Lane, a thoughtful and a sober man. Exhilaration comes but by moments in the happiest of lives – and already he began to remember how very little he had to be elated about, and how entirely things remained as before. Even Lucy; her letter very probably might be only an effusion of friendship; and at all events, what could he say to her – what did he dare in honour say? And then his mind went off to think of the two rectories, between which he had fallen as between two stools: though he had made up his mind to accept neither, he did not the less feel a certain mortification in seeing that his relations on both sides were so willing to bestow their gifts elsewhere. He could not tolerate the idea of succeeding Gerald in his own person, but still he found it very disagreeable to consent to the thought that Huxtable should replace him – Huxtable, who was a good fellow enough, but of whom Frank Wentworth thought, as men generally think of their brothers-in-law, with a half-impatient, half-contemptuous wonder what Mary could ever have seen in so commonplace a man. To think of him as rector of Wentworth inwardly chafed the spirit of the Perpetual Curate. As he was going along, absorbed in his own thoughts, he did not perceive how his approach was watched for from the other side of the way by Elsworthy, who stood with his bundle of newspapers under his arm and his hat in his hand, watching for "his clergyman" with submission and apology on the surface, and hidden rancour underneath. Elsworthy was not penitent; he was furious and disappointed. His mistake and its consequences were wholly humiliating, and had not in them a single saving feature to atone for the wounds of his self-esteem. The Curate had not only baffled and beaten him, but humbled him in his own eyes, which is perhaps, of all others, the injury least easy to forgive. It was, however, with an appearance of the profoundest submission that he stood awaiting the approach of the man he had tried so much to injure.

"Mr Wentworth, sir," said Elsworthy, "if I was worth your while, I might think as you were offended with me; but seeing I'm one as is so far beneath you" – he went on with a kind of grin, intended to represent a deprecatory smile, but which would have been a snarl had he dared – "I can't think as you'll bear no malice. May I ask, sir, if there's a-going to be any difference made?"

"In what respect, Elsworthy?" said the Curate, shortly.

"Well, sir, I can't tell," said the clerk of St Roque's. "If a clergyman was to bear malice, it's in his power to make things very unpleasant. I don't speak of the place at church, which aint either here nor there – it's respectable, but it aint lucrative; but if you was to stretch a point, Mr Wentworth, by continuing the papers and suchlike – it aint that I value the money," said Elsworthy, "but I've been a faithful servant; and I might say, if you was to take it in a right spirit, an 'umble friend, Mr Wentworth," he continued, after a little pause, growing bolder. "And now, as I've that unfortunate creature to provide for, and no one knowing what's to become of her—"

"I wonder that you venture to speak of her to me," said the Curate, with a little indignation, "after all the warnings I gave you. But you ought to consider that you are to blame a great deal more than she is. She is only a child; if you had taken better care of her – but you would not pay any attention to my warning; – you must bear the consequences as you best can."

"Well, sir," said Elsworthy, "if you're a-going to bear malice, I haven't got nothing to say. But there aint ten men in Carlingford as wouldn't agree with me that when a young gentleman, even if he is a clergyman, takes particklar notice of a pretty young girl, it aint just for nothing as he does it – not to say watching over her paternal to see as she wasn't out late at night, and suchlike. But bygones is bygones, sir," said Elsworthy, "and is never more to be mentioned by me. I don't ask no more, if you'll but do the same—"

"You won't ask no more?" said the Curate, angrily; "do you think I am afraid of you? I have nothing more to say, Elsworthy. Go and look after your business – I will attend to mine; and when we are not forced to meet, let us keep clear of each other. It will be better both for you and me."

The Curate passed on with an impatient nod; but his assailant did not intend that he should escape so easily. "I shouldn't have thought, sir, as you'd have borne malice," said Elsworthy, hastening on after him, yet keeping half a step behind. "I'm a humbled man – different from what I ever thought to be. I could always keep up my head afore the world till now; and if it aint your fault, sir – as I humbly beg your pardon for ever being so far led away as to believe it was – all the same it's along of you."

"What do you mean?" said the Curate, who, half amused and half indignant at the change of tone, had slackened his pace to listen to this new accusation.

"What I mean, sir, is, that if you hadn't been so good and so kind-hearted as to take into your house the – the villain as has done it all, him and Rosa could never have known each other. I allow as it was nothing but your own goodness as did it; but it was a black day for me and mine," said the dramatist, with a pathetic turn of voice. "Not as I'm casting no blame on you, as is well known to be—"

"Never mind what I'm well known to be," said the Curate; "the other day you thought *I* was the villain. If you can tell me anything you want me to do, I will understand that — but I am not desirous to know your opinion of me," said the careless young man. As he stood listening impatiently, pausing a second time, Dr Marjoribanks came out to his door and stepped into his brougham to go off to his morning round of visits. The Doctor took off his hat when he saw the Curate, and waved it to him cheerfully with a gesture of congratulation. Dr Marjoribanks was quite stanch and honest, and would have manfully stood by his intimates in dangerous circumstances; but somehow he preferred success. It was pleasanter to be able to congratulate people than to condole with them. He preferred it, and nobody could object to so orthodox a sentiment. Most probably, if Mr Wentworth had still been in partial disgrace, the Doctor would not have seen him in his easy glance down the road; but though Mr Wentworth was aware of that, the mute congratulation had yet its effect upon him. He was moved by that delicate symptom of how the wind was blowing in Carlingford, and forgot all about Elsworthy, though the man was standing by his side.

"As you're so good as to take it kind, sir," said the clerk of St Roque's — "and, as I was a-saying, it's well known as you're always ready to hear a poor man's tale — perhaps you'd let bygones be bygones, and not make no difference? That wasn't all, Mr Wentworth," he continued eagerly, as the Curate gave an impatient nod, and turned to go on. "I've heard as this villain is rich, sir, by means of robbing of his own flesh and blood; — but it aint for me to trust to what folks says, after the experience I've had, and never can forgive myself for being led away," said Elsworthy; "it's well known in Carlingford—"

"For heaven's sake come to the point and be done with it," said the Curate. "What is it you want me to do?"

"Sir," said Elsworthy, solemnly, "you're a real gentleman, and you don't bear no malice for what was a mistake – and you aint one to turn your back on an unfortunate family – and Mr Wentworth, sir, you aint a-going to stand by and see me and mine wronged, as have always wished you well. If we can't get justice of him, we can get damages," cried Elsworthy. "He aint to be let off as if he'd done no harm – and seeing as it was along of you—"

"Hold your tongue, sir!" cried the Curate. "I have nothing to do with it. Keep out of my way, or at least learn to restrain your tongue. No more, not a word more," said the young man, indignantly. He went off with such a sweep and wind of anger and annoyance, that the slower and older complainant had no chance to follow him. Elsworthy accordingly went off to the shop, where his errand-boys were waiting for the newspapers, and where Rosa lay up-stairs, weeping, in a dark room, where her enraged aunt had shut her up. Mrs Elsworthy had shut up the poor little pretty wretch, who might have been penitent under better guidance, but who by this time had lost what sense of shame and wrong her childish conscience was capable of in the stronger present sense of injury and resentment and longing to escape; but the angry aunt, though she could turn the key on poor Rosa's unfortunate little person, could not shut in the piteous sobs which now and then sounded through and through the house, and which converted all the errand-boys without exception into indignant partisans of Rosa, and even moved the heart of Peter Hayles, who could hear them at the back window where he was making up Dr Marjoribanks's prescriptions. As the sense of injury waxed stronger and stronger in Rosa's bosom, she availed herself, like any other irrational, irresponsible creature, of such means of revenging herself and annoying her keepers as occurred to her. "Nobody ever took no care of me," sobbed Rosa. "I never had no father or mother. Oh, I wish I was dead! – and nobody wouldn't care!" These utterances, it may be imagined, went to the very heart of the errand-boys, who were collected in a circle, plotting how to release Rosa, when Elsworthy, mortified and furious, came back from his unsuccessful assault on the Curate. They scattered like a covey of little birds before the angry man, who tossed their papers at them, and then strode up the echoing stairs. "If you don't hold your d—d tongue," said Elsworthy, knocking furiously at Rosa's door, "I'll turn you to the door this instant, I will, by —." Nobody in Carlingford had ever before heard an oath issue from the respectable lips of the clerk of St Roque's. When he went down into the shop again, the outcries sank into frightened moans. Not much wonder that the entire neighbourhood became as indignant with Elsworthy as it ever had been with the Perpetual Curate. The husband and wife took up their positions in the shop after this, as far apart as was possible from each other, both resenting in silent fury the wrong which the world in general had done them. If Mrs Elsworthy had dared, she would have exhausted her passion in abuse of everybody – of the Curate for not being guilty, of her husband for supposing him to be so, and, to be sure, of Rosa herself, who was the cause of all. But Elsworthy was dangerous, not to be approached or spoken to. He went out about noon to see John Brown, and discuss with him the question of damages; but the occurrences which took place in his absence are not to be mixed up with the present narrative, which concerns Mr Frank Wentworth's visit to Lucy Wodehouse, and has nothing to do with ignoble hates or loves.

The Curate went rapidly on to the green door, which once more looked like a gate of paradise. He did not know in the least what he was going to do or say – he was only conscious of a state of exaltation, a condition of mind which might precede great happiness or great misery, but had nothing in it of the common state of affairs in which people ask each other "How do you do?" Notwithstanding, that fact is, that when Lucy entered that dear familiar drawing-room, where every feature and individual expression of every piece of furniture was as well known to him as if they had been so many human faces, it was only "How do you do?" that the Curate found himself able to say. The two shook hands as demurely as if Lucy had indeed been, according to the deceptive representation of yesterday, as old as aunt Dora; and then she seated herself in her favourite chair, and tried to begin a little conversation about things in general. Even in these three days, nature and youth had done something for Lucy. She had slept and rested, and the unforeseen misfortune which had come in to distract her grief had roused all the natural strength that was in her. As she was a little nervous about this interview, not knowing what it might end in, Lucy thought it her duty to be as composed and self-commanding as possible, and, in order to avoid all dangerous and exciting subjects, began to talk of Wharfside.

"I have not heard anything for three or four days about the poor woman at No. 10," she said; "I meant to have gone to see her to-day, but somehow one gets so selfish when – when one's mind is full of affairs of one's own."

"Yes," said the Curate; "and speaking of that, I wanted to tell you how much comfort your letter had been to me. My head, too, has been very full of affairs of my own. I thought at one time that my friends were forsaking me. It was very good of you to write as you did."

Upon which there followed another little pause. "Indeed the goodness was all on your side," said Lucy, faltering. "If I had ever dreamt how much you were doing for us! but it all came upon me so suddenly. It is impossible ever to express in words one-half of the gratitude we owe you," she said, with restrained enthusiasm. She looked up at him as she spoke with a little glow of natural fervour, which brought the colour to her cheek and the moisture to her eyes. She was not of the disposition to give either thanks or confidence by halves; and even the slight not unpleasant sense of danger which gave piquancy to this interview, made her resolute to express herself fully. She would not suffer herself to stint her gratitude because of the sweet suspicion which would not be quite silenced, that possibly Mr Wentworth looked for something better than gratitude. Not for any consequences, however much they might be to be avoided, could she be shabby enough to refrain from due acknowledgment of devotion so great. Therefore, while the Perpetual Curate was doing all he could to remind himself of his condition, and to persuade himself that it would be utterly wrong and mean of him to speak, Lucy looked up at him, looked him in the face, with her blue eyes shining dewy and sweet through tears of gratitude and a kind of generous admiration; for, like every other woman, she felt herself exalted and filled with a delicious pride in seeing that the man of her unconscious choice had proved himself the best.

The Curate walked to the window, very much as Mr Proctor had done, in the tumult and confusion of his heart, and came back again with what he had to say written clear on his face, without any possibility of mistake. "I must speak," said the young man; "I have no right to speak, I know; if I had attained the height of self-sacrifice and self-denial, I might, I would be silent – but it is impossible now." He came to a break just then, looking at her to see what encouragement he had to go on; but as Lucy did nothing but listen and grow pale, he had to take his own way. "What I have to say is not anything new," said the Curate, labouring a little in his voice, as was inevitable when affairs had come to such a crisis, "if I were not in the cruelest position possible to a man. I have only an empty love to lay at your feet; I tell it to you only because I am obliged – because, after all, love is worth telling, even if it comes to nothing. I am not going to appeal to your generosity," continued the young man, kneeling down at the table, not by way of kneeling to Lucy, but by way of bringing himself on a level with her, where she sat with her head bent down on her low chair, "or to ask you to bind yourself to a man who has nothing in the world but love to offer you; but after what has been for years, after all the hours I have spent here, I cannot – part – I cannot let you go – without a word—"

And here he stopped short. He had not asked anything, so that Lucy, even had she been able, had nothing to answer; and as for the young lover himself, he seemed to have come to the limit of his eloquence. He kept waiting for a moment, gazing at her in breathless expectation of a response for which his own words had left no room. Then he rose in an indescribable tumult of disappointment and mortification – unable to conclude that all was over, unable to keep silence, yet not knowing what to say.

"I have been obliged to close all the doors of advancement upon myself," said the Curate, with a little bitterness; "I don't know if you understand me. At this moment I have to deny myself the dearest privilege of existence. Don't mistake me, Lucy," he said, after another pause, coming back to her with humility, "I don't venture to say that you would have accepted anything I had to offer; but this I mean, that to have a home for you now – to have a life for you ready to be laid at your feet, whether you would have had it or not; – what right have I to speak of such delights?" cried the young man. "It does not matter to you; and as for me, I have patience – patience to console myself with—"

Poor Lucy, though she was on the verge of tears, which nothing but the most passionate self-restraint could have kept in, could not help a passing sensation of amusement at these words. "Not too much of that either," she said, softly, with a tremulous smile. "But patience carries the lilies of the saints," said Lucy, with a touch of the sweet asceticism which had once been so charming to the young Anglican. It brought him back like a spell to the common ground on which they used to meet; it brought him back

also to his former position on his knee, which was embarrassing to Lucy, though she had not the heart to draw
back, nor even to withdraw her hand, which somehow
happened to be in Mr Wentworth's way.

"I am but a man," said the young lover. "I would rather
have the roses of life – but, Lucy, I am only a perpetual
curate," he continued, with her hand in his. Her answer
was made in the most heartless and indifferent words. She
let two big drops – which fell like hail, though they were
warmer than any summer rain – drop out of her eyes, and
she said, with lips that had some difficulty in enunciating
that heartless sentiment, "I don't see what it matters to
me—"

Which was true enough, though it did not sound encouraging; and it is dreadful to confess that, for a little
while after, neither Skelmersdale, nor Wentworth, nor Mr
Proctor's new rectory, nor the no-income of the Perpetual
Curate of St Roque's, had the smallest place in the
thoughts of either of these perfectly inconsiderate young
people. For half an hour they were an Emperor and
Empress seated upon two thrones, to which all the world
was subject; and when at the end of that time they began
to remember the world, it was but to laugh at it in their
infinite youthful superiority. Then it became apparent
that to remain in Carlingford, to work at "the district," to
carry out all the ancient intentions of well-doing which had
been the first bond between them, was, after all, the life of
lives; – which was the state of mind they had both arrived
at when Miss Wodehouse, who thought they had been too
long together under the circumstances, and could not help
wondering what Mr Wentworth could be saying, came into
the room, rather flurried in her own person. She thought
Lucy must have been telling the Curate about Mr Proctor
and his hopes, and was, to tell the truth, a little curious
how Mr Wentworth would take it, and a little – the very
least – ashamed of encountering his critical looks. The
condition of mind into which Miss Wodehouse was thrown

when she perceived the real state of affairs would be
difficult to describe. She was very glad and very sorry,
and utterly puzzled how they were to live; and underneath
all these varying emotions was a sudden, half-ludicrous,
half-humiliating sense of being cast into the shade, which
made Mr Proctor's *fiancée* laugh and made her cry, and
brought her down altogether off the temporary pedestal
upon which she had stepped, not without a little feminine
satisfaction. When a woman is going to be married,
especially if that marriage falls later than usual, it is
natural that she should expect, for that time at least, to be
the first and most prominent figure in her little circle. But,
alas! what chance could there be for a mild, dove-coloured
bride of forty beside a creature of half her age, endued
with all the natural bloom and natural interest of youth?

Miss Wodehouse could not quite make out her own
feelings on the subject. "Don't you think if you had waited
a little it would have been wiser?" she said, in her timid
way; and then kissed her young sister, and said, "I am
so glad, my darling – I am sure dear papa would have
been pleased," with a sob which brought back to Lucy the
grief from which she had for the moment escaped. Under
all the circumstances, however, it may well be supposed
that it was rather hard upon Mr Wentworth to recollect
that he had engaged to return to luncheon with the Squire,
and to prepare himself after this momentous morning's
work, to face all the complications of the family, where
still Skelmersdale and Wentworth were hanging in the
balance, and where the minds of his kith and kin were
already too full of excitement to leave much room for
another event. He went away reluctantly enough out of
the momentary paradise where his Perpetual Curacy was
a matter of utter indifference, if not a tender pleasantry,
which rather increased than diminished the happiness of
the moment – into the ordinary daylight world, where it
was a very serious matter, and where what the young
couple would have to live upon became the real question

to be considered. Mr Wentworth met Wodehouse as he went out, which did not mend matters. The vagabond was loitering about in the garden, attended by one of Elsworthy's errand-boys, with whom he was in earnest conversation, and stopped in his talk to give a sulky nod and "Good morning," to which the Curate had no desire to respond more warmly than was necessary. Lucy was thinking of nothing but himself, and perhaps a little of the "great work" at Wharfside, which her father's illness and death had interrupted; but Mr Wentworth, who was only a man, remembered that Tom Wodehouse would be his brother-in-law with a distinct sensation of disgust, even in the moment of his triumph – which is one instance of the perennial inequality between the two halves of mankind. He had to brace himself up to the encounter of all his people, while she had to meet nothing less delightful than her own dreams. This was how matters came to an issue in respect of Frank Wentworth's personal happiness. His worldly affairs were all astray as yet, and he had not the most distant indication of any gleam of light dawning upon the horizon which could reconcile his duty and honour with good fortune and the delights of life. Meanwhile other discussions were going on in Carlingford, of vital importance to the two young people who had made up their minds to cast themselves upon Providence. And among the various conversations which were being carried on about the same moment in respect to Mr Wentworth – whose affairs, as was natural, were extensively canvassed in Grange Lane, as well as in other less exclusive quarters – it would be wrong to omit a remarkable consultation which took place in the Rectory, where Mrs Morgan sat in the midst of the great bouquets of the drawing-room carpet, making up her first matrimonial difficulty. It would be difficult to explain what influence the drawing-room carpet in the Rectory had on the fortunes of the Perpetual Curate; but when Mr Wentworth's friends come to hear the entire outs and ins of the business, it will be

seen that it was not for nothing that Mr Proctor covered
the floor of that pretty apartment with roses and lilies half
a yard long.

CHAPTER XLIII.

THESE were eventful days in Grange Lane, when gossip
was not nearly rapid enough to follow the march of events.
When Mr Wentworth went to lunch with his family, the
two sisters kept together in the drawing-room, which
seemed again re-consecrated to the purposes of life. Lucy
had not much inclination just at that moment to move out
of her chair; she was not sociable, to tell the truth, nor
disposed to talk even about the new prospects which were
brightening over both. She even took out her needlework,
to the disgust of her sister. "When there are so many
things to talk about, and so much to be considered," Miss
Wodehouse said, with a little indignation; and wondered
within herself whether Lucy was really insensible to "what
had happened," or whether the sense of duty was strong
upon her little sister even in the height of her happiness. A
woman of greater experience or discrimination might have
perceived that Lucy had retired into that sacred silence,
sweetest of all youthful privileges, in which she could
dream over to herself the wonderful hour which had just
come to an end, and the fair future of which it was the
gateway. As for Miss Wodehouse herself, she was in a
flutter, and could not get over the sense of haste and
confusion which this last new incident had brought upon
her. Things were going too fast around her, and the timid
woman was out of breath. Lucy's composure at such a
moment, and, above all, the production of her needle-

work, was beyond the comprehension of the elder sister.

"My dear," said Miss Wodehouse, with an effort, "I don't doubt that these poor people are badly off, and I am sure it is very good of you to work for them; but if you will only think how many things there are to do! My darling, I am afraid you will have to – to make your own dresses in future, which is what I never thought to see," she said, putting her handkerchief to her eyes; "and we have not had any talk about anything, Lucy, and there are so many things to think of!" Miss Wodehouse, who was moving about the room as she spoke, began to lift her own books and special property off the centre table. The books were principally ancient Annuals in pretty bindings, which no representation on Lucy's part could induce her to think out of date; and among her other possessions was a little desk in Indian mosaic, of ivory, which had been an institution in the house from Lucy's earliest recollection. "And these are yours, Lucy dear," said Miss Wodehouse, standing up on a chair to take down from the wall two little pictures which hung side by side. They were copies both, and neither of great value; one representing the San Sisto Madonna, and the other a sweet St Agnes, whom Lucy had in her earlier days taken to her heart. Lucy's slumbering attention was roused by this sacrilegious act. She gave a little scream, and dropped her work out of her hands.

"What do I mean?" said Miss Wodehouse; "indeed, Lucy dear, we must look it in the face. It is not our drawing-room any longer, you know." Here she made a pause, and sighed; but somehow a vision of the other drawing-room which was awaiting her in the new rectory, made the prospect less doleful than it might have been. She cleared up in a surprising way as she turned to look at her own property on the table. "My cousin Jack gave me this," said the gentle woman, brushing a little dust off her pretty desk. "When it came first, there was nothing like it in Carlingford, for that was before Colonel Chiley and those other Indian people had settled here. Jack was rather fond of me in those days, you know, though I never cared for him," the elder sister continued, with a smile. "Poor fellow! they said he was not very happy when he married." Though this was rather a sad fact, Miss Wodehouse announced it not without a certain gentle satisfaction. "And, Lucy dear, it is our duty to put aside our own things; they were all presents, you know," she said, standing up on the chair again to reach down the St Agnes, which, ever since Lucy had been confirmed, had hung opposite to her on the wall.

"Oh, don't, don't!" cried Lucy. In that little bit of time, not more than five minutes as it appeared, the familiar room, which had just heard the romance of her youth, had come to have a dismantled and desolate look. The agent of this destruction, who saw in her mind's eye a new scene, altogether surpassing the old, looked complacently upon her work, and piled the abstracted articles on the top of each other, with a pleasant sense of property.

"And your little chair and work-table are yours," said Miss Wodehouse; "they were always considered yours. You worked the chair yourself, though perhaps Miss Gibbons helped you a little; and the table you know, was sent home the day you were eighteen. It was – a present, you remember. Don't cry, my darling, don't cry; oh, I am sure I did not mean anything!" cried Miss Wodehouse, putting down the St Agnes and flying to her sister, about whom she threw her arms. "My hands are all dusty, dear," said the repentant woman; "but you know, Lucy, we must look it in the face, for it is not our drawing-room now. Tom may come in any day and say – oh, dear, dear, here is some one coming up-stairs!"

Lucy extricated herself from her sister's arms when she heard footsteps outside. "If it is anybody who has a right to come, I suppose we are able to receive them," she said, and sat erect over her needlework, with a changed countenance, not condescending so much as to look towards the door.

"But what if it should be Tom? Oh, Lucy dear, don't be uncivil to him," said the elder sister. Miss Wodehouse even made a furtive attempt to replace the things, in which she was indignantly stopped by Lucy. "But, my dear, perhaps it is Tom," said the alarmed woman, and sank trembling into a chair against the St Agnes, which had just been deposited there.

"It does not matter who it is," said Lucy, with dignity. For her own part, she felt too much aggrieved to mention his name – aggrieved by her own ignorance, by the deception that had been practised upon her, by the character of the man whom she was obliged to call her brother, and chiefly by his existence, which was the principal grievance of all. Lucy's brief life had been embellished, almost ever since she had been capable of independent action, by deeds and thoughts of mercy. With her whole heart she was a disciple of Him who came to seek the lost; notwithstanding, a natural human sentiment in her heart protested against the existence of this man, who had brought shame and distress into the family without any act of theirs, and who injured everybody he came in contact with. When the thought of Rosa Elsworthy occurred to her, a burning blush came upon Lucy's cheek – why were such men permitted in God's world? To be sure, when she came to be aware of what she was thinking, Lucy felt guilty, and called herself a Pharisee, and said a prayer in her heart for the man who had upset all her cherished ideas of her family and home; but, after all, *that* was an after-thought, and did not alter her instinctive sense of repulsion and indignation. All this swept rapidly through her mind while she sat awaiting the entrance of the person or persons who were approaching the door. "If it is the – owner of the house, it will be best to tell him what things you mean to remove," said Lucy; and before Miss Wodehouse could answer, the door was opened. They started, however, to perceive not Wodehouse, but a personage of very different appearance, who came in with an easy air of polite apology, and looked at them with eyes which recalled to Lucy the eyes which had been gazing into her own scarcely an hour ago. "Pardon me," said this unlooked-for visitor; "your brother, Miss Wodehouse, finds some difficulty in explaining himself to relations from whom he has been separated so long. Not to interfere with family privacy, will you let me assist at the conference?" said Jack Wentworth. "My brother, I understand, is a friend of yours, and your brother – is a – hem – friend of mine," the diplomatist added, scarcely able to avoid making a wry face over the statement. Wodehouse came in behind, looking an inch or two taller for that acknowledgment, and sat down, confronting his sisters, who were standing on the defensive. The heir, too, had a strong sense of property, as was natural, and the disarrangement of the room struck him in that point of view, especially as Miss Wodehouse continued to prop herself up against the St Agnes in the back of her chair. Wodehouse looked from the wall to the table, and saw what appeared to him a clear case of intended spoliation. "By Jove! they didn't mean to go empty-handed," said the vagabond, who naturally judged according to his own standard, and knew no better. Upon which Lucy, rising with youthful state and dignity, took the explanation upon herself.

"I do not see why we should have the mortification of a spectator," said Lucy, who already, having been engaged three-quarters of an hour, felt deeply disinclined to reveal the weak points of her own family to the inspection of the Wentworths. "All that there is to explain can be done very simply. Thank you, I will not sit down. Up to this time we may be allowed to imagine ourselves in our own – in our father's house. What we have to say is simple enough."

"But pardon me, my dear Miss Wodehouse—" said Jack Wentworth.

"My sister is Miss Wodehouse," said Lucy. "What there is to settle had better be arranged with our – our brother.

If he will tell us precisely when he wishes us to go away, we shall be ready. Mary is going to be married," she went on, turning round so as to face Wodehouse, and addressing him pointedly, though she did not look at him – to the exclusion of Jack, who, experienced man as he was, felt disconcerted, and addressed himself with more precaution to a task which was less easy than he supposed.

"Oh, Lucy!" cried Miss Wodehouse, with a blush worthy of eighteen. It was perhaps the first time that the fact had been so broadly stated, and the sudden announcement made before two men overwhelmed the timid woman. Then she was older than Lucy, and had picked up in the course of her career one or two inevitable scraps of experience, and she could not but wonder with a momentary qualm what Mr Proctor might think of his brother-in-law. Lucy, who thought Mr Proctor only too well off, went on without regarding her sister's exclamation.

"I do not know when the marriage is to be – I don't suppose they have fixed it yet," said Lucy; "but it appears to me that it would save us all some trouble if we were allowed to remain until that time. I do not mean to ask any favour," she said, with a little more sharpness and less dignity. "We could pay rent for that matter, if – if it were desired. She is your sister," said Lucy, suddenly looking Wodehouse in the face, "as well as mine. I daresay she has done as much for you as she has for me. I don't ask any favour for her – but I would cut off my little finger if that would please her," cried the excited young woman, with a wildness of illustration so totally out of keeping with the matter referred to, that Miss Wodehouse, in the midst of her emotion, could scarcely restrain a scream of terror; "and you too might be willing to do something; you cannot have any kind of feeling for me," Lucy continued, recovering herself; "but you might perhaps have some feeling for Mary. If we can be permitted to remain until her marriage takes place, it may perhaps bring about – a feeling – more like – relations; and I shall be able to—"

"Forgive you," Lucy was about to say, but fortunately stopped herself in time; for it was the fact of his existence that she had to forgive, and naturally such an amount of toleration was difficult to explain. As for Wodehouse himself, he listened to this appeal with very mingled feelings. Some natural admiration and liking woke in his dull mind as Lucy spoke. He was not destitute of good impulses, nor of the ordinary human affections. His little sister was pretty, and a lady, and clever enough to put Jack Wentworth much more in the background than usual. He said, "By Jove" to himself three or four times over in his beard, and showed a little emotion when she said he could have no feeling for her. At that point of Lucy's address he moved about uneasily in his chair, and plucked at his beard, and felt himself anything but comfortable. "By Jove! I never had a chance," the prodigal said, in his undertone. "I might have cared a deal for her if I had had a chance. She might have done a fellow good, by Jove!" mutterings of which Lucy took no manner of notice, but proceeded with her speech. When she had ended, and it became apparent that an answer was expected of him, Wodehouse flushed all over with the embarrassment of the position. He cleared his throat, he shifted his eyes, which were embarrassed by Lucy's gaze, he pushed his chair from the table, and made various attempts to collect himself, but at last ended by a pitiful appeal to Jack Wentworth, who had been looking seriously on. "You might come to a fellow's assistance!" cried Wodehouse. "By Jove! it was for that you came here."

"The Miss Wodehouses evidently prefer to communicate with their brother direct," said Jack Wentworth, "which is a very natural sentiment. If I interfere, it is simply because I have had the advantage of talking the matter over, and understanding a little of what you mean. Miss Wodehouse, your brother is not disposed to act the part of a domestic tyrant. He has come here to offer you the house, which must have so many tender associations for you, not for a short period, as you wish, but for—"

"I didn't know she was going to be married!" exclaimed Wodehouse – "that makes all the difference, by Jove! Lucy will marry fast enough; but as for Mary, I never thought she would hook any one at her time of life," said the vagabond, with a rude laugh. He turned to Lucy, not knowing any better, and with some intention of pleasing her; but being met by a look of indignation under which he faltered, he went back to his natural rôle of sulky insolence. "By Jove! when I gave in to make such an offer, I never thought she had a chance of getting married," said the heir. "I aint going to give what belongs to me to another man—"

"Your brother wishes," said Jack Wentworth, calmly, "to make over the house and furniture as it stands to you and your sister, Miss Wodehouse. Of course it is not to be expected that he should be sorry to get his father's property; but he is sorry that there should be no – no provision for you. He means that you should have the house—"

"But I never thought she was going to be married, by Jove!" protested the rightful owner. "Look here, Molly; you shall have the furniture. The house would sell for a good bit of money. I tell you, Wentworth—"

Jack Wentworth did not move from the mantlepiece where he was standing, but he cast a glance upon his unlucky follower which froze the words on his lips. "My good fellow, you are quite at liberty to decline my mediation in your affairs. Probably you can manage them better your own way," said Wodehouse's hero. "I can only beg the Miss Wodehouses to pardon my intrusion." Jack Wentworth's first step towards the door let loose a flood of nameless terrors upon the soul of his victim. If he were abandoned by his powerful protector, what would become of him? His very desire of money, and the avarice which prompted him to grudge making any provision for his sisters, was, after all, not real avarice, but the spendthrift's longing for more to spend. The house which he was sentenced to give up represented not so much gold and silver, but so many pleasures, fine dinners, and bad company. He could order the dinners by himself, it is true, and get men like himself to eat them; but the fine people – the men who had once been fine, and who still retained a certain tarnished glory – were, so far as Wodehouse was concerned, entirely in Jack Wentworth's keeping. He made a piteous appeal to his patron as the great man turned to go away.

"I don't see what good it can do *you* to rob a poor fellow!" cried Wodehouse. "But look here, I aint going to turn against your advice. I'll give it them, by Jove, for life – that is, for Mary's life," said the munificent brother. "She's twenty years older than Lucy—"

"How do you dare to subject us to such insults?" cried the indignant Lucy, whose little hand clenched involuntarily in her passion. She had a great deal of self-control, but she was not quite equal to such an emergency; and it was all she could do to keep from stamping her foot, which was the only utterance of rage possible to a gentlewoman in her position. "I would rather see my father's house desecrated by you living in it," she cried, passionately, "than accept it as a gift from your hands. Mary, we are not obliged to submit to this. Let us rather go away at once. I will not remain in the same room with this man!" cried Lucy. She was so overwhelmed with her unwonted passion that she lost all command of the position, and even of herself, and was false for the moment to all her sweet codes of womanly behaviour. "How dare you, sir!" she cried in the sudden storm for which nobody was prepared. "We will remove the things belonging to us, with which nobody has any right to interfere, and we will leave immediately. Mary, come with me!" When she had said this, Lucy swept out of the room, pale as a little fury, and feeling in her heart a savage female inclination to strike Jack Wentworth, who opened the door for her, with her

little white clenched hand. Too much excited to remark
whether her sister had followed her, Lucy ran up-stairs to
her room, and there gave way to the inevitable tears.
Coming to herself after that was a terribly humbling
process to the little Anglican. She had never fallen into a
"passion" before that she knew of, certainly never since
nursery times; and often enough her severe serene girl-
hood had looked reproving and surprised upon the tumults
of Prickett's Lane, awing the belligerents into at least temporary silence. Now poor Lucy sat and cried over her
downfall; she had forgotten herself; she had been conscious of an inclination to stamp, to scold, even to strike,
in the vehemence of her indignation; and she was utterly
overpowered by the thought of her guiltiness. "The very
first temptation!" she said to herself; and made terrible
reflections upon her own want of strength and endurance.
To-day, too, of all days, when God had been so good to
her! "If I yield to the first temptation like this, how shall I
ever endure to the end?" cried Lucy, and in her heart
thought, with a certain longing, of the sacrament of
penance, and tried to think what she could do that would
be most disagreeable, to the mortifying of the flesh. Perhaps if she had possessed a more lively sense of humour,
another view of the subject might have struck Lucy; but
humour, fortunately for the unity of human sentiment, is
generally developed at a later period of life, and Lucy's fit
of passion only made her think with greater tenderness
and toleration of her termagants in Prickett's Lane.

The three who were left down-stairs were in their
different ways impressed by Lucy's passion. Jack Wentworth, being a man of humour and cultivation, was
amused, but respectful, as having still a certain faculty of
appreciating absolute purity when he saw it. As for Wodehouse, he gave another rude laugh, but was cowed, in
spite of himself, and felt involuntarily what a shabby
wretch he was, recognising that fact more impressively
from the contempt of Lucy's pale face than he could have

done through hours of argument. Miss Wodehouse, for her part, though very anxious and nervous, was not without an interest in the question under discussion. *She* was not specially horrified by her brother, or anything he could say or do. He was Tom to her – a boy with whom she had once played, and whom she had shielded with all her sisterly might in his first transgressions. She had suffered a great deal more by his means than Lucy could ever suffer, and consequently was more tolerant of him. She kept her seat with the St Agnes in the chair behind, and watched the course of events with anxious steadiness. She did not care for money any more than Lucy did; but she could not help thinking it would be very pleasant if she could produce one good action on "poor Tom's" part to plead for him against any possible criticisms of the future. Miss Wodehouse was old enough to know that her Rector was not an ideal hero, but an ordinary man, and it was quite possible that he might point a future moral now and then with "that brother of yours, my dear." The elder sister waited accordingly, with her heart beating quick, to know the decision, very anxious that she might have at least one generous deed to record to the advantage of poor Tom.

"I think we are quite decided on the point," said Jack Wentworth. "Knowing your sentiments, Wodehouse, I left directions with Waters about the papers. I think you will find him to be trusted, Miss Wodehouse, if you wish to consult him about letting or selling—"

"By Jove!" exclaimed Wodehouse, under his breath.

"Which, I suppose," continued the superb Jack, "you will wish to do under the pleasant circumstances, upon which I beg to offer you my congratulations. Now, Tom, my good fellow, I am at your service. I think we have done our business here."

Wodehouse got up in his sulky reluctant way like a lazy dog. "I suppose you won't try to move the furniture now?" he said. These were the only adieux he intended to make, and perhaps they might have been expressed with still less civility, had not Jack Wentworth been standing waiting for him at the door.

"Oh, Tom! I am so thankful you have done it!" cried Miss Wodehouse. "It is not that I care for the money; but oh, Tom, I am so glad to think nobody can say anything now." She followed them wistfully to the door, not giving up hopes of a kinder parting. "I think it is very kind and nice of you, and what dear papa would have wished," said the elder sister, forgetting how all her father's plans had been brought to nothing; "and of course you will live here all the same?" she said, with a little eagerness, "that is, till – till – as long as we are here—"

"Good-bye, Miss Wodehouse," said Jack Wentworth. "I don't think either your brother or I will stay much longer in Carlingford. You must accept my best wishes for your happiness all the same."

"You are very kind, I am sure," said the embarrassed bride; "and oh, Tom, you will surely say good-bye? Say good-bye once as if you meant it; don't go away as if you did not care. Tom, I always was very fond of you; and don't you feel a little different to us, now you've done us a kindness?" cried Miss Wodehouse, going out after him to the landing-place. But Wodehouse was in no humour to be gracious. Instead of paying any attention to her, he looked regretfully at the property he had lost.

"Good-bye," he said, vaguely. "By Jove! I know better than Jack Wentworth does the value of property. We might have had a jolly month at Homburg out of that old place," said the prodigal, with regret, as he went down the old-fashioned oak stair. That was his farewell to the house which he had entered so disastrously on the day of his father's funeral. He followed his leader with a sulky aspect through the garden, not venturing to disobey, but yet feeling the weight of his chains. And this was how Wodehouse accomplished his personal share in the gift to his sisters, of which Miss Wodehouse told everybody that it was "so good of Tom!"

CHAPTER XLIV.

"Going to be married!" said the Squire; "and to a sister of
– I thought you told me she was as old as Dora, Frank? I
did not expect to meet with any further complications,"
the old man said, plaintively: "of course you know very
well I don't object to your marrying; but why on earth did
you let me speak of Wentworth Rectory to Huxtable?"
cried Mr Wentworth. He was almost more impatient
about this new variety in the family circumstances than he
had been of more serious family distresses. "God bless
me, sir," said the Squire, "what do you mean by it? You
take means to affront your aunts and lose Skelmersdale;
and then you put it into my head to have Mary at
Wentworth; and then you quarrel with the Rector, and get
into hot water in Carlingford; and, to make an end of all,
you coolly propose to an innocent young woman, and tell
me you are going to marry – what on earth do you mean?"

"I am going to marry some time, sir, I hope," said the
Perpetual Curate, with more cheerfulness than he felt;
"but not at the present moment. Of course we both know
that is impossible. I should like you to come with me and
see her before you leave Carlingford. She would like it,
and so should I."

"Well, well," said the Squire. Naturally, having been
married so often himself, he could not refuse a certain
response to such a call upon his sympathy. "I hope you
have made a wise choice," said the experienced father,
not without a sigh; "a great deal depends upon that – not
only your own comfort, sir, but very often the character of
your children and the credit of the family. You may

laugh," said Mr Wentworth, to whom it was no laughing matter; "but long before you are as old as I am, you will know the truth of what I say. Your mother, Frank, was a specimen of what a woman ought to be – not to speak of her own children, there was nobody else who ever knew how to manage Gerald and Jack. Of course I am not speaking of Mrs Wentworth, who has her nursery to occupy her," said the Squire, apologetically. "I hope you have made a judicious choice."

"I hope so, too," said Frank, who was somewhat amused by this view of the question – "though I am not aware of having exercised any special choice in the matter," he added, with a laugh. "However, I want you to come with me and see her, and then you will be able to judge for yourself."

The Squire shook his head, and looked as if he had travelled back into the heavy roll of family distresses. "I don't mean to upbraid you, Frank," he said – "I daresay you have done what you thought was your duty – but I think you might have taken a little pains to satisfy your aunt Leonora. You see what Gerald has made of it, with all his decorations and nonsense. That is a dreadful drawback with you clergymen. You fix your eyes so on one point that you get to think things important that are not in the least important. Could you imagine a man of the world like Jack – he is not what I could wish, but still he is a man of the world," said the Squire, who was capable of contradicting himself with perfect composure without knowing it. "Can you imagine *him* risking his prospects for a bit of external decoration? I don't mind it myself," said Mr Wentworth, impartially – "I don't pretend to see, for my own part, why flowers at Easter should be considered more superstitious than holly at Christmas; but, bless my soul, sir, when your aunt thought so, what was the good of running right in her face for such a trifle? I never could understand you parsons," the Squire said, with an impatient sigh – "nobody, that I know of, ever considered me mercenary; but to ruin your own prospects, all for a trumpery bunch of flowers, and then to come and tell me you want to marry— "

This was before luncheon, when Frank and his father were together in the dining-room waiting for the other members of the family, who began to arrive at this moment, and prevented any further discussion. After all, perhaps, it was a little ungenerous of the Squire to press his son so hard on the subject of those innocent Easter lilies, long ago withered, which certainly, looked at from this distance, did not appear important enough to sacrifice any prospects for. This was all the harder upon the unfortunate Curate, as even at the time his conviction of their necessity had not proved equal to the satisfactory settlement of the question. Miss Wentworth's cook was an *artiste* so irreproachable that the luncheon provided was in itself perfect; but notwithstanding it was an uncomfortable meal. Miss Leonora, in consequence of the contest going on in her own mind, was in an explosive and highly dangerous condition, not safe to be spoken to; and as for the Squire, he could not restrain the chance utterances of his impatience. Frank, who did his best to make himself agreeable as magnanimity required, had the mortification of hearing himself discussed in different tones of disapprobation while he ate his cold beef; for Mr Wentworth's broken sentences were not long of putting the party in possession of the new event, and the Perpetual Curate found himself the object of many wondering and pitying glances, in none of which could he read pure sympathy, much less congratulation. Even Gerald looked at him with a little elevation of his eyebrows, as if wondering how anybody could take the trouble to occupy his mind with such trifling temporal affairs as love and marriage. It was a wonderful relief to the unfortunate Curate when Miss Leonora had finished her glass of madeira, and rose from the table. He had no inclination to go up-stairs, for his own part. "When you are ready, sir, you will find me in the garden," he said to his father, who was to leave Carlingford next morning, and whom he had set his heart on taking to see Lucy. But his walk in the garden was far from being delightful to Frank. It even occurred to him, for a moment, that it would be a very good thing if a man could cut himself adrift from his relations at such a crisis of his life. After all, it was his own business – the act most essentially personal of his entire existence; and then, with a little softening, he began to think of the girls at home – of the little sister, who had a love-story of her own; and of Letty, who was Frank's favourite, and had often confided to him the enthusiasm she would feel for his bride. "If she is nice," Letty was in the habit of adding, "and of course she will be nice," – and at that thought the heart of the young lover escaped, and put forth its wings, and went off into that heaven of ideal excellence and beauty, more sweet, because more vague, than anything real, which stands instead of the old working-day skies and clouds at such a period of life. He had to drop down from a great height, and get rid in all haste of his celestial pinions, when he heard his aunt Dora calling him; and his self-command was not sufficient to conceal, as he obeyed that summons, a certain annoyed expression in his face.

"Frank," said Miss Dora, coming softly after him with her handkerchief held over her head as a defence from the sun – "oh, Frank, I want to speak to you. I couldn't say anything at lunch because of everybody being there. If you would only stop a moment till I get my breath. Frank, my dear boy, I wish you joy. I do wish you joy with all my heart. I should so like just to go and kiss her, and tell her I shall love her for your sake."

"You will soon love her for her own sake," said Frank, to whom even this simple-minded sympathy was very grateful; "she is a great deal better than I am."

"There is just one thing," said Miss Dora. "Oh, Frank, my dear, you know I don't pretend to be clever, like

Leonora, or able to give you advice; but there *is* one thing. You know you have nothing to marry upon, and all has gone wrong. You are not to have Wentworth, and you are not to have Skelmersdale, and I think the family is going out of its senses not to see who is the most worthy. You have got nothing to live upon, my dear, dear boy!" said Miss Dora, withdrawing the handkerchief from her head in the excitement of the moment to apply it to her eyes.

"That is true enough," said the Perpetual Curate; "but then we have not made up our minds that we must marry immediately—"

"Frank," said aunt Dora, with solemnity, breaking into his speech, "there is just *one* thing; and I can't hold my tongue, though it may be very foolish, and they will all say it is my fault." It was a very quiet summer-day, but still there was a faint rustle in the branches which alarmed the timid woman. She put her hand upon her nephew's arm, and hastened him on to the little summer-house in the wall, which was her special retirement. "Nobody ever comes here," said Miss Dora; "they will never think of looking for us here. I am sure I never interfere with Leonora's arrangements, nor take anything upon myself; but there is one thing, Frank—"

"Yes," said the Curate, "I understand what you mean: you are going to warn me about love in a cottage, and how foolish it would be to marry upon nothing; but, my dear aunt, we are not going to do anything rash; there is no such dreadful haste; don't be agitated about it," said the young man, with a smile. He was half amused and half irritated by the earnestness which almost took away the poor lady's breath.

"You *don't* know what I mean," said aunt Dora. "Frank, you know very well I never interfere; but I can't help being agitated when I see you on the brink of such a precipice. Oh, my dear boy, don't be over-persuaded. There *is* one thing, and I must say it if I should die." She had to pause a little to recover her voice, for haste and excitement had a tendency to make her inarticulate. "Frank," said Miss Dora again, more solemnly than ever, "whatever you may be obliged to do – though you were to write novels, or take pupils, or do translations – oh, Frank, don't look at me like that, as if I was going crazy. Whatever you may have to do, oh my dear, there is one thing – don't go and break people's hearts, and put it off, and put it off, till it never happens!" cried the trembling little woman, with a sudden burst of tears. "Don't say you can wait, for you can't wait, and you oughtn't to!" sobbed Miss Dora. She subsided altogether into her handkerchief and her chair as she uttered this startling and wholly unexpected piece of advice, and lay there in a little heap, all dissolving and floating away, overcome with her great effort, while her nephew stood looking at her from a height of astonishment almost too extreme for wondering. If the trees could have found a voice and counselled his immediate marriage, he could scarcely have been more surprised.

"You think I am losing my senses too," said aunt Dora; "but that is because you don't understand me. Oh Frank, my dear boy, there was once a time! – perhaps everybody has forgotten it except me, but I have not forgotten it. They treated me like a baby, and Leonora had everything her own way. I don't mean to say it was not for the best," said the aggrieved woman. "I know everything is for the best, if we could but see it: and perhaps Leonora was right when she said I never could have struggled with – with a family, nor lived on a poor man's income. My dear, it was before your uncle Charley died; and when we became rich, it – didn't matter," said Miss Dora; "it was all over before then. Oh Frank! if I hadn't experience I wouldn't say a word. I don't interfere about your opinions, like Leonora. There is just *one* thing," cried the poor lady through her tears. Perhaps it was the recollection of the past which overcame Miss Dora, perhaps the force of habit which had made it natural for her to cry when she

was much moved; but the fact is certain, that the Squire,
when he came to the door of the summer-house in search
of Frank, found his sister weeping bitterly, and his son
making efforts to console her, in which some sympathy
was mingled with a certain half-amusement. Frank, like
Lucy, felt tempted to laugh at the elderly romance; and
yet his heart expanded warmly to his tender little foolish
aunt, who, after all, might once have been young and in
love like himself, though it was so odd to realise it. Mr
Wentworth, for his part, saw no humour whatever in the
scene. He thought nothing less than that some fresh
complication had taken place. Jack had committed some
new enormity, or there was bad news from Charley in
Malta, or unpleasant letters had come from home. "Bless
my soul, sir, something new has happened," said the
Squire; and he was scarcely reassured, when Miss Dora
stumbled up from her chair in great confusion, and wiped
the tears from her eyes. He was suspicious of this meeting
in the summer-house, which seemed a quite unnecessary
proceeding to Mr Wentworth; and though he flattered
himself he understood women, he could not give any
reasonable explanation to himself of Dora's tears.

"It is nothing – nothing at all," said Miss Dora: "it was
not Frank's doing in the least; he is always so considerate,
and such a dear fellow. Thank you, my dear boy; my head
is a little better; I think I will go in and lie down," said the
unlucky aunt. "You are not to mind me now, for I have
quite got over my little attack; I always was so nervous,"
said Miss Dora; "and I sometimes wonder whether it isn't
the Wentworth complaint coming on," she added, with a
natural female artifice which was not without its effect.

"I wish you would not talk nonsense," said the Squire.
"The Wentworth complaint is nothing to laugh at, but
you are perfectly aware that it never attacks women."
Mr Wentworth spoke with a little natural irritation,
displeased to have his prerogative interfered with. When
a man has all the suffering attendant upon a special
complaint, it is hard not to have all the dignity. He felt so

much and so justly annoyed by Miss Dora's vain preten-
sions, that he forgot his anxiety about the secret conference in the summer-house. "Women take such fantastic
ideas into their heads," he said to his son as they went
away together. "You aunt Dora is the kindest soul in the
world; but now and then, sir, she is very absurd." said the
Squire. He could not get this presumptuous notion out of
his head, but returned to it again and again, even after
they had got into Grange Lane. "It has been in our family
for two hundred years," said Mr Wentworth; "and I don't
think there is a single instance of its attacking a woman –
not even slightly, sir," the Squire added, with irritation, as
if Frank had taken the part of the female members of the
family, which indeed the Curate had no thought of
doing.

Miss Dora, for her part, having made this very successful diversion, escaped to the house, and to her own room,
where she indulged in a headache all the afternoon, and
certain tender recollections which were a wonderful resource at all times to the soft-hearted woman. "Oh, my
dear boy, don't be over-persuaded," she had whispered
into Frank's ear as she left him; and her remonstrance,
simple as it was, had no doubt produced a considerable
effect upon the mind of the Perpetual Curate. He could
not help thinking, as they emerged into the road, that it
was chiefly the impatient and undutiful who secured their
happiness. Those who were constant and patient, and able
to deny themselves, instead of being rewarded for their
higher qualities, were, on the contrary, put to the full test
of the strength that was in them; while those who would
not wait attained what they wanted, and on the whole, as
to other matters, got on just as well as their stronger-
minded neighbours. This germ of thought, it may be
supposed, was stimulated into very warm life by the
reflection that Lucy would have to leave Carlingford with
her sister, without any definite prospect of returning
again; and a certain flush of impatience came over the
young man, not unnatural in the circumstances. It seemed

to him that everybody else took their own way without waiting; and why should it be so certain that he alone, whose "way" implied harm to no one, should be the only man condemned to wait? Thus it will be seen that the "just one thing" insisted on by Miss Dora was far from being without effect on the mind of her nephew; upon whom, indeed, the events of the morning had wrought various changes of sentiment. When he walked up Grange Lane for the first time, it had been without any acknowledged intention of opening his mind to Lucy, and yet he had returned along the same prosaic and unsympathetic line of road her accepted lover; her accepted lover, triumphant in that fact, but without the least opening of any hope before him as to the conclusion of the engagement, which prudence had no hand in making. Now the footsteps of the Perpetual Curate fell firmly, not to say a little impatiently, upon the road over which he had carried so many varying thoughts. He was as penniless as ever, and as prospectless; but in the tossings of his natural impatience the young man had felt the reins hang loosely about his head, and knew that he was no more restrained than other men, but might, if he chose it, have his way like the rest of the world. It was true enough that he might have to pay for it after, as other people had done; but in the mean time the sense that he was his own master was sweet, and to have his will for once seemed no more than his right in the world. While these rebellious thoughts were going on in the Curate's mind, his father, who suspected nothing, went steadily by his side, not without a little reluctance at the thought of the errand on which he was bound. "But they can't marry for years, and nobody can tell what may happen in that time," Mr Wentworth said to himself, with the callousness of mature age, not suspecting the different ideas that were afloat in the mind of his son. Perhaps, on the whole, he was not sorry that Skelmersdale was destined otherwise, and that Huxtable had been spoken to about Wentworth Rectory; for, of course, Frank would have plunged into marriage at once if he had been possessed of anything to marry on; and it looked providential under the circumstances, as the Squire argued with himself privately, that at such a crisis the Perpetual Curate should have fallen between two stools of possible preferment, and should still be obliged to content himself with St Roque's. It was hard for Mr Wentworth to reconcile himself to the idea that the wife of his favourite son should be the sister of— ; for the Squire forgot that his own girls were Jack Wentworth's sisters, and as such might be objected to in their turn by some other father. So the two gentlemen went to see Lucy, who was then in a very humble frame of mind, just recovered from her passion – one of them rather congratulating himself on the obstacles which lay before the young couple, the other tossing his youthful head a little in the first impulses of self-will, feeling the reins lie loose upon him, and making up his mind to have his own way.

CHAPTER XLV.

WHILE Mr Frank Wentworth's affairs were thus gathering to a crisis, other events likely to influence his fate were also taking place in Carlingford. Breakfast had been served a full half-hour later than usual in the Rectory, which had not improved the temper of the household. Everything was going on with the most wonderful quietness in that well-arranged house; but it was a quietness which would have made a sensitive visitor uncomfortable, and which woke horrible private qualms in the mind of the Rector. As for Mrs Morgan, she fulfilled all her duties with a precision which was terrible to behold: instead of taking part in the conversation as usual, and having her own opinion, she had suddenly become possessed of such a spirit of meekness and acquiescence as filled her husband with dismay. The Rector was fond of his wife, and proud of her good sense, and her judgment, and powers of conversation. If she had been angry and found fault with him, he might have understood that mode of procedure; but as she was not angry, but only silent, the excellent man was terribly disconcerted, and could not tell what to do. He had done all he could to be conciliatory, and had already entered upon a great many explanations which had come to nothing for want of any response; and now she sat at the head of the table making tea with an imperturbable countenance, sometimes making little observations about the news, perfectly calm and dignified, but taking no part in anything more interesting, and turning off any reference that was made to her in the most skilful manner. "Mr Morgan knows I never take any part in the gossip of Carlingford," she said to Mr Proctor, without any intention of wounding that good man; and he who had been in the midst of something about Mr Wentworth came to an abrupt stop with the sense of having shown himself as a gossip, which was very injurious to his dignity. The late Rector, indeed, occupied a very uncomfortable position between the married people thus engaged in the absorbing excitement of their first quarrel. The quiet little arrows, which Mrs Morgan intended only for her husband, grazed and stung him as they passed, without missing at the same time their intended aim; and he was the auditor, besides, of a great deal of information intended by the Rector for his wife's benefit, to which Mrs Morgan paid no manner of attention. Mr Proctor was not a man of very lively observation, but he could not quite shut his eyes to the position of affairs; and the natural effect upon his mind, in the circumstances, was to turn his thoughts towards his mild Mary, whom he did not quite recognise as yet under her Christian name. He called her

Miss Wodehouse in his heart even while in the act of making comparisons very unfavourable to the Rector's wife, and then he introduced benevolently the subject of his new rectory, which surely must be safe ground.

"It is a pretty little place," Mr Proctor said, with satisfaction: "of course it is but a small living compared to Carlingford. I hope you will come and see me, after – it is furnished," said the bashful bridegroom: "it is a nuisance to have all that to look after for one's self—"

"I hope you will have somebody to help you," said Mrs Morgan, with a little earnestness; "gentlemen don't understand about such things. When you have one piece of furniture in bad taste, it spoils a whole room – carpets, for instance— " said the Rector's wife. She looked at Mr Proctor so severely that the good man faltered, though he was not aware of the full extent of his guiltiness.

"I am sure I don't know," he said: "I told the man here to provide everything as it ought to be; and I think we were very successful," continued Mr Proctor, with a little complacency: to be sure, they were in the dining-room at the moment, being still at the breakfast-table. "Buller knows a great deal about that sort of thing, but then he is too ecclesiological for my taste. I like things to look cheerful," said the unsuspicious man. "Buller is the only man that could be reckoned on if any living were to fall vacant. It is very odd nowadays how indifferent men are about the Church. I don't say that it is not very pleasant at All-Souls; but a house of one's own, you know— " said Mr Proctor, looking with a little awkward enthusiasm at his recently-married brother; "of course I mean a sphere – a career—"

"Oh, ah, yes," said Mr Morgan, with momentary gruffness; "but everything has its drawbacks. I don't think Buller would take a living. He knows too well what's comfortable," said the suffering man. "The next living that falls will have to go to some one out of the college," said Mr Morgan. He spoke with a tone of importance and significance which moved Mr Proctor, though he was not rapid in his perceptions, to look across at him for further information.

"Most people have some crotchet or other," said the Rector. "When a man's views are clear about subscription, and that sort of thing, he generally goes as far wrong the other way. Buller might go out to Central Africa, perhaps, if there was a bishopric of Wahuma – or what is the name, my dear, in that Nile book?"

"I have not read it," said Mrs Morgan, and she made no further remark.

Thus discouraged in his little attempt at amity, the Rector resumed after a moment, "Wentworth's brother has sent in his resignation to his bishop. There is no doubt about it any longer. I thought that delusion had been over, at all events; and I suppose now Wentworth will be provided for," said Mr Morgan, not without a little anxiety.

"No; they are all equally crotchety, I think," said Mr Proctor. "I know about them, through my – my connection with the Wodehouses, you know. I should not wonder, for my own part, if he went after his brother, who is a very intelligent man, though mistaken," the late Rector added, with respect. "As for Frank Wentworth, he is a little hot-headed. I had a long conversation the other night with the elder brother. I tried to draw him out about Burgon's book, but he declined to enter into the question. Frank has made up his mind to stay in Carlingford. I understand he thinks it right on account of his character being called in question here; though, of course, no one in his senses could have had any doubt how *that* would turn out," said Mr Proctor, forgetting that he himself had been very doubtful about the Curate. "From what I hear, they are all very crotchety," he continued, and finished his breakfast calmly, as if that settled the question. As for Mrs Morgan, even this interesting statement had no effect upon her. She looked up suddenly at one moment as if

intending to dart a reproachful glance at her husband, but
bethought herself in time, and remained passive as before;
not the less, however, was she moved by what she had just
heard. It was not Mr Wentworth she was thinking of,
except in a very secondary degree. What occupied her,
and made her reflections bitter, was the thought that her
husband – the man to whom she had been faithful for ten
weary years – had taken himself down off the pedestal on
which she had placed him. "To make idols, and to find
them clay," she said plaintively in her own mind. Women
were all fools to spend their time and strength in construc-
ting such pedestals, Mrs Morgan thought to herself with
bitterness; and as to the men who were so perpetually
dethroning themselves, how were they to be designated?
To think of her William, of whom she had once made a
hero, ruining thus, for a little petty malice and rivalry, the
prospects of another man! While these painful reflections
were going through her mind, she was putting away her
tea-caddy, and preparing to leave the gentlemen to their
own affairs. "We shall see you at dinner at six," she said,
with a constrained little smile, to Mr Proctor, and went
up-stairs with her key-basket in her hand without taking
any special notice of the Rector. Mr Leeson was to come
to dinner that day legitimately by invitation, and Mrs
Morgan, who felt it would be a little consolation to disappoint the hungry Curate for once, was making up her
mind, as she went up-stairs, not to have the All-Souls
pudding, of which he showed so high an appreciation. It
almost seemed to her as if this spark of ill-nature was
receiving a summary chastisement, when she heard steps
ascending behind her. Mrs Morgan objected to have men
lounging about her drawing-room in the morning. She
thought Mr Proctor was coming to bestow a little more of
his confidence upon her, and perhaps to consult her about
his furnishing; and being occupied by her own troubles,
she had no patience for a tiresome, middle-aged lover,
who no doubt was going to disappoint and disenchant

another woman. She sat down, accordingly, with a sigh of impatience at her work-table, turning her back to the door. Perhaps, when he saw her inhospitable attitude, he might go away and not bother her. And Mrs Morgan took out some stockings to darn, as being a discontented occupation, and was considering within herself what simple preparation she could have instead of the All-Souls pudding, when, looking up suddenly, she saw, not Mr Proctor, but the Rector, standing looking down upon her within a few steps of her chair. When she perceived him, it was not in nature to refrain from certain symptoms of agitation. The thoughts she had been indulging in brought suddenly a rush of guilty colour to her face; but she commanded herself as well as she could, and went on darning her stockings, with her heart beating very loud in her breast.

"My dear," said the Rector, taking a seat near her, "I don't know what it is that has risen between us. We look as if we had quarrelled; and I thought we had made up our minds never to quarrel." The words were rather soft in their signification, but Mr Morgan could not help speaking severely, as was natural to his voice; which was perhaps, in the present case, all the better for his wife.

"I don't know what you may consider quarrelling, William," said Mrs Morgan, "but I am sure I have never made any complaint."

"No," said the Rector; "I have seen women do that before. You don't make any complaint, but you look as if you disapproved of everything. I feel it all the more just now because I want to consult you; and, after all, the occasion was no such—"

"I never said there was any occasion. I am sure I never made any complaint. You said you wanted to consult me, William?" Mrs Morgan went on darning her stockings while she was speaking, and the Rector, like most other men, objected to be spoken to by the lips only. He would have liked to toss the stocking out of the window, though it was his own, and the task of repairing it was one of a devoted wife's first duties, according to the code of female proprieties in which both the husband and wife had been brought up.

"Yes," said the Rector, with a sigh. "The truth is, I have just got a letter from Harry Scarsfield, who was my pet pupil long ago. He tells me my father's old rectory is vacant, where we were all brought up. There used to be a constant intercourse between the Hall and the Rectory when I was a lad. They are very nice people the Scarsfields – at least they used to be very nice people; and Harry has his mother living with him, and the family has never been broken up, I believe. We used to know everybody about there," said Mr Morgan, abandoning himself to recollections in a manner most mysterious to his wife. "There is the letter, my dear," and he put it down upon her table, and began to play with the reels of cotton in her workbox unconsciously, as he had not done for a long time; which, unawares to herself, had a softening influence upon Mrs Morgan's heart.

"I do not know anything about the Scarsfields," she said, without taking up the letter, "and I cannot see what you have to do with this. Does he wish you to recommend some one?" Mrs Morgan added, with a momentary interest; for she had, of course, like other people, a relation in a poor living, whom it would have been satisfactory to recommend.

"He says I may have it if I have a mind," said the Rector curtly, betraying a little aggravation in his tone.

"You, William?" said Mrs Morgan. She was so much surprised that she laid down her stocking and looked him straight in the face, which she had not done for many days; and it was wonderful how hard she found it to keep up her reserve, after having once looked her husband in the eyes. "But it is not much more than six months since you were settled in Carlingford," she said, still lost in amazement. "You cannot possibly mean to make a change

so soon? and then the difference of the position," said the
Rector's wife. As she looked at him, she became more and
more aware of some meaning in his face which she did not
understand; and more and more, as it became necessary to
understand him, the reserves and self-defences of the first
quarrel gave way and dispersed. "I don't think I quite
know what you mean," she said, faltering a little. "I don't
understand why you should think of a change."

"A good country living is a very good position," said the
Rector; "it is not nearly so troublesome as a town like
Carlingford. There is no Dissent that I know of, and no—"
(here Mr Morgan paused for a moment, not knowing what
word to use) – "no disturbing influences: of course I would
not take such a step without your concurrence, my dear,"
the Rector continued; and then there followed a bewildering pause. Mrs Morgan's first sensation after the astonishment with which she heard this strange proposal was
mortification – the vivid shame and vexation of a woman
when she is obliged to own to herself that her husband has
been worsted, and is retiring from the field.

"If you think it right – if you think it best – of course I
can have nothing to say," said the Rector's wife; and she
took up her stocking with a stinging sense of discomfiture.
She had meant that her husband should be the first man in
Carlingford – that he should gain everybody's respect and
veneration, and become the ideal parish-priest of that
favourite and fortunate place. Every kind of good work
and benevolent undertaking was to be connected with his
name, according to the visions which Mrs Morgan had
framed when she came first to Carlingford, not without
such a participation on her own part as should entitle her
to the milder glory appertaining to the good Rector's wife.
All these hopes were now to be blotted out ignominiously.
Defeat and retreat and failure were to be the conclusion of
their first essay at life. "You are the best judge of what
you ought to do," she said, with as much calmness as she
could muster, but she could have dropped bitter tears

upon the stocking she was mending if that would have done any good.

"I will do nothing without your consent," said the Rector. "Young Wentworth is going to stay in Carlingford. You need not look up so sharply, as if you were vexed to think *that* had anything to do with it. If he had not behaved like a fool, I never could have been led into such a mistake," said Mr Morgan, with indignation, taking a little walk to the other end of the room to refresh himself. "At the same time," said the Rector, severely, coming back after a pause, "to show any ill-feeling would be very unchristian either on your side or mine. If I were to accept Harry Scarsfield's offer, Proctor and I would do all we could to have young Wentworth appointed to Carlingford. There is nobody just now at All-Souls to take the living; and however much you may disapprove of him, my dear," said Mr Morgan, with increasing severity, "there is nothing that I know to be said against him as a clergyman. If you can make up your mind to consent to it, and can see affairs in the same light as they appear to me, that is what I intend to do—"

Mrs Morgan's stocking had dropped on her knees as she listened; then it dropped on the floor, and she took no notice of it. When the Rector had finally delivered himself of his sentiments, which he did in the voice of a judge who was condemning some unfortunate to the utmost penalties of the law, his wife marked the conclusion of the sentence by a sob of strange excitement. She kept gazing at him for a few moments without feeling able to speak, and then she put down her face into her hands. Words were too feeble to give utterance to her feelings at such a supreme moment. "Oh, William, I wonder if you can ever forgive me," sobbed the Rector's wife, with a depth of compunction which he, good man, was totally unprepared to meet, and knew no occasion for. He was even at the moment a little puzzled to have such a despairing petition addressed to him. "I hope so, my dear," he said, very sedately, as he came and sat down beside her, and could not refrain from uttering a little lecture upon temper, which fortunately Mrs Morgan was too much excited to pay any attention to. "It would be a great deal better if you did not give way to your feelings," said the Rector; "but in the mean time, my dear, it is your advice I want, for we must not take such a step unadvisedly," and he lifted up the stocking that had fallen, and contemplated, not without surprise, the emotion of his wife. The excellent man was as entirely unconscious that he was being put up again at that moment with acclamations upon his pedestal, as that he had at a former time been violently displaced from it, and thrown into the category of broken idols. All this would have been as Sanscrit to the Rector of Carlingford; and the only resource he had was to make in his own mind certain half-pitying, half-affectionate remarks upon the inexplicable weakness of women, and to pick up the stocking which his wife was darning, and finally to stroke her hair, which was still as pretty and soft and brown as it had been ten years ago. Under such circumstances a man does not object to feel himself on a platform of moral superiority. He even began to pet her a little, with a pleasant sense of forgiveness and forbearance. "You were perhaps a little cross, my love, but you don't think I am the man to be hard upon you," said the Rector. "Now you must dry your eyes and give me your advice – you know how much confidence I have always had in your advice— "

"Forgive me, William. I don't think there is any one so good as you are; and as long as we are together it does not matter to me where we are," said the repentant woman. But as she lifted up her head, her eye fell on the carpet, and a gleam of sudden delight passed through Mrs Morgan's mind. To be delivered from all her suspicions and injurious thoughts about her husband would have been a deliverance great enough for one day; but at the same happy moment to see a means of deliverance from the smaller as well as the greater cross of her existence seemed almost too good to be credible. She brightened up immediately when that thought occurred to her. "I think it is the very best thing you could do," she said. "We are both so fond of the country, and it is so much nicer to manage a country parish than a town one. We might have lived all our lives in Carlingford without knowing above half of the poor people," said Mrs Morgan, growing in warmth as she went on; "it is so different in a country parish. I never liked to say anything," she continued, with subtle feminine policy, "but I never – much – cared for Carlingford." She gave a sigh as she spoke, for she thought of the Virginian creeper and the five feet of new wall at that side of the garden, which had just been completed, to shut out the view of the train. Life does not contain any perfect pleasure. But when Mrs Morgan stooped to lift up some stray reels of cotton which the Rector's clumsy fingers had dropped out of her workbox, her eye was again attracted by the gigantic roses and tulips on the carpet, and content and satisfaction filled her heart.

"I have felt the same thing, my dear," said Mr Morgan. "I don't say anything against Mr Finial as an architect, but Scott himself could make nothing of such a hideous church. I don't suppose Wentworth will mind," said the Rector, with a curious sense of superiority. He felt his own magnanimous conduct at the moment almost as much as his wife had done, and could not help regarding Carlingford Church as the gift-horse which was not to be examined too closely in the mouth.

"No," said Mrs Morgan, not without a passing sensation of doubt on this point; "if he had only been frank and explained everything, there never could have been any mistake; but I am glad it has all happened," said the Rector's wife, with a little enthusiasm. "Oh, William, I have been such a wretch – I have been thinking – but now you are heaping coals of fire on his head," she cried, with a hysterical sound in her throat. It was no matter to her that she herself scarcely knew what she meant, and that the good Rector had not the faintest understanding of it. She was so glad, that it was almost necessary to be guilty of some extravagance by way of relieving her mind. "After all Mr Proctor's care in fitting the furniture, you would not, of course, think of removing it," said Mrs Morgan; "Mr Wentworth will take it as we did; and as for Mrs Scarsfield, if you like her, William, you may be sure I shall," the penitent wife said softly, in the flutter and tremor of her agitation. As he saw himself reflected in her eyes, the Rector could not but feel himself a superior person, elevated over other men's shoulders. Such a sense of goodness promotes the amiability from which it springs. The Rector kissed his wife as he got up from his seat beside her, and once more smoothed down, with a touch which made her feel like a girl again, her pretty brown hair.

"That is all settled satisfactorily," said Mr Morgan, "and now I must go to my work again. I thought, if you approved of it, I would write at once to Scarsfield, and also to Buller of All-Souls."

"Do," said the Rector's wife – and she too bestowed, in her middle-aged way, a little caress, which was far from being unpleasant to the sober-minded man. He went down-stairs in a more agreeable frame of mind than he had known for a long time back. Not that he understood why she had cried about it when he laid his intentions before her. Had Mr Morgan been a Frenchman, he probably would have imagined his wife's heart to be touched by the graces of the Perpetual Curate; but, being an Englishman, and rather more certain, on the whole, of her than of himself, it did not occur to him to speculate on the subject. He was quite able to content himself with the thought that women were incomprehensible, as he went back to his study. To be sure, it was best to understand them, if you could; but if not, it did not so very much matter, Mr Morgan thought; could in this pleasant condition of mind he went down-stairs and wrote a little sermon, which ever after was a great favourite, preached upon all special occasions, and always listened to with satisfaction, especially by the Rector's wife.

When Mrs Morgan was left alone she sat doing nothing for an entire half-hour, thinking of the strange and unhoped-for change that in a moment had occurred to her. Though she was not young, she had that sense of grievousness, the unbearableness of trouble, which belongs to youth; for, after all, whatever female moralists may say on the subject, the patience of an unmarried woman wearing out her youth in the harassments of a long engagement, is something very different from the hard and many-sided experience of actual life. She had been accustomed for years to think that her troubles would be over when the long-expected event arrived; and when new and more vexatious troubles still sprang up after that event, the woman of one idea was not much better fitted to meet them than if she had been a girl. Now that the momentary cloud had been driven off, Mrs Morgan's heart rose more warmly than ever. She changed her mind in a moment about the All-Souls pudding, and even added, in her imagination, another dish to the dinner, without pausing to think that *that* also was much approved by Mr Leeson; and then her thoughts took another turn, and such a vision of a perfect carpet for a drawing-room – something softer and more exquisite than ever come out of mortal loom; full of repose and tranquillity, yet not without seducing beauties of design; a carpet which would never obtrude itself, but yet would catch the eye by dreamy moments in the summer twilight or over the winter fire – flashed upon the imagination of the Rector's wife. It would be sweet to have a house of one's own arranging, where everything would be in harmony; and though this sweetness was very secondary to the other satisfaction of having a husband who was not a clay idol, but really deserved his pedestal, it yet supplemented the larger delight, and rounded off all the corners of Mrs Morgan's present desires. She wished everybody as happy as herself, in the effusion of the moment, and thought of Lucy Wodehouse, with a little glow of friendliness in which there was still a tincture of admiring envy. All this that happy girl would have without the necessity of waiting for it; but then was it not the Rector, the rehabilitated husband, who would be the means of producing so much happiness? Mrs Morgan rose up as lightly as a girl when she had reached this stage, and opened her writing-desk, which was one of her wedding-presents, and too fine to be used on common occasions. She took out her prettiest paper, with her monogram in violet, which was her favourite colour. One of those kind impulses which are born of happiness moved her relieved spirit. To give to another the consolation of a brighter hope, seemed at the moment the most natural way of expressing her own thankful feelings. Instead of going down-stairs immediately to order dinner, she sat down instead at the table, and wrote the following note:–

"MY DEAR MR WENTWORTH, – I don't know whether you will think me a fair-weather friend seeking you only when everybody else is seeking you, and when you are no longer in want of support and sympathy. Perhaps you will exculpate me when you remember the last conversation we had; but what I write for at present is to ask if you would waive ceremony and come to dinner with us to-night. I am aware that your family are still in Carlingford, and of course I don't know what engagements you may have; but if you are at liberty, pray come. If Mr Morgan and you had but known each other a little better things could never have happened which have been a great grief and vexation to me; and I know the Rector *wishes very much* to have a little conversation with you, and has something to speak of in which you would be interested. Perhaps my husband might feel a little strange in asking you to overstep the barrier which somehow has been raised between you two; but I am sure if you knew each other better you would understand each other, and this is one of the things we women ought to be good for. I will take it as a proof that you consider me a friend if you accept my invitation. Our hour is half-past six. – Believe me, very sincerely, yours,

"M. MORGAN."

When she had written this note Mrs Morgan went down-stairs, stopping at the library door in passing. "I thought I might as well ask Mr Wentworth to come to us to-night, as we are to have some people to dinner," she said, looking in at the door. "I thought you might like to talk to him, William; and if his people are going away to-day, I daresay he will feel rather lonely to-night." Such was the Jesuitical aspect in which she represented the flag of truce she was sending. Mr Morgan was a little startled by action so prompt.

"I should like to hear from Buller first," said the Rector; "he might like to come to Carlingford himself, for anything I can tell; but, to be sure, it can do no harm to have Wentworth to dinner," said Mr Morgan, doubtfully; "only Buller, you know, might wish – and in that case it might not be worth our trouble to make any change."

In spite of herself, Mrs Morgan's countenance fell; her pretty scheme of poetic justice, her vision of tasteful and appropriate furniture, became obscured by a momentary mist. "At least it is only right to ask him to dinner," she said, in subdued tones, and went to speak to the cook in a frame of mind more like the common level of human satisfaction than the exultant and exalted strain to which she had risen at the first moment. Then she put on a black dress, and went to call on the Miss Wodehouses, who naturally came into her mind when she thought of the Perpetual Curate. As she went along Grange Lane she could not but observe a hackney cab, one of those which belong to the railway station, lounging – if a cab could ever be said to lounge – in the direction of Wharfside. Its

appearance specially attracted Mrs Morgan's attention
in consequence of the apparition of Elsworthy's favourite
errand-boy, who now and then poked his head furtively
through the window, and seemed to be sitting in state
inside. When she had gone a little further she encountered
Wodehouse and Jack Wentworth, who had just come from
paying their visit to the sisters. The sight of these two
revived her sympathies for the lonely women who had
fallen so unexpectedly out of wealth into poverty; but yet
she felt a little difficulty in framing her countenance to be
partly sorrowful and partly congratulatory, as was
necessary under these circumstances; for though she knew
nothing of the accident which had happened that morning,
when Lucy and the Perpetual Curate saw each other
alone, she was aware of Miss Wodehouse's special position,
and was sympathetic as became a woman who had "gone
through" similar experiences. When she had got through
her visit and was going home, it struck her with considerable
surprise to see the cab still lingering about the corner of
Prickett's Lane. Was Elsworthy's pet boy delivering his
newspapers from that dignified elevation? or were they
seizing the opportunity of conveying away the unfortunate
little girl who had caused so much annoyance to everybody?
When she went closer, with a little natural curiosity to see
what else might be inside besides the furtive errand-boy,
the cab made a little rush away from her, and the blinds
were drawn down. Mrs Morgan smiled a little to herself
with dignified calm. "As if it was anything to me!" she said
to herself; and so went home to put out the dessert with
her own hands. She even cut a few fronds of her favourite
maidenhair to decorate the peaches, of which she could
not help being a little proud. "I must speak to Mr
Wentworth, if he comes, to keep on Thompson," she said
to herself, and then gave a momentary sigh at the thought
of the new flue, which was as good as her own invention,
and which it had cost her both time and money to arrange to
her satisfaction. The peaches were lovely, but who could

tell what they might be next year if a new Rector came who took no interest in the garden? – for Thomson, though he was a very good servant, required to be looked after, as indeed most good servants do. Mrs Morgan sighed a little when she thought of all her past exertions and the pains, of which she was scarcely yet beginning to reap the fruit. One man labours, and another enters into his labours. One thing, however, was a little consolatory, that she could take her ferns with her. But on the whole, after the first outburst of feeling, the idea of change, notwithstanding all its advantages, was in itself, like most human things, a doubtful pleasure. To be sure, it was only through its products that her feelings were interested about the new flue, whereas the drawing-room carpet was a standing grievance. When it was time to dress for dinner, the Rector's wife was not nearly so sure as before that she had never liked Carlingford. She began to forget the thoughts she had entertained about broken idols, and to remember a number of inconveniences attending a removal. Who would guarantee the safe transit of the china, not to speak of the *old* china, which was one of the most valuable decorations of the Rectory? This kind of breakage, if not more real, was at least likely to force itself more upon the senses than the other kind of fracture which this morning's explanation had happily averted; and altogether it was with mingled feelings that Mrs Morgan entered the drawing-room, and found it occupied by Mr Leeson, who always came too early, and who, on the present occasion, had some sufficiently strange news to tell.

CHAPTER XLVI.

MR WENTWORTH did not accept Mrs Morgan's sudden invitation, partly because his "people" did not leave Carlingford that evening, and partly because, though quite amiably disposed towards the Rector, whom he had worsted in fair fight, he was not sufficiently interested in anything he was likely to hear or see in Mr Morgan's house to move him to spend his evening there. He returned a very civil answer to the invitation of the Rector's wife, thanking her warmly for her friendliness, and explaining that he could not leave his father on the last night of his stay in Carlingford; after which he went to dinner at his aunts', where the household was still much agitated. Not to speak of all the events which had happened and were happening, Jack, who had begun to tire of his new character of the repentant prodigal, had shown himself in a new light that evening, and was preparing to leave, to the relief of all parties. The prodigal, who no longer pretended to be penitent, had taken the conversation into his own hands at dinner. "I have had things my own way since I came here," said Jack; "somehow it appears I have a great luck for having things my own way. It is you scrupulous people who think of others and of such anti-quated stuff as duty, and so forth, that get yourselves into difficulties. My dear aunt, I am going away; if I were to remain an inmate of this house – I mean to say, could I look forward to the privilege of continuing a member of this Christian family – another day, I should know better how to conduct myself; but I am going back to my bad courses, aunt Dora; I am returning to the world—"

"Oh! Jack, my dear, I hope not," said aunt Dora, who was much bewildered, and did not know what to say.

"Too true," said the relapsed sinner; "and considering all the lessons you have taught me, don't you think it is the best thing I could do? There is my brother Frank, who has been carrying other people about on his shoulders, and doing his duty; but I don't see that you good people are at all moved in his behalf. You leave him to fight his way by himself, and confer your benefits elsewhere, which is an odd sort of lesson for a worldling like me. As for Gerald, you know he's a virtuous fool, as I have heard you all declare. There is nothing in the world that I can see to prevent him keeping his living and doing as he pleases, as most parsons do. However, that's his own business. It is Frank's case which is the edifying case to me. If my convictions of sin had gone just a step farther," said the pitiless critic, "if I had devoted myself to bringing others to repentance, as is the first duty of a reformed sinner, my aunt Leonora would not have hesitated to give Skelmersdale to me—"

"Jack, hold your tongue," said Miss Leonora; but though her cheeks burned, her voice was not so firm as usual, and she actually failed in putting down the man who had determined to have his say.

"Fact, my dear aunt," said Jack: "if I had been a greater rascal than I am, and gone a little farther, you and your people would have thought me quite fit for a cure of souls. I'd have come in for your good things that way as well as other ways; but here is Frank, who even I can see is a right sort of parson. I don't pretend to fixed theological opinions," said this unlooked-for oracle, with a comic glance aside at Gerald, the most unlikely person present to make any response; "but, so far as I can see, he's a kind of fellow most men would be glad to make a friend of when they were under a cloud – not that he was ever very civil to me. I tell you, so far from rewarding him for being of the true sort, you do nothing but snub him, that I can see.

He looks to me as good for work as any man I know; but you'll give your livings to any kind of wretched make-believe before you'll give them to Frank. I am aware," said the heir of the Wentworths, with a momentary flush, "that I have never been considered much of a credit to the family; but if I were to announce my intention of marrying and settling, there is not one of the name that would not lend a hand to smooth matters. That is the reward of wickedness," said Jack, with a laugh; "as for Frank, he's a perpetual curate, and may marry perhaps fifty years hence; that's the way you good people treat a man who never did anything to be ashamed of in his life; and you expect me to give up my evil courses after such a lesson? I trust I am not such a fool," said the relapsed prodigal. He sat looking at them all in his easy way, enjoying the confusion, the indignation, and wrath with which his address was received. "The man who gets his own way is the man who takes it," he concluded, with his usual composure, pouring out Miss Leonora's glass of claret as he spoke.

Nobody had ever before seen the strong-minded woman in so much agitation. "Frank knows what my feelings are," she said, abruptly. "I have a great respect for himself, but I have no confidence in his principles. I – I have explained my ideas about Church patronage—"

But here the Squire broke in. "I always said, sir," said the old man, with an unsteady voice, "that if I ever lived to see a thing or two amended that was undoubtedly objectionable, your brother Jack's advice would be invaluable to the family as a – as a man of the world. I have nothing to say against clergymen, sir," continued the Squire, without it being apparent whom he was addressing, "but I have always expressed my conviction of – of the value of your brother Jack's advice as – as a man of the world."

This speech had a wonderful effect upon the assembled family, but most of all upon the son thus commended, who lost all his ease and composure as his father spoke, and

turned his head stiffly to one side, as if afraid to meet the
Squire's eyes, which indeed were not seeking his, but
were fixed upon the table, as was natural, considering the
state of emotion in which Mr Wentworth was. As for Jack,
when he had steadied himself a little, he got up from his
seat and tried to laugh, though the effort was far from
being a successful one.

"Even my father applauds me, you see, because I am a
scamp and don't deserve it," he said, with a voice which
was partially choked. "Good-bye, sir; I am going away."

The Squire rose too, with the hazy bewildered look of
which his other children were afraid.

"Good-bye, sir," said the old man, and then made a
pause before he held out his hand. "You'll not forget what
I've said, Jack," he added, with a little haste. "It's true
cnough, though I haven't that confidence in you that —
that I might have had. I am getting old, and I have had
two attacks, sir," said Mr Wentworth, with dignity; "and
anyhow, I can't live for ever. Your brothers can make
their own way in the world, but I haven't saved all that I
could have wished. When I am gone, Jack, be just to the
girls and the little children," said the Squire; and with that
took his son's hand and grasped it hard, and looked his
heir full in the face.

Jack Wentworth was not prepared for any such appeal;
he was still less prepared to discover the unexpected and
inevitable sequence with which one good sentiment leads to
another. He quite faltered and broke down in this
unlooked-for emergency. "Father," he said unawares, for
the first time for ten years, "if you wish it, I will join you
in breaking the entail."

"No such thing, sir," said the Squire, who, so far from
being pleased, was irritated and disturbed by the proposal.
"I ask you to do your duty, sir, and not to shirk it," the
head of the house said, with natural vehemence, as he
stood with that circle of Wentworths round him, giving
forth his code of honour to his unworthy heir.

While his father was speaking, Jack recovered a little from his momentary *attendrissement*. "Good-bye, sir; I hope you'll live a hundred years," he said, wringing his father's hand, "if you don't last out half-a-dozen of me, as you ought to do. But I'd rather not anticipate such a change. In that case," the prodigal went on with a certain huskiness in his voice, "I daresay I should not turn out so great a rascal as – as I ought to do. To-day and yesterday it has even occurred to me by moments that I was your son, sir," said Jack Wentworth; and then he made an abrupt stop and dropped the Squire's hand, and came to himself in a surprising way. When he turned towards the rest of the family, he was in perfect possession of his usual courtesy and good spirits. He nodded to them all round – with superb good-humour. "Good-bye, all of you; I wish you better luck, Frank, and not so much virtue. Perhaps you will have a better chance now the lost sheep has gone back to the wilderness. Good-bye to you all. I don't think I've any other last words to say." He lighted his cigar with his ordinary composure in the hall, and whistled one of his favourite airs as he went through the garden. "Oddly enough, however, our friend Wodehouse can beat me in that," he said, with a smile, to Frank, who had followed him out, "perhaps in other things too, who knows? Good-bye, and good-luck, old fellow." And thus the heir of the Wentworths disappeared into the darkness, which swallowed him up, and was seen no more.

But naturally there was a good deal of commotion in the house. Miss Leonora, who never had known what it was to have nerves in the entire course of her existence, retired to her own room with a headache, to the entire consternation of the family. She had been a strong-minded woman all her life, and managed everybody's affairs without being distracted and hampered in her career by those doubts of her own wisdom, and questions as to her own motives, which will now and then afflict the minds of weaker people when they have to decide for others. But this time an utterly novel and unexpected accident had befallen Miss Leonora; a man of no principles at all had delivered his opinion upon her conduct – and so far from finding his criticism contemptible, or discovering in it the ordinary outcry of the wicked against the righteous, she had found it true, and by means of it had for perhaps the first time in her life seen herself as others saw her. Neither was the position in which she found herself one from which she could get extricated even by any daring arbitrary exertion of will, such as a woman in difficulties is sometimes capable of. To be sure, she might still have cut the knot in a summary feminine way; might have said "No" abruptly to Julia Trench and her curate, and, after all, have bestowed Skelmersdale, like any other prize or reward of virtue, upon her nephew Frank – a step which Miss Dora Wentworth would have concluded upon at once without any hesitation. The elder sister, however, was gifted with a truer perception of affairs. Miss Leonora knew that there were some things which could be done, and yet could not be done – a piece of knowledge difficult to a woman. She recognised the fact that she had committed herself, and got into a corner from which there was but one possible egress; and as she acknowledged this to herself, she saw at the same time that Julia Trench (for whom she had been used to entertain a good-humoured contempt as a clever sort of girl enough) had managed matters very cleverly, and that, instead of dispensing her piece of patronage like an optimist to the best, she had, in fact, given it up to the most skilful and persevering angler, as any other woman might have done. The blow was bitter, and Miss Leonora did not seek to hide it from herself, not to say that the unpleasant discovery was aggravated by having been thus pointed out by Jack, who in his own person had taken her in, and cheated his sensible aunt. She felt humbled, and wounded in the tenderest point, to think that her reprobate nephew had seen through her, but that she had not been able to see through him, and had been deceived by his professions of penitence. The more she turned it over in her mind, the more Miss Leonora's head ached; for was it not growing apparent that she, who prided herself so much on her impartial judgment, had been moved, not by heroic and stoical justice and the love of souls, but a good deal by prejudice and a good deal by skilful artifice, and very little indeed by that highest motive which she called the glory of God? And it was Jack who had set all this before her clear as daylight. No wonder the excellent woman was disconcerted. She went to bed gloomily with her headache, and would tolerate no ministrations, neither of sal-volatile nor eau-de-Cologne, nor even of green tea. "It always does Miss Dora a power of good," said the faithful domestic who made this last suggestion; but Miss Leonora answered only by turning the unlucky speaker out of the room, and locking the door against any fresh intrusion. Miss Dora's innocent headaches were articles of a very different kind from this, which proceeded neither from the heart nor the digestion, but from the conscience, as Miss Leonora thought – with, possibly, a little aid from the temper, though she was less conscious of that. It was indeed a long series of doubts and qualms, and much internal conflict, which resulted through the rapidly-maturing influences of mortification and humbled self-regard, in this ominous and awe-inspiring Headache which startled the entire assembled family, and added fresh importance to the general crisis of Wentworth affairs.

"I should not wonder if it was the Wentworth complaint," said Miss Dora, with a sob of fright, to the renewed and increased indignation of the Squire.

"I have already told you that the Wentworth complaint never attacks females," Mr Wentworth said emphatically, glad to employ what sounded like a contemptuous title for the inferior sex.

"Yes, oh yes; but then Leonora is not exactly what you would call – a female," said poor Miss Dora, from whom an emergency so unexpected had taken all her little wits.

While the house was in such an agitated condition, it is not to be supposed that it could be very comfortable for the gentlemen when they came up-stairs to the drawing-room, and found domestic sovereignty overthrown by a headache which nobody could comprehend, and chaos reigning in Miss Leonora's place. Naturally there was, for one of the party at least, a refuge sweet and close at hand, to which his thoughts had escaped already. Frank Wentworth did not hesitate to follow his thoughts. Against the long years when family bonds make up all that is happiest in life, there must always be reckoned those moments of agitation and revolution, during which the bosom of a family is the most unrestful and disturbing place in exist-ence, from which it is well to have a personal refuge and means of escape. The Perpetual Curate gave himself a little shake, and drew a long breath, as he emerged from one green door in Grange Lane and betook himself to another. He shook himself clear of all the Wentworth perplexities, all the family difficulties and doubts, and betook himself into the paradise which was altogether his own, and where there were no conflicting interests or differences of opinion. He was in such a hurry to get there that he did not pay any attention to the general aspect of Grange Lane, or to the gossips who were gathered round Elsworthy's door: all that belonged to a previous stage of existence. At present he was full of the grand discovery, boldly stated by his brother Jack – "The man who gets his own way is the man who *takes* it." It was not an elevated doctrine, or one that had hitherto commended itself specially to the mind of the Perpetual Curate; but he could not help thinking of his father's pathetic reliance upon Jack's advice as a man of the world, as he laid up in his mind the prodigal's maxim, and felt, with a little thrill of excitement, that he was about to act on it; from which manner of stating the case Mr Wentworth's friends will

perceive that self-will had seized upon him in the worst
form; for he was not going boldly up to the new resolution
with his eyes open, but had resigned himself to the tide,
which was gradually rising in one united flux of love,
pride, impatience, sophistry, and inclination; which he
watched with a certain passive content, knowing that the
stormy current would carry him away.

Mr Wentworth, however, reckoned without his host, as
is now and then the case with most men, Perpetual
Curates included. He walked into the other drawing-
room, which was occupied only by two ladies, where the
lamp was burning softly on the little table in the corner,
and the windows, half open, admitted the fragrant air, the
perfumed breath and stillness and faint inarticulate noises
of the night. Since the visit of Wodehouse in the morning,
which had driven Lucy into her first fit of passion, an
indescribable change had come over the house, which had
now returned to the possession of its former owners, and
looked again like home. It was very quiet in the familiar
room which Mr Wentworth knew so well, for it was only
when excited by events "beyond their control," as Miss
Wodehouse said, that the sisters could forget what had
happened so lately – the loss which had made a revolution
in their world. Miss Wodehouse, who for the first time in
her life was busy, and had in hand a quantity of mysterious calculations and lists to make out, sat at the table in
the centre of the room, with her desk open, and covered
with long slips of paper. Perhaps it was to save her Rector
the trouble that the gentle woman gave herself so much
labour; perhaps she liked putting down on paper all the
things that were indispensable for the new establishment.
At all events, she looked up only to give Mr Wentworth a
smile and sisterly nod of welcome as he came in and made
his way to the corner where Lucy sat, not unexpectant.
Out of the disturbed atmosphere he had just left, the
Perpetual Curate came softly into that familiar corner,
feeling that he had suddenly reached his haven, and that

Eden itself could not have possessed a sweeter peace. Lucy in her black dress, with traces of the exhaustion of nature in her face, which was the loveliest face in the world to Mr Wentworth, looked up and welcomed him with that look of satisfaction and content which is the highest compliment one human creature can pay to another. His presence rounded off all the corners of existence to Lucy for that moment at least, and made the world complete and full. He sat down beside her at her work-table with no further interruption to the *tête-à-tête* than the presence of the kind elder sister at the table, who was absorbed in her lists, and who, even had that pleasant business been wanting, was dear and familiar enough to both to make her spectatorship just the sweet restraint which endears such intercourse all the more. Thus the Perpetual Curate seated himself, feeling in some degree master of the position; and surely here, if nowhere else in the world, the young man was justified in expecting to have his own way.

"They have settled about their marriage," said Lucy, whose voice was sufficiently audible to be heard at the table, where Miss Wodehouse seized her pen hastily and plunged it into the ink, doing her best to appear unconscious, but failing sadly in the attempt. "Mr Proctor is going away directly to make everything ready, and the marriage is to be on the 15th of next month."

"And ours?" said Mr Wentworth, who had not as yet approached that subject. Lucy knew that this event must be far off, and was not agitated about it as yet; on the contrary, she met his look sympathetically and with deprecation after the first natural blush, and soothed him in her feminine way, patting softly with her pretty hand the sleeve of his coat.

"Nobody knows," said Lucy. "We must wait, and have patience. We have more time to spare than they have," she added, with a little laugh. "We must wait."

"I don't see the *must*," said the Perpetual Curate. "I

have been thinking it all over since the morning. I see no reason why I should always have to give in, and wait; self-sacrifice is well enough when it can't be helped, but I don't see any reason for postponing my happiness indefinitely. Look here, Lucy. It appears to me at present that there are only two classes of people in the world – those who will wait, and those who won't. I don't mean to enrol myself among the martyrs. The man who gets his own way is the man who takes it. I don't see any reason in the world for concluding that I *must* wait."

Lucy Wodehouse was a very good young woman, a devoted Anglican, and loyal to all her duties; but she had always been known to possess a spark of spirit, and this rebellious quality came to a sudden blaze at so unlooked-for a speech. "Mr Wentworth," said Lucy, looking the Curate in the face with a look which was equivalent to making him a low curtsy, "I understood there were two people to be consulted as to the must or must not;" and having entered this protest, she withdrew her chair a little farther off, and bestowed her attention absolutely upon the piece of needlework in her hand.

If the ground had suddenly been cut away underneath Frank Wentworth's feet, he could not have been more surprised; for, to tell the truth, it had not occurred to him to doubt that he himself was the final authority on this point, though, to be sure, it was part of the conventional etiquette that the lady should "fix the day." He sat gazing at her with so much surprise that for a minute or two he could say nothing. "Lucy, I am not going to have you put yourself on the other side," he said at last; "there is not to be any opposition between you and me."

"That is as it may be," said Lucy, who was not mollified. "You seem to have changed your sentiments altogether since the morning, and there is no change in the circumstances, at least that I can see."

"Yes, there is a great change," said the young man. "If I could have sacrificed myself in earnest and said nothing—"

"Which you were quite free to do," interrupted Lucy, who, having given way to temper once to-day, found in herself an alarming proclivity towards a repetition of the offence.

"Which I was quite free to do," said the Perpetual Curate, with a smile, "but could not, and did not, all the same. Things are altogether changed. Now, be as cross as you please, you belong to me, *Lucia mia*. To be sure, I have no money—"

"I was not thinking of that," said the young lady, under her breath.

"Of course one has to think about it," said Mr Wentworth; "but the question is, whether we shall be happier and better going on separate in our usual way, or making up our minds to give up something for the comfort of being together. Perhaps you will forgive me for taking *that* view of the question," said the Curate, with a little enthusiasm. "I have got tired of ascetic principles. I don't see why it must be best to deny myself and postpone myself to other things and other people. I begin to be of my brother Jack's opinion. The children of this world are wiser in their generation than the children of light. A man who will wait has to wait. Providence does not invariably reward him after he has been tried, as we used to suppose. I am willing to be a poor man because I can't help it; but I am not willing to wait and trust my happiness to the future when it is in my reach now," said the unreasonable young man, to whom it was of course as easy as it was to Lucy to change the position of his chair, and prevent the distance between them being increased. Perhaps he might have carried his point even at that moment, had not Miss Wodehouse, who had heard enough to alarm her, come forward hastily in a fright on the prudential side.

"I could not help hearing what you were saying," said the elder sister. "Oh, Mr Wentworth, I hope you don't mean to say that you can't trust Providence? I am sure that is not Lucy's way of thinking. I would not mind, and I am sure she would not mind, beginning very quietly; but then you have nothing, next to nothing, neither of you. It might not matter, just at the first," said Miss Wodehouse, with serious looks; "but then – afterwards, you know," and a vision of a nursery flashed upon her mind as she spoke. "Clergymen always have such large families," she said half out before she was aware, and stopped, covered with confusion, not daring to look at Lucy to see what effect such a suggestion might have had upon her. "I mean," cried Miss Wodehouse, hurrying on to cover over her inadvertence if possible, "I have seen such cases; and a poor clergyman who has to think of the grocer's bill and the baker's bill instead of his parish and his duty – there are some things you young people know a great deal better than I do, but you don't know how dreadful it is to see that."

Here Lucy, on her part, was touched on a tender point, and interposed. "For a man to be teased about bills," said the young housekeeper, with flushed cheeks and an averted countenance, "it must be not his poverty, but his – his wife's fault."

"Oh, Lucy, don't say so," cried Miss Wodehouse; "what is a poor woman to do, especially when she has no money of her own, as you wouldn't have? and then the struggling, and getting old before your time, and all the burdens—"

"Please don't say any more," said Lucy; "there was no intention on – on any side to drive things to a decision. As for me, I have not a high opinion of myself. I would not be the means of diminishing anyone's comforts," said the spiteful young woman. "How can I be sure that I might not turn out a very poor compensation? We settled this morning how all that was to be, and I for one have not changed my mind – as yet," said Lucy. That was all the encouragement Mr Wentworth got when he propounded his new views. Things looked easy enough when he was alone, and suffered himself to drift on pleasantly on the changed and heightened current of personal desires and

wishes; but it became apparent to him, after that evening's discussion, that even in Eden itself, though the dew
had not yet dried on the leaves, it would be highly
incautious for any man to conclude that he was sure of
having his own way. The Perpetual Curate returned a
sadder and more doubtful man to Mrs Hadwin's, to his
own apartments; possibly, as the two states of mind so
often go together, a wiser individual too.

CHAPTER XLVII.

THE dinner-party at the Rectory, to which Mr Wentworth
did not go, was much less interesting and agreeable than it
might have been had he been present. As for the Rector
and his wife, they could not but feel themselves in a
somewhat strange position, having between them a secret
unsuspected by the company. It was difficult to refrain
from showing a certain flagging of interest in the question
of the church's restoration, about which, to be sure, Mr
Finial was just as much concerned as he had been yesterday; though Mr Morgan, and even Mrs Morgan, had
suffered a great and unexplainable diminution of enthusiasm. And then Mr Leeson, who was quite unaware of the
turn that things had taken, and who was much too obtuse
to understand how the Rector could be anything but
exasperated against the Perpetual Curate by the failure of
the investigation, did all that he could to make himself
disagreeable, which was saying a good deal. When Mrs
Morgan came into the drawing-room, and found this
obnoxious individual occupying the most comfortable easy-
chair, and turning over at his ease the great book of ferns,
nature-printed, which was the pet decoration of the table,

her feelings may be conceived by any lady who has gone
through a similar trial; for Mr Leeson's hands were not of
the irreproachable purity which becomes the fingers of a
gentleman when he goes out to dinner. "I know some
people who always wear gloves when they turn over a
portfolio of prints," Mrs Morgan said, coming to the
Curate's side to protect her book if possible, "and these
require quite as much care;" and she had to endure a
discussion upon the subject, which was still more trying to
her feelings, for Mr Leeson pretended to know about ferns
on the score of having a Wardian case in his lodgings
(which belonged to his landlady), though in reality he
could scarcely tell the commonest spleenwort from a lyco-
podium. While Mrs Morgan went through this trial, it is
not to be wondered at if she hugged to her heart the new
idea of leaving Carlingford, and thought to herself that
whatever might be the character of the curate (if there was
one) at Scarsfield, any change from Mr Leeson must be for
the better. And then the unfortunate man, as if he was not
disagreeable enough already, began to entertain his unwilling hostess with the latest news.

"There is quite a commotion in Grange Lane," said Mr
Leeson. "Such constant disturbances must deteriorate
the property, you know. Of course, whatever one's opinion may be, one must keep it to one's self, after the result
of the investigation; though I can't say I have unbounded
confidence in trial by jury," said the disagreeable young
man.

"I am afraid I am very slow of comprehension," said the
Rector's wife. "I don't know in the least what you mean
about trial by jury. Perhaps it would be best to put the
book back on the table; it is too heavy for you to hold."

"Oh, it doesn't matter," said Mr Leeson – "I mean
about Wentworth, of course. When a man is popular in
society, people prefer to shut their eyes. I suppose the
matter is settled for the present, but you and I know
better than to believe—"

"I beg you will speak for yourself, Mr Leeson," said Mrs Morgan, with dignity. "I have always had the highest respect for Mr Wentworth."

"Oh, I beg your pardon," said the disagreeable Curate. "I forgot; almost all the ladies are on Mr Wentworth's side. It appears that little girl of Elsworthy's has disappeared again; that was all I was going to say."

And, fortunately for the Curate, Colonel Chiley, who entered the room at the moment, diverted from him the attention of the lady of the house; and after that there was no opportunity of broaching the subject again until dinner was almost over. Then it was perhaps the All-Souls pudding that warmed Mr Leeson's soul; perhaps he had taken a little more wine than usual. He took sudden advantage of that curious little pause which occurs at a well-conducted dinner-table, when the meal is concluded, and the fruit (considered apparently, in orthodox circles, a paradisiacal kind of food which needs no blessing) alone remains to be discussed. As soon as the manner of thanks from the foot of the table was over, the Curate incautiously rushed in before anybody else could break the silence, and delivered his latest information at a high pitch of voice.

"Has anyone heard about the Elsworthys?" said Mr Leeson; "something fresh has happened there. I hope your verdict yesterday will not be called in question. The fact is, I believe that the girl has been taken away again. They say she has gone and left a letter saying that she is to be made a lady of. I don't know what we are to understand by that. There was some private service or other going on at St Roque's very early in the morning. Marriage is a sacrament, you know. Perhaps Mr Wentworth or his brother——"

"They are a queer family, the Wentworths," said old Mr Western, "and such lots of them, sir – such lots of them. The old ladies seem to have settled down here. I am not of their way of thinking, you know, but they're very good to the poor."

"Mr Frank Wentworth is going to succeed his brother, I suppose," said Mr Leeson; "it is very lucky for a man who gets himself talked of to have a family living to fall back upon—"

"No such thing – no such thing," said Mr Proctor, hastily. "Mr Frank Wentworth means to stay here."

"Dear me!" said the disagreeable Curate, with an elaborate pause of astonishment. "Things must be bad indeed," added that interesting youth, with solemnity, shaking the devoted head, upon which he did not know that Mrs Morgan had fixed her eyes, "if his own family give him up, and leave him to starve here. They would never give him up if they had not very good cause. Oh, come; I shouldn't like to believe that! *I* know how much a curate has to live on," said Mr Leeson, with a smile of engaging candour. "Before they give him up like that, with two livings in the family, they must have very good cause."

"Very good cause indeed," said Mrs Morgan, from the head of the table. The company in general had, to tell the truth, been a little taken aback by the Curate's observations; and there was almost the entire length of the table between the unhappy man and the Avenger. "So good a reason, that it is strange how it should not have occurred to a brother clergyman. That is the evil of a large parish," said the Rector's wife, with beautiful simplicity; "however hard one works, one never can know above half of the poor people; and I suppose you have been occupied in the other districts, and have not heard what a great work Mr Wentworth is doing. I have reason to know," said Mrs Morgan, with considerable state, "that he will remain in Carlingford, in a very different position from that which he has filled hitherto. Mr Leeson knows how much a curate has to live upon, but I am afraid that is all he does know of such a life as Mr Wentworth's." Mrs Morgan paused for a moment to get breath, for her excitement was considerable, and she had many wrongs to avenge.

"There is a great deal of difference in curates as well as in other things," said the indignant woman. "I have reason to know that Mr Wentworth will remain in Carlingford in quite a different position. Now and then, even in this world, things come right like a fairy tale – that is, when the authority is in the right hands;" the Rector's wife went on, with a smile at her husband, which disarmed that astonished man. "Perhaps if Mr Leeson had the same inducement as Mr Wentworth, he too would make up his mind to remain in Carlingford." Mrs Morgan got up, as she made this speech, with a rustle and sweep of drapery which seemed all addressed to the unhappy Curate, who stumbled upon his feet like the other gentlemen, but dared not for his life have approached her to open the door. Mr Leeson felt that he had received his *congé*, as he sank back into his chair. He was much too stunned to speculate on the subject, or ask himself what was going to happen. Whatever was going to happen, there was an end of *him*. He had eaten the last All-Souls pudding that he ever would have presented to him under *that* roof. He sank back in the depth of despair upon his seat, and suffered the claret to pass him in the agony of his feelings. Mr Wentworth and Mrs Morgan were avenged.

This was how it came to be noised abroad in Carlingford that some great change of a highly favourable character was about to occur in the circumstances and position of the Curate of St Roque's. It was discussed next day throughout the town, as soon as people had taken breath after telling each other about Rosa Elsworthy, who had indisputably been carried off from her uncle's house on the previous night. When the Wentworth family were at dinner, and just as the board was being spread in the Rectory, where Mrs Morgan was half an hour later than usual, having company, it had been discovered in Elsworthy's that the prison was vacant, and the poor little bird had flown. Mr Wentworth was aware of a tumult about the shop when he went to the Miss Wodehouses, but was preoccupied, and paid no attention; but Mr Leeson, who was not preoccupied, had already heard all about it when he entered the Rectory. That day it was all over the town, as may be supposed. The poor, little, wicked, unfortunate creature had disappeared, no one knew how, at the moment, apparently, when Elsworthy went to the railway for the evening papers, a time when the errand-boys were generally rampant in the well-conducted shop. Mrs Elsworthy, for her part, had seized that moment to relieve her soul by confiding to Mrs Hayles next door how she was worried to death with one thing and another, and did not expect to be alive to tell the tale if things went on like this for another month, but that Elsworthy was in-fatuated like, and wouldn't send the hussy away, his wife complained to her sympathetic neighbour. When Elsworthy came back, however, he was struck by the silence in the house, and sent the reluctant woman up-stairs – "To see if she's been and made away with herself, I suppose," the indignant wife said, as she obeyed, leaving Mrs Hayles full of curiosity on the steps of the door. Mrs Elsworthy, however uttered a shriek a moment after, and came down, with a frightened face, carrying a large pin-cushion, upon which, skewered through and through with the biggest pin she could find, Rosa had deposited her letter of leave-taking. This important document was read over in the shop by an ever-increasing group, as the news got abroad – for Elsworthy, like his wife, lost his head, and rushed about hither and thither, asking wild questions as to who had seen her last. Perhaps, at the bottom, he was not so desperate as he looked, but was rather grateful than angry with Rosa for solving the difficulty. This is what the poor little runaway said:–

"DEAR UNCLE AND AUNT, – I write a line to let you know that them as can do better for me than any belonging to me has took me away for good. Don't make no reflections, please, nor blame nobody; for I never could have done no good nor had any 'appiness at Carlingford after all as has happened. I don't bear no grudge, though aunt has been so unkind; but I forgive her, and uncle also. My love to all friends; and you may tell Bob Hayles as I won't forget him, but will order all my physic regular at his father's shop. – Your affectionate niece,

"ROSA."

"*P.S.* – Uncle has no occasion to mind, for them as has took charge of me has promised to make a lady of me, as he always said I was worthy of; and I leave all my things for aunt's relations, as I can't wear such poor clothes in my new station of life."

Such was the girl's letter, with its natural impertinences and natural touch of kindness; and it made a great commotion in the neighbourhood, where a few spasmodic search-parties were made up with no real intentions, and came to nothing, as was to be expected. It was a dreadful thing to be sure, to happen to a respectable family; but when things had gone so far, the neighbours, on the whole, were inclined to believe it was the best thing Rosa could have done; and the Elsworthys, husband and wife, were concluded to be of the same opinion. When Carlingford had exhausted this subject, and had duly discussed the probabilities as to where she had gone, and whether Rosa could be the lady in a veil who had been handed into the express night-train by two gentlemen, of whom a railway porter bore cautious testimony, the other mysterious rumour about Mr Wentworth had its share of popular attention. It was discussed in Masters's with a solemnity becoming the occasion, everybody being convinced of the fact, and nobody knowing how it was to be. One prevailing idea was, that Mr Wentworth's brother, who had succeeded to his mother's fortune (which was partly true, like most popular versions of family history, his mother's fortune being now Gerald's sole dependence), intended to

establish a great brotherhood, upon the Claydon model, in
Carlingford, of which the Perpetual Curate was to be the
head. This idea pleased the imagination of the town,
which already saw itself talked of in all the papers, and
anticipated with excitement the sight of English brothers
of St Benedict walking about in the streets, and people
from the 'Illustrated News' making drawings of Grange
Lane. To be sure, Gerald Wentworth had gone over to the
Church of Rome, which was a step too far to be compatible with the English brotherhood; but popular imagination, when puzzled and in a hurry, does not take time to
master all details. Then, again, opinion wavered, and it
was supposed to be the Miss Wentworths who were the
agents of the coming prosperity. They had made up their
mind to endow St Roque's and apply to the Ecclesiastical
Commissioners to have it erected into a parochial district,
rumour reported; and the senior assistant in Masters's,
who was suspected of Low-Church tendencies, was known
to be a supporter of this theory. Other ideas of a vague
character floated through the town, of which no one could
give any explanation; but Carlingford was unanimous in
the conviction that good fortune was coming somehow to
the popular favourite, who a week ago had occupied
temporarily the position of the popular *bête noire* and
impersonation of evil. "But the real sort always triumphs
at the last," was the verdict of Wharfside, which like
every primitive community, believed in poetic justice;
and among the bargemen and their wives much greater
elevation than that of a district church or the headship of a
brotherhood was expected "for the clergyman." If the
Queen had sent for him immediately, and conferred upon
him a bishopric, or at least appointed him her private
chaplain, such a favour would have excited no surprise in
Wharfside, where indeed the public mind was inclined to
the opinion that the real use of queens and other such
dignitaries was to find out and reward merit. Mr Wentworth himself laughed when the gossip reached his ears.

"My people have given away all they had to give," he said
to somebody who had asked the question; "and I know no
prospect I have of being anything but a perpetual curate,
unless the Queen sends for me and appoints me to a
bishopric, as I understand is expected in Prickett's Lane.
If I come to any advancement," said the Curate of St
Roque's, "it must be in social estimation, and not in
worldly wealth, which is out of my way;" and he went
down to Wharfside rather cheerfully than otherwise,
having begun to experience that pertinacity carries the
day, and that it might be possible to goad Lucy into the
experiment of how much her housekeeping talents were
good for, and whether, with a good wife, even a Perpetual
Curate might be able to live without any particular bother
in respect to the grocer's bill. Mr Wentworth being at
present warmly engaged in this business of persuasion,
and as intent as ever on having his own way, was not much
affected by the Carlingford gossip. He went his way to
Wharfside all the same, where the service was conducted
as of old, and where all the humble uncertain voices were
buoyed up and carried on by the steady pure volume of
liquid sound which issued from Lucy Wodehouse's lips
into the utterance of such a 'Magnificat' as filled Mr Wentworth's mind with exultation. It was the woman's part in
the worship – independent, yet in a sweet subordination;
and the two had come back – though with the difference
that their love was now avowed and certain, and they
were known to belong to each other – to much the same
state of feeling in which they were before the Miss Wentworths came to Carlingford, or anything uncomfortable
had happened. They had learned various little lessons, to
be sure, in the interim, but experience had not done much
more for them than it does for ordinary human creatures,
and the chances are that Mr Wentworth would have
conducted himself exactly in the same manner another
time had he been placed in similar circumstances; for the
lessons of experience, however valuable, are sometimes

very slow of impressing themselves upon a generous and hasty temperament, which has high ideas of honour and consistency, and rather piques itself on a contempt for self-interest and external advantages – which was the weakness of the Curate of St Roque's. He returned to the "great work" in Wharfside with undiminished belief in it, and a sense of being able to serve his God and his fellow-creatures, which, though it may seem strange to some people, was a wonderful compensation to him for the loss of Skelmersdale. "After all, I doubt very much whether, under any circumstances, we could have left such a work as is going on here," he said to Lucy as they came up Prickett's Lane together, where the poor woman had just died peacably in No. 10, and got done with it, poor soul; and the Sister of Mercy, in her grey cloak, lifted towards him the blue eyes which were full of tears, and answered with natural emphasis, "Impossible! it would have been deserting our post," and drew a step closer to him in the twilight with a sense of the sweetness of that plural pronoun which mingled so with the higher sense that it was impossible to disjoin them. And the two went on under the influence of these combined sentiments, taking comfort out of the very hardness of the world around them, in which their ministrations were so much needed, and feeling an exaltation in the "duty," which was not for one, but for both, and a belief in the possibility of mending matters, in which their love for each other bore a large share; for it was not in human nature thus to begin the ideal existence, without believing in its universal extension, and in the amelioration of life and the world.

"That is all they think of," said poor Miss Wodehouse, who, between her wondering inspection of the two "young people" and her own moderate and sensible love-affairs, and the directions which it was necessary to give to her Rector about the furnishing of the new house, was more constantly occupied than she had ever been in her life;

"but then, if they marry, what are they to live upon? and if they don't marry—"

"Perhaps something will turn up my dear," said old Mrs Western, who had an idea that Providence was bound to provide for two good young people who wanted to marry; and thus the two ladies were forced to leave the matter, where, indeed, the historian of events in Carlingford would willingly leave it also, not having much faith in the rewards of virtue which come convenient in such an emergency. But it is only pure fiction which can keep true to nature, and weave its narrative in analogy with the ordinary course of life – whereas history demands exactness in matters of *fact*, which are seldom true to nature, or amenable to any general rule of existence.

Before proceeding, however, to the narrative of the unexpected advancement and promotion which awaited the Perpetual Curate, it may be as well to notice that the Miss Wentworths, who during the summer had kindly given their house at Skelmersdale to some friends who had returned in the spring from India, found themselves now in a position to return to their own proper dwelling-place, and made preparations accordingly for leaving Carlingford, in which, indeed, they had no further occupation; for, to be sure, except to the extent of that respect which a man owes to his aunts, they had no special claim upon Frank Wentworth, or right to supervise his actions, save on account of Skelmersdale, which was now fully disposed of and given away. It cannot be said that Miss Leonora had ever fully recovered from the remarkable indisposition which her nephew Jack's final address had brought upon her. The very next morning she fulfilled her pledges as a woman of honour, and bestowed Skelmersdale positively and finally upon Julia Trench's curate, who indeed made a creditable enough rector in his way; but after she had accomplished this act, Miss Leonora relapsed into one unceasing watch upon her nephew Frank, which was far from dispelling the tendency to headache which she showed

at this period for the first and only time in her life. She
watched him with a certain feeling of expiation, as she
might have resorted to self-flagellation had she lived a few
hundred years before, and perhaps suffered more acute
pangs in that act of discipline than could be inflicted by
any physical scourge. The longer she studied the matter
the more thoroughly was Miss Leonora convinced not only
that the Perpetual Curate was bent on doing his duty, but
that he *did* it with all the force of high faculties, and a
mind much more thoroughly trained, and of finer material
than was possessed by the man whom she had made rector
of Skelmersdale. The strong-minded woman bore quietly,
with a kind of defiance, the sharp wounds with which her
self-esteem was pierced by this sight. She followed up her
discovery, and made herself more and more certain of the
mistake she had made, not sparing herself any part of her
punishment. As she pursued her investigations, too, Miss
Leonora became increasingly sensible that it was not his
mother's family whom he resembled, as she had once
thought, but that he was out and out a Wentworth, possessed of all the family features; and this was the man
whom by her own act she had disinherited of his natural
share in the patronage of the family, substituting for her
own flesh and blood an individual for whom, to tell the
truth, she had little respect! Perhaps if she had been able
to sustain herself with the thought that it was entirely a
question of "principle," the retrospect might not have
been so hard upon Miss Leonora; but being a woman of
very distinct and uncompromising vision, she could not
conceal from herself either Julia Trench's cleverness or
her own mixed and doubtful motives. Having this sense of
wrong and injustice, and general failure of the duty of
kindred towards Frank, it might have been supposed a
little comfort to Miss Leonora to perceive that he had
entirely recovered from his disappointment, and was no
longer in her power, if indeed he had ever been so. But
the fact was, that if anything could have aggravated her

personal smart, it would have been the fact of Frank's
indifference and cheerfulness, and evident capability of
contenting himself with his duty and his favourite district,
and his Lucy – whom, to be sure, he could not marry,
being only a perpetual curate. The spectacle came to have
a certain fascination for Miss Wentworth. She kept
watching him with a grim satisfaction, punishing herself,
and at the same time comforting herself with the idea that,
light as he made of it, he must be suffering too. She could
not bear to think that he had escaped clean out of her
hands, and that the decision she had come to, which
produced so much pain to herself, was innoxious to Frank;
and at the same time, though she could not tolerate his
composure, and would have preferred to see him angry
and revengeful, his evident recovery of spirits and general
exhilaration increased Miss Leonora's respect for the man
she had wronged. In this condition of mind the strong-
minded aunt lingered over her preparations for removal,
scorning much the rumour in Carlingford about her
nephew's advancement, and feeling that she could never
forgive him if by any chance promotion should come to
him after all. "He will stay where he is. He will be a
perpetual curate," Miss Leonora said, uttering what was
in reality a hope under the shape of a taunt; and things
were still in this position when Grange Lane in general
and Miss Dora in particular (from the window of the
summer-house) were startled much by the sight of the
Rector, in terribly correct clerical costume, as if he were
going to dine with the bishop, who walked slowly down the
road like a man charged with a mission, and, knocking at
Mrs Hadwin's door, was admitted immediately to a private conference with the Curate of St Roque's.

CHAPTER XLVIII.

IT was the same afternoon that Mr Wentworth failed to attend, as he had never been known to fail before, at the afternoon's school which he had set up in Prickett's Lane for the young bargemen, who between the intervals of their voyages had a little leisure at that hour of the day. It is true there was a master provided, and the presence of the Perpetual Curate was not indispensable; but the lads, among whom, indeed, there were some men, were so much used to his presence as to get restless at their work on this unprecedented emergency. The master knew no other resource than to send for Miss Lucy Wodehouse, who was known to be on the other side of Prickett's Lane at the moment, superintending a similar educational undertaking for the benefit of the girls. It was, as may be supposed, embarrassing to Lucy to be called upon to render an account of Mr Wentworth's absence, and invited to take his place in this public and open manner; but then the conventional reticences were unknown in Wharfside, and nobody thought it necessary to conceal his certainty that the Curate's movements were better known to Lucy than to anybody else. She had to make answer with as much composure as possible in the full gaze of so many pairs of curious eyes, that she did not know why Mr Wentworth was absent – "Somebody is sick, perhaps," said Lucy, repeating an excuse which had been made before for the Perpetual Curate; "but I hope it does not make any difference," she went on, turning round upon all the upturned heads which were neglecting their work to stare at her. "Mr Wentworth would be grieved to think that his absence did his scholars any injury." Lucy looked one of the ringleaders in the eyes as she spoke, and brought him to his senses – all the more effectually, to be sure, because she knew all about him, and was a familiar figure to the boy, suggesting various little comforts, for which, in Prickett's Lane, people were not ungrateful. But when she went back again to her girls, the young lady found herself in a state of excitement which was half annoyance and half a kind of shy pleasure. To be sure, it was quite true that they did belong to each other; but at the same time, so long as she was Lucy Wodehouse, she had no right to be called upon to represent "the clergyman," even in "the district" which was so important to both. And then it occurred to her to remember that if she remained Lucy Wodehouse that was not the Curate's fault – from which thought she went on to reflect that going away with Mr and Mrs Proctor when they were married was not a charming prospect, not to say that it involved a renunciation of the district for the present at least, and possibly for ever; for if Mr Wentworth could not marry as long as he was a perpetual curate, it followed of necessity that he could not marry until he had left Carlingford – an idea which Lucy turned over in her mind very seriously as she walked home, for this once unattended. A new light seemed to be thrown upon the whole matter by this thought. To consent to be married simply for her own happiness, to the disadvantage in any respect of her husband, was an idea odious to this young woman, who, like most young women, preferred to represent even to herself that it was for *his* happiness that she permitted herself to be persuaded to marry; but if duty were involved, that was quite another affair. It was quite evident to Lucy, as she walked towards Grange Lane, that the Curate would not be able to find any one to take her place in the district; perhaps also – for she was honest even in her self-delusions – Lucy was aware that she might herself have objections to the finding of a substitute; and what then? Was the great work to be interrupted because she could not bear the idea of possibly diminishing some of his external comforts by allowing him to have his way, and to be what he considered happy? Such was the wonderful length to which her thoughts had come when she reached the garden-door, from which Mr Wentworth himself, flushed and eager, came hastily out as she approached. So far from explaining his unaccountable absence, or even greeting her with ordinary politeness, the young man seized her by the arm and brought her into the garden with a rapidity which made her giddy. "What is it – what do you mean?" Lucy cried with amazement as she found herself whirled through the sunshine and half carried up the stairs. Mr Wentworth made no answer until he had deposited her breathless in her own chair, in her own corner, and then got down on his knee beside her, as men in his crazy circumstances are not unapt to do.

"Lucy, look here. I was a perpetual curate the other day when you said you would have me," said the energetic lover, who was certainly out of his wits, and did not know what he was saying – "and you said you did not mind?"

"I said it did not matter," said Lucy, who was slightly piqued that he did not recollect exactly the form of so important a decision. "I knew well enough you were a perpetual curate. Has anything happened, or are you going out of your mind?"

"I think it must be that," said Mr Wentworth. "Something so extraordinary has happened that I cannot believe it. Was I in Prickett's Lane this afternoon as usual, or was I at home in my own room talking to the Rector – or have I fallen asleep somewhere, and is the whole thing a dream?"

"You were certainly not in Prickett's Lane," said Lucy. "I see what it is. Miss Leonora Wentworth has changed her mind, and you are going to have Skelmersdale after all. I did not think you could have made up your mind to

leave the district. It is not news that gives me any pleasure,"
said the Sister of Mercy, as she loosed slowly off from her
shoulders the grey cloak which was the uniform of the
district. Her own thoughts had been so different that she
felt intensely mortified to think of the unnecessary decision she had been so near making, and disappointed that
the offer of a living could have moved her lover to such a
pitch of pleasure. "All men are alike, it seems," she said to
herself, with a little quiver in her lip – a mode of fore-
stalling his communications which filled the Perpetual
Curate with amazement and dismay.

"What are you thinking of?" he said. "Miss Leonora
Wentworth has not changed her mind. That would have
been a natural accident enough, but this is incredible. If
you like, Lucy," he added, with an unsteady laugh, "and
will consent to my original proposition, you may marry on
the 15th, not the Perpetual Curate of St Roque's, but the
Rector of Carlingford. Don't look at me with such an
unbelieving countenance. It is quite true."

I wonder how you can talk so," cried Lucy, indignantly;
"it is all a made-up story; you know it is. I don't like
practical jokes," she went on, trembling a little, and
taking another furtive look at him – for somehow it was too
wonderful not to be true.

"If I had been making up a story, I should have kept to
what was likely," said Mr Wentworth. "The Rector has
been with me all the afternoon – he says he has been offered
his father's rectory, where he was brought up, and that he
has made up his mind to accept it, as he always was fond
of the country; – and that he has recommended me to his
College for the living of Carlingford."

"Yes, yes," said Lucy, impatiently, "that is very good
of Mr Morgan; but you know you are not a member of the
College, and why should you have the living? I knew it
could not be true."

"They are all a set of old— Dons," said the Perpetual
Curate; "that is, they are the most accomplished set of

fellows in existence, Lucy – or at least they ought to be –
but they are too superior to take an ordinary living, and
condescend to ordinary existence. Here has Carlingford
been twice vacant within a year – which is an unprecedented event – and Buller, the only man who would think
of it, is hanging on for a colonial bishopric, where he can
publish his book at his leisure. Buller is a great friend of
Gerald's. It is incredible, *Lucia mia*, but it is true."

"Is it true? are you *sure* it is true?" cried Lucy; and in
spite of herself she broke down and gave way, and let her
head rest on the first convenient support it found, which
turned out, naturally enough, to be Mr Wentworth's
shoulder, and cried as if her heart was breaking. It is so
seldom in this world that things come just when they are
wanted; and this was not only an acceptable benefice, but
implied the entire possession of the "district" and the most
conclusive vindication of the Curate's honour. Lucy cried
out of pride and happiness and glory in him. She said to
herself, as Mrs Morgan had done at the beginning of her
incumbency, "He will be such a Rector as Carlingford has
never seen." Yet at the same time, apart from her glory-
ing and her pride, a certain sense of pain, exquisite though
shortlived, found expression in Lucy's tears. She had just
been making up her mind to accept a share of his lowli-
ness, and to show the world that even a Perpetual Curate,
when his wife was equal to her position, might be poor
without feeling any of the degradations of poverty; and
now she was forestalled, and had nothing to do but accept
his competence, which it would be no credit to manage
well! Such were the thoughts to which she was reduced,
though she had come home from Prickett's Lane persuading herself that it was duty only, and the wants of the
district, which moved her. Lucy cried, although not much
given to crying, chiefly because it was the only method she
could find of giving expression to the feelings which were
too varied and too complicated for words.

All Carlingford knew the truth about Mr Wentworth's

advancement that evening, and on the next day, which was Sunday, the Church of St Roque's was as full as if the plague had broken out in Carlingford, and the population had rushed out, as they might have done in medieval times, to implore the succour of the physician-saint. The first indication of the unusual throng was conveyed to Mr Wentworth in his little vestry after the choristers had filed into the church in their white surplices, about which, to tell the truth, the Perpetual Curate was less interested than he had once been. Elsworthy, who had been humbly assisting the young priest to robe himself, ventured to break the silence when they were alone.

"The church is very full, sir," said Elsworthy; "there's a deal of people come, sir, after hearing the news. I don't say I've always been as good a servant as I ought to have been; but it was all through being led away, and not knowing no better, and putting my trust where I shouldn't have put it. I've had a hard lesson, sir, and I've learnt better," he continued, with a sidelong glance at the Curate's face; "it was all a mistake."

"I was not finding fault with you, that I am aware of," said Mr Wentworth, with a little surprise.

"No, sir," said Elsworthy, "I am aware as you wasn't finding no fault; but there's looks as speaks as strong as words, and I can feel as you haven't the confidence in me as you once had. I aint ashamed to say it, sir," continued the clerk of St Roque's. "I'm one as trusted in that girl's innocent looks, and didn't believe as she could do no harm. She's led me into ill-feeling with my clergyman, sir, and done me a deal o' damage in my trade, and now she's gone off without as much as saying 'Thank you for your kindness.' It's a hard blow upon a man as was fond of her, and I didn't make no difference, no more than if she had been my own child."

"Well, well," said the Curate, "I daresay it was a trial to you; but you can't expect me to take much interest in it after all that has passed. Let bygones be bygones," said

Mr Wentworth, with a smile, "as indeed you once proposed."

"Ah! sir, that was my mistake," sighed the penitent. "I would have 'umbled myself more becoming, if I had known all as I know now. You're a-going off to leave St Roque's, where we've all been so happy," said Mr Elsworthy, in pathetic tones. "I don't know as I ever was as 'appy, sir, as here, a-listening to them beautiful sermons, and a-giving my best attention to see as the responses was well spoke out, and things done proper. Afore our troubles began, sir, I don't know as I had a wish in the world, unless it was to see an 'andsome painted window in the chancel, which is all as is wanted to make the church perfect; and now you're a-going to leave, and nobody knows what kind of a gentleman may be sent. If you wouldn't think I was making too bold," said Elsworthy, "it aint my opinion as you'll ever put up with poor old Norris as is in the church. Men like Mr Morgan and Mr Proctor as had no cultivation doesn't mind; but for a gentleman as goes through the service as you does it, Mr Wentworth—"

Mr Wentworth laughed, though he was fully robed and ready for the reading-desk, and knew that his congregation was waiting. He held his watch in his hand, though it already marked the half minute after eleven. "So you would like to be clerk in the parish church?" he said, with what seemed a quite unnecessary amount of amusement to the anxious functionary by his side.

"I think as you could never put up with old Norris, sir," said Elsworthy; "as for leading of the responses, there aint such a thing done in Carlingford Church. I don't speak for myself," said the public-spirited clerk, "but it aint a right thing for the rising generation; and it aint everybody as would get into your way in a minute – for you have a way of your own, sir, in most things, and if you'll excuse me for saying of it, you're very particular. It aint every man, sir, as could carry on clear through the service along of you, Mr Wentworth; and you wouldn't put up with old Norris, not for a day."

Such was the conversation which opened this memorable Sunday to Mr Wentworth. Opposite to him, again occupying the seat where his wife should have been, had he possessed one, were the three Miss Wentworths, his respected aunts, to whose opinion, however, the Curate did not feel himself bound to defer very greatly in present circumstances; and a large and curious congregation ranged behind them, almost as much concerned to see how Mr Wentworth would conduct himself in this moment of triumph, as they had been in the moment of his humiliation. It is, however, needless to inform the friends of the Perpetual Curate that the anxious community gained very little by their curiosity. It was not the custom of the young Anglican to carry his personal feelings, either of one kind or another, into the pulpit with him, much less into the reading-desk, where he was the interpreter not of his own sentiments or emotions, but of common prayer and universal worship. Mr Wentworth did not even throw a little additional warmth into his utterance of the general thanksgiving, as he might have done had he been a more effusive man; but, on the contrary, read it with a more than ordinary calmness, and preached to the excited people one of those terse little unimpassioned sermons of his, from which it was utterly impossible to divine whether he was in the depths of despair or at the summit and crown of happiness. People who had been used to discover a great many of old Mr Bury's personal peculiarities in his sermons, and who, of recent days, had found many allusions which it was easy to interpret in the discourses of Mr Morgan, retired altogether baffled from the clear and succinct brevity of the Curate of St Roque's. He was that day in particular so terse as to be almost epigrammatic, not using a word more than was necessary, and displaying that power of saying a great deal more than at the first moment he appeared to say, in which Mr Wentworth's admirers specially prided themselves. Perhaps a momentary human gratification in the consciousness of having utterly baffled curiosity, passed through the Curate's mind ·as he took off his robes when the service was over; but he was by no means prepared for the ordeal which awaited him when he stepped forth from the pretty porch of St Roque's. There his three aunts were awaiting him, eager to hear all about it, Miss Dora, for the first time in her life, holding the principal place. "We are going away to-morrow, Frank, and of course you are coming to lunch with us," said aunt Dora, clinging to his arm. "Oh, my dear boy, I am so happy, and so ashamed, to hear of it. To think you should be provided for, and nobody belonging to you have anything to do with it! I don't know what to say," said Miss Dora, who was half crying as usual; "and as for Leonora, one is frightened to speak to her. Oh, I wish you would say something to your aunt Leonora, Frank. I don't know whether she is angry with us or with you or with herself, or what it is; or if it is an attack on the nerves – though I never imagined she had any nerves; but, indeed, whatever my brother may say, it looks very like – dreadfully like – the coming-on of the Wentworth complaint. Poor papa was just like that when he used to have it coming on; and Leonora is not just – altogether – what you would call a female, Frank. Oh, my dear boy, if you would only speak to her!" cried Miss Dora, who was a great deal too much in earnest to perceive anything comical in what she had said.

"I should think it must be an attack on the temper," said the Curate, who, now that it was all over, felt that it was but just his aunt Leonora should suffer a little for her treatment of him. "Perhaps some of her favourite colporteurs have fallen back into evil ways. There was one who had been a terrible blackguard, I remember. It is something that has happened among her mission people, you may be sure, and nothing about me."

"You don't know Leonora, Frank. She is very fond of

you, though she does not show it," said Miss Dora, as she led her victim in triumphantly through the garden-door, from which the reluctant young man could see Lucy and her sister in their black dresses just arriving at the other green door from the parish church, where they had occupied their usual places, according to the ideas of propriety which were common to both the Miss Wodehouses. Mr Wentworth had to content himself with taking off his hat to them, and followed his aunts to the table, where Miss Leonora took her seat much with the air of a judge about to deliver a sentence. She did not restrain herself even in the consideration of the presence of Lewis the butler, who, to be sure, had been long enough in the Wentworth family to know as much about its concerns as the members of the house themselves, or perhaps a little more. Miss Leonora sat down grim and formidable in her bonnet, which was in the style of a remote period, and did not soften the severity of her personal appearance. She pointed her nephew to a seat beside her, but she did not relax her features, nor condescend to any ordinary preliminaries of conversation. For that day even she took Lewis's business out of his astonished hands, and herself divided the chicken with a swift and steady knife and anatomical precision; and it was while occupied in this congenial business that she broke forth upon Frank in a manner so unexpected as almost to take away his breath.

"I suppose this is what fools call poetic justice," said Miss Leonora, "which is just of a piece with everything else that is poetical – weak folly and nonsense that no sensible man would have anything to say to. How a young man like you, who know how to conduct yourself in some things, and have, I don't deny, many good qualities, can give in to come to an ending like a trashy novel, is more than I can understand. You are fit to be put in a book of the Good-child series, Frank, as an illustration of the reward of virtue," said the strong-minded woman, with a little snort of scorn; "and, of course, you are going to marry, and live happy ever after, like a fairy tale."

"It is possible I may be guilty of that additional enormity," said the Curate, "which, at all events, will not be your doing, my dear aunt, if I might suggest a consolation. You cannot help such things happening, but, at least, it should be a comfort to feel you have done nothing to bring them about."

To which Miss Leonora answered by another hard breath of mingled disdain and resentment. "Whatever I have brought about, I have tried to do what I thought my duty," she said. "It has always seemed to me a very poor sort of virtue that expects a reward for doing what it ought to do. I don't say you haven't behaved very well in this business, but you've done nothing extraordinary; and why I should have rushed out of my way to reward you for it— Oh, yes, I know you did not expect anything," said Miss Leonora; "you have told me as much on various occasions, Frank. You have, of course, always been perfectly independent, and scorned to flatter your old aunts by any deference to their convictions; and, to be sure, it is nothing to you any little pang they may feel at having to dispose otherwise of a living that has always been in the family. You are of the latest fashion of Anglicanism, and we are only a parcel of old women. It was not to be expected that our antiquated ideas could be worth as much to you as a parcel of flowers and trumpery—"

These were actually tears which glittered in Miss Leonora's eyes of fiery hazel grey – tears of very diminutive size, totally unlike the big dewdrops which rained from Miss Dora's placid orbs and made them red, but did *her* no harm – but still a real moisture, forced out of a fountain which lay very deep down and inaccessible to ordinary efforts. They made her eyes look rather fiercer than otherwise for the moment; but they all but impeded Miss Leonora's speech, and struck with the wildest consternation the entire party at the table, including even

Lewis, who stood transfixed in the act of drawing a bottle of soda-water, and, letting the cork escape him in his amazement, brought affairs to an unlooked-for climax by hitting Miss Wentworth, who had been looking on with interest without taking any part in the proceedings. When the fright caused by this unintentional shot had subsided, Miss Leonora was found to have entirely recovered herself; but not so the Perpetual Curate, who had changed colour wonderfully, and no longer met his accuser with reciprocal disdain.

"My dear aunt," said Frank Wentworth, "I wish you would not go back to that. I suppose we parsons are apt sometimes to exaggerate trifles into importance, as my father says. But, however, as things have turned out, I could not have left Carlingford," the Curate added, in a tone of conciliation; "and now, when good fortune has come to me unsought—"

Miss Leonora finished her portion of chicken in one energetic gulp, and got up from the table. "Poetic justice!" she said, with a furious sneer. "I don't believe in that kind of rubbish. As long as you were getting on quietly with your work I felt disposed to be rather proud of you, Frank. But I don't approve of a man ending off neatly like a novel in this sort of ridiculous way. When you succeed to the Rectory I suppose you will begin fighting, like the other man, with the new curate, for working in your parish?"

"When I succeed to the Rectory,' said Mr Wentworth, getting up in his turn from the table, "I give you my word, aunt Leonora, no man shall work in *my* parish unless I set him to do it. Now I must be off to my work. I don't suppose Carlingford Rectory will be the end of me," the Perpetual Curate added, as he went away, with a smile which his aunts could not interpret. As for Miss Leonora, she tied her bonnet-strings very tight, and went off to the afternoon service at Salem Chapel by way of expressing her sentiments more forcibly. "I daresay he's bold enough to take a bishopric," she said to herself; "but fortunately we've got *that* in our own hands as long as Lord Shaftesbury lives;" and Miss Leonora smiled grimly over the prerogatives of her party. But though she went to the Salem Chapel that afternoon, and consoled herself that she could secure the bench of bishops from any audacious invasion of Frank Wentworth's hopes, it is true, notwithstanding, that Miss Leonora sent her maid next morning to London with certain obsolete ornaments, of which, though the fashion was hideous, the jewels were precious; and Lucy Wodehouse had never seen anything so brilliant as the appearance they presented when they returned shortly after reposing upon beds of white satin in cases of velvet – "Ridiculous things," as Miss Leonora informed her, "for a parson's wife."

It was some time after this – for, not to speak of ecclesiastical matters, a removal, even when the furniture is left behind and there are only books, and rare ferns, and old china, to convey from one house to another, is a matter which involves delays – when Mr Wentworth went to the railway station with Mrs Morgan to see her off finally, her husband having gone to London with the intention of joining her in the new house. Naturally, it was not without serious thoughts that the Rector's wife left the place in which she had made the first beginning of her active life, not so successfully as she had hoped. She could not help recalling, as she went along the familiar road, the hopes so vivid as to be almost certainties with which she had come into Carlingford. The long waiting was then over, and the much-respected era had arrived and existence had seemed to be opening in all its fulness and strength before the two who had looked forward to it so long. It was not much more than six months ago; but Mrs Morgan had made a great many discoveries in the mean time. She had found out the wonderful difference between anticipation and reality; and that life, even to a happy woman married after long patience to the man of her choice, was not the smooth road it looked, but a rough path enough cut into dangerous ruts, through which generations of men and women followed each other without ever being able to mend the way. She was not so sure as she used to be of a great many important matters which it is a wonderful consolation to be certain of – but, notwithstanding, had to go on as if she had no doubts, though the clouds of a defeat, in which, certainly, no honour, though a good deal of the *prestige* of inexperience had been lost, were still looming behind. She gave a little sigh as she shook Mr Wentworth's hand at parting. "A great many things have happened in six months," she said – "one never could have anticipated so many changes in what looks so short a period of one's life" – and as the train which she had watched so often rushed past that new bit of wall on which the Virginian creeper was beginning to grow luxuriantly, which screened the railway from the Rectory windows, there were tears in Mrs Morgan's eyes. Only six months and so much had happened! – what might not happen in all those months, in all those years of life which scarcely looked so hopeful as of old? She preferred turning her back upon Carlingford, though it was the least comfortable side of the carriage, and put down her veil to shield her eyes from the dust, or perhaps from the inspection of her fellow-travellers: and once more the familiar thought returned to her of what a different woman she would have been had she come to her first experiences of life with the courage and confidence of twenty or even of five-and-twenty, which was the age Mrs Morgan dwelt upon most kindly. And then she thought with a thrill of vivid kindness and a touch of tender envy of Lucy Wodehouse, who would now have no possible occasion to wait those ten years.

As for Mr Wentworth, he who was a priest, and knew more about Carlingford than any other man in the place, could not help thinking, as he turned back, of people there, to whom these six months had produced alterations far more terrible than any that had befallen the Rector's wife: – people from whom the light of life had died out, and to whom all the world was changed. He knew of men who had been cheerful enough when Mr Morgan came to Carlingford, who now did not care what became of them; and of women who would be glad to lay down their heads and hide them from the mocking light of day. He knew it, and it touched his heart with the tenderest pity of life, the compassion of happiness; and he knew too that the path upon which he was about to set out led through the same glooms, and was no ideal career. But perhaps because Mr Wentworth was young – perhaps because he was possessed by that delicate sprite more dainty than any Ariel who puts rosy girdles round the world while his time of triumph lasts – it is certain that the new Rector of Carlingford turned back into Grange Lane without the least shadow upon his mind or timidity in his thoughts. He was now in his own domains, an independent monarch, as little inclined to divide his power as any autocrat; and Mr Wentworth came into his kingdom without any doubts of his success in it, or of his capability for its government. He had first a little journey to make to bring back Lucy from that temporary and reluctant separation from the district which propriety had made needful; but, in the mean time, Mr Wentworth trode with firm foot the streets of his parish, secure that no parson nor priest should tithe or toll in his dominions, and a great deal more sure than even Mr Morgan had been, that henceforth no unauthorised evangelisation should take place in any portion of his territory. This sentiment, perhaps, was the principal difference perceptible by the community in general between the new Rector of Carlingford and the late Perpetual Curate of St Roque's.

VIRAGO MODERN CLASSICS

The first Virago Modern Classic, *Frost in May* by Antonia White, was published in 1978. It launched a list dedicated to the celebration of women writers and to the rediscovery and reprinting of their works. Its aim was, and is, to demonstrate the existence of a female tradition in fiction which is both enriching and enjoyable. The Leavisite notion of the 'Great Tradition', and the narrow, academic definition of a 'classic', has meant the neglect of a large number of interesting secondary works of fiction. In calling the series 'Modern Classics' we do not necessarily mean 'great' — although this is often the case. Published with new critical and biographical introductions, books are chosen for many reasons: sometimes for their importance in literary history; sometimes because they illuminate particular aspects of womens' lives, both personal and public. They may be classics of comedy or storytelling; their interest can be historical, feminist, political or literary.

Initially the Virago Modern Classics concentrated on English novels and short stories published in the early decades of this century. As the series has grown it has broadened to include works of fiction from different centuries, different countries, cultures and literary traditions. In 1984 the Victorian Classics were launched; there are separate lists of Irish, Scottish, European, American, Australian and other English speaking countries; there are books written by Black women, by Catholic and Jewish women, and a few relevant novels by men. There is, too, a companion series of Non-Fiction Classics constituting biography, autobiography, travel, journalism, essays, poetry, letters and diaries.

By the end of 1986 over 250 titles will have been published in these two series, many of which have been suggested by our readers.